Of Yellow Shir.. ... ...

Green Men

Book 1 of The Norwich Chronicles

By

Gene Rowe

ISBN: 978-1-7390872-6-5

First paperback edition November 2024
Cover design by Jonathan Asher

Ministry of Lies
12 Wellington Road
Norwich
NR2 3HT
UK

ministryoflies.co.uk

To the denizens of the Fine City: you know you're weird, right?
Still, never change.

Contents

Prologue 7

Chapter 1: First Contact 8

Chapter 2: The First Lesson 15

Chapter 3: The Second Lesson 22

Chapter 4: Interlude 34

Chapter 5: The Third Lesson 41

Chapter 6: Conspiracy 51

Chapter 7: Instructions 61

Chapter 8: The Credulous 72

Chapter 9: Second Interlude 83

Chapter 10: On Patrol 94

Chapter 11: The Pottergate Incident 103

Chapter 12: Routine 112

Chapter 13: Ghosts 122

Chapter 14: Beer Festival Brouhaha 133

Chapter 15: Third Interlude 147

Chapter 16: Would You Adam and Eve It! 157

Chapter 17: Cathedral Capers 173

Chapter 18: One nil… *again*! 186

Chapter 19: Christmas Crises 199

Chapter 20: Castle Secrets 217

Chapter 21: Fourth Interlude 229

Chapter 22: The Incredulous 245

Chapter 23: Oops, I did it (yet) again 257

Chapter 24: Going Underground   268

Chapter 25: Spies   284

Chapter 26: Goals and Own Goals   295

Chapter 27: Busted?   307

Chapter 28: Fifth Interlude   327

Chapter 29: The Vegan Enclave   340

Chapter 30: The Stirred Pot   356

Chapter 31: Pow Wow   371

Chapter 32: Lost and Found   380

Chapter 33: Into the Lairs   394

Chapter 34: Council of War   412

Chapter 35: I Predict a…   423

Chapter 36: Delia Day Dawns   432

Chapter 37: Into the Box   450

Chapter 38: He Shoots… He Scores?   468

Chapter 39: Autopsy   486

Epilogue   497

Author's Note   499

Acknowledgements   501

About the Author   502

Prologue: Extract from Tom Beresford's 'The Alien Without', unpublished manuscript

There are around one hundred billion stars in the Milky Way – a galaxy that has been in existence for over thirteen billion years. And yet many people seem to believe that humans are the only intelligent life within it.

I mean, *really?*

Others have accepted that 'intelligence' is liable to be more widespread. Some have used an equation – the Drake Equation – to estimate the number of advanced civilisations currently co-existing with humanity. Depending upon the values chosen for the different factors, these savants have come up with different numbers, often in the thousands or low millions.

Ha! Think again!

There are, in fact, close to one billion alien races in the galaxy today with the capability of crossing the space between stars in one way or another, whether in a craft or via some weird kind of ghost-like post-corporeal process.

Seriously.

And who'd have thought that so many of these species would turn out to be such complete and utter arseholes?

Chapter 1: First Contact

Tom Beresford was a thirty-five-year-old waster. He appreciated this fact to be true, and hated himself both for being one *and* knowing it.

Looking at the page of text from the partially written novel on his computer screen, Tom sighed and pushed his swivel chair away from his desk. He had been picking at the book on-and-off for a number of years, although it had only become the prime focus of his life over the last three months… *now that he had time.*

When Tom had started his project, he'd had every expectation that the novel was going to be a science fiction masterpiece, or at the very least, some form of personal salvation, a justification for a life spent doing very little and wasting whatever talents he had – for Tom *did* have some. He had a PhD, and a fine brain – according to many. Well, according to *some*. He had published a number of research articles on how people made decisions, and these had been modestly cited. Though not exactly well known in the research community, he wasn't a complete non-entity. He could probably consider himself a *Beta*. Competent. A man of some insight. But definitely not an *Alpha*. He was not professorial material. He didn't have the drive. He was lazy. He struggled to get out of bed in the mornings. And he didn't like teaching – which was somewhat unfortunate, given that lecturing made up a significant part of his job description.

So, when redundancies had been announced at the University of East Anglia, Tom hadn't been surprised when a brown envelope appeared in his office pigeonhole one day the previous November. He'd managed to leave it untouched for two days. But it had become increasingly difficult to listen to the gossip in the staff common room on who had and hadn't been shafted, and to issue sickly smiles and shoulder shrugs when colleagues asked about his own situation, or worse, congratulated him on avoiding the chop. And so, late on a Thursday, with the department dark and untenanted, he'd taken the letter from the pigeonhole and repaired to the office he shared with Alice Weidner, who'd gone home after a busy week preparing a new lecture course. The letter's contents had been as expected. At least the modest redundancy payment would keep him alive for a few months beyond his notice period while he considered alternative ways to dribble away his unextraordinary existence.

As he'd had no teaching on the Friday, he'd spent the next day in bed. *Alone*, of course. *Might as well get used to it*, he'd thought.

Tom rose from the swivel chair in his 'office' – which was really just a box room adjacent to his bedroom. Four paces took him through his sparse bedroom, with its unmade bed, to a broad top step that separated the two upstairs bedrooms of his narrow terraced house. Down the short, straight flight of stairs, turn right through the dining room, and into the galley kitchen. He looked blankly at the kettle for a number of seconds. The expert in decision making – undecided. *How ironic!* Out through the window, looking at the wooden slatted fence that separated his small plot of land from that of his neighbour, he noticed the top few centimetres in bright sunlight. It looked as though it was going to be a fine, early August day. Go out? Or grab a cup of tea and return to the 'masterpiece'?

No – work!

He lifted the kettle, realised it needed refilling, and set it down again.

Bugger that!

He hesitantly headed back through the dining room – past the steep stairway – to the living room and the front door that led from it. He patted his pockets to ensure he had his keys on him, then opened the door and stepped outside.

Warm enough? Yes? No?

Bum.

He about-turned and re-entered the house to collect his jacket, draped across the room's orange, two-seat sofa. He hefted this, frowned, then lay it down. Picked it up. Then lay it down again. With a shake of the head, a shrug, and a sigh, he turned once more and exited the front door.

***

But he wasn't gone long and was soon back to the book.

I'm NOT a waster, thought Tom, *I'm a novelist.*

Except that he wasn't – even in his own mind.

Tom tinkered with words. He sewed them together into a story. And though he had pretentions to publish, he was a realist. He knew that the famed concept of the slush pile was largely a defunct one now and had

9

been for years. Publishers had outsourced the role of triage to agents, of whom relatively few were interested in his genre of fiction. And both publishers and agents seemed more interested in celebrity than talent. Not that Tom had any appreciable talent, he supposed. He thought he was reasonably competent – but did he have that killer line or zeitgeist concept that would get a bite? Could he ever hope for that slice of luck that might gain him an agent, a contract, a modicum of celebrity, a new career?

Luck? Not if the entirety of his past was any guide to the future. Tom thought he must be one of the unluckiest people alive. And his luck hadn't gotten any better. For now Tom wasn't even an academic, having failed to rouse the interest of any university over his last six months of trying. Perhaps he needed to widen his search? Be less picky? Consider a career change? Become a teacher? He shuddered at *that* thought.

Sat at his computer, Tom sighed, shook his head, and strummed his fingers on the desk. At least he was good at procrastination. *Right.* He moved the mouse and hovered the cursor over the file of his latest chapter, backed up in the Cloud. *Chapter 14: The Deep Speaks.* A double-click, a bit of whirring from somewhere within the computer, and his word processing package loaded up, and then his file. Where had he left it? Ah, yes, his main protagonist had at last made contact with the alien overseer. He began to read from the start, and… *what the fuck?*

DO YOU TRULY BELIEVE?

Someone, somehow, had inserted a comment box at the start of the chapter. It hadn't been him. He was sure of that. Why would he post such an absurd comment in his own manuscript? He rocked the page on the screen up and down with the wheel on his mouse. At the bottom of the page, he noticed another comment.

LOGICAL

This was attached to a paragraph in which one of his characters gave an exposition on the improbability of humankind being alone in the universe. Of course it was logical. Tom still found it hard to comprehend how matters could be otherwise. Sceptics seemed to him to be very shallow thinkers.

Baffled, Tom scrolled further down. There were more comments. Brief. In capital letters. He scrolled to the end to get a sense of how many there were. Half-a-dozen perhaps. And then he returned to the start to read their contents, in turn:

WHAT WOULD THEY WANT?
HOW WOULD YOU KNOW?
HOW WOULD YOU REACT?
WOULD YOU HELP?
And finally, right at the end:
WOULD YOU LIKE TO KNOW MORE? RESPOND TO THESE
COMMENTS AND SAVE IN THE CLOUD

Tom frowned at this last insert and sat back in his squeaky chair. Then, he swivelled his hips left and right, a process that helped him think. What was going on? He wasn't computer savvy at all. He didn't really understand what 'the Cloud' was. To him, it was simply a place to back-up his work so it wouldn't get lost if his computer crashed or got stolen. He paid his subscription and took it on trust that his stored material would be protected. But the privacy issue had initially caused him some concern – mostly because he feared someone might somehow read his embarrassing musings. And now it appeared as though he had been right.

But who would be able to access his work in this mythical other-space? And who would really want to?

He could understand people trying to steal passwords or banking details. He had these stored in other files, also backed up in the Cloud. Maybe he should delete these and change all his passwords?

But back to the novel. Whoever had broken into whatever electronic safe held his work had clearly read the whole chapter. The comments were well-positioned and meaningful. And that didn't sound like the work of a hacker. Unless it was a bored hacker who loved sci-fi. He supposed hackers must be nerds, so maybe that wasn't completely unlikely. But the key issue at the moment was – what was he to do? Look up some sort of cloud helpline and spend a frustrating hour on hold, listening to canned music, and then encountering an uber-nerd who spoke a different language, thence to engage in some unsatisfying exchange that would invariably leave him none the wiser?

First things first.

Tom opened the version of Chapter 14 he'd stored on his hard drive. This was sound and bereft of comments. So, he *hadn't* been imagining things. He saved the Cloud file to his hard drive, giving it a different name. Later, he would find a flash drive and back up his novel on that instead, just in case. But for now?

Tom pulled the keyboard towards him and selected the window containing the altered file. He scrolled down to the final comment, selected the 'reply to comment' function, and typed:

VERY FUNNY. I DON'T KNOW HOW YOU ACCESSED THIS FILE, BUT PLEASE LEAVE IT ALONE

He thought some more, and typed:

THE POLICE HAVE BEEN INFORMED

Weird.

Disturbing, too.

And almost worst of all, a distraction.

Tom saved the file to the Cloud. Then, with his attention and intent disrupted, he did as he always did: he got up from his chair and went downstairs for a cup of tea and to fritter away his time doing something completely different and non-productive.

He truly *was* a waster.

***

Okay. Back to the novel. Tom had squandered Tuesday. On Wednesday, he'd picked at it some more, mostly rewriting a scene in Chapter 13. Now it was Thursday, two days after the peculiar incident. He opened his file again, the one stored in the Cloud, which his computer automatically reached for in preference to the version on his hard drive.

The comments were gone.

Or were they?

Tom scrolled all the way through the chapter, and there, at the end, in answer to his own comment, was another response:

YOUR CONCERN IS UNDERSTANDABLE. I APOLOGISE FOR THE INTRUSION. BUT DO YOU BELIEVE?

Tom frowned. Then he puckered up like a goldfish. Someone still wanted to play. At least they didn't seem to be destructive. Or did they? He returned to the start of the chapter and spent some minutes reading carefully…

Okay – *fine*. There was nothing offensive here. His text hadn't been altered. No surreptitious swear words or other blasphemies had been inserted. And there had been no attempt at humour or sabotage. His main protagonist had *not* been made to say anything ludicrous or corny. In a similar situation, Tom might have been tempted to have Gordon say to the alien contact 'take me to your leader', or some such. But there wasn't even that. So, it wasn't a troll. And there was no demand for a ransom, either. He wasn't being threatened with exposure, or with having other data stolen or abused, which he supposed would have been possible for whomever had the programming sophistication to access his file. So… what then? The message appeared almost humble.

Tom rapped out a tune on the desktop with his knuckles.

What a puzzle!

Where should he go from here?

The prospect of speaking to a helpline still did not appeal. He'd rather visit the dentist. And going to the police? What crime would he report? Malicious respectful communication? Was that a crime?

"Okay," he said aloud. "I'll play along."

Tom added one further response:

OF COURSE I BELIEVE. WHO ARE YOU? AND WHY ARE YOU DOING THIS TO ME?

It wasn't inspired, but he didn't really want to get into a conversation – he just wanted to end this. And yet… he *was* intrigued. He instantly saved the file to whatever mysterious part of the ether such files went and decided to get himself another cup of tea.

Five minutes later, with a steaming brew to hand, Tom settled once more. He opened the remote file again, not really expecting anything, yet somehow excited all the same.

Churn churn.

File downloaded.

Scroll to the end.

Tom jumped – at least metaphorically.

DO NOT BE AFRAID. WE SHOULD MEET. I HAVE MUCH TO IMPART. YOU CAN HELP.

Whoever it was clearly had a lot of time on their hands. Surely they hadn't been waiting these past two days, sat at a keyboard like Tom's, ready to instantly hack, read, and respond? It just didn't make sense. Did he have a stalker? *Him?* Tom actually smiled and shook his head. The very thought! But could it be a joke? A work colleague? Did he have any friends or acquaintances who had the ability to do something like this? Perhaps Manesh? He provided technical support to the faculty. But Tom had rarely spoken to him. What about Brian Francis? Now, he *was* a nerd. He'd embraced new technology to run his research online. Cognitive experiments. Look at this display; record what you see. That sort of thing. And Tom got on tolerably with Brian: they were of a similar age and both utterly useless with the opposite sex.

It was Brian. It had to be. How and why, he did not know. But there was no sensible alternative. Maybe Brian was testing out some newly acquired skills and he was using Tom as a convenient guinea pig? Perhaps there were others? Brian was probably in his office. Maybe he had some sort of alert set up, which was how he managed to respond so quickly?

Okay. He would bite. Tom typed:

FINE. WHERE SHOULD WE MEET?

Save to the Cloud.

Close.

Drink tea.

Check the news. Chris Whitty expected to be made a Duke or something. Biden in hospital again. Markets spooked.

Open file.

Scroll to end.

ST. PETER MANCROFT CHURCH TOMORROW 2PM

Tom smiled. So, whoever this hacker was, who could have been anywhere in the world – Russia? China? – it turned out they knew Norwich well and were able to get to the city for tomorrow.

Brian!

Chapter 2: The First Lesson

To humanity, Norwich was old. According to historians, the city was founded somewhere between the fifth and seventh centuries AD by Anglo-Saxons, close to the older Roman settlement of Venta Icenorum, from which environs had hailed the rampaging Boudicca.

But what is meant by *old?*

To some beings, Norwich's past was still pristine in their individual and collective – biological and synthetic – memories. And these beings knew things that even the best-read historians did not.

For example, they knew the real reason behind the excommunication of the city by Pope Gregory X in 1274 – *apparently* caused by strife between its citizens and the Church's monks. Not only did they know who had *really* started this, but they also knew that the responsible party was neither a scion of Norwich nor even of Earth.

And they knew by what persuasions Robert Kett had been encouraged to lead a famous rebellion in 1549. Some had even felt a touch of alien-analogous guilt on watching the spectacle of Kett's subsequent hanging from the walls of Norwich Castle.

They'd really buggered that one up!

Indeed, these beings knew – both metaphorically *and* literally – where the bodies were buried. *All* of them.

And so they had witnessed the construction of the St Peter Mancroft Church between 1430 and 1455, as well as the various bouts of extension and redevelopment, whether formally recorded or more surreptitiously done. They therefore knew that this rather elegant medieval church, built in the Perpendicular Gothic style, with a long nave and a single tall tower, was architecturally more complex than was currently known to humanity. Indeed, the vicar would have been *most* surprised at what lay beneath his feet…

***

Tom Beresford was an atheist *not* an agnostic. Although he wasn't the most forthright of people, and was more than happy to indulge in the

English pursuits of conflict avoidance, understatement, and use of platitudes, he felt surprisingly strongly about religion and was disinclined to dance around the topic. He knew of others who believed as he did, and were normally much more combative and opinionated, yet who – when faced with religious questions – sought to dissemble: *Believe in God? Well, uh… look over there!*

No, Tom believed in aliens, but not in God. He wasn't *that* crazy!

Although Tom was an atheist, he liked churches. Not what they stood for, but the look of them. They could be truly beautiful. It was astonishing that humanity's primitive forebears had been able to construct such places amid their filthy, stick-and-shit hovels. And so religion, in the end, wasn't all bad. If only they could now re-consecrate these temples to more modern forms of worship – like pubs, as per the converted church he'd once been to in Worcester, or curry houses, like the repurposed place he'd eaten at in Bradford – then the world would be a much better place.

While Tom appreciated churches aesthetically, he didn't really understand them. He knew a few architectural terms, although he couldn't properly define these. The nave was a long corridor down the centre of a church. A chapel was a kind of side room in which the more-dedicated religious nutters could kneel and pray. Pews were seats, with or without cushions. A transept was a sort of cross structure, like the top of a 'T' – he *thought*. And everyone knew that a crypt was like a basement for corpses, and a font was like a little bath for babies and holy water – used to splash people for some incomprehensible reason. Beyond this, well, his knowledge ended. To really understand the architecture of a church would require him to look up information about them online or in a book, which seemed to him a bit creepy and might open him up to accusations of being a secret believer.

Anyway, Tom counted himself fortunate to have ended up in Norwich, which local mythology claimed to have more medieval churches than anywhere else north of the Alps. And of these magnificently picturesque edifices, St Peter Mancroft, perched slightly above and to the side of Norwich's covered market, was one of his favourites. He passed it every week, occupying some central point amid the market, the Art Deco City Hall, the shops on Gentleman's Walk and the Haymarket, the Chantry Place shopping mall, and the Forum (a grand brick building with a vast glass frontage and curved roof that housed Norwich's main library, BBC

TV offices, and other shops and services). The church was also just along from the Garnet – a pub at the edge of the market – from which it could be admired while sitting at an outside table, supping a fine pint of ale.

But perversely, Tom had never, in his dozen years in the city, actually been *inside* the church.

He approached the main portal from the plaza in front of the Forum. The tall, buttressed tower, faced with limestone, had a sheltered porch, with a circular mosaic in black and white set in the stone floor. The entrance here at the west end was of modern glass, with a plaque to the right dedicated to a Mr Samuel Thurston, a notable bell-ringer who'd died in 1841 (as Tom now read, while pausing to gather himself and ensure that he appeared casual to any observer).

With a wry smile, Tom turned from the plaque and pushed open one of the double glass doors. He could already see that there was no one just beyond the door in the small area before the nave and the ranks of wooden seating that faced the altar. Tom paused again here, standing confidently, casting about. Brian was bespectacled, balding, thin, tall, and slightly stooped. He should have stood out. But he didn't. There was a scattering of older people sat on benches to either side of the nave, and an elderly couple heading towards him from the area of the altar. He'd expected Brian to be waiting near the entrance. Tom checked his Seiko. It was eight minutes past the hour. He'd made a point of being a little late, but not *too* late, just to show who was in charge. But was he *ever* in charge? Had he misjudged? He'd actually wanted to arrive a bit early, so that he could surreptitiously view the church entrance from the steps to the Forum's plaza, but he'd mistimed his walk. Had he pushed it too far? Had Brian given up prematurely? Was there another entrance he didn't know about? Or had he been stood up? Perhaps he was being filmed as a joke, and would soon appear in a YouTube video, captioned *Mr Gullible*, or *The Secret Believer*?

Well, he was here now so he might as well have a look. Perhaps Brian was lurking within, maybe behind one of the columns marching towards the altar, or in a side chapel. An image came to mind of a film noir detective in an overcoat with raised lapels and face-shadowing trilby pulled low over the eyes, hunched behind an opened newspaper. That made him smile. He sauntered down the central aisle, continuing to scan from one side to the other, but it was clear that hiding would be difficult:

the church was relatively narrow and had few nooks or annexes, and it was bright from unfiltered light pouring through the tall windows – mostly transparent, with the stained glass having been blown out by the famed Bethel Street explosion in 1647, when ninety barrels of gunpowder had accidentally gone up nearby. The only anomaly in the entire space was an area off to the left of the altar, where a deep blue curtain obscured some minor building works. And there, standing by the curtain, was a man – watching him.

Tom faltered, looked down, looked to the side, then glanced up again. The man had peppery whiskers, a weathered face, and wore a red gilet on which was printed in white, among other words, *The Big Issue*. Tom leant down, pretending to mess about with his knee, as though afflicted by a sudden cramp. *Absurd!* Then he straightened, turning slightly, so that when he took his next steps, he slanted over to the right of the aisle. He tried not to look to the left, but a flick of the eyes revealed that the man – now just three metres away – was still looking at him. Worse, the man now stole forwards – one step, two – and leant casually against a pillar in the empty space near a set of steps leading up to the altar. Tom came to a halt again, now forced to face the man – which he did with a sickly smile. *Not* Brian. Who the fuck…?

"Hello, Tom." The voice was low, calm, accent-less. The eyes were set firm, neither friendly nor unfriendly.

"Uh… hello?"

"The vicar is in the vestry. Quick now. Over here."

"What? I mean… *what?*"

The man turned, stepped over to the curtain, pulled this slightly aside, then looked back. "Please be quick."

The words were somehow compelling. A look back to the entrance revealed no more than half-a-dozen people in the church, scattered through the cavernous space, none showing any interest in him or the other man, none particularly close. And so Tom did as he was instructed, largely because doing otherwise would have involved raising his voice and creating a scene, hence obeying was simply the least embarrassing option.

Tom brushed past the man, who followed close behind. They were now hidden from the rest of the church. Before them, in the whitewashed wall, was a short wooden door with a stone lintel and frame. The man edged past him, produced a large iron key, and opened the door, which creaked ominously. It was dark in the space beyond.

"There is a four-foot drop and no steps, but I have placed a stepladder. Go down backwards, please."

"What?" That was definitely a squeak! "What is that? Where…?"

"The crypt. It is small, but it is secure from observation."

"I'm not going down there!" Tom suddenly found some courage, or at least, resistance, since his fear of dropping into a dark hole exceeded his fear of speaking up. But he kept his voice low, just above a whisper. "And… who are you? What is going on?"

The man was so close he could have given Tom a shove into the darkened space. He was of average height and build, and he didn't look especially strong, but if he moved quickly, he would have momentum and the advantage.

"Please, Tom. I cannot speak here. We must be shielded. Trust me. You will find what I have to say interesting."

There was no hint of threat. And Tom had come this far. "Okay. But you go first."

"Very well. At the top step, pull the door closed after you." The man moved past Tom, turned, and stepped back into the void, found purchase, and then wriggled backwards until he was gone. After a couple of heartbeats, an orange glow came from the space, providing enough light for Tom, now peering in, to see that the sunken room was perhaps the same size as the combined living room and dining room of his house, with a vaulted ceiling and several sarcophagi.

"Fuck!"

"Tom, please be quick."

"What the hell am I doing?" Tom came to the doorway and repeated the actions of the other. At the top step, he pulled the door closed, and only then wondered – in the split second before it clicked – whether it would lock itself or not, potentially trapping him in the crypt with this strange man. Then he stepped back off the ladder and turned rapidly, allowing his two arms to grasp the ladder so that his back was protected.

Only now did the man smile, his face half-lit by a lantern on the floor. The smile seemed functional. It conveyed little, neither pleasure nor sly malice. "Thank you for coming, Tom. I am sorry for the subterfuge. But it is necessary. I must remain hidden – from my side as much as yours."

"Your side? What is going on? Who are you?"

"Please call me *Smith*. I am not what I seem. But then, little is. You suspect this. I have read your work. The notes in your plot files are particularly revealing. You might consider me a *Protector*." Smith moved over to one of the lead-encased coffins and took a perch.

Tom had a thousand questions crowding his mind. He couldn't work out which to voice first, so he started with the mundane. "A… *Protector*? Uh, *great*. Well… well… how did you get into my files? Why?"

Smith's smile disappeared. Was he disappointed somehow? He paused before answering. "We have algorithms that search for interesting information throughout the internet. In emails. In storage spaces, such as the Cloud. The information about you – your profile, your written thoughts – characterise you as someone we think we can talk to. Someone who will believe. Someone who can help."

Tom shook his head. *Hackers!* He'd guessed as much. It wasn't Brian, but someone similar. *We?* Some group? "So… who are you? You still haven't said. A hacker collective?"

"In a way. But much more than that. It is difficult to explain to you in a manner that will enable you to accept it."

Tom was beginning to feel a bit more confident. Okay, he was stuck in a creepy crypt, but he was next to the door and could always shout out if he felt threatened. And he wasn't exactly a weakling. He went to the gym in bouts. He'd studied jiu-jitsu for a year at university as an undergraduate. He wasn't a ninja, but he could probably best the man in front of him, who must have been in his fifties and seemed nothing more than a nerdy hacker.

"Right. But… you still haven't said what you want. If you think I believe in alien conspiracies by the government then, well, *I don't*. And even if I did, I don't see how I could help. If you want me to expose someone… some conspiracy… in my book, then I think you are wasting your time. I'll probably never finish it. And I'll probably never get a publisher to take it on anyway." He smiled sheepishly and shrugged.

Smith observed him for a couple of uncomfortable seconds. At last he said: "This is never easy. Please do not be shocked." He reached behind him and produced a knife – not a particularly big one, but big enough. Tom shrank against the stepladder and opened his mouth to yell, but Smith made no move towards him, and simply extended his left hand, focusing upon it. In horrid fascination, Tom watched as Smith took the knife, rested it upon his open hand, between thumb and index finger, and swiftly drew it down diagonally…

Half of Smith's hand – fingers and all – dropped bloodlessly to the dirty stone floor.

Tom's eyes widened in shock, and he felt his breath catch, rendering him speechless. He looked at the partial hand on the floor, then up at Smith, who swivelled to leave the knife on the coffin, then rotated back to contemplate his mutilated appendage, moving it this way and that, flexing his thumb. Smith then looked up at Tom, but there was no pain in his eyes, and his voice came in the same measured tone.

"Do not be concerned, Tom. I am not in pain. This body is not composed internally the same way as yours. But there is little point in speaking more at present. You need to go away and process this."

At last Tom found his voice. "What the hell! What…?"

Smith leant down and picked up the fallen half of his left hand with his right, which he placed against the site of the amputation. After moving the adjoining flesh around a touch, it seemed to gel. When he took his right hand away, the left was whole again. He wriggled his fingers to check that all now worked. Then he looked back at Tom. "I understand that this is a shock, but what I want from you, Tom, in the first instance, is simply this: *to believe*. I want you to truly believe. Once you do that, we can talk some more. Please leave now. I will be in touch via the Cloud, and next time we can talk more productively."

Tom turned, took two steps up the ladder, vigorously shoved the door open, and scampered from the crypt, his heart beating furiously. He fled from the church without a backwards glance. And once out, it took little effort to decide his next action: he dropped down to Weavers Lane and headed for the Garnet.

Chapter 3: The Second Lesson

It was Saturday, and Tom was still in shock.

No – not shock. Turmoil? Terminal confusion? Meltdown?

What the hell had happened yesterday?

He'd only had a single pint at the Garnet, downed in two minutes, then headed home in a bizarre manner, first ambling, then speeding up, then pausing to sit on an opportune bench, then almost jogging. It had been as though the inconstant meter of his mental processes had somehow transferred to his limbs.

And once he'd gotten home, this staccato rhythm had continued in a more confined space. He'd slouched in front of the TV, then suddenly leapt up to pace to the kitchen. On arriving there, he'd found himself uncertain as to *why* he was there, so he'd returned to the living room. And then he'd bounded up the narrow flight of stairs to his study to scan the news on his computer and check his emails and *think* about opening the latest file of his novel, with finger hovering over mouse button, only to push the mouse away. Then he'd leapt up and paced to the second bedroom – one he hoped to let out one day to help pay down his mortgage – and looked out of the front window onto Muriel Road. After staring outside for ten minutes, he'd returned downstairs to the kitchen, to think about having a tea, start making one, forget about this, return to the sofa, slouch in front of the TV, unseeing, without memory of anything that had been on…

And so on.

He'd not eaten, save for a few salt and vinegar crisps from a packet he'd opened and then listlessly discarded on his small, oval dining room table.

And then he'd gone to bed and tossed and turned.

Eventually, he'd got up to go to his computer. His finger had hovered over the mouse for some seconds, then pushed it away, and he'd returned to bed.

After a little while longer, he'd abandoned bed for a cuppa, but quickly recognised the lack of wisdom of this after the kettle boiled. That would have had him pissing all night! So he'd returned to bed for a bit. Tossed and turned some more. Back to the computer. Open file? Yes. No! *Think think think*. Return to bed…

Now he stood in the galley kitchen, resting both hands upon the laminate, faux-granite kitchen top, looking out the window at the slatted wooden fence that divided his small backyard space from his neighbour's. It was seven, eight, maybe nine. Who knew? God, he was tired.

He desperately needed someone to talk to – but who? He had no one. His last relationship had foundered some years ago. *Eileen.* They'd gotten together as post-docs at Bath University, the relationship managing to survive a further three years following his move to the University of East Anglia. And though he'd initially had something of a social life in Norwich while young enough to associate with the department's post-docs and doctoral students, those years with Eileen had lessened his chances of finding someone new in the happening set, whose members had largely dispersed by the time he was single and available as a consequence of research projects ending and PhDs being completed. And with each churn, each new intake of bright young things, he'd little-by-little become the elder statesman of the group. And then he'd bagged a junior lectureship and found himself perceived as a different creature altogether, no longer quite so welcome in his original circle, expected to socialise with the tenured instead. And this other set was older, usually married, and rarely available for after-work drinks or other activities. Of course, there were a few outliers who didn't quite fit into this mould – like Brian – but that thought made him wince.

In fact, Ged was Tom's last firm friend from the department, but he'd left the previous year on gaining a lectureship at Durham. Now, Tom's social circle had shrunk to two. The first of these was Steve Ritterson – an intense man in his late twenties from whom big things were expected. Alas, Steve worked ferociously long hours and subsequently had little time to socialise, though given he was a bit of a prick, Tom had few regrets about the infrequency of their get-togethers. And the second was Fabio, the 'Italian Stallion', who'd occasionally suggest meeting up to watch football at some sports bar or other, but who only asked Tom because he needed an admirer on whom to shine his knowledge and wisdom, and the Italian knew that Tom was invariably desperate enough to say 'yes'.

So, thought Tom, *I'm a waster* and *a loser.*

No one was going to help Tom decide anything. It was just him and the mysterious Smith: a psychopathic *Big Issue* seller, who possessed a remarkable ability to reintegrate dismembered limbs as well as to hack into hyper-secure internet systems and files. Nothing made sense. The only way this all made sense, especially given Smith's interest in Tom via his nascent sci-fi novel, was that Smith was a…

No!

He couldn't say it.

That was patently absurd!

There was a second explanation, though, which was that Tom was going mad. Had isolation and rejection somehow induced a neurosis? Was he delusional? Dreaming?

But that wasn't right either. Tom closed his eyes and did the mental equivalent of patting himself down, checking for wounds, for something unusual. And there was nothing. Being lonely was his default state, and he'd adapted to that. Oh, sure, he'd once suffered depressive thoughts – for several months after he'd split with Eileen. Split? Well, after she'd dumped him. But he didn't feel now like he had then. Definitely not! So… it seemed he was psychologically sound.

Was there a third option? Nothing immediately came to mind.

What was it Sherlock Holmes used to say? Once you eliminate the impossible, whatever remains, no matter how improbable, must be the truth?

Resolution lay on his computer. It was time to bite the bullet and stop flapping about like a fish on a riverbank. And probably time to stop mixing metaphors and similes. Best leave that for the novel.

***

WHEN YOU ARE READY TO LEARN MORE, REPLY TO THIS

Tom selected the 'reply to comment' function and typed his response at the bottom of Chapter 14, where he'd found the message as expected:

OK

There seemed little need to elaborate.

He saved the file within the Cloud.

How long should he give this? Tom smiled: if he were dealing with some exotic force, then the answer would be 'not long'. He opened the file again – and nodded:

SAME PLACE 2PM TODAY. OK?

That was seriously quick! Whoever had responded – Smith? – must have been literally glued to a computer, opened the file the second it was sent to wherever it was stored, typed with the speed of a professional copy typist, then instantly saved and sent their own response. And they must have already had a plan for how to respond should Tom get back to them.

Again, he typed:

OK

***

Norwich City F.C. were playing at home. As Tom approached the Forum from Bethel Street, passing the Isaac Newton College (a former fire station), the police station, and the city hall, the colour yellow bloomed across his vision. The Canaries fans were out in force in their yellow football shirts and green-and-yellow scarves, often moving in clumps, heading through the centre, making their way to the Carrow Road stadium down by the river Wensum. It was the team's first home game of the season, having won their first game away to Middlesbrough, one-nil. The whole city had a cheery, upbeat air: wending through people in the plaza before the Forum, Tom noticed many smiles and much laughing. Football season had returned, and the city was full of hope.

This time Tom didn't dither. He marched up to the glass portal of St Peter Mancroft, pushed the right-hand door open, and strode into the building. Smith was exactly where he'd been the previous day, lounging by the blue curtain near the north transept. Today, though, the church seemed a bit busier. People praying for victory against Swansea? No – there was not a shred of yellow among the visitors.

Tom's resolve faltered as he approached the man who, as yesterday, was dressed in the red bib of a *Big Issue* seller. As he pulled up to him, Tom diverted his gaze, unable to meet the other's eye.

"Hello, Tom. I am glad you came. There are more eyes today." Smith held up one veined hand. "A moment please. At the sound, *enter*."

"Er, sound? What sou–?"

25

There was a loud clatter from somewhere behind, in the region of the narthex (or 'area at the front of the church', in Tom's limited lingo). It was as though a display board had fallen over – which indeed it had.

Smith twitched the curtain aside. "Quick now."

With a start, Tom resisted looking at the sound behind; he stepped forwards through the curtain, aiming for the scarred wooden door. Smith was right behind him, then quickly manoeuvred in front, key already to hand.

"Great," Tom muttered, "the crypt again."

Smith opened the door, and then turned around to find the stepladder with his feet; he descended from view. As previously, an orange glow appeared in the darkness beyond. Tom followed the other's lead, remembering to close the door as he stood on the second step down.

This time, Tom was somewhat less nervous. He turned about to face the peculiar stranger with less alacrity than previously, and took a step to the right, enabling him to lean against the smooth, cold stone of the crypt, rather than the back-digging rungs of the ladder. The sight of the coffins still creeped him out though.

The two considered each other for some seconds. Tom opened his mouth to speak, but then closed it, unsure of what to say. He waited for Smith to make the first move. At last, the bewhiskered man said: "I have much to tell you, Tom, but I think you need to ask a question first. You know what it is."

"Er… do I? Well, I suppose I do. But I'm not sure how to put it."

"I understand. Take your time."

Tom puffed out his cheeks, looked down, frowned, then looked up and firmed his expression. "Okay, Mr Smith. Who exactly are you?"

"*Who?* Is that the correct term?"

Tom nodded slightly. "Okay. *What* exactly are you?"

"What do you think I am?"

Tom was feeling more relaxed now. Smith was three or four metres away, still rather weak-looking, and there was no sign of a knife. And there was no hint of menace, either. The man rested against a coffin in an easy manner, his expression serene.

"This is getting like twenty questions!"

"I'm sorry, Tom, but I cannot say this thing first. There is no way I can state my truth without it seeming absurd. Or leading. You must volunteer your understanding freely."

"Okay. I kind of see what you mean. I wondered about this moment of meeting in my... novel." Tom's voice dropped slightly in embarrassment, as it always did whenever he mentioned his unfinished pretention. "I think... I think that you are not entirely human."

A smile actually twitched at the corner of Smith's face. "Not entirely? So, partly human?"

This fencing could go on for some time. Tom had earlier decided, back home, to bite the bullet. *So bite!*

"Fine. You're not human at all. You're an al... An al..."

"It's difficult, isn't it? At least, it is for an intelligent man like you. You understand something of nature. Of probability. Of humankind's likely small imprint on a vast universe. I would be more worried if you were able to say this thing easily. In fact, I might suspect you were a touch mad. Yet, still I would like to hear you say it."

Bullet truly bitten: "Fine then. You're an... *alien*. You know and can do things humans can't. Not even Elon Musk. But you look human. And though I believe there is some logic to parallel evolution – that life is likely to repeat similar forms in response to similar selection pressures – your form is far, far too close to ours to be convincing. So, are you some sort of body snatcher?" And as he said it, in the sudden dam-release of words, he whitened and pushed himself back into the wall. *Body snatcher!*

"I knew you were the right choice. Our algorithms are very, very good. Calm yourself, Tom. I did not pillage this body from one of these tombs."

"No?"

"No. It is a synthetic hydrocarbon device, vat-grown and programmed to this shape and functionality. Internally, it is consistent and malleable, which is why I did not bleed yesterday. There are no internal organs. And this device gains its working energy by absorbing its needs from background radiation. In a sense, *I* am not actually here, in this space with you, but elsewhere."

"A spaceship?" Tom blurted.

"You mean, a UFO? Tom, you were doing so well. Please just accept that my true physical form is in another place. And as you recognise in your novel, I am but one being from one species among many." Then he repeated, with unusual emphasis: "*many*."

"Uh, *wow*. So, what… who…?"

"Are you experiencing mental overload? That would not be unusual. It tends to take three of four intercessions before we are able to establish a working relationship. Would you like to return to the Garnet for something to steady your nerves? We can meet again in a few days to carry on."

Tom took several deep breaths. *Alien?* He'd thought it. And now he'd said it. And that somehow made it real. And though Smith looked human – mundanely human – he clearly knew and could do otherworldly things. Tom mentally searched for signs of panic, or shock, or fear, but found nothing. He was barely even *amazed*. Humans had a great capacity to adapt and accept, and he had already done just that. And realising this, his breathing calmed and he gently pushed himself from the wall into which he had momentarily tried to burrow.

"No. I'm fine. In fact, I'm surprisingly fine. Let's carry on."

Smith nodded. "An excellent find indeed! Good. I think we will be able to work together. So, Tom, I need your help. But first, I am sure you have some questions. I can satisfy your curiosity to some extent – *quid pro quo* – though you must appreciate that what I can tell you is limited for your own good, and also for mine."

Tom nodded. "So, you'll not be telling me the formula for immortality or the secret to nuclear fusion or interstellar space travel?"

"You are correct."

Where to begin? There were a thousand questions he might ask and, in a rush, Tom attempted to ask them all at once. "Soooo… why are you here? What do you want from me? What is your purpose? And why are we meeting in this creepy crypt? And… and…"

Smith held up a hand to stem the flow. "Tom, please. *Mea culpa*. This often happens. Perhaps you will allow me instead to volunteer what I can, and then you can ask for clarifications?"

Tom blew out his cheeks. He'd liked being described as an *excellent find* but now feared he might have blotted his copybook through his verbal explosion. *Calm! You're a representative of the human race!*

"Sorry. I'm fine, really. Yes, you go on."

Smith nodded, then momentarily closed his eyes – something Tom had not seen him do before. When he opened them, he gave a gentle smile. "I can start with your last question. This *creepy crypt*, as you call it, is shielded from prying eyes. It is connected to one of a number of tunnel systems that lie under Norwich, built by your forebears many years ago, often secretly. As the vicar has now left the church, we can move somewhere more comfortable."

The man (alien?) pushed off from the coffin on which he had been resting, leant down to pick up his glowing orange lantern, turned around, and took three paces to the far wall. Tom couldn't see what he did, but suddenly there was a faint crack of light to Smith's right – a vertical line from the floor to waist level. The other bent down and turned to look at him. "Follow me, please."

Tom moved up behind Smith as the crack of light expanded dramatically, revealing a hobbit-sized doorway into a well-lit space beyond. Tom followed Smith through to a vaulted corridor, several metres long, with a wooden barrier about knee high, which Tom had to somehow hurdle while bent double. Once he straightened up, he realised that the barrier was actually a section of long bench that ran along the corridor wall and was replicated on the facing side. A long rail of coat pegs stretched most of the way along the corridor too, again on both sides. To Tom's left was a wide, arched, glass window – through which he could see part of the grassy slope of the graveyard – which had a desk before it and a large crucifix upon this. To his right, various boxes and crates cluttered the corridor, sitting upon a thin carpet, with several wooden doors to either side of the space and some double doors at the far end.

Smith had crossed the corridor and now sat on the opposite bench. "We can talk here. Please sit."

As Tom fully emerged from the low doorway, it swung closed, disappearing seamlessly into the wall. He looked about in surprise for a moment, getting his bearings. Then he settled back onto the portion of bench he'd previously stepped over. "What is this place?"

"This is known as a *processional way* or *chancel passageway*. We are under the high altar. This space is out of bounds to the public. It is largely used by the vicar and his staff for offices and storage. Over there…" Smith indicated to his left and Tom's right, "is a larger room that used to be the Octagon Café, built in 1983 as an add-on to this ancient way, closed in

2013 after losing considerable amounts of money, and now occasionally used for various church and community group functions. We should have at least half an hour before there is a risk of us being disturbed. I will let you out the far door when you leave. Is this sufficiently less creepy?"

Tom gave a relieved sigh and smiled. "Yes. This is great. Thanks."

"Good. Now to continue. Among your questions, you asked why I am here. You asked about my purpose. That is easy to answer, or difficult, depending upon the depth of your enquiry. Philosophically, I cannot say for myself or my species. We exist as we wish, not according to the external whim or devices of others, whether Gods..." and at this his face adopted an almost wry expression, and he waved a hand to indicate their surrounds, "or other creatures. And I wish this was true for your species, Tom, although it is not."

Tom frowned deeply. "Sorry. I don't understand. Are you saying that we – humans – *do* have a purpose, or that we *don't?*"

Smith thought for a moment. "What I am saying, Tom, is that humans, unlike my species, *do* have a purpose, it is just not entirely one of their own."

"What is it then?"

"To entertain others. To live, to add nuance and texture to the universe, and then to die and make way for the next generation. In short, you and your species are effectively *extras* in an extremely long movie. But this does not mean that you are unimportant. Far from it. All movies need extras, as well as a few stars. I like to think of you, Tom, and the majority of the human race, as *Betas.*"

Tom startled at this – at the use of a term he had so often used to describe himself. "Extras in a film? I still don't get it. Do we have free will or not? Are we controlled?"

"Not controlled. Not really. Though some Betas are actively *promoted*. They are made to become stars. Or *Alphas*. The benefit of having such a great pool of extras is that sometimes someone does something that stands out and makes those in control – let us call them *Directors* – think 'ah, now this is interesting!' At that point, a person may essentially be promoted."

"Directors? Other species? But not yours?"

"No. Not mine."

Tom wasn't sure how to feel. Or what angle to take. But the mention of *promotion* and *stars* momentarily excited him. Could this be why he had been approached? What were his prospects? He decided to proceed cautiously. "This sounds... incredible. It must be great to be chosen to be a star... an Alpha."

Smith smiled with his mouth only. "Perhaps. But I must give a word of warning. Betas are largely left to chance and their own devices. Alphas may be manipulated in ways that are not always positive."

"What do you mean?"

"Many Alphas are creatives. They are protected because they provide something. Music. Art. Literature. In many cases, they are protected because the Directors wish to collect product. They are the well-fed geese that lay the golden eggs."

Tom frowned in thought. "That doesn't sound negative."

"In general, no. But for some, tragedy can act as a stimulus. Sometimes humans can do astonishing things in response to misfortune, producing great books or works of art, or inspiring some form of crusade. Ironically, is this not one of the assertions made by some of your religions? That God allows human misery because it is a crucible through which a person might emerge, hardened, reformed, and enlightened? In such cases, being in the eye of the Directors is not a good thing. Still, many Alphas are left alone with only minimal interference."

Hopeful nonetheless, Tom continued cagily: "It still sounds like there are more positives than negatives. And who are chosen for stardom?" *Novelists*, Tom thought/hoped, but instead asked: "Great scientists?"

"No. That is a bad example, Tom. The Directors know science, so what would a scientist give them? Alphas are generally influencers. Politicians. Leaders. Celebrities. Or as I said, creatives. You need to understand what it is that Directors are seeking. Think of the question: what do you buy as a present for the person with everything? The answer is not necessarily another expensive car. This is why the human idea of aliens as roving, planet-stealing warriors is absurd. And I am glad that you recognise this in your embryonic book, Tom. When you have the science to cross the gulfs of space, you have the science to do almost anything. Why would any species want someone else's rock when it has access to the immeasurable resources of the galaxy? No. Think more of an all-powerful Gulliver coming onto Lilliput. Would he want to destroy it? Or would he rather observe it in fascination?"

Tom could still hear Smith's words about 'producing great books'. "So… entertainers, not scientists?"

"Entertainers among others, yes. For example, there is a species that collects music from creatures from a thousand planets. They have a particularly high regard for human music. They have intervened on a number of occasions to ensure that certain singers have gained opportunities that might never have arisen, such as by interfering with the voting on talent shows. Leona Lewis is one of their achievements. They love her."

Tom couldn't hide his astonishment. "I always liked her voice. These Directors have great taste! So… where does that leave us? Am I… am I to be promoted? To an Alpha?"

Smith's face adopted a peculiar expression, his eyes moving in a disjointed way. Tom got the impression that the other was working something out. At last, Smith said: "I think, Tom, I may have given a false impression. You recall I said my species was not one of these Directors?"

"Er, yes."

"Well, Tom, here is the issue. This meddling, this promotion of extras into stars, is not allowed. It is illicit. In the prologue to your novel, you correctly anticipate that the galaxy is full of many species. And these species have an agreement. An ethos. Primitive species – by which I mean, *unknowing* species – are not to be disturbed. The great galactic community observe, in fascination, but are not meant to interfere. Alas for some – the Directors – the temptation is too great."

"So, you're not a Director? I am not to be promoted? I am to remain… a Beta?" *Forever.*

"I am sorry, Tom. I did not wish to raise your hopes. But *nil desperandum*. I hope I can offer you something else of value. Something that even the Alphas do not have."

"What's that? A shiny ray gun? A mind-reading device?" Tom knew he was now being absurd and flippant, but he couldn't help himself.

"No. What I offer you is *awareness*. You see, Tom, Alphas have no awareness that the greater galactic community exists. They generally see their advancement as a result of talent. Sometimes they appreciate that luck has also played a role. But they are ignorant in a way that you – already

32

– are not. I cannot promote you to an Alpha, Tom. But I can give you a different position." He suddenly sat upright, and his eyes closed. "Ah. Unfortunate timing. The lady volunteer who helps out is rapidly approaching. I fear we must terminate this session." He stood up. "Follow me. I'll let you out by the Octagon." He started towards the double doors at the end of the corridor.

Tom leapt to his feet and followed. Speaking to Smith's back, he blurted: "What position? What do you want from me?"

They reached the doors. Smith produced a set of keys and attacked the lock, pushing one door half open. He looked back at Tom, whose face was a picture of confusion. "Position? Well, Tom, how would you like to help me thwart these Directors in order to maintain The Agreement? To put a stop to their meddling? Not an Alpha, then, but an *Omega*?"

Tom felt the blood flush from his face. "An Omega? I… I… YES! Er, *probably*. I mean, what would it involve?"

"There's no time now, Tom. She is in the chancel, approaching the stairs down to this passageway. Quick. I will contact you in the usual manner."

Tom jerked towards the door, then straightened, gave the alien a sickly smile, and brushed past him. He found himself on the south side of the church, on a narrow path to the right of the flint-knapped Octagon extension, with a waist-high iron gate at its end. Beyond this was a small plaza, dominated by a statue of the polymath Sir Thomas Browne, but better known for being the location of a McDonald's.

On weak legs, Tom attained the gate, opened it, and escaped the church to the plaza. He turned an immediate left, cutting down Weavers Lane between the church and a short line of shops, to the Garnet. And as he staggered along, the thought that dominated his mind was this: *An Omega… A fucking Omega!*

Chapter 4: Interlude

It was a heads-down sort of day for Jim Taylor…

He'd rowed with Marie last night – and boy, could she hold a grudge! They'd barely spoken this morning, and then she'd sulked off with the kids – to drop them off at school and then continue to her workplace at County Hall. His wife had taken the family car, of course, although that was normal and proper, given that she had further to travel. In any case, Jim didn't mind the modest, half-hour stroll to work (provided it wasn't raining) at the Norwich University of Arts, in a building just north of the city centre. And living in the Golden Triangle – an area of Victorian terraces just west of the centre, *des res* of students and the bourgeoisie – his journey took in some interesting and pleasant urban vistas.

Jim cut down a residential street onto Earlham Road and followed this to its end, where it boomeranged around the gothic Roman Catholic Cathedral before becoming Unthank Road. Here, he took a pedestrian bridge over the inner city ring road, which dropped him onto Upper St Giles – a quaint street of independent shops.

Normally, Jim would have marched confidently, using his umbrella as a walking stick, taking in the enticing sights in the windows of the various delis, coffee shops and galleries. But after the chilled atmosphere at home, he felt rather sensitive and less inclined to risk catching the eye of pedestrians or shop workers in case his expression betray that *here be a cowed man*. Instead, he marched stiffly, with eyes cast down at the pavement, his umbrella clicking time on the concrete. Even so, the view was not bland: the local council and community had been concerned with preserving and beautifying this part of the city – the 'Norwich Lanes' – as part of which a large number of pavement plaques had been emplaced, designed by a local artist to tell the story of the city's industrial and social past. He shortly came across the first of these plaques, depicting a king's head (as from a playing card), the central motif being bordered by small tiles in various shades of green. The tile in the bottom right corner was a stylised logo for the Lanes, and a small inscription beneath the main picture read: *THE KING'S HEAD PH 1760-1914.*

Jim paused to consider the plaque: he must have walked over it a thousand times, and yet he'd never really looked at it. He liked the green tiles, which reminded him of verdigris. So, a public house used to stand here? It had been replaced by a shop called The Plant Den, which held an attractive display of greenery in the front window. Nice – though incapable of quenching the thirst in quite the same way as the bygone pub, which was a shame.

A little further along, he came to a second plaque with a similar, green-tiled outline, this one showing a pair of boots with the title: *JAMES MAY BOOT AND SHOE MANUFACTURER*. Here, the replacement venture seemed an improvement to Jim, for in place of a business of leathered footwear was one selling a tempting array of cupcakes – albeit a shop he'd never previously visited, given he was never hungry on his outward trek, and it was always closed by the time he made his return journey.

A little further, outside the church of St Giles on the Hill, a third plaque showed *ST. GILES WITH HIND*, the eponymous saint being depicted hugging a deer. Jim smiled and tried to put aside lewd thoughts.

Upper St Giles now became just plain old St Giles, and the small businesses here were interspersed with grander edifices. A picture of a set of scales representing the *STREET OF SOLICITORS* was planted near his favourite second-hand bookshop. But more surprising was the plaque after this, in which a collation of compass, set-square and globe was accompanied by the title *NORWICH MASONIC HALL*. This made Jim pause again. Freemasons? In Norwich? And indeed, the broad, stone building, with pillars to either side of black double doors, had signage that declared it to be the St Giles Rooms Norwich Masonic Association. He'd lived in Norwich for over ten years and never known about this. What other mysteries did the city hold?

A plaque with a picture of a telephone was labelled *TELEPHONE HOUSE BY SKIPPER 1906*. This was set outside a grand, baroque building of stone and pillars: the St Giles House Hotel. He'd never been inside the place, which had always seemed rather too plush for him, but hadn't it once featured in a TV documentary series? He vaguely recalled the name: *From Hell to Hotel*.

The next plaque was only a dozen metres further away, outside The Waffle House. This was titled *STREET OF DENTISTS AND*

SURGEONS and showed a wicked looking hypodermic syringe. Jim faltered at the sight of this. While his mood had been gradually lightening with the discovery of new things, there was something about this particular engraving that was somehow troubling. *Discordant.* Jim set himself foursquare to the picture, opposite the glass frontage of the eatery beyond, so that he could fully appreciate the design. It was a devilish looking instrument, which seemed to almost push out from the pavement, seeking to jab him and any others who got too close. And there was something more, something at the edge of consciousness, some other component to the design, another message. Jim frowned and shook his head as though to clear it of some unwanted thought...

Junkies.

His frown twitched and deepened.

Fucking junkies.

What... what was he thinking?

He at last dragged his gaze from the image and took a half step away. Then a young man in a red jacket squeezed between him and the shop front, momentarily obscuring the plaque, and breaking whatever spell Jim was under. Without a backwards glance, he rapidly turned and moved on.

But his brightening mood had darkened. Jim carried on, though quicker than before. He continued to scour the pavement, but with lessened interest in the revelations beneath his feet. There were three more plaques on St Giles: three cupcakes were labelled *JAMES FREEMAN BAKER*, and then a prancing horse was accompanied with the text *BLACK HORSE PH 1763-1970*, while another old pub – the *SUN STORES PH 1839-1889* – was commemorated with a smiling sun. By this time, he was in the centre, with the medieval Guildhall ahead, a building faced in grey flint and ashlar stone. But Jim did not look up; he turned down Lower Goat Lane. There was just a single plaque here, showing two acorns and an oak leaf, with the legend *OAK SHADES PH 1864-1959*. Alas – another long dead pub.

Jim emerged opposite the Strangers coffee shop and another plaque that showed two spools of thread with the caption *THE STRANGERS WERE 15C WEAVERS*.

Strangers? Norwich had had many unusual visitors during its long history, though the Flemish weavers were commemorated more than most in a multitude of local company names and buildings.

Jim kinked left, past the well-regarded Grosvenor Fish Bar, with St Gregory's Church directly ahead forming one side of a small triangle of space – St Gregory's Green – that was also bounded by a low, brick-built pub (currently *to let*) and several small shops. The Green used to be a somewhat dishevelled space, a favoured haunt of the homeless and unemployed, being close to a job centre and hostels (including a YMCA), although it had been gentrified over recent years. The central diagonal paving now bore a large, oval-shaped piece of artwork in a similar style to the plaques, listing the names of many local notables, while the space beside the church had acquired a number of small tables associated with a nearby coffee shop (the Al-Chemista) – a vestige from the Covid epidemic that had led to a growth in the use of outside spaces in the city.

As Jim crossed the Green, he noticed a small group congregated in the corner of the space at the far end of the church next to a tree with pink blossoms. Though gentrification had displaced some of the rowdy elements, it hadn't displaced them all: in spite of the early hour, the trio in the corner held illicit cans of beer and bellowed at each other irrespective of their mutual closeness. Normally, Jim would have shrugged off the sight – if he noticed it at all – but today… today he felt different. The loud, slurred voices grated. Then he noticed that the table nearest to the inebriates held a pair of pensioners, scrunched over their coffees and clearly uncomfortable at the raucous assembly not two metres distant, while the table next to them was occupied by a young woman with a wailing toddler in a pushchair who was trying to calm the child while stealing glances at the men.

Jim slowed and then came to a complete halt. Into his head popped an image: *Syringe.* And suddenly he felt unaccountably *angry*. He whisked his umbrella forwards and back, like the tail of an angry cat. He looked at the trio, and then back at the tremulous people, cowering away from the barrage of swearing and coarse laughter.

Something ought to be done.

Someone ought to do something.

He was someone.

Jim's legs seemed to have a mind of their own. He experienced a moment of surprise as he found himself rapidly propelled across the paving that cut diagonally across the Green and onto the small patch of grass separating this from the blooming tree and medieval church. The men didn't notice until he was beside them.

"It's illegal to drink on the street," said Jim, again surprised at himself. He hadn't planned what words to use; they came naturally. "Please stop. And move on. You're creating a nuisance."

"Eh? Eh? What you say?" The closest man, who could have been anywhere between twenty-five and thirty-five, wore a surprisingly high-quality puffer jacket. Unlike his colleagues, he didn't hold a can, but he was clearly already intoxicated in one way or another. His two colleagues – one in his twenties, the other perhaps in his forties, both stubbled – turned to stare.

The man swayed, then got control of his tongue. "What you sayin' man? Who're you? Fuck off."

"Yeah, fuck off," repeated the man in his twenties. "You can't tell us what to do."

Jim felt his heart beating hard in his chest. This wasn't like him at all – but these words needed saying. "I am asking you to stop and move on. *Politely*."

"Or what?" said the eldest of the trio. "What you gonna do? Call the police?" He laughed and waved his can about. "This'll be gone before the pigs turn up, and then you got *nuffin*!"

The youngest man laughed and leaned in to his colleague to tap cans, which he did more energetically than intended, causing a small amount of beer to fountain out of the top.

"Yeah, and I ain't drinkin!" said the closest man. "It's my human right to be here!"

"Your… *right?*" Jim felt his anger growing. *Syringe.* "Your right to terrify these people?" he waved at the elderly couple off to the side.

"If they're terr-fied, it's their fuckin bag. They can piss off too."

And Jim lost it.

He stepped in, sliding the umbrella along his hand so that he was holding it near to its metal tip, then using the crook to sweep the can out of the hand of the youngest of the party. He then swung the umbrella back to connect with the can of the oldest one – who shied away and managed to cling onto his drink. At the sudden burst of activity, the man in the puffer jacket reared away, staggering unsteadily. The trio were at first too stunned to react, not helped by their mental incapacity. But then the youngest lunged at Jim, emitting an inchoate roar.

The assault knocked Jim back, but without much force, as the other had misjudged the distance: he slid off Jim and onto his face. The older man turned away to protect his precious can, but puffer-man decided he was up for a fight and swung a looping punch, which glanced off Jim's shoulder, twisting him around. There was a shout from behind, and as Jim completed his turn, he noticed the male pensioner – with mouth open wide – now standing protectively by his partner. He also noticed that the Green seemed to have filled in the short time since he had decided to act: people were scattered throughout the space, individually and in pairs, along with one small group of students.

Facing the inebriates once more, Jim saw the youngster clamber to his feet with a curse, and then puffer-man was at him again, his next punch catching Jim in the ear with a sting of pain…

The fight that followed probably lasted less than a minute but seemed to Jim to last an hour. He used his umbrella to fend off the two assailants (while the third shouted insults in the background) as they staggered back and forth across the Green. The crowd around grew, and soon catcalls emanated from it – some encouraging Jim, but others in support of the rogues. Yet it was a largely ineffectual affair: Jim got barged and punched a couple of times and managed to shove the handle of his brolly into the youngster's nose and to deliver a weak, left-handed punch to the top of puffer's head.

At last, the crowd parted, and a pair of constables wearing high-vis vests appeared, at which the combatants instinctively disengaged.

What followed was something of a blur to Jim. There had been shouting, then a policeman had firmly grasped him by one arm. Almost immediately, people from the crowd had surrounded them, volunteering differing accounts of the affair; among these was a young woman with short hair and a nose ring who'd claimed to be a reporter for the *Eastern Daily Press*. Shortly after that, another pair of constables turned up…

Jim was late to work that morning, following an enforced detour to the Bethel Street police station, where he'd been interviewed, formally cautioned, and then sent on his way with a warning that prosecution might or might not follow.

It was close to lunchtime before he slunk into his office, having phoned to say he'd been unaccountably delayed. His work colleagues naturally probed the reason for his absence, though he successfully fobbed them off. But then, mid-afternoon, Jill Swanley excitedly denounced him: apparently, the *EDP* reporter had filmed much of the event on her mobile phone, and the footage was being played on local news channels.

Jim left the second he was legitimately able to. He had no idea what he was going to say to Marie. She probably wouldn't speak to him for a week, although that might not be a bad thing.

Back on St Giles Street, outside The Waffle House, Jim's legs buckled and he nearly fell. There was that plaque again, the one representing the street of dentists and surgeons. He came to a halt, and then deliberately crossed the street. Nevertheless, throughout the remainder of his walk home, there was an image he just could not get out of his head.

Syringe.

Chapter 5: The Third Lesson

"Why couldn't we meet here before, instead of the crypt?" Tom had been let in through double doors that had once provided entry to the Octagon Café, and now followed Smith as they picked their way past boxes on the floor.

"This place is well used. It is also less well shielded from others' eyes – by which I mean, sensory apparatus, as eyes are not the only organ used to see by our multifarious watchers. Please sit." Smith indicated a bench along the wall of the passageway where they'd sat last time. "I wanted to be sure you wouldn't lose the plot and run screaming from the church, which might well have drawn attention."

Tom smiled at this as he settled on the bench under a length of coat pegs. He had, all things considered, remained quite calm during their first two meetings. He felt a momentary pang of pride. Having frankly had little to be proud of in life, demonstrating equanimity in the face of a monumental, life-altering shock surely had to go in the credit column? He rapidly reined in his smile and adopted what he hoped would appear to be a sage and thoughtful expression.

"So, I have passed the test?"

"You have indeed. But neither the crypt nor this passageway is an ideal meeting point, so next time I will suggest somewhere more accessible. But now to business. Matters are afoot, and I need your help."

"Has this got something to do with the Directors?"

Smith gave a wry smile in response – or what Tom interpreted to be a wry smile. Did aliens experience 'wryness'? That was an issue worth further consideration!

"Just so. But first some context. As I hinted last time, there are many species in the galaxy, of many different shapes and sizes, with many different levels of advancement. We are too many, and too different, to form any sort of cohesive body. There is no galactic government, no set of statutes, and no policing organisation. The non-interference agreement I talked about is rather an informal commitment, which most adhere to, and which some believe in more than others."

"But not these Directors? Who are they?"

"It is impossible to fully enumerate or characterise them. They also differ according to the planet under observation. The Directors on Earth are not the same as those on the nearest planet of other Unaware Sentients. It is probably fair to say that Directors tend to be morphologically similar to the species being manipulated – as intelligent beings tend to be most interested and entertained by creatures like themselves. Morphologically similar now or at some time in their past, perhaps before they became post-corporeal, before Transcendence."

"Post-corporeal? Like post-human? Without bodies?"

"That is correct. This appears to be a typical evolutionary path. Most species eventually shuck off the form they had when they first attained sentience. The post-corporeal species are almost impossible to count, and often exist in places invisible or unknowable to the rest of us. And they also tend to be less concerned about The Agreement, or indeed, about anything else the rest of us get up to. They do their own thing and leave little imprint. *Generally*. But there are exceptions."

Smith actually frowned after delivering the last statement. *That's odd*, thought Tom. "Exceptions?"

Smith literally waved this away. "That is a topic for another time. What I want to get across now, is that my species is one of a number that strongly believe in keeping to The Agreement. We consider it our moral duty to species such as yours to allow them to progress unmolested. Unfortunately, in doing so, we occasionally have to interfere ourselves, by recruiting people such as you, Tom. It's all about balance. Of doing a little harm to prevent greater harms."

"And you've chosen me to be one of these helpers? An *Omega?*" Tom still loved the word and the idea. It certainly marked him out as someone beyond the common stock; as special in a peculiar way. And wasn't that really what everyone wanted?

"Yes. We have observed humans for many years and understand you to a high degree. We have sophisticated algorithms to identify useful people who are liable to understand us and help. We are not always right, but we mostly are. And as you might imagine, when we are wrong, there are rarely repercussions."

Tom nodded. "It's about believability, isn't it? There are so many crazies out there, spouting off about UFOs, that no one believes them. And they wouldn't believe me, either."

"Just so. We understand each other perfectly."

"Okay. I get this. It's logical. In fact, some of these are ideas in my book, er… *story*." Tom winced. "But what I don't get is, why *here*? Why are you in Norwich, of all places? Surely there is little of interest happening here? Why not in LA? Or Moscow? Or at least, London?"

Smith gave a gentle smile. "Tom, I have already told you there are many of us. Take the next logical step."

"Ah. Right. If there are many of you then… you *do* have, er, agents – or whatever you call yourselves – everywhere. In LA? Moscow?"

"And London. Bratislava. Hyderabad. Tokyo. In the biggest cities and even some of the smallest villages. Almost every part of this world has its fans. For example, there's a borough of London that has drawn the attention of over a score of species. It's prime entertainment real estate with unbelievable levels of illegal meddling and countermeasures. And there's a rural area in the USA that has several hundred keen observers, and has done ever since a monumental blunder by one species of Directors over sixty years ago. And some of these species just cannot help themselves from further tinkering."

Tom's eyes widened as realisation dawned. "Ah, I guess you're talking about a certain area of New Mexico?"

Smith nodded once, slowly.

"But still, Roswell versus Norwich? It's hard to comprehend why anyone would prefer to follow *us*."

"No, Tom, it really isn't." Smith looked ahead and his eyes seemed to flicker as though reading an invisible script. Then the flickering stopped and he looked back. "Tom, what are the most popular television programmes? Which programmes, in general, gain the greatest audiences – and I mean overall, over time? Views multiplied by length and frequency of programme."

"I get you. You mean soap operas. One-off spectaculars – Royal Weddings, or major sporting events – might get the highest figures for a single episode, but overall it's got to be soaps. Lots of people watch them, and there are lots of episodes. That's what you mean, isn't it?"

"Precisely. And you have been watched, as a species, for so very, *very* long. And tell me, Tom, how often in *East Enders* does an alien spacecraft crash in Albert Square? Or come to that, anything else dramatic take place? A nuclear explosion? Plague? French invasion?"

43

"Er, not often. Well, it couldn't really, could it? Those stories wouldn't be credible. And you could only do them once."

"As you people sometimes say, *bingo*. I like you, Tom. You get things quickly. The Earth and its people are in a soap opera, not a major motion movie. Yet there are some who still like to spice things up and throw in the occasional improbable plot line. Industrial accident. Plane crash. And so on."

"So, what exactly do you want from me? How can I possibly help?"

"The Directors have been frustrated over the last seventy or eighty years. Not much on Earth has happened since World War Two. The Cold War and the Space Race were momentarily fun, but they petered out. Then there were the events in New York on 'seven-eleven'. There have been few really grand events since."

"What about Covid? The pandemic?"

"A good call, Tom. That was different. But was it actually natural? There are some of us who wonder if that might not have been helped along in some way."

"You're kidding!"

Smith actually shrugged. It was a very human gesture. "I cannot say for sure. In any case, there seem to be more and more attempts to tinker with the script – some at a grand level, but mostly at the local level, and that includes in Norwich. So, I want you, Tom, to be an additional set of eyes for me, and occasionally, even a set of hands. I will instruct you what to look out for – how to really see with those eyes of yours. And then you can pass on anything untoward for my consideration."

"Like a kind of spy?"

"Indeed. That is one possible framing. I assume from the excitement in your voice that you are up for it?"

Tom's heart really was racing. He felt like a teenager about to set out on his first independent holiday, arriving at the airport and catching sight of his milling friends clustered around a mound of rucksacks. He'd not felt like this in many years. Yet, he was also aware of a need to appear professional, serious, intelligently detached. His attempts to calm himself couldn't prevent an odd pricking sensation from settling over his scalp or stop his hands from sweating. He licked his lips and croaked: "Mr Smith… *yes*. I am up for it. I am your man."

"Splendid!" Smith now stood up. A set of keys appeared in his hands. "Then let us begin. There is no time like the present. Come. I want to show you something."

***

At the door to the exit by the Octagon, Smith paused with keys in hand, turning to Tom. "We won't go far, as I am somewhat constrained. As I told you, this place is shielded from the senses of a vast number of species, but once outside, I am more visible. This physical form has characteristics that cloak it from the cameras of watchers. But only for six minutes and thirty-two seconds, or thereabouts. So, stick close, keep up, and please follow instructions precisely. Ready?"

"Sure. Let's do this!"

Smith unlocked the door and strode out. He went through the gate at the end of the path, turned left, and left again, and they tracked along the east side of the church, down Weavers Lane. The market opened up before them, but they paused by a red telephone box just shy of it, with the Garnet pub to their left.

"There are phone boxes around town," declared Smith, "and these are also shielded, allowing my form to reset its cloak timer, so if we overstay and I bolt into this, please do not be alarmed."

"A bit like Superman?"

"Perhaps. But let's focus. Tom – I want you to look out for signs. They are everywhere. And some of them are less innocent than they appear. Now, take these." Smith suddenly had a pair of glasses in his hand, which he held out to Tom.

"Sunglasses?"

"Yes. But with a difference. These have a special coating that will aid your sight. I will explain later. Please put them on and go to the edge of the market. I want you to walk up and down, looking at all the different signs along that aisle. Then come back and report."

Tom gave a half smile, accepted the glasses, and put them on. They seemed like a normal pair of sunglasses, giving the world a slightly darkened tint. "Well... off I go."

The stall directly in front, at the edge of the market, sold watches. There were all sorts of messages here, advertising watches, straps, batteries. *FITTED WHILE U WAIT*, declared one prominent headline. Tom spent perhaps a minute just staring, not really certain what he was looking for, taking advantage of the fact that the proprietor had his back turned and seemed to be effecting some sort of stocktake of his merchandise. When the man turned around, Tom hurriedly looked away, turned left, and continued up the aisle. He carried on to the end, not really sure what he was meant to be doing or seeing. To his left was a pizza place set into a long, low stone building, with a shop selling clothes and shoes beside this, and then public conveniences further along; to his right, the covered stalls – effectively grey-green booths with out-jutting striped covers of different colours – sold more clothes, plants, bric-a-brac. Then he came to stone steps that led up one level to a narrow patio of benches and shrubs that ran along the length of the market, with a second set of steps up to the street that ran before City Hall.

He turned around and returned to where he had started, quickly glancing to his right, where Smith stood patiently by the phone box. There were a couple more stalls to that side, which he had ignored first time: these sold all sorts of oddities, from e-cigarettes to perfumes. Forward of this point, beyond a few more stalls lining the aisle, was the pedestrianised Gentleman's Walk and the elegant arches that formed the entrance to the Royal Arcade. And one of these other stalls had a big blue sign announcing *SHOE REPAIRS* as well as a small metal sign on the pavement stating *KEY CUTTING*. Except that it didn't *just* say that: now that Tom *really* looked, it said:

KEY CUTTING
WHAT'S IN YOUR NOSE?

"What the…?" Tom jerked upright from his slouch. Beneath the original declaration, as though hovering over the picture of a pair of keys, the faint question in bold letters seemed to flick in and out of vision. If he'd turned right instead of left at the start of his mission, he would have seen it immediately. He tugged the glasses from his face and the message disappeared. He looked in confusion at a couple who walked past the sign towards him, but they were intent on their own conversation. Then he heard a muttered "excuse me", and he edged to the side to allow an elderly man in a flat cap to get by from behind. As the man passed the sign, he raised a hand to his face and scratched his nose.

Tom looked back to where Smith was waiting, resting against the telephone booth. He was too far away for Tom to make out anything of his expression. Looking forwards again, Tom put on the glasses, and the message was there once more, but somehow fainter. He'd shifted his angle on looking towards Smith. Shuffling left, the image solidified. And then a pair of teenagers brushed past him and continued past the sign; they both raised their hands to their faces, and one shoved a finger deep into his nose to have a good old rummage…

"Yuk!" Tom turned towards Smith again, and this time the other raised a hand to tap at an imaginary watch. "Oh, right…"

Tom hurried over to the alien *Big Issue* seller, who turned at his approach, and without a word, led them back down Weavers Lane.

***

Back in the chancel passageway beneath St Peter Mancroft, Smith indicated that Tom should take his now-customary perch, then he sat down opposite.

"So – what did you see?"

"A sign. By one of the stalls. There was extra writing – like invisible ink – which I could see when I was wearing the glasses."

"What did it say?"

"It said… it said: *what's in your nose?*"

"Good. Did you observe anything else?"

"Er, no, apart from a disgusting youth picking his nose, and… *oh.*" Realisation dawned. "And the man before him… he *scratched* his nose." Tom frowned and looked at his colleague more keenly. "You're not suggesting…?"

"*Suggesting,* Tom?"

"Uh, suggesting that the sign somehow made them, um, attend to their, er, *proboscises?*"

Smith was silent for a moment, his eyes darting over Tom's face, but his expression was neutral. At last, he said: "Would it surprise you if that was what I was suggesting?"

47

"Well, yes. I mean, I don't understand where the writing came from, but whatever it is, I don't buy it being able to have such an immediate effect. That's absurd."

"Is it? Are humans so resistant to influence? What about hypnosis? Do you believe that works?"

"I suppose so."

"Then consider this a variation of hypnosis: messages communicated at a sub-conscious level. The more innocuous the suggestion, the more likely it is to have an effect. A more demanding message would need to be repeated and amplified, and perhaps be attuned to the core beliefs of the individual, or at least take advantage of a person's mood or heightened emotional state, before it could work its magic."

"But where did the message come from? And how is it *there* and also *not* there?"

"Where it came from is easy," said Smith. "I put it there earlier today. But I used a transient 'ink', so it will degrade quickly and be gone by nightfall."

"But not before half the people of Norwich have excavated their nasal passages?"

"Terrible, I know, and rather unhygienic. But the demonstration was necessary. The Directors' messages are unlikely to be so innocent."

Tom rested his head back against the cold wall. He didn't know what to think. "But... how could I see it with the glasses, and why is the message so compelling?" He suddenly felt an urge to attend to his own nose.

"Good question, Tom. How many dimensions are there?"

"Uh, *four*. Three space dimensions, plus time. Although I have heard some physicists claim there are more, but they're probably just showing off."

"Not at all. I'm glad to hear that there are some intelligent people on this planet. In fact, there are considerably more than four. What you saw was a message in what we have designated the seventh dimension."

"Seventh? Hell, why not sixth? Or eighth?"

Smith actually scoffed. "Don't be absurd, Tom. The sixth is an odd dimension of little use to anyone, while you haven't the sensory apparatus to detect anything in the eighth. But you can and do sense the seventh dimension – just not consciously. Sometimes, humans talk about having

48

a *sixth sense*, and in fact they are right. You all have a sixth sense, but it is a vestige of your pre-*homo sapiens* past, like a heightened visual sense. In short, you do see messages in this dimension, and your brain understands them, but rather than flagging them for your conscious attention it sends its translations to the ancient parts of your brain related to instinct and drive, and these can impel a response."

"Like scratching or picking your nose?"

"Yes."

"But… that's terrible. What if you'd written: kill all blondes! Would the streets of Norwich now be awash with Nordic blood?"

Smith looked stern. "Such a message could have been written, yes. And its effects might well prove disturbing. But as I mentioned, more demanding requests are less likely to be fully complied with. You still have a superego guardian within your heads that will resist extreme urges, much as hypnotic suggestions to kill are also resisted."

"So, *not* fully?"

"No. People with a strong, secretive drive might be tipped into indiscretions."

Tom gaped. "Fuck! Then this *is* serious! And you're implying these Directors are leaving messages like this lying around, just to wind people up? For their own entertainment?"

"Just so." Smith stood abruptly. "You still have the glasses, Tom? Good. I'm afraid some cleaners will arrive soon, and we must draw this session to a close. So here endeth today's lesson. Practise using the glasses. See if you can spot any more messages. I need you to be my eyes. Look at everything. Trust nothing. There is some mischief afoot in Norwich, and I need help in figuring out what is going on. Come."

Smith turned and strode to the exit, leaving Tom to scramble to his feet and run-walk after. He only caught up with the alien as he was keying the door open.

"When will we meet again?"

"Soon, but maybe not too soon. I have other affairs to attend to. I'll be in touch in the usual way. Next time, we can meet in the open now that I am sure you will not bolt. You are familiar with the environs of the Guildhall." It was a statement, not a question.

"Er, yes. Why?"

"It's on your typical route into the centre, and it has an undercroft that is connected to here via one of the city's lost tunnels. It's not suitable to meet inside, but I can get in and out without difficulty. Next time, we will meet at one of the benches nearby. I'll tell you which one closer the time. Thank you, Tom. Oh, and do not lose, or show anyone, the glasses, eh?"

"Er, yes. Understood!"

Tom was ushered through the door, which was then firmly and rapidly closed and locked. Smith turned without looking through the door's glass panes and strode back into the shadowy interior.

Tom stood outside for some seconds. At last he shook his head: what had he gotten himself into?

Chapter 6: Conspiracy

Tom saw the advert in *The Golden Guide* – a free glossy mag that occasionally found its way onto his doormat – five days after his third encounter with Smith.

Think aliens live among us? Ever been approached? Come meet fellow fruitcakes to discuss improbabilities over beer. The Alexandra Tavern, from 8pm Wednesdays. You'll know us when you see us.

He couldn't help but smile. It was probably students. Or maybe it was a new strategy to recruit people for the monthly Philosophy Circle the pub occasionally hosted. If only they knew! He finished leafing through the ads – mostly for local businesses and handymen seeking work – then set the *Guide* aside on the arm of his orange sofa, and went off to try to do something more productive.

And failed.

After a frustrating afternoon, in which he struggled to write a single page of text involving the improbable activities of his alien protagonist, V-Garg – whom he was thinking of revamping to make more Smith-like – Tom found himself in the living room again, slouched on his sofa. He picked up a remote control from a small, wooden coffee table and switched on his widescreen TV, which squatted massively in front of the curtained front window. There was little on: some game shows, some 'lifestyle' programmes, and his default at this time of day: 'Nothing to Declare'. He spent an hour or so watching Australian customs officers uncovering drug smugglers and fiends carrying forgotten bananas within their luggage (apparently deadly to all known life on the continent).

As the second episode ended, and adverts came on – each attempting to out-do the next in demonstrating the moral superiority of its brand – Tom shuffled restlessly in his seat and looked around for an alternative source of entertainment. But the room was largely bare: magnolia walls and an embarrassingly dirty green carpet; a tall bookcase in one corner, stuffed full of travel guides and pulpy novels; and a couple of Frank Taylor prints upon the walls – simple yet colourful. Then he noticed the *Guide* on the arm of the sofa and recalled the ad he'd seen earlier. He found the appropriate page and re-read it. *Today* was Wednesday…

As the next episode of 'Nothing to Declare' began its dramatic announcement on what would follow, Tom puckered his lips and looked up to the ceiling, where a maroon lampshade partially obscured a plaster ceiling rose. What was he doing? Over the last week or so, he'd had one of the most extraordinary encounters of his life – one that few others were likely to have had. Not only that, but the affair was like something from a novel. From *his* novel. It should at the very least have been inspirational. If he'd had the passion and ambition of one of his old profs, he would have been putting in fourteen-hour days to complete his book. He could be on the web now, searching out other signs, looking for opportunities. He certainly ought to be energised and excited. Yet here he was, watching repeats of easy-viewing programmes, making glacial progress on his magnum opus, and feeling somewhat puzzled by it all. And then a thought occurred: *my God, they were right to sack me!* This was quickly followed by a second: *I'm going to the pub...*

The Alexandra Tavern was a fifteen-minute walk away through the Victorian streets of the Golden Triangle, over Earlham Road, up Alexandra Road. Although Tom had Smith's special glasses with him – which he'd been wearing whilst out-and-about over the last few days (without seeing anything untoward) – he kept them in his jacket pocket. Well, given the time of day and absence of sun, he didn't want to look like some sort of poseur! He arrived at the pub around 8.10, and momentarily paused to consider which of its two entrances to take. He settled on the main one, accessed through a gap between some wooden benches and standing barrels, which opened into the half of the pub that had once hosted a pool table (now supplanted by extra seating). He suspected the congregation of weirdos would meet in the comfier, carpeted lounge, accessed around the other side of the long bar. On this side, he could order a beer and surreptitiously peer through the entranceway into the other room, committing to nothing. In fact, he wasn't really sure why he was here. Certainly, he had no intention of actually joining the advertised group. He wasn't *that* sad. And yet...

Tom ordered a pint of Ale X from the bar by the opening between the two rooms. While waiting for his drink to be poured, he attempted to nonchalantly peek around the corner. The group would probably be at one of the two bigger tables in the area by the entrance to the toilets. He could see the further of the two tables, but not the one directly around the corner. *Damn!* He sidled around a bit more, hoping that he might at least hear something, for the pub was sparsely populated at the moment. But all he heard was a laugh from a table at the front of the room and the voice of a barmaid speaking to another customer. His beer was presented, and he paid in cash. Then he had a decision to make – which, for Tom, was never a good thing. At last, he determined to casually stroll around the corner to take up a seat at one of the small tables in the centre of the lounge. He *wouldn't* look to his right at the table in the corner as he entered the room.

Tom looked right at the table in the corner as he entered the room.

There were three people there. In the middle, on a bench resting against the back wall, was a tall man in his early thirties with short hair and a mischievous expression who wore a black t-shirt printed with a stereotypical alien – with large, green head, black, oval eyes, and a thin, cartoonish body. Tom was vaguely aware of a younger man sat to one side of the central character, and a bespectacled woman sat to the other. But he found his gaze captured and returned by the man in the middle, whose grin broadened and screamed: *Gotcha!*

Tom faltered and quickly looked away. His hand jerked without volition, and the top centimetre of beer sloshed from his glass. He looked down, inadvertently shaking the glass some more and spilling further liquid onto the front of his jeans and the floor. "Shit!"

He heard a cut-off laugh and then, suddenly, at his side, was the bespectacled woman, holding out a tissue.

"Looks like you might need this."

"I… ah… thank you." Tom gave a weak smile. He placed his pint on the bar, took the tissue, and mopped the front of his thighs.

The woman – of similar age to himself, with straight, brown, shoulder-length hair and a kindly smile – laughed lightly. "Sorry if we startled you."

"Oh. Ah. You didn't. I mean…"

"So you *weren't* looking for us? Do you always spill your beer for no reason? Or do you suffer from the DTs?"

"No, I mean—"

"Why don't you come join us?" This came from the man in the alien t-shirt. He sounded quite jocular. "We don't want to lose you like the others!"

Tom looked at the seated man. "I'm sorry? I was just… well…"

"Don't worry about it, old man. We know what to look for now. I assume you saw one of the ads. Please join us."

The woman smiled. "Yes. Come and sit down. I'm Amanda."

"Ah... Tom. I'm Tom. I'm... sorry. I just wasn't sure...."

"If we were genuine? Of course. Please."

Tom gave another sickly smile, took a step towards the table, remembered his beer, turned to reclaim his pint, then allowed Amanda to guide him the short distance to a chair facing the t-shirt wearer and the younger man next to him. Amanda then sidled onto the bench at the short side of the oblong table, perpendicular to him.

"Hello, Tom," said the man with the t-shirt. "I'm Ed, and this is Simon. We are, well, it's difficult to say what we are. We are people with an interest in the extra-terrestrial, as I assume you are too."

"Um. Kind of. Is this a science fiction society? I didn't know Norwich had one."

Ed frowned. "Well, no, not really. Not... *fiction*. By Zeus, this is hard. We really should have practised what to say, but you're the first person we have managed to get to park his buttocks. There have been others who've pretended that they were here for something else, or who simply bolted – like you were going to. I blame Si. I suspect he scares them off." He gave a lascivious grin at the man beside him.

"Er, yes. And this *isn't* the Philosophy Club?"

Ed shook his head slowly, while Amanda seemed uncertain as to where to look. However, Simon appeared to want to speak, glancing between his colleagues. He was in his mid-twenties with a tousled mop of blond hair and wore a denim jacket that obscured the design of his black t-shirt. He leant across the table and gasped: "It's aliens! They're here! Amongst us!"

Ed's frown deepened. "Yes, thanks, Si. It is aliens, isn't it..."

"What have you seen?" continued Simon, eyes wide. "What have you heard?"

"Si, you're scaring Tom."

"Nonsense. That's why he's here. Just say it. Tell us, Tom. It's easy."

Amanda turned to Tom and rested a hand on his arm. She seemed embarrassed. "Sorry, Tom. Simon gets excited."

"Of course I'm excited! Unbelievable! Spoo...keeee! Come on. Fess up!"

Tom was dumbfounded. They *were* weirdos. How could he extricate himself? He goldfished for a moment, unable to articulate anything sensible.

Amanda stepped in. "*Simon*. Shush, dear. You're not helping." With her free hand she made a calming motion at the young man, while her other hand tightened its grip on Tom's forearm, preventing him from escaping. Once Simon sat back and folded his arms, the woman turned to look at Tom intently. "Let me try. *Tom*. We are simply people who have had some, well, weird experiences. Ed and I have had these for a couple of years. We met by chance. It's a long story. Then we thought we would see if we were alone. A few months ago, we found Simon. Now, I don't know if you know what I'm talking about. You either do or you don't. If you don't, then no problem. We can talk about sci fi and have a drink and then you can pretend you have to be somewhere else in an hour's time, and we can pretend to believe you, and there's no harm done. But if you *do* know what I'm talking about–"

"Don't forget the aliens!"

"*Thank you*, Simon. Yes. Our experiences have been *otherworldly*. But as I said, if you *do* know what I'm talking about, then you may never get a better hearing."

Tom closed his mouth. He had started to lean away from the woman, but she spoke calmly, and smiled nicely, and had an air of sincerity. And she wasn't unattractive. Still. "Ah. Well. I might have seen something. But I'm trying to write a sci-fi novel now…" he winced at this admission, which always felt to him like he was telling a dirty secret, "so maybe I have been dreaming. I… don't know."

"Very cagey, Tom," noted Ed. "That's good. More credible." He now seemed a little excited too, like Simon. Leaning forwards and fixing Tom with a stare, he continued: "Can you say more? What happened?"

They had ignored his mention of the novel, a topic that often caused some excitement… or at least, it did until Tom admitted how little he had completed, confessing that he wasn't a published novelist, at which point the excitement tended to wane to be replaced by smirks and eyerolls. Instead, this lot wanted to know about what he had experienced. But… he couldn't say. Not now. He gave an embarrassed laugh. "Well, I saw, I mean, I was approached…"

"Approached!" hissed Ed to Amanda. "Go on!"

"Approached by a… *man*. And, well, this is stupid really. I think he was a fantasist, though he was kind of convincing, I guess." Tom paused to take a sip of his ale, now sweating slightly under the expectant eyes of the others, which never left his face. He lowered his pint. Amanda's grip had loosened; now it tightened again. "He made this ridiculous claim. He said he was a…"

"Protector?" said Ed.

Tom twitched. If Amanda hadn't been holding his arm, he quite likely would have knocked his pint over. He stared at Ed, who had regained his *gotcha* smile.

***

They continued to talk cagily for some time. Ed bought a round of drinks. Amanda's confidence grew sufficient to allow her to release Tom's arm, enabling him to go to the toilets. There was no rear exit from these, but by this stage Tom wouldn't have taken one even if there had been, for it had gradually become clear that they all shared *something*, to a greater or lesser extent. By the third round, got in by Amanda, they were being quite open.

"So, only Ed's calls himself a Protector?"

"Yes. Mine calls herself a Facilitator," said Amanda. "Simon's is a Guardian."

"Facilitator?"

"Yes. She says she is here to facilitate the observance of the law. To make sure we are left alone so that we can screw up in our own unique way."

"While they watch on," noted Ed with a smirk, "eating their metaphorical popcorn."

"I guess so," continued Amanda. "But mine has never said anything about us being a source of galactic entertainment. In fact, she's never said anything at all about the motives of those breaking the law."

"Haven't you asked?" said Tom.

"Oh yes, lots of times. But she just kind of shrugs and waves her hands about, acts bored, and changes the subject. I've just assumed that the lawbreakers have different and unknowable motives. I mean, they are alien, so who knows how they think."

"What about yours, Simon?"

The young man pouted and nodded sagely. "Experiments. That's what the bad dudes want. They want to examine us. *Probe* us. Vortent said his lot try to stop that. They are part of a league of guardians that stop the bad dudes from kidnapping people. That sort of thing."

"Ah... right." Tom frowned. Simon's contact seemed somehow different from the others. Tom noticed Ed smirking into a hand. "And yours is called Vortent, Simon? What about..."

"Sheila," said Amanda. "Mine calls herself Sheila."

"And mine is called... *Ed*," said Ed. "Well, obviously that's not his real name, but he can't be bothered to think up anything else. He knew my name was Ed, so he decided he'd be Ed too. It could be a piss take. Or an alien attempt to get me to identify with him. But I just think it's a lack of imagination."

Tom thought about Smith's distracted air. Boredom? Otherworldliness? "But... does anyone know why they were approached? In my case, Smith told me they keep an eye on the web. They saw my novel – er, *draft* novel – backed-up in the Cloud, and thought it suggested a receptive mind. What about yours?"

Ed grinned mischievously. "I happen to have certain skills. *Programming* skills."

"He's a hacker," noted Amanda, with a small frown. "Dark web. Mysterious stuff. And illegal, I suspect."

"Not *always*," smirked Ed. "Just think of me as Robin Hood. And if I take a cut, well, I need to live, don't I? But all this is on the sly. You don't have a problem, do you, Tom?"

"Ah, no." Tom raised his hands defensively. "What you get up to is, er, your business. Unless you're arranging hits on people..." Tom gave a feeble laugh. He didn't understand computers really. Even word processing software taxed his competence. He knew he should mind about illegal dealings, but the world was a complex place, and he had enough trouble deciding whether his own actions were ethical or not, let alone trying to judge those of others. All he knew was that he'd been more than willing in the past to complicitly pay tradesmen cash-in-hand for their work on his house, knowing full well that none of the money would ever make it into government coffers.

Ed leered and winked. "No hits… *yet*. Why? Do you want someone bumping off? I could probably look—"

"No! Thanks!" Tom thought, on the balance of probabilities, that his new acquaintance was just joking, but he didn't wish to further test that hypothesis. "Amanda," he turned, "what about you?"

"I'm an influencer. I'm into eco enhancements. You know, ways in which we can live a greener life. I have a podcast. Do some tweeting. Have a few thousand followers. Nothing grand. I was approached a bit like you, via the internet, to help provide certain positive messages about the environment and counter some of the more outrageous claims of the climate change deniers."

"Yeah, she's facilitating veganism," mocked Ed, gently. "I personally think her Sheila is actually one of the Enemy. Once we're all fully vegan, extreme flatulence will wipe out the human race, and *then* they can invade."

Amanda rolled her eyes, giving Tom the impression she'd heard this all before. "He thinks he's funny. Anyway, I'm not a vegan. I'm not even a vegetarian. I'm just careful. I believe in a balanced diet."

"And talking of a balanced diet," said Ed, "come on, Si, get them in. I need to balance another ale with some pork scratchings."

"Ah, right…"

As the young man took his cue and headed to the bar, Tom asked: "And Simon? What's his story?"

"He's a gamer," said Ed, watching his associate at the bar trying to draw the attention of one of the barmaids presently chatting among themselves. "He's never been clear on how he was approached. Plays it a bit close to the chest."

"Ah, I see. A bit hush hush." Tom frowned. "Speaking of which — should we really be talking about this? I mean, between us? It sounds as if we have four different *masters*. Are they of different species, with different motives? Smith said there are thousands of aliens watching us all the time." He suddenly felt uncomfortable. "And maybe we are being watched right now?"

"Can't really say," said Ed. "But I've never mentioned this to Big Ed, and he's never given any indication that he's noticed or is bothered."

"Same with Sheila," confirmed Amanda. "I was also worried at first, but, well, as Ed says, there's never been any come back. I've always assumed we're just small, uninteresting fish and…"

"And our overlords have bigger fish to fry?" smirked Ed, completing the aquatic metaphor.

"Well, *yes.*"

"Still, it might be best not to say anything to your handler, Tom," said Ed. "Especially at this early stage of your relationship. It might be a bit like telling your new bird that you're still flat sharing with your ex."

"Right! I don't want to scare him off… *I think*. But I'm still not really sure what he wants me to do, apart from looking out for seventh dimensional messages. I hope he says more when we next meet."

"At least you've met him," said Amanda. "I've only ever talked to Sheila online, and Ed…"

"I only met mine once. Came round my house, he did. Scared the shit out of me. Thought it might have been Interpol. Or an ex. Or my dealer. Had a fuck of a hangover. Said he was a representative of *The Collective*. I was so shit-faced it never occurred to me to ask why he was at my door in person until he was in my living room." Ed laughed and shook his head. "And then he revealed that he knew everything about my innocent pastime, letting drop certain information that would probably have got me banged up if it had got to the authorities." He gave a resigned smile and raised his hands. "So, I had to listen, and after that it was hard not to believe. Now I'm Big Ed's bitch. Like Amanda, we communicate through the electronic plane."

Simon returned, bearing drinks. He set one down in front of Ed.

"Ta, Si. Now sit. Quick-quick! We've got more important matters to discuss."

"More important than alien interference in human affairs?" said Tom.

"That's right, old fruit. You see, with your momentous arrival, this now makes us quorate. There are now four of us."

"Er, why is that good?" Tom was suddenly suspicious. "Four Musketeers? Fantastic Four?"

"Nah, me old mucker. Four is the minimum number needed for a pub quiz team. So… the Rose Tavern? Next Tuesday?"

And thus The Credulous was formed.

***

Ed really could drink.

By the time Tom staggered home, he knew he was going to be useless tomorrow, and probably have a bit of a headache to boot. But he didn't care. Not only was it now apparent that he *wasn't* going mad, but it seemed as though he might just have – after a lengthy barren period – gained the prospects of a social life.

For Tom, that was worth any amount of grief.

Or so he thought at the time.

Chapter 7: Instructions

As expected, Tom was useless on Thursday and not much better on Friday. He barely left the house, yet still managed to achieve very little. He applied for a job at Caledonian University in the grim north — more than anything to provide some proof of work-finding efforts to the tyrants at the Job Centre — with little anticipation of being invited for interview, and even less of accepting the job if offered it. He finished tidying his spare room so that it was now at least showable when he got around to advertising for a lodger — which would have to be soon, given his dwindling savings. And he wrote a grand total of four pages of his novel, in which he began to hint that V-Garg's motives might not be entirely benign.

What Tom did do, however, was spend a lot of time slouched on his orange sofa with tea to hand, musing on the episode at the Alex. The memory was a comforting one: he had gained some validation of the frankly unbelievable events he'd experienced over the last couple of weeks, and potentially gained a gang. He'd never really had a gang before, having been a loner or part of a couple for most of his post-PhD life, and he was conscious of a need not to muck this up. Amanda was nice and Simon seemed harmless, while Ed — though somewhat louche — also seemed well-disposed towards him and the idea of their secretive clique. And their stories were simply, well, incredible. Just how many aliens were out there, and how many people were like them — aides and confidantes? And if the world really was this extraordinary, how much did it matter that he conform to the norms of society — the treadmill of getting a job, working until pensionable age, eventually getting married and having kids (fat chance), going on one holiday a year, meeting the family at Christmas? Did *any* of it matter? In fact, was this not the ultimate justification for his wastrel lifestyle? Couldn't he just kick back for the rest of his life, smug in the knowledge that all those disapproving people judging him were nothing but ignorant sheep?

Yeah! Sod finding a job! He wasn't a prole: he was an *Omega*!

On Saturday, Tom at last got a message. When he glimpsed the text at the end of his latest chapter, downloaded from the Cloud, excitement and

61

nervousness competed inside him. He hadn't been forgotten, but then again, he hadn't gotten any Omega-type results to report either, so Smith might be disappointed. On his few forays from the house, he'd merely yomped up-and-down the Unthank Road to its parade of shops to grab some over-priced groceries from the convenience stores or some chips for a cheap dinner. And if there wasn't a message in the signage of the shops and services the first time, it now occurred to him, it was unlikely that there would be on the second, third, or umpteenth time thereafter. Strategically, this now looked far from impressive.

The message was succinct: he was invited to meet Smith at noon at a particular bench near the Guildhall beside the northern wing of the City Hall. Tom knew the spot well: it was where he usually sat to eat his market-bought lunch. Coincidence? How long had Smith actually been observing him? He couldn't recall having used the bench for a couple of weeks, and certainly not since he'd first met Smith. *Hmmmm....*

Still, Tom was eager. He fretted at home for an hour until it was time to leave.

Outside, it was a warm, late-August day, somewhat muggy and overcast. Tom carried a small empty rucksack on his back, just in case he decided to do some shopping afterwards. He opened out his sunglasses, gave a wistful look at the clouds above, and put them on – determined to at least show willing.

He headed into town, taking Unthank Road up to the Roman Catholic Cathedral and then the footbridge over the Grapes Hill inner ring road. This dropped him down onto Upper St Giles Street, which led almost directly to the rendezvous site. It was as he was strolling along that something *did* catch his eye. In fact, he was looking downwards, holding the frame of his sunglasses with one hand while using a finger from his other to rub an itchy eye, that he caught a flash of light, a sparkle of unusual and over-bright colour. He juddered to a halt and removed his questing finger to increase his eye power. *What was that?*

Tom stared at the ground, but the light had gone. Instead, there was a carved pavement slab before him, showing a king's head as on a playing card. He looked up and around, but there was no one close by – just an elderly couple further ahead, and a young couple on the opposite side of the narrow road, still some distance away. Tom leant down and looked again, and as he did so caught a flash at the margin of his eye. As he took a step closer, the image seemed to expand and deepen. He stood directly over the plaque, legs to either side, and the floating text clarified. Overwriting the caption of the plaque was the instruction:

BE NOBLE

Tom felt as though someone had injected an icy fluid into his heart. *Be noble?* It was a message! He'd found a message! He took off the glasses and the glowing text disappeared. Or *did* it? He stared hard, trying to focus…

"Lost something, mate?" said a voice.

Tom nearly dropped his glasses. The workman dressed in a yellow bib grinned through a thin beard as he crossed in front of him.

"Ah, no, just looking…"

And then the man was gone with a chuckle.

Suddenly, the street seemed busier, with some people coming from the bridge heading to town, and others making their way homewards, laden with shopping bags. Tom stepped away and rested his back against a black drainpipe in the wall beside the window of a shop. He pretended to clean his glasses and tried to avoid eye contact. When he put the glasses on again he saw… *nothing*. Had it been an illusion? He waited for the best part of a minute for the street to quieten and then moved back to his original position…

And there it was.

He had to be standing at a certain angle. The words resolved once more. *BE NOBLE.* He straightened his shoulders, firmed his expression… and caught sight of a young mother pushing an old-style pram towards him. He smiled at her, stepped off the pavement and onto the road, and found himself sweeping an arm downwards in a universal *after you* gesture. The woman smiled an uncertain thanks and made her way past.

Tom grinned inwardly, then looked back at the message. Be noble? Well, that certainly seemed less mischievous than the nose-picking one written by Smith. Tom scratched at his nose: he still wasn't sure how such messages worked – after all, they seemed to have no effect on him. But time was passing, and so he adjusted the glasses, hitched his sagging rucksack, and carried on up St Giles.

He arrived nearly ten minutes late, full of excitement.

***

"I found some!"

"I'm glad you did, Tom, but it's important to try to be on time. My predictive algorithms suggested a certain window in which I could get from the Guildhall and back without leading to suspicion. Fortunately, I anticipated that you would be late, so I chose an option with a longer interval and left when I saw you approaching – but this might not always be feasible."

Tom's excitement momentarily dipped at the mild rebuke. The alien had been waiting by the stipulated bench under a tall tree – still in the guise of a whiskered man in a *Big Issue* vest. The flinted Guildhall formed a backdrop in the near distance. "Oh! I'm sorry. It won't happen again. But… but…"

"But you have had success. That is good news indeed. Now, tell me quickly and succinctly, for I have less than five minutes."

"Well, there were messages on the ground, written over the top of some pavement plaques. Touristy things. After I found the first, I knew what to look for and found three more."

"And what did they say?"

"The first said *Be Noble* and the next said *Protect the Weak*. A third said *Punish Junkies* and a fourth – just over there…" Tom waved a hand behind him, "said *Punish Drunks*."

"Junkies and drunks?"

"That's right. You know, people who use and abuse drugs and alcohol."

"I know what these terms mean. Importantly, how did the messages make you feel?"

"I'm not sure. The first two seemed quite positive. I didn't really feel any different. The one about drunks…?" He thought for a moment. "No. Nothing, really. But the one on junkies? Well, I did feel a bit *annoyed*. I got an image in my head of a crackhead shooting up. In fact, I still have that image now. *Weird*."

"That's interesting. Was there anything else notable about how and where these messages were written? You said on plaques on the pavement. What did these show?"

"The one about junkies showed a bloody great hypodermic needle pointing right out at me, almost like a weapon. The others were a bit more innocuous. A king's head, a man groping a deer, and a smiling sun."

"Ah, that may explain matters to some degree. The words are only part of the message. They have greatest effect when they take advantage of other cues in the environment – here, a powerful, threatening image. Can I assume that the message about nobility was attached to the plaque showing a king, and the command to protect was associated with the *hugger*?" Was that actually humour in the alien's voice? "But I do not understand the link to the sun picture."

"*Smiling* sun," emphasised Tom. "I suppose it had a rather leering face – just the sort you might feel inclined to punch." Tom frowned: he'd made the last statement with surprising feeling. *Where had that come from?*

Smith was silent for a moment, his eyes performing the strange flickering Tom had seen before. Then he focused on him once more. "Well done, Tom. I am pleased. Now, I must run the algorithms and check the news channels to see if there are any unusual events with possible correlations to these messages."

"Right!" Tom felt a jolt of pride. "So, what next? Do you want me to keep looking?"

"Yes, Tom. But I want you to expand your search. I have noticed that your range has been rather narrow. You have kept to suburbia. But a message is more likely to have an effect if it is placed where many can see it. And it is also more likely to have an effect when it is placed where there is an environmental opportunity: crowds, busy roads, running water, heights. Over the next week or two, I'd like you to get out and about more. Be more systematic. Focus on the city and attempt to quarter it. Do you understand? Perhaps get a map and work out a patrol route. And if you see anything, report it to me at the end of your latest chapter – which I notice is making rather sluggish progress."

Tom looked sheepish. "Yes, I have been a bit slow." He straightened his shoulders. "But what about the messages on St Giles? Do we just leave them there?"

"No. But my six minutes and thirty-two seconds are almost up. I will give you more instructions through the Cloud. In the meantime, if you can find some powerful magnets and get some cans of red spray paint – colour *RAL 3020* – that would be a good start. These will be useful later."

He held up a hand to stall Tom's reply before it could pass through his teeth. "My time is up. Goodbye, Tom." And he abruptly turned and headed back towards the Guildhall.

Tom closed his mouth and watched the *Big Issue* fraud depart. For a moment, he thought of following to see exactly where he went, but then he feared appearing too obvious. Instead, he turned to drop onto the still-untenanted bench by his side and looked up at the leafy branches above. Magnets and red spray paint? There was only one option: *Thorns…*

***

Thorns on Exchange Street was something of a Norwich institution: close to the city's unique department store, Jarrold's, it occupied one entire side of a (small) city block.

"Spray paint… spray paint…" Tom made staccato progress through the shop, threshing his eyes over shelves and displays as he hunted for his prey. The shop was a long, multi-level maze, packed with just about every product one might need to clean, repair, protect, warm, light, or beautify one's home (or garden, or bike, or car…), including canned products of many types. Disinfectants? Brass polishers? Insecticides? Up a half-level, down one, and then his eyes alighted upon a wall of shelves stacked with colourful cans. A young man in his mid-twenties with close-cropped hair stood before this, blocking the creaking-floored corridor, causing Tom to momentarily hold back. He saw the man run a hand along one line of cans, pause, grasp one, consider it uncertainly, shrug, then turn to take his find to a till in an annex close by.

Tom took three steps and planted himself in the same spot his predecessor had occupied. Right. *PlastiKote* paint. Was this the right sort? There seemed a large range of colours, indicated by the plastic lids. He ran his hand along them. *Chestnut Brown. Plum. Sumptuous Purple.* Various blues, greens, greys. And then emptiness. Along an entire little section, above yellow labels that promised *Bright Red, Real Red, Wine Red,* and even *Pink Burst,* there was nothing. And it wasn't as if there was just one can of the non-red colours: the other shades were available in abundance, stacked three or four deep, and so the empty space for his target colour was all the more remarkable. Tom sighed.

He turned around. There were other paints on the shelves behind him, and he spotted more spray cans under a different brand. *Hammerite* metal paint. For a different type of surface? There were fewer colours here – black, white, yellow, blue, gold and... an empty space where the red should have been. *Ridiculous!*

Tom headed to the nearby till, where a somewhat grizzled man with thick, veinous hands had just served a customer – the young man, who was currently stuffing his purchase into a rucksack as he moved resolutely towards the shop's exit.

"Oh, er, hi!"

"Hello, sir. How can I help?"

"Ah, well, I was looking for some paint."

"What type? Masonry? Garden furniture? Garden? Radiator? Primer? Undercoat? Matt? Gloss?"

"Well, I don't really know what it's... for..." Tom suddenly realised that his purpose might easily be misconstrued.

The man gave a sardonic grin. "So, it's spray paint you want."

"Um, yes. But not for what you think."

"I don't think anything, sir. Spray paints have many uses, not just for desecrating buildings and causing urban blight." His smile twitched. "I expect it's for your car, really, but you just forgot that's what you want it for."

"Er, yes." Tom couldn't meet the other's eyes.

"Well, sir, we have a good selection of spray paints just behind you, over there."

"I saw those. But I'm looking for red, and you don't seem to have anything in that shade at all. I just wondered if you have more in stock, or maybe another brand?"

This caused the amused retailer to pause for thought and scratch his head. "Unfortunately, no. Red has been very popular recently. I'm not sure why. In fact, the young gentleman before you must have taken the last cannister we have."

"Oh!" Tom met the eyes of the other briefly before flicking his gaze in the direction of the purchaser – but he was long gone. "How strange." He returned his attention to the other. "Do you know when you'll get more in? Actually, there's a specific colour I need. I think it's something like 'RAL 3020'. Does that make sense?"

The man laughed. "Very good, sir. Is this some sort of prank? Or an internet craze?"

"I'm sorry?"

"The previous customer asked the same question, sir. I couldn't guarantee the shade was right – and in fact, it almost certainly won't be – but he took it anyway."

Tom's eyes widened. He thought *What the fuck…?*, but what he actually said was "RAL? Is it… what is…?"

The man had recovered his composure, and the sardonic expression was back. "You don't know? Well, sir, RAL stands for *Reichs-Ausschuß für Lieferbedingungen und Gütesicherung*, I hope I've said that right, but who knows. What was it Holy Roman Emperor Charles V said, *German for horses*, eh? It's an industry-wide colour standard for paints, coatings and plastics, but perhaps most often used for automotive purposes. So, I'll tell you what I told your friend: your best bet is Halfords." Now he folded his arms and his grin broadened further. "But I'd hurry if I were you, before the lad plunders their supplies too."

Tom smiled lamely. "Ah, thank you for the tip and the, er, education. I'll just…" he twitched a hand to indicate the direction of the exit, gave a deferential nod, and scurried from the other's gaze.

He'd forgotten about the magnets altogether.

***

Tom needed to think. *Halfords* was a bit of a trek past the ring road, and he had no intention of getting into a footrace with an unknown competitor… *if* that's what the man was.

Which he couldn't be.

That was absurd.

It had to be a coincidence.

Tom needed to sit down, have a drink, and contemplate matters. And he needed to calm down, so – a relaxant not a stimulant. A beer not a coffee. But where? He tried to avoid pubs in the immediate centre on Saturdays, which could get busy. So, somewhere just outside, and somewhere he could get some grub. The Coachmakers Arms!

He put on his glasses and quickly assessed where he was. With a nod, he set off, returning to the market and continuing past its stalls and St

Peter Mancroft. Next, he walked up a small incline by Marks & Spencers – with its rather cool living wall of greenery – and into the bowels of the Chantry Place Mall. From here, it was down one level, out onto St Stephens Street, along to a roundabout, through an underpass, and onto Newmarket Road, with his destination just to his right.

The Coachmakers was an old coaching inn, with a paved courtyard that was glassed over, and a low-ceilinged bar beside this. He liked the pub: not only did it have that olde worlde character – wooden beams and ancient brick-and-flint masonry – but it served a good selection of ales from jacketed barrels that covered the wall behind the wooden bar.

As Tom pushed open the door, he faltered and frowned: the explosion of yellow within reminded him that Norwich were away at Preston North End. Their noon kick off meant that the game was certain to be on *Sky*, and the Coachmakers had a clutch of TVs and a pull-down screen to cater for the football crowd. He hesitated in the doorway: a quiet drink was unlikely here. But as he started to turn, he was surprised, and even shocked, to notice a bespectacled man sat at a small table right beside the door.

"Brian?"

"Hello, Tom."

"Uh, what a surprise. I haven't seen you in a pub before. Are you a football fan?"

Brian looked peeved. He had a lugubrious face and thinning black hair. "I am neither a football fan, nor a fan of drinking dens like this." There was an almost-full pint of lager on the table before him. "The fact that I am here is largely *your* fault."

Tom was taken aback: Brian had spoken calmly and matter-of-factly, but there was some hardness in the eyes that assaulted him from behind thick, black-rimmed glasses. "Uh, sorry, what…?"

A thin smile settled on the other's face: in spite of the background chatter and sound of television commentary, his quiet words carried clearly between them: "I think you had better take a seat. You can share my pain."

"Tomaso! You are here!" A new voice cut through the smog of sound.

Tom winced and looked around: a short, handsome man with fair hair wriggled between a pair of gents in canary yellow, returning from the toilets. *Shit!* "Fabio?"

69

"It is *magnificent* to see you again." The Italian drew to a halt at Brian's shoulder: he was a head shorter than Tom, but exuded an aura that somehow made him seem much bigger. "You disappeared. No word! But here you are, still in Norwich, and still alive. Sit sit! You must join us. I will get you a drink!"

"Well, maybe…"

But Fabio had turned and in two steps was at the bar, where he inserted himself into a gap that magically opened before him. He bellowed an order at the barman, oblivious as to whether it was his turn or not.

"Do as the man asks, Tom." Brian's foot pushed at a chair that had been crammed tight under the table out of the way of the busy floorspace; it connected with Tom's knee. He had no choice. He pulled the chair out a bit further and tilted it so that he could squeeze into the small gap between the table and the doorway, all the while under Brain's intent gaze. Once seated, Brian leant forwards and hissed: "Welcome to *my* world. Since you left, Steve and I have had to take your place. *Git!*"

"I'm sorry, Brian. I didn't think… I never realised… I thought you were out of the way."

"No. There has been some reorganisation of office space. I have your old place, sharing with Alice. And you know how Fabio likes the ladies, irrespective of their marital status or availability. Not only does he disrupt my work with his frequent visits, but I have become his new toy."

Guilt and annoyance warred in Tom's head. "Well, that sucks, but it's hardly my fault. I didn't ask to be sacked!"

"I think you got off lightly…"

"Tomaso! Here you go. I know you like this shitty English beer, but they have Moretti on tap, so I got you a proper beer. You missed the first half. It is nil-nil. Brian, move over a bit. Tomaso, have you got fat? Where is the space? The second half is about to begin. Football! The game of Gods!" He actually leant forwards and pinched Tom's cheek. "A beautiful day, beautiful game, and beautiful friends! Ah, the second half – it starts! Quiet now. Watch!"

As Fabio turned his back on Tom, Brian continued to glare.

It was a very, *very* long half, and not only because the dull game ended in a nil-nil draw. But Fabio would not let them leave even then. Tom and Brian had to listen to the Italian's detailed analysis of the match, and his desultory opinion on the flaws of 'the English Game'. Then they were forced to endure the live scores programme for the afternoon matches and Fabio's accompanying commentary and critique – right through to final scores. More fizzy lager was forced upon them…

It was past five o'clock before Tom was able to escape. He was hungry and suffering from heartburn as a consequence of the gaseous brews, with no time to make it to Halfords to fulfil Smith's request.

Chapter 8: The Credulous

It was Tuesday evening at the Rose Tavern.

"Well," declared Ed, effusively, "here we all are then. I hope you've brought your brains, as I have no desire to be bested by these nerds…" he waved an arm to indicate the swathe of people scattered about the pub lounge. Some from the nearest table heard his bold declaration and turned to look.

"Ed – not so loud," hissed Amanda.

"Why not? I call it as I see it; that's my philosophy. You don't mind being called a nerd, do you?" he said, directly addressing the nearest face-turner – a twenty-something man sat next to two similarly aged women. "It's a term of respect, after all. *Here be a brainbox!* What's not to like?"

"Er, yeah, I suppose so," said the suddenly embarrassed man. "We're all nerds here, hey?"

"Precisely! Well, good luck to you and your nerdettes."

"Oh… thanks!" The man quickly turned away, back to his chattering team-mates.

"I'm not a nerd," huffed Simon.

"No, you're right. You – Si – are what I like to refer to as an *uber-nerd*. Nerdious-plus. *Nerd Alpha cum laude.*" He leant across to ruffle the other's already tousled hair. "And I am relying on you to stomp all over this lot should we get a round on *Star Trek*. Surely, no one else here will be able to describe the size and relative dimensions of a Klingon's private parts, eh?"

Tom coughed into his beer.

"Steady on, man," declared Ed. "Need a bib?"

"No… no… really," Tom laughed. Ed was so naughty – a welcome change from the overly serious bookworms he'd known and worked with over the last few years. Indeed, it was Tom's belief that the amount of work expected from tenured academics nowadays tended to cull anyone interesting and original from the pack of post-doctoral candidates, or at the very least, act as a blanket to smother the life from hitherto bright young things once they attained such exalted job security. (*Supposed* job security, Tom reminded himself.) But being around Ed helped him recall his carefree days as a PhD student when life was, well, *fun*.

Ed winked and stood up. "Seems you need a top up, old man." He headed to the bar.

Beside Tom, Amanda shook her head as she watched their implicit leader leave. As Simon excused himself to 'go for a leak', the woman turned back to Tom. "So, any more encounters with Smith?"

"Yes. I saw him on Saturday." Tom paused to give matters some thought. He still wasn't sure how much he should say to his new acquaintances. Surely generalities would be alright? "You know I said he wanted me to search for otherworldly messages? Well, as I was heading to the meeting, I actually saw some. It was a bit of a shock." Should he elaborate? Perhaps it was too soon? Amanda's eyes widened behind her glasses, but she didn't interrupt, and so he continued: "I think he was pleased. Anyway, he then made a weird request, asking me to go and get a particular colour of paint – a very specific shade of red."

"Hmmm. I suspect he might want you to use it to cover over the messages."

"Yes, that's what I've been thinking. But that's not the weirdest thing that happened on Saturday. After I left, I went to Thorns to get some, and they didn't have any. They had every other shade under the sun, but not this one." He hunched forwards, drawing the woman into a conspiratorial huddle. "In fact, they did have *one* can of red – but this young guy grabbed it just before me. And even *more* curious, he apparently asked the cashier about the *exact* shade I needed."

"Wow!"

"And there's more. The cashier told me when it was my turn that they'd had a run on that particular shade, which suggests *others* have been looking for it too!"

"That is… well, I don't know what that is. What did you do?"

"Looked very sheepish. But then I took the cashier's advice and went to Halfords on Sunday. And guess what? Although they did have one can of the correct shade of red, they *only* had one. Apparently, I was lucky, as they'd just got in a new consignment – *specifically* of red spray paints, as these have been flying off the shelf. The cashier said it was a bit of an enigma to them, and she tried to probe me on the matter."

"What did you say?"

"Nothing really. I just mumbled something incoherent, then remembered a bike I used to have that got nicked from the back of my house, and I said it was for that."

"So, you weren't tempted to give an Ed-style answer?"

Tom laughed and looked to the bar, where his teammate had spread himself, occupying enough space for three. "You mean, a perverse exaggeration of the truth? I can just imagine it. *I need the paint to thwart the nefarious plans of alien paedophiles, for whom it is a kind of kryptonite.*"

Amanda smiled. "You've met him twice, and already you've worked him out. Bravo! But this is all a bit odd." She scrunched closer and lowered her voice. "I've never heard of this paint thing before. It's a bit suspicious. I wonder who the young man was you saw in Thorns. Someone like us? And what about the others who emptied the shelves before you and he got there?"

"Has Sheila ever asked you to do any, um, painting?"

"No. All of my work is online, posting positive messages or warnings about fake news. Ethereal rather than physical things."

"Posting a vlog or blog seems quite physical to me."

"Yes, well, I suppose so. But you know what I mean."

"Sure…"

"Someone's pissed all over the floor," said Simon, stomping up to their table and noisily slumping into a seat. Today, he wore a t-shirt with a picture of a dwarfish character wielding an axe. "What time do they start the quiz?"

Amanda touched Tom on the arm and mouthed 'later'.

***

One part of the quiz was a 'table round' involving questions served up on a sheet of A4 paper that were meant to be answered at leisure throughout the evening.

"Tom," said Amanda, "you look like you've seen a ghost."

The table round comprised twenty pictures of places around Norwich, including various statues, carvings, and snaps of partial sections of buildings taken from obtuse and confusing angles. Picture number three was of a hypodermic syringe on a pavement plaque.

"There! *That!* It's… it's…"

"Are you going to blow a fuse, old chap?" asked Ed.

"No. Or maybe *yes*. Picture three is on St Giles Street." He turned to Amanda. "It's one of the places I saw a message on Saturday."

"Message?" Ed frowned.

"Yes. A seventh dimensional one. Using the glasses Smith gave me. It said… it said… never mind."

"Cool!" said Simon. "Let me see the sheet. Maybe there are other places of alien interest on it."

"You mean, like abduction sites?" smirked Ed.

"You never know!"

Tom shook his head and sat back. *Coincidence?* It was amazing how often things like this happened. You'd encounter some odd fact for the first time and then, *bang*, there it would be again later the same day – in an internet news story or a documentary on TV. He glanced at Amanda and noticed that she and Ed seemed to be sharing some unspoken communication, while an oblivious Simon ran his eyes and a guiding finger over the sheet. To change the subject, he cleared his throat and asked Ed: "Anyway, what does this quiz involve? Have you done it before?"

Ed narrowed his eyes in understanding and decided to play ball. "Yes. A couple of times, though not for a while. But I don't know this geezer." He jerked a thumb towards the quizmaster. "Barman said he's a stand-in for their regular john, who's got the shits or something."

"Ah, right." Tom was relieved for the excuse to break eye contact; he looked to the side of the lounge, where the quizmaster was peering at a sheet of paper whilst holding a mic in one hand. The man was a hefty fellow with a scraggly grey goatee. "Okay. But what's the usual form? I guess that will still be the same."

"Normally, there are four rounds of ten that include a themed music round and a themed round on films, plus a table round like the one that nearly made you cack yourself." He gave a wink. "We can play our joker on one of the spoken rounds to double our points. And it appears our host is ready…"

The goateed-one cleared his throat and spoke into his mic. "Hello all, welcome to…" He winced at a screech of feedback and quickly fiddled with the controls of the sound system set on the table on which he was perched. When he continued, the volume was much lower. "Sorry about that. Anyway, welcome to the quiz. The rounds tonight are on words that contain the letter 'X', vigilantes, a music round based on the theme of outer space, and a film round on sci-fi."

"Get in!" cried Ed.

As the quizmaster continued with his instructions, Amanda leant in. "It does seem right up our alley… or at least, *yours*."

"Yours?" Tom was surprised. "Aren't you into sci-fi?"

The woman adjusted her glasses and gave a wistful smile. "Just because I am *the tool of alien oppressors…*" she winked at Ed, "doesn't mean I'm a fan of the genre."

"Nicely put, Mands," said Ed. "But never fear. Maybe there are some unusual vegetables that include the letter 'x' in their monstrous names. Otherwise, I am sure we can carry you just this once, eh? Si – leave that now: we can solve the rest during the interval between rounds. It's time to crush our enemies, see them driven before us—"

"And hear the lamentations of their women?"

"Well remembered, Si. You're in the zone! Now, listen up…"

***

They obliterated the first round. Tom was particularly proud of correctly answering 'Xerxes' to a question on the Persian empire, although he suspected that Ed knew the answer to that, just as he knew the answers to all of the other questions.

"I have a mind like a landfill of rotting knowledge refuse," explained Ed, insouciantly. "But now we're onto 'vigilantes', which is surely something our Amanda knows about. There must be hordes of eco-warriors out there, stealing through the night and taking vengeance upon the unnatural world and those who prefer it to living in dung huts and sodomising badgers, or whatever it is those hippies enjoy." He grinned broadly at the woman. "Spare me, Mands, for I ride a bike!"

Charles Bronson… *tick*.

The Guardian Angels of New York… *tick*.

The Scarlett Pimpernel ("I knew you'd be of use, Amanda, babes")… *tick*.

Kick-Ass ("…and that sexy minx, Hit Girl, eh, Si? Grrrrrrrrr!")… *tick*.

Question nine was about a shadowy group of vigilantes in El Salvador. "Sombra Negra," declared Ed, confidently. "Trust me. Points in the bag."

But the last question stumped them.

"What is the name of the Hero of St Gregory's Green," asked the quizmaster, "who last week stood up to a gang of drug-crazed psychopaths here in Norwich?"

"What-the-fuck!" declared Ed, unamused.

"Something you *don't* know?" teased Simon.

"No, I bloody well don't! Come on, guys, give me a hand here."

"Didn't you see the story in the news?" asked Amanda. "It was on *Look East*, and in the *EDP* the next day."

"No. My horizons are generally broader than the bucolic goings-on in *Naaaarwich*. So, as you've seen the story, what's the answer?"

Amanda shrugged. "I don't know. It wasn't an unusual name, but that's all I can remember. Sorry."

A couple of tables away, an exclamation of delight suggested that someone in the room did know the answer. Two members of the team high-fived.

"Well, they clearly know it," said Tom. "Who are they, Ed?"

The team in question comprised the maximum number of six: three male, three female, all dressed completely in black. Five were young, although their apparent leader – a large man with an immense belly and a thick, black beard – was in his late forties or early fifties.

"Terminus Est," scowled Ed, who'd been keeping notes on their opponents and their scores. "The fat bastard over there reeks of quiz-meisterdom. Probably a member of *The Beast Appreciation Society* who jerks off over a poster of *The Governess* every night in his soulless little bedsit."

Tom nodded, appreciating the reference to participants in *The Chase*, perhaps the premier TV gameshow for quizzers.

"They do seem to be taking this quite seriously," noted Amanda. "Are they really wearing custom t-shirts with their own logo? What does it mean?"

"Terminus Est is the name of a sword in *Warhammer*," declared Simon sagely, tapping his own t-shirt, which bore the name of that very same RPG.

"I suspect it comes from earlier than that," muttered Ed, his eyes still fixed narrowly on the other team. "Name of the sword of the torturer, Severian, in Gene Wolfe's classic novels. *Bastards!*"

"It's only a game, Ed," cautioned Amanda.

"Sure," replied Ed. "But *what* game?"

At the mid-way pause for refreshments, The Credulous were tied for second behind the black-clad team.

***

The music round was a surprise to Tom. They did fairly well – although that was almost entirely thanks to Simon.

"Not really my bag," declared Ed. "Especially this *grungy house* stuff, or whatever the hell it's called. I like music that's actually *musical.*"

Yet Ed still pulled out the best answer of the round in Tom's view: *Jeff Wayne's War of the Worlds.*

They fell to third place afterwards.

"These young wankers all know their music," said Ed. "It's essentially a handicap round for us. *Nil desperandum.* Nothing worth doing is ever easy. I'm sure we'll ace the final round, although I do admit to being somewhat concerned about this table round. Finished it yet, Si?"

The youngest member of their party pouted and swivelled the partially completed sheet for the others to see. "Sorry, mate. No idea where these last ones are."

"Nor me," said Amanda. "Tom?"

"Er, no." Tom still found the image of the hypodermic troubling. He'd had to look at the sheet with a hand over the offending picture. At least he'd been the first to identify the St Peter Mancroft church and the Guildhall, but the other pictures he'd known had been identified by Amanda already, including the Maid's Head Hotel and Pull's Ferry. "But I think others are struggling too. Even Terminus Est. I saw them arguing over the sheet while you were at the bar."

"So, there may still be hope," said Ed. "Here's Chubby Lucifer. Shush!"

Ed and Simon easily answered the final round, including the very last question – one that led to mutterings of discontent around the room.

"Easy," said Ed. "The original was 1956 and the remake was 1978. Oh look, the fat git and his catamites look depressed. Bad luck, sir!" he called out.

"Ed – don't wind them up! They might have the last laugh."

Amanda was right.

"And in second place…" announced the quizmaster, after the final two rounds had been passed over, marked, and scored up in his spreadsheet. "Drum roll please! It's… The Credulous! That means the winners – by two points – are Terminus Est. Well done! Fifty pounds of drink vouchers are coming your way."

"Fuck!" declared Ed. "I thought we might have had them at the end."

"They got full marks on the music round," noted Tom. "I think that's where we lost it."

"And the table round," said Amanda, who held the marked sheet in her hand. "I still don't recognise three of these."

"Hmmm, it was a local theme that did for us, notably, the final question on our joker round and these…" Ed sourly look over the sheet of pictures, which he'd received from Amanda. "And now my wrath is great, and my determination vast. We *will* take down The Est and see them weeping on the beer-soaked floorboards at our feet!" He then handed the sheet to Tom. "There you go, novitiate Tom. I now declare you the expert-designate on all things local. This should be in line with the demands of your extra-terrestrial handler, too. So – revise! Or at least, keep this as a souvenir and look upon it daily to remind yourself what defeat feels like and motivate yourself to never let it happen again!"

"Er, right." Tom took the sheet from a wide-eyed Ed.

But then the other's face creased into a broad smile. "Time for a final round?" Ed declared, in sudden high spirits. "Good show! These are on me!"

***

"Next week?" said Ed, wheeling his bike up to where the others stood beneath the pub sign, dimly illuminated by diffuse light spilling from the pub windows.

"Ah, can't make it, mate," replied Simon. "Got a gaming tournament."

"Me neither," said Amanda. "My… *friend*… is back from Berlin for a week."

"This would be your mysterious *boy*-friend, eh, Mands? A week of banging instead of avenging our sullied honour?" Ed smirked and looked askance at Tom. "Some people have a weird set of priorities."

Amanda simply shook her head and sighed: clearly, she'd learnt to accept Ed's coarse barbs. "I'll let you know when I can next meet up. Tom – which way are you going?"

"Me? Oh. Muriel Road. Down Unthank…" Tom had been thrown by the news from Amanda. He'd had no particular amorous feelings towards her, but still, it would have been nice to at last come into the orbit of a viable target…

"Okay. We can walk part way together."

"Sure."

"Well, cheerio, my credulous companions!" Ed mounted up. "Do not fear. Our time will come! I'll be in touch. *Look to the skies…* or at least to your emails." And he was off.

"Yeah, cheers guys," said Simon, and he set off on foot behind Ed, heading towards Newmarket Road.

Amanda pulled her coat closed and zipped it up. "Well, come on then." She set off down Trinity Street.

They walked together in silence for some seconds, while Tom considered whether he should or shouldn't broach the topic of Amanda's friend. At last, he decided it would have been stranger not to. "So… your boyfriend works in Berlin?"

"Max? Yes, he works for an international environmental NGO. I haven't seen him for over a month. He's often in Brussels, and I'll occasionally take the Eurostar to meet him there."

"Right. He sounds important."

"Oh, well, I don't know about that. His is one of several NGOs in Europe doing similar work, and it's not the biggest, though it does have links to the German Green party, so it's probably got more influence than most."

"Ah, right. And… haven't you thought of going out to join him? I mean, since you are kind of freelance, you can work anywhere, can't you?"

Amanda continued to focus on the ground ahead. "Well, we have talked about it. But I have my life here. I occasionally do things with people from UEA and Cambridge. Besides, Max is, well… let's just say we aren't the closest couple. We have our own interests, and he likes his space." Now she glanced up at Tom. "And there is the Sheila issue, too. I mean, though anyone from anywhere can read my blogs, her interests are in this area, so I try to address local issues in my communications."

"Right." *Not the closest?* "Uh, Smith is definitely focused on Norwich, too. He said that our observers often watch particular communities."

Amanda seemed glad of the change of subject. "Yes, that's why Ed hangs around, too. Well, that and the fact that in spite of his mockery, he actually likes Norwich, particularly being a big fish in a small, odd-shaped pond."

"Right…" Silence descended for several seconds, then Tom laughed nervously. "God, this is awkward."

"Awkward? I'm sure Max wouldn't…"

"No-no!" Tom held up his hands. "That's not what I meant. I meant, well, all this alien stuff. I still don't know what it's all about. What's real. What I can say, and what I can't. Smith told me not to discuss matters with anyone, so I've already broken that trust. What if Smith and Sheila and Big Ed–"

"And Vortent?" Amanda grinned.

"Yes, him too. What if they're all on different sides? What would they do if they found out we were talking? I can't help feeling we must be being watched by someone, something. Or maybe even by *lots* of things."

Amanda's grin disappeared and her expression turned serious. "I know, Tom. It's a conversation I've had with Ed before, when there was just the two of us. You know, he *can* be serious when he needs to be. All I can say, is that we've never had any kind of come back, although we agreed – as we said at the Alex – never to say too much. Never to reveal something that might cause others in the group to change their behaviour, to give the game away. That's fine for Ed, who likes to be mysterious, but I find it hard at times – like you do now."

Tom nodded vigorously. "Too damned right. There's so much I want to talk over. It's an itch I need to scratch. I don't know what to do."

They'd reached the end of the street, emerging onto Unthank Road beside a small Tesco Metro. "I think we part here," said Amanda. She gave Tom a sympathetic look. "Perhaps we just need to take it slow. You mentioned the paint and the messages to us. See if Smith gives any sign

81

that he knows you've been talking. If not, maybe we can speak more next time. I'd also love to get some of this off my chest."

Tom found himself primed by the word: he looked down, then back up quickly, hoping the direction of his gaze hadn't been obvious. "Yes, good plan, I…"

Amanda smiled. "Next time, Tom. Let's wait for the summons from our glorious leader." She turned right and headed towards the centre.

After a moment, Tom turned in the opposite direction.

Chapter 9: Second Interlude

Robert Quigley didn't know why he'd done it – he really didn't. He had absolutely nothing against gay people. In fact, he was a card-carrying member of the Labour Party who believed in gay rights and had even (grudgingly) applauded the Conservatives when they'd legislated for same-sex marriage. Cameron wasn't a *complete* twat!

As he was bundled away by the police in a daze – shielding his head from a furious barrage of colourful placards – he kept asking himself: what the *fuck* had just happened?

***

The Norwich Pride Parade had become an established part of the city's civic calendar, normally taking place towards the end of July. Even when the Covid-19 pandemic had led to its cancelation for a couple of years, it had initially returned in its usual month, though the hiatus seemed to have loosened expectations that it just *had* to take place at that hallowed time. For some reason Robert never caught, it had been moved to the end of August this year.

The timing was certainly not good for him. He'd got back from his summer holiday to Faro with his wife and teenage daughter the previous day, driving back from Stansted Airport in the late afternoon; he needed to get into town today for a bit of shopping in prep for his return to work on Monday. To be precise, he needed some shirts, and as he'd never taken to internet shopping (insisting on trying on clothes before buying) a trip to the centre was required. But he'd forgotten about the rearranged parade, and soon found himself fuming in a stationary car, with roads either closed off or jammed with others who'd presumably also forgotten or else badly misjudged likely conditions.

He eventually found a place to dump his car on a residential street that was supposedly restricted to those with a resident's parking permit – but being fed up, he was willing to take the risk, assuming that the forces of oppression would have their hands full with the parade and hence have fewer-than-normal bodies to patrol the shadowlands in search of parking-fine booty.

Already hot and bothered, the cloying heat – which must have been tipping thirty Celsius – didn't help his condition.

Robert marched briskly to Queens Road – part of the inner ring road – and crossed over near the bus station. From here, he caught strains of music emanating from various invisible bands, rising as he moved closer to the parade. Was that a samba beat? Then that particular rhythm ebbed as the parade continued its unseen way to be replaced by the wail of a brass band. He cut through the bus station, and took Surrey Street towards St Stephens Street – a rather ugly shopping street, unsympathetically reconstructed post-war following German bombing, and only partially redeemed by the building of the Chantry Place Mall. At the junction of Surrey and St Stephens, around the large Marks & Spencers, he saw a wall of spectators sprinkled with pink balloons, rainbow flags and bobbing placards. By the time he reached this bottleneck, it had begun to break up, with the main parade heading down Theatre Street to his left. The shops he needed were in front of him, though it was a struggle to get through the noisy, garish crowd. He attempted to squeeze against the flow, realised he was getting nowhere, then gravitated to the crowd's edge, where immobile shop fronts at least gave him some purchase.

This is bloody stupid!

He probably should have gone into the Mall. He would have gone into M&S, but that was chaos central. The Next outlet was totally out of the question, too, as were the shops fronting Gentleman's Walk and the Haymarket, and so he pushed on down Red Lion Street. The crowds were thinner here: with the street not on the parade route, it acted as a spillway for celebrants and a haven for other unwise Saturday shoppers. What were his options? Primark? *Fuck!*

Even Primark was heaving. When he was a kid, he remembered the retailer and its brand being distinctly unfashionable and low-end. But now, even though its prices were still cheap, the store seemed to have gained an elevated status for many: while still a must for the working classes, it had become ironically totemic for others. *Weird.* One result of this invigorated popularity was that the store was constantly busy, and today was no exception. He spent half-an-hour being buffeted within, and even when he found some shirts he would have liked to try on, the queues to use the changing rooms were prohibitive. And so he left empty handed, this time through the exit onto Gentleman's Walk, which – while still busy – was nowhere near as bad as it must have been previously.

Shortly after, Robert found himself on Hay Hill, a square with a McDonalds to one side, the church of St Peter Mancroft opposite this, and a large, three-storey Next along the third closed side. The space was dominated by a statue of Sir Thomas Browne – seated and holding something up in one hand, in a pose suggesting intense contemplation. Robert knew that Browne was some sort of philosopher, who was the spitting image of a picture he'd seen of King Charles the First, with his 'tache and goatee, wavy hair, and foppish costume. Scattered throughout the square below the raised statue were a variety of sculptures, set in a higgledy-piggledy manner, which were supposed to represent the great man's ideas. Most of these were carved from black stone, sometimes made into angular chairs, sometimes only partially finished, like geodes that had been cut in half to provide a flat surface for seating, or had segments cut from them, like part-demolished and squashed Terry's Chocolate Oranges coated in gravel.

He moved into the square, weaving through shoppers and parade spectators and participants, looking for a spot to rest. As he did so, he found himself – perhaps for the first time ever – really *looking* at the phrases etched onto the artful objects. RELIGIO MEDICI was writ upon the clean, flat surface of one black stone. A couple of the 'Chocolate Oranges' had URNE BURRIALS and VULGAR ERRORS neatly stencilled onto their vertical seatbacks. GARDEN OF CYRUS was written on the flat surface of a low 'table' set in front of the ERRORS chair-sculpture – briefly visible, until a small girl crawled on top of it and obscured the message.

Robert frowned. What the hell did any of this *mean*? He actually felt piqued. It was as if someone were flaunting their intellect in front of him, challenging him, almost sneering at him. Other messages were even more mystifying. He turned and found one of the fully finished stones – a small black seat, with every surface cut into smooth lines – declaring HIDRIOTAPHIA; close by was a similar seat that announced QUINCUNCE. And as he looked at the latter, he noticed beyond it the blocky carving of a section of a human face in white stone laced with grey filaments, with a dead, pupilless eye looking at him. *What the fuck?* Who did the sculptor think he was, the bloody poseur? His pique notched up into annoyance, then further into anger. Everywhere he went, people were thrusting their views in his face. Showing off. Telling him what he could think. Looking down on him like bloody Thomas Browne himself.

And then he got jostled.

Robert turned to look at a man whose face was made up with expertly applied pink lipstick, rouged cheeks, and absurdly long eyelashes. He was wearing a singlet over his muscular physique, along with a kilt in clashing colours that were unlikely to be found in any catalogue of official tartans, as well as a headpiece that seemed to be made of copper and had a crown of rainbow feathers, something like a Native American headdress.

"Watch yourself, dearie," said the man, light-heartedly.

"What? Watch *myself*? You bumped into me!"

The man's smile broadened, and he winked. "If you say so, lover!"

Robert reached up one hand… and swatted the headpiece from the other's scalp.

The man's face registered shock, and he stepped back, reaching one hand instinctively for his missing crown. Behind him, someone swore as they accidentally trod upon the dislodged item.

"Not so smug now, eh?" said Robert. And he felt *good*. *Very* good. And also somehow *strong*, even though it was clear that in any tussle the beefcake opposite would easily best him – a middle-aged mesomorph.

As the man spluttered, and others turned to look at the contretemps, Robert set his shoulders and looked fiercely about. And then, fortified by the lack of challenge, he stepped across to a short-haired woman in a yellow jumpsuit and grasped the blue-and-pink placard she was holding aloft and threw it to the ground, causing a couple of the woman's friends to leap aside.

Robert felt even better! He felt… *relieved*. It was a kind of catharsis, a way to somehow deliver himself from the heat, the press, the thwarted ambitions – not just for a shirt, but for a meaningful career and a purpose in life beyond pushing paper.

As more people turned, more muttered, and some yelled, Robert set off, as though freed from a lifetime's worth of burdens: he barged and skipped and windmilled through the crowd, batting at balloons, grasping rainbow flags from hands and whipping them skywards, tugging banners, shoving drag queens, using a stolen baton – covered in sparkles and tassels – to dislodge wigs and pink cowboy hats and a maroon policeman's helmet…

For a couple of minutes, Robert caused chaos. The crowd was out for fun, not confrontation, and it wasn't until he blundered into a wedge of 'Gay NHS workers', dressed in green but wearing rainbow lanyards, that his rampage was halted, he was firmly held, and soon after delivered into the arms of a couple of constables.

***

Robert didn't have to spend the night in the cells and was allowed home that night. The media must have been tipped off, though, because by Sunday, reporters had come knocking, and he was forced into hiding. Still, the lack of a new shirt proved an irrelevance: he didn't need it after all, as he called in sick on Monday.

Later that Monday, Robert's exploits were the focus of another meeting, held late afternoon at The Castle pub, on Spitalfields. A group of Pride organisers had congregated for a debrief, scattered around a couple of tables.

"Clare, I've never seen you *soooo* angry," said Cathy. Both she and Clare had short-cropped hair, but while Cathy was tall and smartly dressed, having hot-footed it from work, Clare was stocky and still wore an official Norwich Pride t-shirt, with several pins at the breast, denoting her various allegiances to trans, environmental, and other progressive causes.

"I've a right to be angry. We have one day a year and then everyone forgets us. They expect us to disappear in a puff of pink smoke and boiler suits. No, *not* one day a year. They won't even give us that!"

"They?" mused Harry, a late-middle-aged campaigner with a moustache and slicked hair.

"The heteros. The straights. Normal and *decent* society." Sarcasm dripped from her tongue, like saliva from a rabid wolf.

"Steady on, Clare," said Roberto, Harry's slightly younger partner. "It was just one man."

"One man acted, but how many others *wanted* to act? How many would have acted if they'd got the chance?"

"She's right," noted Francis, nodding sagely. He was in his thirties and wore a suit – and hated himself for doing so. "Did you hear about the hassle Billy got?"

"He was near that underpass, wasn't he?" observed Clare. "There's a council estate there. They don't know better."

"Come on, Clare," said Harry, who was turning into the voice of reason. "That's a bit judgmental. Lumping everyone together under one label is what *they* do."

"Precisely! What's good for the goose is good for the... why are you sniggering?"

"Sorry, dear. Did you say, what's good for the *goosed*?" Manny was in his twenties and seemed perpetually aroused.

"Mmmm, I wouldn't mind some of that!" volunteered Steve, Manny's on-and-off partner, in a voice one notch of campness above its usual tone.

Clare shook her head angrily. "Oh, come on. This is serious. *I'm* serious. We need to do something about this. I'm not going to let it stand."

"Do what, exactly?" asked Harry.

"I'm not sure. A march. A protest."

"You mean, another parade?"

"We deserve another parade to make up for this one! But no. What about... a group. An organisation. To patrol the centre. Let everyone know we're still here. That we're not going away."

"Okay," continued Harry, uncertainly. "I hardly think this fellow ruined the entire day, but what you suggest seems harmless enough."

"Harmless?" Clare frowned. "I'm not looking to be harmless. I want action."

"So... a patrolling group. With sandwich boards? Placards?" wondered Roberto.

"Oh, please, no," whined Cathy. "That's so *Socialist Worker*... ah, sorry Clare, I didn't mean to..."

Clare waved the inadvertent insult away. "No. It doesn't have to be so common. Perhaps a style. Something that stands out. Something that's immediately recognisable."

"Headwear's good," mused Roberto. "Someone in a hat always stands out."

"Fine," said Clare. "but what? I know. A beret. That's revolutionary headgear. But–"

"Rainbow!" Manny was suddenly excited, jumping up and down in his seat. "A rainbow beret. That would stand out!"

"*Rain-bow-y beret*...." sang Steve, to the tune of an old *Prince* number.

Clare smiled at last. "Yeah. That's good, that. Everyone who saw us would know."

"I can get them made," said Francis. "Trevor is a dab hand at millinery."

"Excellent! Get on to him. Ask him to make a sample. If I approve–"

"*I?*" Harry looked at the woman with a wry arch to the eyebrow. He wrinkled his nose and waggled his debonair moustache. "Are you taking command?"

"I don't see why not. My idea. Do you object?"

"Not at all... *commandant*. And what do you want to call this new group of yours?"

"Commandant?" Clare clearly liked the sound of the word. "Comm... Comman... Commando! The... Rainbow Commandos!"

"Oh, that is *goooood*," declared Cathy. "Who wouldn't want a piece of *that* action?"

"I'm in!" declared Manny.

Others started voicing their assent. Clare looked around approvingly, then focused on Harry, who clearly held the keys to wider support. "And what about you, Harry?"

"We're not talking about violence, are we?"

"No. We will patrol. *With pride!* And we'll be there to help or defend if necessary."

"Hmmm, okay. That sounds innocent enough. Very well. I'm in."

And so was formed the first cadre of the Rainbow Commandos.

***

Elsewhere in Norwich, at roughly the same time, other portentous events were afoot.

"Jim? Jim Taylor?"

Jim froze and hunched his shoulders. The voice had come from somewhere behind him. He slowly turned and raised his hands in an instinctive act of defence. "I don't want no trouble."

He realised he was in St Gregory's Green – the location of his act of infamy. For a moment, he thought the approaching trio might have been the group he'd accosted a couple of weeks ago – but the first thing he noticed was smiles and an aura of cleanliness. The two men and one woman seemed like normal people.

"It *is* you!" said the statuesque woman, who was at least as tall as the men to either side of her. She wore a long, dark-red leather coat and had shoulder-length hair that was also red. *Amazonian.* "We're *so* glad to meet you."

"Yeah, can I shake your hand?" asked the man to her left – who was dressed in a black bomber jacket and had a neat black beard. "It's great to meet you, man!"

Jim felt compelled to extend his hand, which was eagerly grasped and pumped, not just by the first man, but also by the second, reaching across.

"Me too! Hi Jim, it's a real pleasure!" This man wore denim and bulged at the arms. He too had a beard, though his was longer and tinged with grey, and he was completely bald. "I'm Ken. And this is Tania. And James. We're… well, I suppose you could say, *admirers.*"

"Oh, uh, thanks." Jim felt slightly embarrassed. He quickly glanced off to either side: the Green was moderately busy, with people bustling past, mostly on their way home from work, though the corner by the church, where *it* had happened, was currently unoccupied, with the nearby coffee shop having recently closed, and the rough crew mercifully absent.

"I thought we might be able to intercept you here," said Tania. Her smile was dazzling. "We'd like to talk. We have a proposition. Can we buy you a drink? The Strangers Tavern is just around the corner. Or maybe the Belgian Monk?"

"Might be a bit busy," said Ken. "Could try Micawbers – that's pretty much on his way home."

Way home? How did they know where he lived? "Ah, well, that would be great, but I really ought to get back, or my wife will wonder what's happened to me." *And wonder if I've gone and got myself arrested again,* he thought.

"Please?" wheedled Tania. "We won't keep you long."

She really was stunning: how could he resist? "Well, okay. I suppose I could have a quick half."

Tania bestowed another radiant smile, then took him by one arm and gently coaxed him along. Jim's heart raced. *What would Marie think*? The answer to that was *the worst. Always* the worst…

The two men fell in behind, and the quartet made their steady way down Pottergate. They continued past the junctions with Upper and Lower Goat Lane, moving purposefully, but largely in silence. Soon, they were the only ones present in the street, but their destination wasn't far, and Jim found himself strangely at ease. The pub appeared on their left. They entered and found it empty, having just opened. Ken asked for their orders and was soon in discussion with the landlord.

Jim was ushered into one corner by a window; James moved to sit next to him, and Tania sat opposite.

"It's really good to meet you in the flesh," Tania began. "I'm not sure if you know this, but you've become a bit of an inspiration to us."

"Us?"

"Yes. Ordinary people who have had enough. We work in the centre, so we see it all the time. Every day there seem to be more thugs. Junkies. Drunks. Pushers. Homeless—"

"Not that we have an issue with the homeless," interjected James, looking swiftly at Tania then back at Jim. "We know that many… or at least some… are unfortunate. They can be victims, too. But they're often the fertiliser for villainy. They are definitely part of the problem."

"Uh, right." Jim wasn't sure where this was headed, but he had an uncomfortable feeling about these fine-looking, well-spoken admirers. "It *has* got worse, hasn't it? Norwich seems to have become a bit of a magnet for desperate people."

"It has," said Tania, "and… ah! Our drinks!"

"Here you go!" said Ken. He distributed two pints and two halves amongst the group, then sat next to Tania, diagonally across from Jim, who was now completely hemmed in. "Where have you got to? Have you told him yet?"

"Told me what? Uh, thanks for the drink, but… I still don't know who you are, apart from your first names."

"We are…" Ken paused and looked at his colleagues, almost as if seeking moral support. "We are the Knights of St Gregory."

"Knights?"

Ken gave a somewhat embarrassed smile. "Yes, I know it sounds a bit pretentious, but it's also apt."

"We haven't been formed long," continued Tania, hurriedly. "Less than a week. We know each other from a local rugby club. We were in the bar a couple of days after your fight, and we got talking about your story, and the way the media treated you."

"Typical newshounds," muttered James. "One interview with a supporter, then another with some bolshie progressive type condemning you as the ugly face of an uncaring society, then a third interview with a copper – who of course towed the line of damning you for vigilantism. All in the cause of *balance*. But most right-thinking people are one hundred percent behind you."

"That's right," concurred Tania. "And we decided that it was about time we stood up and did something about things. You know, like a neighbourhood watch, but with teeth."

"And a knightly ethos," said Ken, running a hand over his bearded chin. "You know. Behaving with honour. Protecting the weak. Slaying metaphorical dragons."

"Hence the name," said James. "We are determined to clean up Norwich, once and for all. And it's not just us three. There are about a dozen of us – not just from the club, but others we know. Mechanics, a solicitor…"

"Angus is a doctor," noted Ken.

"That's right. A doctor. And we could recruit more, but we've decided to stay small and keep to the shadows."

"We've done nothing yet," said Tania, now clearly excited. "But we have plans. Nothing violent of course, but… *forceful*. We need to let these people know they're not wanted, and they need to clean up, behave, or leave the city."

Jim smiled weakly. "Ah, those are… noble sentiments. In theory. But how can I–?"

"Lead us," said James. "At least, as our figurehead. Become our Arthur."

"Yes," said Tania. "You're the first… the first among equals. The man who made a stand."

"Yes, join us!" urged Ken. "Be part of something important."

Jim sat back in his seat, resting against the wall, creating distance between himself and the eager trio. He felt slightly appalled and yet also flattered. When was the last time anyone had actually looked up to him, or praised him? Marie still referred to him as a *damned fool*; at work, he was looked upon with embarrassment. The police were still mulling over whether to charge him or not. And all he'd done was stand up to some deadbeats who were making good, ordinary people feel uncomfortable. These three were the first to voice unconditional appreciation, and it felt *good*. He suddenly found himself smiling. He reached down to his half and drained it in three gulps – quaffed in true knightly fashion.

"Jim," queried Tania, "what do you say?"

"I say… I say… I'll have another please, and this time make it a pint! Marie can wait!"

Tania laughed, while James patted him on the shoulder and Ken smiled broadly and rose to his feet.

Chapter 10: On Patrol

It was Tuesday, and already Tom was rueing the absence of the quiz that evening. He'd seen and spoken to no one since last week's event, which – given the unexpected flourishing of his social network over the last few weeks, involving aliens and alienesque humans – seemed like a return to the bad old days.

He'd not met Smith on the Saturday because of a conflict with the Pride parade: a message attached to his latest Cloud-saved chapter had requested that they meet instead on Wednesday at noon 'if he was able to get up in time'. That had seemed an odd construction. Why wouldn't he be able to get up on time? Had Smith been watching him somehow? Was he aware that Tom had been to the quiz last week and woken up late with a slightly throbbing head? Or perhaps the alien had just logged that Tom hadn't accessed his stored novel until eleven that morning and the jibe (was it a jibe? Did aliens 'jibe'?) was referring to that fact?

Tom had written precisely one paragraph all morning. If anything, he seemed to be slowing down. It wasn't that he had writer's block *per se* – he'd come up with some interesting plotlines, and even a putative ending for his story – it was more a motivational problem. For the last week or so, he had gotten into the routine of trying to write in the mornings and then going for a recce in the afternoon, quartering the city (and *eighthing* and *sixteenthing* it too). But his mind quickly wandered whenever he sat in front of his computer: before long, he tended to find himself with multiple opened windows showing local news sites and online city maps, which he took to scanning for interesting or suspicious events while cross-referencing noted locations. He'd not uncovered anything especially noteworthy – a closed shop; the odd brawl; a bit of vandalism – but he still felt that this was a valuable exercise, helping him to gain a greater handle on the city than he'd ever had.

And when not surfing the net, Tom often found himself side-tracked by the spreadsheet he'd created that detailed his routes, with annotations and even a bit of a log:

Thursday: Weather good. Down to Riverside (R3). Mobile hot dog van missing. Past station. Pedestrian footfall light. Yomp to Thorpe St Andrews all the way to

Postwick along River Yare. Nothing to report. Fat Cat and Canary on the way back. Scratchings. Returned same way. Only low-density footfall in the burbs: rethink this route?

And another:

Sunday: Light rain. Northern ring (R2) down Dereham Road to ring road. Norwich Over the Water. To Anglia Square. What a dump. Back via Magdalen Street and Colgate. Should I extend this route to the Courts? Nothing to report.

And again:

Monday: Pissed down. Southern ring (R4) via Chapelfield Gardens to Trowse. Stepped in dog shit. Abandoned. Coach and Horses.

He smirked at that. It was hardly a sign of dedication, but the Coach – which was often patronised by crew and cast from the nearby Theatre Royal after evening performances – was one of his favourite pubs in the city, though one he rarely got the chance to visit, hence his new mission *was* starting to yield some perks.

As he contemplated his intended route for the day (designated R5), the phone rang.

Who was it this time? Microsoft technical support? Amazon? An ambulance chaser calling about the road accident he'd had, wishing to offer their services in pursuing a claim (remarkable really, given that he didn't even own a car)?

He was tempted to let the call ring off. Three rings. Four. Five. Who was he kidding? He leapt from his chair and scampered downstairs, expecting the call to cut off just as he picked up the receiver... but this time he made it.

"Yeah?" he growled, in an un-Tom-like way. "What do you want?"

"Ah! Er, Tom?"

"Mum?"

"Sorry, dear. Have I called at a bad time?"

"No, it's fine. I just thought you might be a man called *Stephen* with a surprisingly subcontinental accent calling to help me fix my non-broken computer."

"Well, I really don't know much about computers. Nor does your father. Should I get off the line?"

"No, mum, I don't need help. It's scammers trying to rip me off. Don't you get these calls?"

There was a slight pause at the other end. "Well, I do get a *few* calls every now and then. The callers seem rather nice, but I think they must be confused. I have to keep explaining to them that I don't have a computer."

Tom rolled his eyes. Thank God his parents had remained in the electronic stone age. *Lambs to the slaughter.* "Never mind, mum. How can I help? I guess dad has gone fishing and you're alone?"

"Yes, dear. I've just phoned for a little chat..."

By the time Tom got off the line it was approaching lunchtime, so there was little point in returning to the magnum opus.

***

Feeling rather guilty at his lack of work in the morning, Tom decided to make recompense by putting in a longer than usual patrol in the afternoon. Yet, the phone call, followed by lunch (a value burger, some own-brand crisps, and an apple), and then a check of various jobs websites (after he suddenly realised he'd shortly have to justify himself to the unemployment benefit people once more) led to further delays. It was therefore close to three o' clock before he left the house.

The first thing Tom did was to slip on his special glasses. At least the weather merited the move: the previous day's spasm of heavy rain had cleared, and it was bright and warm again, befitting the start of September.

He headed down elegant Christchurch Road to Newmarket Road – aka the A11 – which provided the main exit from the city to all areas south, notably Cambridge, London, and Civilisation. There was little to see signage-wise on the early part of this circuit (the R5), which Tom knew from previous experience, given that this was one of the main routes into the city and hence was incorporated into several of his patrols. As such, Tom initially paid little attention to his surrounds. However, he slowed as he approached the old Norwich and Norfolk Hospital and its grounds, and drew to a halt at the junction with Ipswich Road. One of Norwich's colleges lay that way. He'd not been there before: shouldn't he check it out? Nodding to himself, he turned in that direction.

It was a bit further to the college than he expected. Tom passed a couple of junctions, some three-storey apartment blocks, and then various low, brick walls and hedges. And then a pale-coloured college building

96

came into view, shortly followed by 'Gate 3', which comprised a pair of narrow, black gates, presently open to allow access to the grounds. By the road, a couple of small signs welcomed visitors to City College Norwich, declaring this to be the 'main entrance', and providing directions to parking within. Of the college building itself, all Tom could see was one edge of what looked like a prison block, bereft of any significant entry portal. There were surprisingly few people about: he noticed a smattering in the mid-distance, then a small red car slowed beside him and turned into the site. It was all rather unobtrusive, almost ghostly. Was this really the main entrance?

Tom decided to walk on. To his near side was a long, iron fence with a bush behind, and then a line of tall trees that largely obscured the college from the road. However, he soon came to a gap in the trees through which he spotted an entrance of sorts, with access up a small flight of stone steps and a flagpole to one side with a limp blue flag. It was perhaps another couple of hundred metres to the end of the long building, and here – Gate 4 – turned out to be a single lane exit road with a 'no entry' sign. There were a number of other low buildings on the site further along, behind a brick wall, but Tom decided he need go no further. Everything was rather low key, and there seemed little opportunity for surreptitious messaging – at least, *off* site. But *on* site?

The red-and-white no entry sign was only meant for cars, but it still proved deterrent enough for Tom. He retraced to Gate 3 and approached the pedestrian entrance beside it. A blue bin partially obscured one of the entrance signs. And now he looked more closely, he noticed that at the bottom of this was a picture of a yellow triangle with 'CCTV Warning' next to it. He faltered, one foot raised in the air, about to overstep the threshold of the College grounds. And then he heard a cough and looked up. Leaning against some grey railings a short distance away was a young man wearing a dark jacket, his eyes hidden behind sunglasses, his arms crossed.

Tom dropped his foot and stepped back. The other wasn't a security guard, but most probably just a student. He seemed to be waiting for someone or something. Tom gave a guilty grin.

"Wotcha, mate," said the other. "Looking for something?"

"Ah, no…"

"No?" The smile on the other's face broadened. "Well, you coming in, or aren't you?"

No entry.

Warning CCTV.

"Er, actually, I, er, forgot something. I must…" Tom swivelled and headed rapidly up the Ipswich Road, back towards Newmarket Road, his pace not slowing until he regained familiar territory.

***

What had that been all about? Omega Tom, the great investigator, deterred from his duty by an innocent greeting? It wasn't as if he was attempting to break into a bank!

Gutless.

Or was it something else? Perhaps the signs *had* affected him. Were they alien messages of dissuasion? *No.* He had his glasses on, and there was nothing 7D about them. And yet… *maybe.*

He had been sceptical about the impact of subliminal messages like the ones he'd seen in the market and on St Giles. He scratched his nose absently, then frowned at the memory of the hypodermic. But if he had been primed by the gentle warning signs here, then maybe Smith was right. There was power in words and symbols in the right combination in the right place at the right time.

He scratched his nose again and looked up. The old hospital was to his left, while some distance ahead he noticed the sign of the Coachmakers pub… and felt oddly conflicted. He loved the pub (notwithstanding his recent encounter with Fabio and Brian), yet suddenly recalled the leering face of the sun on a pavement plaque and felt a degree of tension. *Drunks…*

But what to do about the college? Students could be a militant bunch: it was prime territory for an alien influencer attack. But he could hardly storm the place and conduct a thorough survey of every corridor and block. And if he did decide that was worthwhile, then he'd need to do it regularly.

Tom came to a halt between two eateries – the Goulash House and the Grill House. He had a decision to make. *Decisions* – plural.

He could not realistically be expected to investigate the interior of every large building – with perhaps a few exceptions, such as the Castle and the two cathedrals. But City College had to be beyond remit; it just wasn't a credible or sensible target for him. So, he would largely continue to roam the streets, parks and waterways *outside*. He nodded to himself: Smith would surely agree. He'd raise the matter with him when he got the chance. But now…

Tom was opposite the junction to Victoria Street. He had planned to extend his patrolling, and now here was a chance. If he nipped down this road, he could negotiate a way to Hall Road, which was a moderately interesting thoroughfare that linked the inner and outer ring roads of Norwich, and what's more, hosted the excellent Kings Arms and Freemasons Arms, which faced off against each other in friendly (and occasionally not-so-friendly) rivalry. And at that point, a break would surely be called for. Tom smiled, then frowned…

Sun.

Drunks!

***

As he couldn't make up his mind, Tom decided to have halves in both pubs. Well, he couldn't show favouritism, could he! He felt better after this. And further, there had been enough road and retail signs *en route* to justify this extension to his R5 patrol. True, footfall had been light, but perhaps just sufficient. Tom gave a last, fond look at the Freemasons, then turned to resume his walk.

He soon rejoined his established route, continuing down Queens Road past Sainsburys to the roundabout at the foot of St Stephens Street, with the Champion pub on the corner, and after that, the crumbling remnants of the old city wall that ran alongside the Chantry Place Mall. Beyond this, he entered the Chapelfield Gardens. There were a couple of children's play areas here, a bandstand, a café, and the sad, shuttered remnants of what used to be the excellent Pedro's Tex-Mex Cantina. But there was a curious lack of signage. Maybe the place would be better targeted during the funfairs, which appeared at various celebratory times during the year?

Finally, Tom had to cross the inner ring road – which at this point was also named Grapes Hill – in order to return home via Earlham Road.

There were essentially three ways he could do this. The first was to do a mad dash across a dual carriageway near a roundabout by the Roman Catholic Cathedral and Temple Bar pub; the second, and his usual, was over the footbridge from Upper St Giles Street, which dropped down opposite the cathedral; and the third was via an underpass further down Grapes Hill accessed by Wellington Lane. He didn't feel like dicing with death, so he eschewed the first, but as he approached the footbridge his eyes flicked over to Upper St Giles. The messages on the pavement plaques had mysteriously disappeared on his last visit – an outcome Smith had shrugged off, suggesting the perpetrators may have returned to remove incriminating evidence – but that bloody *syringe* now came to his mind. Frowning, he carried on past the bridge and headed for the underpass.

And then it happened.

As Tom descended into the underpass, along a wall covered with graffiti, he spotted *something*. He swept off his glasses, at which a single word in gently glowing text disappeared… but reappeared when he put them back on again.

"Fuck!"

***

"I saw something!"

"Very good. Tell me."

It was just after noon on the following day. Tom had made it to his scheduled rendezvous with Smith on time, despite taking a slightly circuitous route in order to confirm his previous day's sighting.

"There's an underpass beneath the ring road – at the end of Pottergate. A spray-painted message says 'Black Lives Matter', but there's a 7D message between 'Lives' and 'Matter', so now it reads–"

"Black Lives *Don't* Matter?"

"Ah, right. How did you… ah, it must be obvious, I suppose."

Smith nodded his be-whiskered head. "Please sit, Tom. I don't want us to draw attention."

"Right. Will do." Tom slumped onto the ring bench beneath the large tree by the Guildhall. At this, Smith – in his traditional *Big Issue* seller guise – walked several paces and also sat, but perpendicular to Tom, so that they might appear like two strangers to any observer. The alien placed his pile of magazines in the space between them.

"Continue to look forwards, please, Tom. I can hear you well enough."

Tom shuffled away and kept his back square against the wooden bench. He waited for the other to continue.

"Good. Now – this message seems far more contentious than the others you saw. I imagine it could cause real antagonism."

"Yes, agreed. It could really stir things up if it were seen by the, um, wrong sort of people. Maybe it could provoke some sort of racist response?"

"I fear we may need to act. And an underpass provides opportunities that a pavement plaque on a busy street does not. Are you willing to now be my hands as well as my eyes?"

In his excitement, Tom had failed to fully think through the consequences of his find. "You mean… you mean the red paint and the magnets?"

"I do indeed."

"You mean, deal with the message?"

"Yes. Remove it completely. I think this is important, Tom." Smith paused as though making some calculation, then continued: "Alas, I fear that whatever species is playing Norwich, it is now attempting to up the ante. Did you hear about the fracas at the Pride event on Saturday?"

"Sure. A man went crazy and tore up a few banners. Sounds a bit like a storm in a teacup to me."

"Indeed. But sometimes, spilling tea can lead to serious consequences."

"Yes, especially if it's scalding hot and drops onto your crotch."

"Nicely put."

"But…" Tom had a lightbulb moment. "Are you saying that alien intervention was responsible for that, too?" He started to turn to look at the other, remembered himself, and turned back.

"I believe so."

"Was it something I missed?"

"Do not worry, Tom. You have a large patch to cover. I do not expect you to catch everything. But now you see why it is important to do something when we do discover a message and there is an easy opportunity to address it. We already have one disgruntled community in

Norwich. What would happen if this new message were to subconsciously incite an attack, leading to outrage in another community, so soon after?"

"I could see Norwich getting panned in *The Guardian* as a den of intolerance. *Shit.* So what exactly do I have to do?"

"I assume you do not have your neutralising equipment in that rucksack of yours. You need to return home to collect it. But that might be for the best anyway. Late afternoon is probably a better time to act, with less chance of being observed."

Inside his head, an image came to Tom's mind of Martin Lawrence declaring to his cop partner, Will Smith: *This shit just got real!*

Chapter 11: The Pottergate Incident

The underpass on Pottergate allowed access to the city centre without crossing Grapes Hill – part of Norwich's busy, multi-lane inner-city ring road. As usual, it was surprisingly quiet – the noise from the traffic above efficiently dampened, as if some magical filter was at work.

Tom approached the underpass from the west and the environs of a small, low-storey council estate. He advanced with trepidation, yet there was no one around – again as usual. And now that he thought about it – and in defiance of the place's subterranean air of menace – Tom had never had any bad experiences here. Indeed, whenever he'd taken this route in the past, he'd rarely seen anyone bar the odd cyclist, and nor had he encountered any of those who used the underpass as a canvas for their graffiti, whom he suspected only came out at night.

He walked down the gentle slope with a supermarket 'bag-for-life' held by its handles in one hand, having eschewed his rucksack on discovering that it was much easier and quicker to draw out his 'weapons' from the bag. The walls were less colourful than they'd been in years past: rather than the usual vibrant hodgepodge of cartoons, slogans, and tags, a long declaration that 'Black Lives Matter' extended a significant length of the underpass along the right-hand wall. Tom supposed that an unwritten code meant that even the free-spirited graffitists felt uneasy at defiling *this* right-on message, leaving them only the left-hand side for their usual experimentation. Nevertheless, he did notice a few small tags within the large, white letters of the declaration, and supposed that these would slowly multiply until, in time, bravery, carelessness, or boredom, resulted in the phrase being completely overwritten.

Tom stopped in the underpass beside the 'M'. It was here that he'd previously seen the seventh dimensional message. He peered intensely through his special glasses – and frowned. The dastardly amendment wasn't readily apparent. Well, it had certainly been present in the morning! Then, he recalled how the messages he'd seen in St Giles Street had needed to be viewed at a certain angle, even with the aid of his magic specs, and so he moved a few feet to his left and jerked his head rapidly in a scanning motion a number of times.

Nothing.

Tom walked a bit further on, turned, and strolled back, trying to keep facing ahead and letting his peripheral vision work, suddenly uncertain as to what had worked on former occasions.

Still nothing.

Nervously looking about to ensure that the coast was still clear, Tom retraced his steps and tried again... and again. At one point, a cyclist whizzed down the underpass from the city side, startling him and causing him to drop his bag. But the cyclist didn't falter or even look at him.

This was getting ridiculous.

He decided to go all the way to the far side of the underpass and descend along the entire message from the 'B'.

No luck.

After ten minutes, trying everything he could think of, there was still no evidence of the pulsing, inter-dimensional word that had amended the message to declare that Black Lives *Don't* Matter.

He was at a loss.

What should he do?

Maybe he'd been mistaken?

Should he just go?

If he did, would Smith be disappointed? He'd never shown such emotion before – but that didn't mean the alien didn't experience human-like feelings. Would he consider Tom inept? Perhaps he'd disengage and seek a better collaborator? After all, this was the first significant thing he'd actually asked Tom to do.

"Fuck fuck fuck!" muttered Tom to himself. "Why am I so *fucking* useless?"

He cast the bag onto the ground, causing the spray can within to roll out and curve around in a semi-circle until it came to rest against the kerb. Making a fierce face, he retrieved it. And once the can was to hand, the resolution seemed obvious. Tom looked at the can, and then up at the wall. The message had been *there*. Spilling over the 'S' and the 'M'. Well, he was here now, and suitably armed. He hefted the can. It was red, as instructed, albeit not Smith's exact designation.

But first, the prep.

Tom knelt and retrieved a large magnet from the bag, holding this in his left hand. Feeling slightly foolish, he began to wave this about over the large white letters where he'd first seen the alien attempt at influencing.

Was that enough?

Smith had suggested that this act would disrupt a 7D message – priming it for overwriting with the paint. But not being able to see the word, Tom couldn't be sure of its effect. He put the magnet down, shook the can, popped off its lid, and began to spray. He fanned the paint from the 'S' and over the 'M' and back, working from the top to the bottom. He was so intent on doing a good job, he didn't notice that he wasn't alone in the passageway until it was too late.

"Nice one, mate! Fuck'em, eh?"

Tom startled and looked around. Two young men were walking towards him from the city side. They were somewhat dishevelled, and one held a can of lager in a heavily tattooed hand. Both wore baseball caps. The beer drinker was the one who'd spoken.

"Oh, er, *no*. It's not what it seems."

"Course not, mate."

The men laughed and continued past, but after a few more metres, the beer drinker turned to look back at the presumed vandal. "I'd piss on it too, if I were you. That'd really rub it in!"

Tom stared at the men's retreating backs. He knew his face must be red – red in a way it'd not been since childhood, when he'd blush in severe embarrassment at, well, just about everything. *Perhaps even RAL 3020 red?* he thought.

"*Fuck!*"

Tom capped the can, grabbed the bag from the floor with his free hand, and with buckling legs, fled in the opposite direction to the men, up the slope towards the city centre, away from his ignominious act.

***

The story even made the news.

Back home, slouched on his sofa in front of the TV that evening, Tom was watching the *Look East* local segment that followed the BBC national news, when the third item made him sit up.

"Meanwhile, in Norwich, a local community is up in arms at an act of racist vandalism. Sally, what's the story?"

The screen segued from the anchor in the studio to a reporter in the field, who – with sombre words – described the deep upset felt by the locals. She was in the underpass with a small group of youths, one of whom – the bottom of his face covered, bandit-like – acted as their spokesperson.

"So, tell me," said Sally the reporter, "what do you think of this?"

"It's disgustin'. We wanted to leave this as a message of support for our black brothers and sisters. The different crews agreed. It wuz sacred. Smudge said he saw a middle-aged geezer at it. Fuckin' racist. Probably an off-duty pig–"

"Ah, yes, thank you, Blitz." The reporter whisked the microphone away from the community rep before he could spew any more obscenities. Behind her, Tom's handiwork was clear – a great red smudge, like a massive blood clot, defiling the message of solidarity. "We understand the police will be making further enquiries–"

"*Fuckin' pigs!*"

"… er, *enquiries*. And with that," continued a flustered Sally, "it's back to the studio."

Tom hid his face behind a cushion and didn't leave the house for two days.

***

"You did *what?*" Amanda was aghast.

"I knew I shouldn't have said anything. Keep your voice down!"

"Tom, I… don't know what to say."

Tom smiled weakly. They were in Heigham Park, strolling on a path between the trellises of the rose garden. It was three days after the incident. With no one particularly supportive to turn to, he'd contacted Amanda, hoping that Max had returned to Berlin and that she was a free agent again (fortunately, he had and she was).

"I don't really know what to say, either," said Tom. "I thought I'd just check to see if, well, you'd heard anything from Sheila about… related matters?"

Amanda came to a halt, turning towards the secret vandal. "No. Nothing like this. In fact, she's been a bit quiet lately. What did Smith say?"

"I, er, haven't spoken to him."

"Perhaps you should?"

Tom looked down, then up and over Amanda's shoulder, avoiding eye contact. "Yes, well, I have mixed feelings about that. I was only doing what he wanted, and now I'm a fugitive from the law, and I've probably made things worse."

Amanda gave a small shake of the head, then took Tom by the arm and began to move again, forcing him into step beside her. "Well, you have to see him to sort things out. I'm sure he'll understand. And maybe your efforts have been beneficial after all."

"What do you mean?"

"If there was a message, you will have definitely gotten rid of it. And what has been the response to the incident? Has there been an upsurge in *anti*-BLM sentiment, or has there actually been *more* sympathy for the cause? Maybe it's a win-win situation?"

"You don't really think that?"

Amanda gave a soft smile and looked at Tom from the corner of her eye. "I don't know. *Maybe*."

Tom shook his head, but suddenly felt some hope. "If only I were competent at using social media. I might be able to check, maybe find something positive to say to Smith. Do you think Ed...?"

Amanda gave a strangled sound, somewhere between a cough and a laugh. Her step momentarily faltered, but then she found her rhythm and continued onwards, hand still through Tom's arm. "Ed? I'm not sure that's a good idea. He could definitely track the trends and the gossip, but..."

"Yes, I know. That's why I thought I'd speak to you first. I don't think Ed will drop me in it, but he'll make me pay in other ways. But now you mention it... could you check instead? You're competent. You know how all this social media works."

"I suppose I could try, but I'd need to be careful." Amanda shook her head gently. "Since meeting Ed, I've learnt all sorts of worrying facts about how we are tracked on the web through our search terms and locations. I wouldn't want to draw attention to myself – or to you by association."

Tom stiffened. "Yes, it's scary. There's so much I don't know. I mean, all this started because I saved my novel as a file in the Cloud and Smith's algorithms were able to access it and analyse it." He came to a sudden halt. "Christ, what if the news I've been looking at has been picked up by some special police unit? Or... the *enemy*? Maybe... maybe I have no choice? I hate it, but I think I'm going to have to speak to Ed..."

***

"You did *what?*"

"Shush! Keep your voice down!"

They were in the Rumsey Wells, a fine old pub on St Andrews Street, with dark wooden floors and a convoluted interior. Though the pub had a pleasant and compact beer garden out back, a cold front had swept over the city in the morning, forcing Tom to seek shelter from the rain. And the best he could find within was a small table to the right of the front door next to the toilets, which wasn't exactly private: a young couple sat at a table a few feet away, between him and the dimly lit bar to the other side of the doorway. Ed had joined him ten minutes after his arrival.

"So, you're *not* proud of your handiwork?" Ed folded his arms and looked hugely amused, the volume of his voice un-tempered. "I always thought those protests were overdone. The fascist cops at the heart of the matter live in another land, thousands of miles away, and those buggers are happy to shoot you if your taillight is out and you don't address them as 'sir' – regardless of whether you're black, white, yellow, or that strange orange colour favoured by US presidents."

"Ed – *please!*" Tom thought he saw the woman in the puffer jacket at the next table stiffen, while her scruffy partner definitely glanced over at them. "Christ, I think they heard!"

Ed waggled his eyebrows, rolled his eyes, and sighed. But he did lower his voice. "Tom, old fruit, I wouldn't worry. News moves on. It was nearly a week ago. People quickly forget."

"They won't if they use the underpass."

"I know the place you speak of. It's hardly a highway, more like a transit zone for crusties and dole scroungers. You're safe."

"And the police?"

"Those muppets? You really think they're dedicating resources to this? The whole of the Bethel Street station, perhaps? Maybe they've also involved Interpol in case you've fled abroad? *Come on*, Thomas. Storm in a teacup."

Where had Tom heard that before?

"But what if they've got CCTV from somewhere? What if…"

Ed grinned and slowly shook his head. "Tom, no, really, it's *not* headline news. I hadn't even heard about it until your bombshell just now. The police don't have the resources. If they told the press they'd look into it, that was just a platitude. *You're safe.* Just don't make a habit of it., eh."

Tom sat back slowly and puffed out his cheeks. The couple at the next table were in intense conversation. The bloke was annoyed, and the woman unplacated. Vicious whispers filled the air. Tom looked at his pint of Ghost Ship, barely touched, then swept it up and took a hearty gulp.

"Better?" said Ed.

Tom lowered the glass. Ed was still smirking. "Yes. *No.* It's not just about getting caught, it's…" Tom waved a hand airily, "it's about this whole business. This *stuff*. It's just not me."

"Then tell Smith you're out. That should be interesting. Maybe, he'll hypnotise you into forgetfulness. Or use some sort of ray gun on your brains. Or accidentally drop a rock-sized meteorite on your head to remove all evidence."

Tom had to smile at this. "Or maybe, he'll just kidnap me and fly me off in a spaceship?"

"That's the ticket. Anal probes all round." Ed addressed his own ale, holding up a warning finger to Tom as he drank. He settled his half-drained pint onto the table. "Right. But seriously. What are your plans? You clearly haven't spoken to Smith. Has he contacted you?"

"Not yet. I thought, well, I thought maybe I would wait until I have a clearer picture of the fall-out. And I thought maybe you could help me here."

Ed rested his elbows on the table, and steepled his fingers over his pint. "I see. It'll cost you. Ghost Ship's good today. I'll soon be in need of a refill. But go on."

"Well, I thought maybe you could do some surreptitious web searches. You know, see if anyone is talking about the, er, *incident*. See if anyone, or any *agency*, is interested. Perhaps put out some feelers. You know, in an untraceable-to-you kind of way." Tom smiled weakly. "I mean, just check out the landscape. I'd especially like to know if some dodgy kind of supremacist group has, um, been encouraged by this."

"You mean, provide you with a fish of sorts to throw to Smith?" Ed pursed his lips as though giving the matter profound thought. But he couldn't keep the front up for long. His ready smile returned. "Of course, old chap. But for that, you'll have to throw in some scratchings too. Hup-hup! By the time you're back from the bar, I'll be empty."

With considerable relief, Tom stood and headed to the bar. But as he passed the young couple at the next table, he failed to notice their conversation peter out, or the pair half-turn, in unison, to follow him with their eyes.

***

"… and there's no evidence of any serious repercussions. I've checked. Spent *days* searching the internet, and–"

The *Big Issue* seller raised a stalling hand. "Tom, calm yourself." Was that amusement in his voice, his expression? "Your actions will have removed the message. The interference has been neutralised. Whatever happens henceforth is a consequence of natural, human actions and not of direct interference. That is tolerable."

They were at their usual meeting place at the circular bench beneath the tree by the Guildhall. It was a Tuesday – the change from Wednesday being at Tom's request. Smith was in his regular guise, wearing his red vest, holding an armful of magazines, standing two feet away. He'd had to wait for a family to finish feeding their toddler in a pushchair and depart before sauntering over from his usual pitch – time that had only heightened Tom's nervous state. But with Smith's response, Tom felt vaguely unsettled. He should have been relieved. But his handler's lack of concern after his anguished week, which had included giving Ed some time to work his magic and report back, instead induced something akin to annoyance. He'd been in dread… for *this*?

"You mean… you mean I've been frantic all this time for nothing? That I could have done almost anything, and that would have been fine? What if the police had caught me, and I'd been arrested?"

110

"That would have been unfortunate, Tom. You cannot aid me in prison. Please be more careful next time."

And that was it.

"I sense there is activity at Riverside," Smith continued. "If you wouldn't mind, I'd appreciate you concentrating your efforts there over the next week or two." He looked about, spotted a trio of lads heading their way, then looked back at Tom. "Thank you, Tom. I am happy with your efforts." Was that another glint of amusement in his eyes? The alien turned and stalked away towards the Guildhall.

Chapter 12: Routine

August had proven quite a month. Tom had been contacted by an alien and learnt some uncomfortable cosmological truths. Then, he'd fluked his way into a group that seemed to not only confirm what he'd been told, but to also suggest that the hidden conspiracy went even deeper – being known about by more than a few humans. He'd spent three-and-a-half decades in complete ignorance, and suddenly experienced an awakening. And then he'd slipped into September and into something else altogether – and he wasn't just thinking about the semi-solid canine-birthed substance that had brought one particular patrol to a premature and messy end.

For the rest of September, Tom attempted to process what he'd learnt, re-frame his thinking about the world, and establish a workable routine. And this proved surprisingly easy. It was astonishing, he thought, how adaptable people could be.

He worked out six different patrol routes, allowing himself one day off a week, and to these he added occasional extensions to cover other parts of the city where footfall was not especially high, yet not so insignificant as to merit their complete abandonment.

He met his colleagues on Tuesdays for quiz-nights, during which they had little chance to discuss otherworldly matters – to his frustration – due to the general noise and hubbub, although they also met in the Alex on one Thursday night, when they were able to talk slightly more freely yet without complete openness. Ed and Amanda were particularly cautious whenever Simon was around, which Tom broached with them when the latter went to get a round of drinks in.

"And now that Simon's at the bar," Tom ventured, cautiously, "I sense you are more, er, *circumspect* when he is–"

"Present?" completed Amanda. "Yes. We suspect his experiences are more, ah…"

"Mental," said Ed, twirling a finger by the side of his head. "By which I don't mean he's a fruitcake. Well, not entirely. Anyone who plays Dungeons and Dragons into their late twenties can't be entirely all-there.

I mean, his experience is in his head, not rooted in physical reality. But you suspected this, old chap – no?"

"Um, right. But then why do you...?"

"We don't have the heart," pre-empted Amanda. "And before you joined us, there were only the two of us with real experiences anyway."

"Yup," confirmed Ed. "He's like a puppy dog. We have no desire to be cruel, plus, he has useful knowledge for the quiz."

"But doesn't it stop you having meaningful conversations?"

"Of course it does," said Ed. "But that might not be a bad thing. Having Si here acts as a filter. It allows us to calibrate what we say and don't say. And if we really need to talk, there's always email – as you found out after your disgrace in the underpass." Ed smirked and waggled his eyebrows.

Amanda nodded and smiled gently. "It was interesting that you only contacted the two of us afterwards, and not Simon. Now... hush! Here he comes..."

And then there were Tom's regular meetings with Smith. Regular-*ish*. They had started as weekly, but as September slipped away and October came upon them, and Tom failed to find any further messages, the meetings became less frequent.

"Do not fear, Tom. I am happy that you are on the case," Smith told him at one meeting in late September. "The pot is still being stirred, but presently only gently. There have been a couple of developments that I am keeping my eye on. But I sense something more dramatic is coming."

***

Then, at the start of October, Tom got an offer he really couldn't afford to refuse.

"I had an RA for a small project," noted the lugubrious Brian, "but he's just cut and run." It was a Saturday, and the two men were sat in a North African coffee shop on St Benedicts Street, opposite one of Norwich's medieval churches. The rendezvous had been arranged the previous day by email. "I have no time to go through the rigamarole of formally recruiting a replacement – there are only three months of the project left."

Tom stirred his White Americano and wistfully appraised the sticky pastries at the counter at the front of the café. These were considerably more sightly than the tall, long-faced, bespectacled academic sat opposite. "Ah, bad luck. But it happens. I'm amazed anyone ever sees out these small projects. Writing up?"

"Yes. He's one of Alice's PhDs. She assured me he would see out my project, but he's had his viva, got an offer, and jumped ship immediately, rather than putting back his new job's start date. *Swine.*"

Tom dragged his eyes from the baklavas, gateaux and eclairs. For Brian, that amounted to full-on blasphemy. "Oh! Dropped you in it?"

Brian waved a hand peevishly. "He was behind anyway. He finished all the experimental work – eventually – but left a mountain of data to analyse and write-up." He peered at Tom intently, sitting as he was under a picture of a man riding a camel. "The project is on financial decision making. It's roughly your area. And the stats are relatively easy – nothing more complicated than analysis of variance."

"Ah!" Tom had been slow on the uptake. He blamed his limited diet – enforced by financial hardship – and its lack of sugar. Frankly, he was getting sick of Asda baked beans, and those pastries… "Right. So, are you saying…?"

Brian looked severe. "Heavens, Tom! Are you still *compos*? Yes, I am offering you some work. It would have to be on a consultancy basis though. A few grand. But I need you to say 'yes' now, and although technically you ought to wait until I get the paperwork sorted, I haven't time, so you will need to start on Monday. You can work from home. I will send you all the project documents and the data."

"Work? I…" Tom sat back in his chair. That was good, wasn't it? His redundancy money was about spent, and he was stretching the patience of Her Majesty's Government's benefits staff. But how would this impact his routine?

"You don't seem enthused." The peevishness deepened. "I thought I was doing you a favour."

"No, I mean, *yes*. Thanks, Brian. It's just a bit of a surprise. I've not found many jobs out there–"

"Young Anthony had no problem."

"Right. Probably going for a different type of job to me. A research post?"

"No. A lectureship. Leicester. Looked right up your street. I'm surprised you didn't apply."

"Apply?" Tom hadn't even *seen*…

"So, is that a 'yes' or a 'no'?"

Working from home? Well, at least he'd still be in Norwich. But he'd have to work with Brian. *For* Brian. He nearly said *no*, but then he saw the proprietor deliver a delicious looking cake to a woman sitting across the room – covered in toasted almonds with a cherry on top. "Tell you what, Brian. Get me one of those," he pointed surreptitiously, "and I'm your man."

***

And thus Tom's routine changed. The story of V-Garg and his machinations – which had only advanced a couple of chapters in September anyway – was largely put on hold. Mornings were now spent attempting to decipher databases on participant choices between conditions related to different financial risk profiles, and then analysing these for statistically significant differences.

And then afternoons changed, too, once Tom realised how far behind Brian's project truly was (no wonder young Anthony had bailed!).

And then so too did early evenings…

Fuck Brian and his fucking poisoned fucking chalice!

Tom did some partial patrols over a couple of late afternoons and then, for a week, nothing at all.

"You haven't advanced your intriguing little story," said Smith, at a Wednesday meeting a week-and-a-half after Tom had accepted his new commission. "Is everything okay?"

Tom had nearly forgotten about the meet up, then contemplated crying off via a message in the Cloud, then decided he needed a break (*fuck Brian!*).

"Sorry. I had to take on some work from a colleague. Unfortunately, doing your bidding for free and trying to write a novel no one will ever see, read, or pay me for, means I'm struggling to feed myself."

Smith turned on the circular bench to appraise him, in breach of his own instructions to the contrary. "There is something in your voice, Tom. Is that tension?"

This time, Tom decided it would be best to continue staring ahead, looking at the market beside the Guildhall. He exhaled noiselessly and attempted to get himself under control. "Maybe. A bit. It's a temporary problem."

"And have you managed to continue with your searches?"

Tom was silent for a moment. Perhaps honesty was the best policy? "Only... only for a few days. Maybe I can do some this weekend."

Smith also fell silent. After several seconds, Tom could bear it no longer: he flicked a glance towards the other, and noticed that the alien's eyes were vacant, focused on some point over his head. Before he could speak, Smith regained control of his eyes and looked down; as ever, his face held no emotion. "I understand. A few days will probably make no difference."

Was he losing him? "I mean, I could probably change my schedule. Go out in the evenings? If only there were some way I could earn some money from helping you. Then I could dedicate more time to things."

"You must live according to your own resources, Tom. Minimal interference. But if you are clever, there may be a way to profit."

"Eh? How?"

Smith suddenly stood. "You were a little late, Tom, and my time is up. All I can say is: keep your eyes open. Opportunities may come your way. We can meet in two weeks." He collected his stack of *Big Issue* from the bench and headed down the hill.

Opportunities – *ha*!

"I could dob you in to the media," Tom muttered to the retreating back of the other. "Even if I'm not believed, it might make a good story. Perhaps *The Sun* would pay?"

After a moment's thought, he headed into the market to get a bacon roll.

***

It took another week before Tom felt he was at last on top of Brian's project.

"Working for *bloody* minimum wage..." Tom scowled at his computer.

And then it occurred to him that even if he eventually completed and sold his novel, any monies he garnered from it would likely remit at an even lower rate per hour than Brian was effectively paying, given the unlikelihood of Rowlingesque success. "So, from self-imposed slavery to indentured servitude," he concluded, as he clicked the mouse to shut down the computer, "and back again!" For now he was off to patrol for Smith *for free*. As he gave his in-desperate-need-of-a-cut hair a quick comb, he concluded to himself in the mirror: "The universe saw you coming, my friend."

It was after seven by the time Tom made it into Norwich city centre. With summer having officially ended, the nights were drawing in rapidly, and the sun had set around half-an-hour ago. His chosen route today was through the centre, around the castle, and over to the Protestant cathedral. As he headed past the silent market it occurred to him that searching for messages now was perhaps not the best idea   and then he realised that, to the contrary, perhaps it *was…*

There were (non-7D) signs *everywhere* – now prominent and visible, rather than obscured by milling shoppers and workers. In the market itself, he was able to stroll up and down the aisles at leisure, inspecting every notice, offer, imprecation and warning (or at least, the ones not hidden behind closed shutters).

Thus, the new routine seemed to have its pros and cons.

He also realised that the special glasses he wore, while appearing otherwise, were *not* in fact sunglasses, and while they didn't aid his night vision, they didn't hinder it via a darkened tint either. He was nevertheless convinced he looked like a prick in them.

Yet, the streets were far from deserted. Though the darkened shopping zone provided few reasons for people to linger, a scattering of pubs and eateries throughout the centre, especially at the fringes, drew a modest crowd at this time – even if too early for the night owls, and too late for the just-finished-work staffers. And one thing Tom noticed quite quickly was that there were eyes *everywhere.*

People looked at him – *really* looked – in a way he'd never noticed before. And their expressions? Doubt. Concern. Suspicion.

First, it was a pair of young women wearing oversized, rainbow-coloured berets, strolling side-by-side in lockstep along Castle Meadow, with the crenelated limestone castle looming off to one side. Neither of the pair said a word: they simply glared at him, causing Tom to avert his gaze in discomfort. Was it the glasses? But if so, why did their eyes hold such menace? Surely, he looked more comical than anything else?

Next – a little further along Castle Meadow, with the ex-Anglian Television building beyond – it was a pair of bearded, middle-aged men wearing leather jackets. He noticed that each had a pin on their jacket's left breast depicting crossed swords and some lettering. An 'S' and a 'G'? Was there a small 't' between these? As he got closer, he realised he'd been staring, looked up, and again found two pairs of eyes boring into him. He looked away. As they passed, one of the men muttered 'good evening', but they were out of earshot before Tom managed to reciprocate the greeting. Was their interest because of the glasses again, or had he drawn their attention by staring at them first?

The third incident took place down Bank Plain, at the foot of pedestrianised London Street, near a small inlet from the main road that allowed cars to briefly park for unloading. There was a large tree here – a *London Plane?* – set in an island of brick paving. And against this, there rested a young man in a trendy Superdry jacket who was *also* wearing shades. This time, it seemed quite possible that the other's interest in Tom was due to his glasses: they stared at each other from a few metres, until Tom broke and looked down. As before, the other's face was firm-lipped, bereft of humour. Was the man annoyed that someone else was roaming the streets with the same style gambit? That did make Tom smile to himself: *me – an agent of cool?* But then a memory came to him that wiped the smile from his face: of a youth leaning against railings at City College. But it couldn't be the same person, could it? Or had Tom truly crashed into middle-agedness, with everyone in their twenties now looking the same?

Tom hurried away, and soon turned down Queens Street, which was livelier, bearing a clutch of bars – Brewdog, Revolution, Revolucion de Cuba, Mr Postle's Apothecary – several of which had outside tables. Here, just about everyone seated in the open appeared interested in him. Tom felt so discomfited, he hurried through the gallery with no attempt to assess the copious signage for evidence of alien intrigue.

Emerging somewhat flustered opposite the medieval Ethelbert Gate, Tom decided to give the cathedral a miss: it was probably closed, and he knew that the grounds around it – hidden behind the Tombland wall – were sparse in terms of messaging opportunities. Yet, in front of the wall

– at an outside table of The Giggling Squid – he found himself under the gaze of two more pairs of eyes: a youngish couple, with tense demeanours, sitting side-by-side rather than opposite one another. The pair looked out at the street, or rather, they looked out at him. *Directly* at him. *Glowering*. And he was sure he'd seen them before, too. But where? They'd been arguing, hadn't they? In a pub somewhere? The Rumsey! What the *fuck* was going on?

Curtailing his route, Tom headed up Princess Street, past the cheerfully glowing Trattoria Rustica, eventually emerging by St Andrew's Hall, the usual venue for the city's beer festival, with Cinema City – the indie cinema mecca – opposite. And then, as he crossed the road, about to return to the centre proper, he nearly collided with a man in a thin, blue jacket worn over a black t-shirt. The shirt bore the legend *Terminus Est*.

Tom gasped involuntarily: "Another!"

"Eh? Wassat?"

"Oh – sorry!" He'd certainly not meant to speak aloud. "I mean, well, you're another person I recognise. I seem to have bumped into a lot this evening."

"Really?" The man frowned deeply. He was actually older than Tom first thought – possibly his own age. He had short, brown hair and a nose that had clearly been broken at least once. "I don't recognise you, mate. Have we met?"

"Ah, well, not formally. I recognise you from a quiz. At the Rose Tavern. Your team won, and we were second. You were all wearing that t-shirt."

The man seemed surprised. His hands were in his jacket pockets; he now brought them together, narrowing the aperture and occluding his shirt's motif. "I'm not sure I've been to that quiz."

"Really? Uh, maybe it's friends of yours then? Members of your club? It was only the once. I don't think you… or your team… have been back since."

"*Riiiiiight…*" The other appeared both amused and bemused at the same time. "Well, I'm off this way…" he gestured vaguely ahead with one pocketed hand, causing his jacket to bulge. "I think maybe you're going the other way? Don't let me interfere with your… patrol." And then he winked, and without another word, sidled past Tom and turned up St Andrews Hill.

Patrol! That was an interesting choice of words! Tom resisted the urge to follow the departing back of the other, and instead walked forwards a few steps until he was between two red phone boxes in front of St Andrew's Church, out of sight of the narrow, brick-cobbled lane the other had taken. Coincidence piled on top of coincidence? But now he thought about it, he was sure that he *hadn't* seen the other man before: the Terminus Est team had comprised five young people and an older man of this one's age, but of significantly greater physique. Unless that other had had a dreadful case of worms, been on the mother-of-all crash diets, or had a gastric band fitted, that quizmeister and this stroller could not be the same person.

And the man was right. Tom had been heading for Bridewell Alley, a lane to the other side of the church. But things had gotten too freaky. Okay, he'd not seen any 7D messages – but this matter concerning Terminus Est was an oddity, and therefore worth further investigation.

Tom risked a peek back around the corner of the phone box and saw the man already some thirty metres distant. Fine. He decided to go for it. He walked past the church and hurried up the brick lane. But as the other was approaching the top of the street – where it came to a mini plaza with a circular bench – Tom had to up his pace or risk losing sight of his quarry. Yet, he needn't have worried, for the man continued straight ahead, between some traffic-deterring bollards to a small, semi-circular set of steps that led into the Cosy Club, which he entered.

Tom was soon at the foot of the steps, looking up at the elegant exterior of the building – the door straddled by four columns set beneath a clock tower that was topped by a weathervane. The Cosy Club had always struck him as a kind of up-market Wetherspoons: like pubs in the latter chain, it occupied a grand, repurposed building, here a former bank. Tom had never been inside, but he'd heard that the interior was as impressive as the exterior. He edged closer – but was startled when the doors suddenly opened to discharge an elderly couple. He couldn't see far through the closing doors, but what he did notice was a desk just beyond the door that seemed to be occupied by a greeter or maître d. There was no way he was going to risk that sort of encounter now – especially as the man he'd been stalking might be anywhere inside, and even facing the door.

Tom stood for some moments, chewing his lip. He'd had quite an evening, and there was much to mull over. It was dark, and he was hungry… and thirsty. Surely he had done enough for one day? He nodded to himself, looked to his immediate right, and smiled: the Wildman pub!

Tom was soon settled on a bar stool with a pint in hand. The pub was well-tenanted, with football showing on several screens throughout, for Norwich were playing away. He had a second, and some crisps.

The result was a scoreless draw. On the way out, he heard one yellow-scarved fan say to another. "Nil-nil? That's becoming routine."

Routine?

Tom almost laughed.

Chapter 13: Ghosts

Tom saw his first ghost a couple of days later.

After a fruitless patrol the previous evening through the newer regions of Norwich, this one brought him to the oldest part of the city to the north of the centre. And it was later, and darker too, and the streetlights seemed to glow with just that little extra sparkle.

As he crossed a narrow section of pavement separating the two halves of Princes Street – between a closed café and a three-storey yellow-brick building – he came to an elbow-like junction. The brick-paved Princes Street continued ahead, while perpendicular to this lay the cobbled Elm Hill, with the medieval St Peter Hungate Church sitting in the pit of the elbow. Elm Hill was reputedly the very oldest street in the city, in existence since the 1200s, though many of its buildings *only* dated from the Tudor period as a result of a disastrous fire that had swept the area in 1507.

In daylight, Elm Hill felt old; at this time of night, with the single-lane street empty of pedestrians, it felt absolutely ancient. As Tom continued down the slope past the menacing church with its black-grey façade and its small, iron-fenced grounds, a chill wind seemed to come from nowhere, playing across the nape of his neck and ruffling his unkempt hair. Beyond the church, in a kink in the road, was a tall, thatched-roofed building of Tudor design – lumpen dimensions, rippling walls, cream plaster and exposed black timber – which he knew to be The Britons Arms, once an ale house, now a more genteel teahouse. And this meant that, instead of being cheerful and bright at this time of night, the building was shut, dark, and spooky.

Just beyond the curve of the lane, three-storey houses lined the lefthand side – again, of irregular, Tudoresque aspect, now run as craft shops and the like – while a small square opened out to the right. The square was dominated by a large tree encircled by an oddly shaped wooden bench, like half-a-dozen individual segments of a circle, attached to each other at mismatched heights on account of the bumpy contours of the ground. Once the tree had been an elm, of course, but thanks to the insidious Dutch elm disease, the current replacement was a plane tree.

By the wickedly posing tree stood a slim iron pump, which in the past would have served the parish's demands for water.

And by the pump was a figure dressed in robes, facing away, shaking its head and raising and lowering a thick book in one hand.

Tom was startled by the sight. He initially thought it was just a man, indistinct in the shadows, which were deep here without streetlights, with the only illumination coming from the upper floor of a house on the square facing the old teahouse. But no sooner had Tom gotten over a mild shock at the sight, than a new and stronger wave of fear settled over him, and he froze.

The figure seemed to blur, then sharpen, then blur again. Then it straightened its shoulders and began to turn…

"Ohhhh… *fuck!*"

Tom instinctively took a step back and raised a hand to his glasses, fearful that they might fly from his face. And as he grasped the frame, the glasses slipped off the end of his nose… and the figure disappeared.

"What the…" Another step away, and Tom felt a sharp stab in his back, which caused him to turn – and jump. He'd come up against a lattice-framed window, beyond which were faces staring at him; *many* faces; *furry* faces…

"Bears?"

He almost laughed in relief. He had reversed into the window of The Bear Shop – his audience nothing more than a harmless cornucopia of stuffed toys.

But then he felt a chill on the back of his neck again and sensed something close by. His right hand, now holding his alien specs, twitched uncontrollably. What was behind him? He closed his eyes tight shut and slowly turned, then squinted one eye open…

Nothing.

There was nothing there.

The figure was gone.

Tom opened both eyes and looked into the darkened square. The tree was there, and the pump, but not the man. He puffed out his cheeks and gave his head a small shake. Then he casually settled the glasses on his nose… and just about wet himself.

By the pump, now facing him, was a monk, his face almost completely in shadow save for his mouth, which twitched with inaudible mutterings.

The figure looked straight at him, with unseen eyes, thumped the black book, and held out a hand towards him.

Tom's knees buckled; recovered; and with a yelp, he turned and fled down the hill...

But didn't get far.

In his panic, he swerved off the narrow pavement and onto the cobbles of the lane, which were tough to run on. He slipped and stumbled and then, after perhaps twenty metres, came to his senses and stepped back onto the pavement, only to clip his ankle against the open end of a drainpipe.

"*Shit fuck bollocks...*"

Tom hopped to a halt several metres further on and leant down to massage his ankle. There was light here beyond the square, which came from a number of widely dispersed yellow lanterns in iron housings set into the walls of some of the premises. After a brief rub, he straightened and turned abruptly to look back. He could see the gable end of the Britons Arms but not the square – and the street was deserted. It appeared that he *wasn't* being chased by the ghostly monk. He plucked off his glasses, gave them a rub, and put them back on.

Still nothing.

He allowed his breathing to regularise, and the pain in his ankle to subside.

Another thirty seconds passed, and still there was nothing untoward in the mid-distance.

He must have been seeing things. *A visual illusion?* Yep. That's what it was...

He now appraised his current location. The brick-built shop to his left declared itself to be Elm Hill Brides; opposite was a Tudor-style building called Elm Hill Collectibles. He noticed a blue plaque on the cream plaster wall just beyond. He took two more deep breaths and said to himself: "Okay – back to business."

Tom limped over the cobbles to the plaque and perused it for nefarious messages.

Pettus House, it declared, giving a brief description of previous owners from the sixteenth century. There was nothing unusual here. He looked further along the street (after a nervous glance back at the Britons Arms) and saw another blue plaque past two windows and a door, all trimmed in black, and the opening to a courtyard beneath a small hanging sign showing a cup and saucer under the legend The Tea House.

He shuffled across to the second plaque, which announced Wrights Court. And something tickled at his memory. Where had he heard that before? He shrugged to himself and read the caption. *The only remaining example of a residential court leading off Elm Hill… blah blah blah… slum clearances… sharing one pump and privy in the yard.* But there was nothing 7D here. He could move on.

It was then that he sensed something odd again: a prickling on his scalp and along his neck. A breeze caressed his face.

Tom jerked his head to look back up the hill. He took half a step, which brought him in front of the opening to the courtyard. There was nothing up the hill, but… he turned and looked left, into the courtyard and there, a few metres distant, standing beneath an iron lamppost, was the flickering shade of an old, stooped woman. As she raised her arms and flowed towards him, Tom turned and ran…

He ran all the way down the hill, which curved at its foot to jink around the St Simon and St Jude Church, and straight into the Glasshouse, a Wetherspoons pub directly opposite on Wensum Street – a more substantial thoroughfare. For once he was grateful that it was busy.

It took two pints of cheap ale to calm his nerves.

And then he abandoned the rest of his patrol and strode home as fast as he could, ensuring he kept to wide roads and beneath streetlights for as much of the way as possible.

***

Tom's attempt to sleep did not go well – his mind awhirl and super-sensitive to every sight and sound, both within his darkened bedroom, and without. Cars; voices; unknown rustling – *was that inside the house!* And that shape at the end of his bed? And in the corner by the wardrobe? And the curtain… *the curtains are moving!*

Ah, no, they're not…

They are! They fucking are!

He'd left the window open. Why had he done that? *Moron!*

He shut the window without looking outside.

Back to bed.

A creaking bed.

There's something under the bed!

No… no there's not. *Don't be an idiot…*

Eventually, he slept, but when he woke he was drained. At least it was Saturday – the one day he had allowed himself off from everything – from Brian's project, the novel, his searches. There was no reason he couldn't have a lie in. Catch up on his missed sleep. But his mind went instantly back to the previous night, and the apparitions he'd seen.

Ghosts.

Or were they?

He tried to reconstruct the order of events. If he'd just seen the monkish figure, well, he might have been able to somehow set that aside – blamed it on work overload, or perhaps an overactive imagination. But there'd been the old lady as well. Two in one night, within minutes of each other? London buses syndrome?

He'd never seen a ghost before – or met anyone who'd made any credible claim to have seen one either. But then again, he'd rarely spent any time in the past walking down deserted olde streets, alone and at night. And now he thought on it, Norwich was known – at least locally – as a pretty ghostly place. He recalled having seen adverts before for 'ghost walks' in the city, and he also recalled that the Maid's Head Hotel was reputed to be the most haunted building in Norwich… and *that* wasn't far from Elm Hill, and in fact, was almost adjacent to the Glasshouse pub! Had he stumbled into spook central? Had something escaped from the hotel, perhaps to visit former, er, *haunts*? And then there was that place where the woman had been. Wright's Courtyard? Wright's Court? That name had also rang a bell…

Tom struggled from the twisted bedsheets and padded across to his boxroom study. The computer was already on. But hadn't he switched it off before leaving? And now he thought back, he was pretty sure he would have shut the window before heading out last night too, but that had been open…

He felt a stippling sensation across his scalp. *Odd.* Just like the ghosts. And just like the weird coincidences a couple of evenings previously. He looked over his shoulder, back into his bedroom… but it was empty. It felt as though the whole world was watching him. He faced the ceiling and loudly declared: "Just fuck off, eh? I'm really not that interesting!"

Tom settled in front of the computer. He typed 'Wright's Court Norwich' into Google and scanned the first couple of pages. Nothing stood out: it was old, listed, a good example of something, had a blue plaque, and so on.

Hmmmm.

Then he added the word 'ghost' and… bingo.

The first entry was headed: 'Most haunted places in Norwich'.

Sitting at his computer, wearing nothing but a pair of boxers, Tom read on. The story he uncovered was somewhat disturbing. There had been a diphtheria outbreak in the late 1800s leading to many deaths, and this had coincided with a gravediggers' strike. *Bloody typical!* Since there'd been no one to bury the bodies, they'd been collected and piled on top of each other in alleyways and courtyards, with eight having been placed in Wright's Court. However, when the gravediggers had gone back to work, the body of an old lady on top of the pile had disappeared. Subsequently, the owners of an antique shop above Wright's Court had claimed to have seen the shadow of an older lady pass by their window, and also reported occasionally hearing the shop door open and its bell ring, only to find no one there. Could it have been the old lady? Was that the woman he'd seen outside in the courtyard?

Absurd! Yet, he *had* seen something.

And what about the monk?

He searched on, and it didn't take long to find the tale of Father Ignatius, a preacher who'd founded a monastery at 16 Elm Hill in 1863. By all accounts, the man had been an aggressive sod who'd cursed any who refused to pray with him. As the people of Norwich feared he was working with the devil, they'd forced him out of the city and made him promise not to come back. Though he'd never returned to Norwich, his ghost had apparently been seen on Elm Hill with a black bible, angrily cursing anyone passing.

Tom sat back in his seat. So, he wasn't mad. Or at least, not uniquely mad. He'd seen things that others had reportedly seen too. He wasn't sure how to take that. It was good, he thought. But also concerning. If his new evening routine took him through this part of Norwich once or twice a week… then what? Had his sighting been a one off, or might he expect this to become routine too? Because he wasn't sure his heart could take many more encounters with ghosts.

Patrolling? It was only then that he thought about his 7D glasses. He'd been wearing them the whole time, hadn't he? Ah, no…

"I took them off, and he disappeared," Tom muttered to himself.

He now recalled that he'd lost sight of the monk on removing his glasses when pressed against the Bear Shop window, only to see him again when he'd put them back on.

Did ghosts exist in 7D?

Did that mean there might be more hanging around the ancient ways of Norwich, just waiting for Tom to blunder into them and give himself the willies? He badly needed to talk to someone about this. In particular, he needed to talk to Smith. But could it wait until Wednesday?

"There's no way I'm heading out again in the evening until I know!"

Tom opened his novel, typed a request at the end, and saved it to the Cloud. Then he went to make himself a cup of tea, still just in his pants.

On his return, Tom was pleased to find a rapid response in the affirmative: three o'clock, usual place, to coincide with Norwich's home-tie kick off. Perhaps in the expectation that there'd be fewer people about? Well, so be it!

***

"I saw some ghosts!"

"I wondered whether you might."

"Wondered?" Tom was aghast at Smith's admission. "What… I mean… how… er…"

"Calm yourself, Tom. This is not a reason to be alarmed."

Tom – *sans* glasses – had reached their meeting bench first, issuing his declaration before the alien had had the chance to sit. "How can I be calm? When I signed up, I thought I was just looking for some glowing messages – I didn't expect to be thrown into the path of ghosts. It scared the crap out of me! It's because of the glasses, isn't it?"

"Yes."

Tom waited for the other to go on, but Smith appeared content with his answer and rapidly lost interest, his gaze flickering over potentially closing pedestrians. "Yes?" cried Tom. "Is that all? Could you explain, please? Do ghosts exist in the seventh dimension?"

Still standing, Smith waited for a family with a pushchair to recede. "Ghosts are not what you think they are." He turned to face Tom. "Do you recall one of our early meetings, in which I told you about the post-corporeal species?"

"Sure. Oh! Are you saying that ghosts are actually aliens? Aliens that just happen to look like dead monks and disease-ravaged old biddies? Come on!"

"The post-corporeal are numerous and frankly unknowable. They literally occupy a different plane of existence to us corporeal species. However, it is clear that one thing they have taken with them into their new phase of being is an appreciation of what your amusingly quaint *Star Trek* television programmes call the *Prime Directive* – not to interfere with lesser civilisations. In short, Tom, we surmise that some of the species occasionally adopt disguises in case they are sensed."

"Disguises?" Tom shook his head. "What – and they also choose to sneak about at the dead of night, when no one is around and there is nothing to see, just to scare the pants off of people?"

Smith stared at Tom for some moments. "Why do you think that, Tom? Why would ghosts only emerge at such times?"

"Because that's when people report seeing them..." Tom's brow furrowed with the effort of thought. "Ah!"

"Yes, Tom. Think things through. Do ghosts – or rather, ethereals – only come out at certain times or...?"

"Or do people only *sense* them at certain times? I see what you're saying. You're saying they're actually around *all* of the time, but people only sense them *some* of the time."

"When it is quiet. When background disturbances are lessened. When atmospheric conditions are just right. Yes."

Tom sat back and blew out his cheeks. It was so obvious. But that meant... he twitched his gaze around, remembered that his glasses were in his jacket pocket, then fished them out and held them under his nose in trembling hands. It meant... "If... if I put these on, am I going to see them here? All around me?"

Smith appeared unconcerned. "It's not impossible, Tom, but unlikely. Ethereals mostly occupy the ninth, twelfth and seventeenth dimensions, rather than the seventh, and most have no identifiable shape anyway. If you could see them in their true form, they would appear as smudges of colour. Only a few mischievous species leak into the seventh dimension and shape their essences into disguising forms. And as I said, to be seen by humans, they need the right conditions."

"Or a set of glasses like mine?"

"That is correct."

"So I *am* likely to see more?"

Smith looked away again, almost nonchalant. "They are harmless, Tom. Do not worry about them. In fact, you might use their presence as an aid to your endeavours, since they are liable to assemble at locations where interesting events are in the offing."

Tom allowed the hand holding his glasses to drop into his lap. "You mean, you think I should actually seek them out?"

"Perhaps not seek them out, but rather pay special attention to any congregations and direct your searches appropriately."

"So that's a 'yes', then. *Bugger!*"

"And now my time…"

"Yes, yes. Your time is conveniently up. You go." Tom slumped back against the bench and made a dismissive gesture. "I'll be fine. *Terrified* as well as *impoverished*, but fine nevertheless."

"Is that sarcasm, Tom?" Smith actually smiled.

And that, in a way, was as scary as any ghost.

***

After Smith departed, Tom roamed the city centre in a desultory manner, glasses on, peering at signs. But as the skies darkened with cloud, he became nervous and hurried home in case it rained.

Or so he told himself.

On Sunday, he decided to do a patrol in the morning, returning early afternoon to do a bit of writing later – in a complete reversal of his normal routine.

Well, variety was the spice of life and all that; it had absolutely *nothing* to do with ensuring that the sun was shining when he was out and about. *Yeah, sure…*

But on Monday, he received a pointed email from Brian asking about progress and wondering why he'd not received an update for some days, forcing Tom to knuckle down and attend to further analysis of project data. It was late afternoon before he managed to finish a tricky piece of stats and work out what the results of this implied. And that meant...

Bollocks!

The sky outside was already darkening.

Come on rain!

But the rain held off, depriving him of an excuse to stay in.

Double bollocks!

With a heavy sigh, Tom set out, glasses on. Nevertheless, he ensured he took a patrol route that kept to well-lit parts of the city where people could be found. He went through the centre, around the castle, and came to the Prince of Wales Road, which descended to the river Wensum and the railway station beyond. By this time, he was feeling more confident and was even able to generate a rueful smile as he looked down the nightclub-festooned street – reputed to be the most dangerous in all of Norfolk. *But not on a Monday night*, he mused.

He walked past fast-food joints, taxi ranks, and clubs that were either closed or rather sedate, still recovering from a rowdy weekend. He came to the Nelson Hotel, crossed a bridge, and arrived at the station – a grand Victorian pile built of red brick and stucco, with slate and lead roofs, an impressive central dome, and a pedimented clock front. Within, were many signs with the potential to influence many people, providing juicy targets for extraterrestrial meddlers. Normally, after perusing the station, Tom would return homewards along a road beside the river that flowed past the cathedral grounds, but he'd already decided he wouldn't risk that particular route tonight.

So, just the station, and then back home the way he'd come. *No problem.*

Or it shouldn't have been.

The station was largely deserted. Platform 6, to the far left, beyond the WHSmith franchise and public toilets, was deeply shadowed. A ticket barrier meant Tom couldn't reach the dingy platform itself (*oh, what a shame!*). But at the barrier, he saw something.

At first, he thought it was a dog.

A stray?

In the station by itself?

The thing shuffled towards him, and funnily, didn't change in hue even when it came within light spilling from the better-illuminated part of the station.

And then it straightened from its hunched posture and looked directly at him.

Facing Tom, from a mere three-metres distance, with large and wicked incisors, was a rat-like creature of improbable proportions, bigger than any rodent he'd ever seen. Then a foul smell assailed him from the creature's breath.

Tom whitened. "What the…!"

He lifted his glasses, and the vision disappeared.

He staggered away from the barrier and would have fled – but retained just enough self-control to pause and lower his glasses, at which the creature reappeared, now far closer than it should have been.

This time, Tom did emit a squeal of fear.

***

Back home, at his computer, Tom tapped away vigorously, quickly finding what he sought: the station was indeed meant to be haunted by a ghost that looked like a 'very large rat-like creature'. He should have done some proper research before he set out. Well, he would rectify that now.

Over several hours, Tom compiled a list of ghostly sightings from throughout Norwich, adding their putative locations to his map of patrol routes. Forewarned was forearmed!

He didn't turn in until three in the morning, and woke late on Tuesday, unrested and desperate to speak to someone.

But not long after, an email arrived from Ed, saying he had to go to London and would miss the quiz that evening. Soon after, Amanda cried off too, and that was that.

"Never mind," wrote Ed later. "Who's up for the beer festival? Starts next week."

Even his mum failed to call, although Tom wasn't sure what he would have said to her about his recent frights. Probably nothing.

And talking to Smith would have achieved zero.

"So, it's just me and the ghosts."

Chapter 14: Beer Festival Brouhaha

The queue to get into the Norwich Beer Festival stretched from St Andrew's Plain all the way along Princes Street.

"You need to join," Ed told his two colleagues, with a hint of impatience. "Then we wouldn't have to queue up with the rabble. We could just go to the front and walk right in."

Tom sensed that Ed was on the verge of going off on one, so he chose his words carefully. "I could be wrong, but I don't think membership lets us queue jump. It just gets us in for free."

"You're a member, too?" asked Amanda, also keen to pre empt their leader. "Why didn't you say so before?"

"It didn't occur to me. But, yes, I've been a member of CAMRA for about ten years. I think it's important to support our traditional brewers–"

"Fuck that," interrupted Ed. "I'm only in it for the discounts and the freebies. You get your membership fee back in Wetherspoons vouchers alone, and I know a couple of pubs that give cardholders 50p off a pint. Plus there's *this*. It all adds up."

Amanda rolled her eyes. "Why am I not surprised at your mercenary motives? Don't you ever do anything just because it's right? Does there always have to be a pay off?"

"What's right for my pocket *is* right. Full stop. If you want to waste money on rip-off 'Fair Trade' sarongs, or expensive organic tofu – or make charitable donations to offset the greenhouse gases that emerge from your butt *after* eating that tofu – then that's up to you. But don't expect me to sub you."

"And you're meant to somehow be a saviour of the human race?" continued Amanda, with some heat. "What are you charging Ed Two for your services? I can't believe you aid our alien overlords for free."

Tom coughed at this and looked around nervously. They were queued behind a party of office workers and in front of a crowd of students. The members of the former were unaware of them, craning to look towards the head of the queue as they shuffled forwards, while those of the latter were largely engaged in a noisy group discussion – although Tom did notice one young man in glasses trying not to look at them. "Er, guys, maybe not so loud?"

"Don't worry, Tom, old bean. No one understands us. No one actually *hears* us." Ed spotted the student standing in their eaves a couple of feet away, angled slightly towards them and apart from his colleagues – who were turned inwards, facing some invisible gravitational social point, excitedly talking over each other. "Isn't that right, mate?"

"Er, I'm sorry?"

"I'm saying," continued Ed to the student, who suddenly didn't know where to look, "that you don't really hear us – no? You didn't catch the bit where my friend was talking about my alien handler?"

"Ah, no. It's a bit loud, innit?"

"Would you like me to repeat?"

"Ed!"

"Shush, Amanda. As I was saying, we were discussing our alien handlers. Mine can be a little shit. Always wants me doing something for nothing. What do you think of *that*?"

"Ah… er… sorry… I think…"

Amanda touched the student on the arm. "Don't worry. Ed is being a prick. Enjoy the festival."

Tom cringed; Ed laughed; and the queue inched forwards.

***

Armed with their half-pint commemorative glasses, Tom and Amanda followed Ed into the old priory building, which was packed to bursting.

Although numbers were meant to be controlled according to fire regulations, Tom often wondered how maximum figures were calculated. In the case of the beer festival, he suspected that this was based on an average-size statistic for humans – which included children, babies, and shrunken old folk – multiplied by the maximum capacity of St Andrews' Hall when empty. Given that there was an age limit of eighteen, that many of the patrons were on the wrong side of 'hearty', and that the Hall was also stuffed with racks of voluminous barrels, this might account for the ridiculous squeeze. The worst part of the festival was thus trying to find a space to stand in that was sufficiently protected from sharp elbows and pushing desperados to enable him to transfer his glass' contents to his own mouth instead of his chest, or embarrassingly, the chest of whoever was closest. Success was always a relative thing: Tom accepted that by close of play, his clothes would be stained with a concoction of ales, perries, ciders, and even the odd wheat beer or other uncategorisable exotica. He'd certainly be running his washing machine first thing tomorrow.

"Here'll do," shouted Ed, over his shoulder.

They had passed through the chaotic main hall, descended some steps, and found themselves in the long, narrow cloisters beneath a vaulted ceiling. This had been set out with tables and chairs, all of which were occupied, although there was space for their small party to rest against a wall between two of these furniture islands.

"Can't see much here," noted Tom.

"Aye, but we're close to the gents," replied Ed. "I'll be needing that soon. Then we can circulate."

"It's fine for me," declared Amanda. "It's less noisy, so we can speak." She took a small sip of her beer and peered at Tom: they both wore glasses, but only hers were prescription. "I got the impression you were keen to talk last week."

"Yeah," concurred Ed. "Something about your emails seemed, I dunno, desperate and needy. So, what's up?"

Tom had momentarily forgotten about ghosts on meeting his friends earlier as they'd exchanged greetings, organised themselves, and focused their thoughts on the festival. And then when he'd remembered, he'd looked at the press around and decided that the queue might not be the best place to discuss such delicate matters... and nor was this place. "It's about some things I saw last week, while I was patrolling. *Unusual* things and, well, frankly, things that were shit-scary."

"Cool!" said Ed. "Vampires? Werewolves? ET pedalling furiously on a bike followed by armed police? Stet that. You said *scary*, and there's nothing scary about that blubber-faced little prick. So... ghosts?"

"Fuck! Keep your voice down!"

"Ghosts?" Amanda's eyes widened. "Really, Tom?"

"Yes, really. I know you're not going to believe me, but... Ed, there's no need to laugh."

"Sorry, my friend, but you're not the first of our little group to come up with that story. Young Si was telling us about them once. He must have been playing one of his RPGs late at night and given himself vivid dreams. Would you like us to humour you in the same way we humoured him?"

"Ah, Simon? No! I mean, I really *did*."

"Ed, I suspect this is different," said Amanda.

"If only our excitable friend were here instead of some gaming dive in St Gregory's Alley, you'd be able to compare notes. That would be interesting. I'm sure he'd match your *spectral postman* with a *Slimer*, and then raise you one *Gozer the Destroyer*." Ed laughed at his own joke. "But Mands is right. Your claims innately possess more credibility."

"Thanks, but…" Tom suddenly noticed that the bearded fellow whose seated back was next to him had stopped talking and leant backwards, holding an oddly stiff pose. *Listening*. "But… I don't really want to go into the matter here. Too many ears. Maybe later, on the way home?"

"Going back a different route, old chum. But I suspect Mands will be going your way, eh? I would say I'm envious of her, but that could be interpreted in a perverse manner. You can *debrief* him later, Mands, and then let me know if we need an EGM at the Alex. Right, pissoir required. Back in five."

Amanda looked darkly at Ed's retreating, leather-jacketed back. "Oh… go play with yourself," she muttered, then louder, to Tom: "Of course. We can chat later if you want."

"That's great. I really need to get this off my chest, and I've had no one to talk to." He smiled sheepishly, mainly because he could see Amanda was still nettled. "I wouldn't take Ed too seriously."

"I won't. I *don't*." Amanda forced herself to smile. "I've known him for a couple of years now. He's like a naughty, mischievous brother. Like family. Which means I've got to bear it and forgive him. But sometimes he can be too sharp. He's wearing."

Tom chuckled nervously. "Yes, and I suspect it's not going to get any easier this evening, especially with Simon absent: it means he's got fewer targets."

"Which is why I'm glad you're here. I wouldn't have come with him alone." Amanda patted his arm.

Tom was cheered by the reassurance. "You know, I have wondered why you hang out with him and Simon so much. I mean, with me, I've never had a large social circle, and it's got much worse since I was made redundant. But you... you must have a lot more friends around."

"Not as many as you might think." Amanda grimaced. "I also spend most of my time alone in my flat, making blogs and vlogs. Most of the people I know in Norwich are friends of Max, and since he moved to Berlin, they're less keen to socialise with me. And as a singleton, it's awkward meeting up with the couples were knew, to be the gooseberry."

"Don't I know it. But I can't believe there's no one else."

"Well, yes, there's Becky, who I meet downtown for a coffee now and then. She works in a charity shop. But she's teetotal, so not much fun in the evenings. And there's Vanda and Michael. They're a couple, but older. They live opposite. I think they see me as a surrogate daughter. Of course, I've also got online friends I occasionally Zoom, but aside from that..." she shrugged, "I'm stuck with you guys."

"Sorry!" Tom gave an exaggerated grimace.

Now Amanda laughed. "No need to apologise. I'm glad you've joined us. It's nice to have someone moderately sane in the group."

"Thanks... but gird yourself. Here he comes." Tom redirected his attention. "Ed, your glass was almost empty when you left. It's now suspiciously full."

"Tom, you wag! I like what you did there. Indeed, I have refilled, but this cost significantly more than a single 'p'. I couldn't wait for you laggards, not surrounded by so many temptations. So, what have I missed?"

***

They had moved position, and now stood beside a different wall in another part of the complex, namely, Blackfriars' Hall, which was the second largest space in the priory, reached via an annex behind the main stage in St Andrew's Hall. This hall was long and thin, with a high, vaulted, wood-beamed ceiling, and walls that hosted tall, arched, stained-glass windows with intricate tracery. Between the windows were paintings, dating from the 16th century, of mayors, sheriffs and benefactors to the city, including one grand portrait of Nelson. One wall was taken up with a long bar behind which lay scores of jacketed barrels, with a temporary stall at its furthest end selling hog roasts, loaded fries and hot dogs.

Ed returned from yet another foray; he was already three halves up on Tom and Amanda.

"You two look like an old couple. If I didn't know you were a pair of lonely losers, I might mistake you for husband and wife – in particular, Roy Orbison and his Germanic second."

Tom looked down in embarrassment, but Amanda rose to the bait. "And you're *not* a lonely loser? In the time I've known you, Ed, you've never had a girlfriend. So: *kettle*, *pot*, and *black*."

To be fair to him, thought Tom, Ed really could take back whatever he gave. The man winked and leered. "That's what you think, Amanda dearest. But I have another side to my life that you don't know about. In fact, *several* other sides. I'm actually a bit of a babe magnet. I just get bored by the morning so have to kick 'em out. No ties. Totally free."

The beer seemed to have gotten to Amanda. She wasn't going to let this one go. "Well, I look forward to meeting your conquest for the evening. Have you got a target yet?"

"What, here? God no! The birds are almost as fat as the blokes. And they've got the same amount of facial hair." He feigned a shudder. "Beer is my sole mistress tonight! On the other hand, some of the punters here are probably on your level if you're pining in the absence of Herr Maximilian. What do you think about that chap over there, resting by the Woodforde's stall? He doesn't look too picky. Great hams on him. Might need help climbing up on you though. A hoist, perhaps?"

"Ed! You complete…"

"Er, time for another, guys?" Tom hurriedly slurped the last of his Landlord and waved around his empty glass. "I think I'll just… nip over…" he smiled guiltily at Ed and glanced at a volcanic-looking Amanda, then turned to head off though the crowd.

"Eyes out, Tom," Ed called after him. "Love is in the air tonight! *I gotta feel…*" and his tuneless Black Eyed Peas rendition was lost in the white noise of the crowd.

Tom continued into the bustle. He decided to pass on the offers in Blackfriars' and head back to the main hall. On stage, a faux-German oompah band started honking and tooting, clearing musical throats before embarking on another barely distinguishable tune. At least it wasn't jazz. Tom *hated* jazz. For music that was meant to be so improvised and original, all jazz sounded the same to him – a bit like the oompah music, but far, *far* more pretentious. One thing Tom decided he liked about Ed was that his new friend was as cynical about jazz as he was. It was just a shame that Amanda was more ambivalent.

At the *Humpty Dumpty* concession, Tom got himself a half of the weakest ale they had. He'd forgotten the name of the thing by the time he took his first sip – a steadying drink, taking away the head before it got jostled off. He set about returning to his friends, but found the path now blocked by a large group of very loud young males, dressed in lab coats. Chemistry students? As it would be difficult to squeeze through them, Tom about-faced and headed to the opposite end of the row. He slalomed and wriggled through revellers until he was near the main entrance, and then he turned to look back towards the stage. As he looked up, he caught a flash of otherworldly light, a glare of unnaturally glowing green…

To his left, and up, there was a large banner affixed to the top of a frame that ran above the row of barrels, visible to all below if they chose to look. The banner showed an advert for CAMRA, proclaiming that the organisation had been: *Campaigning for Real ale, pubs and drinkers' rights since 1971*. But the banner also said a bit more than its designer intended, for scrawled across it in the seventh dimension were the words: *DID YOU.*

DID YOU? What an odd addition! Tom paused, but not for long, as the flow from the entrance caught him and trundled him forwards, occasionally interposing a taller drinker between him and his view of the message.

Was it meant to be the start of a message that had for some reason been aborted?

But then Tom saw an identical banner a few feet further along, and there was another flash of green. As he got closer, he noticed that this bore the superimposed message: *SPILL.*

DID YOU… SPILL? Tom's suspicions were now fully aroused. He was buffeted towards the end of the line, in the shadow of the stage, and there was indeed a third banner, which concluded: *MY PINT*. Without a question mark. *Sloppy*, he thought, with unaccountable annoyance. Even aliens, it seemed, couldn't punctuate properly. *Morons*.

But there was no doubt about it: he'd found another message.

Still shaking his head, Tom swam through the crowd at the edge of the stage, wormed through the annex, and regained Blackfriars' Hall.

***

"I think something's about to happen."

"What?" asked Amanda.

"I'm not sure. I've seen a message. An odd one. But, trust me, I think something's about to kick off, and probably soon."

"You mean, you've seen something with your magic bins?" Ed was intrigued. For a moment, he appeared at war with himself, and then one side emerged victorious – a side that might not have won had it not been for the copious alcohol in his system. "Come on, Tom, let's have a shufti. Lend me your X-ray specs for a mo. I've got to see this for myself."

"Ah, well, I'm not sure I should." Tom suddenly felt like Frodo Baggins being asked to pass over the One Ring, with Ed in the role of an over-eager Boromir. "What would Smith say?"

"Nothing – if you don't tell him. I promise, I'll stay mum."

"*Ed*!" warned Amanda.

Tom frowned at Amanda's concern, but Ed was taller than her and pressing closer. He had a power that wouldn't be denied. "Well, I suppose so…"

Ed excitedly accepted the glasses from Tom's hesitant hand. "So, where exactly is this message?"

"It's… it's actually written over three banners. Go to the entrance and look above the beer racks, then walk along towards the stage."

"Excellent! Back shortly…" and Ed was off.

"Are you sure that was wise?" asked Amanda, directly into Tom's ear. He found the heat of her breath uncomfortably arousing.

"Uh, no. Probably not. But he's incorrigible."

"I know what you mean. Still, this isn't what we agreed – about keeping the fine details secret. About not giving too much away. Not creating waves."

Tom couldn't keep his eyes from the exit to the hall through which Ed had already passed. "Yes, but maybe we *should* work together more. I mean, none of our handlers have ever said anything about us meeting. Still, I can't help wondering if one or more of them have actually been watching us… and maybe are watching us right now."

"Hmmm, yes, that's always been at the back of my mind, too. In which case, don't you think this might cross the line?"

140

"Maybe…"

For several minutes the pair said nothing, with Tom focused on the exit, looking past Amanda as though she weren't there. But with Ed out of range, his power slowly diminished, until…

"Fuck, yes!" declared Tom. "I need to get my glasses back, *quick*. We might be able to intercept him below the last banner. Let's go."

And without waiting for Amanda to respond, or even checking to see if she was in tow, Tom set off. He breasted through the crowd rather roughly, and quickly felt Amanda's hand on his shoulder. They attained the annexe – in which a more permanent bar was set up along the rear wall, which perversely dispensed mostly hot food rather than drink – and had to squeeze against the flow through a relatively narrow door to regain the main hall. As they did so, the volume of music ratcheted up, particularly the muscular tone of a tuba.

They had just made it through the door when they came across Ed.

"Bloody hell, Tom! Well, if I ever had my doubts about you – which to be fair, I didn't – they'd be utterly dispelled now. Here, step against the wall, out of the way." Ed used his extra size to corral his friends out of the main flow, pinning them into an area beneath one of the tall windows. "It's clear as day. *Did you spill my pint.* Want a go, Mands?"

Amanda held up her hands. "No, thanks. I'll take your word for it. I'm not sure we should be encroaching into each other's territory. You should return Tom's glasses."

"Tosh! We're not just slaves to our masters. If they want things from us, they can give a bit in return. And anyway, aren't we all really on the same side? Still, your loss." He handed the glasses back to a relieved Tom, who instantly returned them to his face, unable to silence an internal voice that whispered *my precious*. "So, what's next?" continued Ed. "The message is there, but what's its purpose?"

Tom scrutinised Ed carefully. While he felt happy at having his glasses back, other more-difficult-to-define feelings were vying for dominance. "Well… how did reading the message make you feel?"

"Feel? Aside from a simmering anger at that cunt who knocked my elbow just now…" And then Ed paused. And frowned. And his eyes widened. "You know, I just realised I'm *not* joking. I actually *do* feel pissed off." He looked quickly around, but whoever the jostling miscreant was, he was no longer in view, sucked into the maelstrom of drinkers. Ed shook his head. "I was having fun, but now there is something there at the back of my mind. *Still* there. Something that doesn't want to go. A tension. But you saw the message, too, old chap. What about you?"

"I'm not sure," said Tom. "I don't think these messages have much effect on me." Into his head came a vision of the first sign he'd seen in the market. He absently scratched at his nose. "Maybe I've got some natural resistance... Hey!" he growled venomously, as an elderly man shuffled past, making brief and gentle contact with Tom's beer-clutching arm. "Watch out!"

The man startled and held up a defensive hand. "Sorry!" He smiled in a pained manner and tottered away.

"*Tom!*" Amanda's voice was sharp.

"Eh? Sorry, what?"

"That was a bit harsh!" Amanda looked between the two men; Ed's normally cheery demeanour had turned troubled. "I think maybe you aren't as immune as you think. Maybe we should..."

And at that moment, a loud shout emanated from the area of the stage to their right. The oompah band was finishing off, the tuba giving a long and sonorous honk. Tom looked in the direction of the shout and caught movement at the front of the stage. Someone was climbing up, or rather, clambering to safety. Then there was another shout, then a shriek, and then a fountain of beer jetted into the air.

The chemistry students were nearby: they turned as one to peer towards the fracas. Tom noticed that one of them had a vacant look on his face – a look that transformed into rage when someone beyond their group was forced into them by the pressure of bodies escaping the violent epicentre. The young student opened his mouth and bellowed, then vigorously shoved the man who'd been concertinaed into him. A glass dropped from an invisible hand and smashed; the pushed man would have gone over, had there been physical space for him to fall into. More shouts erupted, and Tom noticed a fist fly from someone short and hidden into the bearded chops of someone taller and visible.

More clambered onto the stage, and the band beat a retreat, with an inadvertent parping of instruments, like the flatus of scared, stampeding animals.

"Ow! *Fuck!*" Ed had been shielding Tom and Amanda within his long arms, his palms resting on the wall to either side of them, but that meant

142

he couldn't defend himself. He was shoved inwards by the melee – at which Tom noticed his face adopt an enraged expression similar to the chemistry student. He pressed back by performing a standing push-up against the wall – and gained the trio some space. But then he swung around, loosed his hands from the wall, and formed them into fists. Tom felt his own anger rise, and found himself transferring his nearly empty glass from his right hand to his left, so that he could load up the *Hammer of Tom* in order to deliver *furious vengeance* upon all beer-jostlers...

But then Amanda was there, in his way. She grasped Ed's right arm and managed to hold on as he started to swing, but at the cost of losing her grip on her glass, which dropped to the floor, fragmenting and spilling its contents across their shoes and legs. "Ed! No! Stop!"

Ed turned, saw Amanda, and the fury in his face bled away. At this sight, Tom felt some of his own tension dissipate.

"Amanda?" said Ed, in something of a daze.

"Ed, we need to get out of here."

"She's right," said Tom. "Stick to the wall..."

They made it out – somehow. Clearly, not everyone had seen the message on the banners: the unaffected led a surge away from the chaos at the front of the room, which the trio rode all the way to the front door and through it.

The excitable crowd outside was torn between gaining safety and staying near enough to ogle the mass brawl inside. But Amanda wouldn't allow her friends to linger, and dragged them to the edge of the plain, where they paused at a circular bench, close to the St Andrews Brew House. Customers at the pub's outside tables were standing and craning to get a look at the bedlam by the Halls.

"Better?" asked a shaken Amanda.

"Yes. Thanks, Amanda," said Tom.

"Yeah, thanks, babe," concurred Ed. "I don't know what came over me... or rather, I do, now." He looked back towards St Andrew's Hall, just as something smashed through one of the ancient windows. "Fuckers! That is... that is diabolical!"

"And all this was caused by your messages, Tom?" said Amanda.

"My messages? *My*... I... ah... sorry..." Tom exhaled and shook away some tension. The rage had nearly taken him again. "Sorry, I'm still somewhat affected. Yeah, *the* messages. I guess so."

"How *dare* they interfere with our holy festival!" Ed seethed, his hands curling into fists and uncurling. "Now, I am pissed. I'm not going to let the fuckers get away with this."

"Ed!"

"No, Mands, I'm fine. Don't worry. I'm not going to do anything now. But these alien shits have crossed the line. I've been taking it easy recently. Now, I'm going deep into the dark web. And I'm going to quiz Big Ed, too."

"Um, without mentioning the glasses!" squeaked Tom.

"Course not. But I'm going to find out which slimeball species is responsible for this." Ed dragged his eyes from the Hall, in which the riot was continuing. "We're not getting back in there tonight, my Credulous chums. So, I'll bid you adieu. I'm going to grab a gallon of coffee and pull an all-nighter. Someone must know something."

As Ed strode off with a peremptory wave, Amanda turned to Tom: "I agree. I think our evening is done."

The pair headed most of the way home together. They discussed messages and the events of the evening, and what they each intended to do about it. By the time they parted, Tom was still wired.

And he never did get the chance to raise the subject of ghosts.

***

"Another crisis meeting, Tom?"

"Yes, because there's been another crisis. You saw the big local story? About the beer festival bust up last night?"

"Don't tell me that you were somehow responsible for that?"

Was that a touch of humour? Last time they met, Smith had actually smiled, and now... *humour?* Was Smith somehow evolving? Getting used to his body? Being infected by human mannerisms? This time he wasn't smiling, so did that mean he was serious? A matter-of-fact question? Surely he didn't *really* need to have it confirmed that Tom hadn't started a major brawl at an iconic Norwich event? "Er, no. Of course not. But I saw what *did* cause it."

"Where was the message?"

"It was on a banner above the beer casks. Actually, it was spread across three separate banners, and it would only make sense if you looked at all three, in turn. *Hang on...*"

"Insight, Tom?"

"I was just wondering how and when the banners could have been inscribed. I'm pretty sure it would have been impossible after they had been put up, which must have been shortly before opening, as there would have been a constant flow of people around. Plus, they were high up. Anyone reaching up to mess with them would have been seen. And that implies they were doctored *before* they went up, but that would also come with difficulties."

"Please explain."

"Well..." Tom scratched his head and looked up at Smith, who was standing and facing him rather than sitting perpendicularly on the bench – seemingly unconcerned about them being seen talking. And that was also new. "Well, whoever messed with them would have needed to be sure that they were put up in the right order, with the top one put up first, the second to its right, and the third to the right of that. And there can't have been any guarantees of that. I mean, they could have been put up going from the right-hand side of the row to the left... or facing different sides, as I'm now pretty sure there was a similar set of banners on the reverse side of the aisle, but I never noticed any messaging on those."

"An enigma, for sure."

Tom grimaced. "You don't seem to be taking this very seriously."

"Oh, I am, Tom. This is clearly a significant escalation. I have sensed that a certain species of manipulators has become emboldened due to recent successes – with their seemingly trivial messages having unexpected and growing effects."

"Trivial messages? The ones I've seen?"

"Yes, Tom. And ones you have missed."

Was that a rebuke? "I'm sorry. I can't be everywhere at once, you know. I've got work to do for Brian and... and the *novel*..."

Now Smith did smile – and Tom didn't like it one bit. Was it mention of his *novel* (God! – he even dropped his *internal* voice to an embarrassed whisper when thinking about it!)? "I understand. But maybe it's time to up the ante. I see you don't have your rucksack today."

"Er, no."

"So, you do not have your magnets and paint?"

"Er, yes."

"Very well. Can I suggest, Tom, that from now on you take these items with you everywhere you go, just like your glasses. Keep them glued to you, in your sole possession, and if you see a message, please attempt to remove it immediately."

"Uh, sure." Tom whitened: what did Smith mean by 'sole possession'? Was he implying he knew Tom had loaned his glasses to Ed? "So, you don't want me to get your approval first?"

"No. That won't be necessary. I trust you."

"Thanks… I think."

It was just a pity Tom didn't even trust himself.

Chapter 15: Third Interlude

It had been a difficult few weeks for Robert Quigley after the *Pride* affair. On sheepishly returning to work at Aviva, he'd been 'invited' to a senior management inquisition. That had been a gruelling encounter – one he probably wouldn't have survived had he not been accompanied by his rottweiler-like union rep. In the end, the company's bosses hadn't wanted to risk an unfair dismissal tribunal, allowing him to escape with a reprimand and an unspoken understanding that his future career in insurance was unlikely to be a glorious one. However, that was only part of the problem: while some of his colleagues had been sympathetic once he'd gotten the chance to relate his side of the parade incident, correcting the sensationalist reporting in the local media – a significant number had decided to ostracise him.

After two months, he'd had enough. But then, on the verge of resigning, he'd tuned into a history programme on BBC2 and had a lightbulb moment. And so here he was – standing coatless on the steps of City Hall on a Saturday morning, at the mercy of a bitterly cold wind sweeping in from the North Sea, exposed before the media. At least he wasn't alone: his empathetic co-worker, Emily, and long-time friend and local Labour Party stalwart, Stan, were with him for moral support.

"Go on, Rob," hissed Stan, who was dressed like Robert in a scratchy old jumper, specifically chosen for its ragged and hairy appearance. "Let's get this started. I'm bloody freezing!"

"Yes, please, Robert," concurred Emily, from behind his other shoulder, "before I catch my death." Her jumper was grey and threadbare at the elbows – having likely come from her husband, who was a keen gardener.

"Right, yes, let's do this…" Robert raised his voice: "Ladies and gentlemen: your attention, please!"

On the steps below, a television camera from the local BBC unit swung to focus on his face. Aside from the cameraman and his reporter colleague, the esteemed Sally Jones, there were four other media reps from local newspapers and radio stations. One of these started to snap away from behind a sizeable camera. Slightly beyond these, on the pavement on both sides of the quiet road that ran between the grand civic building and the war memorial and market below, a growing crowd of curious onlookers had assembled.

"Ladies and gentlemen," Robert repeated, "please listen up! My name is Robert Quigley. As you may know, a couple of months ago, I was involved in an unfortunate incident at the local Pride Parade. To my great shame, I suffered an, um, *momentary brainstorm*, which caused me to run amok. Although no one was physically hurt, my actions may have caused psychological harm to some. Worse, I have been accused of being homophobic, which is *far* from the truth. Nevertheless, I am deeply sorry for the hurt I caused, and the embarrassment caused to my employer, which has stood by me in these difficult times…"

"Nice," whispered Emily from behind. "Margaret will love that."

"…and though I have issued various apologies in the media and online, I have been accused of voicing insincere words. So, to reaffirm my regret, I – with my good friends and supporters, Stan and Emily – have decided to make a more significant gesture. Taking our cue from Henry II, who did penance after his hasty words led to the killing of Thomas Becket, we stand before you in our own hair shirts."

"Don't forget your placard," hissed Stan, who poked that very item into the other's hand from behind, allowing Robert to grasp it without having to look. The placard said: "Down with Homophobia! Gays are Good!"

"So, we will now parade through the city to allow the public to witness my deep contrition." He pulled the placard forward, hoisted it aloft, and declared to the world at large: "Shall we go?"

"Mr Quigley," said the BBC reporter, flourishing a microphone, "do you mind if I ask you a few questions?"

Stan interposed himself between the woman and his friend, and through chattering teeth, pleaded: "Please, love, at the end, eh? Robert – I'm losing all feeling in my hands!"

"Ah, yes," muttered Robert, "that might be best. Afterwards, Ms Jones? Er, excuse me…" He started down the steps, causing the media people to scatter.

The trio followed part of the route of the Pride Parade, from their start on the steps of City Hall and back, through the well-wrapped-up Saturday shoppers. It wasn't a long route, and can't have taken more than ten to fifteen minutes in total, but it seemed to Robert to last forever. Their party had quite a following by the time it completed its circuit.

Once back before City Hall, while Stan and Emily threw on coats and attacked thermoses of hot tea, Robert endured further questions and posed for yet more pictures.

Afterwards, as the trio climbed into a Volvo estate in the subterranean car park of the nearby Forum, Robert muttered to his colleagues: "Thank fuck that's over."

But it wasn't.

The standout image from the event – which made it into several national dailies – was of the trio in their cheap jumpers with erect placards and exceedingly pale faces, passing beneath the glowing blue Primark sign on Gentleman's Walk. One journalist immediately drew a connection between these symbols, dubbing the trio the 'Primark Penitent', and thereby midwifed the birth of another new Norwich movement.

***

The Knights of St Gregory had spent the last few weeks scoping out the city. Their results were now collated on a large campaign map of Norwich that covered an old dining table in their secret lodge (aka Ken's converted double garage in the satellite village of Taverham). On the map, pins of various colours denoted locations of rough sleepers, sites of reported crimes, and reputed and observed zones of drug dealing. And presiding over all, looking down from his raised throne (an old-yet-comfortable reclining armchair set upon a wooden crate), was Grand Master Jim Taylor.

Jim still felt slightly embarrassed by his exalted status – but only slightly. Being a respected ceremonial leader in this place was a damned sight more enjoyable than being at home having to creep around Marie on an invisible carpet of eggshells. Boy, that woman could hold a grudge, having blamed him for their circumscribed social life following his brush with the law. And while it was true that they'd had fewer visits from (her) friends than before, he was pretty sure that was because they were avoiding *Mrs Snappy* rather than any actual enmity towards Jim. In fact, when he'd bumped into Mumtaz at the Tesco Metro the previous week, her concerned query had been about how *Marie* was coping; she'd not asked Jim about *his* state of mind at all. Well – enough of that nonsense!

"So, are we agreed on our target for the night?" Grey-bearded Ken looked up from the map to scan the other occupants of the room. There was a baker's dozen in total: twelve Knights, and their Grand Master. Yet, for a knightly retinue, they were a mismatched lot, mostly clothed in casual attire.

"Yep, let's get this on!" said Adam Jaspars – balding, short, and in his forties. Jim suspected that he had *small man* issues and saw the Knights as a chance to kick back.

"Well, I'm not so sure," said Maurice the dentist. "I still think we ought to do something about the park and estate by West Pottergate. It's a persistent sore."

Ken smiled wryly. "Yes, Maurice, it certainly is to residents in the area… like yourself. But we agreed in our charter to focus on protecting the city, *within* the inner ring road."

"Well, West Pottergate is on the edge of this zone. We shouldn't be pedantic about borders. I found a hypodermic lying on the ground near where children play."

Syringe. Jim frowned and shook his head, the image difficult to dislodge…

"I thought we'd laid this to rest at the last conclave," said black-bearded James. "City centre *first*, then we can extend our efforts later. The current proposal is to hit this area behind Prince of Wales Road. We're pretty sure there'll be dealers there tonight, up on the train from London to supply the clubbers–"

"But the police–"

"The police will have their hands full with the clubbers," sighed Tania. Her long, black leather coat made her look like the badass sister of Trinity from *The Matrix*. "They could do with our help, even though they won't admit it. This is scumville central. We have intel from Sir Ken on where some of the dealers will be, so we need to hit them *now*."

Maurice pouted, and briefly looked over to Jim, clearly with a view to launching an appeal, but after Jim winced and gave a small shrug in response, he threw up his hands and muttered grudging assent.

"Thank you, Sir Maurice," said Ken gravely, without a trace of mockery. "Your quest *will* be undertaken, just not yet."

For the next half hour, the group discussed who would meet where and what they would do under various circumstances. A plan was gradually formed.

"So, two teams," concluded Ken at the end. "James, Tania, Adam and I are Alpha. We'll do the hit. Dave, Pam, Piotr and Maurice will be Beta. But you're not just back-up in case things get hairy: we want you to appear from behind, out of this alley…" Ken gestured at the map, "just after contact. There should be two dealers. They'll probably be bolshie at first, but when they see there are even more of us blocking their escape, that'll likely break their resolve. Got it?"

Jim had been following keenly. This was their biggest operation to date. So far, they had used 'gentle persuasion' to disperse a group of addicts, helped move on a couple of homeless people, and restrained a drunken vandal who'd been caught kicking a bus shelter (their first citizen's arrest). He felt he needed to say something now – a reminder of their moral creed? A rousing and motivational speech? Instead, all he could come up with was: "Er, are we sure about this? I mean, what if one of them has a knife?"

Tania was close; she glided over to him, rested one hand on his arm, and smiled deeply into his eyes. "Don't worry, Jim. Ken and I are proficient at jiu-jitsu. We know how to disarm knife wielders. But we'll be careful. Plus, Sir Adam has his taser, just in case."

"Ah… yes… Sir Adam…" Jim looked at the small man, who was virtually bouncing on the spot, giving the impression that he'd like nothing more than to use his illegal – but morally justified (they'd all agreed) – weapon. "Okay then. I guess… I guess…" he straightened his shoulders and raised his voice, "I approve. Let the Knights go forth!"

The Knights of St Gregory straightened their backs and followed a now- accustomed ritual, resting a hand over the stylised '*St G*' pin each wore on their chest. "As you command, Grand Master!" they cried.

***

"Heh – this'll teach the fuckers," said a ski-mask-wearing Blitz. He gave his spray can a vigorous shake and applied its contents to the statue of the defenceless Sir Thomas Browne. He'd already liberally coated much of the seated figure in a range of colours; now he applied the black paint to its face.

Skid looked up from the foot of the statue, where he was kneeling beside their collection of cans. It was three in the morning, and they were alone. "Christ, B, is that appropriate?"

Blitz looked down. He could barely see his mate in the shadows. "What do you mean?"

"You've done a blackface. Isn't that sort of racist?"

"Is it? Nah! This is symbolic. This is for the brothers and sisters. Remember the underpass and what that racist stooge did to our message of solidarity?"

"Uh, right." Skid stood up and scratched at the straggly beard beneath his own ski-mask; it itched like hell. "But I thought we were doing this as a protest for Baz, who got hassled by those geezers last week, and Stew and Ann and Mags, who got pushed about the night before that."

Blitz frowned, though the mask hid his expression. "It is. That too. It's for all us little people getting hassled by the fascist boog-wa-sie. Can't do this. Can't do that. Can't have a tinnie. Can't have a spliff. Got to get a job. Got to beg for money. *Bastards.*" What he didn't admit, though, was that the straw that broke this particular camel's back was his failure to score three nights ago because his dealer had been warned off by a group of vigilantes. "They want to get rid of all of us who are different. The underclass. Well, they can choke on my fat knob. The fight back starts here." He leapt down from the plinth. "What d'you think?"

"Er, yeah, apart from the blackface, it's cool. This'll piss off the fascists."

"Just one more thing." Blitz leant down and searched through the assorted colours. He found the red and straightened. "They need to know who they're dealing with." On the stonework bearing an inscription about Browne's life and death, he sprayed his tag – a giant *KB*. "King Blitz! Yeah!" Then he mic-dropped the can into the open bag on the ground. "Our work here is done. Let's split. We got a video to make."

***

"Some of you may have noticed a colourful addition to our city centre over recent weeks in the form of people patrolling the streets wearing unusual headgear. Sally – can you tell us more?"

The screens of viewers throughout the East Anglian region showed two images: to the left was Rachel Kettleborough in the BBC studios, and to the right was roving reporter Sally Jones with microphone in hand. "That's right, Rachel. The headgear in question is a rather stylish rainbow-coloured beret, and I have one of the wearers with me now."

On viewers' screens, the studio image disappeared to leave Sally in sole charge. The camera then panned out to reveal that the reporter was not alone: beside her was a severe-looking woman with short-cropped hair and a nose stud wearing a large, multicoloured striped hat of French origin. They were stood before the great glass frontage of the Forum, where the local BBC had its studios, with the outside tables of the Café Marzano to one side. The building lay close to City Hall, the St Peter Mancroft Church, and Hay Hill — site of the statue of Sir Thomas Browne.

"With me here is Clare Ramsay, an LGBTQ+ activist and founder of the Rainbow Commando." Sally turned slightly to face the woman and extended her microphone. "Clare, can you tell us what this is all about?"

"Yeah, sure." Clare stole a look at Harry, moustachioed and debonair as ever, who stood just behind the cameraman. Harry had managed to arrange this gig through his media contacts, and so he'd every right to be here. *Moral support*, he'd told her, but Clare suspected he wanted to keep an eye on her to make sure she kept to the script they'd agreed. "I formed the *Commando* after the assault on our parade. We're here to support the LGBTQ+ community. Our aim is to remind the people of Norwich that we exist; that we don't just come out one day a year."

"So, you're a point of contact?"

"That's right. We're here to help, and to educate. And during the day, we have a safe space set aside in the Greenhouse Trust on Bethel Street, just along from the police station. We're happy for anyone to come in and join us for a chat and a coffee."

Sally nodded. "All this sounds highly commendable. But what would you say to those who have suggested that your organisation has a military demeanour? Is it true that your commandos have been receiving martial arts training?"

Clare's smile twitched. "Well, we are here to defend the community, too. If people are afraid to go to the police — and many have just cause to do so — they can be reassured that there is someone around who'll back them up."

"But you would advocate going to the police first in the case of trouble, wouldn't you?"

"Sure." Clare's smile twitched again as she noticed the deepening frown on Harry's face.

After an awkward silence, and once it was clear that the interviewee was not going to elaborate, Sally changed tack. "And talking about the origin of your group, what do you think of the demonstration last week, by the man who was responsible for the Pride Parade attack? The so-called Primark Penitent? Do you now accept his remorse?"

Clare's half-smile vanished. "Do I accept? Do I...?" She saw Harry gesturing in the background, lowering his hands slowly. "All he did was walk about for a few minutes in an old jumper. That's an easy thing to do. That hardly cancels out a lifetime of homophobia."

"But he's made a number of other public apologies, too. Is there nothing he can do that will lead you to forgive him?"

Clare was tempted to shout 'no'. A leopard doesn't change its spots. She noticed Harry's gestures becoming increasingly frantic: "Well... maybe. But he needs to do more. Much more. He needs to convince us that this isn't a one-off PR stunt to get a free pass so he can go back to his old ways. So, yeah, I'd like to see him do more marches. Show real commitment. Get other recidivists involved."

"I think that's a very clear message! And talking about messages, what do you make of the recent vandalism of the statue of Sir Thomas Browne – in the very square from which Robert Quigley's rampage began? Do you think someone else was sending a message?"

"Well, it wasn't us," bridled Clare, whose short temper was fraying. "And if they were, then so what? I mean, who was this Browne? Yet another white heterosexual male, sitting on a plinth, looking down on us."

"Ah, so you approve of the vandalism?"

Clare noticed Harry waving his hands about as though directing an aircraft to park. Well, he couldn't stop her now. "Yeah, absolutely. Hopefully the first of many. We need to replace these old fascists with more appropriate symbols of our times..."

Harry held a hand over his face.

***

Sally Jones' report the next day came from Hay Hill, just a couple of hundred yards down the slope from the Forum. She wielded her microphone in the shadow of Sir Thomas Browne, who was looking slightly better for a deep clean, though the 'KB' tag was still evident on the plinth.

"Well, the council didn't seem that interested," said Ronnie Waites, a sinewy sixty-year-old with a tan, courtesy of a recent break in Lanzarote. "We pay our council taxes, and what do they do with all the money? *Speed bumps.*"

"That's right," said Colin McArthur, leaning on a mop in the midst of a sudsy puddle. He was of similar age to Ronnie, but had a full head of white hair instead of a Bobby Charlton combover. "This is an important symbol of the city, and we shouldn't have to wait for them to get their arses in gear. So, we felt it was our civic duty to respond. We couldn't leave Sir Tom like this."

The cameraman shuffled around to ensure he captured two grey-haired ladies in the background – Doris and Annie, the men's 'other halves' – as they raised their soapy brushes to attack the final letters of desecration.

"I'm surprised the council sanctioned this," said Sally.

"Weeeeeell... they haven't really," said Ronnie. "We just had a PCSO wander by, but she didn't know what to do so she wandered off again. And in spite of being a catapult lob from the Bethel Street station, we've not seen a real policeman since we started."

"And you're our insurance," said Colin. "I almost want them to turn up and arrest us for interfering with a statue. It would say something about their priorities. It's okay for this 'KB' to come and defile our monuments, but not for us to apply the antidote. I mean, have they even looked into who these people are? They've even left their name, for Pete's sake! KB? Perhaps the *Krustie Brigade* with a 'K'? I doubt these layabouts even know how to spell their own names."

Sally smiled at this. "If the perpetrators are the 'Krustie Brigade', what does that make you?"

"You tell me, Sally," said Ronnie, with a mischievous twinkle to the eye. "Perhaps you can hold a twittery poll, or whatever it is you do nowadays. Let your viewers decide."

"Eh-up," said Colin. "Looks like we've action at last. Hello, officers, how can we help...?"

The interview became confused thereafter, but the police were clearly afraid of bad publicity, and the statue was all but clean, so they allowed it to be finished off and no arrests were made.

***

The *Look East* viewers came up with various names, but 'Thomas Browne's Boys', was the one that stuck.

"Well, I'm not a boy!" said an indignant Doris the next day. She was seated beside her husband, Ronnie, in the large and well-heated conservatory of their friends and co-revolutionaries. "We did most of the work, and you got all the credit. That's just typical!"

"It's just sexism," said Annie. "That's all."

"Sorry, dears," said Ronnie, who clearly wasn't. "I think it's just a play on words. Apparently it's a reference to *Mrs Brown's Boys.*"

"You mean, that horrible 'comedy' show with that Irishman dressed up as a woman?" said Doris.

"That's the one," agreed Colin, who'd seen a few episodes and thought them quite funny in a perverse kind of way. "But what can we do?"

"I'll tell you what," said Annie. "Next time, *we* will do the interview and *you* can do the scrubbing."

"Next time?" wondered her husband.

But of course there would be a next time.

Genies let out of bottles rarely return easily.

Chapter 16: Would you Adam and Eve it!

"The video, which admits responsibility for damage to the statue, was received by the BBC this morning," reported Rachel Kettleborough, in her calming tones. "Before showing it, I should warn viewers that it has been cleaned up to mask language unsuitable before the watershed."

In his small living room, Tom slouched on his worn, orange sofa, nursing a lukewarm cup of tea in his lap. The image on the TV changed from the comely presenter to one of a man in a ski mask sitting behind a desk in a room with lime green walls. Behind him was a banner on which the letters 'KB' were spray painted in red. Tom was reminded of sinister videos he'd seen in the past from the IRA and ISIS.

"Is this [*bleeeeep*] on?" began the figure, uncertainly. "Can I [*bleeeep*] start? So, we is on? Right, listen up, fascists. This is KB and the crew. You need to know that *we* did it. The statue of the fascist imperialist [*bleeeeep*]. We did it for all the underprivileged. The poor. The ordinary people and *independent businessmen* hassled by the state and the pigs and the vigilantes." He leant forwards menacingly towards the camera. "Yeah, the *vigilantes*! We got you clocked, now, yeah!" He stood up, and the wavering camera had to readjust to keep the man's head in the frame. "But most of all, it's to show solidarity with that bird on the TV and her righteous gays, and with the B-L-M. And why have the police still not caught the [*bleeeep*] who [*bleeeeped*] our message of solidarity?"

Tom's leg jerked, and the tepid beverage sloshed over his thighs.

"I'll tell you why: cos it's a conspiracy! They're in on it! So, this is a final warning to *society*. To the *state*. Keep the [*bleep*] out of our lives. Or else this will be the start of a war you can't win." He slammed his hand onto the desk, which was then revealed to be not a proper desk at all, but a board rested across two chairs. "Oh, [*bleeeeeep*]…"

As the board flipped up and the figure began to pitch over it, the video came to an end.

"Fuck!" gasped Tom, and not just from the stain to his trousers.

Back in the studio, Rachel was now revealed to be sitting opposite a smartly dressed senior female police officer.

"Chief Inspector Allenby: a concerning video! What do you make of it? And also, of the allegations about your lack of success in solving the case of the racist graffiti that we reported on in August…"

As Tom mopped at his thighs with a less-than-clean handkerchief, and his eyes flashed from damp trousers to the TV and back again, the words of the police officer only intermittently impinged on his consciousness: "…reassure the public… no place for vigilantes… don't condone… case not closed… following fresh leads…"

"Fuck fuck *fuck!*"

As the interview ended, Tom scrabbled for his mobile phone and fired off a text to Amanda. Then, after a moment's thought, he sent the same message to Ed. He thought some more. Simon, too? But in the end, he withdrew his hovering finger from the *send* icon. "The fewer who know…"

***

The Adam and Eve pub on Bishopsgate – squatting between the extensive grounds of Norwich Cathedral and a bend of the river Wensum – was the oldest pub in the city. The current Dutch-gabled building of brick and flint largely dated from the seventeenth century, although precursors on the site had served customers ever since 1249, when a pub first opened its doors to the thirsty stonemasons building the Cathedral itself.

Tom wove between outside tables, entering through a low doorway between two hanging baskets of red flowers, which provided a cheerful contrast to the drab, naked trees, shivering outside in the autumnal chill. Inside, the low, oak-beamed ceiling made him feel a need to duck his head, even though he wasn't the tallest of men, and in spite of the fact that he had plenty of clearance between it and his crown of overgrown hair (he really needed a trip to the barber's!). He turned from the bar directly ahead, spotting his friends in a small section to his right, where wooden benches lined the walls. Ed and Amanda were both present – Amanda sipping a lemonade, while Ed grasped a pewter tankard.

"Thanks for coming," said Tom, sweeping off his glasses. "I didn't know when we'd meet again…" the quiz had been called off for a third week running, this time because Simon was indisposed, "and I just had to talk." He slumped into a chair next to Amanda, facing Ed. There were a couple more tables in this section – currently empty. "But it's an odd choice, Ed. Why here?" It was mid-afternoon on a Wednesday.

"Convenience *plus* guilty pleasure, Tom, old fruit. I had to drop off a malfunctioning bit of kit at a computer repair place on Magdalen Street, and this is only a wiggle off my route home. Plus, it's a nice pub and they have proper drinking vessels hidden away." He raised his tankard and gave it gentle shake. "But before I am prepared to listen to your latest woes, please get yourself a drink. Amanda is on the pop, and I am not drinking alone."

"Ah, right." Tom scurried to the bar and was soon back with an ale in an ordinary pint glass.

Ed smirked at this. "Tankards are reserved for special people, old chum."

"You mean, for those who actually ask," said Amanda, who wore her hair in a ponytail today, possibly to keep it under control, given that her bulbous orange-and-grey-striped jumper virtually crackled with static electricity. "Anyway, hello Tom. You sound a bit frazzled."

"Oh, yes, hi Amanda. Sorry – don't know if I'm coming or going. I'm glad you could make it, too. Nothing on?"

"Nothing I couldn't rearrange. It's one of the joys of being freelance."

"Indeed, that goes for all three of us," noted Ed. "It's only Simon who's a wage slave, working for The Man." He narrowed his eyes. "Which is why he couldn't make it, eh?"

"Uh, well, to be honest, I didn't ask him. The things I want to talk about are things I've mention to you two before, or things we've experienced personally, so, er…"

"No worries," said Ed, with a mischievous grin. "Perhaps you should begin, then. We are metaphorically all ears."

"Right, first, did you see *Look East* last night?"

Ed started to laugh. "Wager with self – *won*. But it's *you* who should be coughing up, my friend, rather than me having to buy my own rewarding drink. Sure, I saw it. And I thought: well, Tom has probably just soiled himself."

"What am I missing?" asked Amanda, switching her gaze between the two men. "What's so funny? Or not-funny, from Tom's perspective?"

"There was a video from the vandals who trashed the statue of that old philosopher chap," said Ed. "They showed a sanitised version on the news. The masked hombre mentioned Tom's own vandalism as a factor behind their attack, although frankly it just came across as a lame attempt to justify his actions. The problem is, there was a member of Her Majesty's Constabulary on hand to respond. I am assuming the bit about 'new leads' is what has got our Tom all hot and bothered, no?"

"Er, yes."

"*No*, Tom." Ed was suddenly serious. "That was merely a sop. The police don't have any leads, and they stopped investigating about an hour after they recorded your 'offence'. Those are standard words they trot out whenever they're put on the spot. There is nothing to worry about, *capiche*?"

"Um, well…"

Amanda rested a hand on Tom's arm. "I didn't see it, but I'm sure Ed is right. The police don't have the resources to investigate most thefts, let alone who sprayed a bit of graffiti. I mean, it's not as if you actually sprayed anything racist. You merely sprayed over something that someone else had written."

"You mean, over an anti-racist message, which therefore *appears* to be a racist act," said Tom. "You know how sensitive everyone is today about, well, *anything* that could be conceived by *anyone* as… as… *ist* in some way."

Amanda nodded. "Yes, sure. Words have power, and people realise that. And we saw it ourselves last week. But–"

"But here and now, in bucolic Norwich, with our plodding plods, you are safe," confirmed Ed. "In thirty years' time though, things will be different. There'll be fleets of drones and CCTV everywhere, with instant-DNA kits used to irrefutably prove such crimes as who forgot to put the milk back in the fridge, and who left the lights on when they went out. Were we in that future time, you'd undoubtedly be hunted down like a dog, publicly humiliated, and sent to a penal colony on the moon."

"Ed," warned Amanda, "I don't think that's helping."

"Er, no, actually, it is… kind of. You're both right. *Probably*. Maybe I just needed to have these things confirmed by people I trust."

"That's what we're here for, mi amigo," said Ed. "Mutual support. *And* beer. Now, you said 'first'. 'Second' is clearly going to be about the beer festival, which Mands just alluded to. And we should indeed move on to that, for I myself have significant things to impart. But first…" he slid his now-empty tankard over to Tom. "Pint of Jackal, please. Same mug."

***

"So, I started with some diplomatic queries to Big Ed as soon as I got home. He's always accessible. The weird alien chap must never sleep. I suspect it's because 'he' is actually a 'they'. Hive mind? Clones? AI system? Fuck knows. Even the thing I once met in 'person' could have been a puppet, or a stand-in. Big Ed's online presence reveals very little about him – nothing more than an electronic avatar. But I smelt a whole school of blubbery fish as soon as I started speaking to him on Zoom."

"What did you say?" asked Tom, suddenly nervous again. "You didn't mention–"

"Of course not, my tremulous friend! I simply said I'd been to the beer festival and all hell had let loose, and I further suggested that this seemed to be part of a series of odd events in Norwich."

"Series of odd events?" wondered Amanda. "What series?"

Ed shrugged. "I dunno. I was plucking at everything I could think of. The furore at the Pride Parade. The local MP getting roughed up on the train as he arrived at Norwich station a couple of weeks ago. The Lord Mayor nearly getting run down by that angry old biddy the week before that... the one who said her foot slipped, but you could see in the interview that she was steaming. Further civic strife caused by racist graffiti artists–"

"What!"

"Calm down, old chap. I didn't say it was you. Anyway, you asked me what he said, but you should instead have asked me what he *didn't* say."

Tom was too flustered to speak, so Amanda filled in the pause: "So, what *didn't* he say?"

"He didn't say *anything*." Ed leant back, crossed his arms, scrunched his eyes and began a slow nod. "Nothing."

"And why is that important?" continued Amanda.

"Because I'd imparted considerably more information than usual and got considerably less back in return. The big chap is hardly the most voluble, and keeps his cards close to his chest, but he usually provides some commentary, some suggestion as to what data to look at or where to probe. He'd normally encourage me to do something and then report back my findings later. But this time, it was all stony-faced indifference.

And when I wondered about alien interference, he said: 'that's an interesting hypothesis'. And then he instantly switched subject and started asking me whether I'd found any tells in the dark web related to a particular species that seems to be running a gambling syndicate."

"What!" said Tom again, like a stuck record.

Amanda's eyes also widened. "Gambling syndicate? You've never mentioned–"

Ed unfolded his arms and waved the matter aside. "There's at least one species that seems to indulge in illicit manipulations of all sorts of events for betting purposes. This is Big Ed's main concern. I've not told you any details before because we'd agreed to be uber-subtle, but now that Tom has blundered into our lives with his specs of doom and forced me to up the ante with the big guy, it doesn't seem so important to sweat the small stuff."

"Gambling–?"

"Tom, really? Are you still *buffering*? Let that drop. What I'm saying is that I think there *is* something going on, and Big Ed is aware of it to some degree, but for some reason doesn't want me to look into it. *Stupid.* These aliens may be massive science nerds, but psychologists they're not. Naturally, I started looking into things as soon as I cut the connection with him. And it was fascinating what I found."

"Which was…?" prompted Amanda.

Ed held up a stalling finger, picked up his tankard, and drained it. "Thirsty work this, eh?"

Amanda sighed. "You want another?"

"Sure. And Tom could do with another, too, by the looks of it. Tom, close your mouth – you're starting to look like a drooling simpleton."

"Fine," said Amanda, sweeping up Ed's pewter tankard. "And I think I could use something stronger myself."

"That's my girl!"

***

By the time Amanda returned and settled beside Tom, Ed had procured a laptop from a rucksack he'd stashed at his feet. He momentarily ignored the others as he tapped and swiped away.

"Right," said Ed at last, still looking at his screen. "I've been digging deep over the last few days. I've followed two lines of inquiry. First, I've been trying to identify every person that went into the festival prior to our arrival. I've focused on the day we went, as the festival opened a couple of days before that, but there was no grief until our session, hence, I've assumed that the messages must have gone up that same day. And second, I've been hacking into every CCTV camera in the area to try to track the movements of any potential suspects."

"You can do that?" asked Tom – half query, half accusation.

"I can, yes. But it's not easy. Anyway, I eventually got a full list of CAMRA members on the organising team and all additional volunteers. Then I managed to hack into one of their emails and trace their group discussions about who, what, where and when. I eventually found a discussion about their merchandise and promotional material, when it arrived, and who picked it up. Perhaps it's no surprise, but the doctored banners arrived a couple of days before the event, were put up on the first day, and in theory, remained up the whole time."

"So, they were amended *in situ*," said Tom.

"Clever boy, Tom, have a banana."

"But how?" asked Amanda. "We discussed this when we walked home, Tom and I. Surely they'd have had to use a stepladder to access them, and it would have been obvious that they were up to something with whatever magical alien pen they were using?"

"Absolutely right. They shouldn't have been able to… but they did. How? Well, I can tell you: it's that old fire alarm wheeze." Ed grinned in self-satisfaction. "Unfurrow that brow, Tom! Here's what happened. The midday session ran from 11.30 to 14.30, and we know there was no problem during this, so we might suppose that the banners were sound at the time. The evening session didn't begin until 17.30 – giving a three-hour window of opportunity. At around 16.50, the fire alarm went off, and everyone trooped out, as you can see here…" Ed swung his laptop around.

Tom and Amanda craned in to have a look. What they saw was a video of the exterior of St Andrew's Hall from across the road. In the plain, in front of the old priory, a score of people milled about, oozing disgruntlement.

"*Sneaky*," muttered Tom.

"Sneaky indeed! And we can presume that someone didn't leave when the others did, or at least, not before they'd done the dirty deed, going thrice up-and-down a step ladder conveniently left nearby."

"Where did you get this video, Ed?" asked Amanda, still fixated on the barely distinct figures that were at least ten metres from the camera.

"Courtesy of Norwich City Council, of course. I had a bit of luck there. They've been extending their CCTV network, and this camera only went up in April. They probably thought it was about time they kept an eye on the beer-infused revellers from the festival."

"That's great," said Tom. "But do you know who did the act?"

"As to that... not exactly. That's why I haven't been in touch – I've been trying to narrow things down. But I do have a few suspects. The main problem is that there's no CCTV in the priory itself, so I've had to make the most of what I've got. I started by discounting the organisers and brewery reps who were outside during the alarm – and that took some doing. As you see, the shots aren't great, especially of those in the distance. I had to identify every individual and match them to photos I managed to dig out from Facebook and other sites. And that only cut about two-thirds of those with free access to the building. So, I had to then backtrack to see which others from my grand list had entered the building previously and left *after* the earlier session and *before* the alarm. I was partly helped by a CCTV on the outside of what used to be the Dog House pub on St Georges Street, just opposite the west face of the venue. Here..."

Ed reclaimed the laptop, swivelled it to face him, and began clicking and swiping once more.

"Impressive," said Tom to Amanda, speaking low so as not to disturb their intently working friend.

"And illegal," responded Amanda quietly, shaking her head.

"More *sotto* less *voce* please," scowled Ed, still fixed to the screen. "Criminal at work!" He played at his machine for another minute or so, then tamped down on a final key. "*Done.* Now, look at this..."

The laptop was swung round once more.

"What exactly are we looking at?" asked Tom.

"I have isolated eleven possible culprits – people who had the right to be in the hall at the appropriate time, are almost certain to have been there at the end of the first session of the day – as established by rotas in emails, CCTV and suchlike – and who were not seen by me leaving in the interval session. Now, most of these will have actually been absent, and I just haven't been able to get a good view of them on the various cameras, but there's a chance that one is the culprit. So, take a good look. These are the best shots I've got from cameras on the day, or from shots on previous or subsequent days. In two cases, I have no actual photos: for one, I have a Facebook shot, and for the other, a picture from a local CAMRA magazine that had him tagged. Look at the first, then scroll through the rest. Let me know if there is anyone there you recognise."

Once again, Tom and Amanda hunched forwards, leaning in until their heads were almost touching.

The first three images were of men, all hardy in build, none at all familiar.

"The first ones are brewery reps," noted Ed. "You can tell by their clothing. The CAMRA organisers were all wearing speciality beer festival t-shirts and polos under their jackets."

The fourth and fifth were also unfamiliar (the latter highlighted in a magazine clip). But the sixth…

"Hang on!" said Tom. "Him! I know him!" The photo was labelled: Martin Elder.

"Really, Tom?" asked Amanda.

"Yes. Definitely. I'm sure I first saw him outside City College, and then I saw him in the street – in fact, not far from The Halls – a week or two ago. I remember him because he was also wearing sunglasses. That was a weird day. I also saw one of the Terminus Est lot going into the Cosy Club."

"Interesting," said Ed. "I'll look into young Martin further. But carry on." He seemed amused, and also excited, as if waiting for something.

"Right, so…" Tom absently played with his own glasses, which were on the table where he'd dropped them on entering the pub. Pushing them aside, he returned a finger to the mousepad and clicked on.

The seventh was unknown, as was the eighth – shown by a Facebook picture. But the ninth… Tom's brow furrowed. "The woman in the puffer jacket… she seems oddly familiar. But I don't know where from. And there's something missing… Her partner? Is she half of a couple? I just don't know."

"Okay. Teresa Valentin. I'll check her, too. But go on. What about the next one?" Now Ed's eagerness was clear.

165

Tom clicked on.

"Fuck me," said Amanda, rather uncharacteristically. Then her hand went to her mouth. "Sorry!"

Tom shook his head. "I know what you mean. It's got to be him. From the quiz."

"Good!" Ed laughed. "I didn't want to pre-empt you, but I'm sure. There can't be that many fat bastards in Norwich who are that fat. But this time, he's wearing a different XXXXXL t-shirt. Turns out our large friend is called Augustus P. Samson, and he's not only a quiz lord with his own fan club, but he's also a member of the local CAMRA organising committee. Only problem is, I'm not sure this guy could make it up a stepladder. He'd certainly get wedged between the handrails at the top."

Tom laughed… but quickly stopped. "You know, joking aside, you might not be wrong. It wouldn't be easy for him to do the signs. Not quickly, anyway."

"Unless it's a fat suit," noted Ed, mischievously, "and within is a thin alien literally bursting to get out."

Amanda looked up at this and peered at Ed through her glasses. "That's something we haven't thought about. I mean, we've just assumed that someone somehow wrote the message – as opposed to the message having been *materialised* there – but what sort of person?"

"You mean," wondered Tom, "an alien or… what are they called… those servants of vampires in that film, *Blade*?"

"You mean *familiars*," declared Ed, knowingly. "Which I guess is effectively what we are. But I get what you're saying. Are these messages actually being left by real aliens, or by their pets?" He started to withdraw the laptop.

For a second, Tom sat back and watched the machine being turned, but something wasn't right. *Ah!* He raised a hand. "Uh, hang on. Was he the last, or have I miscounted? Was there…?"

"Well-well-well – you *are* vaguely compos, Tom. Yep, might as well see the last…" and Ed tweaked the laptop around with one hand at the top of the screen.

Tom and Amanda peered once more. This shot was slightly different – obviously from a different camera – pointing up the side of the priory towards St Andrew's Plain. Cinema City was visible across the road next to St Andrew's Church, with the St Andrews Brew House on the corner, and a café sporting an orange-coloured façade closer to. Tom knew that next to the Brew House was a zebra crossing, opposite which were a couple of red phone boxes, where he had lurked a while ago when tailing one of Augustus' posse.

Tom shook his head. "Nope. I don't know this guy. But… ha. That's funny."

"What is?" asked Amanda.

"Look. Beyond the bloke. Opposite the café. With his back to us."

"The man in the bib?"

"Yes. It's a red one. Looks like a *Big Issue* seller. It's just like what Smith wears."

"You don't think…?" started Amanda, curious.

"No. It's probably just a coincidence. What would he be doing there? He wouldn't have had access to the festival anyway. Besides, he hangs around St Peter Mancroft and the Guildhall."

"Only?" asked Ed, also intrigued.

"Well, probably no. He's mentioned tunnels under Norwich, and I guess these could pop out anywhere. He also has a thing for… *phone boxes.*" Tom felt a strange unease. "Just like those almost directly in front of this guy, across the road."

"Hmmm. I think it might be worth me revisiting the CCTV outside St Andrew's Church – the one from which I've got most of my intel. That looks straight across to the priory, and it happens to be directly *behind* those boxes. I should be able to get some pictures of the geezer's face. Wouldn't that be interesting, eh? I mean, if it were him?"

"That… yes… that would be interesting. But I don't know what it would imply."

"Okay. For the time being, let's assume it's not him," continued Ed. "I mean, when you saw him after the event, he didn't admit to having been anywhere near the place or to know anything, did he?"

"No. And if he had, I'm sure he would have said so. Okay. Let's assume it's a coincidence. There are at least two, maybe three others who seem suspicious. What of them?"

"Could they be working together?" asked Amanda. "Or could they be working for different masters? Maybe one of them is like us, working for another goodie rather than a manipulator?"

"More good points, Mands," said Ed. "I'll add to my list: check if any of the suspects know each other socially, or are together in any other shots from before or after the event. But if one is working for a *goodie*, as you call our tetchy and graceless overlords, then they appear to be as inept as Tom… or perhaps I should grudgingly say, as 'us', although Tom is the one who's meant to be actively finding and thwarting these demons of disruption."

"Well, inept is a bit strong," said Tom, defensively. "I didn't have my kit with me at the time, so I couldn't have done anything about the messages anyway. I've only started bringing it out with me – on Smith's advice – since I met him after the riot."

"So *that's* what's in that manky looking rucksack of yours," smirked Ed. "Spray paint and magnets?"

"Er, yes. Anyway, it's just occurred to me that even if I had my kit at the time, I still wouldn't have been able to do anything. I mean, I couldn't have sprayed the three banners in front of everyone."

"You wouldn't have had to," mused Ed. "Think: *breaking the chain*."

"Eh?"

"All you would have needed to do was take down one of the banners, as the rest of the message would then have lost its meaning. And as they're portable, you wouldn't have needed to spray it. You know, do a bit of a pratfall. Reach up and grab one of the banners and then go, whoops! Look at me! What a klutz! And pull it down."

"What, and get thrown out!"

"As long as it was only you," grinned Ed, "that would have been a sacrifice I'd have been willing to make. We would have drunk to your health in the knowledge that you had struck a blow for humanity. Light a candle to you once home. And so on."

"Thanks," said Tom, disgruntled.

"No problem. Now, we need to think about what to do next, and I hope you'll agree, I've definitely earned a pint after all this work. What say you top me up? Pip-pip! The post-work crowd seem to be trickling in, but the bloke at the bar's just been served… go go go!"

Tom gave a sigh of resignation. "Amanda – same again? Right…"

He headed for the bar and placed his order. It was only then – while waiting for the landlady to pour his drinks – that he realised what time it was: not late, but given it was early November, it was already dark outside, with lights from within the bar bouncing back off the windows.

Dark.

Well, so what?

Well, it was in the dark that certain things became *apparent.* Tom reached a hand towards his face but paused it half-way. His glasses were on the table. Which was good, he supposed. What he couldn't see, didn't exist. Or perhaps, it did exist, but it didn't matter. And then he realised exactly where he was: the Adam and Eve, the oldest pub in the city. A pub known for... the hairs metaphorically rose on the back of his neck. Tom scrunched his eyes half-closed and scanned his environment. But the space was comfortingly enclosed, beneath a low, wood-beamed ceiling, with a small number of tables scattered over the quarry-tiled floor. There were only half-a-dozen people present throughout, but this still made the place feel crowded. It was definitely non-spooky.

Still...

He carried his purchase back to his friends, a wedged triangle of glasses pressed between two hands. As he set the pints down, he caught Amanda looking up at him, a frown on her face.

"Are you okay, Tom? You look awfully pale."

"It's just the light," said Ed. "It reveals his true colours. Pasty. Unhealthy. In desperate need of a sunbed."

Tom slid into his seat. "Well, there *is* something else. It's something I mentioned at the beer festival, but I never got a chance to talk to you about it."

"Okay," said Amanda, "now's your chance..."

***

Tom related his tale about ghosts. He told of his encounters on Elm Hill and at the station, and repeated Smith's explanation that ghosts were merely disguised, non-corporeal aliens. Amanda listened intently and – to Tom's surprise – so did Ed. In fact, the latter didn't interrupt once.

"And so I've been a bit wary of coming out at night. Or at least, coming to the older parts of the city." His hand twirled his glasses on the table next to his almost-untouched pint. "I mean, even knowing these things aren't going to harm me, and that they're really just–"

169

"Piss-taking aliens?" volunteered Ed.

"Yes. Piss-taking aliens. Even knowing this, they still give me the willies."

"Did you see something at the bar earlier?" asked Amanda.

"No. It's not that. After those sightings, I started looking into other reports of ghosts in Norwich, so I knew where to avoid, and I compiled a list of haunted places. At the bar, I remembered that *this* place is on the list." He reached for his mobile phone, which was in the chest pocket of his blue-checked lumberjack shirt. "Wait a mo." He started swiping at icons and soon found what he was looking for. "Right. Here it is. 'Adam and Eve: the ghost of Lord Sheffield – who was attacked by rebels during Kett's Rebellion in 1549, and brought to the pub afterwards, where he died – is still reputed to haunt the building. So too are spectres of some of the French-speaking medieval monks who lived and worked here.' Blah blah blah. And one monk is believed to be buried beneath us. *Fuck!*" He placed his phone face down next to his glasses. "So…"

"So don't put your glasses on and stay in the light," said Ed. "*Simples!*"

"Doesn't this worry you at all?" Amanda looked across to Ed. "I mean, even a little? I admit, I suddenly feel a bit, I don't know, *sensitive*." She looked about cautiously.

"Yes, it gets to you like that," said Tom. "Once you know, you can't help wondering if every breeze or shadow or—"

"Okay, Tom, that's enough!" pleaded Amanda.

"Sure!"

"Well, thanks for that, my friend," chortled Ed. "A useful heads-up! But if I start getting nightmares and wetting the bed like an incontinent crumbly, I'm sending you the laundry *and* therapist bills. Having now terrorised Amanda and entertained me, what do you expect us to do about your little problem?"

"Do? Nothing, really. I just wanted to talk it out."

"Share the scare?"

Tom gave an enigmatic smile. "Perhaps."

They returned to discussing events at the festival and next steps. These essentially involved compiling a list of things for Ed to do before reporting back. Though they now had several suspicious names, Tom and Amanda agreed that it would not be wise for them to attempt to look into these on the internet for fear of somehow alerting their targets.

"You might somehow be traced," Ed noted. "Whereas I, with my skills in the dark arts, won't be."

With matters resolved and beers not-quite finished, the conversation turned lighter, and then even more beer was had.

By the time they decided to call it an evening, Tom had downed five pints and was nicely soaked and in need of draining. As they all rose, he swept up his phone and returned it to his shirt pocket, pulled on his rucksack, and then picked up his glasses and – with no better place for them – absently put them on.

"Back in a jiffy."

The small gents next to the bar was empty. Tom unzipped and attended his business, swaying slightly as he did so. Five pints on an empty stomach was probably not a good idea. As he continued, he felt a gentle breeze tickle the back of his neck, as though from an opening door.

But the door hadn't opened, and he was still alone.

It took Tom a moment to realise this.

And then another moment to sense someone, or something, over his left shoulder.

He slowly turned his head…

And there, over by the sink, less than two metres distant, was an indistinct, semi-transparent figure, in breastplate and gauntlets, with a cleaver sprouting from its head. But there was no blood, and the figure appeared unconcerned by the part-buried weapon. Indeed, its expression suggested amusement…

Tom yelped.

Turned.

And barrelled through the two doors between him and the lounge.

The table with his friends was close by, but not the closest. He jerkily moved past another small table around which sat a trio of men, who were fortunately engrossed in their own conversation. Ed and Amanda were stood up, waiting.

At the sight of him, Amanda's eyes widened, and then they looked down and widened even more. A hand went to her mouth, but not before the shocked exclamation rang out: "Tom!"

"Ghost! There's a ghost!" hissed Tom. "In there… In…"

Ed couldn't suppress a chuckle. He was also looking down to the level of Tom's waist. "Fuck that! Tom, old mucker, you appear not to have put the little chap properly to bed. Amanda, avert thine eyes!"

Tom's breathing was heavy, which given his current state of exposure only added to the impression of a pervert at large, and most certainly would have led to an arrest had there been any boys or girls in blue around. "What... what do... wha... *fuck*!" Tom hastily turned away, immense embarrassment suddenly flushing fear from his system. He tucked himself away and zipped.

Behind, he heard Ed declare: "Would you Adam-and-Eve-it! Clearly they do indeed give you the willies, Tom, but did you *really* have to demonstrate that to us so explicitly?"

Chapter 17: Cathedral Capers

For several days after the meeting in the Adam and Eve, Tom had been too embarrassed to contact his friends to follow up on their discussions. But the whole team had met up the following Tuesday for the quiz at the Rose. Both Ed and Amanda had smirked on first seeing him, while Ed had occasionally dropped cryptic references to flashers and exhibitionists, but they'd spoken little about previous events – perhaps in part due to guilt about not including Simon in their recent dealings. And when Ed had gotten a chance to say more about his searches for the potential beer festival miscreants, he hadn't.

"Still working on it," he'd said.

And later, more enigmatically: "Surprisingly opaque presences… *like ghosts.*"

Then Ed had warned that he would be offline for a week as he had to go to Antwerp for business – which had scuppered their attendance at the subsequent quiz and left Tom and Amanda frustrated at the lack of resolution of the beer festival mystery.

Tom had pressed on with other matters. He'd made good progress on Brian's project, reassuring his bespectacled tormentor that all would be done by Christmas as planned. And he'd even written a couple of chapters of the novel (no, *manuscript*: a novel was something successfully published, wasn't it?). His alien protagonist – V-Garg – was turning out to have hidden motives, while Earth was being menaced by a host of toad-like creatures that was happy to let humanity survive as long as it ceded all of its planet's shorelines for their habitation. War was brewing, and his hero, Gordon, was hard pressed.

And Tom had continued his patrolling, in evenings when he had to (to newer parts of the city only), but afternoons when he could – as now, on a Saturday.

Today's route took him through the oldest parts of the city, via Elm Hill and Tombland to the Protestant Cathedral. From here, there were two ways into the grounds through the walls: the Ethelbert Gate and the Erpingham Gate. These were separated by a Zizzi's pizza restaurant, the Giggling Squid (a tapas-like place with a large outside section on a wide cobbled plain), a clutch of elegant brick buildings, and a statue of Edith Cavell, famed Norwich citizen and nurse, executed by the dastardly Germans in 1915 for helping downed aircrew escape via her hospital in Belgium (*boo!* thought Tom). It was only a little further down to the Maid's Head Hotel, which was reputedly the most haunted building in Norwich, and thus a place Tom would definitely be avoiding.

Indeed, the gate before him was itself a reminder as to why Tom was here at *this* time, for Sir Thomas Erpingham – who'd been born in Norwich and commanded the archers at the Battle of Agincourt in 1415 – was said to be one of the ghosts that haunted the cathedral. Specifically, it was reputed that on 25th October every year – the anniversary of Agincourt – Erpingham used to visit a close friend now entombed in the Canary Chapel... *and occasionally still did!* And while Tom had missed that supernatural assignation, there were apparently other ghosts to be wary of in the environs – such as the Catholic martyr, Thomas Tunstall, and 'the burning woman'. In short, he'd decided to only visit the cathedral when the sun was out.

The Erpingham Gate was a single, tall arch supported by stone vaulting and decorated with carved saints. Tom walked through, past a niche containing the kneeling figure of Erpingham, and on the other side came to a large, lawned area bounded to the east by the Cathedral, and to the north by buildings of the ancient Norwich School, which dated from 1096. Directly opposite, Tom saw the great doorway at the west end of the nave, with the cathedral's magnificent spire rising above. This had once been the main entrance, but visitors were now directed to enter via a novel-yet-tasteful construction – the 'Hostry Visitor and Education Centre' – along one side of the cloisters to his right.

As Tom took a slanting route across the green, he noticed directly in his path another statue to a local boy – Lord Horatio Nelson. In normal times, this was a plain white colour. Today, however, poor Nelson had been viciously sprayed: he now sported garish, multi-hued clothing and more make-up than an ageing diva. Tom slowed and adjusted his glasses. Well, there was certainly a message here, but it wasn't a seventh dimensional one. The artist had signed their handiwork across the plinth in red paint with the large letters 'KB'. Tom frowned: *KB?* The same crew that had struck the statue of Sir Thomas Browne, led by the masked man who'd attempted to place the blame for their work on Tom himself? *Fuckers!*

Tom sped up again and passed the sorry-looking statue, thinking it best not to be pictured nearby, even though the assault had undoubtedly occurred overnight. As he drew level, something to his right caught his attention: moving towards him were half-a-dozen determined-looking pensioners carrying buckets, rags and scrubbing brushes. *The cavalry?* He decided to leave them to it.

Tom gained the entrance, smiled at a greeter, and wove through a sparsely attended exhibition on 'humanity', mainly comprising abstract art affixed to a forest of temporary white pillars. He quickly passed through the wood-and-glass annex and into the cathedral proper, emerging by the cathedral shop near the old entrance, with the central nave to his right and a great copper font immediately ahead. Having toured the cathedral several times before, Tom was now a dab hand, being familiar with the place's dimensions and likely spots for messaging, notably, the various plaques and verbose memorials inset into floors, or walls, or by sarcophagi. Adjusting his glasses, Tom set forth. He headed down the nave to the pulpit, then to the north and south transepts, then the vestry and the various chapels. He scanned the stained-glass windows in a cursory manner, anticipating that logistics would pre-empt meddling with these. And then, to the south of the choir, he took a wooden door and a short flight of steps down into the cloister – a walkway of vaulted stone that formed a square around a green sward.

Tom hurried along, barely attending his surroundings, knowing that alien light would easily stand out. However, when he came to the west side – beyond the wall of which was the *Hostry* – he encountered something he'd not seen on his last patrol: perhaps related to the exhibition, there were half-a-dozen display boards lined up end-to-end, blocking view of the grassy square.

The mobile displays contained the works of children from several local schools, with each board dedicated to the output from a single establishment. The theme was 'Refugees' – displayed in bold capital letters printed on cards at the top of every board. What was on display was mostly pictures of people of an admirably diverse range of colours (including some not natural to the human species) making journeys away from one disaster or another. Tom noticed a volcano spewing lava in one picture, and an aircraft dropping bombs onto primitive thatched huts in another. Villainous gun-wielders menaced people in several more. One theme was of people aboard various boats and rafts at sea – a sea that occasionally bore pirate vessels with Jolly Roger flags and sometimes the fins of improbably large sharks.

As well as the drawings from primary school children there were written pieces in the form of simple poems, short stories, and letters from desperate people addressed to the PM, the nation, and even the citizens of Norwich.

Tom appraised the boards – not expecting anything nefarious, but merely because they were novel and eye-catching. But as it turned out, the entries on one board possessed colour from a different dimension altogether…

"You've got to be kidding me!" Tom muttered to himself. He swiped off his glasses, at which the image disappeared. Then he put them back on and saw the word: *Parasites.*

And unusually, along with the word in glowing letters superimposed over a succession of pages across the board, was a picture too, of a naively drawn rat.

Tom frowned. Refugees? *Well, they were, weren't they…?*

My God – had he just thought that?

Him – mild-mannered, socially liberal Tom?

Well, okay, he was probably more New Labour than anything (or at the very, *very* worst – when shielded from view in a polling booth and Labour veered too far left – a 'wet' Tory), which made him scum in the eyes of many, but… not this!

And if *he* had just thought this, then what might others think on reading the message subliminally?

What effect might it have on the ambivalent?

Or on, say, an *EDL* supporter?

Fuck!

This time, Tom knew he had to do something. There was no way he could leave this here – not for a second. But how long had this display been up? Days? Weeks?

No. It couldn't have been up that long: judging by the rapid response to the Beer Festival messaging, if this had been up for any length of time, there would have been blood on the streets.

176

Or would there?

He recalled Smith's words about the importance of context. The image of a hypodermic syringe added potency to a message about junkies. The Beer Festival message had worked because it was let loose within a crowded, febrile atmosphere where pint-holding arms were certain to be nudged. Maybe if there were a coachload of refugees having a tour of the cathedral at this very moment, then grief might ensue and an attack might be induced (or, in Tom's case, given how he felt at the moment, a grimace and an unkind word might be delivered). But Norwich was a genteel, out-of-the-way city; it wasn't London. He suspected few refugees who washed up on the country's shores had ever heard of the place, or had any ambition to come here.

So… maybe there was no particular hurry to deal with the matter?

Stop it!

Tom knew what he was doing. He was trying to talk himself out of acting; to justify doing nothing. And if he'd not had his neutralisation kit with him, he almost certainly would have succeeded.

But… *fuck Smith!* He was equipped for metaphorical war; he had all that he needed to stop this here and now.

Man up, Tom!

He exhaled deeply. *Okay. Look around.*

It wasn't that busy. It was a cold Saturday afternoon in mid-November, and Norwich were playing at home, so most locals would be following the newer and infinitely more-popular religion of football. Hence, there was just a smattering of visitors in the entire cathedral, and presently none at all in this part of the Cloisters.

But he had to be sure that this was the only message.

Tom spent a couple of minutes in grateful procrastination as he pored over the six display boards from top to bottom, confirming that the demonic messaging was indeed limited to the one he'd seen.

So – just this: a six-foot-long message spread over five pictures and a pleading letter on behalf of the *Chilren of Ganistan* (sic).

What was he to do? Nothing hasty, that was for sure. He needed to contemplate options – and he was in the ideal venue for such a task. He retired to a stone sill a short distance away, resting his back against a pillar. From here, he couldn't see the message – only the near edge of the first board in the line – which gave him an idea. Maybe all he needed to do was

177

surreptitiously turn the guilty board to point in a different direction. *Hmmmmmmm*. But, if he was going to approach the board again, he should do so as few times as possible to reduce the chance of someone noting his overly keen interest. So…

Tom dropped his rucksack from his back and lay it on the stone floor. He ignored the spray can of red paint and instead brought out the chunky magnet, which had attached itself to the can. A quick look to left and right confirmed that he was currently alone in the walkway. He sprang to his feet and paced to the board, which was the second in the line of six. Another quick left-right, and he brought the magnet up to the 'P', sitting atop a picture of brown people fleeing… *a dragon*? Well, he guessed the people of *Laketown* could also legitimately be considered refugees – so why the hell not?

Concentrate!

He swept the magnet over the glowing letter.

But the letter remained.

So he tried again, this time so close he rubbed the paper.

Then he stepped back.

It was still there.

Then he thought back to the underpass. The magnet hadn't worked there, either. Or had it? That message may have dissolved before Tom had even sprayed it, so in truth, he had no evidence that the magnet *or* the paint worked. Maybe the magnet led to slow decomposition over a period of time? If so, how slow, and did he have the time to wait to find out? Or maybe the magnet was a sort of primer for the paint to work? Or maybe it was the wrong type? Or not strong enough?

Then he heard voices, looked right, and saw a trio of elderly folk shamble around the corner from the perpendicular walkway. He thrust the magnet in his pocket, turned his back to the new arrivals, and sauntered over to his rucksack.

The trio took forever to travel the few metres from the corner to the display, and then even longer to coo over the artwork.

"Come on," muttered Tom under his breath, "they're not fucking Picassos!"

At least the interruption gave him time to calm and think. He realised that turning the board wasn't going to work. If it were at the end of the line, he might have been able to rotate it one-eighty degrees, so that it faced out through the stone arches to the green outside. That would be tricky, but possible, and even if cathedral visitors noticed the result, it seemed unlikely they would do anything about it. He also guessed that staff were unlikely to pass this way often, and even if they did they were unlikely to pause and look. So – that plan might have worked to *reduce* the message impact until he got on to Smith, who could perhaps take it from there.

But trying to turn a middle board risked upsetting those to either side. And switching the guilty board with that on the end would also take more pulling and twisting than he was willing to risk.

So, did that mean it was time for the paint?

The memory of the underpass returned to haunt him. Spraying over *children's* drawings about *refugees* in a *holy* place? That would make his earlier crime seem like, er, child's play.

The elderly trio, arm-in-arm-in-arm, shuffled past, and after a couple more tortuous minutes reached the other end of the walkway and turned the corner.

Tom took the magnet from his pocket and exchanged it in the depths of his rucksack for the spray can, which he then slid into his trouser pocket.

Thank God he'd put on sensible slacks instead of jeans!

Another deep breath, and Tom jolted upright, checked both directions, and returned to the errant board. As he looked at it once more, an image came to him of the three OAPs waving their walking sticks and shouting at a passing person of colour: *Crikey and lawks! Be off with you!* He couldn't help a nervous snigger. And then another thought popped into his head – something Ed had said in the Adam and Eve. What was it exactly? Breaking the chain?

"Ed, I could kiss you," he whispered. "Platonically, of course!"

He didn't need to spray the whole text: he just had to ensure that the message made no sense. For example, if he sprayed the 'P' only, the message would read 'arasite'. Would that induce the hunting down of refugees? He doubted it. But maybe the word was still close enough to the original to be suggestive? And with the rat picture evident, the subconscious might easily fill in the missing letter. Okay. So what about getting rid of a couple of letters in the middle? The 'ra' spread over two pictures: one of people on a raft being threatened by a kraken-like beast with many tentacles, and one a picture of a pair who looked like participants in *RuPaul's Drag Race* fleeing from a tank. If he took down the 'ra', that would leave: 'Pa...site'. Pa site? A place where fathers congregated online? Something like Mumsnet? That would not only defang the message, but potentially make it positive! Could he turn this around completely? Could he induce warm, collegiate feelings in fathers? And maybe the rat would be taken for a hamster. Hamsters were cute and inoffensive. Added context? Yeah!

And now that he thought further, Tom realised he didn't actually need to use the paint. Much like the banners at the Beer Festival, he surely just needed to take down the offending material – to smuggle the two pictures off the board.

Genius!

The pictures were held in place by push pins in a variety of colours. *Simple!* Tom checked again to left and right to ensure that he was alone. And then a thought occurred, and he looked up at the vaulted ceiling with its elaborate bosses: but there was no sign of CCTV. So, he reached up and rapidly plucked out the eight pins by which the two paintings were affixed to the board, returned the pins to now-empty blue felt, and shuffled the pictures together. He stepped back...

Fuck!

The message was *still* there! Somehow, it was on the board itself: rather than overlaying the pictures, it was the pictures that were overlaying the seventh-dimensional message – overlaying and yet not hiding. In effect, the alien message shone *through* the pictures.

Yet, Tom was committed: he'd made a move and was now in the zone. With his heart pounding, he scrunched up the two children's drawings in his left hand and pulled the can from his pocket with his right. Then scrunching the pictures even more within his palm, he used his left hand to pluck the can lid off. Too scared to look, and trusting he still had time, Tom depressed the spray nozzle.

Nothing happened.

Shake it! You need to... Tom shook the can vigorously, but only briefly. He depressed the nozzle again and was rewarded with a fine mist.

"Come on, you..."

Tom shook more vigorously – but now too much. He tried again – and an eruption of paint spurted forth, like a miniature Krakatoa. He slavered the intended letters all right, but collaterally spattered much of the rest of the board too.

"*Shit!*"

Instinctively, Tom brought up the rumpled pictures in his left hand and started dabbing at the excess paint that had over-run the pleading letter from 'Ganistan' and the dreadful Smaug – but only succeeded in smearing the paint more widely and utterly ruining 'Kraken' and 'RuPaul' too.

"Christ alight!" Tom frantically scanned his environs. There was no one in sight but... were those voices? He dropped the children's pictures on the stone floor and paced over to his rucksack. He threw the can into its depth, and then dropped the lid from red-tinged fingers. "Where... where...?"

The voices were coming from his right, from where the shambling trio had earlier emerged, and so he had to go left, and quick. He tossed his rucksack over one shoulder and jog-trotted to the end of the walkway. Before he reached the end, he heard the voices rise in clarity: whoever they belonged to must have turned the corner. But he was close to his own turn, so he just kept going, then jerked to the right to the perpendicular corridor, out of sight. There was another pair of oldsters to this side of the Cloisters, but they were walking in the opposite direction. He made it to an exit on his left and took a short flight of steps up. He was already scurrying through the main nave – face a beetroot red, like his left hand – when he heard a faint shout from somewhere far behind.

But no one stopped him.

He passed the shop, and took the parallel corridor back to the Hostry and the exit, passing within a couple of metres of the desecration, but shielded from the sight of it by the thick medieval wall. Outside, he hurried past the defiled statue of Nelson – which was now being attacked with soap and brushes by the oldsters he'd previously seen – and exited the grounds through the Erpingham Gate.

He kept his left hand buried deep in his jacket pocket all the way home.

***

On *Look East* that evening, following the national news, Sally Jones stood within the cloisters of Norwich Cathedral beside a paint-splattered display board. Off to her right stood a couple of adults, the hands of each resting on the shoulders of a young child. Sally hefted her microphone. "So, tell me, what do you think of this act of vandalism?"

"It's absolutely disgusting," said the first woman. "The kids did all this work," she indicated the board with a twitch of the head, where a picture seemed to show a dragon bloodily massacring a party of fleeing people, "and some idiot comes along and does this!"

"Yes, that's right," said the mum to her side, "it's absolutely appalling. The children spent ages working on their messages of hope, and someone ruins it! Jemima was in tears when she found out." The woman gave her sad-looking six-year-old a shake. "Whoever did this is a monster!"

Sally bent down so she could place her microphone between Jemima and her male classmate.

"Jemima and Ben… what do you think about whoever did this?"

"They're horrible," said Jemima meekly.

"Yeah," said Ben, who appeared far less upset by the matter than the girl, and possibly a little wired on sugar: "dad says they're a scumbag who needs a good kicking!"

"Ah, thank you!" Sally rose rapidly, clearly concerned about what Ben might say next. The camera pulled back to reveal a figure dressed in clerical robes at the side of the parents and their children. "And with me also is the Dean of the Cathedral, the Very Reverend Joseph Lumsden. Reverend, can you give us your thoughts on the events of today?"

The be-whiskered cleric pursed his lips and looked troubled. "Well, Sally, we are all deeply shocked by this unchristian act. It seems as though nowhere is safe from pedlars of hate. It was only last night that the statue of Lord Nelson was vandalised in our grounds, and now this."

"Do you think the cathedral needs to increase security?"

"I really hope not. This is a house of love, not a fortress. In fact, we welcome sinners to come and join the congregation, and to have dialogue with us."

"Even members of this so-called Krustie Brigade – who seem to be the prime suspects in these attacks?"

"Yes, Sally, even them. God is forgiveness."

"Thank you, Reverend." Sally now turned to face the camera. "And with those noble words, we return to the studio, where Rachel has news of another low-scoring game at Carrow Road. Rachel…"

***

"Well done, Tom," said Smith. He'd responded remarkably quickly to Tom's request for a meeting, which had been sent on Saturday evening about an hour after the end of the *Look East* segment at the cathedral: it was 9a.m. on a Sunday morning, at their usual place. As most shops were closed, the streets were deserted.

"What do you mean? I haven't told you–"

"The cathedral incident, Tom. It bore all your hallmarks and correlates well with your urgent request."

"My hallmarks? You mean, incompetence and–"

"Luck, Tom. Incompetence and luck." Smith smiled – an expression he seemed to have begun to master, though in situations where its meaning was ambiguous to Tom. Happiness... or *mockery*? "Given the reported theme of the children's work that you destroyed," he continued, "the logical interpretation is that you defused a potentially major attack on a vulnerable community."

"Yes, at the price of upsetting the children and parents of one school, and the whole Christian community."

Smith's smile remained in place. "Perhaps. But would you rather that potential anger be directed at the vandal – at you, Tom – or at a much larger group? And you have not been identified, so you are safe."

"Seriously?" *That bloody well was a smirk!* "I think you've got the wrong man. Or maybe not the wrong man," Tom suddenly realised that he sounded like he wanted out, which he realised he absolutely didn't, "or the right man with the wrong strategy."

"Nonsense, Tom. I am very happy with all you have done. You are turning out to be one of my best recruits."

"One of?" It was the first time Smith had admitted that he had more than one; and the phrasing implied that he had a whole stable of Omegas. "How many do you have in Norwich? Maybe... maybe if I knew some of the others, we could coordinate?"

"No, Tom. That would be risky. Anyway, I hope you are reassured. Off you go. We'll meet again on the Wednesday after next, yes?"

Dismissed!

Tom looked down. "Yes, sure, okay…" And when he looked up, he found that Smith had already turned and was striding off to the side of the Guildhall that faced the market, to whatever hidden entrance he used.

***

"Well done, Tom," said Ed. It was Sunday night, and both he and Amanda had agreed to Tom's request for an emergency rendezvous at the Alex. Ed had returned from Belgium the previous night and, divining the reason for Tom's urgency, had already trawled the media. "This time you weren't caught. And better still, you seem to have implicated someone else. Bravo!"

Amanda had only just arrived herself. She looked between the seated Ed (already two-thirds through his first pint) and a standing Tom, who'd scurried up to them as she was lowering herself onto the corner bench. Tom had a scarf wrapped around his mouth and dark glasses shielding his eyes. "Not again? Not… *the cathedral?*" She directed wide, spectacle-rimmed eyes at the standing man.

"Shhhhhh!" Tom pulled out a chair and slumped down, drink-less. "It's not what you think."

"You mean," said Ed, "it's *not* a heroic attempt to save the world from some alien devilry that went disastrously awry?"

"Um, no. I mean, *yes.* That's what it was."

"I think you can pull down your scarf, Tom," said Amanda. "It's muffling your words. And it's also drawing attention to you, which is probably the opposite of what you want."

"Yes, thanks!" Tom tugged his scarf down to a more traditional position. He gave a pained smile. "I'm really not cut out for this."

Ed smirked. "Really? Well, go on then. Tell us what happened."

So Tom did.

After, and with all three now nursing beers, Amanda asked: "And you saw Smith this morning? He was okay about it?"

"More than that. He actually seemed pleased. I mean, I caused chaos, and he's happy! I thought our aim was to stop influence, not transform it."

"But you've transformed it in a good way, haven't you?" said Amanda. "From anti-refugees to *anti*-anti-refugees – if you know what I mean. I can't see anyone in Norwich now standing up and saying anything unkind about them. They'd be associated with the vandalism, and crucified."

"Well, I guess…"

"So, everyone's happy," declared Ed. "Except, perhaps, for these Krusties who are getting the blame. And that's somewhat ironic. There they were, citing you as a key cause for their war on statuary and polite society, and now you've inadvertently turned the tables. Karma?" Ed sipped his pint and looked at Tom over the rim of his glass. "Though I suspect they won't take this lying down. Let's hope they don't seek a *terrible* revenge upon you."

***

The response was soon forthcoming, the redacted video being shown on *Look East* the following evening.

"It wasn't us, right!" A ski-masked figure waved a fist at the camera. "We did the statue – Lord whatever-his-name-is. Another aristo, sponging off the people. What did he ever do for us, eh? Inherited a mansion and some slaves probably. So, yeah, we did him. But the cathedral stuff? No [*bleep*] way!"

Behind the figure was a sheet that had been affixed to the wall: it bore a red-painted 'KB' logo. The desk in front of the man seemed rather more traditional and secure than the one from the previous video. "It's a fit-up, right? Someone saw the statue and thought, we'll stitch them up. We love refugees. And kids…." The masked man did a double take, realising what he had just said. "Er, not in a *paedo* way. Not *Jimmy Savile*. We were kids once. We would never…" He straightened his back and regained his composure. "But, yeah, it's clearly a conspiracy. The [*bleep*] pigs are behind it. And probably working with that racist from the underpass. We're not gonna stand for this. Statue dudes beware!"

The man held up a fist in a valedictory power salute… and behind him, the poorly affixed bedsheet fluttered from the wall and draped over him, making it appear as though he were being attacked by a ghost.

"What the [*bleep*]!"

And the video ended.

Chapter 18: One-nil… again!

At the conclusion of the brief meeting on Sunday, Ed had reminded the others: "We're not quizzing this week. Thursday back here instead. It's about time we had another official conclave of the *Society of Alien Tools*. I arranged our usual notification in the *Golden Guide* before I went to Antwerp and I confirmed things with Si – it's called thinking ahead. We need to open a door *and* discuss the festival."

Tom's brow had furrowed at the first part of that last statement, but he'd let it ride and instead asked about the second: "Why not tell us what you found now?"

"I need a bit more time," Ed had replied, refusing to elaborate.

And so here they all were, back at the Alex. They were in their usual corner, tucked away beside the toilets. Ed had arrived well before the others: an empty pint glass sat beside a half-full one next to his opened-out laptop, and he'd set out three more pints around the table in impertinent expectation. Tom arrived second and sat opposite Ed; then Amanda came, sliding onto the bench beside their unelected leader; and Simon arrived almost immediately after – blond hair tied in a ponytail, *Stranger Things* hoodie under his leather jacket.

"You're well prepped, Ed," noted Amanda, eyeing the pint before her suspiciously.

"As always. I'm the only one here who'd have given Napoleon a run for his money. I think you'll find I also correctly anticipated who would sit where, and the tipples should be to your tastes." He broadcast a grin. "But seriously, I needed to guarantee we got this table, and I wanted to ensure I arrived before anyone else – and I don't just mean you lot."

"You mean, the ad in the *Guide*?" said Tom. "Are you expecting someone to join us?"

"Join us? *No.* Spy on us? *Maybe.*"

"Really?" said Amanda.

"Look, there *is* something odd going on in Norwich. There are other forces at work – and it's not just about what Tom has seen and done. Mentions of the city have surged on the dark web, mostly dumb rumours and conspiracy theories, but there are also signs of hackers hacking and snoopers snooping."

Simon nodded sagely. "Yep. Vortent has also grown concerned. Sorry I haven't been around. Stuff to do. What have I missed?"

The other three exchanged glances.

"I think we should talk about the beer festival," said Amanda, cautiously. "You couldn't make it, Si, so we three went."

"Yeah, you mentioned it at the quiz the other week. Said you'd escaped the riot."

"That's true…" Amanda looked to other others for help. "But, well, the truth is, there was a bit more to it than we let on. You see, Tom saw a message with his glasses just before everything went pear-shaped, and ever since, Ed has been trying to identify who might have been responsible."

Simon frowned and looked between the others. "Message?"

Ed nodded. "You've missed nothing, my friend. They left it with me. You know I've been away. But now it's time to report back – and so here you are, fully in the loop!"

"Riiiiiiight. Go on then."

Ed turned to his laptop and spoke as he played with it. "So, we identified several suspects, and I have been doing all I can to track them down. But I've come up with nothing. Or at least, nothing of substance. There's nothing on social media. I got a couple of birth certificates and some school records, but that's it. They have left remarkably little impression – especially the younger ones. And that just isn't right. They're either the most boring people on the planet – snooker-playing Steve Davises on anti-steroids – or they've deliberately kept from the light and had someone with my kind of skills hide them."

"Who are these people?" wondered Simon. "Do you have any photos?"

"Of course, for all the good it will do." Ed turned the laptop sideways so all four of them could see it. "This is the first. His name is—"

"Martin Elder," nodded Simon. "*Easy.*"

For once, Ed was left speechless.

"You *know* him?" asked Amanda, incredulous.

"Sure. He's a bit of a gamer. Bit of a jerk, too. But I don't know why you haven't been able to find any details on him."

Ed recovered slightly. "Tom said he'd spotted him at City College before, so I checked and—"

"I don't know what he would be doing there. I think he's a UEA student. Film studies, or something like that. Doing a Masters? Check there. Actually, I think Martin's his middle name. Got a dumb Christian name, so he doesn't use it. I'm sure you can hack into the uni's system and get something on him."

"Fucking hell!" muttered Ed.

"So, who are the others?" asked Simon. "I mean, just in case."

"Why not?" Ed tapped the mousepad and the picture of the young man in the CAMRA t-shirt was replaced by a woman in a puffer jacket. "This is—"

"Teresa," asserted Simon confidently. "*Definitely*. But I don't know her surname, and it's an odd photo."

Once more, Ed goldfished, leaving Amanda to continue the interview. "Why odd?"

"She's alone. She's almost always hanging around with Ricky. They're a couple. *Sort of*. I don't know how. They're usually arguing. Hmmmm. And she's wearing a Beer Festival t-shirt, too. I know Ricky likes a beer, but she's more into wine. Maybe he talked her into volunteering?"

"So, where's Ricky?" wondered Tom, his gaze darting between the still-goggling Ed and the slowly nodding man with a ponytail.

"That's a good question," said Simon. "I think maybe you need to look harder. This is a CCTV still, isn't it? Haven't you got any shots where she is with him? Tall, scruffy bloke with sideburns."

Ed now found his voice. "No. I only have a few shots of her, and she is alone in them. How the fuck do you know her? Know *them*?"

"Ricky's an occasional gamer. He's more into gigs. *Music*. I often bump into them on St Benedicts Street. He hangs about in Cookes and the record shops, and she's a vegan. Drags him into the Tipsy Vegan occasionally, and sometimes they compromise and go to Slice and Dice. You know – that place near the Ten Bells with lots of boardgames? You can hire a table to play whatever games you like, and they also serve veggie food and drinks."

"The place that's a front for militant veganism?" said Ed, with less brio than usual. "That bribes unsuspecting gamers to attend and then insinuates its doctrines into their subconsciouses? Amanda's sort of—"

"Yes, yes, Ed." Amanda tapped Ed on the arm. "Just show him the last."

Ed looked non-plussed at the interruption, but let it go, tapped, and up came Augustus P. Samson.

"Well, sure, I recognise him," said Simon.

"Another gamer?" asked Tom.

Simon grinned. "He looks like one, sure, but I don't think so. No, he was in that team at the first quiz we went to. You must remember him, too?"

Ed exhaled. "Well, thank fuck for that, at least." He managed to gather himself from the shock. "But that is seriously warped, old chap. I've spent three weeks on-and-off looking into this lot, and I could have just come to you. It's almost suspicious. You sure you aren't double dating us with another gang?"

"Cross-my-heart," said Simon, with a gentle smile.

Ed sat back on the bench to rest against the wall, looking thoughtful. "Gamers? There's certainly game-playing going on, so who better to be involved? And then there's Terminus Est, who sound like gamers – but you say they're not, Si, and there's a black hole in the web around them, and I'm not talking about one caused by Samson's immense mass. You'd think a clique with their own brand would be visible somewhere and somehow, but all I got for Samson is his appearance in CAMRA literature from two years ago. I will expand my searches, and you, Si, keep an eye out, eh?"

Simon grinned and tapped the side of his nose. "*Tradecraft*. I'm on it."

"But that's not all," interjected Tom. "You've forgotten the figure in the bib."

Ed initially appeared not to hear, still lost in thought. Then he shook his head. "Yeah, well, that's also a conundrum." The computer was still side-on to the group. Ed tapped the mousepad and the picture changed. "This is a still from the CCTV on St Andrew's Church, facing The Halls. You just see the edge of the guy's bib in the distance." He tapped again. "And another shot, closer. And another…" He continued to tap. The various pictures showed the bib-wearing man approach St Andrews Street with the St Andrew's Tavern to the left, reach the pedestrian crossing there, and then cross the road. But in every shot there was one or more figure from the festival exodus in the way. There was no clear shot. Then the man was obscured by one of the pair of red phone boxes and… "And that's it. The figure goes into the box – and never emerges. This is the last shot of him: you can see the back of his bib – and it *is* a *Big Issue* bib. I magnified it. Then here's the very next CCTV frame – where two blokes stand directly between the camera and the box. And in the frame after they move slightly…"

"Fuck me," muttered Tom. "He's literally disappeared. And no one around seems to have noticed."

"Could you tell if it was Smith?" asked Amanda.

"Not from those shots," said Tom, peering hard. "There's a bit of grey hair, I think, so it could be him. But I wouldn't put money on it."

"But I bet Si knows him, eh?" smirked Ed. "Come on, amigo, don't let us down."

Simon grinned back. "Sorry – not this one. Shall I get my coat?"

"You bloody well stay where you are," said Ed. "I'll even get you another beer. But this one's on you, Tom. I think you need to be more direct with Smith. Or more subtle. But try and get *something* out of him."

Tom nodded. "Okay. But the last couple of times I've seen him, he's been quite abrupt. I've not really had the chance to ask questions. But I'll try."

Now it was Amanda's turn to reorient the conversation. "Ed – that's the people from the festival. But what about here? You said you thought someone might spy on us. Why? And how could you tell?"

"Tell? Well, I've been keeping my eyes peeled for any lurking non-locals. Do you remember how we gotcha'd Tom? On top of that, I earlier placed a couple of disguised cameras outside, one on Stafford Street and one on Gladstone Street, pointing at the pub doorways. As long as someone doesn't notice them and nick them, I'll collect them when we leave and review their footage back home. That's the *how*. The *why* I can't really explain. It's just a feeling. Tom's been making waves. If there are others like us, and they are as competent and suspicious as I, then they might pay him a bit more attention."

"Shit! I'd never thought about that," said Tom. "And that reminds me: the last time I saw Smith, on Sunday morning, before…" he noticed Amanda suddenly tense. He paused, watched the bespectacled woman flick her eyes towards Simon, and nodded. They didn't want to reveal just how much they'd been side-lining Simon. He continued: "Before… *lunch…* he let it drop that he has others working for him."

"Who?" asked Ed. "What others?"

"He didn't say. *Wouldn't* say. He said it was too risky to tell me, but he didn't explain why."

"You don't think any of these people," Amanda waved a hand at the laptop, "could be in his team, do you? That would be awkward."

"I really don't know what to think. I think… well, I think I need another beer."

"Good call, old chap," declared Ed. "You get them in, and I'm off to the gents – I've had more than you lot and need to make room." He stood. "Meanwhile, you two keep your eyes peeled for subversives."

***

Tom intersected the bar beside Tony – a somewhat grizzled regular – who was in deep conversation with the barmaid, Linda. He waited patiently for the best part of a minute – a pained expression on his face – until Linda at last conceded, reluctantly broke off her chat, accepted his order, and went to wrestle a handpump. Ed settled in at Tom's non-Tony side.

"Need some snacks, old man. Get us some scampi fries."

"Sure." Tom looked up at Ed, and grinned. "Well, that was a bit of a surprise."

"You're telling me! Seems our Si is a bit of a dusky equine."

"Yep. One-nil to Simon, I reckon."

"One-nil?" Ed gurned. "There was I, thinking he's a lumpen defender with two left feet, and he's gone and hammered a hattrick past us."

To Tom's other side, grizzled Tony snorted. "What I'd give for one of the boys to score a hattrick. Or for the us to score more than one goal."

Linda delivered the first two drinks. She heard Tony's disgruntled wish. "Not still sore about the game last night, Tony?" she said. "One-nil to Stoke, wasn't it?"

"Yeah. Unbelievable. Hit the woodwork three times. Three! Mind you, they also hit the woodwork *and* had a goal disallowed. But, yeah, we haven't scored more than once all season."

As Linda gave a sympathetic smile and returned to the other bar from where she'd pulled the drinks, Tony turned to engage with Tom. "I mean, how likely is that? Nearly December, and we've not scored more than one goal in a game!"

"Not good," Tom agreed. He wasn't a huge football fan, but since settling in the city, he'd tied his colours to its proverbial mast, and always kept an eye on the scores. His brow furrowed. "But… we haven't conceded many either, have we? I mean, we are mid-table."

"Good point. Come to think of it…" Tony frowned, "I don't think we've let in more than one, either. Now, that is fucking odd."

Linda returned with two more pints, laying them on the bar and confirming their provenance to Tom.

"I'll take two with me," said Ed, grasping the nearest glasses. "Remember – scampi fries!"

"Right…"

Tom added to his order, paid, and soon rejoined his colleagues, bearing gifts. He tossed a small, green packet of savouries to Ed, who barely noticed, having once more taken to his computer, fingers flying ferociously over the keys. Tom frowned: "What's up?"

"Dunno," said Simon. "You tell us. Something happened at the bar."

"We were discussing the football. Tony was moaning about how Norwich haven't been able to score this season. Is that it, Ed?"

"Yep." Ed didn't look up. "Our hoary friend thought the Norwich scores have been odd, so I thought I'd check. I'm always interested in patterns. Deciphering them is my metier, according to Big Ed."

"So, what are the scores?" asked Tom. "And are they actually odd?"

"Looking right now." Ed tapped some more. "Right, here they are. Norwich results." He mulled over the information a moment, before concluding: "Yep, it's true. The scores are a bit freakish. No side has scored more than one goal in any game involving Norwich. Let me have a quick…" He tapped some more, calling up various other pages. "Okay. It *is* just Norwich. Weekly results show a wide range of scores for the other Championship teams and matches. No other team appears to have had a problem scoring more than one goal, *or* conceding more than one."

"Weird," noted Tom. "But, hang on, they lost that FA Cup game to Fulham. Two-one, wasn't it?"

"Sure. It just seems to be an issue for Championship games."

"Boooooor-ing!" declared Simon. "Who cares? Bloody football. Modern obsession."

"What, not enough *elves* for your liking?"

"Nowhere near enough!" It was clear to Tom that Simon had come to terms with Ed's wit, having learnt that the best ploy was to roll with his attacks, rather than attempt to fend them off. "They play more interesting games," he continued. "Like Quidditch."

Amanda, however, *was* intrigued, even though she generally shared Simon's antipathy towards the national game. Sat to Ed's left, she leant over to peer at the laptop screen. "What exactly are the scores, then?"

"Can you list them?" asked Tom.

"Sure thing. Let me cut and paste. I'll stick it in a Word file. Can't be arsed to play about with a spreadsheet. *Bosh.* Here you go. From the earliest result to the latest." He pushed the laptop around, allowing the others to get a better look.

"It is very… *binary*," noted Amanda.

Tom nodded, muttering softly: "It is, isn't it? It's almost like a piece of code."

"Indeed, it looks a bit like ASCII code," said Ed, sagely.

"Huh? Sorry?" said Tom. "Ass-key code?"

"Tom, you really are a primitive. ASCII stands for American Standard Code for Information Interchange. It's an old character encoding scheme. It essentially allow you to translate computer text to normal text and vice versa."

"Uh, right."

Ed sighed. "Look. It's a code for representing one hundred and twenty-eight English characters as numbers, with each assigned a number from zero to one hundred and twenty-seven. And that magic number, one-two-eight, means all of these characters can be expressed as an eight-digit binary code. Not just letters, but other characters too. And the twenty-six letters actually have two different codes each, depending upon whether they are capitalised or not. Let me show you." He pulled the laptop back towards himself. A quick search on Bing produced a table, listing codes for letters. "So, as you see, uppercase 'A' has a code of oh-six-five, written in binary as 01000001, while lowercase 'a' is oh-nine-seven, written as 01100001."

"Wow. That's interesting!" said Tom. "What would you get if you applied this code to the Norwich scores?"

"Nothing," said Simon, from across the table. While pretending uninterest, he had actually been following the conversation intently. "There aren't enough scores to spell out sufficient letters for a word, let alone a sentence."

Ed frowned. "He's right. *Almost.* You'd have enough to spell 'orc'."

"Or elf," smiled Amanda, unable to help herself.

Simon poked his tongue out at her.

But Tom was still looking at the screen. *There are signs everywhere.* "Still, what would you get if you did assume the codes applied to letters and not to other characters. What would it spell, or start to spell?"

"Okay. I'm game." Ed highlighted the first four Norwich Championship results. "Assuming the sequence is important, and listing the scores as recorded in databases, with home team scores first, we get: 0-1 0-0 0-1 0-0. And this is a… 'D'. Uppercase. Okay?"

"And next?"

"Hold your horses." Ed highlighted the next four results. "0-1 1-0 0-1 0-1. And that is an 'e', lowercase. Means nothing, but interesting that the first letter is capitalised, as is proper at the start of a sentence. I expect this will fall down shortly."

"And next?"

"Now we have: 0-1 1-0 1-1 0-0. And that makes it an 'l'. Lowercase. Then we have: 0-1 1-0 1-0 0-1. And this is an 'i'. Again lowercase. And that is effectively your lot. There are just two more results, so not enough to make another letter: 0-1 and 1-0."

Tom was calculating. "So that gives us D-e-l-i."

"Delicious?" wondered Amanda. "Deliberate?"

"Delinquent?" posited Tom. "Delight? Delightful?"

"Nah. It's *Deliveroo*," smirked Ed. "It's all part of a giant advertising ploy."

Tom shook his head. He couldn't rid the feeling that there was more to this matter, and that it was not just coincidence. "What could the next letter be, er, assuming this is a message. What letters start with… 0-1-1-0."

"Good question. Let me have a squiz. It seems it could be any lowercase letter from 'a' right through to 'o'. They all start with these four numbers. Who watches 'Countdown'? Where's Carol Vorderman when you need her? Useless bint."

"Ed!"

"Sorry, Amanda dear. You know I'm joking. Always had a crush on our Carol."

Tom had meanwhile been rummaging in the pocket of his coat, draped over the back of his chair. He found a small notepad and pen, which he brought out and placed on the table next to his dark glasses, pushing his pint aside to make room. He flicked the pad open and started writing, one word per line:

Delia – Delib – Delic – Delid – Delie – Delif – Delig – Delih – Delii – Delij – Delik – Delil – Delim – Delin – Delio

Ed raised his eyebrows. "I could do that on screen, old fruit. In fact, I will." He set about typing and pasting into his Word file.

"Er, yeah. I know. I just wanted to get it down hard copy. Some of these options aren't viable. *Delii. Delij.*"

Simon now scrunched around from Tom's right. He had no sooner glanced at Tom's list, than he barked out a laugh. "Ha! Obvious! Right in front of you, mate. The first one."

"Huh? Delia…? I don't know any words that start like that. Delia… Delia…"

"No. It's not part of a word. It *is* the word. *Delia.*"

Ed saw it too, on his laptop. "Simon, you dwarf-bothering goblin cleaver. I think you've got it. It is the sainted one. Queen of boiling eggs. The Martha Stewart of the Fens. *Let's-be-having-you.* Etcetera."

"What… Delia?" said Tom. "Delia Smith? Main shareholder of the Canaries?"

"That is classic!" Ed roared. "She's fitted up the league just to spell out her name in Binary ASCII. Well, Tom, fancy putting your money where your mouth is?"

Tom was still somewhat unsettled. It was absurd. But was it any more absurd than a number of other things that had happened over the last few months? He instantly caught Ed's drift. "So… what would the next score be, if the fifth letter is to be an 'a'?"

"I'm afraid we're looking at another 'bloody scoreless draw', as our beer-fuelled colleague at the bar might say, followed by a nil-one score, by which I mean, an away win. Anyone know who we're playing in the next two games?"

They discussed the scores a little more, with Ed expanding on his idea of a grand plot by Delia to take over the world. Meanwhile, more beer was bought and consumed. Amanda left after another half, by which time they were sure they weren't going to be joined by anyone else, then the three men saw it through to last orders. But Tom was quiet and distracted for the rest of the evening, and he was the first to drain his final pint and depart.

As he walked home, Tom found himself patting a rhythm on the coat pocket that held his notepad with its list of five-letter words. *Another nil-nil draw? I wonder…*

He was so focused on the football discussion that he forgot all about their earlier conversation about spies, failed to look out for Ed's cameras, and completely missed the shadowy figure resting on the low wall of a terraced house opposite, *pretending* to look at its phone…

***

That Saturday, Norwich City F.C. were playing at home to QPR. By all accounts, it was a dull affair – the two teams squatting in the middle of the pitch doing little of anything. Outside the ground, at the nearby Riverside complex – which filled the space along the river between the Carrow Road stadium and the foot of Prince of Wales Road and the train station opposite – shoppers, eaters and drinkers were spared the usual buffeting by thousands of voices rising and falling in pleasure and apprehension, and indeed, might have been forgiven for thinking the game had been cancelled altogether. And Tom happened to be amongst these, doing a patrol that he terminated prematurely at the Queen of Iceni Wetherspoons pub. Sitting on a terrace overlooking the river, Tom's phone – set to the live football scores from the BBC – rested on the table next to his glasses.

Thrilling? Apparently not.

Frustrating? Most definitely.

Great saves; last ditch tackles; interventions of the goalposts… none of the above.

Then the final whistle blew.

A collective groan ululated on the freshening end-of-November breeze.

196

And Tom – who'd earlier been to a bookies on London Street – clenched a fist in triumph.

***

The following Tuesday, Tom bustled into the Rose, finding the other members of The Credulous already present.

"It was another scoreless draw!" he cried as he reached the table at which the others sat.

"Put money on it, did you?" said Ed, wearing an amused expression.

Tom felt smug. "In fact, I did. I won eight quid!"

"Tom: the last of the big gamblers! I'd say the beers are on you, except you couldn't afford a single round on that. On the other hand…"

Amanda laughed, shaking her head. Tom looked at her and arched an eyebrow. "You weren't the only one, Tom," she said. "Ed also placed a bet."

Now it was Ed's turn to look smug. "Eight quid, Tom?" He delved into a trouser pocket and pulled out his wallet, which he dropped onto the table next to the beer break sheet – fully stuffed and barely able to close. As the wallet sprang open of its own accord, a chortling Ed whisked a great wedge of notes from its brimming interior. "Times a hundred, old fruit. Go big or go home, that's what I say!"

"Ed? But I thought…"

"Thought me a cynic?" Ed waggled his eyebrows. "There's more to me than meets the eye. Now here…" he proffered a fiver: "go get yourself a drink."

The quiz soon began, and with no sign of Terminus Est, victory was achieved.

As the envelope containing their prize – fifty pounds worth of beer vouchers – was delivered by one of the quizmasters, Ed wrung his hands and gave a faux evil laugh.

Tom smiled and shook his head.

But Simon was more concerned with the future than the present. "Okay, then. What's the next score if the pattern is correct?"

"Nil-one," said Ed, once he'd gotten himself under control. "Fortunately, our next game is away. Unfortunately, it's not a mid-week game. But Saturday isn't too far off. You a convert, my friend?"

"Well… I might have a dabble."

"And you, Amanda darling?"

The team's voice of sanity smiled and shook her head. "I don't believe in gambling. You've had a bit of luck. Don't let it go to your head."

***

"Twenty quid!" cried Tom, the following Tuesday, as he rocked up to his team's table.

Simon and Amanda shook their heads; Ed made a show of looking at his watch as though to berate Tom for his lateness.

His *new* watch.

It was a Rolex.

Chapter 19: Christmas Crises

The aliens had been watching and waiting. Throughout the world, their recruits within the population – aides, spies, dupes, call them what you will – had been at work, gathering intel, provoking, denying, obfuscating, sabotaging. With Christmas on the horizon – a time of holiday, of relaxation – the humans' collective wariness would recede. Attention would be diverted. Opportunities would arise…

They knew this.

They had planned for it.

The time to strike was near.

When humans awoke on that festive day, roused by their eager young, they would find that the presents awaiting them were floods, hurricanes, pestilence, death.

V-Garg looked on and...

"Bollocks," muttered Tom. "What about the Chinese? They won't be gagging on mince pies and tuning in to the Queen's speech."

He pushed his chair back from his desk in disgust.

He'd been unemployed for most of the year, with plenty of time to complete his manuscript, yet he'd managed fewer than a score of chapters, with at least half as many again to write. Sure, he'd come up with lots of intriguing components, but he wasn't sure how to fit them all together, how to solve the puzzle. He hadn't even decided on V-Garg's true status: at the start, he'd cast the alien as a potential saviour, then he'd hinted at its duplicity, and now he wondered whether to cast the duplicity as itself a ruse to confound the other aliens. Perhaps V-Garg would turn out to be a goody after all? Maybe Tom should have taken the plotting of the story more seriously? Done a full storyboard? Identified chapters and critical actions in each of these? But that had seemed too much like hard work. Being a *pantser* was just easier.

Lazy sod.

Waster.

Racist saboteur and desecrator of righteous children's paintings.

Tom chuckled to himself. The year had been about a lot more than fulfilling a (probably deluded) dream. He'd become an Omega – a shield of the human race. How many could put *that* on their CVs? He'd met aliens, discovered ghosts, acquired new friends, and even got a job of sorts… which reminded him that he shortly had a Zoom meeting arranged with Brian. He just had time to get himself a cuppa.

***

"Hi, Brian."

"Hello, Tom." The angle of Brian's camera made him look even more lugubrious than usual, stretching his long face and making it appear horse-like. He peered at Tom from behind thick, black-rimmed plastic glasses. "I got the report last night and went through it. I am impressed."

"Ah, thanks. It was a lot of work, but I got there in the end."

"Yes, it *was* a lot of work. I'd expected it to keep you occupied and out of trouble for longer than it did. But you've delivered it a week early. For you, that is astonishing. Well done."

To Tom's eye, Brian looked far from happy. Sour-faced? Disgruntled? The words were right, but not the expression. That was Brian all over. What more could he say? "Thanks," he repeated.

For a moment, Brian simply stared back through the computer screen – ruminating. Then he said: "Tom – we're having a departmental Christmas dinner next week. I'd like you to join us. You've effectively been a part of the group for the last three months anyway."

"Ah. Okay. Where?"

"Belgian Monk. Monday. Meet at 7p.m."

"Right, and who–"

"Just a few of us. Chris can't make it…." Chris Folkes was the departmental head, and probably the main reason why Tom was sitting where he was now. "But Alice and her husband will be there. And Manesh. Roberta and her partner. And a few others." Was that a sly look?

"Uh, sounds great, but I'm not sure–"

"I really think it would be worth your while, Tom. Both Roberta and Alice have picked up small projects recently, and they want to talk to you about them. They like our MO. And I expect to have more work for you later in the Spring, too."

Tom blew out his cheeks. He really didn't want to return to the fold – certainly not crawling back in this way: the once tenured, now effectively a zero-contract skivvy. But he needed the money, hated looking for a real job, and knew that success in finding one would almost certainly take him away from Norwich, scupper any prospects of him finishing his book, and tear him from his new role as universal saviour. He had no choice. *Fuck!*

"Okay. Thanks, Brian. I'll see you there."

Brian's smile was not a pleasant one. "I knew you'd agree. They had a set menu and we had to pre-order, so I took the liberty of ordering for you. I can't remember what exactly, so it'll come as a nice surprise. I think the starter was something fishy…"

Tom hated fish.

And he knew that Brian knew that he hated fish.

Bastard!

***

The Belgian Monk lay on Pottergate at virtually the epicentre of The Lanes, Norwich's equivalent of Brighton's Lanes (from which it had arguably nicked the name) and York's Shambles. The area was just to the north of the centre, with quirky independent shops in buildings of a variety of styles, interspersed with a sprinkling of the ubiquitous medieval churches. The Monk itself was a three-storey building of mock-Tudor style with a bumpy, plastered exterior of a kind of peachy yellowy hue (to Tom's untrustworthy eye).

Tom loved the approach to the Monk, especially at this time of year – with sparkling Christmas lights strung along the street, and the welcoming glow of yellow illumination spilling through the pub's windows. His approach took him past St Gregory's Green and various favoured haunts, such as the recently re-opened art deco Birdcage pub on the corner of the Green, the well-regarded Grosvenor Fish Bar, and the Strangers coffee shop – the latter two now closed and dark. And a short way further down the lane, past the Monk, was a large old plane tree, which squatted in seasonal nudity at a junction of lanes – a regular pitch for *Big Issue* sellers during the day – and the Thorns wonder shop just beyond.

For a moment, Tom stood outside the pub's wood-and-glass front door and surveyed his surroundings. He could see many people within the pub, though he was presently alone outside. Thorns reminded him of the spray paint, which he carried in his small rucksack along with a large magnet (his glasses being in a jacket pocket). Meanwhile, the Guildhall was almost directly due south, perhaps no more than sixty metres away behind Bagleys Court (opposite the Monk) – a small, hidden courtyard in listed buildings accessed through old wooden gates under an oblong passageway. He wondered if Smith was there, at least in his synthetic human form, or whether he was at St Peter Mancroft, which was perhaps another seventy to eighty metres further south beyond the market... in a direct line.

Tom wrinkled his brow, then swept his mobile phone from another jacket pocket. A couple of quick taps brought up a map of Norwich and confirmed the suspected alignment: you could draw a line with a ruler through the three places from north to south!

Bizarre.

A coincidence?

At least extending the line further north from his current position *didn't* intersect with St Andrew's Hall, site of the now-famed beer festival riot, which was away to the north-east. But the imaginary line *did* intercept Strangers' Hall to the west of that venue on St Andrews Street – a museum of domestic history set in a Grade I listed building, parts of which dated from the fourteenth century, hence a perfect location for ghosts. Tom couldn't recall in his searches finding any reports of spooky manifestations there, but... he took six paces to the corner of the Monk and peered left through an arch between the pub and the Saint John Church: the Maddermarket Theatre was directly ahead at the end of the short alley, announced in big red letters, and that *was* in his file. He recalled that it was meant to be haunted by the spectre of a relatively friendly monk, known for moving about costumes, opening and closing doors, and once saving the life of an actress from a falling light by pulling her out of the way. He was suddenly glad his glasses were in his pocket.

But what did it all mean?

He felt a sudden unease.

And then a voice addressed him from behind, making him jump...

"Tom?"

"Oh, *fuck*," he turned. "Sorry. You scared me!"

It was Alice Weidner, mid-thirties, blonde and elegantly dressed in heels and an expensive-looking coat that reached her knees. By her side was a handsome man with a short, fine beard and amused eyes. Alice also seemed entertained. "I think we're in here, Tom. Were you going somewhere else?"

"Ah, no, I was just…" He smiled lamely.

"This is my husband, Keith. I don't think you've met?"

After an awkward handshake between the men, the three entered the pub-restaurant. They were shown to the upstairs dining area by a waitress, where tables had been arranged to accommodate a number of different Christmas parties. Brian was already there, standing in wait. He greeted them as they entered the room under the wood-beamed ceiling.

"We had a couple of last-minute cancellations, I'm afraid, but we're all here now… bar one." Brian indicated seats for the newcomers at one end of a caterpillar of joined tables. The seated others turned and hailed them. Tom recognised Roberta and her partner Jessica, Manesh the computer technician and his wife Rita, Pavel and Magda, but none of the other three. New recruits? He thought the department didn't have the money to retain its existing payroll, let alone recruit more…

"Here you go, Tom," said Brian, interrupting Tom's confused thoughts. He showed him a place at the very end of one table, next to Alice, diagonal to Keith, with an empty seat in front. *Was that a wicked smile?* Brian then took his own place just beyond Keith, leaving the mystery of the last guest unresolved.

As Tom frowned at the empty space, Alice turned to talk to one of the newbies to her left. This left him no option but to engage with lucky Keith. Tom opened his mouth… but didn't have a clue what to say.

Keith's amused smile returned. He put Tom out of his misery: "So, Tom. I understand you were Alice's former office mate. She never said much about you. And now you're working for the man who supplanted you, eh?"

"Uh, yes. But it's just a small project, and it's all done now. I sent Brian the final report a few days ago, so I guess I'm a free man again," he gave an unconvincing chuckle. "What do you do?"

"I'm a lecturer in the Department of Film, Television and Media Studies."

Tom frowned. Something about that struck a chord, but before he could interrogate further…

"Ah, Tomaso! You were able to come! And you have saved me a seat. This is excellent!"

The mystery of the last seat was solved: *Fabio*! Tom gave a sickly grin at the man whose hand had materialised on one of his shoulders, then he quickly turned to look at Brian – sitting to Keith's other side – to find his expression one of malevolent glee...

***

It proved a painful evening. Tom wasn't sure what he'd done to deserve it, but Brian seemed to have planned the entire event just to torment him. For finishing the project early? That didn't make sense. And he'd done a good job, too, so it couldn't have been from displeasure at his work. Was it something to do with the fact that Brian had inherited his old desk and office? He surely didn't object to sharing with the divine Alice? Tom had never been clear about Brian's sexuality, and suspected that he essentially had none, but that certainly shouldn't have made his office share in any way distasteful. And Tom hadn't sabotaged his old space – left mouldering underpants in the filing cabinet; sealed the desk drawers with superglue; left obscene photographs pinned to his noticeboard. That only left... *Fabio.* And then he recalled the previous accidental meeting of the three of them at the Coachmakers, when Brian had made clear his displeasure at having been adopted by the Italian in Tom's absence. He surely couldn't hold Tom to blame for that, could he? But Brian did have a rather intense, waspish personality, and he was prone to harbouring grudges, so maybe that was it?

Whatever, Brian seemed to enjoy Tom's discomfort immensely, from his reaction to his slimy, fishy starter (what the fuck had that been?), to watching Fabio bombard him all evening with rhetorical football questions and stories, only occasionally interrupted by episodes when the lothario attempted to chat up Alice in complete disregard of the close presence and amused eye of her husband. And then there was the main course...

"I can't remember what I ordered for you, Tom," Brian said, when the waiting staff arrived with the food, one plate in each hand. "We'll just have to see what remains unclaimed at the end."

"Moules mariniere?" queried the last waitress, holding her final dish. "Ah, that must be yours, sir. *Bon appetit!*"

Tom accepted his food glumly, his nose wrinkling at the fishy whiff.

"Gosh, that looks nice," sneered Brian. "I hope I ordered right."

Brian had a delicious-looking steak-frites, as did Fabio. And Brian absolutely knew that Tom hated anything that had spent its life in that giant communal latrine otherwise known as the ocean.

Git.

"Er, well, I'm really a meat eater. I'm not too keen on fish or seafood."

"Really? Oh, I'm sorry. I must have been thinking of Gavin. He left at the same time as you. *Mea culpa.*"

"Ah, Tomaso, do not be like a fussy grandmother. It looks fantastic — eat up! If you do not, I will help, but only after I have finished this excellent steak!"

Brian had even managed to fuck up Tom's dessert order: while most tucked into fantastic chocolatey concoctions, Tom received a texturally dubious fruit tart. And to trump it all, it was only made clear at the very end that the meal hadn't been a gift of the Department or of Brian himself: when the bill came, the bespectacled demon led the charge to split the bill evenly and round-up generously.

Bastard!

The only positive came when Alice confirmed that she did indeed have a small project due to start at the end of January, and that she was keen to employ Tom's services on a consultancy basis, rather than risk a short-term commission with a potentially unreliable research assistant needing extra cash while completing their PhD thesis.

As they stood at the end and began to coat up, Tom found himself next to Keith.

"Well, I enjoyed that," said Keith. "A good job, too, as I'm back on Thursday."

"Uh, why?" asked Tom, dutifully.

"Got another Christmas group do. Just a few of us from my department. Mostly post-grad students."

"Uh, sounds great."

Outside, Tom managed to give Fabio the slip, but only by pretending that he lived in another part of the city. He had to circle the block before doubling back and heading to his actual abode.

***

The next night, the quiz was all over by ten.

"Third!" exclaimed Ed, in disgust. "Undone by the music round again!"

"Sorry, mate," said Simon. "Hip-hop isn't my thing."

"Is it anyone's?" fumed Ed. "Stet that. Clearly the studes and music nerds love it. If I had my way, I'd ban music from any year with a number 'two' before it." But then, just like that, Ed was smiling again and waved off their defeat. "Never mind. In retrospect, any universal deity looking upon this scene will note our score of four out of ten and decide that there are some within our messed-up species worth saving. He… or she…" Ed winked at Amanda, "or it…" he now raised an eyebrow at Simon, "will even now be stocking their heavenly bar with wondrous brews to enable us chosen ones to achieve perpetual bliss in the afterlife."

"And the pitchfork-wielding one will be turning up the barbeque flames for the others?" posited Tom, attuned to Ed's wild imaginings.

"Just so, Tom!" Ed raised his half-empty pint glass in a small toast, took a mouthful, then set it down again. Then, he made a show of looking at the eye-wateringly expensive timepiece on his wrist. "And we still have time for another couple of rounds of the liquid variety. So, not all is bad in the world."

Say what you like, thought Tom, you couldn't keep Ed down for long.

"Aren't you worried about walking around with that thing on your wrist?" asked Amanda. "It must be a beacon for muggers."

"Nah – thanks to the drop in crime rate due to this shadowy band of vigilantes. I'm more worried about how I'll afford my next piece. The Rolex is getting a bit stale after a couple of weeks, eh?"

"Sod!" But Tom was laughing. "So – have you any more tips? Have you cracked the next sequence in the code?"

"Alas, no, not yet." Ed drew forwards – an act that magnetically pulled his companions into a conspiratorial scrum. "The first code word was 'Delia'. We all saw this, eh, though only one of us was confident enough to bet significantly on it." He winked. "We've had a couple of results since then, and both have followed the binary pattern. But we need four to reveal the next letter – which could be anything. And that will still leave a large numbers of possibilities as to what the next will be."

"Unless it's a 'Q'," noted Simon.

Ed pulled back slightly. "You are full of surprising wisdom, Si. I need to keep a better eye on you, my *quizzing* friend. But you are *quite* correct.

Quality insight! *Quod erat* and all that." He smiled at his own cleverness, then leant in again. "But as I was saying, there are still many possibilities, so unless it does prove to be a 'Q', with its almost inevitable sequel, I think we will need to park this matter for now and revisit it later – probably in February. I will continue to update my database of results, and I'll let you know when it becomes interesting once more."

Tom had also started a file with the football scores and suspected Simon had too, though perhaps not Amanda, whose distaste for the game and concern about the evils of gambling was likely to have been inhibitive. But there was something that had bugged him for a while now, and this seemed the time to address it. "Is your confidence something to do with this alien betting syndicate you mentioned? Do you think this could have something to do with them?"

Simon frowned. "Alien betting syndicate? What's that?"

"Ah, sorry, mate," said Ed dismissively. "Something I briefly mentioned the other day. I think you must have been in the loo. Probably a cubicle job at that." He cast a wry look at Tom. "These guys somehow tricked me into breaching our rule on plausible deniability. Like Einstein being scammed by a couple of children. Now, Tom has blundered into it again, so, yes, without going into the sort of detail that would force me to kill you all, there is a species... or actually, a small number of species... that like to do the equivalent of running a book on us humans. Of interfering just to scam colleagues to win bets. I'm sure many illicit Flurbleglurbs, Rigellian dollars, Turkish Lira, and similar improbable currencies, have been won and lost by their actions. Like two bored old men with nothing better to do than wagering on which raindrop will reach the bottom of a pane of glass first."

"So, these aliens," continued Tom, "do you–?"

Ed raised a hand to stall the question. He didn't speak immediately, but the others knew not to fill the conversational space. Ed's expression became more serious. He closed his eyes and slowly rotated his neck. Then, he opened his eyes and pointedly looked at each of them. "I think at some point soon, we might have to lay our full hands on the table. But not yet. So, let me keep my secrets for now, eh? But Tom – the simple answer is, *yes*. The scoring in the Norwich Championship games is quirkily improbable, and I have seen things like this before. So, I admit I was fairly confident about that one-nil score. And I am equally confident that these binary scores are going to continue for a while yet – perhaps to the end of the season. I have mentioned this to Big Ed, who concurs. Whether this is part of something broader going on in Norwich, or separate, I don't know, and that is why we may need to pool our knowledge at a future time. Until then, as I said, leave things with me. Okay?"

The three glanced at each other.

"Sure thing, mate," said Simon.

"Yes. Fine by me," said Amanda. "I'm aware I've not said much either…" and she flicked her eyes to-and-from Simon, "but there is one area in my realm where something odd is happening. But I won't say more now."

"Uh, right," confirmed Tom, glancing at Amanda and wondering what new drama she was aware of. "Whatever you say. But are we still allowed to talk about the beer festival and… *spies?*"

"Indeed," said Ed. "These are matters we have all become embroiled in one way or another." His eyes darted to Simon and back, too. "And I had planned an update today anyway. So, where to begin?"

"Spies," said Tom. "Did your cameras catch anything?"

"I'm not sure. In the time between installing the cameras, half-an-hour before you guys turned up to the Alex, and collecting them, they recorded many different pub punters, but also a few who never made it into our hoppy sanctuary – mainly local denizens heading for the Stafford Street chippie, judging from their appearance, disappearance, then reappearance with white-wrapped parcels. I have a file with about a dozen faces, most, if not all, completely innocent. I have a colleague from the depths of the dark spaces of the web who has some killer face-recognition software that can compare and contrast pictures from photos to the broader web. So, I may at least be able to put names to some of the faces."

Amanda slowly shook her head. "I don't know how much of what you do is illegal, but I'm fairly sure a lot of it isn't ethical."

"All's fair in love and war, Mands. If I could have used my skills in the past to identify that talentless 'artist' from Austria and set up a hit before he became a major world menace, would you have objected then?"

"Well, no. But I don't think we're talking about an alien Adolf."

"True. But I'm also not talking about arranging a hit, merely trying to find out what the fuck is going on and who is responsible. Yes?"

Amanda was clearly not one hundred percent happy. "Okay. As long as we're not talking about blackmailing people or anything like that."

Ed smiled. "But I've always yearned to add Flurbleglurbs to my currency portfolio." He gave an exaggerated sigh. "Still, for you – our moral compass – I will desist. I promise. Nothing egregiously criminal. Okay?"

Amanda managed a gentle smile and a sigh. "Okay."

Tom was more interested in other matters. "What about the people from the festival – the ones Simon identified?"

Ed redirected his attention. "I rechecked, and could find no more pictures of Teresa, and no shots of her with this Ricky character. But I did find some tags of them in other social media posts holidaying with friends, so now I know what Ricky looks like, and that his name is actually Richard Vanian. I also found out that he and Teresa live in a flat over a shop on St Benedicts Street – don't ask, Mands." He coughed out the words "council tax records", then continued: "which explains why Simon sees them there so often. I still don't know what they do, apart from be miserable on holiday together. Christ, in every photo they have faces like smacked arses. Or like someone dumped in their cocktails. Amazing."

"And the others?" continued Tom.

"Augustus P. Samson is clearly not the guy's real name. Still searching. But I found that *Lynne* Martin Elder – seriously! – is indeed a UEA student. But he's not doing a Masters, rather a PhD. He's in the Department of Film, Television and Media Studies."

"No way!"

"Does that ring a bell, Tom?" asked Amanda.

"Uh, yes. You know I went to a Christmas dinner yesterday. Well, it turns out that the husband of my ex-office mate is a lecturer in that very department."

"Hmmm, interesting," said Ed, narrowing his eyes. "And can I ask who this guy is?"

"Well, my ex-office mate is Alice Weidner. Her husband's name is Keith. So… Keith Weidner, I guess."

"Really? That's a shame. *Lynne's* supervisor is a Keith Hardcastle. For a second there I thought we were back in the realm of infeasible coincidences."

"I'm not sure we aren't still," said Amanda. "I think your knowledge of social trends is stuck in the 90s, Ed. This Alice is clearly an intelligent and independent woman. Don't you think…?"

Ed snapped his fingers. "She kept her maiden name. Of course. You guys need to stop this, or I'll have to resign my position as the greatest savant in the group. I'll check later, but I'm now willing to put money on this. I mean, Keith is a bit of a *loserish* name, isn't it? How many famous Keiths do you know? Keith Chegwin?"

"Keith Richards," said Simon. "He's pretty cool."

"Okay – in a now-creepy kind of way, but granted. Who else? No one! Let's call it *Cheggers syndrome*: a desire not to tar your offspring with a name that will get them bullied, tormented and overlooked for the rest of their life. Dr Hardcastle's parents obviously hated their child, and your Alice is doing all she can to disguise the fact that she is associated with a Keith. Shudder!"

Tom shook his head. "This is incredible. You don't think…?"

"That Keith is like the Emperor to young Martin's Darth Vader? It might be worth looking into, eh?"

"How are you going to do that?" asked Simon.

"Fuck! I know where he'll be on Thursday," said Tom. "Where they'll *both* be."

"Say more!" demanded Ed.

"Well, I sat opposite Keith last night. He said his group was coming back to the Belgian Monk on Thursday for their own Christmas meal. So, if he's there, it makes sense that his PhD students will be too."

Ed laughed. "And we've not had our own Christmas dinner yet. Maybe we should organise something for Thursday?"

"Too late, mate," said Simon. "They'll be fully booked."

"Sure, but electronic bookings can sometimes suffer mysterious glitches. Get lost. Get replaced. Etcetera. Who's up for it?"

"Ed – that's not right!" Amanda's disquiet hadn't been fully dispelled. "Christmas dinners are important for lots of people. They're often a highlight of the year. I'm not going to be involved in bumping someone and ruining their Christmas!"

Ed gave an exasperated sigh. "You're no fun, babes. But I still treasure you, my little superego! Very well. I will desist. But it's a wasted opportunity."

"Maybe not," said Simon. "I think you can still go in for a drink if you just want to sit in the bar area. You could turn up and keep an eye on them. *Maybe*. If they're seated upstairs, you might not see much of them, but still…"

"Simon proves his value yet again. You'll soon be appointed High Elf at this rate. I like it. I can do Thursday. Tom, you're coming. Simon? Amanda?"

"Sorry, mate. Got another do then. Fat Cat Brewery Tap."

"And I can't, either. Vanda and Michael have invited me over for dinner. And anyway, I'm afraid this is *it* for me this year."

"Why?" asked Tom, barely able to keep the disappointment from his voice. "Are you going somewhere?"

Amanda smiled gently. "Afraid so. On Saturday, I'm flying out to Berlin to see Max for a week or so, and when I get back, I'll be off to my sister's family for Christmas. And then I've got to tour the country to visit the rest of my family. I might not be back in Norwich until after the new year."

"That's a shame," Tom grimaced. "Well… Merry Christmas."

"I'm not going yet – there's still time for last orders. But I am definitely moving onto the lime sodas."

And so the conversation segued to Christmas and their respective plans. Ed graciously got in the final round, and then a sneaky last pint for himself just after the bell had rung.

As they assembled outside for the last time in the year, and after Simon had bid farewell and left, Amanda turned to the others: "And you two boys – you be careful on Thursday. Remember that we don't have any evidence that any of the people in Ed's photos actually did anything wrong. And they probably didn't. I don't want you getting carried away, and then hearing about a riot or a spray paint attack in the news on Friday morning."

"Of course," said Tom. "We're just going to have a look. Aren't we, Ed? Ed?"

The other gave a devilish smile, but said no more.

***

They'd agreed to meet outside the Forum at 6.30p.m., which in retrospect was not a great idea given the chaotic evening crowds. The huge, glass-fronted, brick-built edifice – festooned with cheerful seasonal lights – was partially open, allowing access to the Café Marzano and Pizza Express within, which were busy. Meanwhile, outside – in the Millennium Plain, which separated the Forum from St Peter Mancroft – an ice rink had been set up, which was doing great and noisy business.

As Tom waited at one corner of the building, he looked over at the church and frowned: it seemed as though he couldn't escape the place. And then, as he panned right past a tunnel of winking blue lights lining the paved area beside the church – which passed through Hay Hill (with the statue of Sir Thomas Browne) to the Haymarket – he fixed his eyes upon a wide, three-storey brick building on the other side of the Plain, the bottom floor of which was taken up by the Television and Movie Store. The similarity of the name and concept to the Department of Film, Television and Media Studies was striking. Another coincidence? A secret HQ? A cosmic warning? Indeed, the shop was still open, taking advantage of relaxed Christmas opening hours. As he looked, a tall figure in a leather jacket strode confidently out of the portals. *Of course.*

Tom intercepted Ed half way across the square, at the side of the ice rink.

"Hey-ho, Thomas! 'Tis bustling and rumbunctious tonight!"

"Hi, Ed. Been shopping?"

"I always nip in t'movie store when I get the chance. Interesting line of t-shirts. Also, interesting line of people. Never seen Si inside before, but it must be one of his haunts." He narrowed his eyes. "And also perhaps the sort of place we might find young Martin." He half-turned and scanned the exterior. "Hmmm, no CCTV – on the outside at least. Never mind." He turned back: "But let's head on, eh? Refreshments and intrigue await!"

They walked between the rink and the frontage of the church, down the short stretch of St Peters Street between the Norwich City Council building (with its abundant yuletide decorations) and the darkened market, sidled around the Guildhall, and took Lower Goat Lane. At the foot of this, the revitalised Birdcage pub provided a temptation, but one they were compelled to resist: they turned right onto Pottergate, and shortly arrived in front of the Belgian Monk. It was crowded inside, but not overly so, with most Christmas diners not having arrived yet. They squeezed in, and managed to find a spot at the short side of the bar, where they could just about see the podium by the front door where new arrivals were intercepted.

Ed ordered a jug of something strong and brown, with two glasses, then invited Tom to do the pouring honours as he retrieved his mobile phone and started to play with it. "Ready!" he declared, after some time, setting his phone on the bar top. "Though, we could really do with getting closer to the action."

"What are your plans?" asked Tom.

"In the first instance, I plan to take photos of young Martin and any of those he is with. If he's a wrong'un, then he might not be acting alone, and it's worth establishing who's in his clique. It might also be worth comparing these blighters to the faces from the festival, and to malingerers from outside the Alex."

"Okay. Sounds reasonable."

"Indeed. And you can help by identifying dearest Keith to me."

"Sure. You said, 'first'. Is there a 'second'?"

"Perhaps," Ed smirked. "Should the chance arise for me to get up close, I might well initiate contact with Mysterious Martin."

Tom didn't like the sound of that. "Right. You mean—"

"Oh, don't worry. I don't mean start a fight or knee him in the groin or anything. Just get up close. Accidentally nudge him; apologise; start a light conversation. Make a joke. Maybe create enough of an impression that if by some bizarre coincidence – *in no way related to stalking* – I bump into him again, I have an 'in'. Know what I mean?"

"Rather you than me."

"Yes, Tom. And better me than you, too. Such a process needs a people person who is comfortable in the company of others. Perhaps not your best suit, my friend."

Tom nodded in grudging acceptance. "Sure."

"But that will only work if he doesn't recognise either of us. Now, I don't see why he should recognise me, but you – Thomas – you have seen him several times before, and he has therefore seen you. If you are nothing to him, a random person from a crowd, then he won't react at the sight. But if there is more to this – that he is aware of you as a potential agent for the other side – then his reaction may be telling. I want to ensure that he sees you and watch his response."

"So, you're suggesting I be a lure?"

"Yes, *lure*. Good choice of word. That's precisely what I was thinking. I definitely *wasn't* thinking 'bait', as in a grotesque wriggling worm. Certainly not!" He grinned, allowing Tom to appreciate that this was *exactly* the image he'd formed.

Tom sighed. "Very well. Wriggle wriggle…"

More people entered the pub-restaurant. Around 7p.m., a major influx began. Soon after, Keith turned up. For a brief moment, Tom wondered whether he'd be accompanied by Alice, but he was with another, slightly older man instead. Tom hunched down – though it would have been difficult for the other to see him through the people lining the long side of the bar.

"That's Keith, with the beard."

"Fuck," hissed Ed, phone now to hand. "I can't get a decent shot from here. We need to get closer if we can."

They had a frustrating half-an-hour. None of the other punters wanted to forsake their space, and indeed, others tried to cram in. They missed Martin's entrance altogether – assuming he'd come at all. Ed began to get tense. Then, at last, they managed to dive onto a vacated table in the narrow area next to the long bar, just a few feet from the greeter's podium. Their view was enhanced, but by now it was clear that most, if not all, of the diners from the various Christmas parties had arrived and trooped upstairs.

So, they sat and drank – which was no bad thing in itself. De Koninck. Grimbergen. Petrus. Ter Dolen. They had several jugs, from which Ed seemed to gain disproportionate measures.

"Fuck'em," slurred Ed, as the evening grew late. "Upstairs in their little restauranty heaven." Then he began to stand. "Right, I'm going upstairs to have a look. Have it out–"

"No, Ed, wait! Remember what you said to Amanda."

Ed swayed slightly and focused on his drinking companion. "Ah, yes, the shrew. No. I didn't mean that. She's a lovely lady. Okay. I'll just… toilet…" and he staggered off.

As Ed headed to the gents, two things happened. The first was that a noisy party began to throng down the stairs, having finished its meal; the second was that one of the barmaids, who'd been watching Ed, cautiously approach Tom. "Is your friend all right?"

Tom had consumed a fair amount too, but not so much as to affect his speech. "Yes… yes, he's fine."

"Hmmmm. Maybe this should be his last one?"

Tom gave an embarrassed smile. "Yes, of course. We were about to leave anyway."

The barmaid wrang her hands and gave a relieved smile. "Ah, great. Well, I hope you had a nice evening," and she continued to the door to wish the leavers farewell.

Tom decided to empty the final jug himself, leaving Ed with just the dregs in his own chalice. On the other's return, Tom instantly stood: "Right, I think we should go. Maybe we'll have better luck next time, eh?"

"Sure thing, bud." Ed swept up his glass and drained it. "There'll always be a next time."

Tom had to guide the other out, and then away from the entrance door. They stood in front of the closed wooden gate to Bagley Court opposite, while Ed patted various pockets to make sure he had his phone.

As they swayed there, a voice hailed them from behind: "Tom… is that you?"

Tom startled, then turned awkwardly: being a head taller than him, Ed was now leaning heavily on his shoulder. A metre away, at the edge of a small cluster of people, stood Keith, wearing the same amused expression he'd worn the first time they'd met. And beside him, with eyes that suddenly – treacherously! – widened, was Martin Elder.

Immediately sober, Tom straightened. "Ah, hello Keith. What a surprise."

"It is indeed!" Keith's expression hardened a touch as he looked between the two men. "But much as I'd like to chat, I think I need to be getting home. Alice will be wondering. Merry Christmas to you and your friend."

"Merry Christmas to you, Keith," and for some unaccountable, instinctive reason, Tom continued, "and to you… *Martin*."

The young man was suddenly tongue tied: he winced, nodded, glanced quickly to Keith at his side, and then began to walk away.

Keith flicked a thoughtful look at Tom, then followed his protégé without a further word.

Beside him, Ed muttered: "*Busted!*"

Chapter 20: Castle Secrets

Christmas throughout the UK had been unseasonably dry and warm, without the snow for which most children and many adults (secretly) yearned. For Tom, these conditions had undermined his seasonal cheer: he normally enjoyed yuletide, but the four days spent at his parents' bungalow in Gloucestershire – doing the rounds, joining them in visiting his brother and sister and their families – had seemed almost fraudulent. Christmas trees, Santa, decorations, and presents, just did not mix with sunshine and green lawns. Even his nephews and nieces had been fractious, as though subconsciously rebelling against this meteorological outrage.

As if to make up for this, at the start of January, Nature sent a cold front from the Arctic barrelling into the island. This dumped a prodigious amount of snow over the east of the country, only to then sweep it away with days of sleet and freezing rain. So, when Tom returned to Norwich for a lonely New Year in front of the TV (*fucking* Jools Holland and his *wanking* Hootenanny!), he found himself trapped in his house by the inclement weather, and at the mercy of a temperamental heating system.

In sum, his life had been on hold for two weeks, in which he'd lazed about mildly disgruntled, writing little, and patrolling not at all. He'd not seen Smith – who'd accepted his online excuses without comment – or any of his friends. Come January 5th, he decided that, sod everything, he was going to head out, regardless of weather, giant asteroids, plague or even Gabriel's last trump.

***

The weather was filthy.

Tom shivered in a heavy coat and woolly hat, with a scarf drawn up over his mouth and nose, the latter making his dark glasses seem all the more incongruous. Having come to the city to perform one of his patrols, he now wondered at the sense of it. The icy wind whipping sleet through the air had scoured the streets of all but hardiest of shoppers: footfall was low, so the odds of alien influencers influencing did not seem high, particularly given that it was difficult to look anywhere but down if one wished to avoid a face full of winter spite. Indeed, as Tom had to constantly wipe his glasses clean of slush, he struggled to fix his attention on any sign, window, object or vista. Worse still, the wind continually ripped his coat's waterproof hood from his head, causing his woollen hat to rapidly become saturated, giving him brain freeze.

He had intended to take his patrol route through the centre and down Prince of Wales Road towards the station, but he faltered in the environs of Castle Mall – the older of Norwich's two shopping centres. *This is insane!* he thought to himself. And then he looked up at the nine hundred year old Norman castle rising behind the mall and hatched a new plan.

***

"Ouch!" said Tom, on hearing the entrance fee.

"Sorry, sir. Inflation!"

The castle had originally been on one of his idealised patrol routes, but since meeting Smith, he'd only been there once, during a time when he'd been feeling especially poor. He'd raised the matter of costs with his handler shortly after, but got the equivalent of an uninterested shrug, after which he'd mentally responded '*fuck you*' and crossed the castle off his list. Indeed, the state of his finances were little better now than they'd been on that previous occasion, in spite of recently receiving payment for Brian's project, which money had merely covered his last few months' living expenses and his Christmas spending. But the weather had forced his hand, and anyway, this was a tourist attraction that had decent footfall at times, and hence was somewhere that seemed a good prospect for alien messaging – just like the cathedral. Tom winced at the latter thought.

"Okay. One ticket, please." It seemed worth the money, just to get out of the sleet.

The castle had undergone a significant renovation a few years previously, thanks to several million pounds from the National Lottery Heritage Fund. The original Norman layout had been reinstated, with work done on all five levels, from the battlements to the basement. Tom started at the top (very briefly, given the weather) and moved down. He wasn't expecting much.

But then, at the lowest level, in a small chamber of little particular interest –perhaps merely buffed in the renovation – he saw it: a message! Well… of sorts. For it was *odd*. Rather than a word or phrase in English, it was a single, convoluted character that could have been Japanese or Chinese.

Was it intended to specifically influence foreign visitors?

Tom smiled to himself, wondering what it might say. Wicked stereotypes came flooding to mind:

Eat noodles now!

Commit seppuku immediately!

Buy Hyundai!

He retrieved his phone and took a photo to enable him to consider it at leisure later, then shook his head at his own stupidity: a glance confirmed that the seventh dimensional writing didn't appear in the picture.

On closer inspection, Tom decided that it wasn't an oriental character after all, being more angular and runic. Was it intended to send modern-day Scandinavian history professors into a berserker rage? But how many nowadays could interpret old Viking runes?

Absurd.

But it was *something*. It was clearly a message of sorts from an alien pen, glowing in the seventh dimension as clearly as all of the other messages he had seen. When he took off his glasses, it disappeared; when he put them back on, it was there.

And not only was it an odd symbol, but it was in an odd location, too. This was hardly Grand Central Station. Okay, so there weren't many visitors around on this early January day with its mega-sucky weather, but even so, at peak tourist season, who would come here, to this corner of this low level of the keep? There was nothing of interest at all, and no reason to look here. It therefore seemed to be a wasted effort.

Perhaps it was no more than alien graffiti? The tag of some intergalactic vandal? And why not? After all, it was clear that aliens in their multitudinous species had all sorts of motivations and quirks. They watched Earth as though it was a soap opera; they committed mischief; they were involved in betting scams. Some seemed noble and conscientious – like Smith, he supposed. So, why couldn't there be others like this so-called Krustie Brigade?

Tom nodded to himself: it was either graffiti, or a meaningless scrawl – the equivalent of a pen test on a scrap pad in a stationery shop. It might be recent or old. Maybe very old. Maybe this place was so far out of the way it had been forgotten by its author and missed by searchers like himself. Regardless, it was here, and Tom's mission was to find such messages and expunge them. He smiled: this time, he could see no peril in doing his job, unlike at the Pottergate underpass, or with the children's paintings in the cathedral. He could wipe this out and report an unmitigated success to Smith.

Tom shucked off his rucksack, still damp from its outside exposure. He knelt to delve within, drawing out a spray can and large magnet – the latter stuck to the former. With a bit of effort, he removed the magnet, which filled his palm. He'd gotten it from Thorns on a second visit, having forgotten to look for it while searching for the elusive red paint on his first. He was about to set it aside – given that it had failed to work on previous occasions – when he had second thoughts. He looked around. There was still nobody about, and in any case, he was in shadow, and would definitely hear anyone approaching. For once, he had time. So, why not?

He straightened and approached the symbol, which was set at chest height. *Here goes nothing.* He brought the magnet to the stone face and… it *clicked.*

What the fuck?

The symbol was still evident, unaffected, but something behind it had responded to his activity. He pressed on the symbol... and the whole wall started to move. Had he *broken* the castle?

No.

Calm.

He quickly looked around, but all was quiet. So, he considered the wall again, and found that he had pushed only part of it inwards, *not* the whole wall. He tried again, and with a gentle scraping sound, and surprisingly little resistance, it moved further. He nodded to himself: it was actually a door in the wall, perhaps one-and-a-half metres in height and two-thirds of a metre wide. And it wasn't that thick, either: shoving further, he found that the door was considerably thinner than the depth of the stone beside it – effectively, a one-inch-thick stone cladding on a wooden door.

Tom left the door ajar and stepped back, suddenly nervous. But it was clear that the shadow in this corner was deep enough that, even if someone entered the room now, they wouldn't see that the wall had been partially depressed. He stepped even further back, then paced off to one side, towards the chamber entrance and a wall light. From here, he *still* couldn't actually see the opening.

He returned to the door, the edge of which he'd pushed in perhaps six inches – still not enough to see what lay beyond. *Time to find out.* He exerted a gentle but continuous pressure, and the door slithered on the stone floor. At around eighty degrees to the wall face, resistance stiffened, and something *clinked.* Tom's exploratory hand revealed a metal ring on the other side – about the height a doorknob might be expected – which prevented the door from folding flat.

And within: blackness.

Total.

Tom stepped forwards into the space, ducking slightly to get under the frame: he took one step, then a second. He felt ahead and to either side – his magnet still clasped in one palm – and touched cold stone. He couldn't see the floor in the attenuated light, but it felt smooth. He needed illumination. Where... *aha!* Tom thrust the magnet in one jacket pocket and retrieved his mobile phone from another. He had a torch app on this, which he found and tapped.

Suddenly, the space before him was revealed: Tom was in a tunnel, which stretched directly ahead beyond the limit of his torchlight.

What now?

One voice in his head said: *leave! What if someone sees you? What if the door slams shut and won't open?*

Another voice said: *testicles, Tom! Grow some! What a discovery!*

Cowardice and bravery vied for mastery, and at last, surprisingly (at least to Tom himself), bravery won. He moved fully inside the tunnel and turned back to the door. Using the iron ring, he tugged at it, closing the portal – but not entirely. In doing so, he noticed the strange symbol again, just above the ring and directly opposite its partner on the front side. Now, that would be the acid test: dare he shut the door completely and see if the magnet activated the hidden locking mechanism from *this* side? The answer: *no!* There was bravery, and then there was stupidity. In any case, it was spooky enough, with almost all of the light from the chamber now cut off, leaving just the insubstantial light from his phone for him to see by. He thought about taking off his dark glasses – even though they didn't actually reduce light from the visible spectrum – just for the psychological impact. But what if there were other messages around? He kept them on.

He turned back to face into the tunnel, still stooped slightly on account of the low stone ceiling.

Onwards, Tom! said the brave/stupid voice in his head.

"What the fuck am I doing?" said Tom in a whisper.

He took a step, then another, and then he was moving – slowly, cautiously.

The tunnel ran straight, like a long stone box. But it wasn't level: he could feel a gradual slope to it, taking him downwards. *Of course!* The castle was built on a mound to oversee the city, so to get anywhere from it would require a descent. Two steps turned into ten, then twenty, then thirty. And with each further step, Tom's resolve faltered. He could no longer see the door behind, with its ever-so-faint silvered outline; it was like he was in a tomb.

Tomb?

And with that thought, Tom began to feel a prickling over his skin, and his heart rate increased. Then, at some indeterminate point ahead, there was a dim light… of sorts. It seemed a haze; a mild glow; a will-o'-the-wisp. He was transfixed by it, unable to move. The light danced up and down, gradually increasing in brightness and definition, until…

Tom was finally able to make out the true nature of the phantasm.

"A *skull*… a *fucking* skull!"

Tom nearly dropped his phone.

As the glowing apparition approached, Tom yelped, stiffened, banged his head on the ceiling, cursed, turned, and crabbed back towards the door as fast as he could. It was still ajar, *thank fuck*. He pulled the ring to open it further, squeezing through the aperture once it was wide enough. Turning, he caught sight of the glowing skull through the still-open door, maybe ten metres distant. How could he close it from this side? There was no handle, and the thing was getting closer…

The magnet?

Tom plunged a hand into his jacket pocket and retrieved the item. He took half a step until he could place it next to the mysterious symbol. *If this didn't work…*

But it did.

As though drawn to the magnet, the door began to slowly move towards him. But Tom wasn't prepared to wait to see if it would complete its journey: he snatched his rucksack from where he'd left it on the stone floor and fled to the exit from the chamber.

He only slowed down once he reached the café, several levels up, leaving bemused fellow visitors in his wake. Here, he managed to compose himself just enough to order a pot of tea, confident that in the light of day, and with a smattering of others seated at tables around him, it was unlikely that he'd be assailed by the demon head. But there was no way he was going back down into the keep.

The weather outside was still terrible – which at least gave Tom a good excuse to break his journey home by hopping from one pub to another, starting with The Murderers on Timber Hill. By the time he made it home, he was saturated by both freezing rain and beer, and quickly fell asleep.

***

The quick response to Tom's request placed at the foot of his draft novel – posted on the Cloud the next morning – proved a bit of an eye opener.

OK TOM. OLD VENUE COMPROMISED. NEW MEETING PLACE ST ANDREWS PLAIN BENCHES, OUTSIDE ST ANDREWS HALL. YOU KNOW THE PLACE. 3PM.

Was this some sort of joke? That was right outside the venue of the beer festival and the very spot where a CCTV camera had captured a Smith-like *Big Issue* seller at around the time the CAMRA banners had been sabotaged. He wasn't sure what to think. Leaving aside what 'compromised' meant, it appeared to confirm that this was a part of the city to which the alien had ready access, and likewise added support to the theory that the indistinct figure discovered in the recorded images by Ed was indeed Smith. One other thought occurred: either Smith was completely oblivious as to how suspicious this looked, or else he absolutely wasn't, and… what? Was he testing Tom? After all, the response clearly stated: *You know the place.* Was he aware of the Credulous cabal and their efforts to solve the beer festival mystery? Was he teasing him? Seeing how he would react? Seeing whether he would make some admission or inadvertent slip? But, if so, to what ends? There was no reason for Smith *not* to tell him if he was aware of Tom's breaches of confidence… so why wouldn't he? Maybe the alien was unsure? Tom would have to be careful.

He immediately typed his acceptance of the rendezvous in five hours' time. But he fretted over matters throughout the rest of the morning and on the walk to the meeting venue. It was cold, but at least the rain and sleet of the last few days had stopped.

Tom arrived five minutes early (a miracle!) and took a seat on a circular bench. This was surrounded by grey bollards against which bikes had been locked.

It immediately struck Tom that this was an odd place to meet. They had so far used two venues that allowed some degree of privacy – albeit St Peter Mancroft required exact timing to avoid staff, and the bench outside the Guildhall was subject to regular passers-by. This venue was usually much busier than those: St Andrews Street was a significant thoroughfare, while the Plain was a natural nexus of activity, lined by the medieval Halls, the St Andrews Brew House (though at this time of year, the metal tables along its outside flank were unoccupied), a couple of cafés, and the (closed) Dog House. Just across the road were two red phone boxes and St Andrew's church – familiar from Ed's surveillance and Tom's patrolling – with Cinema City perhaps thirty metres further up the road. So, it was a crazy place to meet.

Or was it?

Tom's brow furrowed as he scanned the area… and saw no one. The timing was apposite, coinciding with a period where none of the pubs, cafés, churches, or the cinema, were currently patronised, while traversing pedestrians and shoppers were spookily absent (and likely deterred by the cold).

Clever.

While looking about, Tom missed Smith's arrival, and only caught him as he stepped from the pedestrian crossing in front of the nearby pub. With half-a-dozen more strides the bearded 'man' in the red bib was with him. But before speaking, Smith gestured that Tom should shift to another part of the bench that faced away from the pub and towards the narrow, brick-paved Princes Street.

"Hello, Tom. You are keen to meet. What do you have to report?"

"Ah, hi, Smith. Um… where to begin?"

"The start, I suggest," said Smith. And there was that little smile again. "Then progress through the middle part until you reach the end."

"Yes, of course. It was an, um, rhetorical question." Tom wanted to ask about the new venue, and what 'compromised' meant, but time was short, as ever, so: "I went to the castle yesterday and found something. A message. But it was a strange one."

"Strange?"

"Yes. It wasn't in English, or any other human language that I could tell. I thought I would erase it anyway, and this time the magnet worked."

"Excellent, Tom. And there have been no repercussions, as previously?"

"Repercussions?" *Bastard!* Smith *was* smiling. "Er, no. There haven't been. I wasn't seen. But, when I say 'worked', I don't mean that the magnet erased the message. It, well, it seemed to open some sort of mechanism. The sign was by a hidden door in the stone, and behind that was a tunnel."

"I see."

"I mean, the whole wall sort of opened up. I went in, but not far, as I didn't have any light apart from my phone." He decided to skip mention of the ghost for now.

"Okay. And so?"

"I thought you should know. I mean, it's related to alien messaging. But I didn't paint over it, as there didn't seem to be any point, and maybe it would stop the door from opening. I wondered what you wanted me to do. Did you know about the tunnel?"

Smith paused a moment. When he spoke, he gave a tangential answer. "Yes, Tom, I know tunnels exist, as I've mentioned before. There are several under Norwich, constructed many years ago for powerful people, enabling them to move secretly between important places. But even after construction, their entrances were known to few, and these have been forgotten with time. As I've said previously, there is one under St Peter Mancroft, which I use to get to a cellar beneath the Guildhall. I occasionally use others."

"Yes, but did you know about *this* one?"

"Clearly, I do now."

Was that an evasive answer?

Tom suddenly glanced across the road to St Andrew's Church and the phone boxes in front. "And... is there one at the church?"

Smith clearly saw the direction of Tom's gaze, but he chose not to answer directly. "Tom, the tunnels are old and treacherous. You should put them from your mind. There is nothing down there that is of interest to us. There will be no messages there, as no one will be able to see them and be influenced."

"But..."

"And as the message you found isn't human, there is no need to cover it over. I fear all you will do is draw attention to yourself for no good reason. Thank you for the information, but there is no need to explore further. Please focus your activities above ground. I would hate for you to go spelunking and have an accident. No one would find you, and I would be very sad."

Was that a threat? Tom didn't know where to look and ended up fixing on some spot mid-way between the church and the *Big Issue* seller, attempting to decrypt the other's face through the corner of his eye. Smith's tone and facial expression was neutral, as usual. No, *not* as usual. Over their last few meets – and even today – he had started to smile, and Tom suspected that Smith had learnt the reflex so well that he now found it difficult to control. Yet his expression at the moment was old Smith – as blank as blank could be. Too blank? Tom felt the other was somehow holding his newly learned emotions in check. But in that case, exactly *what* emotion was he suppressing?

Tom tried again. "But, maybe this would help explain how the message-leavers are getting around, and why we haven't identified who was responsible for the beer festival... uh..." Tom stiffened. *We? Identified?* That had never been a mission given to Tom by Smith or spoken about between them. Had he implied too much about his extracurricular activities? Fortunately...

"People come and people go," said Smith, with an apparent lack of concern. "Be assured, anyone wishing to leave a message will likely have the capacity to do so. Therefore *who* and *how* are not a concern to us.

226

Merely *what* and *where*. And *where* will almost certainly be above ground. Is this clear?"

"Uh, yes, but..."

"And now my time is nearly up. Continue your patrolling around places of high footfall, Tom."

The alien gave Tom a blank stare, then turned and headed off towards the pedestrian crossing that would take him to his sanctuary.

Tom watched him go, past the phone boxes, heading for one of the alleys to the side of the church, where he became lost to view.

For a moment, Tom sat and ruminated on what he had learnt. He really needed to talk to the guys about this. He nodded to himself: it was time to send some emails to see who else was around.

***

Back home, with emails sent, Tom now had to wait. He wasn't entirely sure who was back in Norwich. Simon – probably. Amanda – possibly. Ed – who the fuck knew? Indeed, he'd not tried to contact his friends before now, since it was Ed who invariably organised their socials; he suspected Amanda and Simon might therefore be waiting too.

In the meantime, Tom had matters to research. The first proved straightforward: in his file on Norwich ghosts, along with those of King Gurgunt, Martha Alden (also known as the Black Lady), and Robert Kett, the castle was apparently home to the ghost of a floating skull believed to belong to Robert Goodale, who was hanged at the castle in 1885 for murdering his wife. Apparently, when hung, his head had separated from his body as though cut off by a knife.

"Well, hello, Robert, or whichever alien has chosen to borrow your shade," muttered Tom. "*You complete and utter git!*"

Next, he took to the internet to look into the issue of tunnels – something he perhaps should have done before now, given Smith's previous admissions. And once he'd cracked the appropriate search terms, he was soon rewarded. He started a new Word file – cutting and pasting texts and links into this. And before long, the file had expanded to a dozen pages, as there were plenty of rumours. Indeed, Norwich was claimed to have the UK's largest collection of undercrofts, many of which were secretly linked. What quickly became clear was that the castle was an important nexus, with tunnels reputed to run from it to places that included the cathedral and a Benedictine nunnery near the junction of King Street and Bracondale (which might or might not be the same as one reputed to run there from what used to be the Three Tuns pub in King Street). There was also reputed to be one running beneath Ponds' Shoe shop on Castle Meadow, another from the cellars of 'a 19th century shop in London Street', and… aha! A tunnel was meant to lead from the castle to the Guildhall near the marketplace – presumably to the 14th century vault below this, which had been previously used as a crypt and a prison. Perhaps the tunnel he'd entered led all the way to Smith's secret HQ?

And the more he looked, the more he found. The cathedral was another node. But other notable names that recurred included St Peter Mancroft, the Britons Arms, and the St Andrew's and Blackfriars' Halls, where the beer festival had taken place.

Tom sat back in his chair and blew out his cheeks. If true, this was incredible. He'd accidentally come across an entrance to the whole network. What's more, if Smith and other aliens were using these tunnels – which might explain how the beer festival had been sabotaged by an unseen person (Martin? Teresa?) –perhaps they all bore a sign like the one he'd come across in the castle, and he might thus be able to open them courtesy of his glasses and magnet.

"Fuck me!"

And then he noticed his inbox tab alerting him to new mail, with a '3' in brackets. He had three new messages. He clicked on the tab to find responses from Ed, Amanda and Simon.

They were all in town and eager to meet.

Game on!

Chapter 21: Fourth Interlude

A high-pressure system had settled over the country in the second week of January, bringing Norwich clear skies and a temperature of nine degrees – a significant improvement on the filthy weather of the new year.

It was also a Sunday.

It was thus a good day for fishing.

And it was a good day for canoeing.

And it was a good day for a family ramble along the picturesque river winding through the city.

The riverside path by the Wensum – from the entertainment complex near Carrow Road, all the way to Fye Bridge (via the train station, cathedral, Cow Tower, and the city law court) – was therefore unusually busy.

And someone – or *something* – had anticipated this.

Along the river were a variety of signs. There were several by the Norwich Yacht Station – a narrow building at river level, by the bridge near the train station, where craft could moor up to access clean water, electricity and other amenities. And there were others along Riverside Walk itself, which gave directions, as well as instructions about acts that were not permitted.

And some blighter had been at these.

In fact, they'd been at just about all of these.

But unless one possessed glasses with particular properties, the messages that flowed across them were only visible at the subconscious level.

But with a lot of people, there were a lot of consciousnesses, and hence, a lot of *sub*-consciousnesses.

Unfortunately, it was the fishing community that bore the brunt of the messages' exhortations.

Push them.

Go on, push.

Just a nudge.

It'll be funny.

Twats in waders.

People found themselves gravitating towards the river's edge whenever they saw anyone with a fishing line or net. But the fishermen (and, yes, they were invariably men) tended not to react, being used to people coming up close to see what they'd caught.

And the people coming up were an odd assortment: youths; kids; couples; whole families; their paths bowing inwards and then, in most cases, curving away.

But not in all cases.

Just down from Cow Tower, Martin Spottiswood had already been nudged by a couple of curious passers-by before a family man knocked into him with sufficient force to send him into the water – spooking the pike he'd been trying to coax onto his line. The family man had been apologetic, and had got a wet leg trying to help Martin back out with the help of his wife. The pair's kids, however, had merely wailed with laughter.

A few minutes later, just around the river bend from Martin's bathing spot, Jed Brodie gained no sympathy at all from the youth who sent him into the cold waters.

By the bridge, a succession of canoeists swerved close to Jezza Armitage, giving him undesired showers with their descending blades and scaring away any fish in the vicinity.

And a hundred metres or so up from Jezza, by Pull's Ferry – a 15th-century flint building that had once been used as a ferry house and water gate – Rod Owens ended up going for a swim – not once, but *twice*.

And they weren't the only ones to suffer.

Perhaps because it was a Sunday, the TV news didn't get the scoop. But the local *EDP* did – after a tip off from the police station about a clutch of complaints – and by the end of the week, the paper had a good story with photos of half-a-dozen disgruntled piscators.

By this stage, the news had been widely disseminated among the angling community, which was up in arms, with various groups meeting across the city. One of these now congregated at the aptly named Compleat Angler, at the foot of Prince of Wales Road by the bridge to the station, not far from where two of the party had been victimised.

"So, what do we call ourselves?" asked one.

"The *Anglers' Army* maybe?" answered a second.

Rod – the serial swimmer – waved his unlit pipe. "What about the *Angliar* Army. A cross between Angler and Anglia. Bit clever, that."

Jezza – the much-splashed-one – seemed less than impressed. "If you say so."

"What about *Fish-Force-Five*?"

The grizzled group turned their eyes upon Junior – who in spite of his sobriquet was a man in his late forties. "Fish… force… five?" enunciated Jezza, with something approaching incredulity. "What exactly is *that* supposed to mean? And why *five*?"

John 'Junior' Bates grinned. "It's a play on Fox-Force-Five. From a Tarantino film. Bit of a cultural ref. Mimetic."

"Aye, well, I don't understand what the blazes *any* of that means," said Jezza. "So, I doubt whether many members will either. And I still don't get the *five* part."

Junior waved it away and slumped back in his chair. "Okay. Forget I spoke."

"Worrabout *Trout Pouters*," said Ancient Reg. "That rings some sort of bell."

"I don't think that means quite what you think, Reg," said Rod.

"Arr, what was that?"

"Doesn't mean what you think," said Rod, much louder now.

Junior laughed. "And you thought *my* idea was dumb!"

"Whassat?" muttered Reg, in confusion, looking between the men.

"Never mind, Reg," said Jezza. "We'll take it on board."

Reg's confusion remained, but at least he now lapsed into silence.

"Okay, what about naming us after this place." Rod waved his pipe again. "*The Compleat Anglers*. It also justifies making this our HQ."

Bernie sucked at his teeth and gave the thumbs up, while Junior murmured assent. Jezza looked sour, clearly wishing he'd thought of this. "Right. I was going to suggest the same. You beat me to it."

Rod merely grinned, raising his pint of ale in salute.

"So, that's sorted," said Junior. "Get a name, and we're half-way there. But what are we going to do?"

Jezza's eyes sparkled. "We're going to mobilise. I'm fed up with the way we're treated and the restrictions we have to put up with. There are over a million keen anglers in this country, and thousands in this area. It's about time people listened to us. Looked after the rivers better. Provided better facilities for us. Stopped seeing us as a nuisance. Stopped abusing us and shouting at us from their stupid canoes. *Lots* of things."

"What about reserving stretches of the river for us on a regular basis?" said Rod. "And that means closing off stretches to water transport."

"Yes, that's a good start," concurred Jezza, grudgingly. "We can draw up a list of demands."

"What, us *five*?" said Junior, with feeling.

"No. More than that. We're all members of fishing clubs. We'll put out some ads in the *Angling Times*…"

"And *Coarse Fishing*," said Bernie. "That's good, too."

"Sure."

"Ads cost," noted Rod. "Who's going to pay?"

"I can call in a favour," said Jezza. "But we might need modest subs…"

The discussion continued right up to last orders. Militant fishing now had a voice, and it was hoary.

***

That January evening, the Knights of St Gregory meant business – or at least, thought Grand Master Jim Taylor, glancing between Amazonian Tania and Napoleonic, stun-gun-wielding Adam – some of them did. Their patrolling had cleared the drunks, junkies and rough sleepers from St Gregory's all the way up to the northern leg of the river Wensum… although arguably, all they'd done was displace the unsavoury activity. So, while this was great for the inhabitants and visitors of the city centre and the Lanes, it wasn't so good for those beyond.

The Knight's tactics had largely involved applying persistent pressure, with an implicit threat of violence to those who wouldn't comply with their firm requests to move on. In the first couple of months, they'd made a number of citizens arrests, too, but the police had seemed annoyed by their actions more than anything, and perpetrators had often been promptly released with nothing more than a police caution. As far as Jim knew, no one they'd detained had actually been taken to court. And so they had ceased the kids' gloves treatment: now, they conducted frisks and confiscated alcohol and drugs when they found these, knowing that their victims weren't liable to run to the police to complain. There had also been an increasing number of 'chastisements' – in the words of Ken – although no one had been keen to explain to Jim what exactly these entailed.

Now, it was time to extend their influence by aiding the people of Norwich-Over-the-Water, and Jim had – at last – managed to persuade his over-protective Knights to allow him to accompany them. This evening, in addition to Jim, Tania and Adam, their team comprised Ken and James (the other originals), plus Keri – a fearsome-looking woman, who was a prop in Tania's rugby club. Ken had led them into what he called 'Indian Territory' (which Jim wasn't entirely sure was politically correct, but who knew these days?): the environs of Anglia Square and Magdalen Street.

Anglia Square was a notorious canker upon the fine city of Norwich – a brutalist, high-rise shopping centre built in 1970, towering over the low-rise north of the city and a nearby flyover of the inner city ring road. Its grim, ever-damp concrete niches and walkways – along with the scruffy area between it and the flyover – were perfect for surreptitious bargaining and low-level criminality; and every exposed concrete surface seemed to be covered in graffiti or human urine (judging by the enduring stench). The place was indeed the latrine of Norwich, and yet, countless plans for its demolition and replacement had gotten nowhere, as council bureaucrats, local politicians and other self-interest groups found one reason after another to appeal and reject developers' plans for their own reasons – and to hell with the local populace.

"Right," said grey-bearded Ken, ducking back behind a concrete pillar, "we're on! Jim, what is it?"

Jim had half-raised one hand to gain attention. "Er, are we safe here? I mean, what about CCTV?"

Ken smiled. "Don't worry, Grand Master. I've plotted a route around the cameras. Anyway, the scumbags also know where these are, and do their wicked business in the gaps in coverage."

"Ah, right, that's a relief."

Ken nodded, then turned to address the rest of the team. "There are four of them out there – a dealer and three others. They all seem a bit wasted, but let's not take any chances, eh? Everyone tooled up?"

"Oh, *yeah*!" said diminutive Adam, uncovering his illicit stun gun. Tania slipped out a rounders bat from within her knee-length leather coat, while James slipped on a pair of knuckle-dusters that were definitely *not* within the bounds of the law. Keri cracked her knuckles and rotated her shoulders, as though preparing to engage in a scrum. Ken – being a jiu-jitsu master – presumably needed no further weapon. Jim goggled at the sight and stepped back a pace, which Ken misinterpreted.

"Yep, Jim, that's good. Keep at the back, and you'll be safe. Now, let's party!"

Ken started around the corner, the others eagerly following, with Jim sticking to Tania's coattails. The targets were about eight metres away, so intent on their business that they didn't notice the newcomers until Ken had reduced that gap to two metres.

"Hello, my friends," said Ken, in a low voice. "What do we have going on here?"

"Eh? Wassat? Who're you?" said one of the four, swaying uncertainly. He had a spliff in one hand and a can of lager in the other.

"What the fuck is this?" said another.

A third – who was steadier on his feet and held several small bags of a powdery substance in his hands, looked about sharply. "Fuck!" And with that he was off.

But Ken was close and started to move too; he caught the man in six steps and swept his feet from under him. Meanwhile, the rest of the group closed to form a circle around the three who remained. Tania took the lead. "Right, you little shits, hand over your gear and fuck off."

"What's that? What? Fuck! Get your own!" said the first.

"Wrong answer!" said Adam. He stepped close and applied his device, at which the junkie let out a shriek and toppled to the ground.

One of the others stared dumbly at the scene in a semi-comatose state, while the third turned and made to run… but didn't get far: Keri moved remarkably quickly for someone of her dimensions, flattening the man in a crunching rugby tackle.

Jim looked around to see Ken frog-marching the dealer back to the others, having already swiped his gear from him. The man on the ground stopped spasming but was disinclined to get up. As Tania held her bat against the chest of the dumbstruck man, Keri roughly hoisted her prey back into the huddle.

"Search them!" demanded Ken – an order with which the others enthusiastically complied.

At last, the four men were on their feet, sullen and frightened, encircled by the vigilantes, with Jim standing a little further back, looking on the scene in – shock? Excitement?

Ken addressed the men: "You know who we are, yeah? Well, this is your first and only warning. The other side of the river is clean, and as of now, so is here. We catch you lot dealing or fucking about around here again, there'll be real trouble. Now, piss off!"

The group was on an adrenalin high on their return back over the water – even Jim.

"How was that, GM?" asked Tania, taking him by the arm.

"Uh, yeah, great. I didn't think you'd go that far but… great."

As they took the Duke Street bridge over the river, Ken tossed the purloined drugs into the Wensum. They continued on through the Lanes until they reached St Giles Street – apparently the Knights' regular route – which took them out of the centre. On the way, they walked over a variety of pavement plaques, including one that depicted a rather large hypodermic syringe…

***

Robert Quigley found himself on the steps of City Hall again, the weather even colder than last time, his jumper more threadbare and itchier. And this time, he didn't have the support of Stan and Emily, who'd each made improbable excuses about having to be somewhere else today (*a party for your son's friend's dog, Emily? Really?*). But he couldn't and wouldn't blame them: they were good people, who'd already done enough – indeed, more than enough, which was why, rather than having two colleagues with him, he now had about a dozen.

"You need to advertise a bit more," Stan had told him. "Give a bit of forewarning. Make yourself seem more serious. Maybe then, you'll get that vengeful lot of Commandos off your back."

Thus, he'd placed a small ad in the *Eastern Daily Press*, and a couple more in free local guides, and this was the result. He'd actually been contacted by more than twice the number around him now, but some hadn't been able to make it today, while others had been from the press, checking on his plans. So, not only had the number of Primark Penitent grown, but the media scrum had too. Sally Jones was there for the BBC, along with other familiar local faces. In addition to these, there were a couple from the national press, a reporter for a Christian evangelical publication, and even a journalist from Belgium. He'd gone international!

They weren't due to set off for another five-to-ten minutes, so Robert turned to consider those around him. There was a fairly even split of men to women, ranging from a woman in her twenties to a man in his seventies, although most were in their forties and fifties. The nearest was a middle-aged woman in a fluffy pink jumper that looked rather more stylish than his brief had recommended. As he appraised her, she gave a shiver and smiled back. "Hello."

"Ah, hello…?"

"Judith. I'm Judith."

"Hello, Judith. What… why are you here today?"

The woman was leaning on a placard, its face turned towards her.

"Well, you see, I've been accused of stealing milk from the communal fridge at work…" She had a thought, and turned the placard around. It declared: 'Milk thief!' "It's all got rather bitter. I've been sent to Coventry!"

"Right. So, you didn't steal the milk?"

"No! Of course not! I…." Her shoulders sagged. "Who am I kidding? Yes, of course I did. It was only a little. At first, I thought no one would notice. Then it became a habit. I mean, no one said anything – until they did." She frowned, but then firmed her shoulders. "So, yes, I *deserve* this. Thank you, Robert, for giving me this chance."

"I'm sure they will forgive you now," said Robert. And suddenly, he realised that all of the others were watching them, having gathered around in a tight semi-circle (probably to gain from each others' body warmth as much as anything else). He broadcast a smile. "Ah… and thank you all for coming. I don't know who…"

"I'm Paul," said the nearest man, accepting the invite. "Overcharged for a gardening job. Feel a bit of a shit now. Poor old lady had a funny turn afterwards. Had to call the ambulance, but she's okay now."

"Ah," said Robert, "I understand."

"And I'm Denzel," said a middle-aged black man. "I've been lying to mum. She means well, and only wants to see me, but, you know, she's a bit boring. Old ways. Always criticising. But I should be more tolerant…"

And so they continued with their brief stories: there were a couple who'd made indelicate remarks that had gotten them into hot water with their employers; a couple more who'd had indiscretions while being in their cups; someone who'd surreptitiously raided their kid's piggybank to pay for a takeaway and then not repaid the money; and someone who'd pissed in the front garden of an annoying neighbour.

The last confessant was a slim man in his thirties in a filthy grey jumper covered in mud, which had probably been applied that morning. "Me? I'm Nigel." The man hefted his placard in two hands, causing the others to pull away. The placard said: 'I'm just sorry, OK!' "I'm not sure what I've done, but I'm sure I've probably done *something* at *some time*. And *someone* is going to find out *someday* when they delve into my various electronic postings. So, here I am: consider it a pre-emptive strike."

It surprised Robert, at first, though maybe it shouldn't have. He mentioned it to his wife later, back home.

"Hmmm, that's a good idea," Jane replied. "Like getting an indulgence. I'm planning on giving Sandra a few choice words next time we meet, the selfish witch. Maybe I'll join your next march to get my punishment sorted early."

"Next march?" Robert huffed. "There's not going to be a next march."

She gave him one of her knowing smiles. "Of course not, dear. But when you do decide on the next date you're *not* going to march on, please check with me first, eh? I'll keep my diary clear just in case..." she giggled, "*Saint Robert.*"

Saint Robert? *Absurd!*

But at work the next day, Robert found himself not only less of a pariah than previously, but also something of a celebrity.

After leaving a meeting with his line manager, Margaret, in which she'd treated him with unusual respect, and almost as an equal, he nipped to the loos – not because he needed to *go*, but because it was a place where (he hoped) he could find five minutes to himself.

As the toilet was empty, he rested his hands on the sink and looked into the mirror.

Saint Robert?

He smiled.

Back home that evening, he started to plan his next event.

***

"Thomas Browne's *Scrubbers!*" exclaimed Doris. "So, we're scrubbers now, are we?"

They were squeezed around the biggest table in the Merchant House, a café on Fye Bridge Street with a pleasant interior of bookcases, greenery, and bric-a-brac. And it was a squeeze, too, for the group's number had grown to a round dozen, although today there were just nine present to discuss the cleaning of the latest victims of the Krustie Brigade (the statues of Samson and Hercules in Tombland) and the media's response to this.

"Well, you do wield scrubbing brushes," said her husband, Ronnie, trying and failing to control a smirk. "So, they are *technically* correct."

"But so do you! And after your interview on *Look East*, the media referred to you – to us! – as Thomas Browne's *Boys*."

"And that's how they referred to us in the TV interview with you last night," sighed Colin. "It's the difference between mainstream media and this social media nonsense. No one can control what people write on Twitter, Facebook, Bingo-Bongo, or whatever else is out there now."

"Yes, but the *EDP* doesn't need to report the rubbish those people write," said Annie, sharing her friend's outrage. With one wrinkled finger she tapped a copy of the offending paper that lay on the table in front of her. "It's sexism, that's what it is. When a man is the mouthpiece, we're noble, but when it's a woman, we're cast as a load of common-as-muck cleaners. It's a disgrace."

"Yes, dear," sighed husband Colin. "I agree, but what can we do?"

"Well, in this case, we can write to the *EDP*," said Doris. "Ask them to apologise and be more respectful in future."

"That's a good idea," said Margery, who happened to be Doris' sister-in-law. "And we should all sign it."

"Yes, good idea," said Colin, in a voice suggesting he believed exactly the opposite. "I'm sure a letter signed by our small cabal will terrify them into a profuse apology."

But Ronnie was less circumspect. "Actually, Col, we are a bit of a force now. I mean, we're not nobodies. We have *presence*. They might well listen. Doris may have a point." He smiled at his wife: it never harmed to stay in her good books.

"And not just us twelve," continued Margery, the most enthusiastic of their new recruits. "There are a lot of people like us who might not like running around with buckets and mops, but who support us in spirit."

"Like John?" grinned Colin. John was Margery's husband – Doris' brother – and he'd been decidedly lukewarm about matters, if not downright mocking.

"Yes. Even John would sign," asserted Margery, crossing her arms in front of her chest, "if he knew what was good for him."

Ronnie was now nodding in thought and looking beyond assuring himself a nice dinner tonight. He tapped his friend on the forearm. "John would. And so would everyone at your Conservative Club."

"And our book reading circle," said Doris.

"And we have lots more acquaintances, some quite senior people," concluded Ronnie. "We could make it like one of these open letters that stroppy academics post in *The Times* or *The Guardian* when they think no one is listening to them. I'm happy to write it, if everyone can start gathering names of people who'll sign in support."

Doris smiled at him, but Colin frowned: "And what would this letter say? Stop calling us scrubbers?"

"Among other things. We could set out a kind of manifesto. Tell people why it's importance to keep the city clean. Retain our heritage. Fight vandalism. And, sure, say something about the disrespect and, yes, *sexism* in some of the media commentary."

"You mean," concluded Colin, "try to bully them to do what we want?"

"Well, that seems to be the way of the world these days," said Doris.

Now Colin nodded. "Well, in that case, I'm all for it. Let's turn the tables on these bounders!"

***

"Heh, heh," chuckled Blitz, with glee. "Those scrubbers won't be able to clean this one up so easily."

The crew were on Opie Street, a short thoroughfare that connected Castle Meadow – which ran beneath Norwich castle – and the pedestrianised London Street, which it joined a few metres up from the elegant Cosy Club. Blitz and Skid had clambered up the iron-grilled gate of the property next door and then onto the roof of the single-storey Café Gelato, on which there was a statue of a cape-and-bonnet-wearing young woman, gazing off in the direction of the cathedral. Meanwhile, Mags and

Mary were at ground level, at opposite ends of the street, keeping a look out. It was three in the morning.

"Yeah," agreed Skid, as he added a bit of green to the statue's face, "those crumblies won't be able to get up here without a Stannah stairlift. But who is this bird?"

"Dunno – but she looks white and privileged," said Blitz. "I'll bet her parents were loaded. Probably owned a sweatshop and had hundreds of servants." He reached down to pick up his special red cannister and signed off with his customary tag. "There!" He leant back: "That's you sorted, *bitch*. Let's scram."

Later, the gang clustered around a TV in Mags' flat off Vauxhall Street.

"… and there's outrage in Norwich tonight," declared Rachel Kettleborough on the *Look East* news at 6.30p.m., "at the vandalism of another of the city's statues. Sally has the story… *Sally?*"

"Fucking yeah!" said Blitz.

Mags and Skid whooped and high-fived.

"Yes, Rachel, I'm here in the centre of Norwich, which has suffered a spate of vandalism over recent weeks. But last night's attack has left the city in shock. With me is local historian, Andrew Reeves, to explain why. *Andrew?*"

The camera pulled back, allowing the graffitied statue to be seen up high, before focusing again on a portly, grey-bearded man standing beside Sally, leaning over her microphone as though it was an ice cream he was about to lick. "Yes, Sally, the statue is of Amelia Opie, a local woman who was a Quaker and a writer. But importantly, she was also involved in politics, particularly in the anti-slavery movement."

"What the fuck!" exclaimed Blitz, suddenly less sure of himself.

"Anti-slavery?" repeated Sally.

"That's right. She helped create the Ladies Anti-Slavery Society in Norwich, which organised a petition to parliament that gained nearly two hundred thousand signatures. And she wrote about the subject too, such as in her 1826 anti-slavery poem, *The Black Man's Lament.*"

"So, this act of desecration is really quite sinister?"

"Aye," said Andrew, "whoever did this is either a massive racist or deeply ignorant of the city's history…"

"Racist!" said Skid, from his place on a cigarette-burned sofa.

"Ignorant!" spluttered Mary, sat beside him.

"... and I have little doubt that the vandals would rather the street had retained its former name and character," continued Andrew, now with a twinkle in his eye.

Sally fell into the trap. "Really? So the name is relatively modern?"

"Relatively," agreed Andrew, trying to stop his treacherous mouth from gurning. "Its name was changed to Opie Street in the 1860s. Before then, it was known as Gropecunt Lane – because of the prostitution, you see."

"Grope..." Sally visibly whitened – in much the same way as Blitz did a couple of kilometres away – "er, yes, thank you, Andrew." She turned back to the camera: "And with that, it's back to the studio!"

The picture on the TV screen returned to Rachel Kettleborough, whose eyes were wide, staring into the camera. Someone must have then given her a prompt through an earpiece, for she suddenly shivered into life, manufactured a sickly smile, and began her introduction to the next section...

Back in Mags' flat, the vandals struggled to process what they had heard.

"Racist!" repeated Skid.

"Ignorant!" repeated Mary.

"Fuck!" exclaimed Blitz.

"Gropecunt," giggled Mags...

***

Cathy enjoyed strolling around the city in her stylish rainbow headgear: not only was she making an important statement in support of her community, but she also looked damned good too; she'd even been complimented on her attire during a generally positive public response. Indeed, in the months since starting the unit, their Commando patrols had frequently been approached by friendly people for a chat – whether by persons from the community itself, or by well-meaning others, who were generally well-spoken and middle-aged. And until now, there'd not been a hint of confrontation – which hadn't really surprised Cathy as, in her experience, the Parade incident had been a one-off, and nothing like the abuse and occasional violence that some of the older members of the group had described from their past. Harry in particular had some harrowing stories from when he was a student in London in the 90s, which made it all the more surprising that he was far more tolerant than half-his-age Clare, whose worst experiences had been occasional insults, name-calling and 'looks' (which she always interpreted as judgmental).

So, today – a fine-if-nippy January day at the end of a fine, rain-free week – Cathy was hoping for more of the same. With her this day were Steve and Manny, who were usually good company, although they were presently in an 'off' phase of their relationship, which didn't seem to affect the irrepressibly camp Manny, but which made Steve snippy. After a leisurely tour of the centre, they went to the Greenhouse Trust on Bethel Street – an environmental art gallery and second-hand bookshop, which served veggie food and coffee. They stayed there longer than planned, gossiping with the clientele and staff, and only left – reluctantly – after Clare turned up and made a pointed remark about the streets of Norwich being left unprotected.

An hour or so later, they found themselves on the bridge on Duke Street, having passed the St Andrews multi-storey car park, with the Premier Inn ahead. As they ambled, they heard voices from behind. Cathy turned to see a troop of six people striding towards them: four male, two female, all scruffy, and moving with purpose. She tapped Manny and Steve on the arm, indicating that they should move closer to the railing to allow the others to pass, and then she gave an uncertain smile at the newcomers.

The leader of the group saw Cathy and slowed.

"Ow – fuck, mate," came a cry from the man behind. "What are you–?"

"Shut it, Zed. *Look!*"

"What?"

The first man – who wore an old, green jacket with a torn pocket and a baseball cap – didn't answer immediately. He continued forwards at half steam, with his company now bunched behind him. When he was a metre away, he announced to the world: "So, what have we got here? More vigilantes?"

"Vigi-*what?*" said the second man – unshaven and wearing a stained hoody. "These?"

"What the fuck are they wearing?" said a third.

"Reckon you'd look good in one of them," cackled one of the women, who was probably in her late twenties, but could have easily passed for someone in their mid-forties.

"Fuck off, Beth!"

"Er, hello?" said Cathy.

But Manny, being Manny, edged in front. "Are you dissing our berets?" He placed one hand on a hip and beamed. "Or admiring them? You can look, but not touch!"

"Touch?" repeated the first man, looking Manny up and down. "You telling me what to do?" His truculence rose a notch to anger. "You giving me orders? You *laughing* at me?"

Manny's expression turned uncertain. "Hey, guy, I'm just–"

"Just *what*? Just taking the piss? You and your lot, trying to run us out of town."

"Er, mate," said the third man, who wore a bobble hat, "I don't think this is the same–"

"They're all the same!" growled the leader. "All cunts. All part of the establishment."

"Really, mate, I think–"

But the leader had ratcheted himself into a rage and wasn't willing to listen. He stepped forwards and grabbed the beret from Manny's head, hurling it into the Wensum. Then, he shoved the stunned man aside and reached for the beret on Cathy's head. She cowered back and raised her arms defensively – in a posture unknown to the martial arts world into which Clare had inducted all her Commandos. She flapped about, but was unable to resist the man, who soon had her beret and a bunch of hair too. The second beret was whizzed into the water to follow the first.

"Stop – stop!" cried Steve, with one hand clutching his own beret.

"Mate!" cried one of the rough squad.

"Jonno!" cried another.

"No – fuck 'em," said the fourth man, who'd not spoken until now. He used the opportunity to sneak a punch into Manny's ribs, doubling him up.

But the altercation was quickly over. Steve's beret joined the others in a watery grave, and he got a thump in the eye to boot. Cathy and Manny held their hands up as they got frisked by the fourth man and the woman called Beth, losing purses and wallets. And then the assault team was off, at a lope, leaving Cathy and her shocked party in their wake.

They dithered as to whether to go to the police or the Greenhouse Trust, both of which lay on Bethel Street. In the end, they decided on the latter, just in case their leader was still present – as she was.

Clare was incandescent: "They want a war," she spat, "the homophobic bastards! Well, we'll give 'em one!"

Chapter 22: The Incredulous

Although the whole gang had been in Norwich when Tom sent his emails after his latest encounter with Smith, finding a meeting time that was convenient for all had proven difficult. In the end, they'd settled for a rendezvous at the Rose for the second Tuesday quiz of the year.

"Thomas, old fruit, you're looking well. Santa been kind to you this year?"

"Hi, Ed. So-so. Usual collection of jumpers…" Tom stood over a seated Ed, indicating the pale blue V-neck he currently wore beneath his heavy winter coat. "What about you?"

"Don't actually know. My parents divorced ages ago and live at opposite ends of the country. In order to show no favouritism, I didn't visit either of them. I suspect, like you, there are various parcels of woollen products still awaiting my attention under trees that should have been taken down days ago."

Tom set his pint upon the small table and sat. "Ah, right. So, where did you spend Christmas?"

"Right here in Norwich, in my flat. Booze and boxsets and not a screaming, ungrateful child in sight. Bliss! Ah, Amanda… and Simon. Arriving together? What is this? At last accepted your true feelings for each other?"

"Same old Ed," muttered Simon, chivalrously pulling out a chair for Amanda. "Anyone need a top up? No? Amanda?"

"Yes, please. You choose." As Simon stole to the bar, Amanda settled into her chair and smiled at the others. "So, here we are agai–"

"*Fuck!* Sorry, Amanda babes, but look who just rocked up."

Amanda and Tom turned to face where Ed was looking. What they saw was a clutch of individuals piling around a table in the corner. As these began to divest themselves of their coats, a uniformity of black t-shirts was revealed.

"Terminus Est," hissed Ed. "*Wankers!* They've come to assert their dominance and steal our beer vouchers."

"We don't have any vouchers for them to steal," said Amanda. They'd been second on their last visit.

"Well, that's because you lot need to up your education. I can't do it all by myself." Ed was still intent on the others. Their obese, black-bearded leader took his seat, his team forming in orbit about him. "Five," he declared. "They're one short. Tom – what's up?"

Tom had flinched at the sight of the others. He turned back to his comrades and scrunched down. "That one at the end recognised me. The one with the nose."

"The chap that looks like an ex-boxer? Eh-up, he does, too. They're all looking over here now. Tom – what did you do?"

"Nothing! It was in October, I think, when I was on patrol. I mentioned it before."

"Did you?"

"I remember," said Amanda. "It was that time you also bumped into Martin. You mentioned it when we were looking at the CCTV shots from outside the beer festival."

"Well remembered, Mands!" exclaimed Ed. "Not just a pretty face."

"Well, now I remember something else, too," continued Tom. "When I bumped into him, I mentioned this place and said I knew his team, but he said he'd never been to this quiz."

"I suspect he was telling porkies. Aaaaand here's Si."

Simon set a pint down in front of Amanda, then settled into the fourth seat around the small table. He followed the direction of his friends' surreptitious glancing, noted the presence of Terminus Est, frowned, and slumped down. He smiled briefly at Amanda's expression of gratitude, then returned to frowning. "More secret plotting, I see."

"Nope," said Ed. "Just sizing up the enemy and casting aspersions at Augustus P. Samson and his crew. It seems that Tom does know one after all. And... *fuck me sideways!*"

The missing sixth person joined the team. He wore a green fleece over his t-shirt and had a small goatee. He rather gave the game away with a quick glance over to their table and a little smile.

"What is it, Ed?" asked Tom.

"Him!" Now it was Ed's turn to scrunch down and draw the others into a huddle. "That guy. He's in one of my camera clips from outside the Alex at our last meeting before Christmas. More than that, he's the main oddity."

"What do you mean?" asked Amanda.

"Well, you know I said I have a mate with face recognition software? I got hold of a copy and ran all the punters through it. I couldn't find a couple of the oldsters, probably because they have no online presence and are still using sundials and abacuses to negotiate life. Others were local. This dude stood out. *Bryson Masters.* Lives somewhere out in Thorpe. He had no business being in our neck of the woods."

"So, that's now three of their team we've encountered," said Tom, "and at least two are suspicious. Samson was at the beer festival, and this guy Bryson was spying on us outside the Alex. But what does it mean?"

"It means," declared Ed, portentously, "that we are not the only game in town, and this lot of herberts are up to something. And though they may be onto *us*, we are now definitely onto *them*. Doesn't it get your juices tingling?"

"*More* players?" said Tom, with an unhappy shake of the head. "On top of Martin and Keith? And the others that Simon knows – Teresa and Ricky? Are you suggesting they're *all* up to something?"

"It does appear to be a crowded marketplace," agreed Ed.

"But what *are* they up to?" wondered Amanda. "Do they all have alien overseers? And if so, are they good or bad? I mean, why would they all be on the side of the manipulators? Maybe Terminus Est are just like us–?"

"I am *nothing* like that fat git," exclaimed Ed, indignantly. "In any case, all three of these cliques had members at the festival. If any are a force for good, why didn't they stop the riot?"

"Maybe they just happened to be at the festival to drink, like you guys?" said Simon.

"I don't believe in that degree of coincidence. It's like the football scores. If it looks like a pig, smells like a pig, and squeals like a pig, then it's most probably a pig. And lard-arse Samson definitely fits all three of these criteria."

"Quizzing tonight, people?" They were interrupted by one of the quizmasters, bearing sheets of paper.

Ed gave an absent nod and beckoned to be given the papers, setting these onto the table without giving them a second glance. The quizmaster frowned uncertainly and headed to the next table.

Tom was the first to continue. "Ah, yes, and this kind of brings me on to why I wanted to meet. I, ah, think I have found out how Smith moves about. And now I wonder whether others like us might do the same. And that could explain how they got into the festival and away without being seen. *Tunnels.*"

"You mentioned before that Smith said there was a tunnel between St Peter Mancroft and the Guildhall," said Amanda, whose memory was ever-sharp.

"Yes, I did. But now I have actually found an entrance. I was in the castle, doing a patrol, and in one of the lower levels I found an alien symbol by a hidden door..." Tom quickly related his tale.

"But where did the passage lead?" asked Amanda.

"Ah, well, I didn't get far. I wasn't really equipped and, er, there was a... well... anyway... I did some internet searches when I got back home, and there's all sorts of rumours about tunnels at the Castle, St Peter's, the Guildhall, the Cathedral... *and* the St Andrew's and Blackfriars' Halls."

"So you stumbled on a way into the network," mused Ed. "Interesting."

"Yes, and there's more. When I contacted Smith to update him, you'll never guess where he had us meet this time?"

"Somewhere near the beer festival venue?" mused Ed.

"Exactly! He came from St Andrew's Church – exactly the place we saw the *Big Issue* seller heading to in your CCTV shots. I'm now convinced it was him we saw in the video."

"And so that makes four at the scene of the crime," said Ed. "The brethren over there, Teresa *sans* Ricky, young Martin, and now Smith. Curiouser and curiouser."

Simon had been following the discussion with a frown, looking between the trio, who seemed to be magnetically drawn together and essentially pulled away from him. "You should have gone to the end of the tunnel, Tom, then we might have known for sure. Why did you turn back?"

Tom looked sheepish. "Ah, well, I saw another ghost."

"Another!" gasped Amanda. "What was it this time?"

"Not Lord Sheffield again," grinned Ed. "I thought he only haunted the cludgie at the Adam and Eve. Or do you think you've now got yourself a post-corporeal alien stalker?"

"No, this was a floating head!"

"Ghosts?" said Simon. "Lord Sheffield? The Adam and Eve?"

Amanda's eyes widened and she quickly broadcast concerned looks to Tom and Ed.

"Er, yes," said Tom.

Simon pushed himself backwards in his chair. "You haven't mentioned this before. To me anyway. But I see you all know what he's talking about. It seems part of a pattern."

"Pattern?" said Ed, with raised eyebrows. "I'm not sure what you mean, old chap."

"The pattern of you lot trying to ease me out. Exclude me. Since Tom joined us, you three have been very chummy and secretive."

"Si – it's not like that," said Amanda.

"Isn't it?"

"A lot of this stems from our trip to the beer festival, my friend," said Ed. "We invited you to join us, but you were too busy playing pin the *Grrrk-lok-aaah* on the Klingon. And when we met up after to discuss it, we didn't tell you as we didn't think you'd have much to add."

"Yeah, still, an invite would have been nice. Anyway, it's not just that. There was that time Tom spray painted that mural, and now you're talking about ghosts as though it's a familiar subject – something you've clearly discussed before without me."

Ed nodded absently: he was still distracted by the presence of their foe, his eyes constantly wandering to their table rather than focusing on Simon, and so he was perhaps less careful than he ought to have been. "Look, it's not personal, Si, but we've had proper things to discuss. There is more to life than the fantasy in your head."

Simon tensed up. "What does that mean?"

"Eh?" Ed seemed to realise that he'd inadvertently spoken out loud. He tried to reclaim the initiative with a smirk. "Oh. *You know.* You have such a vivid imagination. Elves. Tribbles. Vampires. Bug-eyed monsters from the planet Blatto living under your bed."

"I still don't see what you're getting at."

"Oh, come on, Si. *Vortenf?* Really? There is some serious shit going down, and all you can talk about is disintegrating cows and aliens with a fetish for sticking poles up your jacksy!"

"I don't! I've never talked about these things… well, maybe once… but…" Ed's gentle smile was infuriating – at least to Simon. "Oh… *fuck you!*" Simon was suddenly on his feet, and without another word, he turned and stalked through the room to the exit.

For a moment, the remaining three sat in stunned silence. Predictably, it was Ed who recovered first. "Bugger," he said. "That's all we need – especially with the *Terminators* back in town. He could have at least waited until after the music round."

"Ed!" gasped Amanda.

Tom looked down in embarrassment.

"Okay, okay," sighed Ed, raising his hands in a kind of surrender. "My bad! I'll email him later and try to sort this out. Bake up a nice big humble pie on which to gorge. Buy him a *Buffy* figurine from somewhere as reparations."

"Maybe we should, well, bring him in on everything," said Tom. "What harm could it do? I mean, I doubt whether he's going to run off and tell his other friends or the media."

"Yes," said Amanda, determinedly. "We definitely should – even if Vortent isn't real. So, when you arrange to meet him, let's all be there."

"Very well," sighed Ed. "Matters are getting so involved and advanced maybe it is time to be more open about our masters and their whims, and sod it if our activities are noted. But let's focus on the quiz now we're here, eh?"

Needless to say, they didn't win.

***

"Right, I'm here," said Simon, sniffily. "What do you want?" It was a Thursday lunchtime, two days after the quiz, and they were in The Mischief – a large and often boisterous pub on Fye Bridge Street, which was quiet at this hour. They'd chosen this time and place to accommodate Simon, who was the only one of them with a proper job, or rather, *jobs*, as he worked part-time at a comic shop on St Benedicts Street and at a café on Magdalen Street, and The Mischief lay somewhere in between.

Tom and Amanda looked at Ed, encouraging him to take the lead with their eyes. Ed gave an exaggerated sigh. "Very well," he muttered, before focusing on their fellow conspirator and quiz teammate. "Take a seat, Si. We need to clear the air."

"Is that it? Take a seat?"

"Look, Simon, I'm sorry, old chap. I took it too far. But we do need to have a serious chat."

Simon hesitated, clearly wanting to sit, and mollified somewhat at receiving the first apology from Ed that any there had ever heard, but unsure as to whether that marked sufficient contrition. "Chat... about what? About me being a stupid *Trekkie*?"

"Don't make this harder than it needs to be, Si. Look, I got you a drink. And I promise, I won't mock you too much. At least, not today."

Tom smiled and tried to inject some levity. "It's a good offer, Si. Please accept it, or he'll take it out on me and Amanda."

Simon's mouth wriggled with contesting emotions, but his eyes had now found the full pint of ale awaiting him. He pulled out the chair in front of him and scootched in, homing in on the vulnerable glass. "Okay. I'll sacrifice myself. Landlord? Excellent!" He took a drink, then looked between the party sat around two sides of the table. "Right. Go on, then. What's this about?"

"For starters?" said Ed. "It's about Vortent."

"What about Vortent?"

The three looked at each other, wondering who should take on the challenge, but Ed had the floor, so he continued after a pause: "He's... *not real*, is he?"

Simon looked dumbfounded. "I don't know what you mean. He's as real as Big Ed, Sheila, and Smith – if that's what you mean."

Amanda now intervened, speaking softly: "Well, Simon, that's just it. I know you *think* we're playing a game, but we're *not*. Right from the beginning, Ed and I were never entirely sure of *your* story and how much of what you said was legitimate. You remember how we first met up after Ed's advert, and we were all very cagey and no one wanted to say too much, or challenge too hard?"

"Uh, yeah, I remember." Simon frowned, clearly confused by what the woman was implying.

"Well, I think when Tom joined the group that kind of clarified matters for us. When Tom spoke about Smith, the things he said made sense to us, in a way that the things you've said about Vortent haven't."

"I understand him too," blustered Simon.

"No, Simon, I don't think you do," continued Amanda. "Our handlers are *real*. *Really* real, in a way we suspect Vortent isn't. I mean, you've never been clear about what he gets you to do, and sometimes it's seemed to be a copycat of what one of has said, or else it's been fantastical."

Ed nodded: "Your story about *anal probing* kind of broke the camel's back, my friend."

Simon looked at the others, sweeping his gaze across them, not sure on whom to focus. In the end, it was Amanda. "I haven't said much because we *agreed* not to say much. Not to give the game away. Plausible deniability. And the anal probing stuff, well, that was just a joke."

"Joke?" Ed frowned. "*You?*"

"Yeah. You're not the only one with a sense of humour, you know. I was just playing along. You thought I was serious?"

"So… Vortent hasn't got you protecting farms from alien pranksters and cow-haters?" said Amanda. "Or stopping them from making crop circles?"

"No! Well, not the cows bit, but *yes* the circles bit. It's all about messaging, isn't it?"

Tom looked between his three companions. He noticed Ed and Amanda staring at each other, confused, maybe even troubled.

At last, Ed spoke: "So, Si, are you saying Vortent *is* real? *Really* real? As real as, well, this fine pint of ale? So real that, if he were here, I could tweak his nose or give him a Glasgow kiss?"

"Well, I don't know about that. I've never physically met him. He appears as a hologram in the back of the comic store, wearing a cowl, vaguely human shaped. But I already told you this when the three of us first met, and then when Tom joined us. Are you saying you've disbelieved me all along?"

Amanda, as the most diplomatic, took up the challenge. "I guess we have. It's just that Vortent… because of his name, and the way he appears, has always seemed to us like a, well, comic book invention. Do you see what I mean?"

"Maybe that's to be expected?" suggested Tom, cautiously.

"What do you mean?" asked Amanda.

"Well, perhaps the aliens simply take advantage of our expectations… our circumstances. Look, Ed's a hacker, so Big Ed speaks to him through his computer. You're a blogger, so Sheila kind of does the same. Smith approached me through the Cloud, but maybe because I've always been a bit circumspect about the net and all that, he realised he needed to present a physical form to me, and a *Big Issue* seller is a good disguise if you're going to go that way. With Si, maybe it's not a surprise that he uses a comic book persona."

"You might be onto something there," conceded Ed. "But… Si, really? Even though we've had this policy of not saying too much, you've said almost nothing about your activities for months. I thought you'd run out of improbable things to say."

"It's because I've *had* little to say. As I said, *crop circles*. That's his main concern, and they're seasonal. I've not spoken to him for three months, and we might not speak for three months more. He has me chart their appearance and sometimes sabotage them. Have you heard about any recently, in the barren winter fields?"

Ed nodded slowly. "Okay. And the anal probing was a joke? And the cow molesting – that too?"

Now Simon looked a touch sheepish. "Well, yeah, I haven't always had much to say – I mean, I've never had anywhere near the amount of action Tom has been getting – so I used to embellish just a little, and it kind of got out of hand."

"So…" Ed arched an eyebrow. "You are at least *partly* to blame for our *perfectly understandable* mistrust?"

"Ed!" said Amanda. "Don't try shifting responsibility here."

Ed smiled and raised his hands. "Course not, Mands." And then he leant forwards and slapped Simon on the arm. "I accept all blame, from now and forever more. Does that mean we are good? Or do you want me to grovel some more?"

Simon smiled. "Maybe just a little. But what I most want is to hear about what you've been up to and what you've been keeping from me. That would be a good start."

"That is fair. While I get in another round – including another penance pint, Si, so keep your hands away from your pockets – Tom can fill you in. He's the one chin-deep in all of this."

And so Tom reprised all that had happened to him over the last few months, including his incidents at the Pottergate underpass and the Cathedral, his encounters with ghosts, the various messages he'd seen, and the meetings he'd had with Smith. Occasionally, Simon asked a question or laughed.

At the end of Tom's narration, Simon looked between his colleagues. "And you thought *my* stories were improbable?" He slowly shook his head and sighed. "Anyway, where does this leave us now? You've implied that these incidents are somehow multiplying and worsening, but I'm not sure I see that."

"I think it's a combination of things," said Ed. "Maybe it's no surprise that Vortent hasn't said anything to you, given his focus, but Big Ed has also been concerned at the increased chatter on the internet and dark web. There are a lot of angry and determined people out there. Haven't you noticed all these groups of psychos that have sprung up recently? Vigilantes. Vandals. Counter-vandals."

Simon nodded. "Yeah, people in Norwich have been acting a bit weird recently. What about Sheila?" He turned to look at Amanda. "Has she said anything?"

"Kind of. Mostly, she has me countering false ecological information and giving positive advice, which doesn't just relate to Norwich and East Anglia, but more generally. You know, piggybacking on my contacts with the Environmental Sciences department at UEA. But there is one area of concern – something she's alluded to a couple of times – which recent incidents have made me think about. She said she was concerned about the new, er, 'Norwich Vegan Republic'."

"Vegan Republic!" exclaimed Ed. "What Vegan Republic?"

"I didn't know what she was talking about, but something from your research, Ed, and from what Simon said, got me thinking about this woman, Teresa."

"Ricky's girlfriend, yeah," confirmed Simon. "She's a radical. I don't especially like Ricky, but the poor guy is constantly nagged about his diet."

"No wonder he has a face like a smacked arse in all the pictures I've managed to find," said Ed. "But that's just one woman – hardly a republic."

"No, true," said Amanda. "But someone mentioned that gaming vegan place, called Slice and Dice. I was passing it on Benedicts Street the other day and… you do realise that the whole area is virtually a vegan enclave, don't you? There's a vegan shop. There's the Tipsy Vegan restaurant. And if you've explored the streets and shops around, it's amazing how many places do vegan food. *Only* vegan food. Try getting a non-vegan sausage roll anywhere in the Lanes – you've no chance. It's like an anti-meat epicentre."

"Ground zero," nodded Simon.

"Yes, now you mention it, I've noticed the spread of this cancer too," said Tom. "But I don't know why Sheila would be concerned. Surely, this is what she wants? Isn't veganism good for the planet? Lower carbon something or other? Surely she ought to be encouraging it?"

"Fewer farting cows," nodded Ed. "If nothing else, it would help de-stenchify the countryside."

Amanda nodded slowly. "Well, yes, that's true. The problem isn't veganism *per se*. Rather, its vegans themselves."

"Eh?" said Tom.

"Well, have you ever come across a worse advertisement for a way of life? Or worse advertisers?"

"You mean, the smug, supercilious moralising, eh?" said Ed. "As in the joke, how do you know if someone's a vegan?"

"*They tell you*," said Simon, delivering the punchline.

"Well, yes, that's pretty much it," assented Amanda. "Vegans put off more people than they convert. Without their efforts, many more people would probably try the lifestyle. Sheila is convinced of this."

"Your Sheila's not wrong there," said Ed. "Whenever I come across any of the *Holy Ones*, the first thing I look to do is find somewhere to get a burger and then return to eat it messily in front of their horrified pasty faces."

"Exactly," said Amanda. "They need to be stopped."

"Well, count me in," said Tom, who felt the same. He was intrigued by vegan food, but could never bring himself to try it, as though it might be considered a sign of surrender or a signal to any onlookers that *Here Be A Pompous Arse*. If only vegans would disappear, the world could just get on with a transition that he thought was inevitable. He reckoned within fifty years it might be the norm, and without the input of vegans, sooner than that. "But… how does that fit in with other events? And are aliens at the bottom of it?"

"I sense from Sheila that she does think there is some extra-terrestrial meddling involved. Not from a desire to harm Earth, but just to, well, make things in the city more interesting."

"So, can we expect another radical group to form to join the other crazies roaming the streets?" said Ed.

Amanda shrugged. "Your guess is as good as mine."

"But what's the end game?" wondered Tom.

"And how does the manipulation of football scores fit in?" asked Simon.

The group lapsed into silence. There was a lot to think about. A lot of fog.

At last, Amanda said: "Can any of us ask our handlers? Would any of them be straight with us? Speaking for Sheila, I think that's a 'no'. Ed – you're shaking your head. I assume Vortent is the same. What about Smith?"

Tom looked troubled. "Not only do I suspect he wouldn't help, but I also sometimes wonder what his motives truly are."

"Well, if we can't get information from our alien puppeteers," said Amanda, "where else might we find answers?"

"What about the tunnels?" said Simon. "It's something Tom was warned off, but the network seems to be used by Smith, so it's probably used by others too." He shrugged. "I don't know how that helps with the big questions, but maybe it'll help with some of the small ones. *Where? How?* You know."

Ed nodded slowly. "Si, me old mucker, I'm glad we decided to bring you in from the cold. You may have something there. How about it, Tom? Fancy a bit of subterranean exploration?"

Tom gave a sickly smile. In his mind's eye, all he could see was the floating head of the ghost of Robert Goodale.

Chapter 23: Oops, I did it (yet) again

Plans to assault subterranean Norwich were slow in forming – not least because of Tom's reluctance and consequent foot-dragging. On the one hand, he was keen on the project from a theoretical point of view, but on the other, he rather hoped that someone else might do the physical part to save him from having to risk any more ghostly encounters. He saw himself as more a Giles figure from *Buffy the Vampire Slayer* – a Watcher and mentor – as opposed to the eponymous heroine herself. In addition, Amanda had suddenly got cold feet about the expedition once she'd returned to sanity and accepted the limitations of her own claustrophobia. So, there were a number of key issues still to resolve. Who would go? When was the best time to avoid crowds in the castle? What equipment ought they to take?

One week passed, and then a second. And by this time, Alice Weidner had been in touch with Tom to discuss her own small project. Soon after, he had a new six-month contract and a nominal desk in a shared office back in his old department – one that he had absolutely no intention of using.

"Sorry, guys," he reported at an impromptu meeting at the Fat Cat pub, one Thursday evening, "this is taking all of my time at the moment. I have to help with a literature review for Alice. I haven't even managed to write much in the, um, *novel,* either."

And that was true. He'd managed just one-and-a-half chapters in the entire month, although he was quite pleased with what he'd actually composed. Goodies were suddenly bad, and baddies were good. V-Garg's machinations were being gradually uncovered, and Tim – his renamed main hero – was growing a pair and starting to become badass (*Yeah!*) – although Tom did worry a little about the credibility of this transformation. It was clear that Tim was becoming his alter ego, maturing in a way that he only wished he could.

Nevertheless, Tom did manage to largely keep up his patrolling. He continued his routine of doing potentially spooky old Norwich in daylight hours – during afternoons and weekends – and contemporary areas about which no reports of ghosts had ever been lodged during evening stints.

In the first week of February, he found himself doing one such evening patrol in a rather desultory manner, having already nipped into a couple of favourite pubs for fortifying halves. He was now heading homewards between the Forum and St Peter Mancroft – giggling to himself as he contemplated lobbing stones at the stained-glass windows and calling on Smith to come out and play. He crossed onto St Peters Street, which ran past the vast City Hall building that overbore the covered market. To his left was a sign in blue, welcoming visitors to the council building and indicating the way to the 'customer centre' entrance. Beyond this was a flight of steps that led up to three dark doorways, the foot of the steps flanked by a pair of stylised lions on plinths. A long balcony ran along the whole front of the building, fenced with blue railings, while six grand columns rose to roof level, three storeys up.

Tom vacillated at the foot of the steps, not wanting to approach the doors too closely in case this appear suspicious. It was now nearing 9p.m. and the streets were largely deserted: there was no one on St Peters, but there had been people around the Forum, and he noticed several more in the mid-distance, making their way past the Guildhall. He adjusted his glasses and peered at the doors from below the steps, but caught no telltale glare of otherworldly colour. It was probably clear.

Directly opposite the steps, across the road, was a war memorial made of Portland stone, designed by Sir Edwin Lutyens to commemorate the fallen from the First World War. This had originally faced the covered market below but had been turned around at great time and expense some years ago, after the structure on which it stood had been declared unstable. It sat at the edge of a narrow memorial garden with benches and sills, which was an ideal place to sit and eat one's purchases from the market's copious food stalls. As Tom crossed the streetlight-lit road, he almost immediately felt a prickling sensation across the back of the neck and along his scalp. *Fuck, no…*

The faint aura strengthened as he approached. He came to a halt in front of the cenotaph, which rested atop a low screen wall from which protruded a Stone of Remembrance that had gilded bronze flambeaux at either end. Beneath the city's coat of arms on the Stone, over the golden etching of 'Our Glorious Dead', lay ephemeral alien script: *Warmongers.* *Shit!*

Sudden anger surged through Tom. But anger at what? Was the message having its chilling subconscious effect on him? He scratched his nose as he thought back to the other messages he had seen – most of which seemed to have had little effect on him. At most, he experienced a sudden sense of annoyance at junkies. And… did he hold a similar view towards so-called refugees? He dampened down any further thought on *that* matter, unwilling to tread such perilous territory. And now? Well, he certainly felt angry at those who *started* wars, but not the fallen victims… surely? No. He was confident. The anger he now felt was directed at whoever or whatever had done this desecration.

Bastards!

He couldn't let this stand. No way. But… what could he do? In his backpack resided his magnets and spray can. The magnets had never worked on actually deleting messages: their power was rather in unlocking secret doors, such as that in the castle. And the paint? Tom smiled grimly to himself: twice he'd applied that, and both times ended up the subject of local news stories. He turned to look up at the façade of the council building for CCTV cameras – but saw nothing obvious. Still, there was no way he was going to apply graffiti to this sacred object in the heart of the city. Yet, he could not let this message remain: hundreds would pass the monument tomorrow on their way to work or the shops. So, what else could he do to prevent the message being seen? He stepped back and looked around…

Roadworks.

The bane of Norwich.

The council seemed to enjoy tormenting the city's motorists, mainly by closing off roads for works that then didn't start for weeks or months, and – once started – progressed at a glacial pace, invariably at the whim of a single workman with a shovel. It was rumoured to be a deliberate ploy by the Greens on the council to punish car drivers and try to force them to use alternative transport – particularly the expensive bus services. But all this did was lead to cars with idling engines sitting in traffic jams, belching out more CO_2 than they would otherwise have done. Another example, like the vegans Amanda had discussed, where the road to hell was paved with good intentions?

Tom walked to the end of St Peters Street where it joined with St Giles, at the top of Gaol Hill in front of the Guildhall. There was a temporary road sign there, along with several stacks of orange-and-white cones, ready for deployment. On spindly metal legs, the oblong yellow sign declared:

Advance Warning
Road Closed Here
3 February for 1 Week

And there was a phone number to call in case of inconvenience.

The sign was clearly intended for Gaol Hill, but it would take very little effort to move it three metres and reorientate it so that it appeared to apply to St Peters'. Could he at least deflect motorised traffic? He wasn't sure how visible the alien message would be to slow-moving car drivers, and his ploy would likely not remain uncorrected for long, but it was *something*.

Tom scoured the area for strollers, but the environs were empty – it being too late for homewards-bound revellers from pubs and restaurants, which were perhaps not best accessed via this route anyway.

For once, driven by urgency, Tom surged into action: taking hold of the sign, he started to move it – but didn't get far. The hinged bracket at the top of the sign squeaked, and the legs swung back and forth, trapping his fingers.

Owowowowow!

He dropped the sign with a clang.

Stiffened.

Frantically looked about.

Wrung his pained hand.

But he was still alone. So, he picked up the sign again and staggered on a few more metres. Dropped it. Picked it up again – with even greater nervousness. Then, he set it down and stepped away. More anxious scanning followed: but he remained alone and unobserved. *Right.* That was the big move…

Over the next five minutes, Tom edged the sign this way and that, seeking the best position to bar the road to those coming in from St Giles Street. In the end, he set it close to the junction, in the dead centre of the left-hand carriageway.

Yet, this would have minimal effect on pedestrians. But near the sign's original position was the stack of cones…

One-at-a-time, over the course of a further ten minutes, Tom ferried the cones thirty metres up the road to form a cordon around the memorial – not just on the road, but on the footpath, too. Once or twice, he stopped as he caught sight of lamp-lit passers-by at one end of the street or the other, occasionally ducking down, and once falling onto his face. But in all this time, not a single person walked down the road in front of the council building.

At last he was done. Now, any pedestrian approaching – from either direction – faced a hurdle in getting near to the tainted memorial. Tom carefully observed his handiwork from the steps of the council building, from where he was able to see no more than a smudge of *alienese*, which wasn't distinct enough to read.

Job done!

Fuck you, alien meddlers!

And best of all, nobody had seen him – no one at all! Perhaps he was getting good at this?

His heart still racing, but with a broad smile on his face, Tom turned for home. Once back, he sent a message to Smith via the Cloud about what he'd discovered and how he'd countered it, and entreated the other to deal with the matter as soon as possible. With luck, the alien would see his missive rapidly, and maybe even apply his special powers to counter the message before dawn broke.

As he lay down to sleep, just about the last coherent thought to pass through Tom's head was: *One-Nil to me!*

It was a very Norwich City score.

It was also wrong.

Tom had, metaphorically, forgotten about the second half.

***

The next morning, Tom found a response at the end of his latest Cloud-saved chapter, which simply stated: THANK YOU TOM.

Had Smith acted on his intel? Well, he'd done all he could, and the alien had provided no further instructions and hence, in his view, the case was closed. And so, in a cheery mood, Tom spent the day searching databases for relevant articles to include in the review for Alice's project, and then later wrote a page of his novel setting up Tim for more heroics

– now in Norwich, which he'd decided to substitute for London, not being particularly *au fait* with the capital anyway.

Later on, he microwaved to death a Chicken Madras meal-for-one and set this on the coffee table in his living room to watch the evening news as he ate. He'd missed the main news but was in time for *Look East* with its local stories – ironically broadcast from the BBC's studio in the Forum, a few hundred yards from where he'd performed his own heroics the night before.

"Hello, Rachel," said Tom, speaking softly to the screen. "What? Nothing about me today? What a shame!"

But he'd spoken too soon.

"And finally," declared Rachel Kettleborough, smiling gently at the camera, "more high jinks in Norwich. Amid a spate of vandalism against statues and landmarks, last night there was an attempted attack on the city's war memorial." Rachel's face disappeared to be replaced by a camera shot from up high, showing St Peters Street. "CCTV footage shows a man near the memorial, moving cones about…"

Tom started forwards, fork half-raised to mouth, knees banging into the low table. For several seconds, the announcer's words were drowned out by the sound of blood thumping in his ears as he watched a succession of clips of an indistinct figure in dark glasses, with a scarf pulled over the mouth against the cold, wearing a distinctive rucksack – *his* rucksack – moving the street sign, collecting cones, falling onto its face…

"… police say the CCTV operator had been on an extended bathroom break during the episode and missed all the live action. No actual damage was caused, which they believe may have been a result of the man being scared off before he could finish his attack on the monument…"

On the screen, Tom saw himself staring at the monument, hands on hips in satisfaction at his handiwork.

"… and enquiries are ongoing."

The fork dropped from Tom's hand, spilling rice and curried chicken all over his lap. He leapt to his feet. "No!"

Over the next few minutes, Tom gathered up his dispersed jacket, scarf and rucksack, stuffing these into a black bin bag, and then – as a temporary measure – shoving this into the bottom of a wardrobe beneath a pile of old clothes. He was tempted to throw the glasses in with them, but at the last moment retained them, pushing them deep in the back of the desk drawer in his office instead.

There'd be no patrolling this evening… or any other?

Later, he emailed his conspirators, asking for yet another urgent meeting.

***

As Tom slunk into the Fat Cat, he found his three friends already present, clustered around Ed's laptop, focusing upon it with eyes as wide as their smiles. The volume was set low, but an unmistakable tune carried to his ears – one ever-associated with *The Benny Hill Show*, an old-style slapstick comedy show that had run on terrestrial television throughout the 60s, 70s and 80s. His friends were so engrossed, they didn't even notice him standing above them. As the up-tempo *diddly-deeing* continued, first Simon, then Amanda, broke into laughter. Then Ed – sat in the middle of the party – spotted the newcomer…

"Ah, *Benny*, you're here! Take a pew!"

The others looked up: Amanda covered her mouth, while Simon grinned hugely and shook his head.

They were in the oblong-shaped annex to the pub, in the corner furthest from the doorway to the bar. This was a less-convivial space, which largely served for overspill, and consequently tended to be sparsely populated. It was for this reason that they'd agreed it was a more appropriate place to hold delicate meetings – like the one this evening – than the ever-crowded Alex.

Tom slumped onto a chair opposite the trio, his own eyes wide – darting from the laptop, to his friends, and back. "What…? What are you…?"

"Not seen this, eh?" chortled Ed. "An absolute classic, my friend. Apparently, some blighter got up to no good a couple of nights ago, mucking around at the war memorial. Some card on YouTube got hold of the televised footage, and *voila*! Instant classic! Thousands of hits already." Ed moved the laptop forty-five degrees. "Behold!" He pressed 'play' again.

On the screen, under the amused eyes of his friends, Tom watched a speeded-up edition of the CCTV footage shown on *Look East*. Indeed, the producer had somehow got hold of the entire fifteen minutes of film of Tom's activity, condensed it into a fraction of that time, and added the infamous music for effect. On the screen, Tom saw a hapless figure scurrying this way and that, collecting the sign and the cones (one-at-a-time), dropping them, falling down, looking about… Simon snorted with laughter once more, while Amanda looked away and stifled a laugh. Ed merely grinned at him.

"*Fuuuuuuuck!*" said Tom, at last.

"Tom, old fruit," sniggered Ed, "you've really got to stop doing this!" His t-shirt today was white and bore the outline of a flag that might be mistaken for that of Canada (by those unaware of the difference between a maple leaf and the foliage of *Cannabis sativa*).

"That's three out of three, isn't it?" said Simon, whose own t-shirt was plainer, simply bearing the logo of Starfleet Command. "Three strikes and you're… outta here!"

Tom gave a sickly smile. "*Shhhhh*, please!"

"Tom, you muppet!" said Ed. "You should have checked for CCTV cameras."

"I did! Well, I mean, I looked around. I didn't see anything obvious."

Ed sighed. "You'd never make a criminal mastermind, and not only because of your lack of key defining features, by which I mean, a bald pate, facial scar and strokable cat." He attacked his laptop, and after a bout of rapid typing and swiping, he nodded in satisfaction and turned the screen so Tom could see. "Hey presto! And how long did that take, old chum? A matter of seconds."

Tom peered at the screen: this showed a map of the centre of Norwich, in places with pictures of cameras in little blue boxes. "What is… what is this?"

"It's a page on the council's website. It kindly shows you everything they've installed in the city. And as you can see, there is a camera on the southern corner of the council building that provides a wide arc of coverage over St Peters Street, the area around the Forum and Mancroft, and along Bethel Street past the police station. Judging by the clips on *Look East*, it's high up, which may have saved you from being identified. And to top it off, there's a second camera on the Guildhall building at the opposite end of St Peters…" he clicked on an icon, revealing more information, "…on the rooftop. And in fact, there's a third just around the corner, on another side of the Guildhall, although that seems to look over the market place. Ah, the legend claims it's actually on Gaol Hill, so perhaps it's on a streetlight."

"And that's not all," said Simon, still bearing a wide smile. "It's not just the council that has cameras. There are lots of shops with them, too."

"Indeed, Si is right," said Ed. "So, in short, what the blazes did you think you were doing mucking about with a war memorial in the centre of the city on a school night? I think you need a chaperone, *Sir Benny*."

Tom's sickly smile returned. "I know."

"What did Smith say this time?" asked Amanda. At least she had managed to compose herself, unlike the still-gurning men. "Or haven't you told him yet?"

Tom looked miserable. "I haven't told him. Actually, no, that's not quite true. I told him about the 7D message on the memorial when I got home, and I asked him to sort it out. I said I'd, er, taken some temporary measures in the meantime. I've not told him about *this*..." he waved a hand at the laptop. His frown deepened. "But... how did you know about it? I didn't exactly tell you."

Ed laughed. "Elementary, my dear Watson. We've grown accustomed to your alerts. I suspected you'd blundered, and straightaway looked into recent news stories and quickly came to this one. And the guilty figure was easy to identify given your... jacket... rucksack... and glasses." Ed's eyes narrowed, and he nodded in approval. "Though I see you have at least had the sense to retire those incriminating items."

"Especially the specs," observed Simon. "They're a dead giveaway. Sunglasses in winter?"

Tom tensed. Over time, he'd gotten used to the glasses: at the beginning of this affair, he'd only worn them when out patrolling. But eventually, he'd found himself leaving them on when entering buildings — pubs! — to pre-empt the hassle of having to find a place to put them. He now thought back: had he been wearing them the last time he'd come here? What about in the Alex? Or the Rose? And there *was* that time when one of the bar staff — was it here? — had quipped about their inappropriateness given the dreadful weather. He hunched down and again nervously cast his gaze about. If he'd gained a reputation...?

Amanda seemed to sense the reason for his sudden consternation. She patted him on the arm. "Don't worry, Tom. I don't think anyone here will recognise you."

"Yeah, you're pretty nondescript," said Simon.

"Thanks… I think," said Tom.

"But I wouldn't wear the glasses for a little while," said Amanda. "Just in case."

"Indeed," said Ed. "Though this would seem to put the kibosh on your activities for now. At least, in the *visible* realm."

Tom could sense Ed was angling. "What do you mean? Oh…"

Simon caught the drift, too. "Yeah, that's right. No one will see you underground. Well, except for those ghosts."

"Thanks, Si," grimaced Ed. "You were doing *so* well. But seriously, Tom, old chap, when are we going caving? I am becoming increasingly intrigued by this tunnel you found. Perhaps it's time to stop pissing about and get down to business?"

Tom could feel himself being backed into a corner. "Well, yes, but my work, and…" he noticed the others smirking at him. "Oh, *bugger*. Okay. Let me think about it."

Ed suddenly stood. "Fine, old fruit. You think about it. Meanwhile, you have been sitting there without a beverage since you arrived. I will resolve that sorry state of affairs and top myself up, too. So, you've about a minute until I return. Why waste this opportunity, eh? Then we plan."

And plan they did.

***

As the party were getting up to leave at the end of the evening, with Tom's thoughts diverted from his troubles – and even feeling a frisson of excitement about their imminent expedition – Simon made a fateful remark.

"I've been wondering: what do you think Smith has done about the memorial? Do you think he's scrubbed the message?"

Tom's smile crumbled at returned remembrance of the farce outside the council building. "Well, uh… I guess I'll have to ask him. I can't tell if he's done anything unless I'm wearing my glasses, and I'm not going anywhere near the memorial for a while – with glasses or without."

A peculiar expression crossed Ed's face. "Ah, maybe you don't need to, my friend."

"What do you mean?"

"As I earlier established, there are *other* eyes on the memorial than your own."

"The CCTV cameras!" said Tom.

"Bloody hell," said Simon. "Ed… are you thinking what I'm thinking?"

"Yes, Si, I believe I am. Let me hack into the council's systems and I should be able to find out what has been done to the monument since the original desecration, and by whom."

Amanda pulled her thick, brown coat tight. "I don't like the sounds of this, Ed. More illegality?"

"Oh, come on, Amanda. It's for the greater good."

"*The greater good…*" echoed Simon, unable to resist an allusion to a scene from *Hot Fuzz.*

"Uh, not just that," said Tom, suddenly wide-eyed. "Can't you also look *before* my, um, activities? Maybe… maybe you can see who laid down the message in the first place?"

"Fucking hell, Tom, you're absolutely right!" said Ed. "Maybe this is our lucky break. You lot finalise prep for next week and leave this with me. I'm about to go hunting…"

Chapter 24: Going Underground

A couple of days after the latest emergency meeting, Tom found himself at the bench outside the Guildhall – his usual rendezvous spot with Smith. It was early afternoon, and he'd already spent an hour shopping: in his new rucksack – procured from the market – was a strong magnet picked up from Thorns for Amanda's intended use, along with several powerful torches and a compass for the breach team. So far, so good, but he was itching to get the upcoming encounter over with, particularly given the nearness of this locale to his latest debacle – with the edge of the vast council building filling one vista, and the war memorial just a short stroll away. Furthermore – now knowing where to look, thanks to the website Ed had shown him – he had spotted the Guildhall's CCTV camera: an ominous black hemisphere, like a fisheye, attached to a pole that rose from the roof of that medieval edifice. Currently, he sat with his back to the CCTV on the circular bench, with the tall, leafless plane tree forming a barrier to its sight of him. But this meant he was unable to watch the Guildhall itself, and hence see the alien's approach.

"Hello, Tom."

Tom shuddered: he had been peering over his left shoulder, but Smith – in his usual guise as a red-bibbed *Big Issue* seller – appeared to his right.

"Oh… hi… sorry… my heart…"

Smith's expression was neutral – or was it? Had there been the twitch of an amused smile? "Are you okay, Tom?" asked the alien. "I am sorry I could not meet you yesterday. I had other matters to attend to."

Tom swivelled to face the other, who continued to stand, holding a stack of magazines to his chest to complete his disguise. "Ah, yes, that's okay. I'm fine." He paused a moment, then continued: "Actually, no, I'm not. Not fine. In fact, I don't know how to say this, but… we're going to have to take a rain check."

"Rain check?" Smith's eyes went vacant for a moment, as though he were accessing some distant thought; when they refocused on Tom, they scanned him with flickering intensity. "I notice you are not wearing your glasses, Tom. Are these facts connected?"

"Um, yes. I told you about the war memorial online, but what I didn't say, because I didn't know at the time, was that I, um…"

Smith's head jerked about, like a remotely operated camera, focusing on him, then his face, then the tree, then the side of the council building, then past the tree and back towards the Guildhall. "You were detected by CCTV," the alien stated. His eyes returned to Tom's face. "And so you are fearful of wearing the glasses in case you are identified."

"Right. You got it in one. Not just the glasses, but my whole wardrobe from that night." Tom held up one sleeve of his green fleece, the only other jacket he possessed. Unfortunately, this wasn't waterproof, and hence he was feeling distinctly damp in the February mizzle that currently beset the city. "I… it… appeared on the local news, you see. People have seen my efforts. *Many* people." He thought back to the YouTube clip, which he'd accessed this very morning, and concluded: "*Millions* of people." He guiltily looked down and away. "So you see, I need to, um, lie low for a while. Maybe a long while. I mean, the glasses are out of place. Perhaps by summer?"

"Why didn't you report this at the foot of your latest chapter, Tom?" The statement was made calmly, without any evident reproach.

"Ah, I suppose I'm nervous about writing down incriminating things." Tom nodded to himself: especially given what he'd learnt of Ed's capabilities, and therefore what others, including police specialists, might someday uncover. He looked back up and chuckled uncertainly. "But I'm sure *you* won't blab about this to the fuzz."

"Just so, Tom. Still, if you had informed me earlier, we could have resolved this matter easily."

"Resolved? How?"

"Contact lenses. I will manufacture some for you. They will have the same function as the glasses. I would have proposed them at the outset, but I understand some people do not like wearing such things."

"I… *oh!*" Tom wasn't sure how he felt about the matter. Seeing others putting in lenses made him wince: he was squeamish about anything to do with eyes and was undoubtedly one of the 'some people' to whom Smith was alluding "Are you sure? I mean, I've done it again. I'd like to help, I really would, but haven't I been an… um… *disaster?*"

Now the alien definitely smiled – almost slyly. "Tom, I do not understand where you get this idea from. Your performance has generally been excellent. I am very pleased with you. One way or another — admittedly, sometimes in an unconventional manner — you have helped thwart the Directors, including on this latest occasion."

"Really?" Tom loved praise. Who didn't? "Did you... have you dealt with...?"

"The memorial message? Yes. That has been neutralised."

"That's great. How...?"

Smith turned to look away down the slope towards his nearest sanctuary. "There are some matters too complicated to explain, Tom." He looked back and continued: "I will have the contact lenses produced. Let us meet again in about a week. I think the city will be safe for that long. Goodbye."

With the other gone, Tom sat back against the bench. As ever, the meeting with Smith had left him confused. Being wanted was great, but he still couldn't fully delude himself that he was top-notch Omega material. He refocused ahead, and the surrounds suddenly seemed busy with people: a couple pushing a baby in a pram; an elderly man in a hat; a trio of teenage girls... and as they approached or passed, it appeared to Tom that — without exception — they turned towards him and gave him the most peculiar look.

***

Two days later, the team assembled at the iron gateway to the castle, which was set between a pair of small, stone gatehouses. They'd approached this via a brick road that wound past the glass-roofed café extension to Castle Mall and through a thin park that circled the upper level of the millennium-old bastion. The entranceway was wide enough — with gates open — for a single car, though motorised traffic was infrequent, with the road being mostly the preserve of pedestrians.

"Eh-up!" said Ed, arriving last. He paced up to the huddled trio of Tom, Simon and Amanda, only one of whom had had the sense to bring an umbrella against the intermittent rain. Unlike the other men, however, Ed wore a hat to keep his hair dry — an Australianesque affair with a drawstring under the chin. "You look a sodden bunch. Especially you, Tom. Blimey, my friend, get yourself something Gortexy. You look like a waterlogged sheep! Hey-ho, let's go." And without awaiting a response, he strode through the gateway.

"If you'd been on time," muttered Tom to the other's back, "I'd have been somewhat less saturated…"

The road to the visitors' entrance was effectively a bridge over the long-drained moat – now a path between two grassy mounds – which gave access to the ground level of the castle. The ticket office was accessed through a wide, iron-studded wooden door in a squat annex to the three-storey-high medieval keep.

As Tom and the others caught up to Ed, they heard the latter exclaim: "*How much?* I just want to visit the castle, not *buy* it!" The Aussie impostor shook his head and held up a hand to still any argument from the cashier. He fetched out his wallet and flipped out a jet-black credit card. "Take it, then, and with it all my hopes of an early retirement."

As the cashier fussed about with card machine and ticket, Ed turned to address the others over his shoulder. "This better be worth it, Tom, old chum, and not some dingy pothole leading nowhere, or drinks will be on you for the rest of the year."

Tom glanced quickly at the middle-aged woman behind the counter, but she was muttering to herself rather than processing what the awkward customer in front of her was telling his companions. "Uh, yes, I hope so too, but maybe…" he made a patting motion with his hand, which he hoped conveyed the need to dampen down incriminating speech.

Ed smirked, waggled his eyebrows, and turned back to receive his ticket.

***

"So, it's here, is it?" said Ed.

Tom had brought them directly down to the lowest level of the keep. Being term time, there were no children, and nor were there many tourists on such a miserable mid-February day. Indeed, on their descent, they'd passed no more than half-a-dozen people, all of whom had been of pensionable age.

"Yes, it's…" Tom raised his glasses to his eyes and instantly spotted the glowing symbol on the stone wall in the dingy corner. "*There.*"

Simon and Amanda edged towards the indicated spot, while Ed momentarily hung back, appraising his colleague. "Good to see the *bins* are back. It would have been damned inconvenient had you returned them to your handler."

"Uh, yeah, I probably would have, but I forgot to take them. He said he'd make me some contact lenses to use instead."

"And he didn't ask for these back?"

"No."

"That's a bit careless, eh? I mean, leaving alien technology scattered all over the place."

The others had turned to listen to the conversation. "He'll probably do it after he's handed over the contacts," said Simon. "Maybe he hopes you'll keep using them in the meantime."

"And talking of Smith, what did he say about the war memorial?" asked Amanda. "Did he do anything about the message?"

"Well, yes, he said he'd taken care of it, but he didn't say how. He's always conveniently out of time whenever it comes to answering questions on things he doesn't want to talk about."

Ed's expression turned serious. "Taken care of it? Hmmm."

"You seem doubtful," said Amanda.

"Doubtful? Perhaps *puzzled* is a better word. I've been looking at the CCTV from the area: by last night I got up to date. I never saw any crusty old geezer go anywhere near the memorial – and few others, come to that." He shrugged. "Maybe he's had another accomplice sort it out, but if so, whoever did the deed certainly didn't do it with spray paint."

"He probably did it with a ray gun from a distance," asserted Simon. "What about the time before Tom's bumbling? Have you seen who wrote the message?"

"Not yet. That's next on my list of priorities."

"Great," said Simon. "Anyway, are we going to do this or not? We should move while we still can."

"Yes, indeed," said Ed. "Let's strike before the shambling undead descend upon us. So, Tom, what have you got for us?"

"Ah, right." Tom peeled his new rucksack wetly from his back and knelt down with it.

"Nice, Tom," declared Ed, on viewing the rucksack. "But also slightly camp, eh? *Unicorns?*"

"Ah, yes, well…" Tom blushed, though the dim lighting hid this from the others. "I just grabbed the first thing I could from the market. I didn't see the, um, *emblems* until I got home."

"You completely missed the pink unicorns stitched onto the side pockets?" laughed Simon.

"Probably because he wasn't wearing his glasses," mused Ed.

"Anyway…" Tom reached into the bag to distract from his humiliation. He first pulled out a large magnet, identical to the one he carried in his soaked fleece pocket. "For Amanda."

"Thanks." Amanda accepted the item.

Tom then dispensed torches to Ed and Simon and brought one out for himself.

"So, the plan is the same, eh?" asked Simon. "Amanda will stay here and cover our backs, while we go in?"

"Yes, I guess," said Tom, though only after a glance at Ed. "She can let us out if the door closes behind us and I can't open it from the other side."

"I should try the magnet first to be sure," said Amanda.

"You should indeed," said Ed. Now he stepped up to the wall and peered closely at it. After some moments, he declared: "Remarkable. I can't see or feel a join. So, Tom, where exactly is the magic symbol? Here?"

"Uh, close. About six inches to your right, and up slightly."

"Amanda babes – please do your thing."

Amanda moved beside Ed, hefting the magnet in her right hand. She carefully wiped it across the stone in the indicated place – and startled at the sound of a soft *crack*, at which the surface moved slightly. Tom edged back, fearful of what might be lurking behind the secret door, but Ed showed no such trepidation and placed both hands on the stone and gently pressed, at which the door began to open.

"Cool!" declared Simon.

"Well, Thomas, if any of us doubted you before," said Ed, "we don't now." He continued to propel the door inwards. Once it was at sixty degrees, he retrieved the torch Tom had given him, switched this on, waved it about to illuminate the area behind the door, then stepped through. An eager Simon – also armed with a torch – crowded behind him.

Amanda turned to smile gently at Tom. "You too?"

"Uh… *right.*" Tom played about with the frame of his glasses, uncertain whether to retain them or whisk them off.

Amanda clearly divined the reason for his hesitancy. "I don't hear any screaming, so I'm assuming there are no ghosts through there."

"Yes, possibly. *Probably.* But the glasses reveal ghosts more clearly. There might be something that they don't see and I–"

"Tom – get your arse in here," called Ed. "We need to check if you can *both* open the door."

Tom's shoulders slumped. "Very well." He slouched past Amanda and into the opening of the tunnel. The space within was cramped. Simon had squeezed past their leader and was further inside; Ed stepped back to allow Tom to occupy the area closest the door. At least the crowding meant Tom couldn't see past the obstructing men, and so wasn't able to discern anything that might be lurking beyond.

"Push the door closed, then wave your wand," instructed Ed.

Tom did as he was asked, only pausing at the last moment when the door was just about flush. He took a deep breath and pushed it to: the door shut with a surprisingly gentle *click.*

"Now the magnet. Where's the symbol on this side?"

"It's here…" Tom waved his magnet over the indicated spot, then stiffened at the lack of response. "*Fuck!*" He pressed the magnet onto the surface, and this time was rewarded with the soft sound of a lock disengaging, at which the door popped outwards…

They *could* get out from this side.

Well, d'uh!

After the door had been pushed shut again, Ed called from behind Tom: "Right, Mands, we're off. Guard the fort. If we're not back in an hour, then… up to you. I doubt we'll get much phone reception here. Come try to find us if you're brave, otherwise alert emergency services – but only as a last resort. And don't think you can use this as an excuse to be rid of us by blocking us in – or I'll come back and haunt you!"

Amanda laughed. "Okay. Take care, boys!"

***

The tunnel was consistent in dimensions and texture: stone-faced; wide enough for one person; and tall enough for a short man – or possibly, Tom mused, an average-sized man from the past. It was slightly awkward for him and Simon, but for Ed – who was taller – it was a real hassle: "Bloody dwarves!" he muttered. "Hi-*fucking*-ho…"

With Simon in front and space limited, their marching order was fixed, with Tom more than happy to bring up the rear. Marching order – or shambling order? They moved slowly, cautiously, the air heavy and somehow unwholesome, the only sounds coming from their scuffling feet and Ed's low cursing. Simon initially inched ahead – concerned at missing something, scanning the walls constantly – but Ed's exhortations soon had their point-man moving at a steady stalking pace. Tom returned his magnet to his fleece pocket and brought out a compass, holding this in his left hand while his right held a torch. The compass indicated that they were moving north-north-west, and they were clearly descending – though at a gentle gradient.

Time seemed to slow in the tunnel, although it actually took less than five minutes and around sixty paces to come to the first point of interest.

"*Ahhh*," said Simon, softly. "Something's different. Hang on…" He shuffled forward a couple more feet. "The walls disappear. No – it's an opening."

The reflected light from Simon's torch diminished, and suddenly he was gone, and then so was Ed. Tom hesitated at first, and then he heard Ed exclaim: "Thank fuck for that. My back!" The words broke the spell: Tom took three paces and passed through the opening to join the others. He found himself in a small, cavern-like space, with a vaulted ceiling that was low, yet higher than the tunnel – allowing Ed to stand fully upright – and which was perhaps three metres wide. The surface of the cavern comprised a melange of flint, limestone, brick, and mortar that seemed of varying ages – from *just* old to *very* old.

Simon stood next to the far wall some four metres away, running his hands along the surface. "There's a door here," he declared. "It looks old."

"Let's have a gander," said Ed. "Hmm, yes. I wonder what's on the other side?"

"Alien control centre," said Simon, with confidence. "Probably lots of the buggers behind, doing mysterious things with alien computers. Let's give them a shock." As he grasped the iron handle, Ed laid a restraining hand on his forearm.

"Hang on, Si. Let's think about this. Where exactly are we, Tom?"

Tom unhitched his rucksack and felt within. He brought out a map of the city, which he rested on the floor. He then lay his compass on top of it, just above the location of the castle, and then placed his dark glasses next to this. The others turned from the door and came to stand over their crouching friend, shining their torches downwards.

"Thanks," said Tom, now able to rest his torch on the uneven floor and smooth the map with both hands. "Well, I marked the location of the passage before we came, or at least, where I think it is according to its position in the castle. And we have been heading roughly north. See: the compass is aligned with the tunnel behind and it's pointing in the same direction it has been all along."

"We should have brought something to measure distance," muttered Ed. "But we'll know better next time."

Tom said nothing for a moment, tracing their path. Then he nodded to himself. "Castle Meadow. We're under Castle Meadow — a road built over the old castle ditches many years ago. And as I thought, we're roughly here: *Pond's*. Or what used to be Pond's."

"Pond's?" asked Simon.

"Used to be a posh shoe shop," said Ed. "It's something else now. Some sort of charity place?"

"I'll check," said Simon, whipping out his phone. "Or maybe I won't. No reception."

"I'm sure of it," said Tom. "I've been looking into rumours of Norwich tunnels since you lot forced me, I mean, since we agreed to do this thing. Several names came up time and again, and Pond's is one. It's said to be linked to the castle and other places too."

"Okay," said Ed. "Let's assume this is an old tunnel built by humans, perhaps originally as an escape route from the castle. But why would it be used by aliens now? And they clearly do use it, as they've disguised the entrance at the castle and left a marker by it. Ah, but maybe asking about *now* is the wrong question. They could have been using this for many years. Desperate to get quality shoes for their eight humanoid feet-analogues? Absurd. Maybe from before there was a shoe shop here?"

"I think you're overthinking things, mate," said Simon. "It's just a way to get about the city unseen."

Ed frowned. "Okay. But why is there a door *here*? What's behind? A cellar or undercroft in the old shoe shop? But why would no one on the other side think to see what's behind it?"

"I think I see where you're going," said Tom, looking up. "You think they must have another hidden door beyond that one."

Ed was still unhappy. "I don't know. I guess we should just open it and see. Is there an alien symbol next to it?"

"Let me check." Tom swept up his glasses. "No, there isn't. Ah! Not by the door, but there is a mark *there*. About seven feet to its right, where the wall is flatter."

"I see it!" said Simon. He paced to the spot. "It's just flat stone here. None of the flint and other rubbish."

"A second door?" mused Ed. "Another tunnel? Is this a junction?"

"Which first?" asked Simon. He stepped back and swivelled between the wooden door and the bare patch in the mottled wall.

"I vote for the door-door," said Tom, quickly. He got to his feet and assembled his scattered gear, returning the map to his rucksack.

Ed and Simon looked at each other and both shrugged. "Why not?" said Ed. "Go on, Si. Do the honours."

Simon grasped the door handle and pulled. It swung inwards easily, without so much as a squeak of hinges. Beyond, was another four feet of tunnel – slighter wider than the first, and taller, too – and then a wall of rubble. Simon stepped up to this. "It's solid. I mean, it *looks* loose, like scree, but it's actually flat. *Weird*. Bit of a visual illusion."

"Come out, Si. Tom – go in and peer at it with your magic eyes. And maybe wave a magnet at it for good measure."

Tom replaced Simon and did as he was told. An alien icon was indeed there. Tom held up the magnet and the wall *clicked*. "What the...!"

"Tom?" asked Ed, peering from behind with Simon.

"Uh, yes. It's a door. What shall I...?"

"Strewth, Tom! Just go on through. We're right behind you."

As before, the stone door moved freely, requiring little effort in spite of its undoubted weight. Tom now found himself in another smallish space with a vaulted ceiling above and another wall in front, but this was of wood, with a small-yet-sturdy ladder set against it. Ed and Simon were soon with him, their three torches playing across the space like spotlights seeking enemy aircraft in the London blitz. While Tom hesitated again, Simon boldly climbed four rungs of the ladder.

"It's a wooden hatch. Let me…"

The hatch – inclined about forty-five degrees inwards – swung back and slammed against the unseen side of the wooden partition that separated the tunnel from whatever was beyond.

"Shit!" said Tom.

"Sorry!" Diffuse light entered from beyond, casting Simon's head and shoulders into silhouette. "Don't worry," he sighed heavily, after a moment. "There's no one here. It's a small room. There are stone stairs to the right, and a metal banister. I can get…" He wriggled up, twisted to the right, and was gone. Then his face reappeared, and he grinned into their spearing torchlight. "Come on, you wusses. It's perfectly safe."

***

"So where is this?" wondered Ed, speaking low.

They were in a sunken area, with the stairway against the left wall ascending to a closed door. Abutting this, half-way up, was the slanted top of the wooden partition that closed off the secret tunnel, accessed via the small, now-opened hatch through which they'd climbed. Another door near the foot of the stairs was open, revealing an ancient-looking room lit by jerry-rigged lighting, while a further doorway to their left gave access to a sunken courtyard.

"I think," began Tom, "we're in the basement area of what used to be Pond's. The steps probably lead to a door to the back of the place, at ground level with Castle Meadow. And through here…" For once, curiosity got the better of Tom. He led the way through the sunken courtyard – overlooked by grated windows above – into a narrow passage, which kinked one way and led to a narrow white door, presently open. "Ha! What a surprise. London Street. And directly opposite… *fuck!*"

Tom backed into his colleagues.

"Ow! Tom!"

"Sorry, Ed, but…"

"But what?"

"It's the Cosy Club! We're opposite the Cosy Club!"

"Yeah, so?"

"And there's a couple of *friends* out there. From Terminus Est!"

"What!"

"Did they see you?" asked Simon.

"No, I don't think so, but…" Tom urged the pair back along the passage until they were in the courtyard, under dark, late-afternoon skies. "They were talking to each other. A couple of the younger blokes. I mean, what are the chances?"

"Slim," declared Ed, "unlike their *massive* leader. These bozos keep turning up in the wrong place at the wrong time."

"If they're alien pawns, maybe they know about the tunnels too," ventured Simon. "Maybe they use this one? Maybe they'll be joining us shortly?"

"To get their fix of medieval mystery at the castle?" scoffed Ed.

But Simon was not to be deterred. "Well, maybe not the castle. But what about that other hidden door back in the underground chamber? Where does that go?"

Ed frowned. "You're smarter than you look, my Vulcan comrade. Yes. That bears looking into. Well, we now know where this branch leads, so there's no need to go outside. Let's go back and explore what's beyond the other door. Meanwhile, Si, I suggest a quick call to update Amanda, now that you have reception – though whether she will have it deep in the keep, who knows."

***

They retraced their path through the hatch in the slant-roofed wooden partition, which Simon carefully closed behind him from the inside. Then they returned through the stone and wooden doors into the vaulted subterranean chamber. As expected, Tom's magnet opened the second stone door, and he was propelled into the new tunnel by the weight of his friends.

This tunnel was much as the other in terms of size and composition, being similarly cramped and claustrophobic, yet suspiciously well-maintained for something that had presumably been burrowed out hundreds of years ago, possibly for nefarious purposes. At no point did Tom ever feel unsafe, in the sense that the ceiling might collapse and bury them beneath the streets of Norwich, and indeed, the absence of any ghostly apparition gradually eased his nerves, allowing him to move with increasing confidence.

However, this tunnel extended somewhat further than the other. After his first few steps, Tom made a point of trying to estimate their distance by counting his paces. He also continually referred to the compass in his left hand which, after initially pointing east, quickly turned to indicate a northerly heading. The tunnel must have curved somewhat, though it was impossible to tell from within.

After two hundred and twenty steps, they came to an anomaly – another area where the tunnel bulged out, both horizontally and vertically. From about ten metres away Tom caught a telltale glimmer of unnatural radiation on the right wall, opposite the small chamber. He stopped and allowed the others to enter the space and cluster behind him.

"Another door, Tom?" asked Ed.

"Yep. Right here." Tom gestured towards the wall with the torch in his right hand. This time, without being asked, he exchanged the compass with the magnet in his fleece pocket. "Shall I?"

"Knock yourself out," said Ed.

The door opened, and they found themselves in an undercroft. The vaulted ceiling was maybe two metres high, and the uneven walls around were stacked with old crates and several racks of wine.

Ed plucked out a bottle. "Côtes du Rhône – 1996. At this point, I feel I should make some pretentious comment about this being a good year, wax lyrical about the well-balanced mix of Grenache and Syrah grapes, or say something wanky including words like 'mellow' and 'fruity'. But you know what? I know sod all about wine. It's a tolerable substitute in the absence of ale, and that is all." He handed the bottle to Tom. "Nevertheless, I think we have earned a drink, or at least a souvenir, and whoever owns this joint has more than enough to spare. Go on, old chap, stick it in your lucky unicorn sack."

"Uh, okay." Tom wasn't a thief, but he wasn't a saint either, and arguing with Ed was – unlike the wine – a fruitless endeavour. He took the bottle.

Simon had by now made it to the other side of the undercroft, where a sturdy door provided an exit. He found a light switch and flicked it on.

"Bosh!" He turned to face the others. "So, where are we now? And should we, you know, tch-tch…" He used a thumb to indicate the door.

Tom settled the bottle in his rucksack and brought out his map. After a quick scan – under the expectant eyes of the others – he declared: "Somewhere… *here*. I mean, in the area between St Andrews Street, Redwell Street and Princes Street. Uh, in fact, we're probably close to The Halls."

"What!" Ed recognised the implication. "You mean, St Andrew's Hall, site of the beer festival?"

"Er, yes, but I'd guess Blackfriars' instead – attached to St Andrew's – as I remember its name coming up in my searches about tunnels."

"Blackfriars' is the long one, right, with the pictures of the old chaps," said Ed. "There was a bar along one wall at the festival. I seem to recall they were selling the most delicious junk food at one end. It was accessed behind the stage that had that frigging oompah band."

"Yes, that's right."

"So – behind this door is a big medieval church," smirked Simon. "And you two are pilfering from holy men?"

"Um, no, I don't think so," said Tom. "I said I thought we were *near* to The Halls. We're definitely heading in the right direction, but I'm not sure we're there yet."

"So, do we bust down this door or not?"

Ed had been thinking. He shook his head. "No, Si. We're running out of time. I don't want Mands to jump the gun and panic." Simon had been unsuccessful in his earlier phone call, though he had sent a text in case their friend wandered somewhere with 4G access. "We can do some research topside on where this might be. I am now more intrigued by where this tunnel ends – and to see if it really is at Blackfriars'."

***

It was.

The tunnel they returned to continued north about forty more paces, ending in a blank wall with a hidden door that opened into a dark, cupboard-like space that was sealed off from an area beyond by thick, red curtains.

Ed peeked through the curtains, then quickly withdrew his head and quietly updated the others: "It's a brick-vaulted cellar-like room. I vaguely recognise it, even without the slumped forms of inebriates. I think it's at the join of St Andrew's and Blackfriars'."

"Let's have a look then," said Simon, edging forwards.

"Not so fast, my friend. Lights are on, and I thought I heard voices. Does anyone know if this is open to the public at this time? Thought not. Again, more research is required. But we may have found out how the black-clad brotherhood—"

"They've got birds, too," noted Simon.

"Indeed, black-clad brother-and-sisterhood… how they may have got in to sabotage the festival and then returned to their presumed HQ at the Cosy Club. I suggest we return to pass on this news to Amanda while we still can. Agreed?"

Tom was only too happy to concur.

***

"Oh… you gave me a fright!"

Tom smiled sheepishly at their co-conspirator – relieved to see her, relieved to have made it safely from the tunnels, and most significantly of all, relieved to have avoided the ghost of Robert Goodale. "Sorry! I guess we should have, um, knocked or something, in case anyone else was here."

"Yes, we should have thought of that before." But Amanda was clearly also relieved to see them. Her face broke into a smile that made Tom's heart skip. It was just a shame she then directed the very same smile towards Ed and Simon as they squeezed out behind him. "But I'm glad to see you all in one piece, and eager to hear what you found."

"Let us repair from this place to a haven with secluded corners where we can discuss this over an ale," said Ed. "Murderers, perhaps?"

"Okay," said Amanda, "I guess you've earned a drink. But what—"

Ed held up one stalling finger. "Let no one speak until we are seated and sated! I'll just impart this one titbit, dear Amanda, to sustain you until then. Know this: from henceforth, never shall any of us – in the know, and armed with a powerful magnet – ever have to sell our soul, house, car, investment portfolio or trust fund, in order to visit this castle again.

There are other ways of accessing it that don't require breaking the bank. Hup hup!"

Chapter 25: Spies

This time, the call for an emergency meeting came from Ed, via email:

BIG news. Fate-of-the-world stuff. Drop everything. This evening, 6pm.

The location he gave, though, was odd: a residential address in the St Anne's Quarter, just to the south of the city centre, next to the river and across from the Riverside entertainment complex.

Tom lost track of time completing the annotation of an article for Alice's review, and so he arrived at the rendezvous ten minutes past the hour – out of breath, chilled by the cold, and damp from the intermittent rain. He found the entrance to the designated block of flats – a new build, in clean brick – pressed the button for the flat number he'd been given, and was buzzed in. His destination was on the fifth floor.

"Ah, Thomas, it's good of you to join us," grinned Ed. "Please enter my humble abode."

Tom bustled into a neat living room, finding Amanda and Simon seated next to each other on a grey sofa at a low table that hosted a large, opened-out laptop. He noticed a small kitchen area with shining white units off to one side of the broad space. The cream-coloured walls of the lounge were bare, aside from a pair of watercolour paintings of landscapes that bracketed a large, gold-leaf mirror that hung over an antique wooden sideboard.

"Very nice!" said Tom. "Is this yours? But I thought you lived–"

"Yes, Tom. *Lived.* Got my keys to this place a couple of weeks ago. Moving up in the world, eh?"

"You should see the balcony," said Amanda, from her place on the sofa. "It looks out over the river. I'm quite envious."

"Work hard enough, dear Amanda, and one day you too could own a bijou two-bedroom piece of luxury real estate. But we're not here to admire my expensive new pad, or my exquisite taste in decoration and soft furnishings, or indeed, my balcony view – which, in any case, is less 'whelming' than it might be, given the hour and season. No. We're here to save the world, and that is a tad more important. So, Tom, sit your arse down."

"Uh, right." Tom stepped over to one of a pair of pristine armchairs in soft purple fabric, recognising that its twin – settled in front of the laptop – was already reserved for the house master. He slipped out of his damp green fleece and allowed Ed to take this – with a grimace – and ferry it to a coat rack by the door. As Tom sat, he smiled at the seated duo.

"Wotcha, mate," said Simon. "Nifty, eh? But we don't get a drink. Claims he's got nothing in the flat. *Tightwad.*"

"I heard that," said Ed, re-joining the party and taking his own seat. "It happens to be true. Not a drop in the house. Not from abstemiousness – I've simply been so focused on setting up that I've not made it to the super. I've been eating and drinking out for the last week. Happy to get you all a drink later – but you need to earn it first."

Amanda rolled her eyes but said nothing.

"Well, uh, great," said Tom. "But what, I mean, why…?"

"Ever eloquent, eh? Well, let me update you now you're all sitting. Because I don't want anyone to swoon and fall, breaking some *objet d'art*, or smashing a head upon some sharp corner and spilling claret upon my real-wood flooring. Because you would." He pulled the laptop towards himself, the motion of which jolted the screen alive, then clicked the mouse pad to select an already opened window. Then he looked around the rest of The Credulous. "Ready? Now *watch*…" He turned the computer so all could see.

On the screen, a single figure was visible, shot from on high, walking down a deserted street that Tom instantly recognised as St Peters – with the council building to one side, the war memorial to the other, and the coloured roofs of the covered market beyond. It was night, and the only illumination came from streetlights. As the figure got closer, it began to resolve into a man with a short beard, wearing a dark coat overlain by some sort of gilet. In red. No, not a gilet, but a…

"Bib," said Tom, aloud.

Ed smiled slyly and watched as recognition dawned.

"No!" continued Tom. "That's not…?"

"What's he doing now?" wondered Simon. "He's by the war memorial. I can't…"

"Has he got something in his hand?" Amanda had scrunched forwards just like Simon to get a closer look at the screen. "I can't see. He's…"

"Doing something," confirmed Simon. "Waving his hand. Like a magic trick."

"Fuck!" exclaimed Tom. "What... *what!*"

"Fuck, indeed," murmured Ed.

They watched as the figure stepped back and then continued on its way, towards the camera and then out of view: it had come from the direction of the Guildhall and was presumably heading towards St Peter Mancroft, just out of the immediate shot. Ed leant forwards to hit 'pause'.

Simon and Amanda looked at a goggling Tom, waiting for a reaction.

"*Breathe*, Tom," said Ed. "Don't expire in my new armchair."

"*Bastard!*" exploded Tom, at last. "The... *fucking*... bastard!"

Ed reached across to pat Tom on the arm in sympathy. "Done up like a kipper, my friend."

"When was this shot, Ed?" asked Amanda, her concerned eyes still fixed upon Tom's furiously emoting face. "This is from *before*, isn't it? I mean, from before Tom's, um, *involvement*."

"Yep. As I told you at the castle, I found no signs of any physical interaction with the memorial since Tom's handiwork. Frankly, I've been so busy setting up here – installing the *Cray* in my second bedroom..." he waggled his eyebrows, "that I've not had time to check what happened immediately before Tom—"

"Bastard! Fucking... fucking..."

"... before Tom's hapless intercession. This is from two nights before then. I had to reel back through a lot of data to get here. It's amazing how few people approach the memorial. The vast majority walk straight past. I reckon only a dozen ever turned to look at it. Probably an issue of familiarity. After I found this, I went back one more day, but found nothing else. So," Ed concluded, "this is likely it: the moment of desecration."

"Wicked!" exclaimed Simon. "So, all along, Smith has been—"

"Bastard! *Fucking*..."

"Yes, yes, Tom," said Ed, but gently. He patted Tom on the arm once more, then squeezed, drawing the other's attention. "And yet now, my friend, we *have* him."

Tom exhaled and raised one hand to his head. Then he looked into Ed's serious face, and somehow forced a weak smile. "Yes. Yes we do."

"Are you okay now?" asked Amanda.

Tom nodded and looked between her and Ed. "Yes. Absolutely. I'm… fine."

"Thought your head was going to come off for a moment there, mate," said Simon. "Welcome back. Now, what do we do about the sneaky fucker?"

"And *that* is the critical issue, Si, and ultimately why we are here."

"I reckon some serious nipple-twisting is in order," suggested Simon. "Or we could go all *Medieval on his ass.*"

"Si, this is the twenty first century," said Amanda.

"Ah, yeah, you're right. That's so twentieth century, innit."

"Nineteen ninety-four," said Ed, absently. "But no. Vengeance is best served cold."

"So, basically," said Tom, in a controlled monotone, "he's been laying down these messages himself. If I don't find them, then I guess that's not a problem, because it leaves them to have whatever dark influence he intends. And if I do find them, then by trying to erase them, he has got me causing even greater chaos than would otherwise occur."

"It does appear to be a win-win situation for him," concurred Ed.

"D'you think he's got any more patsies in his stable? Uh… sorry, mate," said Simon.

"I remember Tom saying he's admitted to having others," said Amanda. "I wonder how many, though? And I wonder whether they're all, um, used like Tom?"

"Indeed," said Ed. "I've thought about this, too. It could be he has a mix of familiars, some straight, while others are just fall-guys, such as our Thomas."

"Right," said Tom, maintaining his calm admirably, "we can work with this. Sure. We're onto him now. But he doesn't know we're onto him. We know what he's doing, but we still don't know why he's doing it. We need to find out."

"Yeah, he's outed," said Simon, "but what of the others we've been following? Do you think any of these other dodgy dudes are working with him?"

"That's definitely worth thinking about," said Ed. "Maybe we need to reprise what we know about the other potential players in this game."

"What about Big Ed?" said Tom suddenly hopeful. "Do you think he's like Smith? I mean, could he be playing you, too?"

Ed smiled. "Sorry, my friend. I'm sure Big Ed is on the level. There's nothing I've ever done for him that could in itself be harmful to, let's say, the good citizens of this fine city, as opposed to immoral alien tossers and their human intermediaries. But the point holds. Amanda – what about Sheila? And Si – what about Vortent?"

Amanda was quiet for a moment, giving the matter full consideration, and so Simon jumped in. "Nope, not Vortent. As I said when you tried to burn me, he's only a seasonal player, and his main focus is crop circles. Or was. Last time we spoke, he showed some signs of getting with the times and mentioned graffiti. But he's not had me treading down corn stalks or writing anything myself."

"And I think Sheila is also above board," said Amanda, at last. "But I could be wrong. She's got an issue with vegans and also with some of these more radical environmental groups, like Extinction Rebellion. She thinks they do more harm than good, and I agree. But if we're wrong – if *I'm* wrong – then doing anything to undermine them would work against the cause of saving the planet. So, I'm suddenly..." she looked down, clearly experiencing a moment of doubt. But then she looked up, and her expression firmed: "No. I think Sheila is legitimate. And I don't think it's just my ego wishing that."

"If we disagreed with your analysis, then that might be worrying," observed Ed. "But I think we're with you on the damage these well-meaning fruitcakes are causing. And so that, I'm sorry to say, Tom, suggests that it's just Smith who is a servant of the Dark Side."

"Okay," said Tom, grudgingly. "I can buy that. But, as Simon said, what of these other people?"

"Indeed, they are worth deep consideration," said Ed. "So, while we're here, let's complete a review. Let's look at the dubious ones in turn. See how they fit into the scheme of things. So, after Smith—"

"Alien dude," said Simon. "Tom's handler. A devious shit."

"Ah, well summarised!" said Ed. "But we've already dealt with him. Moving on, what about Terminus Est?"

"Cultists with a fetish for black," said Simon, in his element. "Good at quizzes. Led by a fat bloke."

"Possibly connected with the beer festival messaging," said Tom. "But as you found a CCTV shot of Smith nearby at the time, maybe that was him too? Maybe they are innocent?"

"You've just got a thing against them, Ed, because they keep beating us at quizzes," said Amanda. "There's no real evidence they've done anything wrong."

"Keep!" exclaimed Ed. "*Thrice*, Mands. They've only beaten us *thrice*."

"Wiped the floor–"

"Yes, Si, I know they won well, but still only three times. *Wankers.* Nevertheless, Mands, I'm not sure they're in the clear yet."

"Well, you did catch one hanging around outside the Alex," said Tom. "*That's* dodgy. And then the other day, there were two more outside the entrance to the tunnel by Pond's. *And* I've seen them on my patrols – well, one of them, anyway – and he was looking shifty."

"That's enough for me," concluded Ed. "Anyone looking shifty *must* be up to something. But it is true, they do keep turning up at odd times. So, let's keep them on the watch list, eh? Okay, Mands? Thanks. So, next, we have Martin Elder–"

"UEA student," said Simon. "Embarrassing girly first name. Into films and games."

"He was also in the frame for the beer festival ruckus," said Tom. "But again, because of what you've found out about Smith, he might be out of the picture. And if Smith didn't do the festival, then we know Terminus Est hang about by a tunnel entrance that would have allowed them to get to-and-from The Halls in secret."

"True," said Ed. "And yet, you've seen Martin around a number of times, too. And at the Christmas dinner you *gotcha'd* him. Why would he know you? Why would he be following you?"

"Could he be one of Smith's other recruits?" wondered Amanda. "Maybe he's been tasked to keep an eye on Tom? Maybe he helped Smith at the beer festival? It would have taken more effort to sabotage the banners in the hall than it would to desecrate the war memorial on a deserted street at night."

"Yes, good point, Mands," said Ed. "It's a different MO. Plus, there is the fact that Martin's supervisor – *Cheggers Two*, as I shall call him – just happens to be the husband of Tom's ex-office mate, and she is now his boss. This all smells funny to me. It's like they're trying to keep an eye on him. And why would Smith need to do this? He gets regular reports from Tom, and he seems happy with his hilarious ineptitude." He smiled at Tom and gently shrugged: "Sorry, old fruit."

"So, are you suggesting they're involved with *another* faction?" asked Tom, who was starting to become confused.

Ed frowned. "Maybe. But are we agreed, the pair are still suspects of some sort and need to be watched?"

"For real," said Simon, while the others nodded.

"Okay," continued Ed. "That then brings us to this other pair, Ricky and Teresa. Ricky is—"

"Part-time gamer. Music bore." Simon made a whip-crack motion and sound. "Dominated by vegan fanatic girlfriend."

"Again in the frame for the festival," said Tom, "but again reprieved by Smith's possible guilt and the Terminus Est revelation."

"But if Martin and Keith are on a different side to Smith," said Amanda, "then maybe Ricky and Teresa are Smith's accomplices?"

"I don't know," said Tom. "I think we're getting paranoid. Occam's razor. If Smith did the memorial and was around for the festival, then the simplest explanation is that he did everything. The floor plaques on St Giles Street. The Pottergate underpass. The child drawings at the cathedral. And probably other things I haven't seen." Tom scratched at his nose. "And I know for a fact he doctored a sign in the market to say 'What's in your nose'*?* He did it as a demo and told me so."

"So are Ricky and Teresa out?" asked Amanda.

But Ed was not letting go. "Again, if something looks like a shit, and smells like a shit, and makes you slip on the pavement like a shit would, it's probably a shit. And we don't know who wears the hemp trousers in that relationship. Perhaps Teresa is the boss. And there is this growing vegan presence on St Benedicts Street."

"And Amanda did say that lot might be *baaaad*," noted Simon. "Bit like the Borg – assimilating everyone close. First St Benedicts Street, then the Lanes, then a Quorn diet for everyone for the rest of our lives… which won't be long, because the delay in changing our diet caused by reacting against the vegans will push us past a tipping point and… *boom*." He raised his hands to simulate an explosive cloud. "Game over."

"So, *another* sect?" Amanda was clearly doubtful.

"Perhaps," said Ed, also doubtful.

"Okay," said Amanda, now crossing her arms. "And there's the football issue, too: don't forget that. Where does that fit in?"

"Good point, Mands," said Ed. "We've not discussed the football for some time, but we definitely should. I've been keeping an eye on things."

"Me too," said Simon.

"Yep, me three," said Tom, who had been adding Norwich City scores into a separate database ever since their discovery of the bizarre pattern of results.

"Good," declared Ed. "So, you've all seen that the statistically massively improbable scores just keep coming. Since our last discussion, every Championship match involving our beloved Canaries has resulted in a binary score. Has anyone been translating?"

Tom shook his head, but Simon declared: "I have. Not got my notes on me, but the results spell out an 'm' and then a 'u'."

"That's right," confirmed Ed. He turned to his laptop and tapped away, bringing up several windows. "To be precise, the last eight results – over Christmas, the New Year, January and February – have been: 0-1, 1-0, 1-1 and 0-1, which spells an 'm' in ASCII, and then 0-1, 1-1, 0-1, and 0-1, which spells a 'u'. So, the start of the next word is 'mu', and the whole message is: 'Delia mu…' Any ideas what this could be?"

"Delia munches eggs?" posited Amanda.

"Delia muddles through?" wondered Simon.

"Or what about: Delia muffdives magnificently," smirked their leader.

"Ed!"

"Sorry, Mands, couldn't resist. Okay. Here's one for you and your enviro crowd: Delia mulches responsibly."

"Or what about: Delia mumbles inaudibly," said Simon.

"Delia mugs… er, that's all I've got," said Tom, trying to catch up.

"Well, I guess she could have criminal tendencies," said Ed, "though I doubt it."

"So, basically," summarised Amanda, "the message – if there is one – is still unclear. We need more results."

"True," said Ed. "But the sequence we identified is continuing, and given the number of games left in the season, I reckon there is scope for only…" he did some rapid mental calculations, "five or six more letters. As such, options are limited. Think short not long. If the 'm' word is the last of a pair of words then 'munches' or 'mulches' are about the right length, although these don't make any sense. But perhaps the 'mu' word is a short one, and there is one further word after it? And if it's short—"

"Must!" cried Tom, who'd started at the opposite end to his friends, and mentally gone through most of the three and four letter alternatives. "Delia must... something."

Ed nodded. "Yes, that's possible."

"Or maybe mulls," said Simon, muddying the water. "As in, Delia mulls a bid. You know. For the whole club. For another club." He shrugged.

"Again, nice thinking, Si," said Ed, "although I suspect that particular phrase is a letter or so too long. Any more short words come to mind?"

"Mud," said Amanda.

"It's not short, but what about 'murders'," said Simon, leaning forward and rolling his eyes, "or 'mutilates'."

"You lot have crime on the brain," said Amanda, though she struggled to hide a smile.

"Indeed. The Sainted One is not likely to engage in such vices," said Ed. "Perhaps blundering Tom has blundered onto the most likely word. Though whatever 'Delia must' do would also have to be something short. Quit? Hmmmm. Is a resignation in the offing? Let's see, shall we. An 's' would be spelled by 01110011, meaning the next result should be 0-1 – an away win. Aren't we away to Hull City next? Anyone willing to chance another wager?"

It was clear from the sparkle in Ed's eye that *he* was certainly up for this. Tom fancied a small punt himself and guessed that Simon would also sneak down to the bookies at some point. But while this was fascinating enough, he felt a need to bring them back to the core issue. "Well, this is all well and good, but as Amanda said, I'm not sure how this relates to Smith and the others. I can't see how any of them can be influencing the football scores – I mean, we're talking about away games as well as home ones, and I suspect that these, um, *saboteurs*, don't leave Norwich much. We could probably prove it, too."

"I concur, Tom," said Amanda. "This seems like a different matter altogether."

Ed frowned. "I'm not so sure. All this activity around Norwich? I have a feeling this is all building up to something big, and that all these geezers are involved, from Smith down, perhaps with *other* parties we're not aware of working at a higher level. I think we're only seeing part of the picture. We're groping in a darkened room trying to identify an animal within.

Smith and the others are part of a massive hairy arse. The football intriguers are the sharpened tip of a tusk. They don't seem to be related, but in the end, they're all part of the same elephant squatting in the middle of the room. We just need to be wary of 'doing a John Noakes' in its effluent."

Tom nodded in appreciation at the metaphor – and reference to an infamous episode from *Blue Peter* in the distant past. "Er, nicely put. But still, we can't actually do anything about the football. But what about the others? And what am I going to do about Smith?"

"Dob him in," said Simon. "But God knows who to."

"The Intergalactic Council of Alien Wankers," mused Ed, "or *ICAW* as I shall now refer to them. Alas, we don't know their address. No, I suggest we use this intel for our own benefit. So, keep playing along, Tom, but without doing anything else stupid. Meanwhile, we know Smith's main haunts. I'll set up to hack and record all the relevant cameras around St Peter Mancroft, the Guildhall, and St Andrews. Let's see if we can't get an idea what he's up to. See where he goes. See who he meets."

"Yes, good." Tom nodded to himself: it *was* good. More than that, it gave him some ideas for how to advance the plot of his own story, and what to do about the treacherous V-Garg…

"That's Smith," said Amanda. "But what about the others?"

"I will continue monitoring what I can," said Ed, "and flesh out profiles on the others. But more direct observation would be useful. I'm talking espionage."

"Cool!" said Simon. "I'm up for it! I know Ricky and Martin vaguely. I'm happy to take them on. I'm sure to bump into them at Athena Games or The Games Table. Get closer. Maybe do some tailing. *Tradecraft.*"

"Don't get carried away, Si," warned Amanda. "Stalking is a crime."

"I'd hardly call it that," said Ed, "though on that note, maybe it *would* be best if you leave Teresa off your list. Amanda – you and her are kindred spirits. You both believe in hugging trees and saving whales, eh? Would you like to take her on as a project?"

"Well, I'm not sure how I would do that."

"Hang around Vegan HQ on St Benedicts Street," suggested Ed. "Maybe Si can tip you the wink when he sees her with Ricky?"

Seeing Simon give a thumbs up, Amanda sighed: "Okay. I'll do what I can. But don't expect much. And I'm not going to creep about the shadows or do anything sordid."

"Atta girl," said Ed. "And so, Tom, that leaves you. Martin's potential collaborator – *Cheggers Two* – is the husband of your new mistress. *Dig.* Surreptitiously quiz Alice about hubby. Find out if he has any weird solo pastimes not involving the trouble and strife. I'll bet he does. Find out what, where, and when. Forward anything you get to me."

"Sure. I can do that."

"That still leaves Terminus Est," said Amanda. "All we know about them is that they occasionally turn up to the Rose for the quiz."

"And occasionally spy outside the Alex," said Simon.

"And hang about near the Cosy Club," said Tom.

Ed held up a hand to stop any further discussion. Then he tapped his head in thought as the others looked on. At last, he said: "Several things occur. The first is that they probably do other quizzes throughout Norwich, by rotation. Winning and then moving on, rather than making themselves unpopular. I can check out venues and see if I can track their routine. The second is that we have already caught them watching us once. Maybe they are nearer than we think – even as I speak. And if they are trying to watch us, then we may be able to turn the tables. Keep an eye out on your patrols, Tom. I wouldn't be surprised if you occasionally encounter one or another of them. Especially look out for them near the CC. If you do spot them, perhaps send us a quick text and one of us can try to get in range. *Watch the watcher*, as it were."

Simon laughed. "Brutal! I've always wanted to be a spy!"

Ed nodded and clasped his hands before him. "Yes, Mr Bond, welcome to the club."

"I guess that makes you 'M'. So who are they?" Simon nodded towards Tom and Amanda.

"Pretty obvious to me," said Ed. "Welcome, Mata Hari and Guy Burgess."

Tom rolled his eyes. Burgess – the double agent? It could have been worse, though. Given his recent form, Johnny English wouldn't have been a bad shout.

Chapter 26: Goals and Own Goals

Tom met Smith a couple of days later on a Saturday, at which point he was handed a small box containing the promised contact lenses.

"I am sure you can find plenty of information online about how to insert them," said Smith. "They just need to be washed with water between uses. I have given you two pairs in case you lose the first." Something in the alien's voice suggested he believed this was a racing certainty. "Please try not to. Although the technology superficially mimics human technology and would be difficult to tell apart from it, and the lenses will degrade with time, I would rather limit the amount of incriminating evidence laying around. Speaking of which, do you have the glasses?"

"Ah, sorry. I forgot."

Smith looked intently at Tom, who squirmed on the bench under his gaze. At last he nodded. "No matter. Perhaps having them as a reserve is a good idea."

"Um, yes. And when the weather gets better, and enough time has passed, I can go back to using them."

Tom had deliberately left the glasses at home, in the first instance as a *fuck you* to the alien, but the thought had been forming in his mind that they might be of use to one of his friends.

"Very well. Please try the lenses and return to your patrols. I fear the Directors have become emboldened in Norwich, and they are increasing their activities. You are needed now more than ever, Tom." Smith turned and headed back down the slope to the Guildhall.

Tom glowered at the other's retreating back, and muttered, *sotto voce*: "Oh, I'll trial them soon enough, you git, but maybe not in the way you want."

And certainly not today.

His first appointment today was with a betting shop on London Street, after which he planned to search out a pub with a Sky subscription in order to follow the afternoon's football results.

***

The only goal was apparently a comedy of errors. As the Hull City keeper was about to launch the ball from the edge of his area, something distracted him, causing him to squint and air-kick. The lurking Norwich City forward – barely able to believe his luck – slid into the ball, giving it just enough momentum to trickle over the line before the flapping goalkeeper could recover.

The Sky presenter cackled gleefully as he recounted this bizarre event.

In the Wildman pub on Bedford Street – ironically situated opposite the Cosy Club, not far from the exit of the castle tunnel (beneath what used to be Pond's) on adjacent London Street – Tom clenched a fist in triumph.

Ten minutes later, as he was en route to the bookies to claim his winnings, Tom's phone vibrated in his pocket, alerting him to a new text. He correctly guessed its sender.

***

"Ninety pounds!" exclaimed Ed, around an hour later. "Tom, you're really heading nowhere fast, most certainly not to financial independence."

"Well, how much did you win?"

"Oh, I'm not sure I should tell. I wouldn't want to sour your triumph. But it starts with a seven and has another three figures after it."

"*Seven thousand!*" Tom was aghast.

Ed took a pull of ale. They were in the Louis Marchesi in Tombland, close to the Maid's Head hotel and opposite the cathedral's Erpingham Gate: the three male members of The Credulous had just happened to be in the area close to Tom's bookmaker-of-choice, while Amanda had been shopping in the centre. "Go big or go home, my friend!"

Simon laughed and shook his head. "Nice one, mate!"

"And you, Si?" queried Tom, almost afraid to ask.

"Lop a zero off."

"Seven hundred?"

"Well, more like eight."

Amanda shook her head. "Don't you lot think this is going to start looking suspicious?"

"We are committing no crime, Amanda dearest, although you may have a point," conceded Ed. "We should at least ensure that we are using different bookies. Well, when I say 'we', I mean my leather-jacketed friend and I," he slapped Simon on the arm, "not Tom, whose inconsequential wagers are unlikely to cause the faintest ripple of concern within the betting community. And I will certainly start by reducing and spreading my bets. What's next if the third letter in the sequence is indeed an 's'?"

"One-all draw," asserted Simon, nodding. "Can't remember the opposition – not that it matters."

The meeting had been an opportunistic chance to celebrate. But after discussing the football and financial possibilities, with a fair dose of teasing from Ed, and the first signs that a mildly envious Amanda was becoming interested in joining the fun (with Ed's aid, having had no previous experience in the realm of bookmakers), conversation naturally segued to recent issues.

"There are other tunnels, you know," said Tom, leaning over the top of his half-empty pint glass. "I've been kind of neglecting my work with Alice to look into things. Now, I've got a number of targets I want to explore."

"*Want?* Blimey," said Ed, "that's new. I thought you were terrified of the tunnels."

"Well, I was. But our mission went, uh, fine. I'm not sure I'd want to go down there alone, but it wasn't as bad as I thought it would be. And to be honest, this business with Smith has got me steamed up." *Steamed up?* Once he'd gotten home from Ed's posh flat after their previous meeting, he'd set about metaphorically punching walls. He wanted to get his own back, and his earlier meeting today had firmed this resolve. An Omega? He'd show the alien just how good an Omega he could be! And he'd start by tracking down every tunnel and bolthole the alien might be using. "The thing is," he continued, "with the contact lenses and the magnet, I can find these tunnels if I know where to look. Until now, I've not been looking in the right places. Smith has had me looking for messages out in the open where many people might be able to see them, which is of course completely opposite the sort of hidden, unvisited locations where tunnel entrances are likely to be. If I can find one, I can find others. In fact, I've already got a list of targets, and these are *inside* places rather than *outside*."

"Jolly good, my friend," said Ed. "And I'd certainly be up for joining you. However, I've mucho on at the moment – earning my keep, tracking CCTVs, searching for intel on the numerous dodgy characters we've uncovered. And Big Ed has also woken up to the gathering storm." He frowned but didn't elaborate. "And so, alas, I have little time for exploring Norwich's nether regions."

"And I'm not the best one for enclosed spaces," said Amanda, apologetically.

"Don't worry," said Simon, pouting and nodding, "I've got you covered, mate. But unlike the rest of you guys, I gotta work for the man. So, I'm happy to hold your hand, but it'll have to be when I'm free. Lunch breaks. Between shifts. That sort of thing."

"Great, Si – thanks! Let me know when you're available, and I'll prepare."

Tom already had a target in mind, but he'd first have to verify the presence of a hidden doorway there before he could take up Simon's offer.

**

The 'quick celebratory drink' turned into a longer affair, involving several more pubs – at least for the men, with Amanda leaving after a couple more rounds to ferry her shopping home. Tom didn't manage to escape Ed and Simon until last orders, and consequently, Sunday turned into a bleary write-off and his plans became deferred.

Then a new week began, and Tom needed to make up time on Alice's project, though this did bring another goal into range.

The name's Burgess, Guy Burgess, thought Tom, as he rapped on a familiar door in his old department at UEA the following Wednesday afternoon. A muffled voice invited him to enter.

"Tom? Well, this is a surprise," said Alice Weidner, swivelling her chair to face the newcomer.

Tom quickly glanced towards the second desk in the shared office and was relieved to find it untenanted. Brian had been given his old space, though he was currently absent. "Hi, Alice," he ventured, after a pause. "I didn't realise me being on time would come as, um, a surprise."

Alice smiled gently. She was heading into her late thirties, but still handsome, with a heart-melting smile. "I meant, I'm surprised you decided to come at all. It's nearly the end of February and this is your first in-person visit."

They exchanged pleasantries, then Alice showed him the desk he'd been assigned, which was in a room on the same floor several doors away. This held four desks, three of which were allocated to post grads: Fatima, Agneta and Warren – an earnest trio, who were hard at work on their arrival. The residents appraised Tom in a rather cool manner, and indeed, Agneta appeared annoyed at the interruption, which Alice clearly noticed.

"I'll let you introduce yourselves properly at your own discretion," she said. "Let's return to my office to talk shop. Brian's away at a meeting, so we won't disturb anyone."

Tom gave the trio a pained smile and mentally decided he'd not return to this sourpuss realm unless he really, *really* had to.

Back in Alice's office, they discussed the status of Tom's review, and the analysis she wanted him to perform on the articles he'd identified in his literature search. He had to admit, the face-to-face meeting was probably worth a plethora of electronic exchanges. With work matters sorted, and a second instant coffee offered and accepted, Tom attempted a casual segue into the personal.

"Soooooo… how is Keith?"

"Keith?" Alice looked slightly perplexed at the conversational drift.

"Er, yes. Remember – we talked at the Christmas dinner? At The Monk? It was the first time I'd met him. He, um, seems a nice guy."

Alice arched one delicate eyebrow. "Keith is well. Still doing Keith-like things."

"Ah, yes, he's in the Film department, isn't he? I guess he watches a lot of films." That sounded lame, even to Tom. "I mean, he probably *makes* them, too, eh?"

"Yes, he usually has some project or other going on with his students."

Tom grinned. "No major productions though? Something he might need some *talent* for? I've always fancied being in a film."

"Really?" Alice's surprise was genuine. She clearly knew Tom better than he thought: his claim lacked any credibility.

"I mean," he blustered, "not as an *actual* actor. A lead. A *star*. I mean, you know, as an extra in the background." He chuckled unconvincingly.

"You know, *passer-by with coffee. Man on park bench.* Or even *evil henchman number five.*"

Alice's gentle frown turned around. "Ah, yes. I see what you mean. I never envisioned you moonlighting as an extra, but I suppose you have the chance now, given your life of leisure."

She was teasing him! Well, better that than suspecting him. "Yep – I'm happy to go anywhere any when, but I've never had the contacts."

"I could ask Keith if you want. I know he occasionally works with local filmmakers. Or maybe you could ask him yourself. His office is just a short walk across campus."

"Ah, no! Thanks, but I wouldn't want to, I mean, I'm not that…"

Alice's eyes shifted focus – to a calendar that was blue-tacked to the wall. She frowned. "Sorry, Tom, I just realised he's not there anyway. It's Wednesday. He'll be gone by now."

"Gone?"

"Oh, yes. Wednesdays are sacrosanct. He leaves early – home to change and then on to the pub for six. It's his group's social evening. Well, he says it's more work than play, but…" she shrugged.

"Let me guess," said Tom, cannily. "The Fat Cat?"

"No. The Rumsey Wells. St Andrews Street."

"Ah…" Why was he not surprised? St Andrews Street was a continuation of St Benedicts Street, home of the Vegan Mafia, which ran all the way to The Halls, site of the beer festival. Valuable intel! He felt momentarily smug: the team would approve. *Guy Burgess – superspy!* "Anyway, I suppose I should let you work, especially now you've got the office to yourself." He stood, then gave a quick nod at the empty desk. "I suppose he's off somewhere exotic?"

"What, Brian?" Now Alice did laugh – a light and endearing chuckle. "You know he hates flying. No, he sticks to trains. He's actually been away a lot this year. Says he's putting together a large consortium for a major project. He's been on trips every couple of weeks. But you know what a workaholic he is. He generally goes on a Friday so he can have weekend meetings and be back at work by Monday."

"Oh, yes? Where's he gone this time? London?"

Alice stood to escort Tom to the door. "No. Somewhere up north. Where was it? Hull, I think…"

Tom couldn't help emitting a gasp.

***

Tom had to rush downtown after the meeting: Norwich had a mid-week game away to Huddersfield Town, and he had to place a bet. His regular bookmaker was at the end of London Street, which he could have approached via a number of routes, including one that – it now occurred to him – would take him right past the Rumsey Wells, where Keith was meant to be having his weekly meeting with his students. As Tom realised this, his walking slowed, and he quickly looked at his wrist – it was approaching 6p.m.! How... *convenient.* Should he risk it? But perhaps his timing was *too* good to be convincing, and what would happen if Keith spotted him and related this to Alice? He might come across as something of a stalker. No, he decided to save that mission for another time. He sped up, but almost immediately slowed once more, his mind turning to the other matter of concern: *Brian*!

So – the waspish one had actually been in Hull over the weekend that Norwich City F.C. had been in town. That was another bizarre coincidence. Indeed, it was highly improbable, even fantastical. Could Brian somehow be involved in the grand game that at least one alien species was playing with the good folk of Norwich? But Brian *hated* football. The idea of him criss-crossing the country to somehow banjax games just didn't make sense. Tom couldn't see him doing that for any amount of money or cause. And now that he thought about it, he recalled the time when he'd bumped into Brian and Fabio at the Coachmakers on a Saturday – and that was during a Norwich away game. Preston North End? He nodded to himself. *That's right.* So it *had* to be a coincidence – unless antisocial Brian had a partner in crime. *As if!*

And yet...

Alice said Brian was usually away from Fridays for the weekends, yet he was *still* absent today. Huddersfield was up north, too, wasn't it? Could he have stayed on to get across to the second game?

Tom slowed to a halt outside the medieval St Giles on the Hill. This was troubling, but perhaps not worth raising with his friends and conspirators. Not *yet* anyway. He didn't want to muddy any waters, or indeed, introduce yet another variable into their calculations. But this was definitely something *he* ought to look into.

Bollocks!

It would mean another trip to his old department for a manufactured meeting with the sour-faced one, and probably the humourless arseholes who shared his nominal work space, too. He'd rather visit the dentist.

With his mood soured, Tom started up again. He yomped to the betting shop, laid his wager, then returned home the way he had come.

The game was on Sky.

It was an exciting match, for once. Norwich took an early lead and dominated the first half, but just could not score a second. Indeed, the trend continued in the second half, and for most of the game it looked as though Norwich would win. Tom wasn't quite sure how he felt about this. He'd bet on a one-all draw, but would almost take the monetary loss in exchange for the Canaries holding on for the win.

But it was not to be.

In the very last minute, a final Huddersfield press caused the Norwich full back to pass to the goalkeeper for a clearing kick. Unfortunately, the defender struck the ball too well: it flew beyond the keeper's outstretched leg and buried itself into the far corner for an own goal.

Tom sighed.

Frowned.

Then smiled guiltily. Betting against your own side could have its benefits!

The texts began to arrive almost immediately. Little needed to be said, so little was: Simon's emoji was a 'thumbs-up'; Amanda's was a smiley face (so she must have been seduced by Mammon!); and Ed's was a string of dollar signs.

Tom had a hundred-and-twenty big ones coming. He dreaded to think what vast sums the others might have due.

***

But the football was a distraction, as was Alice's project, albeit these were more-or-less profitable ones. In contrast, Tom's novel was an utterly profitless endeavour, and one that not only required time he didn't really have, but a considerable rethink. Having already begun to reveal V-Garg's treachery – perhaps subconsciously driven by his suspicions about Smith – he now worried that pushing this line further might actually cause Smith to wonder whether he'd been rumbled – given that the alien was able to read Tom's Cloud-saved writings, although whether he did any more than look for messages at the end of his latest work, he could not tell. And so progress there stalled.

That left several other immediate goals: to patrol for Smith; to search for more tunnels; to look into the Brian problem; and to follow up on his intel about Keith. Tom decided to set aside the Brian issue until he had reason to visit UEA again, and he had a week before he had to decide on whether and how to eavesdrop Keith (and presumably Martin, too) at the Rumsey Wells, which whittled down his immediate priorities to ones he could perhaps combine – killing two birds with one stone.

And so for three days, from Thursday to Saturday, Tom worked for Alice in the mornings and then inserted Smith's contact lenses (an eye-wateringly unpleasant experience) and went on patrol in the afternoons and evenings. He roughly followed established routes under the assumption that Smith might be keeping some track of him – perhaps in order to plan where to leave demonic messages for him to find and then fuck up (*the bastard!*). He had a number of targeted locations for tunnel entrances, but the main problem was accessibility. His research suggested that the castle might be the location of up to three tunnels, but he didn't fancy paying to get in, and in spite of Ed's bullishness to Amanda, getting back into the castle via the tunnel they had found would not be easy: entry to The Halls was limited to special events (concerts, weddings, business meeting bookings), while the door to what used to be Pond's on London Street was closed and locked when he passed it on Thursday. He was pretty sure of the location of the tunnel in St Peter Mancroft, but he couldn't access that or the location in the Guildhall undercroft – both of which would be locked and might bring him into direct contact with Smith.

But then Tom discovered the Norfolk Museum Pass, which for a steep-but-manageable annual subscription allowed him endless visits to the castle as well as a dozen other museums in Norwich and Norfolk. He bit the bullet and used some of his football winnings to buy this.

On the Friday, he found the entrance to a second tunnel, deep in the keep to the east side.

And on Saturday he found a third entrance facing almost directly west. *The place was a warren!*

He contacted Simon from the castle on Saturday, then had to hang around the café for an hour before the other arrived.

"Bloody hell, mate," said Simon. "I'm going to have to go all-in on tomorrow's game to recoup the cost of that pass."

Tom gave a pained smile. "Sorry, Si, but I think it's going to be worth it. You won't believe what I found."

"A tunnel entrance by any chance?" said Simon.

"Er, no. *Two* entrances."

"Fuck! Well… what are we waiting for? Have you told the others?"

"Not yet. I thought maybe we could have a quick look to see where these head first."

"Sure. I'm up for it."

And so they went for it. Tom had bought another magnet for Simon as well as his glasses so that the other could see the alien symbols too. They tried the east tunnel first, initially checking that the magnets worked, with Simon entering the tunnel and closing it while Tom stood guard, ready to re-open if Simon couldn't get out. When that proved unproblematic, they turned on their torches and took to the hidden passageway, though they didn't go far. After two-to-three hundred metres they came to what looked like a deserted undercroft, which acted as a junction, with one route bearing off north and the other south.

"King Street," declared Tom, confidently, leafing through an A5 notebook he'd magicked from his unicorn rucksack. "In fact, I reckon we're below what used to be The Three Tuns pub, back when this area was a real dive."

"What, King Street? I thought there's only one pub on the street. The Last Pub Standing. *Ah…*"

"Yep, the name says it all. In the past, the whole street was lined with pubs – and several breweries, too. Now there's just the one, which I reckon we'll pass under if we continue… *that* route. North. In fact, I reckon that goes all the way to the cathedral."

"And the other one?"

Tom held the torch over his notebook, read some more, then turned over a page. "I'm not entirely sure, but one possibility is Carrow Priory, off Bracondale. That looks quite a way."

"I reckon both are," concurred Simon. "So, what next?"

"Well, today, I think we should head back and try the other passage. I just want to get a sense of, you know, scale. We can properly explore these routes later with, er, better planning."

"Sure thing. Let's go."

In less than ten minutes they were back at the castle portal. They couldn't hear any noise through the door – but that might have been due to its thickness. In the end, they just had to trust that none of the (few) castle visitors were hanging around the relatively sombre area of stone outside – and they were grateful to find this to be so, exiting into a deserted chamber.

"We're gonna have to find a better way to deal with this," noted Simon. "Might be okay now, mate, but come tourist season, we could come a cropper."

"Agreed!" But Tom was now in his element, and willing to risk one more breach. They headed for the western portal, on the opposite side of the lowest keep level.

As previously, the area was deserted, and they followed the same procedure as before, again not going far.

"This'll do for now," said Tom. They were in a small underground chamber, perhaps two hundred metres from the castle walls. The tunnel carried on into the dark ahead, with another secret door in the wall to one side. "I reckon we're under the Royal Arcade here, and if we carry on this will take us all the way to the Guildhall."

"Guildhall? You mean, where Smith hangs out?"

"Precisely!"

Simon smirked. "You sure you don't want to pay him a visit? Give the fucker a fright?"

"Oh, yeah, I do. But not now. Not until we know where he is. In fact…" An idea occurred to Tom – a way of guaranteeing where Smith would be. But he'd have to talk things over with the crew. Simon gave him a quizzical look; Tom responded with an ambiguous wave, hoping to communicate the concept of 'later'.

They returned to the castle, made it out without being seen, and repaired to The Murderers for a celebratory drink.

***

Norwich F.C. were meant to be at home on Sunday – a midday kick-off against Blackpool.

But late Saturday, there was the first hint on *Look East* that something might be amiss. *Rumours*. The word *norovirus* popped up.

Tom hadn't taken much notice. On Sunday morning, he'd done a couple of hours' work before turning on the television. This time, he wasn't going to be mocked: he'd put two hundred pounds on a nil-nil draw the previous evening after leaving the pub – enough to make the cashier at Betfred raise an eyebrow, but not enough to draw a comment. *Come to daddy*, thought Tom, rubbing his hands in anticipation.

But the programme on TV was not what he expected. There were football pundits talking, but they didn't seem to be at Carrow Road. What…?

His phone vibrated its way across the coffee table. He'd had it on *silent* while working, and had brought it down from his study without checking for messages. On doing so now, he found a flurry of texts. The latest one, from Simon, simply stated: *WTF!*

There were several previous texts from Ed, the gist of which was this: half the Norwich side had caught norovirus and the game was postponed. All bets were off.

But what did this mean for the sequence of results? Had it been broken? Had the aliens been stymied? Were ALL bets now truly off? Had Tom essentially missed the boat?

Testicles!

And yet… it had indeed been a game with no goals.

Chapter 27: Busted?

For Tom, the next few weeks were dominated by the need to service Alice's project, which proved more intricate and time-consuming than he expected.

"I should never have taken it on," Tom muttered to himself on more than one occasion. "I should have followed Ed's lead and bet the house on red…"

But the prospect of winning enough at the bookies to retire, or at least take a furlough, had somewhat receded. The postponed game had thrown a spanner in the works, and on top of this, the conspirators came to an agreement to step back for a while. This was decided at a Thursday meeting at the Alex.

***

"So a 't', to complete the word 'must', would be spelled out by 01110100," confirmed Ed. "Hence, a narrow away win for the boys in the next game – *if* the sequence continues. *Or* maybe it will be nil-nil to make up for the postponed game."

"What do you reckon?" asked Simon, the keenest of the rest of the crew.

"Honestly, my friend, I don't know. I suppose the cunning gambler would bet on both. Given that the odds for such precise scores are likely to be better than two-to-one, you'd win more on the correct call than you'd lose on the incorrect one and so still make a profit."

"But what if the sequence is broken?" asked Amanda. "If a different score comes up, you'd lose on both bets."

Ed shrugged. "Sure. That's why it's called gambling. *Nothing ventured* and all that."

"Hmmm, well, I think I will sit the next one out," said Amanda.

"Yeah, me too," said Tom, to no one's surprise.

"What about you, Si, my dashing amigo?"

Simon pouted his lips in thought and then slowly shook his head. "Nah. Not this time. Anyway, I've been thinking: this could be a signal that we should go easy. Row back a bit."

Ed looked aghast. "*Et tu, Brute!* Where is the real Simon? Has Vortent replaced you with a pod person?"

"Nah, it's still me. I've just been thinking… *Enigma.*"

"Enigma?" Ed looked confused for a moment, but Amanda nodded in appreciation.

"Yes… clever. I see what you mean, Si. I watched the film a little while ago."

Ed looked non-plussed: for once, he was the slow one, and this didn't sit well with him. "Is someone going to explain to this simpleton what you mean or are you just going to communicate in… *code.*"

Tom got it at about the same time as Ed. "I… *see,*" he said.

"Yep," said Simon. "*Code.* When the boffins at Bletchley Park broke Herr Hitler's Enigma code, they had to decide on how best to use that knowledge. They decided they couldn't use it all the time, or else the Nazis would quickly work out something was up. So, they sat on their hands and let the buggers win a few, and only acted when they got a big advantage."

"Right! Got you now!" Ed sought to reclaim centre stage. "So, you're suggesting if we keep betting on every score, someone somewhere is going to get suspicious. The bookies themselves. Or most likely, whatever alien filth are playing this game. Assuming it is one of the little green men betting syndicates, they'll be well tuned to the flow of odds and the pattern of betting. Three or four significant on-the-nail bets in Norwich every time might cause some reaction." Ed smiled at Simon. "I don't know why you keep surprising me, my friend, but you most certainly do."

And so they decided to hold a watching brief for the next few games, with a view to betting big should the sequence continue… as indeed it did.

Norwich did win their next Championship game away to Luton Town one-nil. Then, they drew at home to Wigan Athletic one-all. And then they won away to Coventry City, one-nil, by which time they were into March.

***

Because Simon was busy, there was also a hiatus in Tom's exploration of Norwich's tunnel network. His patrolling, however, did continue – although at reduced frequency. Nevertheless, it took less than a week for Tom with his new contact lenses to make his next discovery of malign intervention.

He was scoping out the south-east of the city one early afternoon, just after lunch. His main focus was the environs of Carrow Abbey, a former Benedictine Priory and Grade I listed building, now something of a conference venue, which lay just across the river from Norwich City F.C.'s Carrow Road stadium. As his online research had suggested this might be the end point of one of the tunnels he'd discovered with Simon, he'd decided to have a look at the place from the outside. But he couldn't get near: a gated road and control booth acted as a deterrent to close inspection. Was there another way in? Had some corporation nabbed the building for its own profit-making purposes? Clearly, he needed to go away and do a more professional job of research.

Returning to the inner-city ring road, Tom took a junction heading back north. Here the A147 became King Street, which extended a couple of miles into the heart of the city, right up to Tombland and the cathedral. At one time in the past, the street had been an entertainment centre and den of iniquity: a plaque on the wall of one building noted how, in the nineteenth century, the street had hosted twenty-six pubs and two breweries, although with the closing of The Ferry Boat at the lower end of the street, The Last Pub Standing (much further up) was the sole survivor of the trade. Still, the street was merely a drunkard's lob away from the river and the newish Riverside complex (which filled the space between the football stadium and the train station), and this provided plenty of options for the hungry and thirsty.

Further up King Street, a number of elegant flat complexes had replaced dives and warehouses, and these were interspersed with old, spalled-brick buildings. However, some vestige of the street's alcoholic heyday had been retained in the names that could be found along its course, inherited from previous pubs and the brewers' art: Polypinn Yard; Malsters Yard; Three Tuns Court; Steam Packet House; Swan Yard. And here also resided one of the city's historical treasures: Dragon Hall. This was a Grade-1 listed medieval merchant's trading hall dating from 1430, which publicity claimed was unique in being the only such trading hall in

Northern Europe to have been owned by just one man. The long, wonky Tudor building, with its vertical dark-wood posts and slightly overhanging upper storey, now served as the National Centre for Writing, although tours of its medieval interior could also be booked. Over its modest front door, a large metal dragon jutted from the upper storey, from which bracket hung a banner that announced the hall's current caretakers and purpose.

As he got near, the first thing Tom caught – from the opposite pavement – was a flash of unnatural colour on the ground floor level. On the cream plaster above the door, and beneath the hanging banner, flowing to a mullioned window, were seventh-dimensional words.

Bugger!

Tom moved opposite the desecrated frontage, but hesitated on crossing the road. From here, he could make out what the message said, or rather, what the *messages* said. Above the lintel was writ:

Use this money to help the poor

And to the side was:

History fetishes cost lives

It seemed that the alien manipulators (Smith?) wanted to stoke the fires of the socially aware and turn them against the preservation of a past which, he had little doubt, most of them despised and wished they could erase.

Well, given the problems in the world, places like this are a bit of a money… drain.

Tom frowned, both inwardly and outwardly. That's not what he truly believed… was it? One of the reasons he loved Norwich was its well-preserved and extensive history, and the sense that he was in a place that had *soul* and *significance*. He scratched his nose. Was the message having an effect on him? Next he would be joining that one-dimensional clique in insisting that space travel, research, art, and just about anything that cost money, ought to be pared back or indeed utterly defunded until all of the homeless were housed and everyone lived in a harmonious, yet utterly dull and pointless world of just-above-subsistence-level beige.

Gosh. Where had all *that* come from?

Tom actually shook his head, as though the physical act would clear it of the debate that raged within: he needed his limited mental capacity to work out what to do now. Given he'd spotted this, Smith would expect him to act. Tom was suddenly aware of the weight of the rucksack on his back – holding his magnets and can of paint.

He quickly looked around. There were people on the street – not many, but a few, coming from both directions. So, he couldn't strike now even if he wanted to. And he *didn't*. He could just imagine the furore caused by spraying over the messages. For a start, those fruitcakes – what were they called, *Mrs Brown's Boys?* – they'd have a meltdown. But then again, those tossers of the Krustie Brigade would probably take the rap – assuming Tom got away with it and wasn't pinged by some hidden CCTV (*well-hidden CCTV*, as a quick scan revealed nothing obvious on the august building).

Actually, suggesting that he didn't want to strike *wasn't* true: Tom *did* want to do something about the message, and that was the killer. Knowing that Smith might be behind it made him desperately want to sabotage the alien's efforts, especially since the message was one he disagreed with (*didn't he? No! Stop that!*), but not at the price of making things worse. If only there were some less-messy way to attend to the matter – as surely there must be. What had Simon suggested – a ray gun? Well, why not? He'd have to look into it. Try to press Smith more forcefully on how he had *apparently* got rid of the message on the war memorial.

And now? Well, there was nothing he could or would do. Yet, if he reported this to Smith later via the Cloud, he was certain Smith would enjoin him to act. And *then* what? So, there was only one solution: do nothing and *say* nothing. Pretend that this had not taken place. Given that in his reports, he tended to give a precis of his route – in truth, mainly to convince Smith of his industriousness – he wondered how Smith would respond.

***

ARE YOU SURE YOU HAVE FOUND NOTHING? I HAVE INTELLIGENCE THAT THE DIRECTORS HAVE BEEN SHOWING INTEREST IN THE AREA AROUND THE RIVER TO THE SOUTH-EAST, WHERE YOU HAVE BEEN PATROLLING. PLEASE REDOUBLE YOUR EFFORTS.

Tom pushed his chair back from the computer. Well, Smith hadn't stated 'go back to King Street' in actual words, but the message was much the same. King Street was the natural route to that part of the city, and Tom had made the mistake of stating that this was where he'd been the previous day (he only updated Smith twice a week). If he hadn't been convinced of Smith's duplicity, this now sealed the deal. But there was also the chance that Tom had said too much himself: in Smith's eyes, his recruit must either be untruthfully embellishing his efforts and claiming activity that hadn't taken place, or somehow be exhibiting extraordinary levels of ineptitude, given that the Dragon Hall message could not have been missed by any ocularly reinforced passer-by.

After a moment's thought, Tom decided that the best of a set of bad options was to admit something else. He pulled himself back to the keyboard and began to type below Smith's message at the foot of his latest chapter, which he had tentatively called 'The Clusterfuck':

SORRY, COULD HAVE MISSED SOMETHING. LENSES CAUSING SOME PROBLEMS. HAVING TO TAKE THEM OUT OCCASIONALLY TO CLEAN AND REST EYES.

Would that be enough? Perhaps not, so he concluded:

WILL RETURN TO THAT AREA AS SOON AS I GET THE CHANCE.

He saved the chapter in the Cloud, waited ten minutes, and heaved a sigh of relief at the absence of any further hectoring. Then he went to make himself a cup of tea.

***

Tom didn't get back to King Street for another four days. This time, he came at the street from its northern end, skirting Castle Mound. He passed The Last Pub Standing, and for a moment fought with himself: *so tempting!* But it was already mid-afternoon. Perhaps a swift half on the way back after he'd done his duty?

A short distance away was 60 King Street, which used to be the location of The Three Tuns pub and was now a complex of flats and small businesses set around Three Tuns Court. The shop at 60 was closed and seemed to be in the process of being renovated, while a locked gate prevented entrance to a small courtyard that was used as a car park. Tom paused a moment. He suspected that the junction of the eastern tunnel from the castle ran beneath the court, with one route north to the cathedral and another south to Carrow Abbey. And by now he was sure there must be an exit here – which would explain how Smith had been able to get to Dragon Hall, a couple minutes' walk away. He needed to go back to explore the tunnel more thoroughly – but would this risk a subterranean encounter with Smith? And there was no easy way in here anyway. Did Smith have a key to number 60, or to the gate?

He moved on – but didn't have to go all the way to Dragon Hall to find devilry.

A short distance further down, the medieval church of St Peter Parmentergate sat opposite the King's Centre, home of the King's Community Church, a small café, and a suite of meeting rooms available for hire for courses and conferences. The Centre provided quite a contrast to the fifteenth century church, being a clean, modern building with a wide glass front and a clapboard design that was elegant even if out of keeping with the brick, stone and flint of the majority of the street's buildings. And over the glass windows there was a long red banner that in human-written script announced *Alpha runs here*, and then, over the top of this, in alien-written script, *Religious wankers.*

Bloody hell!

It seemed as though Smith had been busy. Two messages on the street, left in such a short period of time? Whatever was going on in the city really did seem to be ramping up – and in fact, hadn't Ed claimed that his handler had warned as much?

Well, what was he going to do about *this*? The message was even more direct than the one on Dragon Hall, and more threatening, too. Being an atheist himself, Tom felt a certain sympathy for the message. Religion? *Big-Sky-Fairy-worshipping ignoramuses, poncing about in man-dresses and speaking in that mellow, faux-compassionate tone, then retiring to their secret chambers to bugger choirboys and roll about in piles of ill-gotten gold coins, the bunch of… wankers?*

Uh-oh!

Okay, he wasn't a fan of religion and religionists, but come on! Had this message hit a particular sweet spot that the others hadn't? And if it could create such a surge of negative energy in mild-mannered him, then what might those other messages have done to those for whom they resonated? Might the cathedral message have seeded the ground for future refugee bashing? Would the war memorial message induce Stop the War members to run amok on the right cue?

Tom tried to damp down the spasm of anger. *Stay calm! Think!*

But he was in the same quandary as before: if he acted, he risked making things worse – not just for himself, but for everyone. If he spray-painted the banner, he might prevent other passing atheists from throwing a wobbly, but the subsequent publicity would likely have theists across the city gnashing their teeth and praying to whatever God they believed in to strike him down with thunderbolts. This was getting out of hand. And if he did nothing, what would he say to Smith? That he *hadn't* come to King's Street again (but was Smith in some way watching him from afar?)? Or that he had come, but that he'd somehow missed this second message too?

To give himself time to think and allow his ire against all things holy to subside, he hurried on down the street. It was another two-to-three-hundred metres to Dragon Hall, on the same side of the street as the King's Centre. As he approached, he noted the St Anne's Quarter development rising behind the line of buildings, filling the space between this part of King Street and the river Wensum. He was even able to pick out Ed's new flat up high. He hadn't realised how close it was – in fact, it was probably only a couple of minutes' walk away. *Wow.* A coincidence? Perhaps he could give Ed a call, to see what he thought? But he hadn't brought his glasses, and he could hardly pop out his lenses for the other to use in order to see the alien messages.

Outside Dragon Hall, the message was still there. *Just.* Was it fading, or merely a trick of the light or angle of viewing? He *could* make it out, but had to focus. Was it now faint enough that he could legitimately claim not to have seen it?

For a minute or so, Tom stood on the opposite side of the street, considering options. If he had the glasses, he would have called Ed. *Note to self: never leave house again without them in my rucksack, along with all other relevant gear, including stuff related to caving.* Regarding the messages, he could probably get away with claiming to have only seen one, saying that he was shocked on encountering it and wondered what to do, etcetera, etcetera. But he would *have* to claim *one*. And he couldn't claim not to have his magnet and paint with him, as Smith knew he always carried them after a previous omission. So… what?

As a Norwich great would likely have exclaimed: *a-ha*!

***

PLEASE TRY TO GET MORE PAINT AS SOON AS POSSIBLE. THIS MESSAGE SHOULD BE EXPUNGED. I DO NOT KNOW IF I CAN DEAL WITH IT EASILY.

Tom laughed out loud. In response, he typed:

VERY BUSY WITH WORK BUT WILL TRY TO GET TO THORNS OR HALFORDS AS SOON AS HUMANLY POSSIBLE.

Smith had bought it. *Sucker!* The old 'spray can nozzle fucked' routine. He'd related his discovery of the King's Centre message (but not of the Dragon Hall ones), and claimed to have tried to deal with it, only to suffer spray can failure (*oh what a shame, damn and blast, always happens at the worst time, isn't that typical,* and so on). He'd bought himself some time, but he wasn't sure how much.

***

As it turned out, Tom was soon distracted from the King Street conundrum. He was heading downtown the following day – after spending a solid eight hours working on Alice's project – hoping to get to Thorns before it closed, when the phone in his fleece pocket vibrated an alert.

Got Martin, began the text from Simon, sent to the whole group. *One Life Left, St Benedicts Street. Saw him through the window. He didn't see me. It shuts at 5p.m. Will attempt to shadow.*

One Life Left was a gaming café where you could have a coffee and play a computer game of your choice on a big screen TV. Given that Martin was reputedly a gamer, the location was no real surprise. And this was right in the heart of the action, too, between the Vegan Enclave and The Halls, and close to…

Tom suddenly realised it was a Wednesday, and that meant he knew where Martin would be from 6p.m. The Rumsey Wells was a short stroll from the café, situated just after the junction where St Benedicts Street (or a short stretch of tarmac that was named Charing Cross) became St Andrews Street. But what would Martin do in the hour in between? Maybe he would get to the pub early? Was this an opportunity?

The phone buzzed again. Ed replied: *Go get him!*

Then a moment later it was Amanda: *Be careful!*

Tom was currently on St Giles Street, outside an art gallery. He considered how to respond. Since he was only planning on entering Thorns for the show of it, rather than with the aim of making an actual purchase – as his old can of paint did, in fact, still function – making a detour or omitting the visit entirely wasn't a problem. After all, he wasn't sure Smith was actively observing him – and suspected that he *wasn't*, given the way he responded to what Tom told him in his Cloud messages – but he'd been spooked by the whole CCTV scenario, which had heightened his sense of caution. And what had Smith said during their first meetings? That it was Alphas who were the source of extra-terrestrial interest, whereas he was a secret Omega, a non-entity of little interest to the popcorn-munching alien watchers, and hence, he was probably an unfollowed extra.

Sod the paint deception.

He started typing: *I am close. Where are you?*

Seconds later, the reply came: *Round the corner down the steps. Lurking.*

Tom knew the place. He wended his way to St Benedicts, emerging by the Ten Bells pub. Here, he turned east and strode past the Tipsy Vegan a few doors down, then continued past a succession of specialist shops, pubs, cafés and restaurants. But rather than risk walking by the front of One Life Left, he bore off down the narrow St Margarets Alley onto Westwick Street and yomped to the next junction, turning right onto St Lawrence Little Steps. The passageway here ascended between yet another flint-faced medieval church (St Laurence's – yes, of different spelling!) and a long brick building. There was a small flight of steps near the top of the passage – with a metal banister running up its middle – at the bottom of which slouched a leather-clad, blonde-haired man attempting nonchalance.

"Wotcha, mate," said Simon, as Tom puffed into view. In spite of the chill in the air, his leather jacket was open to reveal a thin, red t-shirt bearing a *Stranger Things* logo.

"Hi, Si. Is he still there?" Tom nodded towards the building on the right-hand corner ahead.

"Think so. At least, he hasn't come out this way, and when I had a peek a couple of mins ago, he was inside."

"Alone?"

"No. With a ginger dude. I've seen him around, but never spoken to him."

"Ah, right." Did that make things better or worse? Tom supposed that if Martin had a friend the two would probably focus on one another when they emerged, so maybe there'd be less 'looking around'. "Uh, have you got the afternoon off?"

"Me? Nah. But the comic shop was a bit quiet, so the boss let me leave early, and I spotted Martin just after."

"Right, so, what's next?"

"Not sure. Pretty new at this spying thing. I guess we just wait for him and see where he goes. See who else he talks to. Take a snap of the ginger bloke for Ed to trace. That sort of thing."

"Well, we know where he'll be at six, as it's Wednesday." Tom had related his intel on Keith during their last meeting at the Alex.

"Ah, yeah – I'd forgotten. The Rumsey."

They didn't have long to wait. Fortunately, Martin and his friend did head Rumsey-wards when they emerged from the café: if they'd turned in the opposite direction, the spies might have missed them altogether. And as Tom surmised, the two men were speaking to each other as they passed the head of the alley, oblivious of the pair watching from below.

Tom and Simon looked at each other for a moment in indecision, but then Simon winked, held a finger to his lips, and started up the steps. Tom followed close behind.

They allowed the two men to gain a lead of maybe twenty metres.

At one point, Simon turned back into Tom as the ginger man swivelled to check the traffic before crossing to the other side of the road, with Martin hidden beyond his bulk. Simon paused for a moment with his back to the action. After a moment, he whispered: "Are we good?"

Tom's heart returned to his chest. "No! No… Yes! Let's cross." And the pair resumed their stalking.

They didn't have far to go: art supplies, musical instrument shops, record shops, antiques, barbers, restaurants… and opposite a pedestrian crossing (where the street thinned to a single lane), the men turned right and disappeared up St Gregorys Alley, passing in front of a red phone box set before the iron-fenced grounds of the eponymous church.

"Quick!" said Simon. "I know where they're going." He started forwards again at a jog, startling Tom into similar activity. At the foot of the alley, by the French café on the corner, they peered… just in time to catch the back of Martin following his friend into a building half-way up, nearly opposite the church tower.

"Athena Games," stated Simon. "Of course!"

"Another shop?" said Tom. "But won't that close soon? Five thirty?"

"Nope. It's not just a shop, it's a gaming centre. It's open until ten-thirty. I bet Martin stays until he has to leave to meet Keith at the pub in…" he checked his watch, "an hour and a quarter."

"What now? We can't just follow him in, or we'll be seen."

"*You* can't," said Simon, with a smirk. "He knows you're up to something. And he's seen you with Ed. But he's not seen you with *me*. I won't stand out inside. I'm *known*." He puffed out his chest. "Maybe I can scope him out. Listen in. Say 'hi' even."

"Er, yes, good idea. You should do that."

"We can meet after. Why don't you find a spot out of the way nearby, and I'll text you when Martin moves, then I'll follow him. Make sure he goes to the pub. Then we can meet and compare notes, yeah?"

It was clear that Simon was enjoying himself. And Tom couldn't deny he felt a frisson of excitement, too. He tried to mask this with a serious expression: two spies, on a mission. "Good. Then I'll… I'll… check out the Rumsey. Yes. Check out where they might meet. See if there's some corner where we might be able to hide from sight and watch them. That sort of thing. As long as you keep me informed about Martin, and I'm gone before six, it should be alright."

"Great," said Simon. "We have a plan." He raised a hand for a high-five, which – after a moment's hesitation – Tom self-consciously gave. Then Simon turned and headed up the paved alley.

***

It was only a hundred metres or so further along the road to the Rumsey Wells. The pub was a large, yellow-brick building with a double doorway at the front, which was arched with a deep-blue stone surround. Although a fine pub with a good selection of ales, it just happened to be slightly too far from Tom's home (and the centre via the Lanes) to be a regular haunt for him, with so many nearer pubs to entice and pre-empt. In fact, the last time he remembered visiting was several months ago, when he'd met Ed to tell him about his blunder at the Pottergate underpass, which was hardly a memory he enjoyed recalling. But now he was here, he broke into a smile: dim lighting, wooden floors, various asymmetrical sections, a cellar bar that was only open on weekends, and a covered beer garden out back – a proper pub!

Before exploring further, Tom headed to the long bar – dissected into two by an intervening pillar – with its multitude of glinting hand pumps, backlit by yellow lights that sparkled off the optics on the wall behind. He ordered a pint of Adnams Mosaic, and as it was being poured he looked about. It was only then that he realised the walls around were coated in white beermats, like tiling. There were hundreds of them, originally plain, but clearly intended to be used like non-stick post-its, which the pub's punters had filled in over the years with messages, signatures, and drawings.

"Here you go, mate," said the barman, who sported dreadlocks. "That'll be…"

Tom absently handed over the requisite sum, then moved over to the left hand wall, where a long wooden counter ran beneath a partition window looking over a stairwell leading to the cellar bar. There were two or three tall seats here: Tom settled into one and started to read the mats tiling the area above and beside the window. There were one or two decent sketches, but in the main, the pictures were drawn in shaky (drunken?) hand, and the messages were trite, or boastful, or ambiguous.

And then he spotted: *Ricky ♡ Teresa*

WTF!

That could only be the dodgy pair they'd been following – especially given the unconventional, h-less spelling of Teresa's name. So – the place was a definite haunt of the couple, which was perhaps no surprise, given that they weren't far from the Vegan Enclave. Tom was nevertheless unsettled: he cautiously peered about. In spite of the relatively early hour, there were at least a dozen people scattered throughout the various spaces around. But none of them resembled the dubious pair. His shoulders sagged in relief. It was absurd to think that they would be in this very place at this very time.

Tom took a drink, then turned back to the wall and scanned some more. And then… *junkies*. The word came to his mind with a surge of emotion, for on one mat there was a sketch of the plaque with the hypodermic needle from St Giles Street, where he'd encountered an alien message.

Fuck!

Was this a joke?

He continued to scan, now giving each and every mat intense inspection. And then he shifted from his chair and stood, peering up at the mats that lined the wall above the bar and to its side. And then he crossed the room to examine the cardboard tiling on the opposite wall.

Terminus Est appeared on one very old mat in a high corner.

There was a picture of an entrance to the Pottergate underpass on another, with the legend *BLM* above this.

There were several aspects of the cathedral, as well as naïve sketches of other places in the city – statues, sections of buildings, vistas...

So – some were places where he'd found messages; maybe others were places where messages had been left before his time, or perhaps during his time but which he hadn't found? The clincher was a still-pristine card – clearly recently emplaced at the end of a row – that stated *King's Centre* and was surrounded by floating crucifixes.

And it wasn't just the drawings that were of mystical interest: throughout the patchwork were various cards that contained apparently meaningless numbers and letters. Co-ordinates? Codes? And in a couple of places there were even binary sequences of eight numbers, just like the letters in the ASCII coding they'd uncovered related to the football scores.

What was this place? An information nexus? An HQ of the nefarious?

Tom was so intent, he barely noticed the brief vibration of the phone in his fleece pocket.

And he certainly lost all track of time.

Then...

"Hello, Tom. This is a surprise."

Tom's pint-holding hand trembled: had his glass been any fuller, he would have showered the floor. He hunched his shoulders and turned slowly. "Ah... hello, Keith."

Alice's husband stood before him, an arch expression on his handsome, finely bearded face. "Are you usually in the pub at this time? What would your employer say?"

"Ah, well, no, not usually, I mean..."

"So, maybe you're looking for someone? Someone like me, perhaps? Alice did tell me you'd taken an interest in my activities."

"Did she?" *Fuck!* Tom reddened. "Ah, no. I mean, I was just making small talk. I wasn't really…"

Keith laughed. "My dear wife tells me everything. Or at least, she does when I ask her about her latest project and her new employee. You were my suggestion, by the way. I'd heard good things about you. Still, if you're an early boozer, where's the problem as long as you do the work? And I can hardly talk, eh? So – what are you having?"

"Me? No, um, I can't…" Tom was too flustered to think straight. "I was just going to have one, and then–"

"Nonsense. You're here now, so I insist you join me." Keith flicked his head over one shoulder. "There's a table over by the door. You settle in. What's that?"

"Um, Mosaic."

Tom shuffled over to the indicated table and put down his near-empty glass. How was he going to get out of this? Then he looked at his watch: ten-to-six. Keith was early, but only just. *Why didn't… ah!* He fetched his phone from his pocket. He had a text message waiting from Simon: *Martin and Ginge about to leave. Will follow.*

As Tom's uncooperative fingers and mind struggled to compose a response, Keith returned from the bar, placed two pints on the table, and sat across from Tom. Then the front door opened…

"What the *fuck* is he doing here?"

"What the fuck indeed," replied Keith, levelly. "I was thinking that maybe we should try to find out. Sit, Martin. Trevor…" he addressed the ginger-haired man, who was in his late-twenties, "fetch Martin a drink, please, and then join us."

As a frowning Martin settled in next to Keith, his partner disappeared to the bar.

Tom gave a pained smile at the newcomer. "Oh, hello. Martin, isn't it?"

"You know damned well it is, as you revealed at the Belgian Monk. And now you're here."

"Maybe it's time to dispense with the pleasantries, Tom, eh?" said Keith. "We both know that something is up. It seems that we have each been keeping an eye on the other." He paused to drink, but his eyes – peering over the top of his pint glass – never left Tom's face.

"Well, I suppose that's true."

Keith settled his pint slowly and smiled. But he didn't speak. *Waiting.* The silence quickly became uncomfortable. Martin also remained silent, flicking his gaze between the two men.

Tom broke first. "I... don't know what to say."

"Clearly."

"Well... you followed me first. I mean, Martin did. I saw him – at City College. And then elsewhere. So why were *you* following *me*?"

"Why do you think, Tom?" asked Keith.

"I don't know. I mean, I'm just a regular guy, er..."

"Except you're not, Tom." Keith tapped the table with one finger. "You are far from regular. Or ordinary. And what you have been doing is hardly innocent, eh?"

Tom puffed out his cheeks. "I'm not sure what you mean." He looked up: the man named Trevor had returned. The new arrival dispensed his purchases then sat in the seat next to Tom. It was only then that he appreciated the ginger-haired man's size: he was so broad of chest and shoulder that Tom had to turn slightly to the side to stop their arms from touching, pressing him against the wall. The new man turned to smile at him.

"Ah, Tom. Meet Trevor. The third musketeer. I'm surprised you don't recognise him. He's been on your tail for some time now – ever since Martin was rumbled."

"Wotcha," said Trevor, then: "*traitor!*"

Tom froze and looked between the smiling – snarling? – man, and the group's apparent leader. "Traitor?" he squeaked. "What do you mean? I'm not–"

"Come now, Tom," said Keith. "Don't play the innocent. We know what you have been doing. We've been following you, hoping to interdict when possible. What we don't know is *why* you are doing it. Money? Some sense of importance? Has the Thruvian offered you anything else?"

"Thruvian?" *Smith!* "You mean... um... what do you know? Who *are* you?"

"At least he's not actually denying it," said Martin.

Tom felt his phone vibrate in his pocket again. Undoubtedly Simon. Where was he? Outside?

"I… I'm not saying anything." Tom stiffened his shoulders. Trevor was menacing, but they were hardly going to start slapping him about in a public place. And Simon must be near – maybe even watching from some shadow. "You already seem to know something about me, but I don't know anything about you. Quid pro quo. *You* go first."

Martin was about to speak, but Keith rested a hand on his arm to stay him. "Okay, Tom. I'm not sure how much you know about the grand scheme of things. Maybe a lot, but maybe not so much. I have been in this game for quite some time – my colleagues less so. Trevor is a former student of mine and Martin, as you know, a current one. I suspect your experience is also relatively short." He moved his hand from Martin's sleeve and folded both hands together behind his sparkling pint glass. "We are perhaps best described as guardians of the status quo. We attempt to track attempts to upset the balance and interfere with the normal course of events. Does this make any sort of sense to you?"

Surprisingly, Tom had started to feel calmer. His bout of bravado had come off; he felt on a more equal footing, even though outnumbered. "Kind of. But you're hedging. You've not said the, er, 'a' word."

"It's difficult to say, isn't it, without sounding crazy or absurd?" Keith actually smiled. "But okay, I'll say it. We aid an *alien* species to uphold the compact of non-interference. There. Satisfied?"

Tom nodded. "Yes, I guess so. But I, well, I thought you were somehow on the, um, dark side."

"Us!" exclaimed Martin. "You're the bad guy here. You're the one running around causing chaos. Do you know what you're doing? Do you have any idea of the potential consequences?"

"I'm not bad!" exclaimed Tom. "I'm just, well, not intentionally. I was deceived. I thought I was doing good."

"Past tense, Tom?" asked Keith, now with some doubt. "*Deceived? Thought?*"

"Yes! But I only realised a few weeks ago that not all was, um, as it seemed." He didn't know how much he should say. There had been no mention of his friends yet. Were they known about, too? And what about Simon?

"Hmmmm," pondered Keith. "The war memorial episode?"

"Shit!" said Tom. "You knew that was me? Then why didn't you drop me in it?"

Keith smiled grimly. "That was considered. But in the first place, you hardly committed a crime – wanton cone-moving? You wouldn't have got more than a police caution for that, although the embarrassment might have put you off further mischief. But then we decided that would probably just lead the Thruvian to recruit someone else who might be more enthusiastic. More competent. Better the devil you know, and all that."

"We left you on the end of a line," said Martin, with some relish. "Like a fish on a hook."

Keith nodded. "Indeed. And we've tried to keep you close, so we can keep an eye on you and increase our chances of reducing the damage you've been doing."

"The job with Alice?" said Tom. "Is that part of the play?"

"Of course. Once I realised you were Alice's ex office mate, and quizzed her about you, it became clear what we had to do. I ensured you were invited to the Christmas meal and given the work you have now, although I'm not sure how effective any of this has been at thwarting your activities."

"And is Alice…?"

"No!" Keith was firm in his response. "Alice doesn't know what we are about. I have been involved for over ten years, and I am sworn to keep matters secret from the unapproached, even my wife. Please do not try to bring her into this. In any case, she is far too sensible to believe you."

"I won't. But what happens now? You say you're not bad, and I believe you." He paused a moment in thought. It was true: he *did* believe them. After all, it had never been entirely clear what Martin and Keith were doing that was wrong, apart from being in the frame for the beer festival sabotage, but that had probably been done by Smith, whether acting alone or with assistance. "I admit I have done some, er, things that seem a bit, um, *off*. But you need to believe me, I haven't meant any harm. Smith – the *Thruvian*? – told me I was helping. My job was to find messages–"

"That *he* had written," interjected Martin.

"Yes, that he had written, although I didn't know that until recently. Um. Yes. So, find messages, and then erase them. With red paint and a magnet. But the paint just made things worse, and the magnet didn't work."

"Magnet?" said Keith. "Ah, again I think you have been misled. The messages he leaves naturally decay over time – the evidence of his interference erases itself within a few days. If they didn't, then other species would notice before long and cause a fuss. Magnets actually help revivify the message. They were working, Tom, but opposite to how you thought."

"The sneaky fucker," chortled Martin.

Tom simply shook his head. He was not at all surprised. Still, the magnet apparently had another effect that presumably Smith had not intended him to discover, and which might ultimately be to his detriment. "And the paint?"

"No effect at all," said Keith. "Or rather, plenty of effect when sprayed over sensitive locations. More enduring, for a start. There is still seething resentment in some quarters about the defacing of the BLM mural and the refugee posters at the cathedral, which we assume was also you."

"Um, well…"

"Plus, it's entertaining for the watchers," added Trevor, in a gruff voice, "and provides an alibi for the Thruvian, as in, a more visible explanation for why people are starting to act crazy."

"So what now?" asked Tom once more, grimacing in embarrassment. "Pax?"

Keith and his comrades shared glances, as though telepathically communicating. At last, Keith ventured: "Provided you cause no more harm, yes, pax. In principle. But we don't trust you yet. We need proof that you are reformed."

"Okay. What do you want me to do?"

"Carry on your searching, but let us know as soon as you spot something, for we do have a device that will genuinely erase alien messages."

"What device?"

The others exchanged looks again, then Keith answered cautiously: "I think we'll keep that to ourselves for now. Until you've provided suitable *bona fides*. As I said, let us know what you find, and we'll deal with it as quickly as we can."

"Right. But how should I contact you?"

Keith thought a moment. "Not by email. Our adversary will likely have his talons in your computer accounts. You can visit your old office and leave a note there. I often meet Alice for lunch. Leave a note in the top drawer of the desk we chose for you."

Tom suddenly broke into a nervous smile, for he saw an immediate opportunity to shine. "Fine. But there's no need to wait. I can give you something now. Were you watching when I went to King Street...?"

***

"What the fuck, mate?" said Simon, as Tom walked through the door of Strangers Tavern on St Benedicts Street, less than a minute's walk from the Rumsey Wells. They had managed to arrange the rendezvous via text as soon as Tom escaped from 'the Musketeers' to go to the toilets. That was almost an hour ago.

"I have much to tell," said Tom. "I think we have been wrong about Martin and Keith. We may have allies."

Chapter 28: Fifth Interlude

"Great march, Robert!"

"Was it?" Robert Quigley grimaced at the Penitent who was wearing a threadbare navy jumper. His name was Andy, and according to the placard he leant on, he'd slammed the door in the face of a charity canvasser. He was something of a brown nose, too, in Robert's brief experience, having sucked up to the *primus inter pares* on their first meeting, and accompanied him like a lieutenant ever since. "I had over one hundred promises, but we can't have had more than ninety."

"Still, it's the biggest yet, isn't it?"

Robert nodded assent, then mumbled something about needing to talk to someone and edged away, looking for a more profitable encounter.

He saw the *Look East* reporter, *whatsername*, but she was busy interviewing a man who had gone spectacularly overboard in his attire – a frayed straw hat, shredded trousers, and a single shoe being added to his symbolic hair shirt. He moved towards the pair, putting himself in easy reach of the reporter for when she was done.

While lingering nearby, he appraised the nearest marchers. He recognised a couple of attenders from last time (Glen and Hazel?), who were in such an intimate huddle it suggested to him that 'betraying my current partner' was likely to be added to their tabs next time. And then there was his wife, Jane, cheerfully nattering with a couple of friends she'd encouraged to attend in order to make a day of it. None of the trio had tried that hard: Jane's small placard proclaimed 'I've been a bitch', while her friends' banners both simply stated 'Me too!'. They'd already covered their musty jumpers with much more stylist overcoats.

"Is it always like this?" asked Margaret, sidling up to him. She'd already folded away her banner, which had proclaimed: 'Mean boss' – a truth to which he could testify, since she was his line manager.

"Always?" said Robert, restively, glancing briefly at her and then away, looking for the journalist from *The Sun* he'd bumped into at the start. "It's only the fourth but, yes, it's pretty typical."

Margaret gave an uncertain smile. "Certainly cathartic," she posited. "And we've been lucky with the weather."

Robert's head snapped around. "Lucky?" They were in the middle of a mild spell. "This isn't meant to be a party, *Margaret*. On the last march, the weather was *much* more suitable." The heavy rain had provided fantastic optics, hence the even greater attendance and media presence at this event. He then glowered: "Penance shouldn't be easy!"

"Ah, sorry, I see what you mean." Margaret winced and bowed her head slightly: her meanness to Robert had abated over the last few months as the man's reputation had grown. "I'll have to come again when it is properly dreadful."

"Yes, you will." Robert turned his back, dismissing her.

"*Saint Robert!*" came a call from somewhere behind the crowd that currently blocked the road in front of the city council building. From somewhere near the war memorial? "*Saint Robert!*"

Robert stretched up his neck to see over those nearest. The crowd began to part. A group of three people was working its way towards him – cameraman, sound technician, and reporter. *Channel Four News* had turned up late. *Highly unprofessional*, he thought. They ought to join the next march just for that! Well, they were here now…

He began to smile, but then remembered himself. Prophets didn't smile.

It proved a profitable discussion. It turned out that *Channel Four* not only wanted an interview, but to talk to him about doing a documentary and following him around for the next few months.

Later, at home, Jane actually snuggled up to him on the sofa as they watched the news. "You look great, Rob," she said, resting her head gently on his shoulder. "I think the girls are quite envious of me."

Robert laughed. He did look rather magnificent on the screen. The reporter had got him to muss up his hair so it looked wild, and the practise he'd been doing in front of the bathroom mirror had paid off, for his wild-eyed stare and ferocious aspect looked almost biblical, like a furious Moses bellowing out the words of God. No wonder the media wanted a piece of him! He turned to speak to the top of his wife's head: "Envy is a sin, you know."

"Oooh, yes. They can put that on their banners next time."

Robert thought some more. *Only ninety*. He needed more. Many more. "Yes… next time. And what of your other friends? And *their* friends?"

"Oh, I guarantee they'll all want a piece of *this* action."

Robert nodded in satisfaction. By summer, who knew? Maybe he'd be able to bring the streets of the city to a standstill. And that *would* make great TV.

***

The so-called Krustie Brigade had continued its assault on well-to-do Norwich at a persistent though low-key level.

Its graffiti had extended from areas where it had been tolerated – mostly around the Pottergate underpass and the walls of the merely decades-old social housing blocks nearby – to places where it was seen as an intolerable blight, viz, older dwellings and buildings in the Lanes. And being wise to CCTV, its urban terrorists had generally gotten away with their vandalism, wearing ski masks and acting quickly whenever they knew they were likely to be caught on film. But though the group's activities had regularly featured in the local *EDP* paper, it had done nothing big enough to get on TV since the embarrassing episode with Amelia Opie's statue.

Nevertheless, what Blitz *had* achieved over the last couple of months was to act as a focus for wider discontent. The KB Crew had assimilated other drug users and dealers from its members' acquaintances, and then a sizeable proportion of the homeless population (constituencies that overlapped to some degree), and then… *others*. And while Blitz was stoked at the growth of his shadow force from a mere half-a-dozen to several score – all of whom looked up to him as their leader, boosting his ego to stratospheric levels – he had to admit that there were some cons, too.

The biggest problem was that many of the new members were less driven by Blitz's politics of grievance than by their own specific grudges against respectable society, which brought conflict with other groups. For the first few months, aside from the under-resourced and indifferent police, all Blitz had to worry about was the whinging of Mrs. Brown's Boys, or whatever they were called. But that was hardly a game of cat and mouse and more one of naughty dog and despairing owner: the crumblies had their hands full cleaning up the KB crew's messes, without having the capacity to actually track them down. Now the KB had to contend with the Knights of St Gregory too – who were far more energetic – and with them it was a case of hiding in the shadows. But worse still was the beef with the Rainbow Commando – for while Blitz and his originals were full-on supporters of the community, some of the new recruits had rather more prehistoric views…

"Leave the gays alone!" he'd bellowed at his assembled troops at their last meeting in the ground floor of a derelict building to the north of the city. "Their cause is just, yeah? They're antifascists, just like us. They're our brothers and sisters!"

But he'd seen the smirks, the laughing asides, and caught the odd derogatory remark. There was one clique that had apparently made a habit of collecting the colourful berets of the Commandos as trophies, seeing this as no more than an innocent game. But Blitz knew that the severe-looking woman who led that group wasn't laughing.

With ego inflated, Blitz needed more. Daubing his tag on yet more colourful plaster walls of historic buildings was no longer doing it for him. He wanted something bigger, *needed* something bigger.

"So, what we gonna do, B?" asked Skid. The small group was in the graveyard of St Peter Parmentergate on King Street, clustered around Blitz, who currently perched upon an old stone tomb. Like a number of other medieval churches in Norwich, Parmentergate had been repurposed – but nothing so genteel as the antiques emporium at St Gregory's, or the hands-on science centre at St Michael's, or the café at St Simon and St Jude's. This place was rather edgier, having been converted into a radical skateboard shop called The Drug Store.

"It's gotta be spectacular," said Blitz.

"Well, what about Dragon Hall?" said Mary, scratching an arm vigorously with one tattooed hand. She'd passed the place the other day and for some reason couldn't get it out of her mind, to Blitz's annoyance. "Maybe spray the whole fuckin thing. *That's* big."

"Big for Norwich," scowled Blitz. "I want something that'll get on the news, like, everywhere. Not just friggin' *Look East*. I'm talking national news. *International*."

"We haven't done any of the churches yet," said Mags, who cast a menacing look towards the King's Centre, visible through the stone entrance to Parmentergate. "The churches are rich. You know, built on the labour of the people. They claim to care about the poor, but have you been in one? Full of crumblies wearing pearls. We could do the cathedral.

Reckon that might cause the Archbish of Cunterbury to have a seizure, yeah?"

Blitz nodded. That was better…

"Or what about the war memorial?" said Jonno. He was a newer recruit, but full of enthusiasm and fire. He had something to do with the Socialist Alliance, although Blitz couldn't get his head around the politics of that organisation. It seemed there'd been something of a schism recently: some had thrown in with the Rainbow Commando, but Jonno's faction claimed the Commando represented white middle class concerns and had instead chosen to back Blitz's group. *"Fuckin' warmongers."*

"That's been done," said Skid.

"No, it hasn't," Jonno scowled. "Some drunk geezer moving cones about isn't the same as doing the thing properly. They spent millions doing it up. Just think how much bread that could have bought to feed the proletariat!"

Blitz nodded slowly. "Yeah… some good ideas there. We need to keep thinking. Hold a watching brief."

"*Watching briefs*?" said Mags. "Wot are they? Pants with cameras in? I don't understand."

"No, it just means we sort of keep an eye out for stuff," clarified Skid. "Think a bit more. That sort of thing."

Jonno scowled deeply. "Hell, why not do *all* of these places. *Simultaneously*. A day of action. Rise up against all the capitalist pigs and their edifices of power. Start a real revolution."

Blitz caught the glint in Jonno's eye, and he liked what he saw *and* what he heard. "Fuck! You know what… yeah. Maybe. That sort of thing. If we could pull that off, we'd be headline news every-*fucking*-where!"

"I reckon we'd need more crew than we got to do that," said Mary, who seemed less convinced.

"More than we have *now*," said Jonno. "But we can get more. *I* can get us more."

More? For Blitz, that was the magic word.

***

The so-called Krustie Brigade wasn't the only informal organisation to have grown over the last few months. Thomas Browne's Boys (aka Mrs.

Brown's Boys, aka Thomas Brown's Scrubbers) had also expanded its membership. From its origins as an indignant pair of elderly married couples, the group had grown to first include various friends and relatives, and then members of sub-groups of The Norwich Society who wanted to preserve the city's heritage, and then a corps of members of the local Conservative Party (who were mainly acquaintances of Colin). The Merchant House café on Fye Bridge Street had therefore ceased to be large enough to accommodate the totality of outraged elders.

"Order, order!" called Colin McArthur, sitting at a table at the head of the meeting room on the first floor of The Halls. The Erpingham Room – a tidy space with lime green walls, a fireplace to one side, and a whiteboard behind him – was intended to accommodate no more than two-dozen, although they'd manage to squeeze in a few more (the excess currently standing at the back of the room, occluding the light from its pair of arched windows). In short, they'd even outgrown this venue.

"Well, they don't'," continued Hector, ignoring the Chair's call. "They really don't!"

"I said *order*!" For the umpteenth time that evening, Colin wished he had a gavel. Instead, he had to make do with thumping one hand onto the white tablecloth, causing the water in the jug – and in his and Ronnie's glasses – to tremble, as though presaging the imminent arrival of a stomping T-Rex. "Hector – please! Wait until you are recognised by the Chair!"

The tonsured gent harrumphed and sat back down. From the row in front, a jacket-and-tie wearing man with thick glasses turned around to face the miscreant. "If the police don't do anything," he said, "it's because they don't have the resources to do so."

"I thought that's the way you like it," said Ronnie Waites snidely from Colin's side, ignoring his friend's attempt at re-establishing due process. "Minimal public services."

"You can't blame us for this," retorted the man, Timothy Kendrick, looking back. "There's not been a single Conservative on the council for ages. The police are funded from local monies. You need to *own* your own mess here, Ronnie."

"Well, that's because the council has been underfunded by central government for years…"

Colin sighed and banged his hand on the table once more. Though it was nice to have a bigger group, it meant there were various cliques within it, and contrary to the belief of millennials, old people weren't all of one mind. Ronnie, for example, claimed to be a Liberal Democrat, though Colin suspected he leant further left than this. And so sometimes the group's members squabbled like nursery children – unbelievable for persons of their supposed maturity and wisdom. "Can we just stick to the issue, please, and save the politics for after?"

"Okay, well, if the police won't do anything, or *can't* because of a lack of resources, then what about this other lot?" continued Hector. "The Knights of St Gregory. Can't we make common cause with them? They seem a righteous lot of–"

"*Vigilantes*," said Timothy.

"Okay, vigilantes. But at least they're doing something socially responsible. Filling a gap. Don't say you haven't noticed the clean-up of the area around St Gregory's and this side of the water."

"Yes, but at what cost," said Doris, Ronnie's wife. "Harassing the homeless?"

"The poor dears!" enjoined Annie, Colin's better half. The two women were in militant mood themselves, having been demoted from the top table ("There's only room for two of us, dear," Colin had explained to Annie earlier).

Colin tapped his hand less vigorously this time, but he couldn't hide his frustration. "Again, ladies, I am sure we all accept that many of these homeless are unfortunates suffering for no reason of their own…" He noticed Timothy fold his arms and glower but chose to ignore him. "But Hector is right – the area is now less threatening."

"And they've also had a big effect on petty crime," Hector continued.

Colin hated to concede to the disruptive one, but he had a point. "They have, haven't they. Maybe… maybe there is something to this?"

"Aye," said Ronnie from beside him. "We need some foot soldiers of our own. More sprightly people. People who can act. Can get there on time. Can apprehend the villains."

"That's just typical," said Margery, sitting behind her sister-in-law, Doris. "You men always want to turn things into wars, talking about soldiers and the like."

"Well, how else are we going to stop the blighters?" asked Hector, re-directing his attention.

Other voices rose to agree or contest. Colin closed his eyes and leant back, leaving them to it.

The debate continued for some time. But an idea has been formed, and it had legs.

***

Although the Knights of St Gregory had also grown in number over recent months, they had done so *virtually* rather than physically, having only accepted two new members since the start of the year. As Ken had explained to Grandmaster Jim Taylor, being a knight was a prestigious position, and shouldn't be open to just anyone. But for Jim, there was a sense that they were now a much more significant organisation than they had been, with a range of hidden supporters as well as sponsors from the local business community.

"New intel," said Ken, standing up from the computer desk at the side of the annex. "Inspector Blue has the address of a place off Cowgate."

"What is it this time?" asked Tania, looking particularly badass today in her long, red leather coat and combat boots. "More junkies?"

"Nope. Bloke's a burglar. Record as long as your arm – and mine too. Got out of prison two months ago. Police suspect he's back to his old ways, but they've got nothing definite on him, and until he slips up, they can't justify a stakeout or raid."

"So," said Jim, cautiously, "is he our next target?"

"Reckon so," said Ken, approaching the campaign map of Norwich laid out over the old dining table in the converted double garage in Taverham. He plucked a red pin from amongst a forest of these at one edge of the map and – after a moment's consideration – pushed it into the map at the relevant location. As he did so, others sashayed over from the scattering of comfy chairs and sofas by the walls to have a closer look.

"Just off Magdalen Street," confirmed Tania. "Not far from that possible doss house off Bull Close – the one Sergeant Orange alerted us to."

"Isn't that where James is at the moment?" said Jim, looking at the close positioning of the white pin and the red. All these colours got confusing. In retrospect, maybe they should have chosen a different class of things to use for the names of their secret sympathisers in the local constabulary. Animals perhaps? Sergeant Warthog? Inspector Lion? Constable Giraffe?

"No. Sir James, Sir Maurice and Dame Keri are at the station. Remember – we got that tip off about some scumbag coming up on the train from London. County lines courier. But it does make sense to send another quest off to this general area here – kill two dragons with one lance, as it were."

"What about Vicky's PCSO patrol?" asked short-arsed Adam, as he fiddled nervously with his taser. "I thought she said her beat was around Anglia Square today."

Ken nodded. "Yes. Well remembered. Perhaps we should get her on the radio and ask if she'd swing by. Get a sense of the area. Take some photos." He turned to look at Jim. "Grandmaster?"

Jim smiled. "Of course!" He manoeuvred around the map and paced over to his 'throne'. Standing nearby, Sir Piotr manipulated the controls on their radio, setting the correct frequency. Then he gave a small bow and handed this to a now-seated Jim, who held the sole authority to command. Jim especially loved this bit. He'd been allowed to choose the codewords and, well, what was that most knightly of weapons? It was only natural for *his* call sign. And after that, no one had objected to his other choices.

Jim opened connection and began: *"Broadsword calling Danny Boy, Broadsword calling Danny Boy... over..."*

A week later, they received a delegation from Thomas Browne's Boys, and the Knights' power and influence rose further.

***

Cathy leant forwards until her head was almost touching Harry's. "In truth, this is all getting a bit tense."

Harry beetled his brows and raised a hand to slowly caress his neatly trimmed moustache. He'd come alone to the Greenhouse Trust to browse the books and gallery and have a pot of tea, but Cathy had homed in on him, desperate to talk to someone. She still wore her rainbow-coloured beret, having just returned from a patrol. "Tense?" he repeated. "You surprise me."

But it was clear to Cathy from the glint in Harry's eyes that surprise was the last thing he felt. "Well, yes, when I say *tense* I mean a bit mental... um, wrong choice of words. I'm not trying to mock the impaired, but..."

Harry held up one calming hand. "I understand. And I assume you are talking about our beloved Commando, which I admit I have rather avoided recently. Tell me more."

Cathy hunched even closer. "Yes. It's Clare. She's gone all Margaret Thatcher in a kind of left wing way. Right bossy and a little bit extreme. I can't talk to her, and she won't listen to anyone else. Maybe you, Harry? You've always been the voice of reason."

"You'll be telling me I'm a kind of father figure next, Cathy dear. I'm not sure I approve of that. There's still life and lust in this old dog yet. But before I speak to her, I need to know what exactly is going–"

Cathy's eyes widened as they redirected towards the opening door. "Oh, *bum*. Look out."

Harry turned to see Clare enter in deep conversation with a youngish man with a severe face and crewcut, both wearing the distinctive berets. Clare noticed the seated couple, gave a brief nod, but continued her discussion unchecked. The newcomers headed to a table at the opposite end of the room.

"See!" hissed Cathy.

Harry turned around. "See what? There's no clear evidence of psychosis to my eye."

"Do you know who that is?" Cathy didn't give Harry a chance to respond. "That's Stuart. He's not gay. He's not even *bi*."

Harry grimaced. "Cathy – if we have supporters from the straight community then–"

"He's Socialist Worker. Or one of those groups. He's like their local leader. Thing is, it's not just him. There's loads of them. And last week, she was canvassing Fran from Stop the War. She's also straight. And she's onboard too."

Harry's frown deepened. "Onboard? Do you mean, a beret-wearing colleague?"

"Yes! That's right! Since you came to the last meeting at The Castle, after we were attacked, she's been like a woman possessed. She's had us do double martial arts training, bought a crate of pepper spray from a dodgy source, and been recruiting. There are now more militants in the Commando than members of the community itself. It's crazy."

"That's… concerning. I did question the motives of this group at the very start."

"Yes, Harry, I remember. I'm afraid of where this might end. Clare and Stuart and Fran, well, they've been having these secret top-level meetings, and she's not telling us anything. I don't know what they're up to, but I suspect it's a lot more than just patrolling, and supporting, and giving advice. I think *targets* are being identified. People and things that she thinks are homophobic. Or were homophobic. Or might become homophobic at some time in the future. And that's pretty much *everything*. And Stuart and Fran scare me. There's a sense of violence with them. I mean, all this stuff – it's just not us. We're a peaceful community."

Harry slowly sat back in his chair. "I remember marches. And riots. I thought we'd got beyond all that. At least here, in sleepy Norwich." He shook his head. "Ah, the perversity of human nature. I've always thought, if you want to find a sinner, look for someone deeply religious. If you want to find a bellicose individual full of hate, go to a pacifists' march. And I hate to say this, but if you want to find someone who abhors diversity and tolerance, go seek anyone marching with a banner demanding those very things." Then he sighed, looked down, and saw his cup of tea, which was no longer gently steaming. "Okay, Cathy. I'll try to have a word with her. But I can't promise she'll be upfront with me, or even listen to my concerns."

And Harry's doubt proved well-founded: when he eventually found an opportunity to chat to Clare, she wasn't and she wouldn't.

***

"Oh, look," sneered Jezza Armitage, "it's the *splitters*."

Rod Owens and John 'Junior' Bates, ex-members of the Compleat Anglers, had to pass by Jezza's table to get to the bar. Rod seemed unperturbed: he waved his unlit pipe. "Evening chaps!" Then he nodded at those old colleagues amongst the group he recognised. "*Bernie. Reg. Martin.*"

"You've got some cheek coming in here," said Jezza. "This is our manor."

"You can't bagsy the entire pub, Jezza," said Junior. "We're by the river. It's a natural place to meet. So it's the Angliar Army's home too."

"Nick our concept *and* our pub," muttered Bernie.

"And you nicked the name," said Junior. "Rod came up with it in the first place!"

"Jointly!" squawked Jezza. "It were in my mind; he just spoke it first!"

Rod gave a gentle grin through his beard. "Doesn't matter, Junior. Let it go. They're welcome to it. I'll get these in – you join the lads, eh?"

Junior nodded, winked at their former comrades, and headed further into the pub.

"Good riddance," muttered Jezza. "I'm only surprised you didn't go with the idiot boy's name. What were it? The Fishy Five or summat? That's about the number of members you've got, isn't it?"

Rod frowned. "First, Junior is forty-eight and far from an idiot. And second, we now have eighty-three members. Today's meeting is just for the committee."

"*Eighty-three*," spluttered Jezza. "Eighty... ah, well, novices, I guess."

Like the fish in the river recently, Rod decided not to take Jezza's bait. He tucked the unlit pipe into the side of his mouth and continued good-naturedly: "I take it that's more than you've recruited? Never mind. There's plenty of fish in the river... if you know how to catch them."

"Not with the worms you use!"

Rod frowned. "Steady on, there." This was one of the reasons for the schism. "They work better than the maggots you use."

"Ha! Shows how much you really know," spat Jezza.

Rod took a deep breath. "Look, Jezza, we're not your problem. It's the bleeding *Watersporters* we need to worry about." After the public announcement of the formation of the Compleat Anglers, a group of canoeists and boaters had quickly gotten together to form their own counterweight organisation – and they'd already been on to the council and other authorities to press their case for better facilities, and to plead for further restrictions to fishing the Wensum within city limits.

"Them buggers are here too," seethed Jezza. "They're meeting downstairs as we speak!"

338

"Are they? Cripes! This place is getting crowded. Well, I must push on. Ale to procure. Good day to you all."

As he turned back for the bar, Rod caught the muttered words: "*Judean People's Front...*"

He couldn't help but smile: *No, we're The People's Front of Judea...*

Chapter 29: The Vegan Enclave

"…so, they aren't bad after all," concluded Tom. "In fact, they seem just like us."

The quartet were meeting at Ed's fifth-floor flat in the St Anne's Quarter one evening, a few days after Tom's encounter at the Rumsey Wells. As before, they were seated around a coffee table on which Ed's laptop formed a centrepiece.

"So you say," said Ed. "But what evidence did they provide to back up their claims? Si, did you see or hear anything of interest during this confab?"

"Nah. I could see them through the window from outside, but they were next to the door, so there was no way I could get in without being rumbled. I had to wait for Tom to escape before I got a rundown on what was going on."

"Well, I'm willing to give them the benefit of the doubt," said Amanda. "After all, we haven't actually caught them doing anything wrong."

"Exactly!" said Tom. "And given that Smith is responsible for at least some of the bad messages, it's possible he's responsible for them all. I've been thinking: the plaques in St Giles are in easy reach of his base at the Guildhall. The war memorial lies between St Peter Mancroft and the Guildhall. We saw him near the beer festival, which he could have accessed from the tunnel we found that went to The Halls, maybe going from his HQ via the castle." He paused and looked at Simon, who today was wearing a *South Park* t-shirt bearing a smug-looking Cartman. "And Si, that other new tunnel we found? I did say I thought the junction was below King Street, where the Three Tuns pub used to be. So, Smith could have taken that from the castle and emerged onto King Street not far from Dragon Hall and the King's Centre."

Simon pursed his lips and nodded. "Sure. And you also said you thought the northern branch of that tunnel goes to the cathedral. So, the tricky geezer could have used that to go there and leave those message on the children's drawings that you fucked up."

"Er, yes, thanks for reminding me of that." Tom turned back to Ed. "And finally, these Musketeers also knew that Smith is a bit of a villain.

They called him a *Thruvian*. It seems Keith has been involved in this game for quite some time – probably longer than any of us. So, that kind of validates them in my eyes."

"Stop making such a persuasive case," Ed scowled. "I don't like thinking well of others unless absolutely necessary, particularly if they're called 'Keith'! Very well. But it would still be good to verify that all these tunnels do exist and go between the places you suggest, adding weight to the Smith hypothesis."

"Well, I'm happy to explore further if Si is willing to come along."

"Sure, mate. But if Smith does use these tunnels to get about, don't we run the risk of bumping into him down below?"

"And maybe not just him," said Amanda.

Tom frowned. "What do you mean?"

"I can't believe Smith is the only one of the many aliens apparently watching us to know about the tunnels, or to use them. And maybe not just the aliens, but their familiars, too."

"Good point, Mands," said Ed. He turned a smirk upon Tom. "Indeed, I've more to say on this anon. In any case, my old mucker, you've proven Amanda's point yourself with that ghoul you encountered on your first descent into the underworld. Or perhaps we should say 'post-corporeal alien'? And that is one hit out of a total of, what, four short expeditions? Not that I'm trying to scare you away from further searches or anything."

"Well, you're doing a good job of it!"

"I'm not bothered about ghosts," said Simon. "But it would make sense to ensure Smith is somewhere else when we do hit the tunnels again. Fix that dude in place somehow."

Ghosts very much did worry Tom, and he suspected Simon might not be so blasé if he'd actually encountered one. But he had come to a similar conclusion about his handler. "Yes, I agree about Smith, and I've been giving the matter some thought. Two solutions come to mind. The first is that some of you guys go into the tunnel instead of me while I'm meeting up with him. And the second is that I arrange a meeting, but don't turn up, and go with Si instead. But I'm not keen on that one, as I don't know how Smith would react to me not showing, and I don't want to give him cause to doubt me."

"Well, the odds must be pretty good that he won't be in any tunnel on any particular visit," said Simon. "Especially the ones furthest from his base – like the one you think goes to the cathedral."

"In fact, I'd give you better odds than we got for Norwich's nil-nil last time out," muttered Ed. They'd all placed a bet on that game, since it was the last one for which they were fairly confident of the result, but the bookmakers' odds had been so low that not even Ed had made much money.

"So, where does that leave us?" said Tom. "Do you really want more proof, Ed?"

Ed struggled to answer. In the end, he gave an exaggerated sigh. "No. I take your various points, old chap. But you should arrange another meeting with these Musketeers and get them to cough up more. I'd particularly like to know whether they know about the tunnels, or whether they have any intel on Ricky and Teresa, or Terminus Est–"

"Or the football," added Simon.

Ed looked doubtful. "Well, maybe keep schtum about that one, just in case it's merely a fluke of the universe."

"You mean," said Amanda, with a small smile, "just in case they don't already know about it, and Tom's revelation leads them to start betting too, increasing the risk that whoever is manipulating the scores realises that someone has found out about their game, leading them to stop, thereby reducing your potential winnings?"

Ed returned the smile and raised it. "You're too sharp for me, Mands. I swear you and Si have received intelligence boosts from being in my presence all this time. It's just a shame that poor old Tom is still bumbling about like a barely sentient neanderthal."

Tom was unbothered by Ed's latest jibe, although something else weighed heavily on his mind: "Er… you said I should meet them, but I was thinking that maybe we should *all* meet them. Then you can appraise them yourselves, plus we might benefit from all the extra, you know, *heads.*"

Ed raised a cautionary hand. "You said they don't know about us yet, right?"

"Er, no. Well, they mentioned 'my friend from The Belgium Monk', but when I failed to bite, they let that lie. To be honest, I'm not sure they're the most sophisticated spies. Apparently, Martin was following me until I noticed him a couple of times, then Trevor took over. But they have their normal lives too, so they've not been tailing me all the time. I suspect it's mainly been at weekends and the occasional evening. And I'm almost certain they haven't been hacking me, as Keith seemed concerned about Smith's skills in this area."

"If they're worried about Smith," said Ed, somewhat smugly, "then they should be terrified of me. Anyway, I'd still play it cagy for now. After all, you say they have a device that will genuinely erase these messages, but they're keeping that from you – which is hardly playing nice. So, keep up your searches and then let us – and them – know next time you find something. You can use that intel to leverage more from them. And then… we'll see. Knowledge is power and all that, and I'd like to retain what little power we do have. Agreed?"

They discussed the matter a few minutes more, but with Ed having effectively made a decision for the group, none were desperate to contest it. Then Ed procured some bottles of beer from his fridge – for himself and Simon – and made coffee for Tom and Amanda. Afterwards, they talked about the football some more, before moving on to Ed's online searches.

"I have managed to hack into the CCTV of various pubs throughout the city," Ed began. "And I've been checking their clientele on quiz nights. And lo, I have indeed come across our meaty friend and his demonic crew, blasting all comers out of the water. But apart from making me feel better – in not having found anyone else able to beat them – I'm not sure about the value of this effort. I've identified eight individuals in total who interchange in the team, but they limit themselves to between four and six for quizzes, in accordance with the particular quiz rules or, I guess, availability. Anyway, I've decided to knock that effort on the head."

"What about the Cosy Club angle?" asked Tom.

"That's been my other line of enquiry. I found CCTV at a couple of nearby places with views of that establishment – but interestingly, there's no cameras in the CC itself, or at least, none I've managed to access. From these other cameras, I've clocked all eight of the black-clad twats entering the place at one time or another, but Monday seems to be sacred. They all turn up that day, usually just before 7p.m., and then they leave between eleven and midnight."

"They're having meetings!"

"Yep, Si," said Ed. "That is the logical deduction. But here's something I want you all to see, which I believe confirms the dubiousness of this clique and a hypothesis Amanda made earlier." He had been playing with his laptop in the meantime. Now he clicked on the mousepad and turned the device so the other three could see it.

On the screen, Tom watched a scene play out in the area in front of the Cosy Club, shot from off to the side, possibly Bedford Street. From the Wildman pub – or was the angle wrong? What was shown was a pair of vaguely familiar people – one male, one female – crossing the street from the pub's entrance to... "The door to the passage leading to the tunnel under Ponds!" he gasped.

"Indeed," said Ed. "Not only that, but–"

"They've got a key!"

"Bingo bongo, hole-in-one-go. They go in... and they don't come out. At least, at no point until I find one of them enter the CC three days later from a different direction."

"They must be using the tunnel!" exclaimed Amanda.

"Yep, though on this occasion, perhaps merely as a lazy short-cut. But I did find a second occasion where a different pair opened the door and entered the passage and then returned a couple of hours later. Which begs the question, where did they go, and what did they do? Visit Smith? Do something else dodgy? I will amass further evidence of times and places and people, and then attempt to correlate my findings with other intel." He sat back and folded his arms. "You may now praise my efforts."

All three murmured their appreciation.

At last, Ed continued. "So, while I keep on the trail of Terminus Est, and continue to try to track Smith – although with little hope, as I suspect almost all of his activities take place below ground and out of sight – the last string to pluck at is Teresa and Ricky. Amanda, darling, how would you feel about following up one last discovery I've made?"

Amanda reached up to play with her glasses. "Well... that depends. What have you found?"

"This is perhaps no big shock: some evenings, our Teresa waitresses at the Tipsy Vegan. As such, a reconnoitre sounds in order. Now, I know this is a terrible ask – as it would involve having to eat vegan food – *the horror, the horror!* – or, at least, pretending to. Personally, I'd take a doggy bag and drop the revolting lot within, but that would require a certain sleight of hand. The alternative is small bites, swallowing whole, and constant swilling with a flavoursome beverage. Interested?"

Amanda took some persuading, but in the end, Ed proved irresistible.

***

It took over a week before plans to infiltrate the so-called Vegan Enclave were finally in place. Before then, a number of other notable events took place.

First, the Canaries won their next away game one-nil (or formally 'nil-one'), and then their following home game, also one-nil. This sequence – 0110 – could have formed the start of any letter from 'a' to 'o' in the ASCII code, which wasn't especially helpful for the gamblers among them.

Second, Tom stumbled upon another alien message – one that most definitely was within Smith's roving zone. On Hay Hill, site of the statue of Sir Thomas Browne, almost opposite St Peter Mancroft, was a small McDonalds occupying a neat, three-storey building with an ornate, white-arched doorway. And to the right of this was a large symbol of the golden arches that had been extra-dimensionally banjaxed in a rather ironic way, given the current concern of Tom's team: the 'M' had been incorporated into a 7D message that declared: *Meat is murder.*

Tom's jaw dropped open at the sight – both figuratively and literally. *Jesus H. Christ!*

It was early afternoon on a weekday, and the restaurant was typically busy, as was the square itself. Assuming the message had been left overnight, how many had seen it during the morning? *Hundreds* could have been exposed!

The only positive in Tom's book was that this was such a busy position there was no way he could get at the message or be expected to deal with it now. But Smith would undoubtedly expect him to remove it when he could – likely in the early hours. So, what was the alien's game plan? A day of subliminally enraging people about meat-eating, and then having Tom smear the golden arches with red paint. *Like blood.* He could just visualise that drama playing out in the press: perhaps animal rightists crowing and claiming the act for themselves, followed by legions of outraged Maccy-D fans up in arms, and then, worst of all, vulturine American corporate lawyers 'suing the ass' off everyone. And probably using financial muscle to hire a battalion of private eyes to hunt down the perpetrator of the vandalism – Tom himself! – to rendition him to Guantanamo Bay, or somewhere even worse.

Bollocks!

He had to let people know, and quick. Alerting his friends by text was easy. But informing the Musketeers was rather more difficult. In the end, he took a bus to UEA and didn't arrive at his old department until mid-afternoon.

***

As soon as Tom entered his new shared office, three pairs of eyes swivelled towards him – those of Fatima, Agneta and Warren.

"Ah, hello. Um, don't let me disturb…"

Warren raised a hand in brief recognition, then turned back to his computer; Fatima twitched a smile and then did the same; Agneta glowered at him as though he had murdered her pet, shook her head, and returned to perusing a paper copy of an article she'd been annotating by hand.

Tom tip-toed over to his desk. He'd left a notepad in the top draw. As he pulled out the draw it creaked, and someone sighed. "Sorry!" he whispered. Then, he slid back his wheeled chair, which squealed, and sat – with more creaking. A louder sigh came from someone else, along with a disapproving hiss. Somehow, the others' activities were performed noiselessly – keys caressed, pen slipping across paper like an ice skater – yet Tom's every motion resulted in a wave of exaggerated noise. In pencil, he wrote an explanatory message addressed to *Athos* (he was proud of himself for this touch), which somehow made a sound like fingernails drawn down a blackboard. He felt like a child with ADHD let loose in a classroom of slinking uber-ninjas who were practising gliding lightly over rice paper.

He finished his message and put this away according to Keith's instructions. The desk drawer thudded shut, then Tom's chair rolled backwards and clanged into a metal filing cabinet, and he muttered an involuntary expletive. At this, Fatima dropped her head onto her arms,

Warren violently struck the return key on his keyboard, and Agneta, amazingly, managed to snap her plastic Bic.

Without another word, Tom fled the office.

The door slammed on his way out.

**

"Ah... *Brian*."

"Hello, Tom. You sound surprised. I guess you are looking for Alice. She's currently giving a lecture."

It had occurred to Tom, after exiting his shared office, that Keith would somehow need to be alerted to his departmental visit. In retrospect, they should have devised a better method of communication. As it was, Tom's only option was to pop in to say 'hi' to Alice, in the hope that she would mention this to her husband, who'd claimed she told him everything. Of course, that meant any message wasn't likely to be picked up until tomorrow, unless Keith was able to find an excuse to come in later that evening – but Tom wasn't sure how that would work. He'd bet his entire football winnings that one or more of the industrious trio would still be here, working late into the night, and he wasn't sure how Keith would explain a visit and a rummage in Tom's desk...

"Um, yes," Tom responded, after a pause. "Er, can you let her know I stopped by?"

"She won't be long. I would estimate..." Brian turned to peer at a wall clock through his thick lenses. "Eight minutes."

"Right..." And then Tom realised: *it's Brian*! Another mystery for Guy Burgess to look into? But a whole eight minutes in the presence of the prissy one? He had to strike fast and leave! "Well, I really have to go. Um – bus to catch. But good to see you again and I, er, hear you've been touring the country."

"Touring? Hardly. A few meetings, that's all."

Tom attempted a disinterested and off-hand: "Hull, wasn't it?"

"Yes."

Silence.

Brian wasn't playing.

So, he tried again: "Right. Just Hull? I heard you were gone for some time. I didn't know Hull was that interesting."

"It's not. I went to Halifax afterwards." Brian gave a smile that had no humour in it. "I thought you had a bus to catch?"

"Ah, yes, I do. Well, please tell Alice and… I'll be seeing you."

Tom fled the office. He then had to wait twenty minutes for a bus. As he chilled his buttocks on a cold bench at the bus stop, he thought: *Halifax – not Huddersfield.* So, it probably *was* a coincidence that Brian had been in the same city as the Canaries for that earlier away game, and he hadn't been to Huddersfield for the subsequent game.

It was only later, at home, that Tom had second thoughts and looked at an online map.

The jury, it seemed, was still out: Halifax was only five miles from Huddersfield.

***

"Thanks for coming, Tom," said Amanda, drawing to a halt in front of him. She was girded against the cold in a thick brown coat, multi-coloured scarf, and over-sized, purple woollen hat, looking like a frumpy bear at a children's party.

"Hi, Amanda. You look, er, *nice.*" Was that going too far?

Her smile suggested otherwise. "*Thanks.* Well, shall we go in?"

Tom's attendance this evening was the price of Amanda agreeing to a sortie to the Tipsy Vegan, for she'd objected to dining alone and appearing a sad-act singleton. Ed had regally proclaimed that Amanda's wish should be granted, leaving Tom little choice, although it had been apparent to all that this did make sense. In the first instance, it meant more eyes to look out for oddities, but more importantly, as Ed had noted, throwing Tom into the den (under the bus?) seemed more likely to provoke a reaction than Amanda would on her own – just as his presence during the Belgian Monk episode had with Keith and Martin.

The restaurant lay on lamp-lit St Benedicts Street, almost directly opposite The Little Shop of Vegans, with the (vegan) board-gaming shop Slice and Dice a further fifty metres away, past the Ten Bells pub: they had truly entered 'The Enclave'!

At the door, a *non-Teresoid* waitress showed them to a table. Tom allowed a quickly defrocked Amanda to settle on a purplish banquette against the wall, and then he took a spindly chair across from her. Soft orange lighting created a warming ambience, glittering off small mirrors and framed pictures on the green, wood-slatted walls.

"Well, this is nice," said Amanda. "If the food is anywhere near as good as the décor, we should be in for a treat."

Tom grimaced. "I really hope you're right. This is a first for me. What about you?"

"I'm not sure I've ever specifically ordered anything vegan before, but I've had plenty of vegetarian meals. I don't really see why it should be that different. Anyway, it's not the food that's bothering me, it's the other thing." Amanda leant forwards and lowered her voice. "I don't see her, but then, I've only ever seen her in CCTV shots. You've seen her in the flesh. Is she here?"

Tom surreptitiously scanned the room, then twisted in his seat to look at the bar area. It was early evening, Thursday, and the place was two-thirds full. The clientele was heavily female, comprising small parties of friends/work colleagues and a few same-sex couples (mothers and daughters?); Tom only noticed one other hetero pairing. One waitress was currently delivering food to a group of three young women, while a second stood at the bar, chatting to a young man with a trim beard who was polishing a wine glass. "Nope. Not yet, anyway."

"Maybe she's in the kitchen? I hope Ed hasn't got it wrong, and this turns out to be nothing more than a wild goose chase."

"Ed – wrong?" Tom smiled sheepishly. "I guarantee, whether he is or isn't, he somehow *won't* be... if you know what I mean."

Amanda laughed lightly. "Yes, I do. It will be entirely our fault, probably because Teresa saw you first, and either bolted or hid until we left."

They were interrupted by the waitress from the bar – young, enthusiastic, her fair hair tied in a ponytail. They ordered drinks and perused menus. Tom allowed Amanda to choose something for him which – in her opinion – wouldn't offend his tastebuds too much.

But after a few sips of beer, Tom felt more comfortable. Teresa's no-show was perhaps no bad thing, for here he was, on his first date for longer than he cared to remember... although 'date' wasn't exactly the right word. He inwardly frowned. It was time to bite the bullet and get the appropriate pleasantries out of the way as quickly as possible.

"So, uh, how is Max? Still in Berlin," he chortled, "trying to save the world?"

Amanda's brow furrowed. "Max?" She put down her wine glass and directed her attention to its stem. "Yes. He's still there."

"Oh, sorry." *Great start, Tom!* "Have I said something wrong? You're missing him?"

She looked up with a pained smile. "No, Tom. I'm not. *Definitely* not." She sighed. "The truth is, we've decided to take a break."

"Break… oh!"

"Yes, that foolish euphemism. A break. A time out. A period apart. What was that line from those celebrities – a conscious decoupling?"

"Ah. I've definitely put my foot in it. You don't have to…"

Amanda adjusted her glasses and tried to fix Tom's elusive eyes. "Maybe I do. Or should." She sighed again. "To be honest, I've suspected Max has been playing away for some time. He's joked about having an open relationship before. Or maybe *half*-joked. I mean, he's away in Germany, surrounded by temptation. Lots of little eco-frauleins flirting with the big man – as he sees himself. I've always had doubts about his ability to resist." She shook her head. "But.. no. I make it sound like he's been seduced away, but I suspect he's been the seducer more often than not."

"I'm sorry. Are you…? How do you…?"

"How do I feel? Don't worry, Tom. I'm not pining away. I think I'm *annoyed* mostly. *The big rat.*"

Tom's heart went straight from second to fifth gear. While at one level, he felt sorry for Amanda, he was, after all, a dastardly male, and one who lived in a world of few opportunities – at least, few given his mild temperament and circumscribed social life. Maybe there was hope…

"But *this* is great," Amanda continued. "Perhaps it's just what I need. Time out with a platonic friend of the opposite sex. No stresses and strains. No need to worry about how I look, or what I say, or what you might be thinking, or where you might be looking."

Or maybe not…

"Right. Sure." Tom couldn't keep the disappointment from his voice.

And Amanda clearly noticed: her eyes widened, and her mouth twitched. Then she reached across the table to touch his hand. "But let's not talk about silly relationships now, eh? And, please, say nothing about this to Ed. Now, tell me more about your latest find."

What was that about? Tom liked the feel of Amanda's hand on his and was disappointed when she withdrew it. Maybe not *no* hope? But he was relieved to be able to change the subject. So, he started to tell Amanda about the message he'd found the day before yesterday at McDonalds.

"…but I've not told Smith yet," he finished. "And I've not heard back from Keith, either, so I don't know if he got my note, or whether he's been able to do anything about it. The problem is, we didn't think hard enough about a feedback mechanism. With luck, he's already obliterated the message with his invisible ray gun, or whatever he has."

"You haven't been back to check?"

"No. I don't know if Smith hangs around St Peter Mancroft, peering through its stained glass windows, but that's definitely one of his main bases. I don't want to risk him seeing me near there. It'd reduce the credibility of me denying having seen a message just across from it."

"Hmmm, maybe I can swing by tomorrow morning? I've got to go to the centre for an optician's appointment anyway, and I need to get a birthday present for Val, too. What are you going to do next?"

"Well, I'm *not* going to tell Smith and be forced to try to erase the message. I don't want to end up in Guantanamo… er, sorry. Extrapolation gone mad. And I really don't want to go back to my office to leave another message and risk meeting Brian and the ghouls. So, I guess I'll have to stop by the Rumsey next Wednesday, when–"

"Hi!" said a waitress, appearing suddenly, a plate of food in each hand. "I've got one oyster mushroom and chorizo linguini, and one buffalo burger with parmesan chips, who's…"

Tom and Amanda looked up at the waitress, who seemed to have lost her voice.

Teresa.

"Oh. The linguini's mine," said Amanda, with a start.

Tom stared at Teresa.

Teresa stared back at Tom.

Then the waitress jerked forwards, placed one plate before Amanda, the other in front of Tom, looked at Amanda and muttered: "Enjoy your meal," and abruptly stalked off.

After a moment, Amanda swapped the plates around. "Well, she certainly recognised you. That was quite a reaction."

Tom puffed out his cheeks. "Yes, especially as we've never formally met. Or spoken to each other. But apart from confirming that there's something odd with her, I'm not sure what else it tells us."

"Nothing yet," agreed Amanda. "But the evening is still young. And *this* looks nice."

While they resolved to keep an eye on Teresa and her activities, particularly noting who she spoke to – other staff or customers – they were soon distracted by the food.

"Wow," said Tom. "This is actually quite nice. I suspect if I got this in a normal restaurant and wasn't told it was vegan, I wouldn't think twice about it. Maybe the texture is a little different. And there's a taste that could be from the sauce… Oh, *fuck*!"

Amanda laughed as Tom put his head in his hands, as though distraught. "And let's definitely not tell Ed about this," she said. "He'd probably suggest Teresa put some alien chemical in it to cause an addiction and turn you."

"Yes, and suggest it only worked was because I am weak-willed, but that he would have been able to resist. But…" A thought occurred, and Tom sat back in his seat and peered at his food more intensely.

"Tom? What is it?"

"Well, I just wondered… maybe my reaction *is* alien inspired. Remember the message at McDonalds? Is my reaction genuine, or have I subconsciously been influenced? I mean, it *is* good to think I'm eating something that hasn't been cruelly slaughtered just for my own selfish and venal desires… *Oh, shit.* That's definitely *not* me!"

"What, you mean you *do* actually like to think your food has been tormented just for your pleasure?"

"No. Not that. I've just never *thought* about it before."

Amanda peered at Tom, doubt in her eyes. "That could just be because of the environment you're in now. The context. It's only natural."

"Yes, I get that. But I said that with real feeling. *Real* feeling. I mean, I'm not as *anti* as Ed, but even so."

"Okay. But how would swaying people towards vegetarianism or veganism be an evil thing? Sheila thinks that's good for the planet and ultimately should be encouraged; it's just the MO of the believers she thinks is counterproductive."

"I'm not sure. Maybe people like me aren't meant to be the main target of the message. Look, if it made even me feel a bit emotional, then maybe it'd cause true believers to go into meltdown. Maybe even over the edge. Maybe even spur them into violence."

Amanda shook her head slightly. "I'm not sure that works. Given the position of the message, you and fellow omnivores are likely to be the main victims – customers of McD's itself. For that plan to work, the message would be better placed somewhere around here. The Enclave."

"Yes, that makes sense, I guess. But from this perspective, wouldn't that make Sheila a more likely source for the message than Smith?" He held up his hands. "I know she doesn't do this sort of thing, so that's not a serious suggestion. I'm just struggling with the motivation here."

"Just don't let the struggle ruin your meal."

Tom smiled back. "I'll try not to. I'm now keen to risk the dessert. I remember something about Greek doughnuts with 'honey' and pistachios."

As they finished their main courses and ordered further food and drink, they tried their best to keep a watch on Teresa, and even managed a few faux selfies that caught her in the background. But their target didn't approach them again, and another waitress dealt with them thereafter. And then it was time to settle the bill and leave.

Outside, the cold was bracing. The pair stood about awkwardly.

"Well, that was actually quite nice," said Amanda. "I mean, the food. Though the company wasn't bad either."

Tom felt his heart miss a beat. "Yes. I also strangely enjoyed it. But we didn't learn much, so from that perspective it was a bit of a write-off." He looked about and his eye caught a pub sign a short distance away. "Ah… but maybe we should think a bit more about these matters while they're fresh in our minds? Perhaps one for the road?"

Amanda laughed. "Okay. Just one."

Tom led the way to the Ten Bells. They entered through a door into a small annex furnished with a sofa and some comfy chairs, then turned right towards the main bar. The place was lit by orange lamps and the light from various TVs, showing football with the volume low, while *Don't Fear the Reaper* played on some unseen music system. At the bar, Tom perused the beer pumps.

"A pint of Wherry for me, please. Amanda? I think they're big on cocktails here."

"Are you trying to get me drunk? Thanks, Tom, but I'd better just have a half. Wherry is fine. Oh… and look at that."

Tom completed his order, then turned to see what had caught Amanda's attention. On the wall directly facing the bar, not two metres away in the narrow room, was a mural in black on white tiles. "Wow. It's her majesty!"

"With her famous words, too."

The mural showed the image of Delia Smith – Norwich City F.C. supremo and renowned chef – with mouth open, shouting into a mic. Next to the image was written her famed exhortation – delivered at half-time in an attempt to rouse the fans during a match against Manchester City after the Canaries had squandered an early lead: *Lets be having you*!

"You know, they renamed a street near Carrow Road to honour the event," said Tom. "The city now has a Letsby Avenue."

"Really?" laughed Amanda.

"Yep. Absolutely true. Look out for it next time you're near the stadium."

Their drinks were poured, Tom paid, and they left Delia to her imprecations. They returned through the annex with the comfy seating and entered a larger room to the left of where they'd entered the pub, finding a booth that had just been vacated.

Amanda was still amused by the mural and Tom's revelation. "It's amazing, though. Coincidences everywhere. I mean, with all the football results and everything."

"Yes, absolutely. And we still don't know what 'Delia must' do. Shout? Scream? Bellow? Cry? I think 'cry' would work, given the limited number of games remaining in the season. Ah, and speaking of coincidences…" Tom leant forwards. "The three women in the booth behind you were in the Tipsy Vegan earlier."

Amanda half turned, but as it was awkward for her to look at the party directly, she turned back to watch Tom's face. The group had left the restaurant half-an-hour before them, clearly following a similar routine: they'd had a drink and were now standing up to leave.

"Yeah, that's right... twelve-thirty at the Forum," said one. "We've just got time to do it in our lunch break."

"Make sure you take your banner, yeah?" said a second.

"Don't need to," said the third. "Teresa said she'd have it."

"Lucky you," continued the second. "And you're closest, too, working at the council. I barely have time to get there and back, and I won't have time for lunch. Wendy can be a real dragon about timekeeping."

The third woman sounded apologetic. "Sorry, babe. Just do your best. If you're late for the speeches outside the Forum, go straight there. It's just down the hill."

Various exclamations of 'love' followed, and the three women moved off.

Tom and Amanda stared at each other for a moment, lost for words. At last Amanda said: "You don't think...?"

"Yes, I bloody well do!"

Chapter 30: The Stirred Pot

Amanda called at Friday lunchtime.

It was quite a shock for Tom. No one apart from his mother ever phoned him. But it was nice to hear her voice.

"They're here, Tom," she said, with chanting in the background. "Teresa *and* Ricky. He doesn't look happy. There are about forty them. They're outside McDonalds."

She hadn't seen any messages scrawled on the walls of that edifice – which was hardly a surprise, given she lacked the appropriate alien filters. Nevertheless, she remained to give running commentary for a while, until she had to head off to meet her charity-shop friend for lunch.

The story made it onto *Look East*, which Tom caught later that evening, slouched in front of his TV. Rachel Kettleborough had been there: in her report, she recounted the vegans' 'beef' with all carnivores, most clearly represented in their minds by the cow-murderers from across the Atlantic.

Tom couldn't supress a chuckle at what he saw on the screen, for in one clip was Ricky, standing beside his amour, hefting a banner demanding 'Human rights for cows!' and looking utterly miserable.

But as the protest passed off peacefully, and the number of protesters was small, the BBC editor clearly decided that the story merited little time: Rachel's piece was quickly wrapped up, and the studio presenter moved on to another story about argy-bargy on the banks of the Wensum between a group of fishermen and some canoeists.

Tom wasn't sure what he had expected. A wholesale riot? Hay Hill awash with the blood of burger-munchers, battered by vegan fanatics? In retrospect, that had never been likely: the impact of the alien message was sure to be more subtle and long-lasting.

He rose to his feet and scurried to his galley kitchen to make himself a sandwich for lunch. Ham and cheese? He absently returned the pack of ham to the fridge unopened and stuck with the cheddar, which he garnished with some cheese-and-onion crisps. *Mmmm, crunchy!* Then he returned upstairs to his office, determined to complete another scene for his book, with his interest in that project suddenly revivified.

***

One side effect of recent events was that Tom suddenly found himself with more time on his hands. The revelation from Keith about why he'd gotten Alice's job – i.e. that it was just a means to keep him otherwise engaged and out of trouble – had undermined his interest in that project. And the revelations about Smith and why Tom had really been chosen as an Omega – i.e. that he was little more than a fall-guy – had diminished his interest in patrolling, with its risks of finding alien messages that he would then be expected to address. With this extra time, Tom had indeed found a renewed interest in his novel, and for the last couple of weeks had made astonishing progress. This was also in part a consequence of having a wealth of new ideas inspired by current circumstances.

"Right," Tom muttered to himself, appraising his latest work, "V-Garg, you little toad, how am I going to fuck you over?"

In Tom's mind, his alien provocateur had become indistinguishable from Smith. He found the character he was writing transforming in ways that were perhaps inconsistent with quality writing, but he convinced himself that he could justify the changes as a kind of evolution – in the same way that Smith had been evolving since Tom had first met him, with his deadpan face now often twisted into sardonic smiles and his Vulcan-like objectivity giving way to evident appreciation of human emotion. "I can pull it off," he said to the monitor screen once. Or at worst, he could tweak the alien's early characterisation in the next draft. And in fact, Smith's latest response at the end of his Cloud-saved work was a case in point:

I AM SORRY ABOUT YOUR DECREASE IN PATROLLING. BUT I SEE YOU HAVE WRITTEN TWO WHOLE CHAPTERS QUITE QUICKLY. YOU APPEAR TO HAVE REGAINED YOUR MOJO. WELL DONE.

Mojo? Had Smith really just used that word? Would he have done so six months ago?

"I'll show *you* mojo," muttered Tom.

But he had to be careful: Smith had certainly read Tom's first few chapters, as he'd annotated them in order to start a dialogue with him, but was he still doing so? Why would he? The quality of the prose? The excitement of the plot? *As if!* In short, Tom was careful not to incriminate himself via insinuation. So, having unveiled V-Garg's treachery previously – and before Smith's subterfuge had been confirmed, his subconscious perhaps more on the ball than his conscious mind – he now had to row back a bit. And so he'd had V-Garg (*the snake!*) come up with an excuse that seemed to satisfy Tim. *Seemed* to. But the increasingly heroic Tim hadn't bought it and was working his own double-cross.

"Oh…oh… he goin' down!" sniggered Tom, in some weird melange of accents, as he thrashed away at the keyboard.

And in parallel with V-Garg's switch, another main group of alien protagonists – who he'd set up as the villains initially – was now being revealed as secret allies of the human race, in a reverse that both complicated and enhanced the plot.

So, although this whole affair with Smith had delayed his completion of the novel, Tom was in no doubt that the insights he'd gained had far improved the story. Now, he just had to decide what to do with the shadowy Black Coats, a cell of human operatives whose motives he still hadn't fully clarified in his own head (a fact that he felt actually enhanced the story further: after all, if *he* didn't know what the fuck was going on, how could any reader work it out?).

Tom looked at his latest work on the screen. It was now time to progress the story of The Black Coats – an organisation that just happened to be led by a huge man with a large, black beard, called Trajan T. Hercules. *Just what,* he wondered to himself, *is your game going to be?*

In his latest chapter, he realised further revelations were needed…

***

The crew had been busy over the weekend, and Ed couldn't make the Tuesday pub quiz, so Tom didn't see his friends and collaborators for some days. He avoided the city centre during this time, fobbing Smith off with a further update declaring that he was so busy with Alice's project (a lie: he'd been at the novel) that he was unable to do any patrols – although he promised he would try to restart his routine later in the week. By Wednesday, Tom just had to know: had Keith received his message about the McDonalds graffiti, and had he and his team done anything about it?

He waited until ten past seven, then strolled through the entrance of the Rumsey Wells. He saw the Musketeers in the corner of the room: Keith, Martin, ginger-haired Trevor and... *WTF!*

Agneta was there, sitting beside Trevor, glaring at him. As her mouth moved, Trevor redirected his gaze and the two men with their backs to the door turned in their seats.

Tom faltered, but then recovered and took the few strides necessary to reach the table, raising his hand in tentative greeting.

"Tom!" said Keith, his mouth fighting a smile. "Nice to see you. Join us. Pull up a chair."

Tom smiled nervously and did as requested. He had to sit at the perpendicular edge of the table between Agneta and Martin, with Keith sitting opposite Trevor. As he sat, Agneta hissed: "Don't make yourself too comfortable. You won't be staying long."

"Uh, hello, Agneta. I'm sorry to disturb you. I didn't know..."

Keith's mouth had given up the fight; his smile was now broad and mischievous. "You didn't know Agneta was with us? Well, why would you?"

"I thought there were only three of you Musketeers."

Agneta frowned and looked to Keith; the latter shrugged. "That's not our name, Tom," said Keith. "Did I make such an analogy? Ah... and now I understand the reference: *Athos*, the leader of the Musketeers. Very slow of me. But now I think of it, quite apt."

"Yeah," nodded Martin. "And that would make Agneta D'Artagnan."

"I'm not a worthless man!" hissed Agneta. Martin whitened and pulled away slightly.

Keith was still amused. "Aside from the gender insult – unintended, Agneta, I'm sure – that maybe isn't a bad analogy. Agneta is our latest recruit – in fact, recruited by Trevor under orders from our patron."

"King Louis XIII?" wondered Trevor.

Keith laughed. "Why not! Let us refer to him as 'the King', at least in Tom's presence."

"And does that make the Thruvian Cardinal Richelieu?" continued Trevor.

"Men, men and more men," snapped Agneta.

"We could refer to our patron as 'the Queen', if you wish," said Keith, consolingly. "After all, sex or gender is not a clear and obvious distinction for many of the alien species."

Agneta waved the offer aside, her focus back on Tom. "I don't like him being here. Now, he knows about me. What else are we going to tell him?"

Tom had been watching the tense exchange with fascination: this lot seemed to lack the esprit of The Credulous. "Ah, I'm only really here to check that you got my message."

"As you can see," said Agneta, "we did."

With a small frown and quick glance at Agneta, Keith confirmed: "Yes, Tom, we did. Thank you. And we dealt with it that very night. It is now gone, or at least, degraded enough to cease to be a problem."

"Ah, great. That's a relief." Tom decided to focus on Keith, but he sensed Agneta's glower, which seemed to heat up the nearer half of his face as though he were sitting close to an electric fire. "So, it was gone before the demo on Friday? That was our main concern – that it might enrage the vegans into some sort of fury."

Keith cocked his head slightly. "*Our? Not your?*"

"Um, figure of speech."

"Really, Tom?"

"Maybe he means the tall guy from the Belgium Monk," said Martin. "Is he involved, too?"

"Er..." Tom could feel four sets of eyes boring into him, with Keith's asquint with suspicion. "*Maybe.*"

"Is he an *approached*," asked Keith, "or just a friend you've let in on your secret?"

There seemed no point in denying this one thing, as they clearly wouldn't believe him otherwise. "Okay. Yes. I mean, in your terms, he is an 'approached'." Then he added hastily: "but not by Smith, I mean, the Thruvian. By another. A *goody.*"

"Interesting," mused Keith. "So, how did you two meet? Randomly? No. That's not credible. And does he know you are a–"

"*Traitor!*" hissed Agneta.

"I was going to say," Keith continued, after a wry glance at the woman, "servant of one of the manipulator species. And if he does know, and you've told him, where does he stand on this? How is he your friend?"

"I'm sorry, but I don't think I should say any more." A flustered Tom started to rise. "I've admitted my mistake, and given you proof that I'm reformed. But you've given me nothing back. I think I should just—"

"Tom – no!" Keith was half out of his own seat now. "It's I who am sorry. I think maybe we should be more trusting, or at least, less distrusting."

"*Mistake*," muttered Agneta.

Keith frowned at her. "Maybe it is, Agneta. But weighing the odds, I don't think so. He already now knows more about us than we do about him. For a start, he knows who we are and where we meet and where we work. Yet, he's not alone – and we didn't know that. Clearly, our surveillance has been lacking. If Tom was truly deceived by his patron, then maybe we can work this situation to our advantage, eh? Who will have better contact with the Thruvian than him? We have never managed to get so close."

Tom hesitated and waited for the dispute to resolve. At last Agneta nodded, though she looked far from happy. "Okay. But with caution, please."

"Of course." Keith looked at Tom again. "Please, sit. I'll get you a drink. Mosaic, isn't it? While I'm at the bar, everyone, please play nice. And please don't discuss anything significant until I'm back."

And so for two minutes, not knowing what else to say, the four sat in uncomfortable silence.

At last, Keith delivered Tom's drink and sat. "All friends now? Hmmm, perhaps not. Tom, while at the bar, I was thinking: it's silly of us being so coy with each other. You do believe we are 'goodies' – in your phrasing – do you not? And we dealt with the message you found, presumably saving you from having to report it and deal with it yourself, with potentially disastrous consequences – yes? So, maybe you should tell us a bit more about your friend?"

Tom had spent the last couple of minutes thinking hard – mostly about how he could escape alive, especially from Agneta, who really did seem to have it in for him. "I can't, honestly. Not yet. I mean, we all agreed that I wouldn't—"

"*All?*" hissed Agneta.

Keith's frown returned. "More secrets, Tom? Just how many of you are there?"

Tom groaned, and not just inwardly. "I really can't. Not without—"

"Two others?" suggested Martin, peering into Tom's face closely.

"More like three," rumbled Trevor. "I think if it were just two, he would have stuck with 'we'. The word 'all' suggests a bigger group. I bet there are at least three others."

"Fuck!" hissed Tom. "Maybe I should just go before I say too much."

"Whoa, Tom," said Keith. "Wait! *Quid pro quo*. Here's something from us. The messages? Our patron – let's stick with 'the Queen' – has given us a torch that emits light in a certain spectrum. This has the effect of disrupting seventh-dimensional messages, allowing us to act from a distance. Are you satisfied?"

"Oh! Well, thanks. Do you have, er—"

"Yes, we have a couple, but no, Tom, we can't afford to give you one. The Queen would disapprove, and we need it logistically."

"Right..." Tom thought some more. "And... how do you see the messages? I have glasses..."

"*Giveaway*," muttered Agneta.

"... but now I've got contacts. What about you?"

Keith nodded. "The same. Contacts. We all have them. And so that's *two* bits of information from us." He leant forwards. "So now it's your turn. Is it two, three, or even more colleagues? And are these others also servants of Belgium Monk's patron? Do they belong to another grouping, like us 'Musketeers'?"

Just how much could he say? The compulsion to reciprocal altruism made him gasp out: "*Three*. And they all have different patrons. *Shit!*"

Trevor made an odd gesture with one hand that essentially translated as: *booyah!*

Keith kept up the pressure. "Three? That's astonishing. How on Earth did you all come together?"

"I've already said too much. Ed is going to kill me. *Fuck!*"

"So, one of them is called Ed," sneered Agneta.

"Name rings a bell," said Martin. "Is that Belgium Monk Guy? It is, isn't it!"

Every time Tom opened his mouth, he gave something away. He even made Johnny English appear competent. "It's complicated. We agreed to say nothing for now, but I did suggest we should be more open. Don't ask me anymore. *Please.*" Did that sound too whiny? "I'll talk to them. See if they'll agree to, um, come out of the shadows. Okay?"

Tom was surprised when it was Agneta – apparently already second-in-command, in spite of being junior – who threw him a lifeline. "Yes," she murmured, somewhat cautiously. "That sounds reasonable. I think we should accept this, Keith. Allow him a little time to bring the others to us."

"Yeah, and I've said before, we're too few in number," said Trevor. "This could help – especially now."

"Thank you, Agneta, Trevor. I'm glad you approve. Okay, Tom. I won't press you on your colleagues any further." He paused to collect his thoughts. "But now something else occurs to me – perhaps some intel you can exchange instead. Earlier, you mentioned the vegan demo. I can't recall your exact words, but it seemed like you knew it was going to take place. You said something about fearing the message's effects on them. We didn't know about the demo, although we do have some suspicions about that community. What–"

"You mean, Teresa and Ricky?" Tom was glad to change the subject, and this seemed safe and potentially milkable. "Do you know about them?"

It turned out the now-called Musketeers didn't, so Tom was more than willing to fill them in, concluding: "But we don't know who they work for. Amanda says... *fuck*!"

Keith and Trevor exchanged knowing looks, the latter making scribbling signs in mid-air as though writing an invisible list.

But tension in the group drained away over a second round, until Martin was dropping quips and even Agneta mellowed, albeit a smile never crossed her face.

"...yeah, there's a lot of shit going on," said Trevor, summarising events in Norwich over the last few months.

"We know Smith is to blame for some," said Tom. "Then there's Ricky and Teresa. Then the foot... ah..." Tom coughed. "The foot...soldiers of the... Black Coats..."

"Sorry, Tom," said Keith, alert once more. "Who are these Black Coats?"

"Um. Sorry. I call them the, er, Black Coats. Er, from something I, er, *read*. It's just that they usually wear black. Um, but they call themselves Terminus Est. Do you know them?"

"*The Mercenaries!*" hissed Agneta, suddenly agitated.

"Ah, they sound like bad dudes, as Si would say… oh, *bollocks!*"

"House!" declared Trevor.

Keith made a calming motion with both hands but grinned at Trevor from the side of his face. "Indeed, Tom. The Mercenaries, or Terminus Est, or the Black Coats, whatever you want to call them, are bad dudes. I take it you have no special intel on them?"

Fuck fuck fuck, thought Tom, then: *why don't you just reveal the PIN of your credit card as well?* Instead, he said: "No. We just know they like to hang around the Cosy Club. But we're not sure what they've actually *done*."

"Well, then settle back and listen," said Keith, "and consider this the 'quo' for your information on Teresa and Ricky. The mercenaries are a group that have been around for a long time, Tom. Very long."

Tom puffed out his cheeks, still trying to recover. "What… decades?" But seeing Keith shake his head, he continued: "Centuries?"

"Millenia, or at least millennium."

"A thousand years!"

Keith nodded solemnly. "Indeed. Tom – how good is your local history? Did you know, for example, that the entire city was ex-communicated by Pope Gregory X in 1274 because of strife between its citizens and the church's monks?" When Tom shook his head, he continued: "That was down to them. Or at least, they facilitated it."

"No!"

"But you must have heard of Kett's Rebellion? In 1549, during the reign of Edward VI, Robert Kett was encouraged to start a revolt against local landowners. Much pushing and shoving followed, and it did not end well for Robert. Who do you think was in the wings then, spreading rumours, using church bells as earlier-time message dispensers?"

"Terminus Est!"

"They have had their fingers – in one way or another – in most of the significant events in the city, from the Great Blow in 1648, on the eve of the Second English Civil War, when a riot led to an explosion that wrecked most of Bethel Street, to the burning down of the old library – where the Forum now sits – in 1994. They are a society that has many patrons amongst the meddlesome species, and yet no masters. They are guns for hire. They are the ultimate pot-stirrers.''

"Wow!" Tom's mind was awhirl. He had to somehow get all this in his book. Could he insert something portentous in an early chapter?

"That's right. And over the last few decades, they have held their conclaves in what is now the cellar vault of the Cosy Club, a place so well-shielded that no human or alien surveillance device can penetrate it.''

"My God! Wait until I tell the others…''

"Ed, Amanda, and Si,'' whispered Trevor to Agneta.

"…they'll freak. Oh, shit!''

Keith immediately spotted Tom's dilemma. "Well, you'll have to tell them sometime, Tom. Remember, you did agree to consult them about potentially coming out to us. Given the undertones raging through this city, I suggest that happens sooner rather than later.''

When they broke up soon after – with Keith worrying about Alice's reaction should he return late – Tom promised to talk to his friends and leave a message with Agneta back at UEA once he had something to report.

***

Football games were coming thick and fast in this latter part of the season, with prospects for promotion and relegation starting to clarify. And Norwich City were suddenly in a run of form. On the Saturday after the vegan demonstration, they won their third match on the trot, again by a single goal, this time away at Blackburn Rovers. (*I wonder where Brian is?* Tom had thought, on learning that result.) In electronic exchanges, Simon had quickly noted that this reduced the possible letters starting the third word in the alien code to a 'd', 'e', 'f' or 'g' (all beginning with 011001). And then on the Wednesday of Tom's meeting at the Rumsey, a nil-nil draw at home confirmed the letter to be a 'd'.

"So, 'Delia must d…'?" mused Ed, at a meeting in the Alex the next evening. "*Dab?*"

"Part of a victory dance at the end of the season to celebrate promotion?" mused Simon. "Or maybe *dip*. A metaphor for us getting relegated?"

"Or alternately, *dig*, as in *dig for victory*?" said Tom, who couldn't get the idea of tunnels entirely out of his mind and felt happy discussing football and postponing for a while revelations about the Musketeers, Terminus Est, the message outside McDonalds, and his loose-lippedness.

"Or *dig into her pockets*," said Simon. "Spending some of the moola the board continually sit on rather than spending on new players."

"Well, none of those phrases is the answer," said Ed, "as they're all too long. In fact, I've been thinking about the nature of the third word." He paused to take a pull of beer and allow tension to build. He lowered his glass to the table and continued. "Now, we all appear to have accepted that it'll be a three letter word, not two. This confirms it: 'Delia must do' is the only meaningful option, and that's so vague I think we can dismiss it. But even three letters initially seems to be a problem."

As Ed paused for effect again, Amanda took the role as chief chivvier-upper. "Please explain."

"Okay. It's like this. There are twenty-four teams in the Championship, meaning each side has to play the other twenty-three teams twice, making a total of forty-six games. But each ASCII letter comprises eight binary digits, and hence a complete set of letters or a phrase must be a factor of eight digits. And that means–"

"We're going to the play-offs!" exclaimed Simon.

"Indeed," said Ed, with a hint of disgruntlement at being pre-empted. "If we finish anywhere from third to sixth at the end of the season, our glorious yellows will have a two-leg playoff – home and away. That's the good news. The bad news is–"

"Then we're gonna get *fucked*," said Simon, mind racing ahead. "We won't get a forty-ninth game – the playoff final – so we won't get promoted."

Ed sighed. "Si, you're cramping my style, my friend. You've not only stolen my thunder, but also my lightning, torrential rain, and sodden, fist-waving pedestrians too."

"Sorry!"

"But maybe any further game won't matter, as long as the sequence is completed?" suggested Tom. "Maybe the aliens will relinquish control once their message is spelled out, so there *could* be another game after?"

Ed arched an eyebrow. "Really, Tom? Given the neatness of all this, do you honestly think that's the case? Anyway, I think there is too much uncertainty at the moment to bet on the next letter, which surely must be a vowel. Fortunately, we don't have long to wait to get an update, as Saturday will soon be upon us."

Try as he might, Tom just could not bring himself to raise the matter of the Musketeers. And then Amanda had to nip off after only a couple, and being less than quorate, and not wishing to make any revelation without Amanda being present (which might annoy her and reduce his, um, *chances*), he held fire.

And two days later, on the next Saturday, Norwich pulled off yet another one-nil victory – this time away to Bristol City. Alas, the '01' pairing was the first two digits of all of the conventional vowels plus the ambivalent 'y' (and indeed, all twenty-six letters, as Ed subsequently realised later   in embarrassment   meaning they'd missed the chance at a dead cert winning bet), so that turned out to be somewhat uninformative – at least, football-wise. But…

"Brian?" said Alice, the next time Tom popped in with a message for Agneta (which simply and untruthfully said: *Discussions with team ongoing; update soon*). "Oh, yes, he was having a meeting last weekend with people from the University of West of England."

"UWE? Isn't that in–?"

"Bristol, yes."

***

"Hello, Tom," said Amanda, the following Monday. "Well, here I am!"

Tom lurked near the bandstand in Chapelfield Gardens – a small park directly north-west of the Theatre Royal and Chantry Place Mall. The park stretched along the inner-city ring road up to a major roundabout close by St John's Cathedral (the city's smaller Roman-Catholic one). Unusually, he'd arrived early, and spent the previous ten minutes pacing around. He was now sweating within his fleece, for it was the cusp of April and fine, unseasonal weather had settled over the city, a boon to all except those lacking sensible outerwear.

"Oh, hi, Amanda. I'm glad you could make it."

Amanda's green woollen coat was also meant for winter, but she didn't seem phased by the weather, and indeed, had it buttoned closed. She even wore a purple tea cosy hat of the same fabric. "Oh, it's no problem. I just had to post a vlog on how to save on heating costs, and then I had to do some tidying. I'm still finding pairs of Max's underthings at the bottom of drawers." She smiled: "he just won't go away!"

"Want me to exterminate him for you?" joked Tom (*joked?*).

"Thanks, but no, because you'd definitely get caught and be sent to prison, where you'd be much less fun. So, what's up?"

"Ah, well, I needed to talk to someone about a sensitive matter."

Amanda rolled her eyes behind her glasses and shook her head in faux-despair. "You've done it again, haven't you? What is it this time? Was there a message on the Oxfam shop window? Have you struck a blow against those fighting third world poverty and hunger?"

Tom's worried smile became more genuine. If Amanda could tease him about this, then he might still be able to get out of this affair with prospects undimmed. "Maybe next time. No, it's..." And as they strolled around the park, he related his meeting with Keith and the Musketeers and his inadvertent over-sharing. He was relieved at Amanda's mild response.

"Tom – you're a bit of a disaster, aren't you."

"Guilty as charged. In fairness, it was a very useful meeting. But..." He shrugged.

"But you're worried about Ed. Simon won't be bothered, but Ed is likely to be annoyed."

"And you're not annoyed?"

"Well, I am *slightly* annoyed." Amanda flashed him a quick smile. "I thought you were going to take me to lunch."

"Oh!" Tom reddened. But once he found his voice, he was more than happy to fulfil Amanda's expectation at the nearby Georgian Townhouse, where they talked tactics.

***

"You knew!" said Ed to Amanda. "He told you in advance!"

The next evening, the four members of The Credulous were at the Rose for the quiz. In the absence of Terminus Est, they won, leaving Ed buoyant – just as Amanda predicted. And so, when she'd invited Tom to tell all during the post-quiz, last-pint interval, his revelation had merely nudged Ed's mood down to disgruntlement, with his first words being to Amanda, not Tom.

"Well, yes," confirmed Amanda. "He used me as a sounding board, realising that I wouldn't be so dogmatically negative."

Ed sighed. "Look, it's not that I object *per se*. It's just that this complicates matters. We've been trying to play this whole thing softly-softly in order not to alert our respective puppeteers. The bigger we get, the more people who know, the greater the chance that someone's going to slip up and we're going to get noticed. Now, Big Ed has been clear that my work is meant to be hush hush, need to know, etcetera. This is why I have been especially schtum about my activities. I've assumed you lot are the same. As members of a quiz team, we four have a credible front for meeting. Joining up in a clandestine encounter with another group in some shadowy dive might start to draw attention."

"Are you sure this isn't about diluting your influence?" said Amanda. "I mean, by bringing in an experienced other group with their own leader, you might face a challenge for supremacy."

Simon said nothing, but his smirk suggested he thought Amanda was on to something.

Ed sighed some more. "Not at all, Mands. You might think I am an egotist – and I have sufficient self-awareness to know that I sometimes appear this way – but that really isn't my main concern. In any case, if Cheggers is their leader, I will have no problem in supplanting him and enlarging my own empire." He smirked and raised his eyebrows. *Same old Ed.* But then the waggling stopped, and he became serious once more. "No. My main issue here, is that we agreed not to do this now, and yet Tom has gone and done it anyway."

Tom looked downcast. "I'm sorry. *Really*. I didn't plan to. It just sort of slipped out."

"Either Cheggers *et al* are experts in the arts of the Gestapo and Torquemada, or you – my dear chap – did your usual banana-skinning. I'd lay long odds it was the latter. But I know you are kosher, so don't worry, my friend, I don't blame you. It's like leaving a child in a kitchen with a boiling pot of water then being surprised when you have to take a trip to A&E." Ed gave Tom a gentle smile. "Never mind. What's done, is done. Yes, we need to meet Cheggers and his chums. But before we do so, let's agree rules of engagement, eh? And, Tom, I suggest that when we do meet up, you leave the talking to me, okay?"

Tom smiled in relief. "Don't worry – I'm more than happy to."

Chapter 31: Pow Wow

It had taken over a week to organise a suitable meeting place for the two groups, as nowhere in the city seemed private enough. In the end, Keith had booked a large meeting room at UEA close to his department. Most of the Musketeers – as well as Tom – were academics, giving them due cause to be on campus, while Amanda had an association with the School of Environmental Sciences, justifying her presence.

The Credulous gathered in the concrete square by the Students' Union building one early evening in April, from where Tom led them to the venue. Once outside the booked room, Ed turned to issue a last word of warning. "Remember, chums, perhaps it's best if you let me lead. Chip in when necessary, though without giving away too much, okay… *Tom*?"

Tom smiled sheepishly but said nothing. He opened the door for Ed, noticing with a quick glance that the Musketeers were already present, seated at the far end of a large table, facing the door.

"Hello, *Keith*," said Ed as he led his team into the space, smirking as though at some private joke.

Keith Hardcastle, husband of Alice Weidner, responded with a faint smile of his own. "And hello to you. I think we've met once before, outside the Belgium Monk, but we've not been formally introduced. Now, I'm pretty sure you're not 'Amanda', so it's a toss-up between 'Ed' and 'Si'. I'll go for Ed."

"Exactly so! Well done! And that means you can probably work out who my colleagues are. You already know Tom, the double – or is that triple? – agent. So let me introduce you to *Simonella* – the one in the dress – and the androgynous *Amanda*, today styling a *Star Wars* t-shirt and leather jacket."

"Ed – really!" Amanda's rebuke was half-hearted. She turned a more genuine smile onto Keith and his colleagues. "I'm Amanda," she said, "and I'm pleased to meet you all."

"Yep, me too. I'm Simon," said the definitely non-androgynous one. "Hi Martin," he continued, focusing on the youngest of the others. "Surprise-surprise."

"Simon? No!" Martin somehow managed to look both shocked and embarrassed at the same time.

As Ed took a seat and Tom, Simon and Amanda arranged themselves around him, Keith concluded the introductions – after a quick sideways glance at his PhD student. "Well, it seems some of you know Martin. The other Musketeers – in Tom's vocab – are Agneta and Trevor."

Trevor muttered a greeting; Agneta glared between Ed and Tom; and Martin continued to goggle.

"Good," said Ed, immediately taking control. "That's formalities sorted. Now, let's cut to the chase, shall we? We know from Tom that you all serve one of the puppet-masters."

"*Queen of France*," blurted Trevor, with his own quick glance at Agneta.

"Ta, Trev. The Queen she is. And Tom suggests you lot are on the level, that is, non-Sith-like jolly good fellows and fellowesses." Tom had forewarned Ed about Agneta's sensitivity – something he suddenly suspected he might regret. "Now, I and my troop," continued Ed, "for I guess I am the head honcho... are happy to take Tom's word for this. For our part, we serve four different masters – and perhaps mistresses, for who can tell what these freaky aliens really have dangling-or-not between their metaphorical legs?" Again Ed cast a sly grin at Agneta, who Tom feared might shortly leap up to lamp him. "So, all we need say for now is that three of our overlords-stroke-overladies are also forces for good – or at least non-bad – and then we have Tom's, who has played him like a violin, and I'm not talking about a Stradivarius."

As Ed paused for breath, Keith made a claim for at least some of the spotlight: "The Thruvian. Yes, we are aware of him. But what we're not clear on, is how you four came together in the first place."

"That? Ah, there's no great mystery. I was beginning to doubt my sanity, as was Amanda. We found each other through the medium of small ads, then Simon responded to another, and we became three. But Mands and I had some doubts as to Si's *bona fides*," Ed looked aside and winked at Simon, "...an embarrassing misunderstanding that needs no further discussion. So, I guess, we continued to advertise in our own mystic manner in order to try to establish whether it was Simon who was the loon, or the pair of us instead. Tom then came out of the closet, and with his accession to the group we came to the firm conclusion that we are all, in fact, sectionable." Ed leant forwards and tapped the table with one finger: "And with a good number for a pub quiz team, that is where we decided to stop. While finding fellow travellers is in some sense *nice*, we are not here to form some uber-lovey-dovey group and risk alerting our jealous keepers to our breaches of confidence."

Keith nodded. "I understand. Yet here you are. And I don't think your presence today is just to say 'hello and goodbye', is it?"

"You're not just a beard with a pretty face, Keith, me old mucker." Ed placed both hands on the table. "We're mainly here because, to be bluntly Anglo-Saxon, we're not entirely clear what the fuck is going on in Norwich. It's something big, and complicated, and it's coming to a head. And I hate to say it, but we – The Credulous – may need a little help in order to save the human race, or at least, the web-fingered part of it that resides in this fine city. As such, we're prepared to accept a *pax* on a limited-run basis. You show us *yours* and we'll show you *ours*."

Keith continued to nod gently. "Well put. This is precisely why we wanted to meet you, and so I guess this place…" he opened his hands to indicate their present space, "must qualify as 'behind the bike sheds'. We are willing to share what we know, within limits."

Ed squinted at the other, pursed his lips, and nodded slowly in return. "I couldn't have expressed that better myself. You are a man of rare wit. As such, I think we can do business. So, let's begin. First, tell us…"

***

The discussion began on what each side knew of Thruvians, and here Keith made a shocking revelation: "The one you know as 'Smith' has other irons in the fire. In fact, there is at least one other *Big Issue* seller who works for him, plying her trade in the Lanes, and we have suspicions about a second. The Thruvians seem to have appreciated the possibilities here. After all, what could be better than taking advantage of supposedly homeless people, who are out on the streets all day, able to observe places and people and events, looking for opportunities to influence, as well as doing a bit of message dissemination themselves."

As Keith paused, Ed probed: "Message dissemination?"

"*The Big Issue* itself," said Simon. "Obvs!"

"Exactly!" Keith nodded approval. "We've found that they occasionally insert small messages in the copies they sell – similar technology, dissolving after a few days. I presume Smith edits these before distributing them to his minions. They probably don't know he is an alien manipulator. Maybe they just see him as their contact with the organisation. Anyway, Trevor has become a regular customer of the Lanes seller, an Eastern European lady. He picks up copies of the magazine to enable us to keep an eye on what messages they are broadcasting."

"Yeah, it sucks," said Trevor. "Even though you know the intent of the messages, you can't help being affected by them. If there were a march tomorrow – either for or against social policies related to homelessness, unemployment, or drug or alcohol misuse – I'd have to keep well away. I'm not sure I'd be able to stop myself from smashing things up."

"What do you mean, 'for or against'?" asked Amanda. "Surely you mean policies in *support* of the homeless?"

"Nope," Trevor shook his head slowly. "That's the problem. They're playing both sides against each other. Sometimes there are messages that dig at the homeless. You know, using terms like 'wasters', 'freeloaders' and 'layabouts'. And sometimes they dig at the establishment: lots of 'Tory scum' and 'fascists'."

"Indeed," said Keith. "Some messages work better with some people, and other messages with others. They want to tweak the emotions of everyone who reads their copy."

"That's terrible!" concluded Amanda.

"It is," concurred Keith. "And in line with everything else, the frequency of these messages is increasing. We used to find one every month, then one a week. This week, Trevor found two messages in the last copy he bought."

"Like a clock counting down," mused Tom, louder than intended.

"Yes, Tom," said Keith, turning to him. "A countdown. Or count *up*. But the problem is, not only are we unclear about the alien endgame, but we're also not entirely sure what clock they're using."

Tom gave a pained grin. And then a thought occurred to him at the exact same time it did to his colleagues. "Clock? Ah, well, about that..."

Simon started to laugh.

Amanda exclaimed: "You don't think?"

And all three turned to look at Ed, who merely muttered: "*Bollocks!*"

"Well, Ed," said Amanda, "you've got to come clean now. Are you going to tell them, or am I?"

"Desist, dear Amanda. Grudgingly, I admit you are right." Ed folded his hands on the table before him and slowly looked between the Musketeers. "Okay. If you are sitting comfortably – boys, girls, and others – let me tell you a tale of the beautiful game; of improbable results; and of devious codes. Hold onto your hats, and quite possibly also your bowels. We first noticed…"

***

"No *fucking* way!" exclaimed Trevor. "Manipulating football games? I mean, just *one* would take some doing, but *every* game Norwich have played this season, home *and* away?"

"The results are available on any news site for you to peruse at your leisure," said Ed. "And you can find the ASCII codes online, too. By all means, check. But if you're in doubt, I'm happy to indulge in a little wager. Funnily enough, we've had quite a decent run of luck recently." Ed twitched his wrist ostentatiously, drawing attention to the expensive Rolex thereon.

"You've been using this information to bet on results?" Keith's tone clearly indicated disapproval. "Do you think that's wise?"

"Wise? If done incautiously, obviously not. But a man's gotta feed himself, so we have indeed been careful."

"And the message says 'Delia must d…'?" said Agneta, through a frown.

"That is correct, my dear," said Ed, patronisingly. "Though we can now make a good guess at the next letter."

"Yep. It's an 'i'," said Simon. "Gotta be."

"My strange friend, Simonella, is correct," said Ed. "Since we last debated these affairs, there have been a couple of one-nil results for Norwich – a home victory and an away defeat. This makes the first six letters of the code: 011010. Now, there are four possibilities from here: nil-nil would make the next letter an 'h', nil-one an 'i', one-nil a 'j' and one-all a 'k'. Of these options, only the vowel makes sense, and hence you can bet your mortgage that on the coming Saturday, our glorious chaps are going to go down to an ignominious home defeat to Brentford."

"So, the message becomes 'Delia must di…'?" continued Agneta, successfully biting down on her annoyance. "And you say there can only be one more letter? So, what does that leave?"

This time Ed refrained from snapping back a response, and he and Simon exchanged frowns. Tom had been so intent on his novel and this meeting that he'd completely forgotten about the mid-week game last night, but even so the solution was obvious. "*Fuck*," he muttered.

"Yes indeed, Tom. Fuck."

"Maybe it's 'dig'," said Simon, with more hope than expectation. "Or 'dim', as in, she loses her, you know, *lustre* as supremo."

"That's pretty *dim* itself, mate," said Ed. "And you can *dig* all you like. I have thought hard about this during the day, and I do not believe the alternatives to *the obvious* make a lot of sense. 'Din'? Make a racket? 'Dio'? As in, supplant that much-lamented hard rocker on a tour with his ex-band, *Rainbow*? 'Dip'? To avoid a low beam, perhaps? 'Dis'? But who would she slag off? Or at a stretch – 'DIY'? In any case, there are separate codes for capital letters, so that could have been coded with fidelity. And that leaves the 'oh fuck' option."

"*Die!*" said Trevor, Agneta, Keith, Amanda and Martin, almost as one, in manners ranging from disbelief to shock.

"If the inevitable one-nil away win is followed by the sequence: 01100101, then the message would indeed state that 'Delia must die', though we must hope and pray that this is nothing more than mischievous word play rather than a statement of intent."

***

"I still don't believe it," said Trevor. "Killing Delia?" He looked at his fellow Musketeers for confirmation: "I'm not aware of any case where an alien species has been involved in actual homicide."

"Nah – they just get others to do their dirty work for them," said Ed. "There are plenty of examples of that, and you know it."

Keith nodded glumly. "You are correct. This has been happening for centuries."

"But who would do *this*?" persisted Trevor.

"What about Terminus Est?" asked Tom, cued by Keith's mention of their past skulduggery. "You told me they've been involved in many of the past crises in the city."

"Involved – yes," confirmed Keith. "But as agitators, not assassins."

"Then that just leaves, well, *the people*," said Tom. "The citizens of Norwich. Or maybe just football fans. They can get a bit, um, *feisty* at times. But we're doing well this season, and the code implies we're at least going to the playoffs."

"Fair point that, old man," said Ed. "I don't see why it'd be our fans, while the oppo in our final game should be happy with a win. If they were Ipswich fans then who knows, but I can't see anyone else being fussed."

Agneta had been silent for some time, cogitating. Now, she said: "Perhaps the people could be persuaded to do it if the conditions were right. If Delia appears at the wrong time and place after the defeat. There is a lot of tension in the city. Maybe the result could be the spark for something more widespread?"

Keith ran a hand through his hair. "I don't know. There is still much we need to learn. If the football season is the clock counting down, then everything will come to a head in about a month?"

"Late May," nodded Simon.

"Okay. So, we still have time to uncover the means. The process. For a start, I think we need to keep an eye on all these angry groups that have sprung up."

"Agreed," said Ed. "Plus, we need to keep eyes on the various gits who are driving this, not least Sir Lard Arse and his spawn. You appear to know a lot more about them than we do. Given the difficulty of somehow affecting football results, and the number of these wankers, do you think they are responsible?"

Keith looked around his colleagues unhappily. "I suspect so, but maybe not alone. This is so big, I can't help thinking that the Thruvians are involved, too – perhaps as their paymasters, or at least as part of a collective of manipulator species. Even so, I just don't know."

"Maybe Teresa and Ricky are also involved," said Amanda.

"Yes, perhaps." Keith was still troubled. "But maybe there are even more. Others we don't yet know about."

"Oh!" A thought occurred to Tom, who couldn't stop his hand from automatically rising to his mouth.

"Tom?" said Ed, with beetling brows. "What is it now? What have you done?"

"Me? Nothing! But it just occurred to me that there might be someone else involved..." he looked at Keith. "Someone you know. Someone close to home."

"Alice? Don't be ab—"

"No. Not Alice. *Brian!*" Tom set about explaining all he knew about his ex-office mate's peculiar movements. He concluded: "...it's suspicious, no?"

Keith sat back in his chair, too stunned to speak.

Ed gave an exasperated sigh: "Really, Tom? Is this all? Or have you more intel you're sitting on, waiting for a dramatic moment?"

"No – none. I swear. It's just, well, Brian *hates* football. Absolutely hates it. I saw the correlation, but just couldn't credit him with ever going to a game of his own free will."

"Might be a ruse," suggested Simon. "Or maybe it isn't, and it's his way of hitting back by sabotaging lots of games. But I don't see how he could be doing this alone."

***

The discussion veered back and forth for another hour. For the most part, Tom let the more voluble speak – mainly Ed and Keith, with occasional input from Trevor, Simon and Agneta. He only really piped up when Norwich's lost tunnels were mentioned: it turned out the Musketeers were aware that these existed, but didn't know exactly where, and had never used them. They were astonished by Tom's revelations, although uncertain as to how this knowledge might best be employed.

At last, Ed attempted to bring the meeting to a close. "To summarise," he said, "we'll unite our efforts until this stable is swept. You'll take on the footie, we'll keep an eye on the vegans, and we'll both up our game with the Wankers in Black and the Thruvian."

"Sure," said Keith. "Trevor is a season ticket holder, and he can get Martin in, too. They can try to find out how the games are being fixed. Now we know about this, I suspect we'll find several mercenaries in attendance at the games."

"I'll try to get to an away game, too," said Trevor. "I haven't been to one in ages."

"What about Brian?" said Tom. "Who's going to watch him?"

"I think you can leave that to me in the first instance," said Keith. "I can subtly query my darling wife, and perhaps be more sociable with him when I go to meet her. Plus, Agneta is on the spot."

"Great!" sighed Tom, relieved that this excruciating chore had been taken from him.

"Though, of course," Keith continued, "it wouldn't hurt for you, Tom, to look in on him when dropping off messages to Agneta."

"Oh!"

"And Tom will act as the go between, yes?" said Amanda.

"Indeed," said Keith. "He can use Agneta, or come to us at the Rumsey on Wednesdays. I agree with Ed that we should be careful about using any electronic communication: the Thruvians are deeply immersed in the internet. And watch out using your mobiles, too. I'd hate for our entire group to be identified from someone's intercepted call."

Ed smiled and turned to Tom. "Communications discipline, eh, old chap? Don't let the side down."

Tom noticed that all had turned to look at him, mostly with wry amusement. It was only as he was half-way home that the meaning of those final moments struck home, and an image came to his mind of that legendary dragon, Anne Robinson, sneering at him: *You are the weakest link: goodbye...*

The cheeky fuckers!

Chapter 32: Lost and Found

And thus did Brentford slay high-flying Norwich City F.C. at their own manor, causing the Canaries' fans to suddenly wonder whether they had done enough to gain one of the Championship play-off spots, or whether they might still be pipped to the post.

"The place was swarming with them," said Trevor, at the Musketeers' subsequent Wednesday meeting at the Rumsey Wells, which Ed had encouraged Tom to attend. "I saw at least four of them – and Martin spotted Sophie, too. They were wearing yellow, rather than black."

"Where did they go?" demanded Agneta. "What did they do?"

"It was difficult to keep track of them all," said Trevor. "I only saw them in a group once, outside the stadium. They didn't stay together. I noticed Samson in the Geoffrey Watling Stand under the Directors' box, and one of the others was in the Barclay Stand."

"We think they had seats in all of the stands," added Martin. "But we couldn't move around to check. We were in the Barclay."

"But what did they do?" asked Keith. "Could you see?"

"Not really," said Trevor. "But get this: one – Tristan, I think his name is – was dressed as a steward. He could have got up to anything."

"Did you see any messages?" asked Tom. "Were you wearing your contacts?"

"We were," said Trevor. "But as you know, 7D messages need to be seen from the right position, the right angle. They could have been all over the place. I wouldn't be surprised if there were some on the pitch-side advertising boards, and maybe even some in the changing rooms. Then only the players would have seen them up close."

"What about the game itself?" asked Keith. "We know the result, but it wasn't on TV, so we couldn't watch. What was your impression?"

Trevor and Martin looked at each other; frowned; shrugged. "It was… definitely odd," said Trevor, resuming. "For the whole of the first half and most of the second, both teams seemed afraid to attack. It was like the penalty boxes were, I dunno, *electrified*. There was lots of neat passing and pointless shooting from range. But whenever one side got into the box, they seized up and seemed afraid to shoot. And they were *so* slow on the ball, they got tackled and lost possession."

"Yeah, and then there was the penalty," said Martin. "Or *non*-penalty. We should have had one. The stadium went mad. Our forward got clattered, but the ref waved play on. Pity Championship games don't have VAR."

"That's right. And then, from about the seventieth minute, Brentford came alive for ten minutes, scored, then sat back. And we did fuck all. Game over. Nil-one. It was just *strange*."

"Aren't you a season ticket holder, Trevor?" asked Tom. "How did this compare to the rest?"

Trevor had the decency to look embarrassed. "Well, I am, but I've been busy with work and, you know, this other stuff. I've only been to three games this season. We did okay in them. None were great. They were all, well, forgettable."

"Because of the lack of action?" said Keith.

"Yeah, I guess."

The five around the table fell silent for a moment, toying with drinks, or staring off into the pub interior. Tom kept an eye on Keith, who seemed deep in thought. At last, the latter shook his head, looked up and around, and declared: "Well, I think that's settled. We haven't paid much attention to the Mercenaries as they haven't appeared active, but it seems they've been busy all along. I didn't know they were fans of football."

"Generally, they're not," said Trevor.

"Okay. That makes their behaviour all the more odd. And we've confirmed the unusual pattern of results. It looks like you and your team were right, Tom. Nil-one, just as predicted. Hence, 'Delia must di...'."

"Ah, yes," said Tom, "and that brings us to the reason I'm here, uh, well, apart from wanting to hear your update. I have a message from Ed."

"Go on," said Keith.

"Well, you see, after our last meeting, Amanda and I thought you might be right about drawing attention to ourselves through betting, so we decided not to. But Si has been cagey, so I guess he did. And, well, so did Ed. He placed a big bet."

Keith tutted and shook his head; Agneta hissed: "*Stupid!*"

"Yes, well, be that as it may, when Ed went to collect his winnings on Saturday evening – he used a Coral on Prince of Wales Road – you'll never guess who was already there?"

"One of the Mercenaries?"

"Yep. The big cheese himself: Augustus P. Samson."

"I would swear if it were in my nature," said Keith. "No, I will anyway: *fuck*." He turned to Trevor. "This isn't my thing, but I thought there were bookies at the stadium itself. Why wouldn't he use one of those?"

"There are a couple, but they'd probably be busy. And maybe he's had to spread out where he's placing his bets."

"A bit like Ed," said Tom. "Makes sense."

Keith pushed back from the table and his long-empty pint glass. "A sideline? I suppose the Mercenaries are, after all, fundamentally *mercenary* – so why not? They serve their alien masters, receive whatever fee they are offered, and make a bit extra too."

"Or maybe the betting wins *are* their payment," suggested Agneta.

"Good point." Keith's eyes suddenly narrowed, and he looked hard at their guest. "Tom – it seems some of your colleagues are benefitting in the same way as the Mercenaries. Just between us, here and now, how sure are you of their motives? And Ed's in particular?"

Tom shook his head, at first vigorously but then more slowly. An image flashed into his mind: the sight of Ed's expensive new apartment in the St Anne's Quarter, viewed from King Street, a very short distance from Dragon Hall and a couple of the latest alien messages. Always close to the action. Always in the know. Surely Ed was above board?

Surely?

***

"Still nothing, Tom?" asked Smith the following day, at their usual rendezvous by the Guildhall. The mid-April weather was fine, almost balmy, and the plane tree by the bench was starting to look chipper.

"Er, well, you see," lied Tom, "it's this new project I've got, back at my old department. I'm being worked like a dog. I hadn't realised what a taskmaster Alice is."

"Yet, I see you have made good progress with your novel. You're having quite a creative spurt."

"Ah, yes, but you see, I'm working on this in between things for Alice. It's not like I'm working all day on work-work and then the evenings on, er, *non-work* work."

Smith tilted his head in an oddly human way, allowing him to examine Tom from a slightly different angle. "Really? So, you've had no time to explore the cathedral environs as I asked? That's a pity."

Tom gave a lame shrug. "Sorry. Maybe tomorrow?"

In fact, he had been to the cathedral the previous day, and so he'd seen the outrageously homophobic 7D message scrawled over the famed Samson and Hercules statues that stood to either side of the front portal of that eponymous 17th century house in Tombland – which, after many changes of use, was now a mortgage advice centre. And he'd also seen the 7D desecration of the signage to the privately run Norwich School, within the cathedral grounds, which suggested its pupils were radiant in 'white-privilege' and that their teachers were 'nonces'. But the only ones he'd told about this were the Musketeers via Agneta.

"Tomorrow may be too late. I hate to say this, Tom, but I think we must up our game. I have reports of increased manipulations."

"Ah, okay. Well, let me know, and I'll really *really* try next time." And then – to add substance to his little play – he shook a hand to the heavens. "Curse you, Alice!"

Smith gave him a *very* human look – the sort one might give a madman. "Goodbye, Tom." He stalked off to the side of the Guildhall facing the market.

Tom waited for a minute or so, and then rose from the bench and headed the same way. He ambled up to Sir Toby's Beers – a licensed stall at the market's edge that sold craft beers in cans, bottles, presentation packs, and on draft through a couple of kegs.

"He went in the side door," said a woman there, perched on a bench by the side of the stall, nursing a half-pint glass of something yellow. She spoke low, from the side of her mouth.

Tom ignored the woman, ordered himself a half, and then went to sit beside her. He stared straight ahead.

"Hi, Amanda. Do you mean the big door?"

"Yes. The one in the middle, under the arch with the four shields, between the buttresses. It was locked, but he had a key."

Tom had been doing some research. "There's definitely some sort of undercroft or crypt there. Apparently, a Christian martyr – Thomas Bilney – was held there before being burnt at the stake in 1531."

Amanda quickly glanced at him. "Not another ghost, Tom?"

"Ah, no. I don't think so. I've not found anything spooky related to the Guildhall."

"Thank goodness for that. But what now?"

"I guess we wait."

It took longer than expected, and in the end Tom felt compelled to get a second drink while Amanda continued to nurse her near-empty glass. Tom jumped when his new phone went off – his burner phone.

"Yes!" he said, in an unintendedly high pitch.

"It's true, old bean," came Ed's voice. "Comes out in the cathedral, as you predicted. Some subterranean chamber: empty – and dark as Satan's a-hole. But the door out isn't locked. We're going to exit here rather than risk a return journey."

"Oh, er, good. Any problems?"

"Aside from constant muttering by Buck Rogers about missing a shift at the comic book store, no." The voice became muffled: "Yes, Si. You got that camera set up yet? I'm just…" then the voice came back stronger. "We'll swap stories next debrief. Toodle pip."

"Everything good?" asked Amanda.

Tom gave a relieved smile. "No. Nothing's good. But at least, nothing's bad either."

Amanda suddenly rose. "I'll leave first. See you later, Guy."

"Roger that, Ms Hari."

***

Two days later, on Saturday, Tom encountered a happier Simon. "No problemo, mate," the latter had said, on their meeting outside the castle gate. "I still don't know what Ed actually does to earn his money, but some of us have to work, and I like my jobs and want to keep them. But today's kushti."

They were now deep within the castle's nether regions, in a chamber that held one of the three secret doors Tom had found in the ancient edifice. He wore his fraying fleece, while Simon wore his usual black, leather jacket – beneath which peeked a well-worn *South Park* t-shirt bearing a picture of Cartman issuing an insult and announcing a plan to immediately return to his own abode. But unusually, Simon wore a pair of glasses over his fine-boned face – a pair he'd borrowed from Tom at their last meeting prior to his caving expedition with Ed. And, like Tom, he also bore a backpack, although his was way cooler, with lightning flashes rather than pink unicorns.

"Have you got the cameras?" asked Tom.

"Yup. At least, the ones we've got left. We managed to place seven last time. They're really cool. I don't know where Ed got them as he wouldn't say, but they look like serious, military-grade hardware."

"Seven!" exclaimed Tom. "How…? Where…?"

Simon smirked. "We put one by each door in the castle the north, west, and east exits. Then we took the east door as you instructed. And beneath the King Street node, under The Three Tuns, we put two there. You said the southern passage goes to Carrow Priory, so we ignored that and explored the northern passage. A bit further up, we found another doorway to a passage heading east again. We just checked the magnet opened the door, then installed a camera on the other side, but we didn't follow that route. I reckon it goes towards the river. Might be the Pull's Ferry tunnel you suggested from your research. Then we carried on north until we got to the cathedral, and we put the seventh camera there."

"Wow. That's great. And they all work?"

"S'pose so. They're wireless. Ed's recording everything back in his pad. He's not mentioned any problems."

"Right, so…" Tom looked at the wall in the corner, where his contacts picked out a faint glow by the secret door. "Are you're saying there's a camera here? It must be inside, yes?"

Simon grinned broadly. "No bananas. It's here. Right in front of you. Told you they were cool. It's that bulge there, in the shadow of the ceiling. No, mate: a bit further left. Bit further still. About three metres."

At last, Tom thought he saw it. *Just*. It was tiny, black, and could have passed for a minor blemish on the stone wall. "Again, wow!" Then another thought occurred, and Tom swiftly turned to the runic mark by the door. "But talking of things that shouldn't be here, I wonder why the entrance sign is visible. If it's in 7D, I thought these were meant to fade quickly."

Simon shrugged. "Maybe cos they're different from the messages? Perhaps those are done in a different paint to ensure the evidence quickly disappears, but the door markers aren't a threat, so they're in, y'know, permanent ink?"

Tom frowned. "I guess so. Anyway, shall we go before the crowds arrive?" They had arrived at the castle at opening time, the very first visitors.

"Yup. Make it so!"

***

Tom and Simon took the tunnel that led from the north of the castle. This was the one that passed beneath what used to be Pond's shoe shop. They left a camera here by a brick archway; this would capture shots of anyone entering from London Street and the Cosy Club opposite. They placed a second camera at the undercroft they'd previously found further north — and this time chose not to pillage the wine that had been left there (neither being particularly partial to the product of the vine). And then they installed a camera at the terminus in Blackfriars' Hall, but this time…

"Simon!" hissed Tom. "Where are you going?"

"Let's have a proper nosey," the other replied, half-way through the thick, red curtains that closed off the cupboard space that hid the secret door. "We should see where we are. There might be an easy exit. The cathedral was a cinch." And then he was gone, across the stone floor and over to an old wooden door.

Tom nervously followed, then paused half-way: "What's that noise? It's… Si!"

After placing an ear to the door, Simon had decided that all was okay. As the door was already unlocked, he passed quickly through.

Tom scurried after, finding himself in a short passageway, the rising hum of a crowd as a backdrop. "Wait!"

But Simon was off, blond ponytail swaying from side-to-side. He took several paces to a small flight of steps, ascended to another door, then opened this a smidgen to peer through. The sound of human voices rose further. Simon turned to face Tom and smiled: "It's the main hall. There seems to be a record fair on."

Tom would have happily left matters there, but Simon wasn't through with slinking. And it was a good job, too. In a vaulted, galleried area, beyond the toilets, they found another small room with an unlocked door and steps down into dinginess… and another secret door.

"The whole place is like a warren," gasped Tom.

"But the rabbits are bigger," said Simon. "Come on!"

There was no use arguing, so Tom followed. After a pause for Simon to set up another camera, they followed this tunnel in a roughly north-eastly direction (according to Tom's compass). There were two further side passages leading to spooky undercrofts. Tom guessed that one of the exits was in or near the Briton's Arms on Elm Hill, and the second was at the Augustine Steward House in Tombland – where they nearly blundered into an active Escape Game. The latter was suspiciously close to the Samson and Hercules house that had recently been graffitied. And the terminus of the tunnel…

"Fuck me," said Simon, leading the way. "We're back at the cathedral. But it's a different door."

After setting a final camera, they escaped the tunnel system and headed off to a pub to get lunch, and then to a second for a liquid dessert, and then, well, neither had much else on, so they sought a third with sports channels on TV so they could follow the live football scores – this being an important day for the Canaries.

The Murderers on Timberhill was crowded, though they found a spot in one corner with an oblique view of one of the TVs.

"So… a one-nil away win?" queried Tom.

"Yep. They'll be partying in the city this evening."

"Have you, uh, got a bet on?"

Simon smiled and took a sip of his IPA. Lowering his glass, he confirmed: "Do Vulcans have pointy ears? Yeah. Just a small one, though. I can't help wondering if things might still go tits-up. I mean, if we can see what's going on, and Martin and his lot know now, maybe it'll somehow get to the enemy and they might, I dunno, shift tactics. I don't want to go all-in and lose my current winnings."

Tom nodded. "I've been worried about the pattern changing ever since the start. I mean, we know what the results are going to be. We *really* do. But I still can't help thinking this is too good to be true, and I just know

I'm going to get shafted. I guess I'm just a bit more risk averse than you and Ed."

"Ed laughs in the face of danger, mate. He's still going full tonto. He mentioned hiring a car for the day so he could hit every bookie in a twenty mile radius." He laughed and shook his head: "What a guy!"

Tom pouted his lips and scrunched his brow. Cautiously, he repeated, "Yes, what a guy. He's certainly making the best of a bad situation. I mean, whatever happens, he'll probably come out on top."

Simon shrugged. "Sure. Some people are like that. You just gotta admire them."

"Ah, so, you admire Ed?"

"Well, I guess so. I mean, he can be a bit of a prick at times. And a bit of a sexist. I think Agneta's going to rip him a new one at some point, and Amanda would have done so already, but she's too nice. But he's a doer. And charismatic. Anyway, don't tell him I said any of that, or he'll rag me for weeks."

Tom gave a weak smile and nodded acquiescence. But he was troubled. He'd thought Smith was on the level, but he'd been played for a fool. Surely this wasn't strike two? On the one hand, he doubted whether his friend was fully on the dark side, but on the other, he wasn't entirely convinced he couldn't be turned for the right price. Damn Keith for putting the doubt in his mind!

Inevitably, Norwich won.

"I hope Trevor and Martin aren't in yellow," laughed Simon. "Otherwise, they're not going to get out of Reading alive tonight."

And with other results going their way, a place in the play-offs was virtually assured: it was now a case of where they would finish, and that would depend upon the result of their final home game (which they knew would be a one-nil victory) and the results from other matches.

"Third or fourth," concluded Simon, after scribbling on the back of a flyer that had been left on the table. "Makes sense. Third plays sixth and fourth plays fifth. But in both cases, the first playoff leg will be away, and the return leg will be at home. Mid-May."

"Our last game of the season," mused Tom. And then he thought: and maybe Delia's last game ever…

***

The next day – a Sunday – Tom and Simon met up again, but later. The castle didn't open until 1p.m., but that deadline was missed: for one reason or another their rendezvous got pushed back to nearly half-three.

"Ah, hello," said the middle-aged woman at the ticket desk. "Back again?"

"Um, yes," said Tom, flourishing his museum pass. "We, er, like castles. A lot."

"Clearly! I didn't see you leave yesterday. I thought you might have gotten lost."

"I, er, guess you must have been on a break."

"I suppose so, although I never go far from this desk. Anyhow, have a nice visit."

As the pair hurried into the keep, Tom whispered: "maybe we should try to be less conspicuous?"

"Why?" asked Simon. "I doubt whether she's one of them. She probably just thinks we're like trainspotters. And, mate, I'm a *gamer* – so I'm used to people giggling and making assumptions."

"Okay. But we definitely need to leave by the front door today. The castle closes at five, so she's likely to be here until the end."

Tom suspected that the main reason *he* had been so tardy was subconscious resistance, for he was distinctly nervous today. The team had explored the north and east exits from the castle over the last week, which meant today it was time to reconnoitre the tunnel beyond the west exit, which his research suggested led to the Guildhall. He didn't want to risk bumping into Smith, but with matters rushing to a head, Ed had persuaded him that it was pretty much now or never.

In the lowest level of the castle, they found the secret door in an empty chamber. The castle wasn't busy at the time, with most visitors congregated on the levels above, at a number of exhibitions spaces and the café.

"Here goes!" exclaimed Simon, excitedly. Today, he wore a Minecraft t-shirt under his jacket, presumably to remain in keeping with their subterranean mission. He used his own magnet to open the door and was rapidly through, a torch in his other hand.

Tom was more than happy to let Simon lead. With the tunnel so narrow, he struggled to see beyond the man in front, and equally, anyone beyond would be unable to clearly see him. This meant that, should they run into Smith, he might still have the chance to turn run for it, retaining his anonymity. He had tentatively voiced this to Simon, who'd given a knowing smirk, but otherwise seemed fine with the option, as neither of them expected Smith to turn violent and fry the lead person or engage in any sort of close combat.

Soon, they came to a small underground chamber, a couple of hundred metres from the castle. The pair had been here before, a few weeks previously, shortly after Tom had discovered the three castle exits. At that time, they'd stopped here and gone no further. Tom had predicted that the secret door in the wall to one side led to a space under the Royal Arcade. This time they went through the door, but the side passage didn't go far and was blocked by rubble.

"Not sure it's worth wasting a camera here," said Simon. "I wonder what's... hang on..." He raised a hand for silence.

Tom tried to still his breathing, then he heard it too: a gentle plashing. "Water? Is that running water?"

"Sounds like it. Drains? Are we close to the sewers?"

"Perhaps," mulled Tom. "Or else it's the lost river."

"The what?"

Tom nodded as Simon turned to face him, blinking as the other's torch shone directly into his eyes. "Lost river. It's rumoured there's another river that runs under the city. Given all the other rumours that have turned out to be correct, it wouldn't surprise me if there's truth to this one, too."

"I wonder if the river had something to do with collapsing this tunnel?"

"Er, yes." The thought of tunnel collapse suddenly concentrated Tom's mind. "I think we should get out of here – just in case."

Back in the chamber, Simon edged in front, and they set off down the main passage. Tom's compass indicated that they were heading almost due west. At each step, he tried to visualise where they might be in relation to the area above. "We must be under the market now," he said, at one point. Then, after a little longer: "This isn't right."

Simon stopped and turned around, this time directing his torch at Tom's chest. "Whassat, mate?"

"I was just thinking, I'm not sure this is right. Wait." He knelt down and retrieved his city map, laying it on the stone floor between them. He pointed: "See *here*. This is where I reckon the west door is. And we've been heading almost directly west. That takes us under the Arcade, *here*. Then the market. But we're not curving… or if we are, it's slightly to the south, whereas the Guildhall is to the north a bit."

"So, where else could we be heading?"

Tom thought a moment, then tentatively stated: "The Old Swan Inn, perhaps?"

"Eh? There's no such place."

"Not now, no. But there's rumours there was a tunnel under an old pub that was knocked down some years ago. It was on St Peters Street, near the corner where the Forum is now."

"Near to the war memorial, too?"

"Yes. That's right. And there's an undercroft beneath the monument, but at the level of the market itself."

"Right – cos the market sits in a depression, and St Peters runs a couple of metres above it. Well, let's carry on and find out. It can't be more than another thirty metres from here."

Tom folded his map and returned it to his rucksack. He took a deep breath. "Okay. Lead on."

It was only another fifty or sixty crabbed paces to the next point of interest – a widened chamber, with brick vaulting. From here, an open tunnel curved off to the left – roughly south – and another led almost directly to the right, or to the north. But unlike the south passage, the north one had a wooden door… and it was open.

"Fuck!" hissed Tom. "I don't like the look of this."

Simon turned down the illumination on his torch and took a half-step back to stand next to his partner. "What is it?" he whispered, taking his cue from Tom. "This seems about right. Under the Forum?"

"Yes. But if it is, then the left tunnel must lead to St Peter Mancroft, about twenty to thirty metres away, and the right almost certainly leads to the Guildhall… maybe one hundred metres away. Meaning—"

"Meaning that this is the bad dude superhighway!" exclaimed Simon. "It's how Smith gets from the church to the Guildhall."

"And we're right in the middle. He could come by at any time. *And why is the door open?*"

"Whoa, mate, calm down! He's not likely to be wandering about at this very moment. And he probably doesn't shut the door—"

"Because he's just opened it!"

Simon tried to give a reassuring smile. "No, Tom. It's probably because he uses it a lot and doesn't need to shut it to keep people out. *Simples*. So – what now?"

"Cameras," wheezed Tom. "Put up cameras *quick*."

"Don't you want to–?"

"No!" Tom tried to calm his breathing. After all, what was there to *really* worry about? Smith had the form of a wizened old man. He had never mentioned controlling alien sentinels or hordes of demons, and there was no reason to suspect that he did. Indeed, the alien relied on humans to do his bidding.

After a worried glance at Tom, Simon went to set up two of the tiny cameras, and then tested their connectivity with his laptop. He needed to be close to pick up their output; only Ed, with his monstrously powerful machine at home, was able to receive, collect and collate the data from the different cameras from any significant distance.

"Right, all done," said Simon, after what seemed an age. "Are you sure you don't want to have a quick peek while we're–"

"No! Really! We've ridden our luck so far. Besides, we have to be out in... *shit*. Twenty minutes!"

"You should have led with that," smirked Simon. "That's a decent excuse. Then you wouldn't have seemed such a wuss."

They quickly vacated the chamber and headed back towards the castle. But they were soon in for a bigger shock...

They passed the door to the collapsed shaft and were approaching the exit to the castle, when Simon, in front, suddenly stiffened... and whimpered.

Tom ran into the other's back and dropped his torch. "Si, what?"

"G... g... gho... *ghost!*" Simon was suddenly leaning back into his partner.

Over Simon's shoulder – which now nestled under Tom's chin and was steadily forcing him backwards – Tom was able to make out a bright light, some five metres ahead, hovering in the air. It was small, and not unfamiliar to him: the glowing, ghostly skull of Robert Goodale, a hanged wife murderer whose execution had gone so awry his head had popped from his body. *"Ohhhhhh crap..."*

And yet the skull was going nowhere: it didn't advance or emit any tortured wailing; it simply hung in the air, just before the exit to the tunnel. If Tom hadn't frozen in place, Simon might have backed them all the way up to the opposite end of the tunnel. But, unable to move, and with no clear threat, Simon's shoulders de-tensed and he rapidly regained his composure.

"I didn't believe you, mate," he whispered hoarsely. "Sorry!"

"No problem," gasped back Tom. But having a human shield helped him to regain a degree of calm too.

"What now?" asked Simon. "It's not doing anything, and we *have* to get through that door."

"I know. But—"

"*Why are you whispering?*" The words came from the direction of the ghost, though its jaws did not move. The voice was male and mellifluous.

"Uh… I think I just crapped myself," said Simon.

"Me too."

"*Do you wish to pass?*"

"Oh, fuck," muttered Simon, then, more loudly, "er, *yes*. Yes, please, Mr Ghost."

"Please, Mr Goodale," squeaked Tom. "Let us through."

The skull didn't respond for a moment, and then declared: "*Goodale? Yes, this guise is his. We saw his end. But that is not who I am, Tom.*"

"Shit! You know my… you know…"

"*Of course. We – the post-corporeal – are everywhere, unlimited by physical constraints, unlike those who watch your species from above.*" The voice paused again. At last it announced: "*We play our games, and the meddlers play theirs. Who is to say what is moral? But the Thruvian goes too far.*" And then the skull began to retreat, to fade. It reached the stone door… and sank into it. The last words to come to them were: "*Good luck, Tom.*"

"You may have *lost* control of your bowels, mate," muttered Simon, after a shocked moment, "but I reckon you might have just *found* a very spooky friend."

Chapter 33: Into the Lairs

It was a week before the totality of the forces of good were able to meet again – a week during which messages had flown back-and-forth between the Musketeers and The Credulous via Tom, who had also managed separate meetings with individuals of his own team – though not all three at once. As the forecast was fine for the current Saturday – some cloud cover and a modest fifteen degrees – they had settled on meeting in the morning in Chapelfield Gardens near the city centre.

Keith was the last to bustle up to the congregation, which had picked out a patch of grass in one corner, away from the main paths through the park and other early visitors. "Sorry," he declared, slightly out of breath. "I had to give Alice the slip. She thinks I'm shopping for a present. I haven't got long. What have I missed?"

"Missed?" said Ed, who lounged on the grass, resting on one elbow. "Almost nothing. In fact, I'd just said to my speleological chums: 'No *fucking* way! It spoke to you?' And here you are before they've had a chance to reply."

Keith gave a strained smile and dropped into a crouch between Trevor and Agneta, both of whom sat cross-legged, as did Martin beyond. "Didn't you know about their adventures? Tom debriefed us on Wednesday."

"I *knew* knew, yes," said Ed. "But I've been out-and-about for the week. This is the first time I've spoken to the ghost-whisperers." He turned to look between Tom and Simon, who sat to either side of Amanda, completing a semi-circle that faced off against their erstwhile allies. "And I'm still awaiting a response."

"Really not much to tell," said Simon, sitting with one leg stretched out in front of him. "Spooky floating skull; inadvertent bowel movements; and then best wishes to Tom. Oh – and the ghost dissed 'the Thruvian', so they're clearly not chums."

"Have your lot come across these ghost imposters before?" asked Ed, turning back to Keith. "You've been at this lark for some time."

"No, we haven't. The Queen has mentioned post-corporeals before, but she's never expressed any interest in them, or concern about them."

"Hmm," mused Ed. "What I'm trying to angle at is this: are these white-sheets potential allies? Can we make use of them somehow – especially since Tom appears to have a fan?"

Keith shrugged. "I'm not sure what you expect. It seems these post-corporeals are continually watching, but if they have any concerns they don't appear to act on them. Then again, it seems odd that one actually spoke to your friends. So – who knows. Tom?"

"Ah, well, I really couldn't say." Of the various critical matters to discuss today, Tom had rather hoped that this wouldn't be amongst them. Indeed, he feared what conclusions might be drawn, and in particular, that he might be asked to seek out further meetings with the Goodale phantasm or others of its kind. Okay, once it had been clear that the skull wasn't going to race at him and spray him with ectoplasm, he had managed to settle his nerves: but every time he'd encountered a ghost, it had filled him with an initial terror that was hard to get across to the others – although Simon had clearly experienced something similar. Maybe the fear he'd felt was the result of a deliberate mechanism – perhaps chemical – to keep people away? Or maybe it was just for laughs? Who knew...

"Tom?" said Amanda, at his side. "*Hello?*"

"Oh... sorry... lost in, um, thought. What did you...?"

"Keith asked whether you thought they might respond to a request for help."

"Ah. Help? Well... you know as much as me. I doubt they would physically help, even if they had the, um, limbs to do so."

"But maybe they'd be happy to supply some intel?" wondered Keith.

Tom gave a sickly smile and shrugged. "I, er, would rather not ask. Not unless we really *really* need some help." He noticed Amanda giving him a compassionate look.

"Quite possibly we might, old fruit," said Ed, with no sympathy at all. "But let's bank this for now as *Cheggers* – ah, sorry, *Keith*, my mind was elsewhere – needs to get back to she who wears the leather trousers. With our glorious team's final league game this afternoon, I'm keen to hear more about their match last Saturday."

Trevor accepted the commission. "As before, really. Martin and I caught the train to Reading. Bloody horrendous journey. Delayed departure from Norwich; signalling problems near Manningtree; hassle crossing London from Liverpool Street to Paddington. We barely made it in time for kick-off. I initially thought we'd struck out, but then we saw Jules in the queue for the gents, and then Martin spotted Tristan again…"

"Yeah, dressed as a steward," said the name-checked one. "I don't know how he managed that."

"Little prick," muttered Trevor. "Anyway, we hung around after the game for an hour or two, but we didn't see any more of them. Then we headed back to London – another nightmare. The train broke down and we sat in the suburbs for ages. We only just managed to catch the last train to Norwich. I thought we were going to get stranded in the capital."

"Thanks for the travelogue," said Ed, sarcastically. "But what about the game?"

"Similar to before. The teams seemed terrified of each other's penalty areas, and I've never seen so many mis-hit shots from range. But right after half time, our boys just clicked, like someone hit a switch. They attacked like demons for twenty minutes, got a goal from a rebound, and then reverted to scaredy cats. One-nil away win – as you predicted."

"Was the lard mountain there?"

"Samson? We didn't see him."

"Probably hoovering up all the half-eaten pies from the stadium bins," muttered Ed. "Okay, I guess you chaps deserve a pat on the back, except… what about Brian?"

Trevor frowned. "No, but then that's not really a surprise. Neither of us have seen him in the flesh. We only have a couple of dodgy photos from Keith taken at socials with his wife. He doesn't even have a proper mugshot on the UEA website. So… he could have been sat next to us at the ground and we might not have recognised him."

"Well, I have some news on this matter – of sorts," said Keith. "I picked Alice up from her office three times last week, and she was alone on each occasion. At first, she was puzzled by Brian's absence. It was only yesterday, when I mentioned the matter again, that she revealed he's apparently on holiday."

"That's odd," said Tom. "In all the time I was at the department, I never knew him to take a holiday. Apart from being away for conferences, he was in the office almost every day, including bank holidays. If they hadn't shut the department and locked it up, he probably would have gone in on Christmas Day too."

"What a sad act," murmured Ed.

Keith's frown deepened. "That's pretty much what Alice said. She'd initially assumed he was away at a meeting and just hadn't told her. It was only a chance discussion with the departmental secretary that resolved the matter. But as to where he went or what he is actually doing…" Keith gave a shrug, "that is something of a mystery."

"I don't like this," said Ed. "I smell a whole sewer full of rats. A potential villain goes AWOL at this juncture? How convenient. Are there any more freak coincidences that we should know about?"

"Yes, there is." This time it was Amanda who spoke. Tom had managed to snare her for a coffee at Al-Chemista's off St Gregory's Green on Tuesday, and another at Strangers coffee shop on Pottergate on Thursday. She'd taken to 'Rowling-it', as she put it: doing her research and writing on a laptop in various cafés around the so-called Vegan Enclave, beginning to take her spying role seriously. "I saw Teresa yesterday." She paused to consider her next words.

Ed only allowed her a second, before an impatient chivvying: "*And, Amanda dearest?*"

"And I followed her. The weather was like today, so I sat outside at Sahara – you know, the North African coffee shop and deli on St Benedicts. They were allowed to put tables outside during the covid pandemic and then keep them there afterwards."

"Close to One Life Left," noted Simon, "and the comic shop where I work."

"Yes. That's right. It's not as close to the Enclave as I would like, but it gives the best views down the whole street. Anyway, Teresa walked past me in the afternoon, and as I'd finished my drink, I thought *why not*, so I followed her." For the first time since Tom had come to know her, Amanda actually seemed excited. "She went all the way down to The Halls, then up St Andrew's hill, to the little plain outside the Cosy Club and…" she paused to look at the mobile phone she'd been clutching in her hand, then swiped at it: "Look!"

The others crowded around – leaning in, or scootching forwards, until Amanda was at the centre of a circle of craning heads. The image on the phone was of Teresa bent forwards in conversation with…

"A *Big Issue* seller!" exclaimed Tom, who was to Amanda's immediate side and had the clearest view. "Not…?"

"Yep," said Trevor, almost directly opposite and having to view the screen upside down. "That's her. The Thruvian's stooge."

"*Other* stooge," said Agneta quietly, peering at Tom.

Amanda swiped to reveal a succession of largely identical images.

"What's she doing there?" asked Simon, at one point.

"They talked for a bit. Not long. Then the seller gave her a copy of the magazine from the *bottom* of her pile. Teresa didn't pay her anything, and then…" The final picture was skewed diagonally, showing the bottom half of two pairs of legs and the paved street. "Sorry. I thought she was going to see me, so I had to quickly, um…"

Ed straightened his back, having risen to stand behind Amanda and then bend to see her photos. "Well, well, well. I'm not sure what surprises me more: confirmation that Teresa must be a member of team Smith, or the daring of our very own Mata Hari." He returned to his original spot as the others peeled back from the picture show and slumped onto the grass. "Bloody well done, Mands!"

As others muttered their appreciation, Amanda appeared unsure where to look. "Gosh. Thanks. But it was a bit embarrassing. I couldn't follow Teresa afterwards, as I remembered I hadn't paid for my coffee, so I had to rush back to Sahara. Fortunately, the owner is a nice man, and as I've become a regular he hadn't phoned the police. But I thought it best to order an extra pastry as a kind of tip."

Tom found himself smiling broadly at the woman, and only withdrew slightly from where he'd encroached for a better view, leaving his arm almost touching hers.

"So," said Ed, with authority, "where does this leave us? I think it's clear that Smith is at the bottom of pretty much everything. He and his familiars – who we now know include Teresa, and almost certainly her whipped beau – have been leaving inciting messages across the city, and coincidentally gulling Tom into making matters even worse. This other *Big Issue* seller is something of a go-between, linking the alien not only to Teresa, but also to The Blob and his Blackshirts. Which means Smith is either wholly or partially behind the football scam. And it's possible nobby-no-mates Brian is also part of his team. The central role of Smith, the Thruvian, also seems to be confirmed by Tom's new disembodied BFF. Thoughts?"

Keith cleared his throat. He was now standing, having declined to return to his awkward crouch. "I agree. This seems to be one big conspiracy. I just hope we've identified all its members." From where he sat, Tom caught Keith's side glance at him, and his subtle head jerk towards Ed. "And we also know the clock is counting down. There's today's match, which we expect Norwich to win, and then the first play-off game next Saturday, at some away venue. And then there is the return fixture – which Trevor tells me will be two weeks from today at Carrow Road. So, we have two weeks to stop whatever is *going on* from *going off*."

"Surprisingly well put," said Ed, approvingly. "And that leaves us… where?"

Silence descended. Tom looked around. He had been mulling over this very issue, for he'd come to a place in his novel where a similar question needed answering. And the answer he'd come up with was an uncomfortable one for him and his colleagues. He had no choice but to speak. "I, er, I wonder whether we've been playing this right." Feeling the eyes of the others upon him, he continued: "I mean, we've been very secretive, trying to make sure we remain hidden from everyone else. But maybe we should now reveal what we know?"

Ed shook his head: "We've been through this before, old chap. The police, media, normal rubes – they'd all think we're loons. It's what the alien interferers rely on for our silence."

"No, I don't mean *reveal* reveal – like to the general public. I mean, well, and I hate saying this, but reveal what we know to the bad guys – like Terminus Est. Let *them* know that *we* know they're up to something. Maybe it'll stop them in their tracks. I mean, we're all playing this game quietly so as not to alert the greater community of alien watchers, so maybe if we confront them, they'll back down rather than risk exposure?"

Ed pursed his lips and shook his head again, but less vigorously. "If we do that, my friend, we'll also uncover ourselves. We're in the same boat, and in a way similarly guilty. We're not meant to know what's going on either. It would at the least embarrass our handlers – if embarrassment is actually an emotion bug-eyed creatures can experience. If so, I'd have thought a look in the mirror would be enough for that, but hey-ho."

"Maybe that's a price worth paying anyway?" said Amanda.

"Maybe… maybe yes, maybe no," said Keith, clearly caught between confusion and perturbation.

"I'm not talking about a big public outing," clarified Tom hastily. "You know, something more subtle that might not be seen by the watchers – although we could threaten wholesale unmasking if they won't play ball."

Ed frowned; Simon and Amanda looked down in thought; the Musketeers looked among themselves. Then Keith asked his team: "Thoughts?"

Agneta scowled: "The turncoat might have a point."

"But who are we talking about?" asked Trevor. "Everyone involved… including the Thruvian?"

"Maybe not him," said Tom. "I mean, that would give the game away totally."

"It'd expose *you*," noted Simon. "And you're our secret weapon. So, if we did this, you couldn't be there – we'd have to make it seem as though the mystery had been solved by others, like the Musketeers. If Teresa does work for Smith, she'll spill the beans. Ditto Terminus Est."

"How convenient," muttered Agneta. "You get to hide, and we get to take the risk of exposure."

"Sod that anyway," said Ed. "I'm not letting this lot take all the credit. When the Man with Ten Bellies gets taken down, I want him to know that we were involved in it."

"You seem to have a grudge against Samson in particular," noted Keith.

"Ed's just a sore loser," smirked Simon. "Pub quizzes. Don't ask."

"Regardless of our friend's motives," said Keith, raising his hands before Ed could compose a suitable riposte, "we are out of time and must do something. And I am out of time, too. I do not wish to invoke the wrath of my dear wife who, for all her many great qualities, doesn't count patience amongst them – eh, Tom? For want of a better plan, I agree with Tom. If you've got the time now, perhaps you can think about who should be confronted, where, and by whom. Trevor… er, *Agneta*," he shifted his attention. "Perhaps you can speak for the team. You have my full confidence. Now, I must go…"

As Keith headed off, the rest of the group looked at each other. The real haggling was about to begin.

***

400

There were four in Team Alpha: Ed, Simon, Trevor and Agneta. Tom and Amanda had been designated Team Bravo; they waited a short distance from the Cosy Club, sitting on a long curve of bench at the end of pedestrianised London Street, close to Tom's regular betting shop. This area used to be a meeting point for undesirables – particularly in the darkened hours – but had been 'sterilised' by the Knights of St Gregory, so the pair felt moderately safe even at this time of evening. They were there as back-up: to record and observe and – in the worst case scenario – contact the police.

"*Breach breach*," reported Simon excitedly – his voice coming to the couple through earpieces supplied by Ed. The pair watched jerking images on a laptop that had been supplied at the same time – in fact, two images in separate windows, which came from bodycams worn by Simon and Ed.

"Si – mate," came the unmistakable voice of their leader on the same channel, "hold the dramatics. Strewth! This is hardly the *Wolfsschanze* – lair of that mono-testicular bad boy from Austria." Tom could easily imagine Ed rolling his eyes and giving one of his world-weary sighs.

"Nah, mate. These dudes are *worse*. Consorting with aliens to assassinate our saint…"

The wobbly pictures showed the elegant interior of the Cosy Club. The camera bearers had passed a greeter sat at a desk to one side of the entrance, and were now in a high-ceilinged room, beneath a grand, glass dome and small, cylindrical chandeliers, with Corinthian columns and wood flooring, a long bar to one side, old portraits and stuffed stag heads on the walls, and tall, spindly plants in stone vases. The room was split into two by a partition on which the vases rested: to the right were small tables with mustard-yellow sofas and upholstered chairs; to the left were more tables, but with banquettes and chairs in green leather.

The hulking form of ginger-haired Trevor filled the screen of one camera and stern-faced Agneta the other.

"Now what?" asked Trevor loudly, his voice coming through the mic.

"Now you stick close to me," came Ed's voice. "You're the muscle here. I want to make best use of your steroid abuse. Keep quiet; look menacing; and crack your knuckles occasionally… what's that, dearest Agneta? Was that you *hissing*? I don't know. This place is a bit of a warren. Downstairs, I reckon, but there's also a small meeting room to the side, and a larger one at the back, so I suggest we check… yes, I did a brief recce yesterday in the mid-afternoon…"

Though he could only hear half of the conversation, Tom smiled to himself: he could well imagine Agneta's curt questioning.

The images started moving again as Team Alpha peeled off to the left of the entrance. A small doorway declared 'The Oval Office'. Ed told the others to wait, as space was tight: his camera showed a small-but-elegant room with a dark, oval table that would have perfectly suited a cabal of the size of Terminus Est, but which was unoccupied. Ed then retraced, leading the party further into the den. There was indeed another annex at the back of the main room, visible through a couple of doorless entrance ways. Being a Monday, the main pub-restaurant was only sparsely populated, as was the back room that quickly came into view. As the party reached their destination, the cameras revealed the ceiling in the annex to be low, while its rich patterned wallpaper – in various shades of red – was covered in framed Union Jack flags and copious small pictures of fish, flowers, old motor cars, and a plethora of other items. A dozen-or-so small tables dotted this space, with only three occupied, none with persons in black.

"Would be a decent place to meet," muttered Simon. "Think we're too early?"

"No. As I said, I think they're downstairs in the converted bank vault. *Yonder.* The loos are downstairs, too. Hear that, Tom? That's for your info. Now, follow me."

There was another doorway to the left of those leading to the annex: a sign over this announced that the vault and toilets lay this way. Ed led his team down several flights of stairs, his camera showing red-mauve wallpaper and more of the small prints of mundane objects. At the bottom of the stairs, past the toilets and a tiled pillar, they came to the end of the basement space – and found an iron-gated door, presently open. The door here was only wide enough for one person to pass at a time.

"The door, Mongo," came Ed's voice. "Enter, then fold your arms across your pecs like a pissed-off bouncer. Let me do the talking."

Ed followed Trevor into the room. Once through the doorway, his bodycam revealed a small bar to one side, a scattering of comfy armchairs, a long oval table, and a back wall hung with several wooden boards on which were scribed names – reminiscent of the honours board in the pavilion at Lords. At the table were seated eight people, mostly young, all wearing black t-shirts bearing their allegiance. After a moment, Simon joined the pair (followed by Agneta), allowing Tom and Amanda a double-barrelled view of the table's occupants, who stared at the lenses with a mixture of anger, annoyance, and trepidation. Both cameras flickered about until they focused on one very large, bearded man, struggling upright from a leather-bound chair…

"Ah, Augustus P. Samson. Pleased to meet you in the *mountainous* flesh. I'd sit down if I were you, or you'll end up giving yourself a coronary… who the hell we are is *your nemesis*. You and your gang of fetishists are busted."

"Yeah… *busted*!" came Simon's enthusiastic echo.

"Thanks, Si. No, Samson, my bulbous amigo, let me speak…" the camera showed an outraged man, mouth opening and closing – but emitting words too far away from the mic to be picked up. Then, Ed's voice continued, slightly louder, overriding the other. "Enough! Let me speak and then we'll depart and leave you to your orgy. Where's the goat by the way? Being lubed up in a back-room? Fun fun fun! Anyway, hear this: we four represent the forces of light. We have several masters… *and mistresses*… of the bug-eyed and tentacled variety, and I don't mean *Cthulhu*, although our laser-wielding superiors could easily turn that *mother* into sushi… no, shut up! I'm in the zone! Trev, wedgie to within an inch of his life the next nerd who tries to get out of his chair!"

One camera swivelled to focus on a couple of the nearer opponents – both young men – who'd risen in their seats, but who now peered uncertainly off to the side and subsided at the sight of something threatening and presumably ginger.

Ed continued, his camera returning to its prime objective: "As I was saying, we're onto you. We've seen your messages and wiped many of them. And we know all about the footy – indeed, we've been following you around for the last few matches. What's that, blubber guts? Oh, yes. Let's just say we know you'll be having a jolly up to Derby next Saturday, and we know that Delia's boys are going to miraculously triumph there one-nil. Thanks for that, by the way. And we also know you'll be back at Carrow Road to ensure the second leg doesn't end so well for the lads. I am assuming they'll get knocked out on penalties after a one-nil defeat, eh? And then…"

Now the large man in the centre of both camera shots *smiled*. Samson appeared to have recovered from the shock of the intrusion. He responded, his mouth working slowly. Ed paused while the other delivered his reply…

"You think you're protected?" said Ed, at last. "You think you're untouchable? We know the police can't touch you, but the watchers… yes, yes, they'll see us too, but we're noble and… and fuck you, too!" Ed's voice revealed rising anger; he was clearly not getting the response he'd hoped for. On the laptop screen, Samson looked smug, his large arms crossing his chest and resting on his huge belly. Still his mouth worked…

"Bring it on? *Bring it on!*" exclaimed Ed. "Do you think you're members of a Californian high school cheerleading troop or something? I mean, sure, I wonder whether some of your team wouldn't rather be wearing tutus… *yes, Si…* Okay… it may be beside the point but it needs saying. Oh, and now…" A savage index finger appeared in one window, aimed directly at the foe's leader like a pistol… "…now you've riled me. You are going down, Jabba! Got that? Your demise is going to be spectacular."

The camera shot swung as Ed turned, briefly showing a close-up of a t-shirt stencilled with a stylised Martian from a Tim Burton film framed by a leather jacket, then a view of the outer chamber. "Come – my legion of purity!"

The second camera showed two more fingers superimposed over the form of Samson, both of the *middle* variety – a parting salute. Then this shot also revolved to focus on the retreating back of Agneta…

Back on the bench on London Street, Tom and Amanda sat back from the screen. Amanda popped out her earpiece and winced at Tom. "I guess that's a 'no', then."

Tom winced back. "I guess so. But it was worth a try. And I can't believe this won't get some sort of response from TE."

"Hmmm, yes. But let's just hope it won't be a response we come to regret."

***

On Tuesday, around lunchtime, Tom, Amanda, Ed, Trevor and an impatient Agneta, formed a huddled knot on the short, brick-paved Opie Street at the London Street junction. The Cosy Club entrance was a mere ten metres around the corner, and just in front of this – in a widened triangular area where three essentially pedestrianised streets merged – was a circular bench. It was near the bench that their next target stood.

"Go on, Ed," said Amanda. "You can afford it. Give her the money."

"I don't see why I should be punished for my financial acuity. Or why we should pay out at all. Surely, the ginger monster can just threaten her?"

"No, Ed!" said Amanda, firmly. "We're not going down that route."

"Then why am I here?" asked Trevor, equally unhappy.

"Because you're a familiar face. And to back up Agneta."

"So I *am* meant to act as muscle."

Amanda had the decency to look troubled; it had, after all, been her idea. "Well, I guess so, in a sense. But *non-threatening* muscle. You have some sort of rapport with her. You just need to look a bit stern. I hope the shock of discovery will be her biggest motivator."

"Let him go alone, then," said Ed, who'd dug out his wallet and now held a handful of twenties, "and let me keep my winnings from the clutches of this harridan."

Agneta's glower turned into a wicked smile and she held out a hand. "No. Amanda is right. We're not robbers, and you have profited enough. Come on. I need to get back to work."

With a sigh of exasperation, Ed handed over some of the notes and then, when Agneta's hand remained outstretched and her eyes hardened, all of the rest.

"Okay, Trevor, let's get this done." Agneta turned and stalked around the corner, with Trevor reluctantly trailing. The three members of The Credulous edged to the corner to peer at the action – Tom pulling a woolly hat down to his eyebrows and ensuring his scarf covered most of the rest of his face.

They watched the Musketeers approach the *Big Issue* seller. Agneta was soon beside her, leaning her head forwards, while Trevor loomed behind. From their position, the observers could see the seller's face take on a startled expression, then nervously twitch between the two confronting her. After some seconds, an exchange was made: a fistful of notes for the entire pile of magazines in the woman's arms. Then Agneta raised a warning finger, and the red-bibbed woman took a step away, smiled uncertainly, and turned to stalk past the Cosy Club, heading towards the city centre.

Agneta and Trevor re-joined the others, then they all moved a few metres down the street, pausing by an iron gate under the gaze of Amelia Opie's statue.

"No problem," announced Agneta. "We told her we knew what she was doing, warned her off Smith, then paid for her stock."

"*Handsomely*," muttered Ed.

"Fair recompense for ceding her pitch for the next two weeks," corrected Agneta.

"Do you think she'll stick to the bargain?" asked Tom, still wrapped in woollen anonymity.

"Yes, I think so. We applied both stick and carrot–"

Ed burst into laughter. Fixing his grin on their erstwhile enforcer, he elaborated: "Don't you mean *carrot* and carrot?"

"Ha-bloody-ha," said Trevor.

"Okay, pony up those mags," said Ed. "I paid for them. Maybe I can recoup some of my losses."

"Sorry, Ed," said Amanda. "Give then to Tom. He needs to check for messages, and then destroy them if they have any…"

And as Tom found out back home that afternoon, they did. *Many* of them – on almost every page. Indeed, by the time he'd gotten through just one magazine, he was bubbling with anger at both the homeless *and* uncaring society *at the same time*. He slammed the whole stack into the blue recycling bin outside. Given that Trevor had reported that these magazines usually only held a single message, the infestation here seemed yet another sign that the endgame was near.

***

On Wednesday, Tom joined the Musketeers at the Rumsey Wells, arriving late, having spent the afternoon touring the nearby streets. He had some noxious 7D graffiti to report for removal – in fact, three different sets.

"In a way, we've been doing some graffiti ourselves," said Keith. "You know, in all this time, we never realised that our own HQ might have been being used as a message board for the foe. We didn't know about the beermat walls until you told us. Anyway, why don't you fetch yourself a pint of Mosaic and see what I mean."

Tom headed for the bar, and quickly discovered Keith's meaning: there were several newly emplaced beermats in the cardboard tiling in the bar area.

One declared: *Teresa, we are watching you*, writ above a large, lidless eye.

A second stated: *Ricky, we are wise to your games*, with a picture of a fingertip flicking over a king chess piece.

A third declared: *Terminus Est – you are terminated*, with a picture of a Schwarzenegger-type cyborg (rather well drawn, Tom thought).

He also noticed that the *Ricky ♡ Teresa* card had been amended, with: *Or does he?* added at the bottom.

When Tom returned, he said: "How did you manage all this?"

"We're regulars on Wednesdays," said Trevor. "Plus, me and Martin come here a lot, too, as it's close to the gaming places. So, we know a couple of the bar staff. One was happy to give me a job lot of beermats and let me replace a few of the faded cards. I didn't tell him about the ones I wrote over."

"Ones? I saw the Ricky and Teresa one. There are more?"

"Hell, yeah," confirmed Trevor.

"Hopefully, we have disrupted some coded messages," said Keith, "but our own inserts should reinforce the fact that we are onto our enemies. Now, Tom, quick: where are these 7D messages you discovered? I'm keen to erase them immediately."

***

On Thursday, it was Simon's turn to become involved. He'd been emplaced at the castle, arriving after a shift at the comic book store on St Benedicts during a long lunch break.

"They're at the tunnel entrance under Ponds," declared Ed, from his command centre in the St Anne's Quarter. "Go go go!"

"Are you sure?" said Simon, replying on his burner phone. Because reception was poor, he was currently at the level of the castle entrance.

"Si, just get to it. I've been logging the use of the tunnels since we installed the cameras. They've used this route twice in the last five days, at about this time, which is why you're here now. I don't think they *need* to use the tunnel, or that they're up to no good at present, it's just a shortcut for Jules and Sophie. They're taking the piss."

"Okay, I'm on it." Simon scurried down several levels and found the largely ignored lower chamber where the entrance to the western tunnel was. He only just made it in time…

The door *clicked* and opened a tad. Being in shadow, no one in the chamber would have known what was going on unless they knew where to look and what the sound signified. Simon assumed that those within used a small camera of sorts to poke out to check the coast was clear. He pulled his head back around the room's entrance and waited.

Several seconds passed, and then there was a slight scraping sound as the stone door opened and then closed. Simon knew the others would have to pass him in the corridor to get to the stairs up or to the other secret doors on this level, and so he lounged against one wall as coolly as he could.

A moment later: "Wotcha, Jules. Hi, Sophie. Going somewhere?"

"Fuck!" exclaimed a young man in a leather jacket not dissimilar to that worn by the lounging interceptor. "What… what are you…?"

"What am I doing? Well, mate, I'm just having a rest after inspecting this wall." He turned to tap at the wall with one fingernail. "Very solid! But now I'm done. Where are you headed? Cathedral, I expect. I don't know how you managed to rent a pad in Cathedral Close… oh, sorry, I wasn't meant to spill that intel. Anyhow, mind if I tag along?"

"Fuck!" repeated the one called Jules, while denim-jacketed Sophie muttered an even fouler invective. The pair looked at each other, then Simon, then back at each other again: speechless and undecided.

"Come on – I haven't got all day."

Rather than attempt to squeeze past the man in the corridor, the pair came to an unspoken agreement and returned the way they'd come.

Simon followed, leant against a wall within the chamber, and crossed his arms. "Off you go then. Or would you like me to open the door for you?"

Scowling, Jules revealed a magnet, not unlike the one in Simon's jacket pocket, and the pair returned to the tunnel.

Hurrying back to the entrance, Simon phoned Ed. "Good intel, mate. That's put the cat among the chickens."

At the other end of the line, Simon heard a weary sigh.

***

On Friday, Tom headed to meet Smith outside the Guildhall in the early afternoon.

"The slippery-one is on his way," said Ed on his burner. "He passed the junction below the Forum a few minutes ago. Same as last night. Since he returned the same way later that evening, it suggests to me he dosses down at Mancroft not the Guildhall. I'll confirm what the devious little shit gets up to once he's through with you."

"Roger that. Ah, coming up to the rendez… *fuck*! He's already waiting! That's a first. Must go." Tom snapped off his phone.

"Still nothing, Tom?" This time there was real exasperation in the alien's voice.

Tom sank onto the bench beneath the tree. "Ah, well, blasted Alice put a press on. Then I was going to go scouting, but I lost one of the contact lenses. I thought it was gone for good and didn't dare tell you in case you got mad. But then I found it this morning, behind my bedside table. Eureka! So, I'm up for it now, and, um, yours to command."

Smith stood unmoving, his piggy eyes fixed intently upon Tom in his green fleece – a fitting garment for once, with a North Sea front throwing cold weather over the city. "You humans can be somewhat unreliable, as well as insufficiently cautious."

"Incautious? Um, sorry, what did I…?"

Smith waved his free hand irritably; his other hand clutched a stack of *Big Issues* thicker than any Tom had seen him with before. "Not you, Tom. Well, it cannot be helped. But, Tom, listen to me: I have news from my clique of protectors that there will be a serious effort by the Directors next week to cause problems."

"No! *Really?*"

"Yes, really, Tom. It is imperative that you patrol as much as possible in the next few days. More than that, if you discover any message, I want you to deal with it straightaway. You do not need to wait to consult with me on the matter. I am afraid that this will require some late-night action. Do this, Tom, and perhaps I can see to your advancement."

"Sorry – *what?* Advancement? You mean… to an Alpha?"

"I may be able to arrange that."

Tom shook his head, not knowing what to think. "But… I thought you said being made an Alpha isn't all it's cracked up to be? That sometimes people could be made to suffer and—"

"Yes, Tom, that may be true for some." Smith seemed impatient – presumably because his time was running out. "But in your case, as you have nothing to lose, then nothing could be taken away. You'd need to achieve something first. Perhaps a best-selling novel? I note that your novel is now largely set in this city. Perhaps you could become a grandee? The Sage of Norwich?"

"Uh… wow! Really?"

"I will be busy for the next week or so. This will be our last physical meeting for a while. But I will send details of targets to you through the normal route. Goodbye, Tom. Be proactive. Earn your laurels." Then Smith turned and stalked away.

Tom stared at the other's retreating back in something of a trance. It was his ringing phone that brought him around.

"Yep, Tom, old mucker, he's just passed the camera going back to Mancroft. That's his HQ. How did it go – did you manage to successfully dissemble?"

Tom paused for a moment, uncertain what to say. Then, in a croaking voice, he declared: "He tried to bribe me. The wanker tried to bribe me!"

***

On Saturday, Norwich won the first leg of their Championship semi-final play-off against Derby, by one goal to nil.

The Credulous had assembled at Ed's to watch the game live on his recently installed seventy-five inch mega TV.

"So, Terminus Est weren't deterred," said Amanda.

"Seems not," said Ed, trying to hide a smile. "What a pity."

"You placed a bet!" said Amanda. "I thought you said you were going to stop. You told Keith—"

"I told Cheggers what he wanted to hear to stop him from bugging me. Sure. But you don't get a TV like mine without a bit of daring. Also, I'm owed for you lot stiffing me over payment to Smith's satanic bride."

Tom looked at Ed uneasily, but Simon smiled and shook his head: "Gotta give it to you, mate: respect! Even I cried off. You're surely not going to bet on the decider though, eh?"

Ed scrunched his eyes in an attempt to look mysterious. "We shall see. Sometimes betting against your own side can yield benefits – your side wins and you're happy but a bit poorer, they lose, and you're disappointed but considerably richer. Nice to guarantee some sort of silver lining with a bit of hedging, eh?"

"Ed!"

"I didn't say I definitely was, Amanda dearest! I said *maybe*. And if so, only a little one – something to take the edge off the inevitable despair. But let's look beyond that. We've got one week to sort things out, eh? Maybe we can still thwart Smith, save Delia, and help our boys to victory at the same time?"

While Amanda and Simon voiced their assent, Tom chewed on his bottom lip and wondered…

Chapter 34: Council of War

The stars had begun to align.

Norwich's second-leg Championship playoff game was due for a Saturday in mid-May. Whether by chance or infernal design, other events had been arranged for the city that very same day.

First, there was a march by the Primark Penitent, which had been officially sanctioned some time ago. The city's policing supremo had already allocated a number of shepherding officers to this (from the limited number remaining to her, given that most were needed for the football). The previous Penitents march had seen a significant ramp-up in numbers, but having tapped into some zeitgeist, and with extensive press interest, this next one was expected to be a break-out event. Buses had even been laid on to transport members of new chapters to the city. A four-figure turnout was quite possible.

Next, was a demonstration planned by the Rainbow Coalition – a new grouping around the Rainbow Commando, which took in several flavours of Socialist Workers, Stop the War, and other radical grievance groups. Norwich for Refugees had decided to join them – a novel group that had taken umbrage at the sabotage of refugee-supporting children's drawings at the cathedral some months previously – as had the Virtuous Vegans. The policing supremo had baulked at allowing *this* march to go ahead, until her deputy warned that barring it would liable get her and the entire force tarred with a great many 'ist' labels. Her deputy had furthermore noted that the truculent leader of the Commandos was likely to go ahead anyway, permission or not. Already the supremo was tearing up rota worksheets and holiday requests and starting to wonder at the overtime pay she'd have to approve to cover the deployment of officers on the streets.

A day after the Coalition request, Thomas Browne's Boys had announced that they too planned to march on this particular Saturday. And although the Boys had only grown to a couple score members, they'd linked up with various historical and cultural organisations, plus a hodgepodge of others, including charities for the aged and various right-wing nationalist causes clustered around the local Conservatives club. The supremo would have *loved* to have quashed this so-called Coalition of the Righteous – being left-leaning herself, and well supported by a red-green council – but to allow a grouping that was largely left wing to march and then deny one that leant to the right would have gone down about as well as a shower of shit at a barbeque. Besides which, the leaders of this clique knew – *and were friends with* – the mayor. On top of this, there were rumours that the Knights of St Gregory would join them to act as outriders and defenders in case of any argy-bargy. While the supremo was against the Knights and their vigilantism and would have liked nothing better than to lock them all up, she was aware that many of her rank and file were secretly sympathetic, and that some of her officers were actively (and assuredly illegally) feeding them intel. But by this stage, she rather wished she could deputise the Knights, instead, she'd gotten on the phone to other forces, begging to borrow any spare officers they might have.

And that wasn't all. Absurdly, the Compleat Anglers had decided to take advantage of all the publicity being generated to do a march too. But they were being sneaky about things. After she'd categorically told them 'no way', they'd gone quiet. But they'd not been deterred. There were some avid fishermen (yes, *men*) among her senior team, who'd suddenly become quite shifty. She'd only managed to get an insight into their plans on cornering one of her DIs by the coffee machine and browbeating him into submission. He'd revealed that the Anglers were planning on assembling in small groups (as well as hiding among other marches), and then unfurling their banners and coming together 'organically' at a certain time and place. Worse still, it appeared that the Angliar Army (who the DI had cursed as 'splitters') had decided to march too, without formal permission, as had the Watersporters. The supremo had started to really sweat at this point, throw her spreadsheets into the air, and considered going to pray. ('You can do that at the march,' the skewered DI had said, with a touch of retributive mockery. 'I hear an interfaith group are also planning to attend, sick of all the graffitiing of their buildings. They'll be with the Boys.')

And to top this all off, as the day approached, dire rumours began to circulate that the Krustie Brigade and their new allies (some other Socialist Alliance cadres) were planning a touch of civil disobedience to protest their right to drink, take drugs, and vandalise in peace. CID had been tasked to find out more, but they were currently overstretched and had learnt very little.

And so the supremo looked at her calendar each morning, and marked off another day, counting down to what the local press had already declared 'D-Day' – with the meaning of the 'D' being heavily debated on social media. But with football being paramount, and perhaps of interest to most of the denizens of the city and county (being supported by young and old, and those from left and right), it was soon being referred to as Delia-Day.

***

On an early Wednesday evening in May, the Musketeers arrived at an apartment in the St Anne's Quarter. They were buzzed in and met at the door to a top floor flat.

"Ah, you've found my lair. Well, to rip off the late, great JRRT, speak 'friend', and enter."

"We haven't time for this," scowled Agneta.

But Martin held up a hand and boldly proclaimed: "*Mellon.*"

"Of course! I forgot young Martin is a fantasist, just like our Si. Very good. Come in. And the rest of you, too: Scary Agneta... Mongo... Cheggers..."

Behind Ed, the rest of The Credulous issued greetings, and before long, the modest lounge – dominated by a dining table bearing a map of Norwich, with chairs and sofas pushed against the walls to create space – was filled. A gigantic TV dominated one wall; a sideboard held a collection of soft drinks, bottles of beer and wine, and an assortment of glasses.

"I would say make yourselves comfortable," said Ed, "but my humble abode was not meant for such a horde, so grab a drink, slouch into a chair – or find somewhere to prop yourselves – and let's get started."

After a couple of minutes of milling, drink-getting, and exchanging pleasantries, Ed knocked on the table top. "Right, fellow conspirators, let's start. Since Tom stitched me up and invited you Musketeers to my pad – by the way, no sticky fingers please, all *objets* have been documented and counted..." he winked at Keith, "I will MC." He paused for effect, folded his arms, and slowly scanned the room's occupants. "Ready? Good. It seems, then, that we are in agreement: this is 'it'. On Saturday –

in a mere three days' time – all sorts of shit is going to hit all sorts of fans, and I don't only mean those wearing the noble yellow of our Canaries. The crazies are coming out to play. *All* of them. What are we going to do about it?"

"My assumption," began Keith, "is that our opponents will leave messages across the city to prime the various marchers to explode, and then wait for the spark."

"You mean, the football?" said Amanda.

"Yes. I suspect these marches will comprise a lot of people who are already tense and angry who'll then be subliminally made tenser and angrier by messages along their routes. I'm guessing that once the football result becomes known, or maybe once the disheartened supporters leave the ground and come into contact with the marchers, then…" he raised his hands in the air.

"Boom!" hissed Simon.

"Like mixing two elements that are stable alone, but explosive together," said Trevor.

"This makes sense," said Ed, nodding slowly. "And these messages – already present, or to be laid?"

Tom shook his head. "No. Not yet. They fade."

"That's right," said Keith. "They generally last two-to-four days. In order to remain viable for late Saturday, and also reduce the risk of setting people off early, I expect they'll be laid down over the next couple of days. Or should I say, evenings and nights, as the scribes will require peace and isolation to work."

"And on Saturday, the Mercenaries will be at Carrow Road," added Trevor, "so if they're responsible for any of the writing, it'll be done by then, or confined to the stadium."

"I'm not sure how many of the messages are down to them, though," said Tom, cautiously. "I suspect Smith has been the main writer. And maybe Teresa and Ricky?"

"What about Brian?" asked Amanda.

"Still AWOL," said Keith. "At least, he was as of Monday."

"And he wasn't in today," said Agneta. "I walked past Alice's office a few times. I've no real reason to talk to her, but before I left, I did stop by to complain about Tom." She looked at Tom through slit eyes. "Brian wasn't in then, and his computer was switched off and his desk was clear."

"Well, we can't do much about that particular ghost," said Ed, turning a smirk upon Tom. "But the others… maybe. I suggest we place teams at critical locations about the city. I can direct you from here – just call me *generalissimo*. My camera network will allow me to follow the scumbags if they use the tunnels. Indeed, I've been keeping watch since Tom's last meeting with Smith, and I've picked up some interesting movements. Let me show you." Ed reached behind him, where his laptop occupied an elegant chair of purple fabric; it was attached by cable to the TV. As he leant down and toyed with this, the TV came on, and the picture from the laptop played on the giant screen. "Behold…"

Ed played a series of clips, the times and dates of which appeared at the bottom right of the screen. He had clips from each of the last four days – all involving Smith. "He's been a busy boy, travelling the tunnels, always leaving from St Peter Mancroft and returning there by the end of the day. He's taken pretty much every route we've mapped."

"Just Smith?" asked Keith. "Not the others?"

"Nope. I guess they mostly stay above ground. Maybe Si's intervention a few days ago spooked the Terminals for good."

"In other words," summarised Keith, "you can likely direct us to where Smith is going, but for these others, we need physical eyes-on. *Arse*… ah, excuse my French."

Amanda had been examining the map: without looking up, she said: "Maybe rather than chasing them, we should wait where we think they're likely to leave messages? I mean, do we know where the marchers will be marching? Logically, the messages will be placed along those routes."

"Yes, Mands, *on the ball* as ever," winked Ed. "And not only do we have intel there – for I have been doing some research – but we have the perfect strategist to take advantage of it. Si – time to shine."

Simon approached the map-covered table and set a tin upon it. He opened the lid, revealing the container to be full of small, metal gaming figurines, colourfully painted. He looked up and grinned: "I've brought my *Lord of the Rings* collection. Always useful. Um, right, now, where is…" He started searching among the contents until he found a particular figure, which he plucked up and placed on the map at their current location in the St Anne's Quarter. "Right, here's Ed: Gandalf."

Ed nodded smugly. "Good call, my perspicacious friend. Continue."

Simon returned to delving, and shortly found a dark-cloaked figurine, which he placed on St Peter Mancroft, followed by eight similar ones, which he clustered on London Street by the Cosy Club. "Ah, this isn't going to work. The map's not big enough."

"I think one will have to do," said Ed. "I am assuming this Nazgul here is meant to be Smith, and the eight others are Terminus Est. I would suggest just selecting the fattest one to represent our Evil Billy Bunter, but all of the Nazgul appear to be in need of a good feed, so any one will do."

"Right. But I'll put the rest at the edge as a reserve in case TE split up and we need to represent that."

Martin was eying proceedings keenly – indeed, Tom thought he saw lust in his eyes at the sight of Simon's collection. "You've only given Ed a character. What about us?"

"Yep. I thought we could be other characters from the fellowship. I'm bagsying Legolas."

"Yeah, you even look like him," said Martin. "I want to be Aragorn."

"Sorry, mate. I think Keith gets to be Aragorn. I'll let you be Boromir, okay? Then Trev can be Gimli. The rest will have to be hobbits. Sorry, guys… and girls."

"Typical," muttered Agneta. "Where are the female characters?"

Simon placed the named characters plus three hobbits in a cluster around Gandalf/Ed. They currently covered all of the Riverside complex. "You can fight over who is who. Now…"

Over the new few minutes, Simon plucked out other figures and, with Ed's direction, placed them elsewhere on the map. At last he stood back, and all viewed the scene.

Ed cleared his throat. "Right, let me summarise. Here, at Carrow Road, we have the fans, looking like a bunch of tooled-up yokels…"

"*Shire battle company*," hissed Simon to Martin.

"Then," continued Ed, "in the grounds of the cathedral, we have a host of grey, ghoul-like things, which is meant to be Thomas Browne's Boys and their cadre of crumblies. 'Warriors of the dead', Si? Good choice, as most of this lot are probably little more than a sneeze away from the afterlife. And the cathedral is where their march is due to start. Then, by City Hall, we have this rabble, who are meant to be the Penitent…"

417

"*Hobbits of the Shire*," said Simon, quietly.

"…and in Chapelfield Gardens, we have the Rainbow folk, rather ungenerously represented by orcs. You could have chosen something more colourful, eh, Si? Then, we have some rough old coves here, by the train station and the Compleat Angler – apparently 'Sharkey's Rogues', whatever the fuck they are; I must have missed them in the book – representing some of the fishermen loons, whose secret electronic plotting has frankly been beneath my skills to unravel, but probably far above the skills of the plods. And finally, here in the Vegan Enclave, we have this spidery thing. Shelob? Presumably, that's Teresa. No character for Ricky? Well, we've not seen him up to anything by himself – he seems little more than a shit on Teresa's stilettos. I guess we can find a spare 'tosser of evil' from Si's stash if necessary. Are we missing anything?"

"What about the Krustie Brigade?" said Tom. "I saw something in the *EDP* yesterday. There's rumours they're going to cause trouble."

"Yes, thanks, old man. My own delving into the dark web nether regions has suggested that they will initially collect around Anglia Square. Simon, if you please…"

"Uruk-hai," said Simon, placing half-a-dozen more brutish figures on the map.

"Good," said Ed. "Now, behold the field of play. What we do know is that the marches are all timed to go off early-to-mid-afternoon, in some cases to allow participants to assemble from afar, and in other cases deliberately to coincide with the football, in the knowledge that Her Majesty's Constabulary will largely be picketing Carrow Road. All of the marches are planned to converge on Millennium Plain outside the Forum, though there's no way all these people will be able to get in – like trying to squeeze Augustus P. Samson into a yoga teacher's leotard."

Keith had been leaning on the map, taking everything in. "That's right," he muttered. "It'll be bedlam – even without the effects of any messages."

"Sure," said Ed. "There'll be thousands of psyched-up people bellowing at each other and then, bang, here come the depressed fans, streaming up from the stadium, perhaps pushing Delia in a cage, ready for a sacrifice outside the Forum. You know what – maybe I'll give the city a miss this weekend and head for somewhere quieter. Beirut? Grozny?"

"So, what's the plan?" asked Tom, who couldn't take his eyes off the spooky miniature that rested on the map above St Peter Mancroft.

"Si," said Ed, "with your gaming hat on – proceed."

Simon's eyes roved the map. "Right. Here's my thoughts. We need two teams of spotters to keep an eye on Terminus Est and Teresa, just in case. And one flying squad, ready to follow Gandalf's – er, Ed's – shout when he sees Smith on the move. Let's say Amanda and Tom…"

"The lovebirds," grinned Ed.

"…watching Teresa, as Amanda knows the area best." He moved two of the hobbit figurines to St Benedicts Street, near to Shelob. "Then maybe Martin and Trevor should watch Terminus, somewhere near the Cosy. Also, they're close to The Halls, so if Smith goes there, they can be redirected." He moved Boromir and Gimli to a spot near the Ringwraith on London Street. "And the flying squad should wait near the Cathedral. I think this is likely to be Smith's first target. Carrow Road can wait until the day of the match, and if he takes the Pulls Ferry tunnel and leaves messages by the river, we can probably deal with those in daylight as the area shouldn't be too busy then." He looked at the figures he had left, then with a rueful smile took the Legolas model and the remaining hobbit. "That means it's me and Agneta in the flying squad – as I'm guessing Keith might not be able to make it?"

While Ed chuckled at Simon's discomfiture and Agneta muttered a curse, Keith nodded: "Yes, Simon, you are right. I am somewhat astonished that I am the only one married here – but it does make matters trickier. Nevertheless, I shall try to concoct some excuse so I can do my bit on Thursday or Friday evening. But I'm not sure I agree with one thing you said, about Carrow Road and waiting until match day."

"Agreed," said Ed. "It'll be chocka on Saturday, and no one will be getting in without a precious golden ticket. I suppose Mongo here will be able to get in with his season pass, but no one else. That means he'll have to face-off against God knows how many others. In spite of his impressive musculature, I do not see how he can follow them all and interdict their mischief – even if he is able to leave his seat."

Trevor frowned mightily. "Yeah. That has occurred to me. But will they really be painting all the messages then? Surely, they'd be seen doing it? I think it's more likely they'll have done them beforehand and then somehow uncover them on the day. Like revolving advertising or something like that."

"Good point," said Keith. "And here maybe I can play a role. Give me a day to work on things, but I do have some contacts with Carrow Road and I may be able to offer them something *quid pro quo*. After all, UEA is an important city institution, and I am in the Department of Film, Television and Media."

"Special project," snapped Trevor. "Of course! Do you think they'll let us do some filming at the stadium?"

"On the day itself, probably not," replied Keith. "But beforehand? I know how to frame this. *Charting historic events. Symbiosis between two important cultural elements of the city.* Yadda yadda. I can take some of my students, and Martin too. I'll try for Friday, as late as possible. The Mercenaries will probably have all their set-up done by then. If we can find and take out those messages, it'll leave them reliant on their manipulations on the day – and for that, I'm afraid, we'll be dependent on Trevor."

Ed looked thoughtful. "Yes, just Trevor…"

"Ed?" said Amanda, noticing his distraction. "Something on your mind?"

"Oh… no. Nothing really. Just ruminating. But I like this plan." He looked up from the map and smiled, then turned to Simon. "You know what to do, my friend!"

Simon took the figurine of Aragorn and placed it by the armed Shire folk at Carrow Road. Then he pulled back and appraised the map. "Stonking! But I nearly forgot about Ed. He can cover King Street, if Smith goes this route, as it's just outside his pad."

"Agreed," said Ed. "Thanks, Si. That's the people and places sorted, but there is still the issue of *equipage*. We don't all have the means to see these seventh-dimensional messages or – having found them – do anything about it."

"I thought of that, too," said Simon. "Tom has his contact lenses, which is why he is with Amanda. Trev and Martin both have contacts, too, and so does Agneta, which is why I'm teamed with her. Keith is also sorted. You're the only one who's blind, so you'll have to borrow Tom's glasses. They're in my rucksack."

"And in terms of *disruptors*, my team has two," said Keith, "including a spare." None of The Credulous had yet seen these miraculous devices, and Keith seemed keen to keep it that way. "These should go with those most likely to need them tonight. Agneta can take one for the flying squad, and Trevor can hold onto the other. If necessary, his team isn't too far from Tom and Amanda and can get to them within five or ten minutes."

Ed mused upon the map a moment, then looked around the assembled group. "I think not-so-simple Simon has a decent plan – obviously open to adaptation. I say we go with... ah! *It begins*." An alert caught his attention on his laptop. "I see Smith is on the move – he's just passed the camera below St Peters Street. I suggest the various squads head out now. Before you go, I have a job lot of burner phones to dispense to our noble allies. Let's see what this evening brings and reassess before tomorrow evening – perhaps a midday Zoom meeting?"

Equipment was dispensed and the party members, bar Ed, hastily made their way from the flat to their allotted positions in the city.

Once outside, in the plain at the foot of the flats, Keith held Tom back. "Tom... a quick word."

Tom grimaced, looked over to Amanda – a few metres away – and received a shrug. "Yes, Keith."

Keith watched the other pairs move away, raised a hand towards Amanda to suggest she remain where she was, and turned slightly so his face was hidden from the woman. He leant in. "We have a decent plan, I think. But I admit, I am slightly troubled by Ed's centrality in this. You understand what I mean?"

"Um, yes, sure. But I don't know what to say. I... trust him."

"You paused there, Tom. Are you really that confident?"

"Er, yes. I am. He's been upfront throughout."

"He's got a nice place. Nice toys. Doing well for himself. Just saying."

"He's a clever man. And I guess ace hackers are always going to get well paid... somehow."

Keith was silent for a moment, his eyes flicking over Tom's face. "Okay, Tom. If you say so. But please, for me, take a step back. I wouldn't want you to be played again. Ed is probably above board, in his own peculiar way. But this is too important not to be cautious." Then – with a final nod – he turned and walked away.

Tom returned to a curious Amanda. She didn't need to speak to ask a question. He considered a white lie, but quickly realised he'd be as transparent as clingfilm. With a sigh, he admitted: "Keith still has doubts about Ed. He thinks I – we – need to be cautious."

"What did you say?"

"I said I thought he was genuine."

This time it was Amanda who scanned his face. She said nothing, but simply nodded, and put a hand between his arm and side and started to lead him away.

Chapter 35: I Predict a...

On Wednesday evening, very little happened.

Tom and Amanda saw Teresa do a full shift at the Tipsy Vegan before returning directly home to the flat she shared with Ricky, which was a short distance further along the street above an art supply shop.

Those watching the Cosy Club had a fruitless time too, not seeing a single member of Terminus Est.

And while the flying squad did follow-up on Ed's alert that Smith was heading to the cathedral via the castle, this proved to be their only mission: Ed recorded Smith returning to the tunnel after a very short sortie and then going directly back to Mancroft without emerging again that night.

"We only found one message," reported Simon, the next day at noon, during the pre-arranged Zoom meeting set up by Ed. "It was on the west entrance to the cathedral. There are a couple of statues either side of the door – saint dudes probably. The message was written over the figures and apparently said FUCK CHRISTIANS and included an Arabic phrase associated with, um, certain naughty Islamists. Of course, I had to rely on Agneta to see and remove the thing as Ed has my glasses. She deleted it with her cool, double-barrelled torch thing – or said she did."

"Said?" hissed Agneta. "Don't you believe me?"

"Sorry, yes, of course. Chill, mate! I'm uber happy to be in the flying squad with you."

Agneta seemed surprised by this admission, and her fierce expression gentled.

"Hmm," said Tom, clearing his throat. "That's interesting. When I got home last night, I found a note from Smith at the end of my latest chapter in the, um, novel, telling me to go to the cathedral urgently. He obviously wanted me to find that message and deal with it."

"And had you done so, my gullible chum," said Ed, "that most certainly would have raised the temperature of quite a few of the nutters in Mrs. Brown's clique and made it into the evening news – perhaps being pinned on the fall guys of the Krustie Brigade. And as it'd take a few days to repair your vandalism, it would have served as a nice *hors d'oeuvre* for the marchers starting at the cathedral, reminding them of why they are so angry."

"Yes, and if I didn't do anything," said Tom, "it would incite subconscious Islamophobia."

"That alien really is a sneaky shit!" concluded Ed.

***

Thursday followed a similar pattern to Wednesday. Teresa worked all evening and then returned home; the Cosy Club remained devoid of any black-clad miscreants; and Smith made just a single trip – this time to The Halls. On this occasion, Simon and Agneta initially struggled to find any message, until Tom checked his Cloud-saved novel (accessed through his phone) and found a note from his duplicitous handler directing him to St Gregory's Green.

"Is there another tunnel from Blackfriars' Hall that we don't know about, heading west from there?" wondered Ed, at noon on Friday during their final online debrief. "Well, we haven't time to search for it now."

The flying squad reported having duly found the message. "Another set-up," said Simon.

"This one was written over the names in the pavement in the diagonal strip across the Green," said Agneta.

"You know," said Simon, "the list of famous dudes with some relation to the city – people that most of us have never heard of. There are about twenty of them."

"And the message was?" asked Keith.

"GAMMONS," replied Agneta.

"Well, you've got to give it to Smith," said Ed, "he's certainly up on contemporary insults."

"Isn't that an odd place to leave a message, though," said Amanda. "I mean, it's not near any of the march starting points, and I doubt it's on any of the marching routes."

"I believe you are correct, my dear," said Ed. "But let me have a quick gander at the campaign map." On everyone's screen, Ed turned to contemplate something off to his right, his eyes twitching and brow furrowing. At last, he turned back to his camera. "Okay, Mands, you're right. But it is well located for through traffic. On Saturday morning, a lot of people are likely to shamble past the Green on the way to their different first tees, so a message there would have had the potential to impact quite a few – fortifying 'progressives' with malicious glee and riling everyone else. And, of course, red-painted vandalism from Tom would have invoked further wrath, mostly from the cultural-protection brigade, while drawing forth Ms Kettleborough of the BBC, to further enhance her chances of a 'Reporter of the Year' award."

But their main collective concern was the absence of Terminus Est.

"Mind you, the buggers don't actually live at the CC," said Ed, "it's just their HQ. Indeed, during my research, I've managed to garner the blighters' addresses, ready for our letter bomb campaign later – only joking, Mands! Well, I have addresses for all except Sampzilla. It's amazing how someone so large can simply disappear into thin air. Anyway, if they haven't been to the CC, I'll wager they've been to Carrow Road."

"Yes, you would *wager*, wouldn't you," said Keith, pointedly. "And you've no coverage there? That's a shame. But I do have some positive news, which is why we need to wrap up quickly." He cleared his throat. "It's taken a day of effort, and I've had to call in lots of favours, but we're *in*. Carrow Road. We're doing some *vox pop* with staff at the ground, to talk about the season and what it means to them, plus we're on for a quick tour to allow us to take some promotional film of the stadium. But I've a narrow window to collect my team and equipment. Oh, Martin – you need to be outside the stadium shop at three. Make sure you bring along a disruptor."

"Yes, Keith!"

"That's fantastic," said Amanda. "Well done!"

"Thank you, Amanda. But there's more. I hinted at a desire to gain an interview with Delia herself on match day, and I let drop that Trevor would be at the match and might be available to do this – rather fudging his current affiliation with the Department."

"Wow!" said Trevor. "Really?"

On screen, Keith held up his hands. "Maybe. I won't know until tomorrow morning, perhaps only a couple of hours before kick-off. I'm going to sketch out a series of questions to forward to Delia's staff for approval – just in case."

"Keith, I may have said some indelicate things about you and your squad in the past," said Ed, "but I'd like you to know that these were never personal and comparing you to that dubious icon Keith Chegwin was only done in jest. I think I would like to have your children, though perhaps by surrogacy – up for it, Agneta?" It was a good job the namechecked-one was not in striking distance. Ed winked into his camera. "In any case, you are definitely excused tonight. But for the rest of us, this is *it*. Go big or go home. Last chance saloon and all that. Perhaps siestas are in order, for I fear we will be busy later."

***

…and they were, for Friday proved a completely different 'kettle of poissons' (as Ed would later put it).

Nevertheless, the conspirators started the evening in good spirits.

"Yes, we found their messages, and deleted them," said Keith, speaking to Ed on his burner phone. "And the Delia interview is on, too. I've got some things to sort out for that, while Martin has to get himself and his disruptor over to Trevor, so a full account will have to wait – perhaps a quick Zoom call in the morning? Meantime, pass on the good news."

Which Ed did, although the positive update was received by some with a tinge of frustration.

"I wonder what they found?" said Amanda.

"Yes, it's intriguing," said Tom. "Martin was there, which means he knows, and so Trevor will know soon too. And I bet they update Agneta, and so Simon will get the facts as well. Which means…"

"We'll be the last to know," harrumphed Amanda. "Typical!"

But Tom and Amanda soon had other things to worry about.

Shortly after, they spotted Teresa and Ricky leave their flat together. After a brief-but-sharp argument on the street outside their front door, the pair headed to the Plough directly opposite, leaving 'the hobbits' (Ed's words again) lurking in the shadows across the road at the far side of St Margaret's Church (another medieval edifice on St Benedicts Street). The lack of CCTV in the area ensured that they were safe from being reported to the police as potential addicts or troublemakers, though the spot provided little cover, or indeed, any reason for dallying. The only positive for Tom, was that this gave him an excuse to stay intimately close to

Amanda, enabling them to pass off as a canoodling couple if necessary. And better still, Amanda didn't seem at all bothered by this.

After around an hour, Teresa and Ricky emerged from the pub. Tom and Amanda pulled back behind railings, from where they caught the sound of Teresa's voice, raised in rebuke. Shortly after, when they dared peer in the direction of the voices, they noticed the pair heading down the street, past the Tipsy Vegan towards the Ten Bells.

They moved up to the Norwich Arts Centre, housed in yet another Medieval church (St Swithin's), which lay opposite the new pub, and here found better cover down a small flight of steps on St Swithins Alley. But this didn't make further waiting any less irksome or stressful.

After an impatient forty minutes, Tom wondered: "Where are they?"

"Having a drink?"

"Well, yes, I know that, but... well, you know what I mean."

"Sure. And it's getting cold. There's nothing for it..." Amanda pulled her coat closed and moved towards the steps.

"Amanda... what... wait!"

"Come on, Tom. There's no point lurking here. Let's go inside and watch up close. If they do see us, we can play dumb. They don't know who I am, and they've seen you in the area before, so it's not that suspicious. And even if it is, so what? Surely it doesn't matter now."

"Uh, right."

But Teresa and Ricky didn't see them, because they were nowhere to be found within the pub.

Tom returned from the gents. "He's not there."

"And she's not in the ladies."

"How could they have gotten away? There's a small beer garden at the back: maybe they climbed over the wall to Ten Bells Lane? But they couldn't do it without being seen. And why would they do it unless they'd clocked us?"

"If they left even five minutes ago, they could be almost anywhere by now."

Tom shook his head. "What a cock-up. Let's have a drink while we think this through."

"Good idea. Get me a half, and I'll nip outside and phone Ed. He might have an update."

It was now mid-evening and the pub was busy. Tom squeezed up to the bar between two young men dressed for an evening of clubbing. By the time he'd collected a couple of halves of Wherry, Amanda was back.

"Smith's on the move," she half-shouted into Tom's ear. "And it seems Terminus Est have come out to play. *All* of them. That means Trevor and Martin are busy, too. Ed's frantically trying to juggle lots of balls… Oh! That's ironic!"

As they vacated their space at the bar – Tom holding two half-pint glasses sloshing with brown fluid – they found themselves next to a narrow, wooden shelf on which a number of candles burned. Above this, on the white-tiled wall, was the black-etched mural of Delia Smith beside her battle cry: *Let's be having you!*

But Amanda, wearing normal glasses, couldn't see what Tom, wearing his alien contacts, could.

Tom did well not to drop his beer.

"*Fuck!*"

"Tom – what is it?"

"The mural. Over it. There's a message. A 7D one."

"Really? What does it say?"

"Er, just one word: *DIE.*"

The message really shouldn't have made much of a difference: it simply confirmed what they knew from the pattern of football results. But the instruction was nonetheless ominous.

"It won't work on us, Tom," consoled Amanda, two minutes later, once outside, after Tom had chugged his drink *and* Amanda's (she'd had a single sip). "If these subliminal suggestions are like hypnotic ones, they won't be able to get people to do extreme things out of character. I'm not sure anyone has ever been successfully hypnotised to commit a murder."

"Yes, but these are *alien* messages. I suspect they're more potent. Anyway, I'm not really concerned about us harming Delia – although it's probably best not to let Trevor see this before he interviews her tomorrow. I'm thinking about really passionate fans. Or away fans. In the right circumstance – you know, bitter disappointment, and maybe being affected by other messages – who knows?"

Amanda looked severe. "You're right. We've got to call the others and get one of these disruptors over here to delete this. Trevor and Martin have one. I'll get on the phone to alert Ed."

***

Martin did eventually join Tom and Amanda, but not for half-an-hour.

"It's crazy out there. All the Mercenaries turned up at the Cosy Club, then three pairs left a bit later. It's impossible to follow them all. We could only tail one lot, and Ed's been trying to keep track of the others on CCTV, but Norwich doesn't have as many cameras as other cities. Less reason to, I guess. Anyway, Trev's still on the case. I've got to sort this, then get back to him."

"Is that it?" asked Tom. They were across the road from the pub, next to an iron fence, with the Arts Centre set back from the street behind a strip of grass. He pointed at the tubular device held by Martin. "Can I see?"

"No time now. Also, Keith's a bit possessive. Best you leave this to me."

Tom directed Martin to his target, and then he and Amanda waited for another five minutes or so. At last, Martin bustled out.

"I couldn't get a good shot at first as there were people in the way. You need to play the disruptor over the message for some seconds. Fortunately, it doesn't emit visible light, so I just looked a bit odd, standing in front of the mural waving my designer 'torch' about. But it's done, and I'm off..."

"Wait!" said Amanda. "What happened earlier? At the stadium?"

"Sorry, Amanda, I really have to go."

And then Amanda's burner phone rang, and as she answered, Martin escaped down the street.

"Where?" said Amanda, as Tom watched and listened. "Okay. But we'll only be able to mark any messages, not delete them – we briefly had a disruptor, but Martin's taken it back. *Fine*."

Tom raised a querying eyebrow.

"He wants us to forget about Teresa. We're to head up to the Guildhall and St Peters. One of the Terminus Est pairings is up there, making all sorts of weird gestures at buildings and walls."

***

And that was how the evening went.

Tom and Amanda hurried along to their new patch, where Tom was shocked at what he saw – messages everywhere. He had to describe the position of these to Amanda, who couldn't see them, although she'd had the foresight to bring a notepad and pen: all they could do was log them for others to erase. They even caught sight of a pair of the Terminals once, looking shifty before disappearing down a side street.

They had to follow other events via updates on the phone – mainly from Ed, but also from Simon, who took pity on them after a while and began relating what he and Agneta were up to, and – when he had the intel – what Trevor and Martin were doing.

"Mongo is at Anglia Square," said Ed at one point. "Obviously, the foe is trying to ensure the Krusties get suitably jacked. But it's a bit of a dead end. With luck, they'll curve back, and then our lads can cauterise that particular wound before continuing after them."

"We're passing the castle," said Simon, a bit later. "It's on at least one marching route. And boy have they gone to town. Agneta's spraying her invisible rays like she's Jesse 'The Body' Ventura in a *Predator*-infested jungle armed with a rotary machine gun."

Comms from Ed went dark for an hour or so just after midnight. When he came back online, he explained: "Sorry, folks. Smith popped out of the King Street tunnel, and I thought I should go have a look. Amazing specs, Tom. But like you, I've just had to take notes to pass on for others to action. The flying squad are edging this way, but I may be able to get Gimli and Boromir to you at some time…"

Around 2a.m., Simon phoned a latest update: "The fuckers just won't stop."

"Where are you now?" asked Amanda.

"By the river. We've just cleansed the area outside the train station. There's CCTV here, so Ed spotted another pair at it. This is psychotic. Trev and Martin have been through the cathedral. Agneta says they're heading your way. We're off to Riverside next, and then Carrow Road. Ed then wants us to come back via King Street…"

And on and on.

It was close to 4a.m. by the time the various miscreants finished their work, having essentially painted the city 'red' – or rather, a non-colour from another dimension.

Ed called Amanda a final time. They were presently outside the Roman Catholic Cathedral – at the meeting of Unthank and Earlham Road – which had been given a couple of sprays, presumably because it would be passed by city dwellers heading from the Golden Triangle to the centre. Trevor and Martin had just yomped off, having made use of their alienesque mop. Amanda put the speaker on and held out the phone so Tom could also hear.

"Right, my little hobbitses, I'm calling it. Smith is tucked up in his alien bed, and the Nazgul have returned to their crypts. I've not seen Shelob at all. Maybe she's been feasting upon the husk of Ricky in some dark cave somewhere? Go get some sleep and set your alarms. New plan: meet at mine at eleven, Delia Day. Oh, and one final thing. Your messages. Can you confirm they were like everyone else's? I've rather assumed they were but haven't asked."

Tom and Amanda looked at each other, deciding who would speak. Amanda nodded at Tom, as she hadn't actually *seen* a single one of the nefarious scripts.

"Apart from the message in the Ten Bells, they were all the same," said Tom, after a pause. "Just one word, repeated over and over: RIOT."

Chapter 36: Delia Day Dawns

Delia-Day dawned. By mid-morning, the clouds had parted and warm May sunshine bathed the city.

"Shit," said Tom, as he wearily trudged down Unthank Road towards the centre. A torrential downpour might have helped quell ardours, dampen expectations, deter attendances. Had the aliens manipulated the weather too, or was this just coincidence? Indeed, was anything that had happened recently 'just coincidence'? As it stood, the conditions couldn't be better for marching – neither too hot nor too cold: full-Goldilocks! "And chanting…" muttered Tom to himself, irritably. "And waving placards. And being all self-righteous." As far as Tom could see, none of those out and about today deserved this weather.

It took another twenty minutes to get to the St Anne's Quarter, through the centre, past the castle. Tom was knackered by the time he reached his destination and was buzzed on up: he'd not got to bed until 5a.m., so an 11a.m. meeting was really pushing it.

"So, here we are all," said Ed, "now that Tom has arrived – last but by no means least. Find a pew, old fellow."

"Sure, thanks." Tom smiled weakly and sought a place to sit. The various chairs and sofas pressed against the walls were occupied, including armrests, while Ed's special purple armchair was reserved for his opened-out laptop. He saw Amanda, who returned his smile and patted the arm of the leather, two-seat sofa she shared with Agneta. He squeezed past the table with its campaign map and Middle-Earth figurines to reach her.

"I don't know how you're so bright, Ed," said Amanda, making space for the latecomer. "I feel how Tom looks… how *most* of us look."

"That's cos he didn't have to criss-cross the city all night," said Simon. "All right for some. You had a cushy number, mate."

"Perhaps I didn't burn the physical calories, Si, but certainly the mental ones," Ed tapped his head. "It took some effort, following all the cameras and directing you lot here and there. Besides, I did have to foray out once to check that alien scumbag's invasion of King Street. But enough of my heroics. It's time for you lot to do some work." Ignoring the disgruntled looks, he turned to Keith who stood nearby, leaning against one wall, looking neat in a pristine white shirt and dark suit. "Keith – are you and the Honey Monster ready?"

Keith grimaced and glanced at Trevor, who simply shrugged. "I believe we are."

"Good, now, the rest of you–"

"Hang on," said Amanda. "What is Keith going to do? Some of us are still in the dark about today's plan. And I still don't know what happened at the stadium yesterday."

"That's right," said Tom. "No one's told us a thing."

Keith arched an eyebrow. "Ah, I'm sorry. I thought someone would have updated you by now, but I guess we've all been a bit busy. To cut a long story short, Martin and I – and some of my students – had a good tour of Carrow Road, where we did some filming and talked to staff about the season. Martin, perhaps you can take it from here?"

"Uh, yes, well, it turns out there were messages *everywhere*, especially in the changing rooms. On the walls of the home room were messages like 'lose' and 'fear'. In the away room they were different: 'caution', 'one is enough' and 'score and hold'. And there were more on the advertising boards, like 'Canaries fail' and 'Delia die'."

"Indeed, the word 'die' was quite liberally scattered about," said Keith. "It was rather disturbing, and I admit, it made me clench my fists at times."

"And wish some of your numpty students dead?" wondered a smirking Ed.

"You say that in jest, but I did come very close to snapping on a number of occasions. And the staff we talked to were clearly perturbed and even skittish, presumably having been infected too."

"Yeah, but I think we got most of the messages," said Martin. "Or at least, we dealt with those we came across; we didn't see every executive box, or the officials' room, so…" he shrugged.

"And today?" asked Amanda.

Now Keith did smile. "A bit of a coup, there. Trevor and I have been given privileged access. We'll be joining the directors and their friends at half-time in one of the lounges. I'm not sure which one – there was some mention of 'renovations and revamping'. And then we've seats in the Director's Box to watch the game itself, courtesy of some last-minute absentees. More, we've been promised an interview with Delia herself afterwards."

"You are moving in exalted company, Keith old fruit," said Ed. "Don't let that go to your head and keep your eye on the ball."

"Oh, we plan to. We'll get to the stadium by two with our camera, meet a few people, and then we'll see."

"What about Terminus Est?" said Amanda. "The whole group may be around, and they'll surely see their messages have been deleted."

"Indeed," conceded Keith. "But they'll have little opportunity to replace them. Certainly, doing so in the players' changing rooms or at the pitch-side advertising will be exceedingly difficult. I'm not clear what they can actually do. Maybe they'll just be turning up to enjoy the result of their handiwork? In any case, we can do no more at present, save play it by ear."

"Thanks, Keith," said Ed. "Satisfied, Mands? Tom? Now, moving on, I suggest the rest of you stick together and retrace the marching routes, just in case the forces of darkness realise their evil has been undone, and attempt some last-minute replications. After all, you only have one message annihilator – assuming Super Trev retains his at the stadium in case of need."

"Fair enough," said Keith. "I recommend Agneta take charge, as she has the disrupter and my trust."

"Are you fellows okay with this?" asked Ed, looking about. "Tom clearly enjoys being under the stiletto, as Amanda can so-vouch; young Martin is used to taking orders; and Amanda is ever-so-sensible. That leaves you, Si. You fantasists have a fetish for strong women, especially wearing leather and carrying improbably large weapons, yes?"

"Fine by me," said Simon. "Aggie's cool."

"Aggie!" Agneta's face contorted, though it seemed to Tom that the expression she was most intent on suppressing was a smile. "Well, okay, then."

"And what about you, mate?" asked Simon. "What are you going to be doing?"

"Me?" Ed gave a sly smile. "Oh, I'll be here, continuing to monitor the tunnels, the marches, social media gossip, you name it. I'll let you know if I see anything significant and you need to act. Okely-dokely?"

When no one objected, Ed declared: "Then can I kindly request that you go forth from my abode this instant and save our fine city from carnage... or die trying!"

***

Tom, Amanda, Simon, Agneta and Martin left Ed's flat together. It was still shy of noon, with most of the marches not due to start until 2-3p.m. At Simon's suggestion, they crossed the Lady Julian Bridge to the Riverside complex, and strolled to the Queen of Iceni – a large Wetherspoons pub by the river. The Carrow Road stadium was visible from here, rising above rooflines a few hundred metres away. There were already a few policemen about, wearing yellow bibs as though in sympathy with the Canary fans' yellow replica football shirts. In contrast, there were few signs of the blue away strip of Derby F.C. supporters, but with the train station close, these were sure to multiply between now and kick-off.

They found a table outside, at the edge of a large terrace next to the river. Breakfasts and brunches were ordered and duly delivered. As they tucked into various shades of fry-up, their conversation was low key, with everyone still weary from the previous night.

After a while, Amanda sighed: "All this feels very reactive. The manipulators do their thing, and we scurry after them, trying to clean up. It's a shame we can't do anything positive." She stared sombrely at her coffee. "If only we could actually help."

"Yes, I know what you mean," said Tom. "I've been pushed and pulled about for the last few months. It would be nice to get a blow in first for once; do something they don't expect. We're merely trying to reduce the harm they're causing, rather than–"

"Making people feel better?" Amanda looked up and smiled, but Martin stifled a laugh. She turned a disapproving look on the young man. "I don't see why that's funny, Martin."

"Sorry, I wasn't mocking. I mean, it's just that–"

"Martin!" hissed Agneta, in warning.

"Ah, I wasn't..." he stuttered, "I mean, I was just saying–"

"Saying *what?*" Amanda was suddenly alert. "That there is a way? That there *is* something we can do?"

Simon had been cogitating; he looked between the pair of Musketeers. "The disruptor?" he said. "That's it, isn't it?"

Martin looked ill under Agneta's glare. "Well, I can't say."

"It works in 7D," continued Simon. "So, if it can delete messages, what happens if you *reverse polarity*?"

Agneta muttered a curse and Martin tried to look everywhere but at his colleagues.

"Ha – busted!" Simon made a peculiar wrist-flicking gesture, then looked slightly abashed. "Sorry, Aggie. Not trying to dis you or anything."

Agneta's mouth moved in a peculiar way, undecided how to settle. At last, she sighed: "Okay, yes. You're right. The disruptor can be set to write messages too."

"I see," said Amanda. "That's why Keith hasn't let us handle them. That's why he's insisted on only your team using them."

"Guilty," said Agneta. "He isn't entirely clear on your loyalties," her eyes narrowed, "or at least, on *all* of your loyalties."

"You're talking about Tom the turncoat," said Simon, grinning and giving his friend a nudge.

"Not just him," said Amanda, looking at Tom for confirmation. "Ed too, yes?"

"That's right," said Agneta. "In fact, Keith was expecting one of you to work it out before now. His money was on Ed, though."

"I'm hurt, Aggie," said Simon, in faux afront. "He thinks Ed is more intelligent than us?"

"Maybe in a different way. He has an unconventional intelligence."

"Well, er, that's true," said Tom, who had no doubt as to their unelected leader's faculties. And suddenly, he wondered: if Simon had got it, maybe Ed had worked it out too, but had just not said anything.

"Well, this is good news," concluded Amanda. "Maybe, rather than just looking to erase bad messages, we can leave some counter messages instead. Maybe… ah…" Her enthusiasm drained as quickly as it had risen.

Agneta peered at her closely and nodded gently. "I think you see it. We can't use the disruptor this way. If we did, it would make us as bad as the manipulators. It would make *us* manipulators – just ones trying to write a different storyline."

"I see that," said Amanda, unhappily. "Yet, I still don't think it's exactly the same thing. We're not starting anything – we're merely trying to repair a situation already set in motion. We may have doused a lot of the sparks last night, but there are still a lot of angry people who are going to be marching, shouting, and egging each other on. None of this would have happened without alien intervention. We'd simply be restoring the balance – wouldn't we?"

"And then there's the Delia situation," said Tom, determined to help out. *Delia must die?* We can't sit back and let that happen."

"Delia isn't going to die," said Agneta, without conviction. "Keith is sure that's just a symbolic expression. People aren't complete automatons. No one's going to suddenly decide to kill her from out of the blue."

"Sure," said Simon. "But there are a lot of crazies out there. True fans can be the worst of all. Who knows what one might do? And it might not be intentional, either. Y'know, someone might instinctively give her a push down some stairs or in front of a bus."

"Thanks, Si," said Amanda. She focused on Agneta: "Can we really take the risk?"

"But Delia is at Carrow Road," said Agneta. "She's out of our reach, and I can't see the marchers storming the stadium to get at her."

"Maybe not," said Amanda, with growing resolve. "But we can't just sit back and watch. Even if we did get all of the messages last night, and we intercept any new ones, these groups have already been primed. It won't take much to set them off. A riot is still likely to happen. People are still going to get hurt."

Tom nodded, feeling a peculiar sense of pride in his friend. "I think Amanda's right. It's not like we'd make a habit of this. It's a one-off for today, to repair what's already been done."

"C'mon, teamie," said Simon to Agneta. "Let's do what's right." As he leant back, his t-shirt was exposed beneath his leather jacket: it showed a picture of wizened Yoda with the caption: 'May The Force With You Be'.

Agneta looked at Martin, doubt in her eyes. Martin gave a shrug: "I'm not so precious about this, but Keith will kill us if we misuse the disruptor."

"All this talk of killing," muttered Agneta. "Delia's not going to die and Keith is not going to kill anyone. But what The Queen makes of all this may be a different matter."

"We've got our masters too," said Amanda, "so in a way, we're in the same boat. But we can deal with that later. I'm not sure how Sheila could complain anyway. She's effectively getting me to manipulate people to be environmentally aware – she's just getting me to do it *au naturel* without using any alien tech to do it. And Simon," she turned, "when Vortent gets you to do whatever it is you do with crop circles, isn't that really the same, about acting against other alien interests?"

Simon raised his hands. "Hey, you've already got me. It's Aggie you've got to persuade."

Agneta scowled, but her determination was clearly crumbling. "Well… maybe if we do this, and don't tell Keith and Trevor, they'll escape any blame from The Queen and it'll just be on us."

"But for a good cause," said Tom. "And these aliens aren't all saints – I doubt whether it's just Smith who is, um, morally ambiguous. So… sod them. Sod them all."

Agneta gave a wry smile. "So, you want me to become a turncoat, too?" She closed her eyes, thinking, while the others watched and waited. At last, she opened her eyes and looked at Amanda. "Oh… all right. I just hope we don't come to regret this."

Simon pumped a fist. "Alien dudes – prepare to reap the whirlwind!"

***

Robert Quigley had arrived outside the City Hall building early, dropped off by his wife, Jane, who'd gone on to meet a posse of her friends at one of their homes to 'get ready' for the march. 'Getting ready' should have required no effort at all, and indeed, the opposite of effort, but Robert knew the women would spend an age on make-up and accessories to accompany their matching 'hair shirts' – a kind of deshabille chic. While this attitude irked him, he'd managed to hold his tongue, partly from guilt, as he'd spent considerable time that morning himself, prepping his image to look just right, taking on board the quiet suggestions of the Channel 4 documentary makers who'd been following him around. These were currently a short distance away by the war memorial, interviewing Penitents with the best costumes or most titillating or outrageous confessional banners.

Brown-nosed Andy – his self-appointed lieutenant – scurried up to him, dressed in a woolly Christmas jumper that was missing a sleeve. "The Ipswich chapter has just arrived, Saint Robert. They marched up from the station. There's over thirty of them, and they've really made an effort. They're filthy!" He waved a hand in the direction of the Forum, barely able to suppress his excitement. "And the coaches from Nottingham and Leeds have just got in, and they're packed!"

Robert struggled to keep a smile from his face. This was *it*. They'd reached some sort of tipping point, and everything had gone exponential. The last march had been attended by about a hundred, but there were over treble that number around him now – and they were still ninety minutes from the off. They already blocked St Peters Street, which had been closed by the police just for this… for *him*! He got his treacherous mouth under control. "That is… satisfactory. What about—"

"Sorry, Saint Robert. A moment." Andy raised his left hand to stall him, while his right went to an earpiece. "It's Margaret…" He looked down and his tone changed. "Yes… go ahead… ah-ha… right… that's great. I'll tell him." He looked up. "Colchester are here, too, and they've got so many Penitents they've had to hire *two* coaches!"

"I guess they're particularly sinful in Essex," said Robert, portentously. He had been trying to keep a tally all the while – but decided to give up. His last estimate was four hundred and seventy, but with these arrivals, and with pledges from at least a dozen more newly formed chapters yet to arrive, there seemed no further point. A thousand? It might be considerably more – and *should* be more. He inwardly scowled at the thought of the competing marches: many of the attendees of which bore significant sin and probably deserved their own special circles in hell.

"Saint Robert?" A voice came from behind his right shoulder. "A word? I'm from the *Guardian*…"

Robert momentarily stiffened, but then remembered his self-training, straightened his back, set his face into a magnificent frown, arched his eyebrows, and ponderously turned to glare at the newcomer. *The Guardian*? He'd truly arrived…

***

Colin McArthur and Ronnie Waites stood at the centre of a small clique of self-appointed grandees from the Coalition of the Righteous. Their wives – Doris and Annie – were also present, as was Timothy Kendrick of the local Conservative Association, Rajan Singh of the Inter-Faith

Alliance, Pamela Smythe of the Norwich Historical Society, Hector McMahon – a self-invited twat-without-portfolio (in Colin's eyes) – plus a trio from the Knights of St Gregory: Grand Master Jim Taylor, plus a couple called Ken and Tania, who seemed to act as Jim's protectors and mouthpieces. They stood near the statue of Nelson in the Cathedral grounds, amid their placard-waving legions.

"Well, I think we should start early – in half-an-hour," said Doris, who'd been determined not to be sidelined by the boys. "It's a bit warm, and some of the elderly are going to struggle if we hang about much longer."

"That's right," said Annie. "Most of us are here now. I don't see why we need to wait until three."

Colin sighed. "Ladies – we have to wait. We need to follow procedure. We arranged a start with the authorities at 3p.m., so that's when we must go."

"That's right," said Timothy. "As believers in order and the rule of law…" he gave a quick sideways glance at the trio of Knights and frowned, "we must act as exemplars to the rest of the rabble in the city today. In any case, our liaison officer hasn't arrived yet, and nor has the full complement of constables. I understand the police have been hard pressed to find the numbers."

"Blasted police," muttered Hector. "What do we need them for anyway? To protect the city from our ferocious cohort of respectable citizens? Or defend us from the other mobs? We've got the Knights for that." He gestured towards the trio.

"Er, yes," said Grand Master Jim. "Defend? Right…"

Tania put a hand on Jim's arm to stay him. In spite of the weather, she was wearing a knee-length leather jacket in red and black and had added black streaks to her red hair. She even made Colin's long-atrophied libido stir. "We'll do our best, but there's only thirty of us. Remember that."

"That's right," said goateed Ken. "Much as I think the police are pretty useless, they're needed for crowd control, although they won't be much use in a fight if the Krusties or Socialist Wankers kick-off," he turned a quick smile on Doris and Annie, "sorry, ladies, excuse my French! Anyway, we'll form a protective curtain when we all move off – Sir James is organising the troops as we speak." He cracked his knuckles and smiled, exuding excitement.

"Oh, well, thanks for that," said Colin. "We appreciate your attendance today. But... softly, eh? We don't want any violence."

"Of course not!" declared Tania. "We're a purely protective organisation."

Colin frowned. Somehow he didn't quite believe her.

***

Chapelfield Gardens was full of colour. Rainbow flags flew everywhere along with the occasional transgender flag – with its light blue, pink and white additions – and others that were entirely red. Indeed, most of the hundreds who milled around the park were colourfully dressed, often bearing multi-hued banners and balloons. But the iconic berets of the Rainbow Commando were only worn by a select few – for bespoke manufacturers Francis and Trevor had been unable to keep up with demand. However, all of those currently clustered beneath the conical roof of the central bandstand possessed them, though one held his beret in his hands.

"What's the matter, Harry," said Stuart of the Socialist Workers, with something approaching a sneer, "you don't seem keen to put it on?"

"Me?" Harry's eyebrows beetled in surprise. "Oh, I'm happy to – in principle. I was just wondering what it now represents, and whether that's the same thing it did when I was presented with mine... which was some time before you got yours, Stuart." He smiled and waggled his moustache, hoping to emphasise good-naturedness. The gesture didn't work.

"Sometimes it takes new blood to get things moving," Stuart replied, without humour.

"Old school," muttered Fran of Stop the War, and she clearly didn't mean this in any positive sense.

Even Clare frowned. "You don't have to be here if you don't want to be, Harry. I think we've got this covered."

"No. Harry should be here," asserted Cathy, linking arms with Harry. The pair were quite a contrast: the young woman wore purple tie-dyed pantaloons and a bright yellow halter top, while the man was neatly dressed in chinos with a white button shirt and a pink jumper tied about his neck. "Most of the community look up to him. I certainly do."

Clare's frown deepened. "Sure. But maybe you should stay out of the way, amid the rear echelon."

"*Echelon*, Clare?" said Harry. "That's a rather militaristic term. This is meant to be a peaceful march, isn't it?"

"It'll be as peaceful as the pigs, the capitalists, and the gammons allow," interjected Stuart – who wore jeans and a combat jacket which, like Clare's beret, was covered in metal pins depicting various militant causes.

"And warmongers," said Fran.

"And carnivores," said Liza, of the Virtuous Vegans.

"And the racists and fascists," said Derek, of Norwich for Refugees.

Clare nodded. "That's right. We are going to march peacefully, Harry, but we're demanding our voices are heard. We won't be silenced. Or stopped. As long as the homophobes and their allies keep back, we'll all be fine. But we're ready if they don't."

"Too *fucking* right," said Stuart.

Harry shook his head and looked at the beret in his hands. Sadly, he declared: "It was such a noble idea. How did it come to this?" He gently disengaged from Cathy's arm and made to leave.

"Not staying?" smirked Stuart.

Harry looked back grimly. "Oh, yes. I'm staying. We need someone with a cool head today. Rear echelon? Fine. I'll fetch Roberto and Manny. Cathy, please join us later." He stalked off.

Clare rolled her eyes, then turned back to talk tactics with her new friends.

***

"It's ruddy heaving, Jezza," said Bernie, coming up to report to the president of the Compleat Anglers. They currently stood on the riverside footpath between the eponymous pub and Pulls Ferry. With them, blocking the path for some distance, were around two-dozen others, all wearing waders. "I reckon we should have got here earlier."

"Thanks for that, Bernie," scowled Jezza Armitage. "If only you'd suggested that before."

The bad-news messenger held up his gnarled hands defensively. "Sorry! But there's more. I saw Rod over there. I didn't know the splitters would be at the pub…"

"*Splitters*," hissed a couple of those nearest Jezza.

"…and there's the football crowd, too. *And* I saw Tom Potts as well."

"Potts?" said Ancient Reg. "Ain't he one of them waterboys?"

"*Watersporters*," corrected Bernie. "That's right, Reg. He was wearing a captain's hat. You know, with the little anchor on the front. I saw a couple more wearing the same caps. I reckon they've nabbed the lower level of the pub. They've got a few canoes tied up outside."

"So, let me get this straight," said Jezza, barely able to control his temper, "it's *our* pub, 'cos we formed first, but now we've been squeezed out by these newcomers and the fans? Makes my blood boil!"

"Yeah, well, it might be for the best," said Bernie. "It'd take an age to get a round in. Plus, there are loads of police outside. They seem to be waiting for something."

"Yes, they are," said Gerald Rice, who stood beside Jezza. He was a fifty-something police inspector, counting down to retirement and the prospect of peaceful days staring at the river over the top of his rod. "I told you: the Chief got a tip-off. Er… don't know who from." He crossed his fingers behind his back. "Anyway, I think we should go up Ferry Lane past the cathedral rather than up Prince of Wales Road. I know she's not got enough officers to cover every city approach."

Jezza sucked on his teeth. "Arr, maybe you're right, Gerald. I'm glad we've got *someone* competent in the group." He looked askance at Bernie, then refocused on the detective inspector. "So, you're suggesting if the splitters leave, they'll get rounded up?"

"Hmmm, that's difficult to say. If they leave in groups of six or less, they'll be okay. Same with the Watersporters. But they're probably safe anyway; they can get away by river and paddle somewhere else – maybe up to The Ribs by Fye Bridge, or down towards Carrow Road – and then they can do their march from there. The Chief hasn't got a navy, so she won't be able to stop them."

"Well, we need to work out where they're *both* going, or else we can't, um, let them have it," said Bernie, instinctively reaching down to the small, maggot-filled tub in the pocket of his flak-jacket – something they all carried.

"If the worst come to the worst," said Gerald, "we can just head over to the Forum. That's where all the marches will be ending today. It's logical they'll be there, too."

Jezza ruminated some more. In truth, he wished Rod was with them. He was a bit of a know-it-all, but he had brains that were rare amongst the Anglers. Still, that was also the reason why he and the splitters needed to be taken down a peg or two, along with the boating twats. He came to a decision: "Right, lads. Make sure you got your banners. We'll head for the Ferry."

***

Blitz scanned his troops, clustered in the dingy area beneath the overpass of the inner ring road, near to Anglia Square. There weren't as many as he'd hoped – about thirty all-told. Since the meeting at the Drug Store off King Street, there'd been lots of bold words, but very little direct action. His extended crew had talked the talk but frankly weren't prepared to walk the walk. In the end, what most of the crew really wanted, was to be left alone to shoot up, doss down, or paint their tags in peace, not to conduct large-scale unrest that would bring the pigs down upon them. But this day had seemed too good an opportunity to miss.

In fact, Blitz had only half of his force here: the other half – comprising Jonno of the Socialist Alliance and the worst of the Neanderthals – had already moved off. Their target was the Rainbow Coalition. To Blitz, it was clear that Jonno's beef was with the Socialist Workers rather than any of the other progressives – an internecine thing about some trivial disagreement over whether Trotsky would have kicked Stalin's ass in a fight or not. Something like that. And the thugs who'd gone with him just thought the rainbow folk were easy game and that it would be a bit of a laugh to spoil their day and see them 'mincing about in terror'. Blitz shook his head at recollection of *that* expression. In truth, he was glad they'd gone as they were little better than the fascists…

"Hey, B," said Skid. "We just gonna chill here, or what?"

Blitz shook his head and frowned. "Nah. It's time to move. The crumblies and the fascists have it coming. Everyone tooled up?"

The dishevelled lot – almost all of whom had the bottom halves of their faces covered with scarves – gave a muted response, with some holding up spray cans. The paint, though, was just one of three weapons they had today. Most also carried several water-filled balloons (innocuous enough to suggest that they were festive marchers), while others held glass vials of noxious-smelling fluids – essentially stink bombs – that had been concocted by Einstein, his crew's 'chemist'. They were mild enough weapons, as the plan wasn't to cause serious hurt, just to disrupt the so-called Coalition of the Righteous – to scatter their march and show the world that King Blitz was still around.

And, of course, to get them on TV.

To get *him* on TV.

"Right, let's go. Stay in small groups, yeah? Hide your gear, and watch out for the pigs. We'll re-form at the cathedral."

"We gonna hit them there?" asked Mary, nervously.

"No. I just want to tail them from a distance. I want maximum coverage, so we'll strike when they're all together. Probably by the Forum."

"Outside BBC HQ," nodded Mags. "Cool!"

Blitz adjusted his own face-covering, then in a muffled voice called: "Move out!"

***

They'd taken a convoluted route through the city, hitting key landmarks and following the planned marching routes. They'd first ventured to the football stadium via King Street, then taken the riverside footpaths to Pulls Ferry and beyond, exploring the grounds of the cathedral and the area around Tombland. Then they'd continued up to Anglia Square via Magdalen Street, and returned via the area around Colgate, crossing the Wensum by the Playhouse then pushing on through the Lanes, past The Halls and St Benedicts Street, back to the area around the castle. During this long loop, they'd encountered the odd extra-dimensional message, which they'd deleted, and they'd begun to leave more uplifting messages instead.

As Agneta had control over the disruptor and knew how to 'reverse polarity' – as Simon had put it – she had the dubious honour of breaching her oath of non-interference first. She'd done so by writing   PEACE, in relatively small letters, on the outside of Dragon Hall.

Soon after, she'd ceded control of the device to Martin, allowing him to dirty his hands, too. As these were the only two with alien contact lenses able to see the script (bar Tom, whom Agneta still viewed with a degree

445

of suspicion), they had to be the ones to write, but in order to be inclusive, the whole party took it in turns to make suggestions as to *what* to write.

LOVE, suggested Amanda, which Martin had written on the wall of a building at the lower end of King Street. Then JOY on the pavement of Carrow Bridge, en route to the stadium.

Simon's first suggestion was GOOD VIBES, which Martin followed with CHILL OUT – both written on a wide gravelled area outside the stadium.

Tom had been tempted to suggest something insulting about Smith, but instead proposed DON'T WORRY and below this BE HAPPY – channelling his inner Bobby McFerrin.

As they'd continued, a competition developed to find the most quirky exhortation of positivity, leading to messages such as PEACE OUT, DON'T SWEAT!, and RELAX DUDE.

"Come *on*," Agneta had muttered at one point. "Be serious!" But she'd said it with a barely suppressed smile, and hadn't been able to stop herself giggling at some of Simon's proposals.

At first, there had been relatively few people about, and the writers had been able to make their invisible marks unmolested, with little more than the occasional curious glance from passers-by, perhaps wondering what some loon was doing waving an oddly shaped torch at a wall or pavement. But as the crowds got bigger, the team started to shield the writer in a semi-circle of bodies, enabling them to complete their work without attracting too much attention. And as time passed, among the growing numbers wearing yellow replica tops, they'd begun to come across people hurrying to the different marches – Penitents in threadbare jumpers carrying placards admitting to (usually trivial) sins; people in Rainbow berets or other colourful clothing; grumpy elders wearing rosettes or badges or carrying neatly-painted boards demanding respect for history, culture, faith, or some other worthy concept. Near the river, they'd run into a wedge of hoary elderly men sweating in the sun in bulky gilets and rubber waders. On Magdalen Street, they'd had to step into the road to allow a group of heavily tattooed and pierced people – carrying strings of bumping balloons – to pass.

Slowly, the yellow shirts had begun to be outnumbered by others, until there were very few left – just patriots who'd not been able to get a ticket to the game but still wanted to show their support.

Soon after, as they passed behind the castle once more, heading towards Cattle Market Street, a long, low sound carried to them on the light breeze from down the hill.

The party stopped and looked in the direction of the noise, though the stadium was well hidden from view.

"That doesn't sound good," said Tom.

"We know we're meant to lose one-nil," said Simon. "I'm guessing that's the 'one'."

They carried on, and by around 3.30p.m. found themselves on the pedestrianised Haymarket, close to Hay Hill, the market, and St Peter Mancroft. By now, they were all somewhat frazzled from the long walk under an increasingly hot sun. The streets were busy with shoppers and waylaid marchers. They had to halt for some minutes here, squeezed against shop fronts to allow the grim-faced Primark Penitent to trudge past with their police escort in yellow visibility bibs.

"What a miserable-looking lot," said Amanda to Tom.

"Yes – and look! It's their leader, Saint Robert. What a scowl!"

"Face like a smacked arse," noted Simon. "I think he's infected his whole posse. He's probably had words with them. Probably reminded them that this isn't meant to be a jolly, and any smiles will mean bigger banners with more lines next time."

"Well, let's see how they look on their return after passing our messages," said Amanda.

"The bigger issue is whether they'll actually see them," said Tom. "Maybe those on the outside will, but those in the middle won't see much."

"True. But happiness can be infectious," asserted Amanda. "Let's hope they all get a dose."

Once the last of the killjoys shambled past, the team proceeded to Hay Hill and sidled up to one of the larger sculptures, crowding around Martin. He wrote HARMONY, at Amanda's suggestion, ending with a flick of the wrist.

Agneta nodded in approval and reclaimed the disruptor. "Good. What now?"

"We've not been to Chapelfield Gardens," said Amanda. "Maybe we should head there? We didn't do it last night, as it was too spooky and we didn't have time, so there could still be messages there."

Tom frowned. "Er, okay, but what about here? This is the centre of everything." He eyed St Peter Mancroft on the edge of the little square.

"You think Smith is close by?" said Amanda. "Do you think he'll get up to something?"

"Well, this is his HQ. He could be around here now, or on Millennium Plain, and we wouldn't necessarily see him. He could be leaving last-minute messages as we speak. Or he could come out at any time in the next hour and still cause problems."

"We need to head him off at the pass," said Simon. "Bottle him up. Don't let him out."

"Sure," said Agneta. "But if we all just sit here and he stays where he is, we're missing a chance to do more good." Having reluctantly agreed with the plan to leave messages, Agneta had become fully invested. "The atmosphere is still tense. You can feel it."

Tom nodded. "Agreed. But it would help if we knew where Smith is." They'd not heard a thing from 'Gandalf' in HQ all afternoon.

"I'll give Ed a ring," said Amanda, who was the designated intermediary. "Hang on. It's a bit noisy here. Let me find a quiet spot." She wandered off to the glass shopfront of Next, and there hunched over in an effort to shut out the noise. After a minute or so she returned.

"No luck. He's not answering."

"In the john," assured Simon. "Always the way. Give him five minutes."

Amanda tried again a few minutes later, but still got no response.

"Obviously having a *number two*," said Simon.

"Well, we can't wait for him to finish wiping," said Agneta, matching Simon's grin. "So, are we moving on or not?"

Tom looked at the church opposite and made a decision. "Okay, let's go. Or rather, you go: I'll stay here and try to contact Ed again in a bit. I want to keep an eye out here. I don't trust Smith to behave, and I know which exit he uses."

"Just you?" said Amanda.

Tom winced. "Yes. I'm worried Smith might be somewhere close, watching. I don't think he knows about you lot. If he just sees me, well, maybe he'll come by and set me a task, which I can pretend to do instead of letting him succeed in doing it himself. Or something like that." He shrugged. "I'll probably join you soon though."

"Well, okay," said Amanda, doubtfully. "If you're sure."

And so the party split. Agneta led the group towards Chapelfield Gardens, while Tom headed for the front entrance of St Peter Mancroft. *This is it*, he thought. *Twist and win… or bust.* The time of maximal peril was at hand: Norwich were losing; the marchers were tetchy — even if not as tetchy as they might have been as a result of their efforts — and the whereabouts of Wildcard Smith was unknown.

Everything could still go downhill from here.

Fast.

Chapter 37: Into the Box

Keith and Trevor had arrived at Carrow Road at the requisite time and place outside the Directors Entrance. There, they'd been met by a club official, who'd led them to their seats in the director's box in the Geoffrey Watling Stand. They'd arrived relatively early, though the stands soon filled, as did the seats around them – with people who were generally smartly dressed, though draped in the yellow and green scarves of the club.

"I'm not sure any of this lot would be capable of harming Delia, even if they wanted to," said Trevor, speaking low.

"You'd be surprised at what even the most feeble human can do when properly enraged," replied Keith. "Hello, here is her majesty!" He caught the eye of Delia Smith and gave her a smile and a small nod, receiving a wave and a silent 'hello' in return.

"You know her?" asked Trevor, slightly awed.

"Not well, no. But over the years – given our interests in TV and filming – our paths have occasionally crossed. And of course, she's aware of our desire for an interview afterwards, if we can find the right opportunity."

"Still, that's cool. But *hello*. Who is… *shit*."

"What have you seen?"

"Look. Down there. Pitch side, over there. It's Tristan – wearing orange. And… who's this? Josh? He's also dressed as a steward."

"They must be legitimate stewards," said Keith. "Otherwise they'd get challenged, surely?"

Keith focused on the two members of Terminus Est below. After a moment, he broke into a smile. "The Mercenaries don't seem best pleased. In fact, it looks like they're arguing."

Trevor snorted a laugh. "You're right. They're clearly not happy. Do you think they're saying something like 'where the fuck have all our messages gone'?"

"Let's hope so!"

After a couple of minutes, the pair stalked off.

"Well, I wonder what mischief they're up to?" said Keith.

Trevor looked about unhappily. "Whatever it is, we'll not be able to find out until it's too late. We're hemmed in here."

"Yes," agreed Keith, scouring about. "Still, I've seen no alien messages since we arrived, and the Mercenaries' activities are going to be limited too." Both Keith and Trevor were wearing their alien contact lenses. "Let's hope that those two are engaged in their paid jobs, and nothing more."

"You mean, shouting at fans to sit down?"

It was another ten minutes before the players took to the pitch, and several more before the whistle went and the game began.

On the pitch, Derby County seemed up for it, and began pressing immediately. It was largely one-way traffic until the fourteenth minute when…

"*Nooooooo*," a collective groan ran through the stadium. On the pitch, a Derby player in blue ran to the nearest corner flag, chased by joyous teammates.

"Shit! It's happening!" said Trevor. "One-nil down. Does that mean no more goals until penalties? But I thought we'd got rid of the messages?"

"Maybe we did," mused Keith. "Maybe this is just *organic*. Let's watch."

And indeed, the game continued apace and was soon end-to-end, with both sides throwing themselves forwards. And then, in the twenty-ninth minute….

"*Ooooooooooooh!*"

The crowd groaned once more, but now with frustration, as a Norwich midfielder clipped the post with a shot from the edge of the box.

"Well, that was close," said Keith. "How does this game compare to the others you've watched?"

"Definitely more action," said Trevor. "A lot more. Maybe we did succeed?"

"And maybe we'll now lose four nil," said Keith, wryly. "Sometimes be careful what you wish for."

Then, just before half-time, a Norwich striker rose in the box, met a cross and…

"*Goooooooal!*"cried the crowd, with almost one voice.

In spite of himself, Keith found he was on his feet too, a wordless roar in his throat. But almost immediately, the joyous mood in the stadium dampened, and there was at first confusion, then anger.

"What?" said Trevor. "*What?* A foul? No! You've got to be…"

On the pitch, the referee was surrounded by players in yellow. It took some time before the figure in black managed to extricate himself. On a big screen in the corner of the stadium, between the South Stand and the Barclay Stand, the incident was replayed. The murmuring of thousands of voices rose.

"Where's the foul?" said Trevor.

"Indeed," said Keith, leaning in so he could be heard. "Contact seems to be minimal."

As play restarted with a free kick, the mood of the crowd darkened.

"I wonder where the Mercenaries are?" said Keith. "Holding the officials' next of kin hostage nearby, perhaps?"

It was still one-nil at half time. The whistle blew, and fans got to their feet to stretch and seek bladder relief or sustenance. Below them, Delia and her husband, with a small set of others, were quickly up, heading for the designated lounge for a drink. Keith and Trevor stood to follow.

In the hospitality room, a table along one side had been laid out with hors d'oeuvres and drinks; Delia stood chatting in a small group at the far end. Keith and Trevor had no sooner found themselves a spot by the opposite wall when…

"Fuck me!" Trevor nudged Keith, who looked to see…

"The Mercenary! Augustus P. Samson!"

"In an XXX-L Canaries top," muttered Trevor. "That must have been custom made."

The leader of Terminus Est stood near the door, seemingly oblivious to the pair, a drink already in his bulbous hand.

"Has he seen us? Does he recognise us?"

"Hmmm, perhaps not," said Keith. "He's never seen me, although I believe he has definitely seen you… *Mongo?*"

"Don't you start!" said Trevor.

But the shocks weren't over. As they continued to covertly watch their adversary, who was himself keeping a surreptitious eye on Delia and her clique, a waitress came over with a tray of refreshments. "Would you like a drink? Red or white?"

"Oh, thanks… *what*!"

Trevor's exclamation caused Keith to turn and look. Through their contact lenses, both men were able to see the seventh dimensional message on the tray, which seemed to shine through the glasses resting upon it. The words were crystal clear: DELIA MUST DIE.

Keith looked up just as Trevor gasped: "Teresa!"

The waitress stiffened. "Sorry… what? Who are…?"

Trevor grasped one edge of the tray and refused to let the woman withdraw it. "Oh no you don't!"

Keith moved closer to the pair, attempting to shield proceedings from eyes elsewhere in the room. "Listen to me, Teresa," he said, low but firm. "We know who you are and what you are up to. And we can read the message on this tray as clearly as the name on your badge. Like you, we are not quite what we seem."

"I don't care who you are," hissed the woman. "Let go of the tray."

"So that you can incite the others in this room to turn upon our host?" said Keith. "I think not."

Teresa glowered at Keith, then back at Trevor, and tugged some more, making the remaining glasses twitch. But the ginger man held firm. "If you don't let go I'll…"

"What?" said Keith. "Make a scene? Go on. That might distract the others. At least it would draw attention to you. But you work in the shadows, don't you? So, go on – it might be for the best."

Teresa glowered some more and then, suddenly, relaxed. She stepped back and let go of the tray, causing Trevor to nearly drop it. Then she smiled. "Okay. Take it then. My work here is done." She turned and strode from the room, passing an oblivious Augustus P. Samson.

"Fuck! What now?"

"Now, Trevor, we drink up and get rid of this tray. Put it on the edge of the long table – upside down."

But they soon saw what the woman meant about her work 'being done'. For as they approached the table, they caught the tell-tale glow of extradimensional writing… and found that along its length, glowing through small plates of nibbles and carafes of water and wine, was the same message as on the tray, repeated half-a-dozen times.

And then Keith looked up and noticed the other patrons in the lounge. Like Samson, their attention seemed less focused on immediate colleagues, and more upon the short-haired woman in the corner wearing her team's colours, who was currently chatting merrily with her husband and another couple. And those staring eyes were *hard*.

Keith leaned in. "Trevor – let's move closer to Delia. Act as barrier just in case anyone gets a funny idea."

"I don't know about the others," replied Trevor, "but I may have to defend her from myself. I'm afraid I'm not feeling especially well disposed towards her at the moment. It seems I'm not immune to the messages."

Keith looked over at the woman, and found himself thinking, *how can she appear so happy when we're going to lose*! And then he realised he wasn't immune either.

They were only in the lounge for another five minutes before they had to make their way back to their seats. But for Keith and Trevor it seemed much, much longer.

***

St Peter Mancroft was where it had all begun. As Tom approached the glass door at the west end, beneath the tower, he recalled the first time he'd visited last year, when he'd entered the church in trepidation and bemusement, expecting to be the butt of a joke – absurdly, in retrospect, by the humourless Brian (and where was *he* now?). Once again, he hesitated before pushing the door, this time feeling a sense of foreboding. Would Smith be within, sitting on a pew, watching him – perhaps holding a brain-melting device, or sat amid Replicant killing machines disguised as little old ladies pretending religiosity?

Of course, there was no such waiting committee. In fact, the church interior was a soothing environment, cooler than outside, and far less fraught. There were five or six people in the entire edifice – from what Tom could see. The nearest trio comprised an elderly couple and a balding, middle-aged man, who was speaking to the pair with authority and gesturing towards the ceiling. Some sort of guide? Tom made his way down the nave towards them. As he got close, he heard the guide say: "Yes, that is a peculiarity. The corbels – the carved figurines you see sticking out from the wall, providing support for the ceiling – are usually human in form. Saints and the like. So, that one is a mystery."

Tom had to slow down to manoeuvre around the party, who hadn't seen him and so weren't budging.

The elderly male raised a hand above his eyes as though that might somehow aid sight. "I can't really see…" He pointed. "That one?"

"Yes, that's right," said the guide. "It's like a cross between a pig and a man. Definitely non-human. Some have joked that it's an alien…"

Tom faltered as he tried to follow the guide's direction, *en passant*, and stumbled into a chair by the nave, causing it to scrape on the floor.

The trio turned to look at him in surprise.

"Ah, er, sorry."

The elderly couple grimaced, but the guide smiled benignly. "No problem."

Almost without volition, Tom squeaked the word in his mind: "Alien?"

"Eh?" said the guide, momentarily perplexed, then: "Oh, the corbel? Just a joke we have. I mean, nobody knows what aliens really look like, eh?"

"Humph!" harrumphed the elderly man. "There's no such thing as aliens. What nonsense!"

"Er, yes, of course," said Tom. He smiled weakly, nodded at the party; and scurried past.

There was little further to go; the church wasn't particularly spacious inside, and he was already at the altar. What to do next? To his left was the curtained area with the small wooden door that led into the crypt, where he'd first spoken to Smith. He knew there was at least one secret door within that dingy chamber, as Smith had opened it. Previously, Tom had been at a disadvantage – but not now, for he currently wore his otherworldly contact lenses and would be able to see any alien signs. And even better, in the unicorn-adorned rucksack on his back, he had a magnet that would open any revealed portal.

The door that Smith had used previously led from the crypt into the chancel passageway under the altar; but could the crypt also be the location of a door into the tunnel network that ran beneath the city? That seemed likely to Tom. But last time, the wooden door from the nave to the crypt had been physically locked, and while Smith had a key, Tom didn't.

But Tom could – if he wanted, and he wasn't sure he did (well, no, actually he was very sure that he *didn't*) – access the crypt from the other direction, namely, through the passageway that led to the now-closed Octagon café. But though the café could be accessed from the Hay Hill square outside, that door would again need a human key to unlock it, hence, Tom faced a similar problem. He paused to think for a moment. Yes, there *was* a viable way in: to his right was a small staircase that led down, the entrance to which was cordoned off with a *terrifying* red rope.

What was he doing?

He hadn't really thought things out, but he knew one thing for sure: Smith needed to be stopped. *Somehow*. And if the alien was here, this was where that might happen. But Tom wasn't sure of Smith's whereabouts, and he'd received no update from Ed since leaving the flat this morning. *Okay*. He tried to contact Ed one last time, standing next to the red rope, and was unsurprised when his burner phone rang and rang and then went to an irritating message about the caller being unavailable…

Bollocks!

What now? Give in? Return to the others? Or he could just man up. Be like Tim, in his, um, *draft manuscript*. After all, what was the worst that could happen? He looked around frantically, his mind in overdrive: there were, of course, a host of things that could – and likely would – go wrong.

Suddenly, Tom found himself alone. The church was empty save for the trio, and these were now at the far end of the nave near the main door.

"Oh, *fuck*! Here goes…"

Tom stepped over the drooping rope, and quickly descended the stairway, running his hands along handrails set into the white-painted walls. He found himself in the chancel passageway on a thin yellow carpet in an area with modern wooden doors, cheap-looking shelves, and a couple of offices for clerical staff. Turning left, he saw the old passageway with benches along the walls, like a school changing room, at the end of which was a wide stained-glass window that looked outside, in front of which was a table bearing a crucifix.

Tom paused a moment to listen. There wasn't a sound, and he sensed emptiness. There were no humans present – or aliens.

He continued to the spot in the wall he remembered as being the location of the secret door to the crypt… and there it was: through his contacts, he could see a glowing alien rune. He retrieved the large magnet from his rucksack and stood with it in front of the hidden portal.

Don't think – act!

Tom applied the magnet, heard a click, and saw the faint outline of a low door over the top of the bench. Without allowing any time to talk himself out of the insanity, he crouched, pushed, and clambered through the opening into the dark and dusty chamber.

Dark... but empty!

Tom allowed the door to swing shut behind, leaving him in the claustrophobic crypt.

He felt his heart thumping in his chest, and for a moment stood paralysed with indecision and not a little fear. But then he realised the chamber was too small for any unseen lurker, and it wasn't entirely dark, or at least, it wasn't for his enhanced eyes. His heart-rate slowed, and he was able to consider the scene more calmly. Though there was no light in the spectrum used by humans, he noticed patches in a bluish colour where there was seventh-dimensional alien script – not one, but *three*.

The first patch was just at his left shoulder, where he'd entered.

The second patch was against the opposite wall, and presumably marked the expected entrance to the subterranean tunnel network.

There was no mark at the far end, where the old door led to the church, but now that he thought of it, that was unsurprising: the door between nave and crypt was no secret at all, just infrequently used. No, the third patch was on one of the stone sarcophagi by the walls.

In total, the light was sufficient that Tom didn't feel a need to use the torch function on his phone.

He stood a moment, listening, but the crypt was eerily silent.

What now?

If Smith wasn't here, he was either outside or in the tunnel network. But if outside, he would only have six-and-a-bit minutes before becoming visible to alien watchers – apparently. (But could that have been a porky too?) Anyway, Tom had been faffing around in the church for longer than that and he'd not seen him, which implied that if the alien *Big Issue* seller was out and about, then it was elsewhere, and if not, then he must be in the tunnel, hence, somewhere behind the door in the opposite wall.

As an excuse to delay more than anything, Tom took a few steps over to the tomb. Was it the one Smith had sat on during their first meeting here? *Probably.* Tom hefted the magnet in his hand and looked at the alien rune set mid-way along the oblong box, just below the stone lid.

What the hell.

He applied the magnet and heard the lid click – and only at that moment did the thought pop into his mind…

Vampire.

He jerked back as though a cube of ice had been dropped down his back. What had he… what if…?

The silence remained.

Nothing moved.

Maybe that was because Smith was sleeping within the box, arms folded across his chest, perhaps eyes open yet unseeing, with outrageous fangs now protruding from his upper jaw?

More deep breaths.

And still no sound or motion.

"Get a grip, Tom," he muttered to himself.

He approached the tomb and touched the lid – and jumped, as it slowly began to rise of its own accord.

He might have fled at that, but he was too scared to move. Instead, he closed his eyes, counted to three, then slowly opened one eyelid and squinted… and gave a huge sigh of relief.

Within the tomb was no vampire, or empty bed of black silk or alien earth, but a narrow tray, about six feet long by three feet wide, faintly illuminated by red light along its perimeter. Within was a number of unusual metallic implements.

"Cool!"

Tom bent to examine the metalwork. There was nothing particularly pointy and torture-y or kill-y, so that was good. But the things were completely incomprehensible to him, except…

"Hello, mama!"

Tom selected one of the instruments and hefted it. The thing – which fit neatly into one hand – looked like a double-barrelled torch with a couple of switches to one side, almost identical to the disruptor that Agneta and Martin were currently wielding in Chapelfield Gardens. A sly smile spread across Tom's face. If Smith didn't have his toy, he couldn't cause further damage, could he?

Tom swung the rucksack from his back and placed the device therein, pulling the drawstring at the top tight and then fastening the two catches.

"Fuck you, Smith!" he muttered to himself.

"Are you sure that's wise," said a deep and mellow voice behind him.

Tom nearly lost his Wetherspoons brunch through his bottom…

He slowly turned to see, floating a short distance away by the still-closed door to the tunnel network, the glowing skull of the spectre of Robert Goodale.

***

As the second half wore on, Norwich City began to dominate, and yet, they just could not get the ball in the back of the net. It was as if they'd forgotten how to do so, not having scored more than one goal in any Championship game during the entire season.

As Trevor fretted and groaned in tune with the home crowd, Keith focused on other matters. He kept a close eye on the excitable Delia, sat three rows down and to their right, in the very corner of the partitioned box, as well as on the dour supporters around her. There was a palpable hostility in the air, like a small black cloud hovering over those fans who, Keith noted, stole malevolent glances towards Delia at the end of every failed attack. He also kept an eye on events around the pitch, focusing on the brightly bibbed stewards scattered about, most of whom stood with their backs to the game, watching the crowd for misbehaviour. As such, it was he, not Trevor, who made the next shocking discovery…

"Ah, Trevor," he bellowed, trying to be heard above the crowd noise. "I think we have a problem. *Another* problem."

"*Ooooooooooo*," said Trevor, gasping with the crowd at another near miss. Without taking his eyes from the game he leant towards Keith and bellowed back. "What do you mean? Are Tristan and Josh back?"

"No. Someone else. Look down there. Right below. By the entrance to the tunnel. The tall man in a yellow vest, laughing and joking with two others – one in yellow and one in orange."

"The tunnel? I see… *fuck*! It's Ed!"

"It is indeed."

"What the hell is he doing here? He's meant to be in his flat, playing at being Big Brother."

"But that's not all," shouted Keith. "Look who he's with. Not the bruiser with the shaven head, but the other guy."

"I don't know him. But… he looks vaguely familiar."

"Let me give you a clue. You bumped into his partner not long ago."

"Ricky?"

"Precisely. So, what is Ed doing with Ricky, both dressed as security staff, standing by the tunnel to the teams' changing rooms *and* the officials' room – which we weren't shown on our tour yesterday?"

Trevor's eyes widened in fury. "Messages left in the refs' room? No wonder they're against us! I'll…" he looked about. But they were stuck in their seats. There was certainly no way they could get to the aisle and descend towards the pitch without being challenged. And then… a roar.

The men's view below was obscured by those in front leaping from their seats in celebration.

Brief celebration.

"Not a-*fucking*-gain!" raged an elderly man in the row below, as he twisted his yellow-and-green scarf in his hands.

"Offside?" cried others around them. "No way was that offside!"

But the decision stood. The atmosphere in the stadium darkened, and those in the box glowered at the backs of the club-owning couple even more intensely.

"There's nothing we can do about them now," yelled Keith. "We just need to keep an eye on Delia and intervene if necessary, though I'm hardly cut out for mortal combat, so I'm afraid it'll be up to you to play the knight in shining armour."

By now, Ed and Ricky had disappeared.

The game continued at a furious pace, but Norwich could not score, and eventually the final whistle blew. Over the two legs the score was now an aggregate one-all, and so extra time would be played.

"It's all going to plan," said Keith, during a momentary decrease in volume, as those around caught their breath. "Unfortunately, not to *our* plan."

Below, they watched a couple of the officials disappear into the tunnel. Quick toilet break? In truth, Keith didn't know what the form was for football. He knew the referee and linesmen left the pitch at half-time along with the players, but he'd not seen many games go into extra time. If the officials went back to their sanctuary, did that mean they would soon receive more subliminal instructions? He muttered a curse.

"So, now we just wait," said Trevor, bitterly. "For two goalless halves of extra time, and then penalties and defeat."

"Alas, I fear so. And then we may need to move quickly in case the fans around us take the messages they've encountered rather too literally."

The officials returned; the teams took their positions; and the game began anew. Naturally, the first fifteen-minute half was goalless, with both teams sizing each other up. But then, in the second half of extra time, from out of the blue...

"*Goooooooooal!*"

And the stadium erupted – in both fury and joy.

***

"Ah... um... what...?"

Tom's behind was pressed firmly against the tomb, his rucksack on the floor at his feet. The skull floated just two metres away, close enough that should it wish to suddenly swoop in and bite off Tom's nose with its naked teeth he would have been unable to stop it. But though Tom instinctively expected such a move, he *knew* – in one small part of his brain where rationality still resided – that this wasn't about to happen.

The voice came again, though the spectre's mouth remained lockjaw tight.

"I do not know your motives, Tom, but there are too many of those devices in this city. Far too many."

"I... uh... don't plan to actually use it. *Au contraire...*"

"You wish to deny its use by the Thruvian? Fine motives, perhaps, but we have seen today how dangerous such devices can be in the hands of humans, regardless of their intents."

"Right, okay, then I'll just put it..."

"I did not suggest you do that, Tom. You are not mine to command. And I do not wish to influence you one way or the other." The disembodied voice paused. When it continued, Tom sensed a change of tone, and even a hint of uncertainty. "This affair has led to many moral conundrums, not only among humans and watchers, but even among us."

Tom had managed to calm himself. His shoulders gently sagged, and he pressed away from the tomb. This was the third time he had seen this particular ghost – among others – and on each occasion the initial fright he'd felt had waned increasingly quickly. Robert Goodale's hijacker was

461

not a threat. And now curiosity drove Tom's response: "You're not meant to talk to us, to *me*, are you?"

"No. But then many are doing things today that they are not meant to be doing. Ultimately, the only physical peril as a result of these breaches will be to humans. And that is not right."

"Yes. And that's what we – me and my team – are trying to prevent."

The voice paused again. *Thinking?* At last it continued: "I know where the Thruvian is. It might help you to know this. Do you want me to tell you?"

"Yes! Definitely!" Sod Ed – Tom had Turbo Ghost Assist!

"Very well. The Thruvian has been checking his theatre of operations, and trying to contact his various helpers, with little success. As I speak, it is taking the western tunnel from the castle. I predict it is heading this way. If you leave now and take the thing you call a disruptor, it will be inconvenienced. But not completely. There are other instruments in that compartment behind you, and elsewhere in this place, which might still enable it to cause mischief."

"Right, so maybe I should try to… to stop Smith getting here?"

"I will not advise. But decide quick, Tom, while you still can." And the skull floated off to the side, leaving open a path to the second hidden doorway – the one that undoubtedly led to the tunnel network.

"Can't advise, my arse," muttered Tom. The ghost had all but issued an invitation. "Okay. I'll stop him." He grasped his rucksack and swung it onto his back, then paced across the stone floor to the alien rune, applied his magnet, and watched the wall nudge back with a gentle scraping of stone. He nodded thanks to the glowing skull and pushed the door open.

He'd only taken a half-step into the narrow tunnel, however, when a voice emanated from the direction of the skull: "Good luck, Tom. But be careful. The Thruvian is – in your peculiar jargon – *pissed off.*"

To Tom's credit, his step barely faltered.

Within three paces, the faint alien light from the crypt faded to nothing, forcing Tom to whip out his phone and select the torch app. The light revealed a tunnel much like the others he had been down: grimy, stone-lined, wide enough for a single person only, and seemingly built for dwarves. *Or hobbits*, thought Tom, remembering the figurine chosen for him by Simon.

It was only a short distance to the junction beneath the former location of the Old Swan Inn on St Peters Street and the brick-vaulted chamber that Tom and Simon had come across when exploring the western tunnel from the castle. On that previous occasion, they'd not followed this particular branch to St Peter Mancroft, as Tom had been spooked by an open door directly opposite to it and perpendicular to the tunnel from the castle. And indeed, as before, the old wooden door stood open.

Tom's confidence – which had risen following his easy encounter with the ghost – now began to dip again. He alternated his glance between the open door, and the tunnel to the castle to his right. If Goodale was correct, Smith should be emerging very shortly from that direction; in fact, he could be there now, just beyond the shadow line of his phone-torch, watching him from the dark. And he still had no actual plan beyond…

"Tom. What a surprise."

This time Tom did jolt in shock. Smith emerged from his right into the chamber – which was perhaps four metres by three and tall enough for a normal human to stand up in, having likely been an old undercroft.

"Ah… sorry… you made me jump. I wasn't expecting…"

Smith emerged fully into the room to stand opposite; his face was neutral, emotionless. If the alien was indeed pissed off, it was doing well in hiding it.

"You weren't expecting me? Then what were you expecting, Tom? And why are you here?" Smith's eyes seemed to be trying to look into the passage behind Tom. "From your positioning, you must have come from the church of Mancroft. Interesting." And now the alien's face did register something akin to human emotion: its mouth pulled down into a frown.

"Yes, well…" What could Tom say? He considered the alien: Smith was dressed as usual, in a red *Big Issue* seller's bib. But he had no weapons to hand, or even a torch, presumably because he could see in the dark or had access to other weird alien senses. He looked unthreatening. Yet there was something about his bearing that suggested tension; he didn't stand straight, but rather in a slight crouch, as though ready to spring. Tom drew himself up, now that he could fully straighten his back: though not an especially tall man, he was still taller than Smith's human guise, and he found some evolved confidence in this. He cleared his throat and puffed out his chest. "Well," he began again, "that's not strictly true. I mean, I have been expecting you. I have been on to you for some time. I know what you have been doing. And I know you've been playing me for a fool. Getting me to do your dirty work."

Smith remained stock-still, save for his eyes, which narrowed. "That explains some things. Your increasing ineptitude and lack of diligence. And now I think about it, the change of focus and tenor of your novel. About how London and New York got changed to Norwich and Great Yarmouth; your main character's increased truculence..."

"Truculence!" That wasn't how Tom wanted Tim's evolution to come across!

"...and the machinations of your alien protagonists. It was there all along. I should have allocated more attention to that. It seems that I have underestimated you."

"Yes. You have." Tom wasn't sure how to feel about that. Being underestimated was never really *that* good. Just how much of a useless cretin had Smith thought he was? "Anyway – the game is up. We know what you're up to. It's time to stop."

"We?" Smith still seemed calm, but his eyebrow rose, Roger-Moore-like, reinforcing the fact that he'd become rather more human than perhaps even he appreciated. "You have friends in the know? How interesting. In any case, it matters not. Tom – please step aside. I have important work to complete."

"Work?" Tom widened his stance and folded his arms, and then unfolded them – as the effect had been to cover his torch screen and plunge the chamber into weird, disconcerting shadows. "Ahem. Work!" he tried again. "You mean, cause chaos in the city. Start a humongous riot. Set men against, er, other men. And women. And, er, probably trans-persons too. If you know what I mean."

"Noble sentiments, Tom. But this is an imperative that needs expressing. Your lives have become rather mundane: all this – and I don't know how much you understand – is simply an attempt to add a little spice to your lives. Your city will remember this day in the future with great enthusiasm in a way that it, and your people, would otherwise not, bathing instead in a beige and pointless existence. It is a harmless distraction."

"Harmless!" spluttered Tom. "*Delia must die?*"

Now, Smith's equanimity did waver. He frowned in a deep manner that Tom had not seen before. "You worked out that code? That is...

astonishing. Truly, I have underestimated you, Tom, and for that I am sorry." He paused and looked at Tom more closely, then muttered: "remarkable." Then, after another pause, he continued: "Even so, you must realise that this expression is not meant to be taken literally. We wish no harm to any human being. We – as you must appreciate – are manipulators. We are not murderers, or assassins. We do not seek human pain, discomfort, or misery in any sense. And we especially do not wish any harm to come to your respected icon."

"What you wish, and what you get, may not be the same thing," said Tom, now heatedly. "If your plans come off, there's going to be a riot. People – real people – are going to get hurt. And Delia herself is at risk – if she goes left instead of right, or gets a little too far from those who would protect her, then she could get seriously hurt. So don't pretend you care so much. You want drama at whatever cost. And drama usually involves pushing and shoving and kicking and punching and the letting of claret..." Tom paused. That wasn't bad, that. He'd have to remember that line for his protagonist, Tim! "So, I'm not going to let you do it. Whatever *it* is. You'll have to zap me with your death ray to remove me." Tom spoke with brio, but the moment the words left his lips, he felt a surge of doubt. Death rays? He'd rather not!

"So – we are at a stalemate," said Smith, calmly. "You occupy the tunnel, and though I could possibly force my way past you with this body, to do so is not our way."

"Yeah, right," said Tom, suddenly relieved. "So... fuck off! Go back to your flying saucer."

"Fuck off?" Smith almost looked offended. "Flying saucer? That is most un-Tom like."

"You seem to think that *Tom* is a bit of a muppet – a docile, gullible muppet..." Tom paused: that was it; that was *exactly* it; that was how he'd been seen. "But I'm *not*. I'm now a completely different creature. And though I'm not a man of violence, I will..." *what was it Simon had once said?* "... go all medieval on your ass if you try to pass."

Smith actually looked perturbed. "I... *see*." And then he did something completely unexpected. He turned around and, with a sprightliness that should not have been possible in such superficially aged legs, bolted in the opposite direction through the open door leading towards the Guildhall.

For a moment, Tom stood still, stunned, confused. What had just happened? Had he just bravely faced down an alien terror? His faced twitched into a smile. But then he thought: *where the fuck is Smith off to... and why?*

He had to find out!

Tom started after Smith, catching a glimpse of the alien disappearing up the tunnel. But he wasn't shambling like Tom, but instead loping like a chimpanzee, using his hands like a second pair of legs, making much greater speed in the enclosed space. Within a second, his quarry was out of view, lost in the dark. "Shit!"

Tom made the best speed he could. The tunnel to the Guildhall wasn't that long – perhaps two hundred metres? Less? He could have jogged it in less than a minute if he could have stood upright, but it took considerably longer with his awkward gait. It certainly gave him time to consider options. Did Smith have a second stash of kit at the Guildhall? It was, after all, his secondary base. But why would he do so? He would have never expect a situation like this, and it was only a short distance away from his HQ, thus it seemed an unnecessary risk, distributing embargoed alien tech about the city. So, if it wasn't a supply depot, maybe Smith's plan was to outflank him? Emerge at the Guildhall and then return to Mancroft 'overland'. Though with the crowds now gathered in the area outside – crowds that, ironically, Smith had been responsible for – his going would be tortuous. Indeed, it might well take Smith longer than his self-proclaimed six-minute limit before he could make it.

Then what?

Tom slowed. There was something, another option, but he just couldn't get...

The end of the tunnel came into sight – blocked, as expected, but with an alien rune shining in extra-dimensional blue. Tom waved his magnet and was rewarded with a customary 'click'. He cautiously pushed open the 'door', or rather, a piece of wall in what was revealed to be another undercroft, presumably in the basement of the Guildhall. The space he emerged into had shadowed alcoves and seemed to be being used as a store room. A thick wooden door off to one side was ajar, with a gentle light spilling around its edges.

Tom fully emerged, crouched, and then gingerly waddled up to the door. As he approached, his frown deepened. This wasn't right. What was Smith's gameplan? Maybe...

He swivelled, realising the ploy at the last moment, but too late.

Smith slid out from an alcove, cast a malign smile at Tom, and scuttled back through the tunnel towards Mancroft.

He'd been scammed!

"Oh... BUGGER!"

There was no way Tom could keep up. Smith would beat him by a couple of minutes, and have time to collect his appropriate mega-disruptor, or whatever it was he was aiming for, and be long gone before Tom arrived.

Fuck!

But then Tom looked at the phone in his hand, emitting a bright light from its screen.

Phone.

Maybe...

He dimmed the torch and checked: he had reception, albeit faint. He tapped in a number, put the phone to his ear, and waited. Six, eight, ten rings... he was waiting for the inevitable 'user unavailable' message when the receiver picked up.

"Tom?"

"Amanda! Thank God! I know this is difficult but... where are you? Chapelfield?"

Amanda gave a gentle laugh. "No chance. Can't you tell from the background noise... or lack of it? We couldn't get there. We suddenly ran into a line of police and the Rainbow marchers, and when we turned back, we got squeezed between the Penitents and the Righteous. It's quite spicy out here. I think it could go either way."

"So, where are you?"

"The Forum. It's relatively peaceful here, as all the shouty people are outside, and normal visitors are avoiding it. Why? Where are you?"

"Thank God!" The Forum was separated from St Peter Mancroft by the Millennium Plain. *Ground zero.* But it was only maybe fifty metres distant. "Amanda, listen, I need you to..."

Chapter 38: He Shoots… He Scores?

At Carrow Road, the fury had been from the away fans; the joy from the yellow army.

"No way!" gasped Trevor.

They waited for the groan of thousands of disappointed voices; for a late linesman's flag to be raised; for the referee to wave his arms while whistling to indicate foul play. Instead, the referee peeled off and pointed to the centre circle. Anxiety dripped from the crowd. But then the kick-off was taken, and it was too late to go back: Norwich had indeed scored.

"One-all," said Keith, loudly. Then again, as if he didn't quite believe it: "One-all!"

"The sequence is broken," said Trevor, daring to take his eyes from the game in order to look at his colleague. "Does that mean the curse is lifted?"

The burner phone in Keith's breast pocket vibrated. He raised a finger to stall Trevor, retrieved his phone, noticed an icon that indicated he had a text message, tapped this… and began to laugh.

"What is it?"

"It's from Ed," said Keith. "It says: 'Apparently Delia must dig', and there's a smiley face emoji."

"What does *that* mean?"

"A one-all draw must change the ASCII code from an 'e' to a 'g'. How long do we have left?"

"About five minutes."

"I don't understand what Ed's game is, but let's hope he's not being premature. In any case, another goal by either side will break the entire code, as two isn't a binary number."

"Even so," said Trevor, "we'll have to convince those around us in the box that there's been a mistake and Delia is not due to meet the Grim Reaper."

"I suspect that may not be a problem," said Keith. "Without the spark of defeat, the message becomes a piece of meaningless fluff. But cross your fingers tightly for the next four minutes and thirty seconds."

"Plus stoppage time."

"Indeed!"

***

Robert Quigley was uneasy. The march had started well: he'd given a speech from the steps of City Hall using a loudspeaker conjured up by the Channel 4 team, in which he'd emphasised the seriousness of what they were doing. "This is penance!" he'd roared. "Not a tea party!"

And that seemed to have worked: the few smiles he'd caught on placard-bearing listeners had quickly dissipated, and he was pleased to see even Jane and her friends adopt a suitably downbeat demeanour.

Then they'd moved off for their long, slow, ponderous trudge around the centre of the city. And that had been great. Their silent progression had acted as a black hole of anti-joy, like a giant hand pressed to a pair of massive lips, rebuking the frivolous shoppers and stray marchers they'd passed: *SHHHHHHHHHH!*

But that was at the start. He'd expected the negative vibe to self-reinforce, as it had during the previous march, with Penitents growing more severe and intolerant of gaiety as they progressed; of increasing their level of miserabilism to Cromwellian levels. Instead… the reverse! It was like a gentle ripple flowing through his serried ranks, starting at the front, and indeed spreading from marchers on the outside in. By the time they were on the return sweep, the silence was under constant attack – gentle titters and the odd cut-off laugh. Smiles. Winks. A balloon had appeared at one point, a stray from one of the other marching cohorts he guessed, and soon that was being batted about by his own placard-hoisters as though a beachball amongst the tanked-up spectators at a one-day cricket international. *Outrageous!* When it had gotten close to him, he'd grabbed it and squeezed it until it burst – an action met with a low groan from those around.

And now they were back on St Peters, heading towards Millennium Plain and a thin wall of police. They'd been allowed to occupy Bethel Steet, between the northern face of the Forum and its car park and the police station and City Hall – but not the plain itself. The plain had been bagsied by one of the other marches – Robert could now see colourful rainbow banners raised high over the heads of the already squeezed police – while Hay Hill and the area around the market had been ceded to others.

Robert made his way to the very front of his troops, where his television company enablers had raised a small stage for him in front of the police line. But progress was slow: he had so many followers, he feared they'd not all fit into their allocated zone.

***

While Robert Quigley forced his way to his stage, Harry and his friends were nearby in the Plain in the middle of the Rainbow Coalition marchers – a centre of tranquillity and good humour surrounded by banner-wavers who'd been rather shouty and fierce during their procession around the city. *Had been.* For there had been a peculiar shift in the demeanour of the multi-cellular Rainbow organism. Fiery speeches at the outset in the park had succeeded in winding up people who were ready to be wound up; then the banging of drums, hooting of klaxons and chanting of slogans had helped to maintain a kind of martial ardour. But then…

Passions had dampened. Shouters had become hoarse. Drummers had become tired. And the scowly outriders had perhaps got face ache. And all the while, Harry and his clique had remained upbeat, colourful, cheerful, spreading gaiety outwards. By the time they made it to Millennium Plain, the perilous atmosphere had – to the clear chagrin of the cabal of beret-wearing leaders at the front of the march – dissolved. But not completely. There was still an underlying tension, continually stoked by the main triumvirate of Clare, Socialist Stuart and Anti-War 'Kill anyone who disagrees with me' Fran, and matters might still go downhill quick.

"This is when it could go off," muttered Harry.

"What do you mean?" said Cathy, who'd been enjoying herself, having managed to get the grim orchestra nearby to beat a number of anthemic community tunes.

"Until now, our more bellicose members have been shouting into a vacuum," explained Harry. "But now they've come up against the supposed foe, especially over there on Hay Hill, and those are people who are likely to shout back. So, there is now something for them to react against."

"What are we going to do?"

Harry smiled. "Do what we do best, Cathy dear. Do you still have the band twisted around your little finger? Then let's get ready to party!"

***

Grand Master Jim, Sir Ken, and Lady Tania had been squeezed out of Hay Hill and onto Weavers Lane, a narrow passage between the east side of St Peter Mancroft and a row of shops that faced onto Gentleman's Walk. The lane led past the Garnet pub to the covered market.

"Damn and blast," shouted Ken over the hubbub. "We can't do any good here."

"Yes, but we've got a good view of the, er, grandees," said Jim. For indeed they had. directly opposite, in the packed square – separated from the larger Millennium Plain by a blocky retail building containing a Next – they could see the statue of Sir Thomas Browne and the bobbing heads of the leaders of the different cliques of the Righteous clustered about it. The leaders were raised above the crowd by virtue of standing on a flat level at the top of a tier of steps. "And no one's going to get close to them there."

In fact, Jim mused, no one had gotten menacingly close to them during their entire march – something for which he was grateful (a view not necessarily shared by the other Knights). Which wasn't to say that there'd been no threat at all: they'd been shadowed most of the way from the cathedral by several rough-looking groups, holding balloons, who'd stayed just beyond their line of police escorts. And whenever Ken had directed Knights in the direction of these packs – using his walkie talkie – they'd retreated a sufficient distance to avoid confrontation.

"It's the periphery we have to watch out for," said Tania. "The lefties are up the hill, and there's only a shallow line of plods separating them from us. And God knows where the Krusties are. I don't like it."

"Me neither," said Ken. "We're kettled up. Now's the time for our enemies to strike."

"Let's go uphill past the church to the front line," said Tania. Without awaiting approval, she took off, edging past the low, flint-faced octagonal building – once the church's café – against which they'd been standing.

They'd barely moved, however, when they bumped into a pair of young people squeezing their way through the crowd.

"Ah, excuse me," said a geeky looking man, "we're just…" he waved a hand at a short path beyond an iron gate set in railings that separated the church and its octagonal add-on from the square. The area beyond the rails – and the path itself – was clear of marchers.

"No problem," said Ken, moving aside. "But you know the café's closed, don't you?"

"Oh, we know," said the man's partner – a severe-looking woman hefting a strange, torch-like device. Her face twisted into a wicked grin: "And we plan to keep it that way."

Jim watched the pair go through the gate and cross to the closed and darkened doorway of the ex-café. He noticed his colleagues also watching intently. But the pair seemed harmless, so Tania shrugged and led them onwards.

**

"Fuck! We can't get anywhere near them," muttered Blitz.

As the Righteous swelled into the area around Hay Hill, screened off by police in yellow bibs and clandestine individuals in sunglasses with stylised 'St G' pins on their jackets, it had left Blitz's brigade no place to go. They'd syphoned down Briggs Street onto Rampant Horse Street and found themselves at St Stephen's – another flinted medieval church. Blitz's whole team now clustered outside the church – with the Marks and Spencers away to one side, and the paved area before an entrance to Chantry Place Mall to another. *Whole team?* Blitz looked sourly at the score that remained – for a third had been afflicted by some strange mellowness that had led them to down balloons, stink-vials, and spray cans, and go off to enjoy the sun (and perhaps the odd spliff) somewhere else instead.

"Yeah, it's a pisser," said Skid, though in a tone suggesting that he wasn't quite as downhearted by matters as he should have been. "Maybe we should, you know, bail? It was a good idea an' all, but, you know…" He shrugged his shoulders.

"No!" said Blitz. "We need to strike at the fascists!" But there was a surprising lack of vehemence in his voice. *What has happened to me?* Maybe it was the fine weather. Maybe it was a case of the chase being more thrilling than the kill. After all, the stalking had been quite fun. And did he really want to stampede the old codgers? One of the head honchos of

The Boys suddenly reminded him of his own grandad. He shook his head vigorously. Time to sort himself out! Time to…

"Here, who are they?" asked Mary.

Trooping towards them – up the path through the cemetery from Rampant Horse Street – were about thirty men, looking like an ugly stag party. Resting with his back to the church wall, Blitz wondered sourly (and louder than intended): "Who's the poor git getting married?"

The troop in waders, gilets, and assorted slouch hats came to a halt. A grizzled elder at the front frowned at him. "What was that, sonny? Married?"

Blitz crossed his arms. "Stag do, no? So who's the geezer getting hitched?"

"No one's getting hitched. Damn fool!"

"So why are you in fancy dress?" laughed Mags.

"Fancy dress!" spluttered the elder.

"We're the Compleat Anglers," said a fifty-something man to the elder's side.

"Whassat? The Complete Wankers?" grinned Blitz.

"Bloody cheek!" scowled the elder. But the younger man's grin wasn't a challenging one, and the elderly fisherman found himself grinning too. He'd been grinning for quite a lot of the last hour or so and wasn't entirely sure why. "No, sonny. The Complete Wankers are another lot. *Splitters…*"

"*Splitters,*" echoed a number of his colleagues, though in an almost perfunctory manner, bereft of any real emotion.

"You don't 'appen to know where they are, do you?" he continued. "Got themselves lots of banners with pictures of fish on."

And then one of Blitz's crew rushed up from the direction of the mall. "Oi, Blitz! There's more marchers behind us. Looks like two lots. Dunno who they are, but one lot are wearing those fucking stupid little sailor hats. They're squaring up. Might be a barney."

"The Watersporters, Jezza?" said the fifty-something man.

"Aye, might be, Bernie. And Ron's lot, too. Let's go see."

The two groups filtered into each other and headed up the narrow path between the gravestones: it seemed as though the day might not be a complete loss after all.

***

After his rapid phone call to Amanda, Tom started back down the tunnel to Mancroft. In the brick-arched chamber where three tunnels met, he found the spectre of Robert Goodale waiting. This time, he didn't so much as flinch.

"Tom," cried a deep voice, from the approximate location of the floating skull, "you must hurry. The Thruvian is assembling a projection device."

"A what?"

"A highly illicit instrument. It is essentially a version of the device you have in your backpack. It will allow the Thruvian to write messages in the air, like the sky messaging from stunt planes using smoke, albeit in a dimension only visible to the human subconscious."

"But won't something that obvious be visible to the alien watchers?"

The skull bobbed up and down, as though nodding. "The message will last a very short time only, but yes, it might well draw the attention of the watching species. That the Thruvian would risk doing so suggests it has much invested in this game, and that it is desperate."

"Uh, right. So, I need to stop him. Got you."

The skull slid aside and Tom scurried down the last section of tunnel to the crypt of the church.

The stone wall at the tunnel's end soon yielded to Tom's magnet and slid aside.

Somewhat out of breath, Tom squeezed through the opening gap, holding his surrogate torch before him. The crypt was empty, though the tomb from which he'd pilfered Smith's disruptor was open, and he could see that several of the other indentations were now empty of their devices – presumably parts of the projector thingy. Assembling these must have taken some time, so Smith couldn't be far away – surely?

There were two other exits from the crypt, but the wooden door set half way up one wall was liable to be locked, and it would be difficult to access without a stepladder anyway, and so he took the secret door in the wall he'd used earlier. He entered the chancel passageway, bright from light spilling through the window that closed off its north end. He turned in the opposite direction, past the offices, heading towards the old octagon café and the door to the outside – and pulled up in surprise.

Martin and Agneta stood there, firm expressions on their faces, arms crossed like a pair of bouncers.

"What…?"

"You just missed him," said Agneta. "But we were in time… just. Smith got a shock when he opened the door and found us blocking the way."

"Yeah," laughed Martin. "Especially when Agneta told him to 'fuck off back to Thruvia'. He ran back inside without locking the door."

"We waited a few seconds before deciding to come in," said Agneta. "But now we're here – what next?"

"Er, *great*. Well, he didn't pass me, so he must have gone up a level into the church. Stay here in case he comes back."

"Righto!" said Martin.

"Go go!" hissed Agneta.

Tom about faced, and within five paces was through another internal door and at the foot of ascending steps, which he bounded up. At the top, he stepped over a red rope and looked about. He was next to the altar; the church seemed utterly deserted. He started down the central nave towards the exit beneath the belltower – and saw shadowy figures behind the glass door ahead, which opened to reveal…

"Tom!" It was Amanda. "He was just here – literally five seconds ago!"

Simon was at the woman's shoulder. "Yeah, mate. He looked right at us and didn't fancy it. Then he went *that* way…"

Tom and the pair came together, just inside the doorway. Simon had indicated an area to his right – Tom's left. There, set within a large pillar, was a narrow spiral stairway, going up.

"Into the belltower," said Tom.

"Trapped," nodded Simon. "We can pen the wanker up and wait until everything plays out. He can't do anything now."

"Er, that's not *quite* true. After I phoned you, I bumped into Goodale's ghost again. He said Smith has a device that will let him write in the sky. A kind of projector."

"So, if he gets high up, or onto the roof, he can still cause chaos," said Amanda. "That's not good."

"Quick mate," said Simon, "after him! We'll stay here in case he throws you out of a window and comes back."

"Window! Oh, shit!" But there was nothing for it: Tom entered the stairwell and started to climb.

It wasn't far – just a few turns, perhaps no more than ten metres vertically – to the surprisingly spacious ringing gallery. He emerged onto a red-carpeted floor, with commemorative plaques on the walls, and a stone arch to one side that was closed with glass and gave a view over the nave of the church and the altar at its end. A number of bell ropes hung through the wooden ceiling, a couple of which swayed as though recently jostled.

For a moment, Tom paused and considered the ropes. Smith was clearly going to the top: maybe he could just stay here and start tugging at one of these? The noise above would surely be disabling – assuming Smith heard in the human auditory range. But bell ringing was meant to be a complicated task, wasn't it? In any case, ringing one of the bells would draw attention – not only of 'the authorities', but also of those outside. "Yeah right," he muttered to himself. "Tom the patsy, one last time. *Hi, everybody, look up here, into the sky. I've got a message for you!* Fuck!"

He found a small wooden door, which opened onto more spiral stairs that continued up. Groaning, he stepped through.

It was further this time – long enough for him to get out of breath. And then he came to another old wooden door with a message on the outside saying 'Keep Out'. "Sod that!"

Tom cautiously opened the door. What he saw was a confused space of walkways, handrails, and bells, with light spilling in through the upper arches of grimy windows... and then a flash of red. It was Smith's bib in motion.

Tom sidled into the chamber, gulped hard, and shouted: "Smith! Stop!"

The alien paused some five metres away and turned. "Tom? You are certainly persistent."

Tom came fully into the space, gingerly stepping onto the narrow beam on which the alien stood. He saw that there was another door at the end of the walkway, presumably giving access to the roof; he also noted that Smith held a bulbous metallic object in one hand. *The projector?* He had to stop him getting outside.

"Yes. I may be inept, but I'm definitely persistent. So, give up, *please*. I'm not going to let you do whatever it is you plan to do."

476

Smith actually smiled. "But for that, Tom, you have to catch me first." He turned and crabbed towards the door.

Tom rocked back on his heels in surprise, but momentarily only. He took a cautious step forwards, and then a second, and… slowed. For Smith had reached the end of the walkway, grasped the door handle, pulled and… *nothing*.

The door was locked.

As Tom edged within reach, he could barely believe his eyes: an interstellar traveller defeated by a rough old door made by human hand and an ancient iron lock! He couldn't help but giggle: "Got a problem? I thought you had the keys to this place?"

The alien stopped scrabbling and turned around slowly, the projector device pointed at Tom's chest. "Alas, Tom, I don't have a key for this one. I've never needed to access the roof before."

The two stood facing each other. Tom's heart rate rose as he looked upon the levelled, gun-like device, but then he exhaled deeply and gestured at the projector. "Are you planning on messaging me to death?" And then he grinned: given the perils of social media, that was perhaps not an entirely absurd analogy.

"Sorry? This? No. There is no threat intended – the positioning is simply a result of your human anatomy." Smith lowered his hand until the 'weapon' was pointing down. "And so we have a stand-off. Are you sure you won't allow me to create a little–?"

"No! Not one!" And then Tom's burner phone rang. He'd shoved it into the front pocket of his shirt. Not taking his eyes off Smith, he retrieved the phone and groped a thumb towards the 'accept call' icon, then brought it to his ear.

"Tom!" It was Simon. An *excited* Simon. "You not dead yet? Great! Get your arse back down here quick. I think it's too late for him."

"Uh, sorry, what?"

"We won! We *fucking* won! Well, no, actually we drew, but you know what I mean. I'm looking out the front door. It's going crazy out there, and not in a bad way either…"

Simon's voice was suddenly lost in a sea of noise. Tom returned his phone to his pocket and grinned broadly at Smith. "And now the game is definitely over. *Check mate.*"

***

When the final whistle blew, the atmosphere in Carrow Road utterly transformed. Arms were raised; yellow-and-green scarves were waved; and a huge roar reverberated around the ground that would carry on the wind most of the way to the city centre. The fans were instantly on their feet; in surprisingly quick time the stadium started to clear. During this exodus, Keith and Trevor quickly lost sight of Delia and her entourage.

"She's getting away!" shouted Trevor.

But Keith smiled and gave a gentle shake of the head. He leant into the large, ginger-haired man and shouted back: "Don't worry. I think she's safe. Look around."

The other occupants of the Directors Box were on their feet, streaming out too, and their demeanour had also transformed: if any were looking towards, or could even see, their patron saint, then their glances were drained of all enmity.

As they shuffled to the end of the row, Trevor replied: "Well, she's safe as long as she keeps away from the Derby fans. What now?"

They hadn't been entirely forgotten. A PA waited for them as they left the light and entered the stadium interior. They followed the woman down a side corridor.

"Delia sends her apologies. It's quite hectic now. Would tomorrow be okay? We can keep hold of your camera and equipment – you left them in a cupboard by the media centre, didn't you?"

"That's fine," said Keith. "Thank Delia again for her time and for remembering us – and pass on our congratulations."

The young woman smiled, winked, and bustled off.

They were soon outside.

By the Directors Entrance they came upon a bizarre sight.

"Check him again!" said a tall, fair-haired man wearing an orange steward's bib and a pair of familiar glasses. "He could hide every piece of cutlery from the entire stadium in those blubbery folds."

A shaven-headed brute in the yellow bib of club security began a more rigorous pat-down of a huge-bellied, black-bearded man wearing a tent-sized replica top who stood with his arms out.

Augustus P. Samson did not look impressed.

Keith and Trevor moved aside and waited for the frisk to conclude. The brute then revealed a small teaspoon as if by magic, causing the bearded one to splutter in outrage and protest his innocence.

"Good find, Bad Angus. Take him inside and do a proper search – full body cavity and all that." The tall man directed a scornful look upon the detainee. "And you're looking at a revocation of privileges at the very least, my big-boned friend. Maybe even prosecution." Then he winked at the grinning security guard, made a peculiar hand gesture, and walked over to the waiting men.

"What-ho, chaps! Fun and games, eh?"

"Ed – what was that all about?" asked Keith. "In fact, no, let me rephrase in terms I wouldn't normally use: what the *fuck* is going on?"

Ed slipped out of his bib and slung it over one shoulder. "Let's not hang around here, eh? I don't want anyone to ask too many questions. Walk with me. Let's follow the joyous horde downtown – and see whether our amigos have managed to do their part, or whether the streets are full of burning tyres, barricades and people hanging from lampposts."

"Ed!" reiterated Keith. But he struggled to keep a smile off his face, and Trevor had to cover his mouth to prevent laughter escaping.

"Ah, well, the specific is that, ever since we found out about the football manipulations, I've been on the case. I've been grooming Bad Angus for a couple of months – in a non-sexual way, of course. It's amazing what deep, dark secrets security personnel often harbour, and given their miserly pay they're often not averse to a bit of sidelining. Or is that moonlighting? *Whatever.* Anyway, Angus got me a one-off gig, and I've made a contribution to the *Bad Angus Charitable Fund.*"

"So, you've stitched up Samson?" said Keith.

"In a manner of speaking. It wasn't planned, mind you, but when I saw the humongous git, I couldn't let him off scot-free. The thought of him getting a stadium ban somehow leaves me all tingling."

Trevor blurted out a laugh, receiving an eyebrow waggle from Ed.

"And the rest?" said Keith. "I particularly want to know what you were doing with Ricky, and how you managed to swing the game… assuming you had some part in that."

"Ah, Ricky Ricky Ricky! I had two motivators there. The first is the filthy lucre. Or effectively so. He has a fetish for collecting records that far exceeds his means and his bar-staffing salary. His social media

479

accounts revealed the extent and nature of his lust. I picked up some limited edition recordings through certain, ah, *contacts*. But you know what? I probably needn't have bothered." He drew to a momentary halt and looked at his fellow yompers: they'd made it to the riverside and were well on the way to the Prince of Wales Road. "Tell me, chaps, what is the one feature of just about every photo and video we've seen of Ricky and Teresa together? Big Trev – fancy a go?"

Trevor shook his head. "I don't know. Just, well, they never seem especially happy."

"Hole in one for the Honey Monster! Bravo." He turned and started forwards again, drawing the others with him. "The pair always look as miserable as sin. They have a love-hate relationship. Or perhaps that should be a hate-hate-love-hate-hate relationship. Teresa wears the denims. And Teresa is Smith's acolyte; Ricky is merely a hanger-on. Anyway, turns out he would have probably helped just for the joy of getting one over his oh-so-superior girlfriend." Ed turned again. "By the way, did you know he hates vegan food? Absolutely makes him barf." He carried on. "And I needed Ricky to get access to Teresa's *disruptor* – or maybe I should say, *writer* – since you wouldn't let me borrow yours."

"Writer?" said Keith, innocently.

"Oh come on, Keith! Did you think I wouldn't work it out? It took me about thirty seconds to realise that something that could erase would likely also be able to write."

Keith sighed. "Of course you did. Go on."

"Not much else to tell. Ricky brought Teresa's *tool* along, let me use it, and now he's rushed off home to return it to the bottom of Teresa's lingerie drawer before she knows it's been borrowed. When she returns – probably fuming – he'll be listening to *The Boss* on his record player with a knowing look upon his pimply face."

"But what did you do with it?" asked Trevor.

"What I could. Which was limited. With Tom's specs, I could see that you'd done a good job removing pitch-side and changing room messages. But you never got to see the refs' hangout, and after that first half farrago it seemed clear that they'd been nobbled. Of course, I couldn't get in at half-time, but I did manage to in the second half. Sure enough, the walls were covered with alien filth – specifically directed against Norwich. I erased all that and replaced it with more positive messages. Had Derby scored in extra time, I think you would have found the goal would have been disallowed. And had anyone wearing yellow stumbled anywhere near the Derby box, a certain white spot in the centre of their box would have received a good-and-proper pointing-at. Fortunately, we didn't need the assist, as our goal looked a good-un to me."

They were now coming up to the bridge over the river with the Compleat Angler pub visible on the other side of the road.

They paused for a bit as they negotiated the road crossing, and then found themselves in a noisy knot of fans.

At last, Keith was able to continue his interrogation. "Okay. I guess congratulations are in order. But what I don't understand is why you've been so secretive about this. You haven't said a word."

"Hmmm, yes. Well, much as it pains me to say this, you might have noticed I don't take defeat well. In the first instance, I didn't know how all this was going to go down. There are plenty of places where my plans could have come unstuck, and I'd rather not have to wipe an omelette from my face. But second, old fruit, I didn't want to risk lectures and arguments – whether from the saintly-yet-naïve Amanda, unamused by my use of bribery, to general disapproval of my own manipulations. I suspect your Agneta would have chewed my todger off if she'd thought I was going to write any messages." He gave a sideways smile. "And I'm also mildly surprised that you haven't had a meltdown yet."

Keith frowned. "Well, yes, frankly I need to process this. You're right, I wouldn't have approved. But now it's done, it's done."

They had joined a cheerful stream of yellow, heading towards the top of Prince of Wales Road.

"Well, I'm jolly glad to hear you've come out so darned reasonable. I just hope you can forgive me this next act. Ah, here we go. Wait for me, won't you."

They were outside a Coral betting shop.

"Ed!" said Keith. "What have you done?"

"Ah, well, you see, in the end, I couldn't resist. So, I placed a little bet. One-all after extra time. *Quelle surprise!* Drinks are on me!"

***

481

Outside, it was bedlam, albeit of a good sort. Though the Plain was meant to belong to the Rainbow Coalition, people from other marches had squeezed through the permeable, under-staffed police lines. Yet, instead of strife, a bizarre positivity infused the square and streets around – partly instilled by the Rainbow band, energetically conducted by a young woman in tie-dyed purple pants and a yellow halter top, and partly by the news from Carrow Road about Norwich City's triumph, which spread through the close-packed mob like a supervirus.

The party left Smith in the church and dived into the good-natured scrum, initially intent on getting to Chapelfield Gardens to meet their colleagues from the stadium there. But – in horse racing parlance – the going was soft. *Extremely* soft. Indeed, *mud-bath*, thought Tom. It wasn't just the numbers, but their enthusiasm. People were either dancing or else huddled in excited conversations, often waving balloons, banners, and increasingly, yellow-and-green Norwich City scarves.

They made it to the St Peters Street frontline and saw the raised platform on which stood a man with wild hair, a cameraman attempting to film proceedings beside him. The man was clearly unhappy – his mouth working, his eyes wide, his arms waving. But whatever he was saying, he was being ignored. Indeed, this frontline had dissolved completely, with the only sign of the thin-blue-line being an occasional policeman's helmet, bobbing in isolation within the colourful human sea, sometimes topped with a donated rainbow beret.

They came to a small area like trodden-down stalks in a field of rape, where Penitents and Rainbow folks were kneeling together and laughing: some of the former seemed to have undergone colourful makeovers, and in return they were sharing their placards…

"I've not had enough men," cried one especially camp male. "That's a sin. Put that down."

"Manny, my dear, *au contraire*! I think you've had far, *far* too many!"

"I suppose I can be a bit smug," shouted another woman, kneeling beside a trio of middle-aged ladies in patchily threadbare pullovers, who were using marker pens to amend their placards, which they'd rested on the ground. "Maybe meat *isn't* murder, just serious assault and battery."

"That's the spirit, dear," said one of the women. "Go on, Jane, add that."

"You see – it's quite cathartic isn't it!" said the pen-wielder, completing the modification. She looked up in the direction of the bellowing messiah. "And I'm going to add to mine – *Panders to husband too much*," and then she raised her voice and shouted: "Oh, do shut up, Robert!"

"We'll never get through there," shouted Simon into Tom's ear. "Bethel Street is rammed. Might be better crossing the Plain towards the Mall."

Tom merely nodded and allowed Simon to turn the group about and head back.

Eventually they traversed the Plain in front of the Forum, passing one huddle of beret-wearers…

"Okay, maybe Trotsky wasn't *all* bad…"

"Lots of good people here. Maybe we're obsessing too much about a few bad apples?"

…and were forced with the flow towards Hay Hill.

The eastern front had also dissolved, with the police here having apparently given up completely and withdrawn.

Near the statue of the looming Sir Thomas Browne, a clutch of well-dressed elderly folks were in animated conversation with a half-dozen younger people…

"He wrote about fake news? What, this geezer?"

"Effectively, yes," replied one besuited man, leaning on a placard demanding the saving of history. "That's what 'vulgar errors' means – you know, the words written on one of the stones over *there*. One of his books was about debunking false beliefs."

"I didn't know! That's useful. Well, maybe *his* statue can stay…"

"Thank you, young man," said an elderly woman, dabbing a neat handkerchief at her over-heated brow. "But there's something to be said for *most* statues, even if the people depicted weren't always that nice. And of course, we'd be very happy for there to be statues to more diverse people, like that nice Stephen Fry. He's a local chap and one of yours, isn't he?"

"Too far!" shouted Simon. "We don't want to get funnelled onto Brig Street. Swim with me past Maccy-D's. Come on!"

And with effort, the party fought back up the slope, attained the corner of the fast-food mecca, and were then spat through the narrow gap between it and Next, with the church of St Stephen – sun sparkling off flint – visible ahead.

The human current swept them fully over Theatre Street – their objective – and onto the path through the church towards Chantry Place. Simon yelled for a halt, but Tom and Amanda weren't able to respond, linking arms so as not to get separated, and the others had to follow. It was as though they were in a tube of toothpaste, being squeezed through the nozzle, unable to turn.

And then they were spilled into another plain, with the sloping glass frontage of Chantry Place Mall ahead, and eateries fencing the two perpendicular sides. Through the churchyard, amid gravestones, and within this pool, there were other strange beings with different garb and placards hosting more mundane demands.

"Go on, Ron, give 'em a go," said one man in waders, handing a tub of small, white wriggling things to a man sucking on an unlit pipe.

"I have, but they've never worked for me, Bernie. But thanks. I will try again. No use being dogmatic."

"Just don't tell Jezza that, eh?"

"This is bonkers," shouted Simon to Tom, catching at Agneta's arm to prevent her being ricocheted off, while she in turn had hold of Martin.

"No, it's not so bad here," yelled back Tom. "If we get into the Mall, we can drop down a level and escape onto St Stephens Street."

And so that's what they did, wriggling like Bernie's maggots through a throng of people who seemed intent on swapping hats – fishermen's slouches for captains' caps and vice versa – amid placatory words…

"You don't get enough credit for ensuring the river stays clean…"

"… doesn't bother the fish that much…"

"… room for everybody!"

And more ambiguously, between two men with tattoos, piercings and oddly bumping balloons: "Throw it here? No way! I'll be lynched."

On St Stephens, Amanda phoned Keith, and they agreed to meet in the underpass where St Stephens met Queens Road. Indeed, both parties had been so delayed they arrived almost simultaneously.

"Ed!" declared Simon. "What the fuck! I didn't know you were with Keith and Trevor. And what's with the orange bib?"

Ed smirked. "Now, there's a tale and a half. But it's not one I plan to tell in this dingy hole with its faint whiff of human urea. Just above ground there are two most excellent hostelries — the Champion and the Coachmakers. Slightly off the immediate track of the yellow army. And if we can't get into either of these, we're not too far from the most excellent Trafford Arms. I have earned a beverage or two, and it sounds as though you have not disgraced yourselves either. In my wallet, I have a generous donation from Mr Coral. Coming?"

Tom smiled and shook his head — and noticed Amanda smiling too. They were still linked, arm-in-arm. Nothing more needed to be said.

Chapter 39: Autopsy

So, that was it.

Tom slept all of Sunday morning, suffering from cumulative mental and physical exhaustion. When he did wake, just after noon, he lay in bed a while longer, his head throbbing mildly from alcoholic excess, going over events in his mind. Had he really been involved in all that? While certain memories made him smile to himself, he still felt, overall, vaguely unsettled. The story seemed at an end, but of course, it wasn't really. Not like a novel. Not neat. Read 'The End' and close the book. His life continued. He was still a mid-30s waster, without a proper job, and without a proper girlfriend. And then there was the aftermath of what he and his colleagues had done. Were his friends and collaborators even now being carpeted by their respective handlers for breaching rules? And what of his own – of Smith?

Tom rolled out of bed. He went next door to turn his computer on, then, still wearing just his pants, descended to his galley kitchen to make himself a cup of tea and find some paracetamol. When he returned to his computer, he opened his email. There were a number of messages from Alice, the last titled 'Tom – are you still alive?' As he'd done nothing on Alice's project for the past few weeks, he decided to leave reading and responding to those for later. Then he turned to the news websites – but wasn't entirely clear what he expected to see. And indeed, there was little on the situation in Norwich – for how could there be? They'd succeeded. Failure would have seen reports of riot and perhaps even football-directorcide. Whatever, it seemed his own efforts would likely remain hidden from the people of Norwich and the wider world. And that somehow got him thinking of his 'novel'.

Tom opened his latest chapter, stored on his hard drive, and read through it as he sipped his milky tea. He was very close to the end. Just bits and pieces to tie up before having to start the onerous process of revision. And reading, he was suddenly filled with doubt.

His main protagonist had not only undergone a name-change part way through, but something of a personality shift, too. Tim had started off somewhat ineffectual – much, Tom supposed, like himself. Then he had started to become badass. Or rather, a little bit badass. But not full-tonto badass. And as Tom mulled over what he'd written, he realised that the secondary characters he'd gradually introduced had grown and developed and, in truth, it was a number of these that had done most of the heavy lifting in countering the alien menace. In the end, Tim had become an enabler and narrator, rather than the central hero. Tom mentally frowned: was that going to fly with a publisher? In films, mild-mannered Clark Kents invariably transformed in the most improbable ways, flinging off glasses and developing biceps upon their biceps. Having worried at the modest transformation of his own hero, he now worried that he'd not, in fact, transformed him enough. People *did* grow and change, but not usually by much. In trying to retain some degree of realism, had Tom shot himself in the foot? After all, he was trying to write popular fiction – not mainstream. Perhaps he'd have to heavily rewrite to ensure that it was Tim who kicked down the final door and came out with the killer Schwarzeneggeresque put down, *not* Tim's allies?

And then there was Tim's love interest. This was the main loose end he needed to tie up. Should Tim get the girl? Did he actually *deserve* to get the girl? And had he been romantic enough to make getting the girl even vaguely credible? In this case, he knew exactly what readers would expect. But looking now at what he'd written, he winced. Was this really the sort of thing Tim would say or do?

Tom deleted the offending paragraph.

Then, in exasperation, he saved and closed the file.

No girl then.

None for Tim, and none for Tom.

But then he noticed a new email – this from Amanda. Ironically, it was also labelled: 'Tom – are you still alive?' If she'd sent him an email, it was likely because he'd not answered a text. Where had he left his phone? And his burner phone? They must be downstairs.

But the sight of the email made him smile. He wasn't completely forgotten. He chewed on his lip and nodded with resolve.

He'd deleted the offending paragraph, but he had a back-up stored in the Cloud.

Tom addressed the keyboard, found his last-saved version in the ether, scrolled down towards the end where he'd parked the romance paragraph, and…

"Fuck me!"

HELLO TOM. YESTERDAY WAS QUITE A SURPRISE. SHALL WE MEET UP – ONE LAST TIME? 2PM TODAY AT THE USUAL PLACE?

"No-*fucking*-way!"

Was this a trick? A trap? Was he about to be assassinated by an alien on a Sunday afternoon in... forty-three minutes?

Forty-three!

Of course, he had to go. Whatever this was about, he had to go, to get some kind of closure. "Come on, Tim," he said to himself. "Kick the door down ..."

He typed a quick response, saved the file, then went to put on some clothes.

***

Tom bustled up to the bench that circled the plane tree in front of the western end of the Guildhall. He was six minutes late – surely too late, given that Smith had only six minutes and thirty-two seconds before becoming detectable to other watching species... or so the alien had claimed.

Yet there he was, waiting. And he seemed different, too. Tom was used to seeing him standing straight, arms clutching a pile of *Big Issues* for cover. Though his garb was the same – wearing his customary red bib, jeans, and walking boots – he now lounged on the bench, one arm resting across its back, with not a copy of the magazine to be seen.

For once, it was Tom who had to stand. When he'd sat in the past, he'd always felt in an inferior position, supine, over-borne; yet now that he stood, he felt no better, and perhaps even worse – a supplicant approaching a king seated upon his throne. *Weird.*

"Hello, Tom."

"Ah... hello. Sorry I'm late. I didn't get your message until, well, um, and I know you have to go very soon."

Smith waved the hand of his resting arm dismissively. "It is of no matter, Tom. I may now be visible to watchers, but only if looked for. If seen, my presence will likely be recorded as a displeasing anomaly, but since this is my final manifestation at this place, and in this form, that makes little difference to me. The bigger risk is to you."

"What do you mean? They wouldn't… abduct me, would they?"

"And probe your anus?" Smith's bearded jowl contorted into a smile. "You humans have some very odd ideas. But no. No abduction. No probing. No ray guns. No mind wipes. But you might find yourself of sudden interest to viewers – you, and any of those you associate with. Does that thought not make you feel uncomfortable?"

"Uh, well, yes, I guess so." Tom looked about as though he might see aliens peering around corners or staring over the tops of newspapers. "So, maybe we should, um, get…"

"Get this over with? Indeed. We do have some unfinished business." The alien dropped his arm from the top of the bench and held out his hand. "The device you took from my store case, please."

"Okay. Fair enough." The disruptor was still in Tom's rucksack, where he'd placed it yesterday. He swung the rucksack from his back, retrieved the desired item, and handed it over.

"Thank you, Tom. And can I also have your glasses and contact lenses, please."

The request irked Tom. He hadn't been sure what this meeting was actually for, and though he understood the issue with the disruptor, this further request just seemed petty. He'd forgotten to reclaim his glasses from Ed last night, though he was currently wearing the contacts – which he'd put in habitually and unthinkingly before leaving the house. With a touch of petulance, he said: "Ah, sorry. I think I lost them."

Smith looked at him askance. "Really, Tom? You have become quite rebellious. Very well. Keep them. But do not try to advertise or sell them. Your science will not be able to detect the seventh dimension and therefore the secret of the lenses will be indecipherable. And even if you were to find a suitable savant to try them on, you know our messages decay rapidly, cannot be photographed, and are generally innocuous and written in English. Further, their subconscious effects are not detectable with your blunt psychometrics. At best, anything you reveal is likely to be seen as a trick. So – will you at least agree to keep them secret?"

Tom smiled cautiously. The lack of menace – while in keeping with Smith's demeanour since he had known him – was still a relief. In actual fact, Tom had not thought about what to do with the *oculars* until now: his push-back had been instinctive. "Sure. I promise. Cross my heart."

"And hope to die?"

"Er…"

Smith twisted his mouth into a smile. "Relax, Tom. You must realise by now that we do not, or will not, directly act to harm humans. This is not our inclination. And in any case, though the non-interference compact between alien species is informal, there are some quite dogmatic beings that would probably act if they thought harm were being caused by otherworldly hands… or claws… or tentacles – as characterised in your novel, Tom."

"Yes, well, bizarrely, I do trust you on this. But I'm surprised at your magnanimity."

"I'm not sure why. None of what has happened has been personal, Tom. My species is a very old one that simply seeks entertainment. And I must say, recent events have certainly entertained me, and not-a-few other watchers, too. It's just a shame that my intended audience never got to see the rousing denouement I had planned." Smith placed his hands on his thighs and pushed himself up. "But now I must go."

"Go? You mean, back to your base at St Peter Mancroft?"

"No, Tom. This play is done, and my cover has been blown. I cannot function here any longer; it is time to move on."

"To Alpha Centauri?"

"Very droll, Tom. No, not so far. Perhaps elsewhere in Britain, but maybe further afield. And with a different shell." Smith raised his hands and looked at them. "This one will be retired."

"So… more mischief elsewhere?"

"The watchers need their entertainment, as do I. Next time, I hope to find more reliable and compliant staff. But enough: my time is up. This is goodbye – and good luck. I sincerely wish you well, Tom."

"And I, you." Tom realised he meant it.

The *Big Issue* seller gave an uncharacteristic wink, and for a final time turned and headed for his lair.

***

It was Tuesday evening.

At the Rose Tavern, three members of The Credulous occupied a table in the corner of the main lounge, having arrived well before the start of the quiz in order to nab a decent spot. Tom bustled in last. He smiled apologetically, and sat opposite to Ed and Simon, next to Amanda. A full pint awaited him.

"Last but not least," chuckled Ed. "I'm nearly ready for a top up! And what reason do you have for your tardiness today? Fending off an alien assault group?"

"No, nothing that exotic. I'm so far behind in my project with Alice, I've had to, well… I'm working like a dog to catch up." He frowned and flicked his gaze around the others, lingering on Amanda, who looked especially nice today, with her hair in a ponytail. "In fact, I'm not sure I'll ever have another alien encounter, unlike you lot."

"But aren't you still wearing your contact lenses?" asked Amanda.

"Ah, no. The funny thing is, they've suddenly gone all *squishy*. I don't think I can use them anymore."

"Smith probably beamed an auto-destruct sequence," suggested Ed. He magically produced a pair of glasses. "But here are your bins. I managed to neither lose them nor sit on them. Count yourself fortunate."

Tom received the glasses gingerly. "Thanks." They were his last link to the hidden secrets of the world. They seemed intact. He put them on; looked about; then whisked them off again. He wasn't sure what he had been expecting to see: their alien nature only became clear when a seventh dimensional message was in range, and it was no surprise that there were none in the pub.

Ed nodded sympathetically. "Furl up that pouty lip, my friend. You are still part of the club. The Credulous. Or perhaps we should rename ourselves, given our heroics: 'The Alien Fuckers'. No, Mands? Perhaps you're right. Bit too suggestive of xenophilia. Ugh! 'The Alien Arse-Reamers'? Ah, same problem."

"What about 'The Galactic Avengers'," suggested Simon.

"Except, Si, old chum, we're hardly avenging the entire galaxy. Or even the entire human race. And 'The Norwich Avengers' sounds a quantum lame."

"I think The Credulous will do," said Amanda, firmly. "After all, it's about what we know as much as what we do, and Tom knows as much as the rest of us, even if he might not do so much in the future."

Tom noted Amanda's concerned look and gave a sheepish smile in return; the others seemed to have quickly divined what was going on in his head, something he hadn't clearly articulated to himself until now. "Thanks. I mean, it's not as if I've actually enjoyed running around looking for, uh, alien clues, and I've *definitely* not enjoyed being played by Smith, but… well… you know… for the last few months, I've felt like I've justified my existence."

"Like *Red Dwarf* and *The Inquisitor*," nodded Simon. "Good call, mate."

"Yes, maybe. Now, I'm back to being just Tom – an unemployed academic and, er, novice writer." *Author* sounded too pretentious; he just couldn't say it.

"Well, you're more than that, old chap," said Ed. "Consider yourself investigator without portfolio. A freelancer. Keep your super-enhanced eyes peeled, as I'm sure we could do with a warning if spooky messages start to reappear. And I'm sure Cheggers' crew wouldn't mind a heads-up, too."

"Yeah, mate. And there's still mysteries that haven't been solved," said Simon. "Like, what's happened to this Brian character and was he was involved in the football banjaxing."

"And Terminus Est need watching," suggested Amanda.

"That's right," concurred Ed. "They're proper villains according to Cheggers. Smith was just a recent paymaster, but they seem to be well known to the alien twaternity. Indeed, young Thomas, do you not recall that I mentioned awhile back that Big Ed was worried about an alien betting syndicate? Bit of education for you here: syndicates *aren't* individuals. So, it seems that Smith was piggybacking on some other arseholes." Ed paused and scrunched his face. "A disgusting image just came to mind there. Shudder! Anyway, the point is this: given the football links they have, its odds-on that Augustus P. Megabuttocks and his slimy cabal are still on a retainer and more mischief is in the offing. It wouldn't surprise me if they end up having a jolly to Wembley shortly for the play-off final."

Simon snapped his fingers. "Of course! And I bet we'll win. And then next season–"

"Armageddon!" exclaimed Ed. "I see what you're thinking, Si. It's amazing, isn't it, how often we win the Championship playing like lions, then get relegated the following season, getting thumped by absolutely everyone – including the promoted teams that we beasted the year before. How likely is that, hmm?"

Amanda shook her head. "I sense there are more bets to come."

Tom nodded. Simon and Ed had identified a real anomaly, which given recent events now seemed incredibly suspicious. But this talk of mysteries had got him thinking. There were other matters that seemed worth investigating. Like what had happened to all of that particular shade of red paint he'd been tasked to get hold of by Smith at the outset, and who had been buying it, and why. And he was still intrigued by where all the Norwich tunnels went, and who else might be using them. And then there were the ghosts: were they truly hands-off, or did their occasional appearance signal some other game afoot? Maybe the others *were* right and there *was* still a role for him. Maybe he was, in a sense, *not un*-special...

"Okay, right, enough of being Tom's agony aunt," said Ed. "More important matters are afoot. The quizmeisters seem to have become animated, and I see them roving the tables with table round sheets. And with our nemeses absent – probably licking each other's, er, *wounds* – that means victory and free beer await."

But things didn't go exactly according to plan.

***

"Second!" exclaimed Ed, as the scores were read out at the end of the quiz. "Who beat us?"

"It's those two," said Simon. "In the corner. The guy looks familiar."

"The one with the goatee? Chubby Lucifer? Fuck! Wasn't he the stand-in quizmaster at the very first quiz we attended? And... who's he with? It's just him and a young girl!"

"Apparently, she's his daughter," said Amanda. "I overheard him telling the quizmaster while you were at the bar."

"Beaten by a team of two," continued Ed, disgruntlement personified, "and by just one point! It was that question on *Rammstein*, wasn't it? I blame you, Si. Metal is meant to be your oeuvre. And don't you shrug at me like that. Un-*bloody*-believable!"

But Ed's outrage was more than a little faux: the wide eyes and flaring nostrils directed at Simon quickly dissolved into a wry grin. "Oh, well. Let them enjoy this moment of glory... *for it shall be their last!*"

"That's the spirit!" said Simon. "Now, one for the road? Ed? Tom? Amanda… no?"

"Sorry, boys. I've got a busy day tomorrow."

"Oh," said Tom, with an inadvertent exhale. "That's… a shame."

"Oh, for fuck sake, Tom," said Ed. "Stop being such a pussy."

"Uh, what?"

"Your interest is clear. Amanda babes," Ed turned to face Amanda, who'd risen. "Tom would very much like your company for a date. I want you two to get this over with so I don't have to suffer any more little glances and sighs. So, let's say tomorrow."

Tom winced and looked down, so he didn't see Amanda's response, though he heard it. "Oh! Tell Tom I'm sorry. I'm busy tomorrow," she paused. "It'll have to be Thursday. When he gets back from wherever he is now, ask him to text me to say where and when. See you all. Bye!"

Amanda had turned by the time Tom looked up, but he followed her back with his eyes all the way to the door.

"Thank God that's over with," said Ed. "And if you're running short of ideas, maybe you can arrange a double date with Si and the delectably bitter Agneta."

Simon gaped: "How did you know!"

"Me?" said Ed, smugly. "Oh, I know everything."

"Except about *Rammstein*," muttered Tom, but with a degree of affection.

***

"Hello, Tom. So – here we are." Amanda came to a halt in front of her date, who for once in his life had been early. Twenty minutes early.

Tom flushed at the sight of the bespectacled woman wearing a denim jacket over an ankle-length, green patterned dress, her shoulder-length hair tied in a ponytail. "Ah… hi. I'm glad you came. Uh, not that I thought you wouldn't. I mean, we've been to dinner before. On that mission, remember?"

"Yes, we have, haven't we. In fact, just over there…" Amanda nodded in the direction of the Tipsy Vegan, perhaps fifty metres down the road from where they stood outside St Lawrence's Church on St Benedicts Street, near to the One Life Left gaming café. She seemed amused, struggling to control her mouth. "But this isn't quite the same thing, I hope."

"Uh, yes. I mean, *no*. I mean, I thought we'd just meet here as it's familiar territory."

"Not because you wanted to return to that restaurant to visit Teresa?"

"No! In fact, God, I'd forgotten about her working there. I… ah… you're teasing me!" Tom broke into a gentle smile. "I'd have expected that from Ed, but not you. I mean, you're too…"

"Sensible?"

"No, I was going for *nice*." Was that too much? Tom had been out of the game for so long, he really didn't have a clue.

"Nice? You've got a PhD and you're writing a novel, and out of your vast vocabulary the best you could come up with is 'nice'?" She gave an exaggerated sigh. "Well, there are worse things to be called, I suppose."

"Oh, yes, definitely!" Had he blown it? No, he didn't think so. Still… "If everyone in the city were like you, we wouldn't have had the problems we've just had. Bugger – you know what I mean. I'm making a hash of this. I'm sorry."

Amanda smiled more broadly and edged closer. "No, Tom. You're doing just fine. But, I had no lunch and I'm intrigued as to where we're going. Not the Tipsy, surely?"

"No. I was thinking, what about something a little different. Maybe a quick drink first then… have you been to Turtle Bay?"

"The Caribbean place? No, I haven't. But I'm happy to try."

A little way further along the street, at the corner of St Gregory's Alley, they stopped for a drink at the Maker's House – a pleasant French bistro. But it was most definitely a 'quick one', as Amanda wanted to eat. Afterwards, they carried on up the Alley towards St Gregory's Green, past Athena Games.

"It's a small world," murmured Tom as they drew level with the gaming centre, which was still open.

"Sorry, Tom?"

"Oh, it just occurred to me how all around us are places where important things have happened over the last few months. It's like the centre of our universe. I remember tailing Martin and Trevor here with Simon before we knew they were goodies. And then there's the church here where Norwich vigilantism started. And... oh! Look at that!" He took several steps up the alley, drawing Amanda with him.

Where the alley narrowed before disgorging onto the triangular Green, a bright sprawl of graffiti ran across the church's flint façade beneath two arched, leaded windows.

"The Knights aren't going to like that," said Amanda. She started to laugh: "Though I think the message could have been better thought out."

Tom also started to laugh. The message included the tag of the city's premier vandal – a man who'd once appeared on TV in disguise to condemn Tom's handiwork in the Pottergate underpass. It read:

KB – STILL REVOLTING

But that wasn't the end of the surprises. As Tom turned to look at Amanda, he caught sight of a bespectacled figure emerging from Athena Games just five metres away and – with head down – turn left towards St Benedicts. The laughter froze on Tom's face, his mouth wide open.

"Tom... what?"

"Behind you!" he hissed. "It's Brian!"

Amanda turned to look, but only saw the back of a man wearing a dark overcoat with a visible bald patch disappearing around a corner. "Is it? I can't... Did he see you?"

"No. He was looking down, like he was distracted. He was in Athena. I didn't know he was a gamer."

"Well, you didn't know he liked football, either."

"He doesn't." Tom shook his head. "What a mystery!"

A smile stole across Amanda's face. "A mystery worth investigating by Tom – freelance alien detective?"

Tom grinned back. "Ah, well, yes, as long as he can do so with his trusty side-kick."

"I think you mean 'partner'."

"Exactly! I mean, if you're really up for it. It would involve a bit of stalking."

"Tom – are you trying to corrupt me?" Amanda sighed. "Okay. I suppose I can resist the hunger pangs a little longer. Lead on. Let's see where he's going."

Steel entered Tom's eyes. The story wasn't over after all...

Epilogue: Extract from Tom Beresford's *still* unpublished manuscript 'The Alien Without'

So, the alien wankers had been thwarted.

Tim gazed out over the golden sands of Great Yarmouth from the Britannia Pier, nodding gently to himself. The pink-fleshed multitudes didn't know how close they had come to oblivion; how much they owed to Tim and his heroic comrades back in Norwich. But that was okay: the rewards he'd gained from this grand affair were enough. He turned to smile at the bespectacled woman beside him and thought: *more than enough.*

"What are you thinking, Tim?" asked Alice. "About V-Garg? About where he might strike next?"

"Eh? I guess so. Amongst other things. But mainly, I was thinking about what a funny species we are…" he waved an arm to indicate those sunbathing on the beach, kicking about footballs, eating ice creams on the promenade, and wading in the dirty brown sea, "and about why any alien would really be interested in us in the first place. I mean, don't they have better things to do with their unnaturally elongated lives?"

"I guess not. But as they are interested, we have to be vigilant."

"Yes. The world might not know it, but its fate depends upon us." He took hold of the woman's arm to lead her away. "But enough of that. I want to try to forget about little green men for a while. Let's go get some doughnuts."

THE END

Author's Note

Right, there are two important matters I desperately need to discuss with you all – matters that might seem to undermine my authorial credibility. But they don't. Let me explain.

The first is apostrophes. I have a thing about these devilish little blighters. You see, I *understand* them. 'Should think so, too!' I hear you cry. But believe me, the number of otherwise bright people who don't get them is extraordinary. From a long career in academia, I can tell you that a significant proportion of 'doctored' people are also clueless about them. Now, I'm not a monstrous pedant in general, but about these seemingly innocuous punctuation marks I'm prepared to make an exception. People: it's not hard! They generally arise in two situations: to indicate possession (Tom's; the General's; the dogs' – note the apostrophe follows the 's' when plural), or word truncation ('it is' becoming 'it's'). I suppose the only anomaly is for possessive pronouns, hence, his-hers-its, rather than his'-hers'-its' (or should that be, hi's-her's-it's?). That's all, folks. NOT. DIFFICULT. Strewth!

Right, now here's the rub. Throughout 'Yellow Shirts', the keen reader will likely notice errors aplenty. Maybe even think: *what a moron! Author? Hah!* But any such blunders are nothing of the sort: they are intentional and represent commonly accepted spellings. For those with a mathematical bent, think 'error carried forwards'. I am, of course, speaking predominantly about the names of retail or service outlets and of streets. Thus, much activity in the book takes place on or around St Benedicts Street. That's right – the street of St Benedict, hence properly, St Benedict's Street. Road signs, however, have an allergy to the apostrophe. Maybe this is understandable. Imagine the fiddlyness otherwise. But the thing is, venues that exist upon such streets by-and-large give their addresses in sympathy with the road signs – viz, no apostrophe. In this case, I have conceded to the norm (while punching myself vigorously in the thigh). But perhaps what is truly annoying is how, sometimes, proper convention is followed. Other key locations in the book are St Andrew's Hall and adjacent Blackfriars' Hall. Now, these tend to be written with appropriate apostrophes – generally, but not always (look online and you'll see what I mean) – in counterpoint to adjacent St Andrews Road and St Andrews Street. Sigh!

In short, I have attempted throughout to follow the predominant norm, and be consistent in apparent inconsistency. Some might argue that in some particular case I am incorrect in what is the norm – and I can live with that, as long as none accuse me of misunderstanding the bloody apostrophe. Right? Suggest otherwise, and I'll put a curse upon you (as the great Micky Flanagan would say).

The second issue is geography, in particular, civic geography. I have attempted throughout the book to stick close to reality in my descriptions – but it's astonishing how quickly things change. My main regret is the revivification of Hay Hill, the scene of numerous important events in the book. Up until a short time ago, the place was exactly as described in various chapters. I have laboured under some delusion (perhaps) that the book might prove a hit and lead to the descent of hordes of tourists upon our fine city – to snap themselves in key locations; sup from notable boozers; search out the mysteries of graffiti, pavement plaques, and artistically amended beermats; even hunt down the precise seats at Carrow Road occupied by some of the heroes in one of the later chapters. But the blighters from the council have gone and dug up Hay Hill and moved the weird sculptures that once resided there, and it's not clear to me that the statue of Sir Thomas Browne will remain, either. Meanwhile, other outlets have since changed name or moved (most recently, the Tipsy Vegan!). *Bugger.* Just trust me on this, okay? Most of the locales are still the same, and where I am wrong, I wasn't originally. But by all means, come along to check, bring your wallet, and give fine old Norwich a look-see. I don't think you'll regret it.

Acknowledgements

I have plenty of people to thank for this one, some of whom provided significant early commentary, while others read much later drafts and merely spotted the odd typo or two. Nevertheless, I appreciate the efforts of all of my readers, even if they provided little except positive feedback. So, in alphabetical order, my thanks are due to Paul Beacon, Carl Burrage, Adam Carpenter, Jack Dainty, Adrian Deasley, Phil Nicholls, Alexander Mo, Natalia Perez, Andrew Schofield, Paula Smith, Martin Webb, and Gary Wortley. As ever, any errors are entirely down to me.

About the Author

Gene Rowe was born in Bedford in 1966 (the glorious year!), although he didn't stay there long, having to move around a lot as a child thanks to his father's job in the United States Air Force (his father is a Mainer). He read psychology at Bristol University and subsequently completed a PhD at the Bristol Business School. Years of toil as an academic followed before he transitioned into a self-employed consultant. He now seems to spend almost all of his time scribbling stories in Norwich, where he lives with his partner and two increasingly large children.

Of Yellow Shirts and Little Green Men is his fourth solo novel and the first of the Norwich Chronicles (to be followed by *Of Spilt Ale and Alien Revenge*). His other books include *The Greater Game, The Price of Freedom Part 1: Ghuraj to Arkon*, and *The Price of Freedom Part 2: Velasia*. He is also co-editor of the British Science Fiction Association's (BSFA) *Fission* anthologies (with Eugen Bacon).

Printed in Dunstable, United Kingdom

68538065R00285